RUNE WARRIOR

FRANK MORIN

ISBN: 978-0-9970233-3-6
A Whipsaw Press Original
Edited by Joshua Essoe
(http://www.joshuaessoe.com/)
Cover art by Christian Bentulan
(https://coversbychristian.com/)
Book design by Kate Staker
(https://katestaker.com/)
First Whipsaw printing: May 2016

Created with Vellum

OTHER WORKS BY FRANK MORIN

Find all books on www.frankmorin.org

The Petralist Series

Set in Stone, Book One

A Stone's Throw, Book Two

No Stone Unturned, Book Three

Affinity for War, Book Four

The Queen's Quarry, Book Five

Blood of the Tallan, Book Six (release in late 2020)

When Torcs Fly, A Petralist Origins novella: Tomas and Cameron

Game of Garlands, A Petralist Origins novella: Anika

The Facetakers Series

Saving Face, Book One

Memory Hunter, Book Two

Rune Warrior, Book Three

Aeon Champion, Book Four (release in September 2020)

Short Stories

"Odin's Eye," included in *A Game of Horns: A Red Unicorn Anthology*

"The Essence," included in the *Dragon Writers: An Anthology*

"Only Logical," a purple unicorn story

"The Seventh Strike," included in *Cursed Collectibles: An Anthology*

ACKNOWLEDGMENTS

Every book is a major undertaking, and *Rune Warrior* had its own special challenges.

Thanks to my family, who continue to rally behind every book I write. Your enthusiasm is inspiring. Jenny's deft touch as an editor, and her insightful feedback were invaluable. Kate and Kyle as always were as blunt as they were supportive. I wouldn't have it any other way.

Thanks also to Eve Ledesma and Joe Morris for great beta reads and excellent comments. And thanks to my fantastic editor, Joshua Essoe. You never pulled any punches, but you were always fair, and the story shines because of it.

Jared Blando, thanks for the epic runes. And finally, thanks to Christian Bentulan for a fantastic cover. You nailed it.

RUNES

Rune Warrior Rune

Healing Rune

1

When I read a good book, I wish this life were three thousand years long.

~EMERSON

SARAH ENTERED A SIMULATED OPERATING ROOM, complete with beeping monitors and the smell of antiseptic. She verified both empty gurneys were in position, and that the Sotrun machine was masked by a white sheet.

"Relax, everything is ready." Eirene entered, dressed in a doctor's white coat. She wore her light brown hair in a simple braid that accented her beautiful face.

Even Sarah struggled to note the tiny signs that Eirene's athletic body was not her original form. Eirene looked maybe thirty years old. That was some fantastic aging. No one who didn't already know Eirene was a facetaker would believe she had lived since the times of the Roman republic. Only when one looked closer, noted the depth of her gaze, might they sense there was more to her.

Sarah shrugged. "I can't help it. I'm excited we're actually going to do this."

"Piece of cake."

"Only if it's abomination cake," Alter said, already frowning as he followed Eirene into the room, trailed by Sofia, an actual surgeon on Quentin's medical staff. The Italian woman was the only real medical staff in their sham operation.

Sarah met Alter's angry stare calmly. He had argued against the procedure, even though it was such a desperately needed service. The handsome young hunter still struggled to see beyond his strict upbringing.

Eirene gestured to Domenico, an Italian enforcer who loved to laugh. Today he was pretending to be an orderly. He saluted and left to fetch the patients.

Alter approached and took her hands, his deep, black-eyed gaze intense. In his mid-twenties and in fantastic shape, she considered him a good friend. He also helped teach her to fight. They sparred together every day, so she could have read his emotional state even had he tried to conceal it.

He didn't try. Alter was not a master of subtlety.

"Sarah, you barely know these people. You can't condone ripping out their souls."

"We're helping them." Tired of the argument, she grabbed his sleeve and led him to the side of the room just as Domenico returned with an elderly gentleman and a young man. The two were engrossed in conversation.

"Watch and learn," she whispered. When he tried to protest again, she added, "And be quiet."

"Hello, Walter." Sarah turned her back on Alter to greet the younger of the two patients. His face looked too mature for the body and Sarah easily picked out the signs of misalignment along his jaw.

Walter grinned. "Sarah, my dear. So good to see you again."

The elderly gentleman greeted her warmly and kissed her hand. "It is such a pleasure to finally meet you. You're even lovelier in person."

"I bet you say that to all the girls." Sarah was used to getting hit on, but not by guys so old. As a top-ten model for Alterego, she'd maintained a waiting list of over eighteen months of renters eager to live in her body for a while.

"I'm glad you two have already met. Have you signed the transfer order?" she asked.

"With pleasure." His name was Leandro Blickensderfer, a Swiss billionaire. Sarah had spoken with him a few times on the phone and studied his online profile in detail.

"It's easy when we both win," Walter added.

"I'm glad you feel that way." She cast a glance back at Alter. "We're ready to begin."

Alter frowned but made no move to interfere.

Sarah gestured to the gurneys, and Domenico helped the two men get positioned with Sofia's help. Sarah breathed a sigh of relief that no last-minute issues had come up. She had met Walter and his dear wife Gladys after the destruction of Alterego. Walter was one of the unfortunate clients who had lost his elderly body in the fire and been left living as a thirty-something man.

His wife had been returned to her aging body, leaving the two of them generations apart. To make matters worse, the family of the deceased convict whose body Walter ended up in sued him for child support, and they had been caught up in court battles for months.

With Alterego destroyed, the secret to the marvelous technology that allowed the transfer of consciousness between bodies was lost. Sarah had learned the truth, that the technology was worthless unless powered by the ancient soul gift of the facetakers. Most people lived in happy ignorance of the truth, but Sarah had fallen into their world, where arcane dangers were very much alive.

She had managed to escape Alterego with body and soul intact, but had felt driven to help those who had not been so lucky. Now the secret facetaker council was led by Eirene and her husband, Gregorios. They controlled the machine that had survived Mai Luan's fiery death, and Sarah had convinced them to help her restore what victims of Alterego they could.

Walter was the first, and he might just be the last. Although almost twenty couples had ended up in similar circumstances, he alone sought to join his wife in old age. Most of the other couples split by the generation gap had filed for divorce. The younger partners hadn't wanted to be saddled with a spouse generations older. The break-ups were usually ugly and Sarah found the lack of fidelity heartbreaking.

All the more reason to help Walter. Sarah smiled at him as Sofia injected a fast-acting tranquilizer into his arm, then into Leandro's.

Instead of charging the couple their usual exorbitant fee to grant them new lives, Eirene had agreed to perform this soul transfer free of charge. She'd said, "It's a small price to pay to wrap up the final threads of that abomination."

Phrasing it that way had helped sway Alter. "Abomination" was one of his favorite words, and his entire life as a hunter was dedicated to removing such evil from the world.

"See you on the other side," Walter muttered before sleep claimed him.

Leandro lay back, a radiant smile on his face, his lips moving in a whispered prayer.

Usually identifying bodies for use as transfer vehicles fell to the consignment team. Their activities sometimes skirted and even crossed the line of what Sarah considered morally acceptable. Besides, Alter would have tried killing them all if the facetakers had attempted to procure a new body for Walter using their regular means.

He'd finally relented when they found a willing transfer vehicle. Leandro had been more than willing. When approached, he'd eagerly agreed to the terms. He would not only paying to settle the outstanding lawsuits, but would provide Walter a generous compensation package. The two men would switch bodies, both getting what they wanted.

Eirene moved to the head of Walter's gurney and placed her hands over his face, her fingers curling around the line of his jaw. She took a steadying breath and her eyes began to glow like purple LED lights as she activated her nevra core, the source of her soul power. Purple fire rippled along her fingers as she drove them through the skin around Walter's jaw.

The process of soul transfers still amazed Sarah. Although she had undergone more than all but the eldest facetakers, during most of them she had lain blissfully unaware of what was really happening. She had since witnessed several transfers, but still shuddered to see it.

She risked a glance at Alter. He watched the procedure with a frown and with clenched fists. Had Gregorios been performing the soul extraction, Sarah doubted Alter could have refrained from interfering.

His relationship with Eirene was complex and slowly deepening. Although shocked to learn that Eirene was really his long-deceased great-grandmother, he was coping by small degrees. Eirene seemed willing to invest however long it took, and Sarah sometimes caught her smiling with radiant joy at him.

Sofia shifted quietly to stand beside Alter. Sarah noted that the doctor didn't seem disturbed by the soul transfer. As a staff member working for Quentin, she must have seen soul transfers before, and would be well aware of the marvelous rune enhancements worn by enforcers.

With her fingers deep under Walter's skin, Eirene began to pull. Walter's face peeled away from his skull with a wet sucking sound, like the dregs of a milkshake worked by a child.

Sarah hated that sound. It dredged up horrific memories of the terrifying memoryscape battle. Images flashed into her mind of Asoka melting into the floor and of Mai Luan's chest vaporizing under the blast of Sarah's gun. She forced the memories down, refused to turn away from the sight and be ruled by her nightmares.

The skin of Walter's face sloughed off, revealing his shimmering, translucent soulmask as it disengaged from the underlying bone structure of his skull. The gap widened and the soulmask broke free as the last pieces of loose skin slipped away.

Eirene lifted the soulmask high. The eyeballs shrank to half-spheres, sucking in the dangling nerve clusters. The soulmask thinned, trailing rainbow mist, visible tendrils of the man's soul. On the blank skull of the body he had just abandoned, the skin flowed together until it looked like a department store mannequin, unbroken but for a thin slit where the nose should be.

Sarah's heart pounded and she wiped her hands on her slacks. At least Eirene didn't throw her head back in silent ecstasy as she took Walter's soul the way Mai Luan used to. The fact that Eirene didn't revel in the process helped Sarah see this as the good deed it was.

Domenico accepted Walter's soulmask from Eirene, who moved to Leandro to repeat the procedure. Before she began, Sarah pulled up the left side of the sleeping man's shirt.

"What are you doing?" Eirene asked, hands poised to begin the extraction.

"A little gift," Sarah said.

Eirene cautioned, "He can't know about runes. We're only barely holding the illusion as it is."

"I won't tell him what it really means. He can still just enjoy it in ignorance." Sarah said. She turned to Sofia, who was already proffering a scalpel. The woman was very good.

"Sarah, this is not wise," Alter protested as he drew closer.

"These are good people. Come activate this for me," she said.

"No."

"Come on," Sarah pleaded. "Try helping a little instead of just opposing everything. It'll help you feel connected with what we're doing."

"Why do you think I want to feel connected to this?"

"Because we're restoring balance to their lives. Isn't that what hunters are supposed to do?"

The hunters were a secret organization, concealed within the Jewish population for centuries. Their rounon powers granted them marvelous enhancements through their rune markings, powered by the force of their souls. They were dedicated to eradicating the heka, or kashaph as they called them, from the world. Heka shared similar rounon powers but stole the force of other souls to power their enhancements.

"We don't work this way," Alter said, but edged closer.

"Just try it," Sarah urged. She took his hand to draw him to the gurney and he gripped her hand tightly, his skin warm against hers.

"There is no guarantee he can bond to it."

"What's the worst that could happen?"

"If it doesn't bond, the cuts heal in a few days," he conceded. "But what if it's a partial bond?"

Sarah hadn't thought of that. Those were supposed to be very dangerous. "How often have you actually seen a partial bond?"

"Well, I've heard of them."

She squeezed his hand. "Walter's already experienced one soul transfer. I feel it, Alter. This is the right thing."

She couldn't explain why, but she couldn't deny the strength of her conviction. Runes called to her in a way nothing else did. They made *sense*. This made sense.

Eirene said, "Whatever you're going to do, get on with it. Walter will come around any second and I don't want him experiencing true dispossession."

Sofia spoke softly in her slightly accented voice. "He is aged, but stable. I do not believe the attempt will threaten his health."

Sarah flashed her a grateful smile. "I'm doing it, Alter. You decide if you're going to help or just keep sulking."

2

You are a little soul carrying about a corpse. Some may carry more than one on their journey, but the end is the same.

~MARCUS AURELIUS, FOURTH LIFE OF EMPEROR NERVA

"LET ME MARK IT," Alter offered.

"No, I've got this," Sarah told him.

Alter was a runesmith, an expert at designing runes, marking them onto living flesh, and activating them by virtue of his rounon gift. That soul power somehow allowed runes to bond to the soul of the person who wore them.

He'd helped Sarah design her first rune, a beautiful, custom symbol that had turned out to be the same design Eirene had developed generations ago while living under cover among the hunters for one of her many lifetimes.

"Figure it out, children," Eirene said, her eyes beginning to glow.

Alter was the expert, but Sarah intended to give Walter the healing rune she'd developed for Tomas. She felt a deep connection with that rune, and felt confident she could mark it accurately. She felt an intense desire to be the one to do it. Besides, she was already holding the scalpel.

While Eirene removed Leandro's soulmask, Sarah inscribed the complex rune into the left side of the body, just above the lowest rib. She had memorized the rune that terrifying day when it had saved Tomas' life.

With the sharp scalpel, she easily cut the skin. That day she'd cut it into Tomas' side around that ghastly knife wound, her hand had shaken so badly, she'd barely managed to complete the work. Today she worked with careful precision, with both Alter and Sofia hovering close, watching her work.

Despite feeling acutely aware of the scrutiny of the others, Sarah completed the rune just as Eirene pressed Walter's soulmask into place on Leandro's empty body.

The rune didn't look very good yet, with the lines still bleeding, but Sarah pressed Alter's hand over the mark. "Hurry."

Alter sighed and focused over the mark. The skin of his hand grew hot against hers. She'd never held his hand while he activated a rune and was fascinated to feel that there was a physical effect of using his rounon gift. She wished she could feel more, feel the process of bonding the rune to the soul. She loved studying runes, but hated that she was still an outsider to the heart of the process.

There was no guarantee it would work. Many souls lacked the fortitude to bond runes, but she suspected Walter did. The skin of the blank skull flowed over the soulmask as it fused with the underlying bone structure, altering the shape of the skull slightly to best fit the new owner.

The face shook like water in a pond on a windy day for a moment. Eirene maintained her hold for several additional seconds, smoothing the connection between the soulmask and the host body, erasing the scarring, wrinkles, and bumps along the jawline and forehead that often resulted from slight misalignment to a new host.

Sarah and the rest of the team held Walter down as he began to shake. Bonding a soul to a new body could be a traumatic experience. The first time Sarah had experienced a new bonding without first having been tranquilized had been an overwhelming experience. Every muscle, every nerve had clamored for attention as her soul took possession.

Walter only shook for a few seconds. His mind was still asleep, easing the transfer. Plus, he'd only been dispossessed for a short time. The longer the dispossession, the harder the transition.

Sarah bumped Alter with her shoulder. "That wasn't so bad, was it?"

"I don't know how you talk me into these things," Alter grumbled.

"Because you can't resist me."

She had intended it as a light-hearted tease, but his expression changed and she easily read his desire. Standing so close, she became far too aware of their proximity and edged away.

Alter leaned after her. He'd been attracted to her since the first day they'd met and had resented her deepening relationship with Tomas. Usually he kept his feelings in check while studying runes or sparring with her, but they were always there, simmering just under the surface.

By the time Walter blinked his eyes open, Eirene had already pressed Leandro's soulmask onto Walter's recently-vacated, younger body.

"How are you feeling?" Sofia asked as she helped Walter sit up.

He took stock of his elderly frame and grinned. "I feel old. It's wonderful."

Leandro woke up a few seconds later and shouted with the joy of renewed youth. "This is amazing!"

"Enjoy it, son," Walter said.

Leandro pumped his hand, then swept Sarah off her feet into a twirling embrace. "You're my angel deliverer!"

Sarah avoided the kiss he tried to plant on her lips, letting him peck her cheek instead. He was taking to his new youth with style.

"I'm glad you're satisfied," Eirene said as Alter approached, looking like he wanted to punch the young-old man for handling Sarah like that.

"Thank you, doctor!" Leandro hugged Eirene too. "If you ever need anything—*anything*—call me."

"I'll remember that," Eirene said with a gracious smile.

"I mean it. I'll be traveling the world for the next few weeks, but call me any time."

After he left, laughing with the joy of new vitality, Tomas wheeled Gladys in to see Walter. Sarah met Tomas' gaze and gave him the smile she reserved only for him. He grinned back and winked.

"Oh, Walter, you look wonderful," Gladys exclaimed.

He stood to show off his new form. "Hey, what's with the glowing tattoo?"

The healing rune on his side was glowing blue-white. Sarah silently exulted and smiled her thanks to Alter. Sometimes runes took hours or even days to bond. That the bond came so quickly was a good sign.

"It'll fade soon," Sarah told him.

Gladys said, "I'm glad you only have one tattoo. That last body was covered with them."

"This one is a symbol of your commitment to each other," Sarah explained, and on one level that was true. "It'll help you return to a normal life. In fact, I recommend you get one too," she added to Gladys.

"What would I do with a tattoo?" Gladys chuckled, waving away the suggestion.

"Trust me, this will help," Sarah pressed. Gladys was in poor health. The upgraded healing rune wouldn't reverse aging, but it could ensure several more good years at least.

Eirene gave Sarah a warning look and Alter ground his teeth together. She ignored them both. This was her moment. She felt close to this wonderful old couple and she wanted to help them. If she could see one family restored to a better place after so much struggle and horror, it would help her cope.

The old couple exchanged questioning looks as Sofia took Gladys' pulse. She said, "In my professional opinion, the tattoo Sarah is offering will not cause harm, and might indeed become a symbol of your renewed commitment to each other."

That seemed to help ease Gladys' worry. Walter took her hand. "Sarah's responsible for everything we've achieved today. I trust her."

"Oh, Walter, of course you're right," Gladys said.

Sarah didn't waste a moment. With the help of a willing Tomas and a scowling Alter, she eased Gladys onto a gurney and took out her scalpel.

"Wait, I thought tattoos were made with little needles," Gladys protested.

Sarah said, "This is different. The tattoo is a medical symbol and needs to be inscribed differently. It won't hurt much. Please trust me."

Gripping her husband's hand, she nodded. Sofia again stepped in to help, distracting Gladys by checking her blood pressure while Sarah carefully marked the same healing rune. Gladys barely winced.

Sarah pressed a cloth over the symbol and felt it clearly against her skin, as if she could sense the marks through the fabric. That was a first, and she love it and took it as a good sign.

A sudden feeling of exhaustion surprised her. She hadn't realized how much of an emotional toll the moment would take on her.

The feeling passed quickly, and Alter joined her beside Gladys. After a final angry look, he raised his hand to the symbol. Sarah removed the cloth, and just as Alter touched the symbol, it blazed with blue-white light.

Gladys gasped.

Walter exclaimed, "What is it, dear? Does it hurt?"

"No. I feel good. Better than I have in ages." Gladys laughed and gripped Sarah's hand. "Oh my dear, what did you do?"

Sarah said, "There are some proprietary components to the procedure, but I'm glad you're feeling so good already."

After the two of them left, Sarah gripped Alter's hand. "See? Wasn't that wonderful?"

His smile had faded to a thoughtful look.

"Is it so hard to admit this was a good thing?" Sarah asked. Tomas moved to her side and she slipped an arm around his waist, happy to feel him beside her.

Alter spoke, his voice distracted. "It's not that. The rune activated too soon. I barely touched it."

"You're more efficient than you thought," Sarah teased.

"Maybe. But I hadn't even started concentrating over it."

Eirene said, "Well, your rounon was already active. You'd just used it on Walter."

"Maybe that's it." He didn't look convinced.

Tomas clapped him on the shoulder. "Don't worry about it, Alter. Mission accomplished. Well done."

"Come on," Eirene said, linking arms with her great-grandson and leading him from the room. She had a date with Gregorios that evening, but she continuously worked the relationship with Alter with the care of a master builder.

"Thanks for all your help today," Sarah told Sofia.

"It was my great honor to witness the good you did today," Sofia said. Quentin sure knew how to find good help.

Sarah turned to Tomas and gave him an enthusiastic kiss. She loved his new look, had been thrilled to learn this muscular, godlike figure was the real Tomas. Everything about who he was now felt so right, she could have kissed him for an hour.

"I'm happy to see you too," he said when she let him breathe.

"Wasn't that awesome?" She squealed with delight and kissed him again.

"You've had a good day." He wrapped an arm around her shoulders as they headed out of the room.

"How was yours?" she asked.

"It's looking up. We've got a fix on that heka woman we've been tracking. We're going to pick her up in the morning."

Tomas was captain of the Tenth, the facetakers' elite company of enforcers with origins dating all the way back to the days of Julius Caesar. They had been hunting members of Mai Luan's heka cell ever since the explosion a couple weeks ago.

"That's wonderful. Let's get some dinner."

"You're coming tomorrow. I need some cover. You're it."

"Are you saying I'm fat?" she teased with mock severity.

"Not that kind of cover," he apologized quickly. "You're my date."

"I'll be your date tomorrow, but only if you take me out tonight. I feel like celebrating."

"Deal."

3

The arrogant Romans regard us as a tumultus of slaves, lacking nobility and generosity of spirit. They shall learn to their dismay that honor is won not only in the arena. When my sword strikes down the legion that disparages my very existence, my glory will eclipse that of the pompous Glaber. Rome will quake with fear, and Eirene shall rue the day she took my Iltea's life. I will be avenged!

~SPARTACUS

EIRENE STOOD at the top of the steps leading into the imposing temple of Summanus, facing north across ancient Rome. The early morning light outlined in sharp relief the other grand buildings clustered atop the peak of Palatine Hill. The nearby Capitoline Hill was still visible, but most of the distant Quirinal Hill was obscured by a dark pall of smoke.

The dream was very old, but still as sharp as a dagger in her mind. It usually started in a different moment, but she recognized it as soon as she took in the panoramic view of the ancient skyline the day the eternal city fell.

That and the distinctive feel of Iltea's face layered over her own.

"They have breached the wall, just as your augury predicted."

Flamen Titus stood to her left. He wore the battle garb of the priests of Summanus, with the addition of the dyed black crest that proclaimed him flamen. In honor of the day, Eirene wore a hooded, crimson robe and black leather mask. He was wise enough not to ask about it.

"It was no augury," Eirene said through her layered sets of lips. That day had been the first time she had attempted to wear another soulmask atop her own and it proved a challenge.

Titus shrugged. "Do not disparage your gifts, priestess."

He always addressed her with strict formality. It was the best way to pressure her to respond in kind. He was the youngest facetaker and his ambitions blinded him to the truth of his appointment as high priest.

"It was simple logic. I knew Spartacus' supporters would find a way to open a gate. It was just a matter of time," Eirene said.

"As you say, Priestess."

Eirene barely paid attention to the conversation, one she had re-lived hundreds of times. This time she was actually looking forward to the upcoming confrontation. Vanquishing her oldest enemy always soothed her nerves.

Your very breath defiles my lips. Iltea's mind-voice growled with hatred in Eirene's head.

Cease interfering or you'll die knowing he was only moments away.

The Thracian woman's consciousness faded to sullen silence. She had fought savagely to reclaim her lost body when Eirene first restored enough connection to allow the flesh to seal over their stacked soul-masks. Although Iltea had been born in the body, Eirene had worn it far longer. Still, the struggle had been taxing.

A lower priest rushed up the steps to report. "The Visigoth hordes are approaching at speed."

Titus spared a surprised glance at her. Despite how many times they re-lived the moment, it always amazed her that he never believed their temple would be singled out during the sacking of the city. Then again, for him it was always the first time he faced the nightmare.

She had seen Rome fall more times than she cared to count. Modern historians considered it an example of a restrained event, but they had not lived it. There would be nothing restrained about the upcoming confrontation.

In less than half an hour, even as most of the Visigoths still pillaged around the distant Salarian Gate, a force of over one hundred heavy infantry approached at a quick trot. At their head ran a powerful figure who she recognized instantly, despite the distance.

Spartacus.

Their animosity spanned centuries, all the way back to the waning days of the republic. Their struggle in many ways defined the history of Rome.

Today during his victorious conquest, she would finally vanquish him.

Iltea's consciousness surged against Eirene's restraints as the woman caught sight of her long-separated love. *It's him! Oh I've missed him.*

Eirene squashed the resistance. *Keep to our agreement and he will live.*

The woman quieted, but her powerful emotions still radiated across the connection to Eirene's mind. The heat of her love boiled like the heart of Mount Vesuvius. That pure emotion was the reason Iltea still lived.

Eirene was a sucker for a good love story.

Better yet, it would prove the downfall of both of the Thracians.

Eirene smiled as she slipped back across the wide portico supported by Corinthian columns of delicate white marble. The first volley from catapults concealed in outbuildings near the base of the steps launched their deadly barrage of caltrops and stone shot. Distant screams confirmed the hits.

She stopped in the grand entrance and surveyed her forces. Although lacking the glory of earlier days before the Christians began usurping power from the elder gods, the temple to Summanus still demanded respect. More than its high granite walls or columned porticoes, the reputation of the priests of the god of nocturnal thunder ensured continuing devotion.

Unlike standard legionnaires, her forces wore armor of alternating plates of black leather and iron, fastened in overlapping horizontal sheets. White lightning bolts ran across the shoulders and down both arms. They wore simple iron helms and carried rounded parma shields painted black, with crisscrossed lightning bolts.

If any other force of forty-eight soldiers faced Spartacus and his enhanced century, they would be destroyed in minutes. Even her well-trained force was destined to fall, but they would make it a Pyrrhic victory, whose importance would be lost to history.

None of it mattered. All of their sacrifice was but the backdrop for the real contest.

As the Summanus devotees moved forward to take positions at the top of the steps, Eirene scaled a rope ladder to a wooden platform concealed in the shadows atop the fifty-foot columns. Each of the nineteen raised platforms held four sagittarii, bows at the ready, arrows already knocked.

Eirene crouched beside one young archer who quivered with eagerness to join the fray. The air up there smelled of clean marble and wisps of lingering smoke from last night's cook fires.

Spartacus' forces had passed the catapults and begun to climb the steps, rectangular scutum shields at the ready to ward off the expected missile barrage. She frowned as she scanned their lines. Every other time she had returned to this memory in her dreams, the catapults had winnowed a full tenth of the attackers. Not this time.

Spartacus led at the center of the front rank, a powerful presence that drew the eye. Most superstitious citizens would attribute the almost-tangible weight of his presence to the favor of his patron god, Quirinus.

They knew nothing of his singular enhancements. He pointed at Titus with his signature oaken spear and his enhanced barbarians howled battle cries and surged up the long granite steps.

They were armored much the same as any Roman legion, with breastplates or chainmail coats. In addition to the scutum shields, many carried thrusting spears known as hasta. The rest waved swords over their heads. Those swords were half a foot longer than the typical Roman gladius and were much preferred by the barbarians.

"Pilum and martiobarbuli," Eirene ordered, her voice calm.

Her caller, who perched on the ladder just below her platform, whistled four sharp notes.

Battle priests all down the line at the top of the steps launched their javelins or barbed darts at the onrushing horde. Spartacus, who carried no shield, batted several missiles out of the air with his thick-hafted spear. Many of his men were not so lucky.

Most of the javelins were blocked by raised shields, but still served their purpose. They were designed to drive into the shields before the shaft broke off, leaving the heavy iron head embedded and nearly impossible to remove. The weight made the shields unwieldy and more than a few frustrated Visigoths dropped them instead of dealing with the hindrance.

The lead-weighted darts proved more deadly. They could be thrown much farther than the pilum, and with fantastic accuracy. The barbed tips pierced faces, necks and legs, and soldiers fell screaming from the ranks. Many of those men would cut the darts free or simply rip them from their flesh, trusting to their tattoo-like runes to heal them before blood loss claimed them.

Strangely, as the two forces closed, and despite the many fallen from Spartacus' host, the barbarian lines looked undiminished.

Time to change the odds.

Eirene spoke again. "Sagittarii."

Two shrill, whistled notes. Composite bows thrummed from the concealed raised platforms. Arrows whistled down past Titus and his force and drove into the unsuspecting barbarians just four strides below the top of the steps. The front ranks of Spartacus' force wilted under the onslaught. He caught five shafts himself, although three of them glanced off his heavy armor. One drove deep into his left bicep and the other gashed his neck.

That was unusual. Always before, Spartacus was struck in the arm only.

No! Iltea shrieked. *You said he'd live!*

He's not dead yet, but if you don't remain silent, that will change.

She didn't usually have trouble shielding her thoughts from Iltea. This time Titus did not wait for her to whistle the next order. He led the charge that descended upon Spartacus' confused mass of barbarians in a coordinated strike. Spears and swords drove into the barbarians and cut down the second line.

Instead of pressing the advantage, Titus' little army retreated back through the portico, leaving three dozen barbarians dead or wounded. Eirene descended the ladder with the sagittarii and led the retreat. Her movements were a little jerky as Iltea fought against her control.

You lied to me! All we ever wanted was freedom.

Then you should have taken more care who you believed, Eirene retorted, severing all but the final shred of connection between Iltea's soulmask and their combined form. *Lies can never set you free.*

Iltea fought with greater determination than usual. By the time Eirene regained her composure, the enemy had already re-formed ranks and advanced into the portico, their numbers again restored.

That was definitely wrong. It was as if someone was tampering with her dream, even though she wasn't walking this memory through the machine. That meant her own mind was twisting the memory. Why would she do that? The question unnerved her more than she cared to admit.

There was no time to figure it out. Time to bring this dream to an end. Eirene spoke a command. Despite a look of surprise, her caller whistled the order.

Titus looked angry, but he obeyed. Their little army abandoned their positions and retreated again, across the outer sanctum and through the wide doors on either end of the heavy, interior partition wall. The outer sanctum had been cleared and was little more than a rectangular room one hundred and fifty feet wide and fifty feet deep, paved with smooth tile.

Spartacus and his forces gave chase and, despite her concern about the twisting of the dream, Eirene still paused to enjoy the next part.

Four ballistae were waiting in the doorways. As soon as her forces flowed past, the giant crank crossbows fired five-foot shafts as thick as her forearm. They missed Spartacus but shattered at least twelve of his men.

Screams echoed in the empty sanctum and the scent of fresh-spilled blood filled the temple. As the assault faltered, Eirene drew her small force to the far end of the inner sanctum. They could have held the doors for a while, but none of that mattered. She felt irritated and wanted to finish it.

The inner sanctum was a huge vaulted room lined with more columns and paved with an intricate mosaic in the form of their god with lightning bolts raised. Eirene's forces gathered on the final set of stairs that led up to the immense propylaeum, the gateway to the secret heart of the temple that only priests were allowed to enter. It was upon those grand steps that her force would make their last stand.

Eirene moved off to the side and breathed deep to settle her mind. Despite the strange alterations to the dream, she knew what to do and the outcome would not change. The air held a hint of roses above the ever-present incense that Titus insisted on burning just because this was a temple.

Spartacus' forces charged across the huge open expanse, howling like barbarian berserkers. In his greatest moment of glory, Titus led the counter-charge. He had embraced his nevra core to motivate his troops and instill fear in his enemies. His eyes burned with purple fire and flames danced along his fingers.

Sagittarii filled the air between the forces with waves of arrows, while the relocated ballistae blasted enemies off their feet. Screams rent the air and echoed endlessly in the cavernous space, while the copper scent of blood clung to everything. The armies came together with a crash of bodies and they began hacking at each other with wild abandon.

Eirene ignored all of that and focused on Spartacus, who had detached himself and approached with an implacable stride, oaken spear half-raised. His eyes remained fastened on her mask.

"You cannot conceal yourself from me, daughter of the gorgons."

"Concealing was never my intention."

And thus I bequeath my promised gift.

Eirene unfastened her crimson robe and let it fall. Beneath it, she wore only a leather halter-top and short skirt. The outfit left her midriff, arms and legs bare. The silvery runes inscribed on her flesh glowed bright in the dim light.

The sight of his beloved always drove Spartacus to impetuous fury. "You have dishonored her too long!"

He charged, spear raised to deliver the killing blow.

Eirene removed her mask and loosened her hold on Iltea's soulmask.

"Spartacus, my love!"

His assault faltered and he stumbled to a halt just out of reach. His spear fell to his side and he gazed with incredulous joy at the face of his beloved.

"Can it be?"

He took a faltering step forward.

"I've missed you!" Iltea cried. Eirene allowed Iltea to rush them forward and embrace her long-separated husband. He wrapped them in his arms and kissed her fiercely.

That was the worst part.

Although his lips didn't really touch hers, Eirene still felt the pressure of them on Iltea's, felt the woman's rising passion burning against her soul.

I told you I'd reunite you. She sent the thought to Iltea, then seized control again.

Their body convulsed and Spartacus drew back just enough for Eirene to grab his face while embracing her nevra core.

She ejected Iltea's soulmask. Since they shared the same body, ejecting it took only a fraction of her focus. The flesh of her face flowed back, allowing it to slip free. Spartacus gaped and grabbed for it as it began to fall. The rainbow mist of her soulmask caressed his powerful hands.

Eirene dug into the skin under his jaw with hands burning with the purple fire of her nevron. She had realized in the final years leading up to the fall of Rome this one way to defeat Spartacus. It had taken a long time to orchestrate the perfect moment.

Some things were worth the wait.

"Together you will greet the eternities."

She drove her nevron into his soul. His eyes widened in terror, but she owned him now.

Then for the first time, she didn't.

Instead of extracting his soulmask as she had hundreds of times before, something blocked the soul strength of Eirene's nevron. The invisible force formed a protective barrier around his soul.

Spartacus snarled and lifted Eirene off the ground with one hand. His enhanced strength was terrifying. With his other hand, he held aloft his wife's soulmask. It was glowing like quicksilver.

Eirene gasped. He was using the life force of his beloved to fuel a new rune, one with the power to hold Eirene at bay.

"Thus do we, united, take our revenge!"

He dropped Iltea's soulmask and, even as the protective barrier around his soul began to fade, he drove a dagger up through Eirene's jaw. Pain exploded through her as Spartacus sawed with the dagger, severing her face from Iltea's body.

She couldn't stop him.

He thrust his face close to hers. "Your world is about to end."

Eirene snapped awake as she tumbled out of bed, hands burning with purple fire. The cool night air of her own room in modern-day Rome caressed her sweat-soaked skin. It took several gasping breaths to calm her racing heart.

She sagged back onto the bed and fingered her jaw where the dream knife had driven into her skull. Nothing like that had ever happened before.

On the other side of the bed, Gregorios was sitting up and wiping sleep-rimmed eyes. "You all right, love?"

"I'm not sure. I had a new nightmare."

That woke him up. "What happened?"

"Spartacus."

He grimaced. "I hate that man."

She spread her hands and shrugged. "Nightmare, remember?"

"Thinking about him is going to ruin my day."

She flopped onto her face to allow him to massage her back. Her knotted muscles slowly released under his practiced touch. Then he slid his hands further and her lingering worry from the nightmare faded to new emotion.

She rolled over and pulled him down for a passionate kiss.

She gave him that special smile a minute later. "Let's think about something else, shall we?"

Gregorios grinned, and she decided to forget about the strange dream.

After all, it was just a nightmare.

4

The soul is the captain and ruler of the life of mortals.

~SALLUST, ROMAN HISTORIAN, 40 BC

"THIS IS GREAT," Sarah gushed as she exited a cramped taxi and joined Tomas on the curb.

On the far side of a wide plaza filled with picture-snapping tourists reared the Colosseum. The ancient ruin still awed with its sheer size and lingering hints of former glory.

Tomas chuckled as he paid the driver then took her hand. "You never get tired of it, do you?"

"Are you kidding? I'd visit every day if I could."

She had taken the Colosseum tour three times, and every time she learned something new. A sense of history hung over the ancient structure so thick she could taste it.

She decided it would taste like gelato.

"Well I'm glad we could combine work and pleasure," Tomas said.

That was a nice way to remind her to focus. She kept her smile on her lips and a little bounce in her step, but began to scan the plaza like he had taught her. Before they crossed half the huge expanse, she had already picked out most of Tomas' team, and their mark.

The suspected heka was a woman of average height who blended in with her Mediterranean good looks. She wore cotton slacks, and a light jacket that hid any telltale runes and concealed any potential weapons.

The enforcers were surprisingly easy to spot. None of them had been clever enough to bring along girlfriends, and they really should have. Not that they were overt in any major way, but she was learning what to look for. They were dressed like rather conservative tourists, with closed camera cases that did not hold cameras. They moved independently through the crowds, converging on the Colosseum. The problem was that a bunch of young, buff, good-looking guys wandering the square alone drew the eye.

She worried the mark would spot them as easily as she had. Sarah had to admit Tomas looked like a captain. Simple tourist clothes failed to conceal his broad shoulders and well-muscled torso, and the two of them drew more than a few admiring stares. She had dressed simply in Capri slacks and a blue cotton blouse, but she had not been a top-ten model for nothing.

The mark didn't change pace or direction, but joined the crowd pouring into the Colosseum's many entrances. The intel on her was supposed to be pretty solid. Tomas and his team had been trailing her for the past couple of days, and had planned to capture her at a more remote location. When she'd headed for the Colosseum instead, Tomas had decided to close in, despite the risk of a confrontation.

"She doesn't look like she's running," Sarah commented.

"We can't lose her," Tomas replied.

Three weeks ago, they had defeated Mai Luan in a terrifying memory battle in the secret lower levels of Hitler's World War Two Berlin bunker. Since then, they had not apprehended any of the cui dashi's escaped team. The bomb that had destroyed part of the secret facetaker headquarters building and killed several of the aged council members had facilitated the heka team's escape.

Pressure was growing to run the heka to ground. There were unanswered questions about Mai Luan's activities, and worry that surviving members of her team might possess dangerous information. Tomas wouldn't normally risk a run-in with police, but they needed this capture. They didn't have any other good leads.

Sarah didn't like referring to the nameless woman as "the mark." It was too impersonal. She decided to think of her as Rosetta, after an infamous female mob boss.

Sarah and Tomas entered the Colosseum about a hundred feet behind Rosetta, with the rest of the team trailing, spread throughout the crowd. Most of the eight-man team would remain positioned near the various entrances in case Rosetta lost Sarah and Tomas and tried to escape. One of the two enforcers flanking Tomas and Sarah was Anaru, the hulking Maori who served as Tomas' scowling second.

Sarah patted the small can of mace in one of her pockets. It was more a feel-good weapon than anything. All of the enforcers carried dart pistols powered by quiet compressed air that delivered fast-acting sleep drugs.

Undoubtedly they all carried traditional firearms too, but if Rosetta was as enhanced as they suspected, normal bullets would not easily stop her. The plan was to drug her and whisk her away before the effects wore off. A second team of enforcers, dressed like paramedics, was standing by.

For a tense minute, they lost sight of Rosetta in the press. The Colosseum was one of the most famous landmarks in Rome and eager tourists packed the plaza and crowded the entrances. The chorus of voices was a constant din, a melody of many tongues, making a counterpoint to the sing-song speech of the many Italian tour guides. The air in the packed passages smelled of clashing colognes and perfumes, overlaid upon the scent of old stone and sweat.

Tomas was just starting to issue orders to his dispersed team through their tiny, radio ear pieces when Sarah grabbed his arm. Rosetta had slipped through the crowd and stood at the rail of the observation platform on the western side of the inner arena, overlooking the ruins of the lower levels. That was Sarah's favorite place to stand and imagine what the amphitheater must have looked like all those centuries ago.

She had not yet visited the Colosseum in its heyday, but it was on her to-do list.

"We have her cornered," Tomas said softly as he and Sarah closed on Rosetta, who was staring out at the ruin like any other tourist. "Moving in for first contact."

Sarah's pulse increased as they drew near. The few times she had faced Mai Luan or one of the rune-enhanced heka had all been terrifying.

The last few weeks of heavy training with Tomas and Alter had given her a solid foundation of close combat skills, while her own unique enhancement rune provided another edge. It increased her strength, speed, and reflexes to the point where she could nearly hold her own against her far stronger and more experienced sparring partners.

At that moment, knowing all that didn't help as much as she had hoped. As her tension mounted, Sarah slipped a hand into her pocket and fingered the ancient Spanish silver piece of eight that Eirene had gifted to her. The pirate silver, a relic of the swashbuckling life Eirene spent sailing the Caribbean, had become a good luck charm for Sarah and helped center her mind for the upcoming action.

Tomas eased a hand into his camera case and moved into position just a few feet behind Rosetta. He would fire the dart through the specially designed outer shell of the case once he got around one final fat French lady. When Rosetta collapsed, they would call the paramedics and be gone before anyone realized the truth.

Everything was falling perfectly into place.

That should have tipped her off.

Rosetta turned and looked Tomas right in the eye.

Sarah's heart nearly stopped. Rosetta had known they were there. Had she been planning a trap of her own? Sarah had seen enhanced heka charge through a hail of bullets and still attack with terrifying strength. Rosetta could turn the quiet platform full of unsuspecting tourists into a deadly battleground.

She did not.

She leaped over the rail.

Tomas lunged to catch her, but missed by a fraction of an inch. Tourists around them cried out in alarm, and everyone rushed to the rail to see the woman fall.

Rosetta was already running. She headed left, between a pair of ancient, crumbling walls that curved away and provided cover if Tomas or his team decided to fire down on her.

Tomas remained remarkably calm. "We're blown. Engaging in pursuit."

He vaulted the rail.

Even as more tourists gasped, Sarah leaped after him. One helpful fellow tried to grab her arm and pull her back. She avoided his grasping hand and pushed off against his arm.

The look of shock on his face was priceless.

Sarah exulted in the weightless free-fall. It was like bungee jumping, but without the hassle of the safety rope. They were committed now. They had to take Rosetta, and fast. The polizia would swarm the area in minutes and haul them all off to prison if they didn't escape.

Sarah landed hard but caught herself on enhanced legs. Having even temporary enhancement runes was simply awesome. Plus, she had wanted an excuse to explore the lower levels of the Colosseum since the first time she visited.

Ignoring the tumult of alarmed tourists and enraged tour guides on the platform above, Sarah ran after Tomas, who was already sprinting after Rosetta. They raced down the curved lane, but Rosetta had disappeared. Tomas slowed and Sarah caught up to him.

"I need a visual," he said into his earpiece.

The ancient stone wall to their right creaked ominously and an eight foot section broke free and fell toward them.

Sarah dove into a forward roll, bounced to her feet, and turned back.

Tomas had caught the wall.

His muscles stood out in sharp relief as he strained to keep the heavy wall from crushing him. Sarah had known he was inhumanly strong, but she hadn't realized just how much strength he could bring to bear.

"Don't you realize how old this place is?" Tomas grunted as he heaved the loose section of wall back up into place.

Sarah had been so surprised by the unexpected attack she hadn't thought through the ramifications of fighting down here. They had to get Rosetta before she wrecked the priceless historic landmark.

Rosetta barked a laugh from the far side of the wall and a dull thud echoed through. Again the wall began to fall and Tomas braced it.

"I'm really starting to hate her," he muttered.

Sarah ran for the first rough doorway in the wall. She jumped through and sprinted back up the far side. It was time to teach Rosetta a lesson on civic responsibility.

Rosetta was gone.

Sarah ran past the section of broken wall, back toward the observation platform where tourists madly snapped photos of Tomas' heroic efforts to save the ancient wall.

A chorus of startled cries from the platform gave Sarah her only warning. She dove forward again and just barely avoided Rosetta, who dropped from above. Rosetta slammed her leading knee into the ground so hard it sunk three inches into the packed soil. She must have leaped right over the wall.

Up close, Rosetta looked more intimidating. Although she stood several inches shorter than Sarah, she wore an expression of such hatred, it twisted her features into an ugly scowl.

Rosetta stalked forward, speaking in a heavy Italian accent. "I kill you now and leave present for your boyfriend."

Sarah punched her in the throat.

She caught Rosetta by surprise and the blow staggered the woman back, gagging. Sarah pressed her advantage and tackled Rosetta to the ground. The two grappled and jabbed at each other with fists, elbows, and knees. Rosetta struggled like an insane cat to free herself, while Sarah tried to hold her down until Tomas could arrive.

The woman was wearing a surprisingly gentle fragrance that clashed with her enhanced strength and the steady stream of Italian profanities she shrieked as she fought. Sarah raked Rosetta's back, feeling for the concealed pack many heka wore containing the dispossessed soulmask they consumed to fuel their enhancements. She was surprised to feel nothing.

"I'm coming!" Anaru, the giant Maori enforcer landed nearby with a thud that shook the arena. He charged and filled the entire passage. He'd be able to collar Rosetta like an unruly kitten.

Rosetta gouged a nail into Sarah's eye. She jerked away, cupping her face to protect it from the excruciating pain.

Rosetta kicked her so hard she launched into the air right into Anaru's path, tripping him. He fell onto her like a tree trunk, nearly crushing her.

"Sorry." He hoisted her up, but it took a few seconds for her vision to clear. Despite the strength of her enhancement, her body ached from the abuse.

"Where's Rosetta?"

"Who?"

"The mark."

Anaru pushed Sarah east, toward the far side. "She ran. Captain's in pursuit."

As they sped across the bottom of the Colosseum, sirens wailed outside, announcing the imminent arrival of the polizia. The sound motivated Sarah to run faster between the ruined walls of the lower level to the far side. She arrived just as Rosetta vaulted onto the top of one ruined wall and leaped from there up to the wooden decking that covered the eastern edge of the arena.

Tomas followed several seconds later, but she was already sprinting with unnatural speed toward the wide-open gate in the outer wall. It was known as the Death Gate in ancient days because funeral processions for fallen gladiators always exited there.

Tomas drew his dart pistol and fired several times.

Sarah had never seen him miss when they practiced together, but Rosetta never slowed. She did stagger a little just before rounding the outer wall and disappearing from sight. The sleep darts were extremely fast-acting and could drop even men with basic enhancements in a couple seconds.

When Sarah and Anaru reached the eastern side below that platform he asked, "May I?"

"Please."

He grabbed her by the waist and *threw* her. She soared in a graceful arc all the way up onto the wooden decking and landed running. Four seconds after she landed, the platform shook under Anaru's weight. She didn't bother to look back.

Sarah sprinted out the Death Gate, expecting to be met by a crowd of angry polizia, but the way was clear. She caught sight of at least a dozen uniformed officers pushing through the crowd at a distant gate. They must be still responding to the initial report of someone jumping off the far platform. Hopefully the delay would grant Sarah and the team enough time to bag Rosetta and get away.

Tomas was easy to spot as he sprinted through the crowd, heading west around the southern curve of the building. The bulk of the Colosseum blocked Rosetta from view.

Sarah gave chase. With her temporary enhancement, she ran faster than most Olympic sprinters, but Tomas still drew farther away. Anaru passed her, his face locked into an expression of angry determination.

Tourists scattered out of his way and Sarah followed in his wake. They rounded the Colosseum and she spotted Tomas across the long plaza, near the Arch of Constantine. He slowed to a stop and waited for Anaru and Sarah to catch up.

"Are you all right?" Tomas asked her. He didn't even look winded.

"I almost had her. Where'd she go?"

Tomas grimaced. "A car picked her up. I've already dispatched the mobile team to track it."

Anaru muttered a curse and spoke into his earpiece. "Extract. Rendezvous with mobile team."

A chorus of acknowledgments sounded from the other team members who had gotten caught in the crush of the crowd.

Anaru cast one angry look at Tomas, but suppressed it quickly. The two had been slowly developing a cordial working relationship, but Sarah wondered if Anaru would ever really get over the fact that Tomas had beaten him.

Anaru had lost the fight for leadership of the Tenth. For someone who wore his honor so tight, that had to be hard to cope with.

Tomas and Anaru discussed strategies for cornering the elusive heka while they waited for the team to arrive. Then Tomas' cell phone rang.

He listened for a moment. "On our way."

"Anaru, you're in command of the chase. Hunt her down."

The huge enforcer came to attention but managed to not salute in public.

Tomas clapped him on the shoulder then turned to Sarah. "We're needed at Suntara. The machine is ready."

Her frustration at losing Rosetta faded under a thrill of nervous excitement.

"I hope we get a happy memory this time."

5

GREGORIOS ENTERED the secure basement vault via a reinforced steel door, guarded by a pair of enforcers and biometric retinal scans. Built into the lowest level of the Suntara Group headquarters, the vault was the most secure location in the building. Moving off-site was a risk Gregorios would not accept.

The Suntara building, situated close to the Vatican and the Sistine Chapel, had housed the secret council of the global facetaker organization for centuries. The bomb that had destroyed part of the fourth floor and killed four aged members of the council had also helped kill Mai Luan. On the bad side, Gregorios had also lost a couple of experienced enforcers and an entire medical team.

The vault was a long, sparse room sheathed in gleaming stainless steel. The ten-foot ceilings sported rows of lights that kept the room painfully bright. Alter liked it that way, and his role was vital so Gregorios resisted the urge to break a few bulbs.

Two machines sat in the middle of the room. The first one, recently used in Sarah's philanthropic attempt to right the world's wrongs, gleamed in the light, its smooth steel casing unmarred. The other huddled nearby, the charred and dented casing gaping open as if it had been disemboweled. Snarled masses of wires and internal electronics threatened to spill onto the floor.

Alter crouched beside the ugly machine with the team of engineers Gregorios had assigned to help him.

"So, you've given that thing another life?" Gregorios asked as he approached.

The young hunter leaped to his feet, grinning. "Yes! We got it working."

Barely twenty-five and just starting his first life, Alter was so sure of himself Gregorios got a headache just thinking about talking with him. He stood a little over average height, with dark hair and a permanent, eager expression.

The fact that he was a hunter made things very interesting. Gregorios agreed with the clan's eternal mission to rid the world of heka and cui dashi. Their penchant for removing facetakers whenever possible complicated things.

Alter harbored a particular hatred for Gregorios after he'd left Reuben, Alter's brother, dispossessed for so many years. The decision to bring Alter to the heart of their headquarters had been difficult. Gregorios was still not entirely convinced he'd made the right choice. One more reason for the two enforcers stationed just outside the vault.

Gregorios approached the beat-up machine that Alter and his team had cobbled together from parts salvaged from the machines damaged in the bomb blast. If he ignored the battered casing, he could almost believe it would work.

They had attached a new monitor and keyboard and replaced the thick cables of twisted wires that ran from the machine to a pair of blocky helmets. The helmets were battered, scarred originals that had survived the blast.

The faceplates were intact, if blackened. The unique apparatus looked a lot like an optometrist's phoropter, but with jagged edges. When closed over the face of the one wearing the helmet, those edges dug into the skin and helped link the victim to the machine via the nevron of the facetaker who powered it.

It was an ingenious device that helped filter mental dissipation caused by too many soul transfers, and supposedly reversed soul fragmentation as well. Gregorios didn't pretend to understand exactly how the filtering worked. From what he'd learned from the surviving members of the council, Mai Luan had spent decades perfecting it.

The promise of that technology had trumped the aging council members' good sense. Mai Luan had promised them the one chance at eternal continuation of their fading lives and they'd gambled everything on that chance. That foolish choice had nearly doomed the world.

Mai Luan's secret agenda had combined that marvelous technology with a unique set of runes engraved on the machines, the helmets, and the faceplates. Those runes allowed the second helmet wearer to act as a passenger in the victim's mind and walk through their memories with them. That had been the real danger. A facetaker's memories were not things to trifle with.

Most of the machines had been destroyed in the blast, and every machine they knew about was accounted for. Still, he couldn't shake a lingering worry that someone else had access to the memory technology. That worry fueled the increasing pressure on Tomas and his team to track down the surviving heka from Mai Luan's team.

Gregorios and Eirene had taken turns testing the one good machine over the past weeks. Everything had gone smoothly and they'd brought Tomas, Alter and Sarah along as passengers in turn. Together they'd learned much about the limits and benefits of the marvelous technology, but still Gregorios worried.

On more than one occasion he could have sworn he'd felt a whisper of resistance in there. Despite all their precautions, despite exhaustive searches of the memoryscape, he'd found no solid evidence that another machine might exist. Even so, something felt not quite right. Something just beyond the periphery of his senses.

He had learned from long experience to trust his instincts. Impatient facetakers did not live many lives.

Now the second machine was on-line. Most of the team knew nothing of his vague worries, but perhaps with all of them walking a common memory he could determine if his concerns were justified or just old habits of paranoia.

The vault door opened to admit Tomas and Sarah. Her long brown hair looked a little disheveled, but on her the look just added to her allure. Sarah was tall and graceful, with perfectly proportioned curves and a beautiful face. She possessed a strong soul and remarkable bravery for a first-life girl.

Gregorios had lived over two thousand years, but a man would have to be dead and buried not to notice Sarah. It still amazed him that Tomas has snared such a catch, and wearing Carl's wimpy body at that. He'd never understand women.

But he'd always love one of them.

Eirene entered behind the two young ones and her smile affected him with undimmed intensity.

"They're ready?" Sarah asked, eagerly approaching the machines.

"Yes," Alter responded quickly.

As always, his face lit when he looked at her. He lacked the guile to attempt to hide his infatuation. So far both Sarah and Tomas had ignored the hunter's attentions, but Gregorios hoped Alter figured out soon that he didn't have a chance.

Gregorios motioned the group to him. "Well done, Alter. With two machines, we can do a full test."

"Who's going to test it?" Sarah asked.

"There are five of us but only four helmets," Eirene said.

Alter grinned. "Actually, I figured out how to add a second passenger to the original machine. The drain will be more severe, but it should work."

A new voice spoke from near the vault door. "Good thing there are more of us to share the load."

Three newcomers entered the vault and Gregorios smiled to see his children. His son led the way, wearing a fit body in its thirties, flanked by the girls, who looked stunning in forms that couldn't be more than eighteen. They always did prefer cycling lives at the same time.

Alter frowned at the newcomers and turned a questioning look on Eirene. "I thought you and Gregorios would be running the machines."

She patted his hand in a maternal way although in her current form she looked more like his older sister than his great-grandmother. Despite Alter's lingering hatred for Gregorios and facetakers in general, he had become devoted to her.

She gave him a warm smile. "If we ran the machines, whose memories would we walk?"

Alter gave that a moment's thought. "But can we trust them?"

Gregorios smiled. "Who can you trust if not family?"

"Of course. I thought they looked familiar," Sarah said with a grin.

He should have expected her to figure it out. She was a quick study, and her sensitivity to runes and facetakers was unrivaled for a non-gifted soul.

"Correct," Gregorios said, extending a hand toward the newcomers. "I'd like to introduce our children."

Bastien made an extravagant bow, a habit he'd picked up centuries ago at the French court, and planted a kiss on Sarah's hand. "Enchante, mademoiselle."

Even Sarah appeared impressed by Bastien's suave demeanor. He'd always been good with the ladies.

Francesca and Harriett waved to Gregorios, embraced their mother, hugged Tomas, and were soon chatting with Sarah like old friends.

Harriett shared around pieces of her newest pie creation. Chocolate hazelnut toffee cream. Gregorios declined a piece, but the others soon learned why her pies had been loved for decades. Within minutes, everyone but Alter seemed at ease.

Scowling, he ate three slices.

He looked like he wanted to run for his gun with so many demons in one room, but he couldn't kill any of them yet. He should have thought of that when he agreed to work there.

Sarah turned to Eirene. "So when facetakers have kids, they inherit your powers?"

"Not usually. No one knows exactly how the talent passes from one generation to the next. The council launched several studies over the years, but we still can't determine when and how people are born with active nevra cores. It seems completely random."

Gregorios said, "There has to be an underlying reason. Our bloodlines do seem to give us a little bit of a higher statistical average."

Alter seemed intrigued by the conversation despite himself. "But you sired three demons."

Francesca picked up on his word choice and sauntered closer to Alter, a sparkle in her eyes. "Ooh, we've got a hunter in the house. The last couple hunters I met I had to spank with their own guns to make them behave."

Alter stammered, red-faced, unable to figure out a fitting response.

Gregorios rescued him. "He's part of the team, Francesca, so no spanking."

"Pity," she said with a lingering gaze over the flustered young man. Alter was in for an entirely different kind of test of his hatred for facetakers if Francesca decided to take an interest in him.

"And yes, Alter, we did sire three children with active nevra cores," Gregorios added to return the conversation to topic. "By playing the odds."

Eirene added, "We had lots of kids."

"How many?" Sarah asked.

Gregorios shrugged. "I lost count centuries ago."

Eirene punched him on the arm. "Liar. Let's just say it's a pretty big number."

"Like how big?" Tomas prodded.

Gregorios slipped a hand around Eirene's waist. "How many kids do you think you could have over the course of seventy lifetimes?"

Sarah gaped. She was still early in her first life, trying to decide if a relationship with Tomas was going to work out. Who knew when she'd start her first marriage? Seventy was probably more than she could comprehend.

"Receptions get old," Gregorios added.

Eirene punched him again, but the blow lacked strength since he still held her in the crook of his arm.

He leaned close to her. "But always worth it."

"Oh, please," Harriett said with mock dismay. "Will you two cut it out?"

Bastien gave Eirene a hug, then lifted Gregorios off the floor in turn. "It is good to see you, Father."

"It's been too long, Son," Gregorios agreed.

During the decades he'd been on the run from the council, he'd seen little of his family. Keeping his distance had helped them stay safe. Seeing them all reunited filled him with a sense of *rightness* that had been absent too often from his last life.

The girls finally got around to hugging him, and Gregorios wrapped them both in his arms. "Dinner tonight's on me. We've got too much catching up to do."

"I choose the restaurant," Harriett said immediately, which started an argument about the venue.

Gregorios let them work it out, smiling to see their good-natured bantering. He noticed Sarah had taken Tomas' hand, and the captain was looking a bit nervous, as he had more often of late.

Alter looked like he wasn't sure how to react to demons acting like normal people. He frowned again, turning to Eirene. "So my great grandfather..."

She took his arm. "He got a lifetime all his own."

"How does that work?" Sarah asked. Then she blushed as if realizing how personal that question was.

Eirene wasn't fazed. Little could faze her. "We look at our lives differently than even most other facetakers. I believe it's what's helped keep our faculties from dissipating as quickly."

"I think loving you just keeps me young," Gregorios said.

She winked at him. "Each lifetime we choose to commit to each other, we hold those vows sacred. When our responsibilities force us to take actions that might invalidate those vows, we begin a new life, one in which we have not made that commitment."

"But you're still you?" Sarah looked uncomfortable with the idea.

Gregorios explained, "It's a matter of perspective. We choose to take the view that some moral obligations are tied to the life of the body. Others are linked to the soul."

"That doesn't make sense," Alter said.

"Think about it, dear." Eirene patted his hand. "It will eventually."

"Know the difference. Stay true in each life, and things work out," Gregorios said.

Sarah asked, "But what did you do if you didn't like what you looked like in one of those lives?"

Gregorios shrugged. "Never happened."

Eirene added, "One thing most first-life mortals don't realize is that the body doesn't really matter. It's the soul that endures. It's the soul that counts. That's the fount of a person's true beauty."

Sarah grew thoughtful, and Tomas turned their attention back to the mission at hand. They quickly agreed that Bastien would power the gleaming Sotrun machine and the girls would take the Franken-machine, linked with a power-sharing rune.

"And we'll see if we can get both machines to work together and drop us into a shared memory," Eirene added.

She moved toward the Franken-machine. She had reached the same unspoken realization as Gregorios. Better she test that one first. Alter would be motivated to keep her safe instead of being tempted to allow an "accident" to dispose of Gregorios.

Sarah and Tomas joined Gregorios next to the Sotrun III machine. Alter joined Eirene next to the Franken-machine. They arranged reclining chairs around the machines and settled back.

Bastien, the oldest of the facetaker children, and Francesca, who was several hundred years his junior, began preparing the helmets. She paid particular attention to Alter, who looked uncomfortable with her hovering close by his head.

Sarah asked, "Who's picking the memory?"

"I will, dear," Eirene said.

"Please make it a good one."

"But not too good. We don't want to get distracted again," Tomas added.

"Hey, Ksiaz Castle was a good memory," Gregorios protested. He'd planned that trip especially for Sarah.

"It was," Sarah agreed quickly.

"I'll take care of everything," Eirene said. She glanced at Gregorios. "I always loved Florence in the spring."

"Sounds good to me." If his suspicions were groundless, they'd still have a great time.

If not, it would prove an excellent place to hunt.

6

That men do not learn very much from the lessons of history is the most important of all the lessons that history has to teach. The rest is facetaker propaganda.

~ALDOUS HUXLEY

SARAH HATED THE FACEPLATE.

Francesca, in her trim, teen-aged body, gave her a reassuring smile before folding the phoropter-like plate into position. The jagged inner edges dug at Sarah's face around the eyes and along the line of her jaw, as if they were clawed extensions of a facetaker hand.

She shivered. It still amazed her that she had lain unawares under facetaker powers hundreds of times without seeing through the smokescreen of the technology.

"Engaging the machine now." Bastien spoke with a smooth French accent that helped ease Sarah's worries. She should try to get Tomas to talk to her in a voice like that some time, maybe over dinner.

A humming filled the dark helmet as the machines came to life. An acrid smell tickled her nose, then the cool metal of the faceplate warmed.

Seconds later, searing heat rippled across her face and the jagged edges dug in deeper. They never left a mark after a memory walking sequence, but it always felt like she would arise with bleeding scratches.

The heat flowed along her jaw just as it would if the facetakers were preparing to remove her soulmask. Instead of intensifying like it would in a full soul transfer, that heat dragged her mind down into darkness.

Darkness abruptly changed to light.

Sarah blinked against the illumination of an early afternoon sun. The awful helmet was gone along with the machines and the entire vault.

Now she stood in an open square filled with people dressed like renaissance reenactors. In front of her reared an imposing, fortress-like building with a single, square tower that rose several stories above the roof. Near the building stood a statue she had longed to visit for years.

David, by Michelangelo.

The incredible marble statue stood a full seventeen feet high. From that height, David looked out over the square with a rather stern glare, as if warning everyone to behave.

"Not bad, huh?" Tomas asked.

"Not bad? He's amazing."

"You wouldn't be so excited about him if he was wearing a loincloth."

Sarah gave Tomas a sly smile. "He's gorgeous, but cold stone statues aren't what get me excited."

He actually blushed. She loved that puritan streak, but she did find it frustrating. She'd dropped several hints that it was past time they take their relationship to the next level, but he'd always changed the subject or pretended not to understand.

His initial hesitation made sense once she'd realized he was wearing another man's body. After returning to his own spectacular form, he'd been far more comfortable around her. Even then, he hadn't wanted to go any farther than a few passionate kisses.

She couldn't understand why he wouldn't commit. Her life had been shaken to its foundation when she'd stumbled into the secret world of facetakers and heka assassins. He was one of the few solid pillars she could cling to, and she feared losing him.

Arm in arm, they joined Gregorios and Eirene at a small table outside a ristorante. Several plates of fruits, sweetbreads and breakfast meats awaited them, along with six different beverages. The two facetakers clinked glasses, looking like locals.

Eirene wore a beautiful, red silk dress with puffy, blue sleeves that left her shoulders bare. It lacked the heavy, multi-layered look of many of the other women in the square, but still blended well. Gregorios wore a form-fitting, black doublet that laced up the front, and gray pants tucked into tall boots.

They had dressed Tomas much the same as Gregorios but with a blue doublet. Sarah wore a cream-colored dress that hugged her torso and flared into a long skirt. She wished she could take it with her when they woke up.

"I love this city," Eirene said with a contented smile.

"You had a good life here," Gregorios said.

She nodded. "The Medici were excellent patrons."

Alter joined them and dropped into a chair, already glaring at Gregorios. "Why do I get the ridiculous tights?"

He did look ridiculous. He wore a pair of hugely flared pantaloons of a garish green, gray tights, and soft slippers of pale blue. He tossed his floppy hat onto the table.

"Just going for some variety," Gregorios said with a straight face. He speared a sausage and took a huge bite.

Eirene spoke before Alter could make an angry retort. "It appears the machine you repaired is working perfectly."

Gregorios nodded. "I was drawn to the joint memory without a hitch. Good work."

That mollified Alter a bit and Sarah hid her smile before he glanced at her. He did notice Tomas' smirk, and that nearly started the argument all over again.

Gregorios drew them back to the mission. "We've tested the single machine enough to have a pretty good idea of how to mess with physical laws inside a memory. That's not the point today. Eirene and I are going to alternate taking over some of the memory details from each other to mimic an actual memory duel."

"Memory duel?" Sarah asked. That sounded exciting.

"He always has to name things," Eirene explained.

"I like it," Tomas said, and Alter nodded agreement.

Men. Everything got simplified into a contest or, better yet, a fight.

Sarah asked, "You want to test the effects of losing details to another mind? Won't that generate monsters?"

"It will," Gregorios said.

"Why bother? We own all the machines," Tomas said.

Eirene gestured with a glass of deep, red liquid. "All the ones we know about. It pays to understand the full extent of the technology."

Alter spoke up. "I've discussed what we witnessed in the Berlin conflict with my father. The clan runesmiths have expanded our original theories about why we saw those monsters in the memory."

"We talked about that," Gregorios said. He didn't look happy that

Alter had discussed the memory battle in such detail with his family. "Bad things."

Alter said, "It's more than that. They suggested that the root of the issue is that everyone remembers the same memory differently. In complex memories, hundreds of details may vary. As two minds struggle to control a joint memory, they win by degrees, by applying details of the moment as they remember it."

Eirene nodded. "That's about what we figured. That's exactly what we were going to test."

"I know. Hear me out. It's when you lose some of those details that cause problems."

"How?" Sarah asked. She was intrigued and wanted to understand how to limit the likelihood of running into monsters. Walking a pleasant dream like this was fun. Walking with nightmares, not so much.

Alter was happy to talk directly to her. "Say Eirene loses a detail of the memory today."

"Fat chance," Eirene said, throwing a challenging look at Gregorios.

"Just imagine. That bit of your memory is ripped loose. It becomes a fragment that latches onto your subconscious and takes a new form."

"It's an angry bit of memory, is that what you're saying?" Tomas asked, looking amused.

"Wouldn't you be?" Sarah asked.

Alter nodded. "Correct. That's why those fragments generally manifest as monsters. They are inherently the product of trauma so they latch onto nightmares and fears from your subconscious."

Gregorios' expression turned thoughtful. "That's why some of the monsters in Berlin were ones I recognized right away. Others were different, things I wouldn't have thought about. Those had to come from Asoka."

"Exactly. The anger is directed toward the one who broke the integrity of the moment."

Tomas said, "So the more we win control over the memory, the more monsters appear to fight us from the losing mind?"

"That doesn't sound fair," Sarah said.

Eirene said, "Actually, it presents some interesting opportunities. In an actual memory duel, we could purposefully cede portions of the memory to our opponent in order to trigger more monsters to help fight them."

"I like that idea," Tomas said.

"But wouldn't that just mean we'd have to fight another monster once we took that detail back later?" Sarah asked.

Eirene shrugged. "If it's unimportant, we don't necessarily have to take it back."

Gregorios swallowed a huge bite of a pear and said, "We'll test it. Let's pay attention to what details we choose to fight over. It's not just a mental arm wrestle."

This was sounding complicated and more than a little dangerous. The thought of facing more monsters dredged up the terror of the bunker battle against Mai Luan. Sarah wouldn't willingly join a conflict like that again.

Eirene glanced up at the fortress-like building towering above them. "Change the color of the Palazzo Vecchio there, love."

The huge structure changed from brown stone to pink marble in a blink.

"Wow, that's ugly," Tomas said.

A bronze statue, set back under one of the archways of a nearby building behind Gregorios, began to move. It was another nude sculpture, but held a sword in its right hand and the decapitated head of a defeated enemy in its left. It dropped the head and jumped down from its pedestal. Its eyes burned with amber fire and it charged Gregorios, sword raised.

Sarah blinked in surprise as she struggled to accept what she was seeing.

"Incoming!" Tomas vaulted the table to intercept the onrushing statue of living bronze. He covered the thirty feet in two seconds.

The statue swiped at his neck with its sword, apparently intending to add his head to its collection. Tomas ducked and threw his weight into its midsection. Even though he was flesh and blood against bronze, his strength and speed were enhanced to superhuman levels by his bonded enhancement runes.

Bronze lost. The statue tumbled backward, crashing into the facade of a nearby building. It landed on its feet and resumed its charge.

Gregorios was already standing, a grenade launcher appearing in his hands.

"You can't fire that thing at such close range," Eirene said.

"Good point." The launcher disappeared, replaced by a backpack holding three green canisters. A long nozzle dropped into his hands, connected to the pack by a hose.

"Stand back," he called as he pulled the trigger.

A stream of super-heated flames gushed out the end of the nozzle, shot across the twenty feet to the charging statue, and enveloped it with liquid flame. The air grew hot and Sarah covered her face with one hand to block some of the brimstone-like stench.

The statue kept coming, despite the continuous stream of fire that turned its upper chest and neck red hot.

Alter shouted, "I need an axe!"

A huge, double-bladed monstrosity appeared in his hands.

As the statue closed on Gregorios, sword held high, Alter shouted, "Clear!"

Gregorios cut off the stream of fire and the flamethrower disappeared, replaced by a heavy shield. He caught the statue's sword on the shield, but the impact drove him back three steps.

Alter struck from the side, and his heavy-bladed axe sheared right through the softened metal of the statue's neck. As soon as the head left the statue's body, it crumbled to dust.

Low growling spun Sarah around. A wolf-like creature stood barely ten feet away, already crouched to spring.

She had seen something similar in the Berlin nightmare so she knew what to do with it. Tomas' forty-five caliber pistol appeared in her hand.

The beast launched into the air at her. She raised the gun, and for a split second, she felt strangely light, just like she had when she had fought Mai Luan.

In that memory battle, her body had turned partially insubstantial, allowing her to pass through things. She hadn't managed to replicate the feeling in their memory walks since then, and she didn't want to lose it. She needed to understand how it worked.

She decided to let the monster dive right through her.

Before she could see if it would work, Alter's axe spun past her shoulder and smashed the beast out of the air. It fell to the ground as a pile of sand.

"I had that under control," she complained, giving Alter a vexed look.

"Didn't look like it," Alter said.

Tomas joined her, not even breathing hard. "Are you all right?"

"Are you kidding me?" She turned to Gregorios. "What was that all about?"

The table full of food disappeared, along with evidence of the statue turning to life. Its pedestal was still empty, though.

"I guess we just proved Alter's theory," Eirene said.

"Let's think that through a little more next time," Sarah said.

Gregorios said, "A bronze statue, really? I thought we were starting small."

Eirene shrugged. "I can't control what the memory fragment manifests as, love."

Alter said, "It wasn't a monster, though. This is the first time we've seen the fragments manifest as something not nightmarish."

"It think it was pretty scary," Sarah muttered.

Eirene said, "Perhaps it was because I don't hate Gregorios. I've always thought Perseus a particularly fine hero."

"The second beast was nightmarish," Tomas pointed out.

Alter nodded. "Smaller too. Probably appeared in response to the weapons we summoned. Those were small breaks."

"But important ones. No one in these times had flame throwers or pistols," Eirene pointed out.

"All good points," Gregorios said with more good cheer than Sarah felt was appropriate. He rubbed his hands together, a look of anticipation on his face. "Let's test the limits."

7

For so many years, the ultimate desire that fueled all my industry, every success, was acquiring enough wealth to secure a second life. I've gained everything I ever wanted, but have nothing that really matters. Why did I never see that lingering beyond the short span of years of everyone I love is a burden my heart was not prepared to bear? How others manage the transition, I cannot understand. Please help me learn to live this new life with peace of mind.

~COSIMO I DE'MEDICI, GRAND DUKE OF TUSCANY, IN A
LETTER TO EIRENE, 1575

OVER THE NEXT TWENTY MINUTES, they crisscrossed Florence, exploring the limits of the memory duel. They left the Piazza della Signoria and the fantastic statue of David. Eirene never did restore the color and facade of the towering Palazzo Vecchio.

Sarah was happy they instead started with small changes. Several blocks north, they stopped to gaze at the incredible Basilica di Santa Maria del Fiore, or the Duomo, as Gregorios called it.

Eirene said, "Don't mess with the Duomo. It's too important a landmark."

"As you wish," Gregorios replied with a grand bow. The gesture would have looked sarcastic in modern clothing, but seemed perfectly appropriate in medieval attire.

Sarah, Tomas, and Gregorios faced off against Alter and Eirene in a game of capture the flag. Eirene set her flag somewhere near the Duomo.

Gregorios' team headed south, crossed the beautiful Ponte Vecchio bridge that spanned the Arno River, and set theirs in the Boboli Gardens behind the magnificent Palazzo Pitti.

Sarah loved every minute they spent exploring the beautiful city. Florence was in the midst of its heyday. Gregorios said they were walking in the year 1570. Everywhere she looked, Sarah spied another incredible building, statue, or fountain.

"We need to visit here in real life," she gushed to Tomas.

"Then we'd have to worry about not breaking things."

"Don't mess with the David."

He shrugged. "It's a memory. Doesn't matter."

"It does to me."

"I'll try." He actually sounded sincere.

Then Eirene and Alter launched their first assault for the flag and his promise evaporated in the face of a heated running battle. They fought their mock confrontations back and forth across the Ponte Vecchio, with both sides using the unique parameters of the memoryscape to their advantage.

Bending the laws of physics didn't seem to adversely affect the integrity of the memoryscape. Sarah could easily vault thirty feet to rooftops and break right through solid stone walls. None of that triggered the rise of nightmarish creatures.

Tomas and Alter pushed the limits even further, their repeated encounters growing more and more intense as they both fought to outmaneuver the other. The rules of the game gave advantage to the defending side, but the aggressor did not have to relent and return to his side until the defender landed three solid strikes.

At one point, Sarah paused to admire the grand statue of Neptune in the Piazza della Signoria. Without warning, Alter landed atop the huge, white statue, a longsword in his hand. Tomas jumped off the roof of the still-pink Pallazzo Vecchio, firing a pump shotgun as he fell.

Alter leaped away in a graceful arc that covered most of the square. Slugs shattered part of the statue, while buckshot ricocheted off the surrounding bronze sculptures.

"No modern weapons," Alter shouted before racing away around the corner.

Tomas blew the head off a long, scaly serpent that exploded out of the waters of the fountain. "Have to test the limits, right?"

"So you proved summoning modern weapons breaks the integrity of the memory. What about not breaking anything?" Sarah raised an eyebrow.

"I'll be careful."

Then they both had to race for cover as Alter returned to the square carrying a belt-fed machine gun.

"This thing triggered an actual vampire," Alter shouted above the roar of his gun.

"He takes research too seriously sometimes," Sarah muttered.

"I've got this," Tomas grinned while they hid behind yet another statue that was getting chewed apart by Alter's bullets. "You go for the flag."

He leaped away and crossed the square in a flash, with bullets sparking off paving stones behind him the entire way.

Sarah left them to the duel and ran north toward the Duomo. She tried not to worry they would take things too far. Minor injuries in the dream world could be ignored, and Gregorios and Eirene had the ability to heal severe wounds.

The catch was that the drain on the facetakers running the machine would grow exponentially. And if not healed immediately, injuries sustained in the memoryscape radiated back up to their sleeping bodies. She didn't want to wake up to find everyone covered in blood and needing a hospital.

Also, the locals that inhabited historical Florence were starting to take notice. At first, the dream people had ignored them, but they were starting to look hostile as the damage to the city grew.

Through their memory journeys, they had learned that the more dramatic the changes to the remembered locale, the more response from the locals. Syncing the memories of multiple facetakers through different machines appeared to work similarly.

It also mattered who made the changes. Gregorios and Eirene were the only ones who could alter major details of the memoryscape, but the others were not completely helpless. They could make small changes, particularly personal things like their outfits or weapons. But the effect of Sarah summoning a pistol was more severe than if Gregorios summoned it for her.

As Sarah ran up a cobbled street between shops overflowing with bright-colored fabrics, she suddenly felt like she was being watched. She slowed and looked around. The street was busy and most of the locals who passed close to her scowled, but the feeling was emanating from something else.

After a moment's consideration, she oriented on a man sitting on a nearby bench. A wide-brimmed hat that did not quite fit with the styles of the day, covered his face. Sarah slowly approached, despite a growing feeling of unease. Something was definitely off about this man.

As she approached, he slowly raised his head. In a moment she would get a glimpse of his face, but suddenly she didn't want to.

Alter raced around a nearby corner, startling her out of the momentary lapse.

"Need to move faster than that to keep ahead of me, Sarah!" A weighted net appeared in his hands and he threw it.

Sarah leaped straight up to a nearby roof, frustrated and relieved at the same time by the interruption. Alter leaped after her, so she imagined a large brick in the air just above his head.

Alter crashed into the brick and the impact knocked him out of the air. He tumbled to the pavement just as Tomas appeared around the next corner.

Tomas charged, a baseball bat appearing in his hands. He caught Alter in the chest with the first swing, and the blow swept Alter off his feet. He flew right through a nearby window.

Several locals jumped Tomas from behind.

He fought them off and shouted, "Go, Sarah! We don't have much more time."

She raced north across the rooftops but glanced back to the spot where the strange man had sat. He was gone. Good. She didn't really have time to worry about that.

She exulted in the experience of racing across the tiled roofs toward the towering Duomo, and bent her thoughts to figuring out where Eirene would have hidden the flag. Only one location made sense.

So she launched off the end of the last roof and soared across the piazza to the Campanile di Giotto, the square, free-standing tower that stood adjacent to the Duomo. It reared almost three hundred feet above the stone-paved piazza and was the fastest route up. Hiding the flag on the roof would be just like Eirene.

So was waiting a hundred feet up the side of the tower in ambush.

As Sarah ascended the outside of the tower by leaping up the side from one precarious handhold to another, Eirene dropped from her concealed perch above. Sarah barely registered movement out of the corner of her eye before Eirene's weight ripped her from her perch and the two of them fell toward the cobbled piazza fifty feet below.

"Nice try dear," Eirene said with a wink.

Air rushed past and Sarah braced for the brutal impact. Before they hit, a huge airbag inflated underneath them, like those used by stunt men in movies. They landed on the cushion and Sarah pushed away from Eirene before she could land the required three strikes.

She rolled off the edge of the air cushion just before it vanished. Eirene had rolled off the far side and stood twenty feet away. She paused to dispatch a bat-like creature, and Sarah seized on the moment of distraction.

She could never fight past Eirene. She needed a smarter strategy. As she ran for the basilica, she got an idea and threw all her focus into making it reality.

A bright red jetpack materialized directly in front of her. It sounded like a hundred weed whackers had been bottled inside the central canister that stood six feet tall and two feet in diameter. Two turbines were mounted on either side of the central unit, with the pilot's framework on the front. The entire machine stood on two flat runners.

Sarah settled into the pilot harness and glanced back at Eirene. The facetaker had paused to stare, just as she had hoped. Eirene had been unincorporated during most of the recent technological revolution. She was catching up fast, but Sarah doubted she'd ever seen anything like the jetpack.

Sarah had gotten a chance to try one out the year before during a swanky event thrown by Alterego. It could fly her to the top of the Duomo in seconds.

She had forgotten about the monsters.

The ground directly under Sarah's feet began to buckle, then fall into a dark pit that yawned open just beneath the jetpack. Sarah gunned the motor, and the whine of the machine turned into a scream as the turbines sped up. It lifted off the ground just before the entire section of the piazza fell away into a widening hole.

An actual minotaur leaped up from the pit and grasped at Sarah with its clawed hands.

In that second, the same strange ethereal feeling she had felt while fighting Mai Luan rippled through Sarah. The claws passed right through. It was as if she was becoming intangible. All through the memory duel, she'd been trying to figure out how to trigger that feeling.

She didn't have time to figure out how it worked. The monster's claws might have passed through her, but they caught the framework of the jetpack. The extra weight slowed her ascent even though Sarah maxed the throttle.

The minotaur bellowed right in her face. Its head was like a demonic bull and its breath smelled like rotten meat. It slammed its horned skull forward.

She was no longer insubstantial.

Sarah had no idea how to control the change and, strapped into the jetpack, she could do nothing to defend herself.

The horned head pounded into her with the force of a battering ram. All that saved her sternum from rupturing was the same steel framework that prevented her from escaping.

The metal bars bent under the impact, absorbing the lion's share of the hit. The fraction of the blow that she felt drove the breath from her lungs. It crushed her back with such force that she nearly blacked out.

Her hand slipped off the controls and the jetpack dropped out of the air. One skid landed on solid ground while the other fell into the hole. Together Sarah and the monster tumbled into the pit.

She screamed as they fell ten feet before crashing into solid rock. The minotaur landed under the machine and took the brunt of the fall. It bellowed again and threw her and the heavy jetpack off. The machine tumbled several times before bouncing off the wall of the cave.

Sarah tried to extricate herself, but she was still having trouble breathing and her head was spinning from the wild tumble.

The minotaur put its head down and charged.

No way she could escape.

Tomas dropped into the hole and landed right in front of the monster, a six-foot spear in his hands. He planted the spear against the ground and angled it toward the beast. The minotaur impaled itself before it could stop, driving the shaft deep into its chest.

It fell in a heap with Tomas. Despite the terrible injury, it clawed and bit at him. Instead of trying to escape, Tomas beat on the monster with unrestrained fury. Hammers with spiked heads appeared in his hands and he pounded at the creature, shouting like a berserker.

Alter and Eirene dropped into the pit. While Alter rushed to Sarah, Eirene leaped into the fray, slender daggers already slashing.

"Help Tomas," Sarah cried as Alter worked to pull her from the twisted wreckage of the machine.

"I am."

"What are you talking about? The monster's over there."

"It's not the monster that's important."

With his help, Sarah slipped free of the jetpack. She tried to run to help Tomas and Eirene, but Alter grabbed her by the waist and threw her up out of the hole.

Gregorios caught her.

"Let me go! I have to help."

"Settle down," he said, restraining her. "And look before you leap."

She leaned over the hole, his arm gripping her tight. Alter had joined the others and hacked at the monster with the axe he favored. Together, they overwhelmed the monster and beat it to dust.

When he vaulted out of the hole, Tomas was covered in blood, but she couldn't tell how much of it was his.

He threw his arms around her. "I'm glad you're all right."

"I'm fine. What about you?"

Alter scowled, "What were you thinking? A jetpack? Here?"

"Just pushing the limits," Sarah snapped, still angry that he hadn't trusted her to help them. "Isn't that the excuse you used for that machine gun?"

Eirene interrupted. "Drop it, kids. Time to go."

Only then did Sarah notice the square was packed with an angry mob. Scowling locals, led by several well-dressed lords shouting for justice were fast working themselves into a frenzy.

Gregorios held up the crimson piece of cloth that was Eirene's flag. "Perfect timing."

"How'd you get that?" she demanded.

He winked. Then he closed his eyes and spoke loudly, "All right, Bastien. Take us home."

The shattered piazza faded from view as the angry mob surged toward them. The last thing Sarah noticed was the still figure of a man standing behind the crowd, face concealed by a wide-brimmed hat.

8

It is rare that the mortal world can produce delicacies fit for a palate refined over so many lifetimes. When I do, I salute, and I savor the moment.

~JOHN, FACETAKER COUNCIL MEMBER, WHILE
DRINKING A BOTTLE OF 1811 CHÂTEAU D'YQUEM

SARAH WAITED IMPATIENTLY for Francesca to slide the faceplate open so she could remove the helmet. She rubbed at her aching jawline, but her fingers came away clean. No blood.

When she stood, she noticed Francesca looked exhausted. The other facetakers looked little better.

"Are you all right?" Sarah asked Bastien, who had powered the Sotrun machine.

"I will be if you allow me to enjoy that chair of yours, yes?"

Sarah scurried out of the way for him.

Harriett dropped into Alter's chair with a sigh when he rose. "What were you doing in there? The drain was a lot worse than we expected."

"We were testing the limits," Gregorios said.

"And what of our limits? Another minute and we might have lacked the strength to draw you out," Bastien said.

"Nearly crisped our crust," Harriett added with a tired shake of her head.

Tomas said, "Another minute and there might not have been much of us left to pull out. The locals were getting angry."

Sarah asked, "Can you blame them? With you and Alter shooting up the Neptune statue and throwing grenades?"

"They probably weren't happy when we toppled the David," Tomas admitted.

"Hey, I told you to leave that one alone!"

He pointed at Alter. "His fault."

She rounded on him, but he cut her off. "Who was it that called a jetpack into the Middle Ages?"

Gregorios interrupted. "Did any of you experience anything weird in there?"

"You mean weirder than running battles through the streets of medieval Florence?" Tomas asked.

"Exactly."

Sarah thought back to the strange figure in the wide-brimmed hat. "You're worried someone else is still walking the memories, aren't you?"

"It is a possibility."

"I doubt it. We have the only working machines," Alter said.

Gregorios responded, "The only ones we're aware of. We haven't captured Mai Luan's heka cell yet so we have no confirmation there weren't more."

"We'll get them," Tomas assured him.

Gregorios said, "Until we do, keep your eyes open. The risk is small, but I don't like surprises."

"Well not those kind of surprises," Eirene said with a slow smile.

Sarah didn't like surprises either, and she felt a lingering sense of unease about that hat man. She opened her mouth to tell them about him, but the vault door swung inward and John strode inside.

He was tall, with salt-and-pepper hair that might have made him look distinguished if not for the scowl he always wore. John was one of the aged facetaker council members who had survived the bomb, and he was impatient to gain access to the machine.

"How dare you initiate a test without me present?" John demanded as he marched up to Gregorios.

Gregorios wasn't ruffled. "Would you have preferred we hook you up to an untested machine?"

He gestured at the cobbled-together machine. Although she trusted Alter, Sarah had been secretly glad she was not the first person to use that one. It looked like it could more easily fill someone's mind with rust than reverse mental dissipation. She was looking forward to examining its rune configuration.

John's belligerence faded as he surveyed the ugly machine. "Well, you should have called me down anyway."

"I was just about to, so your timing is good. First test was successful. It's your turn."

John beamed, eager as a child at the fair. He glanced from the ugly machine to the pristine Sotrun. "Since you already have experience with the rebuilt machine, it is probably best I use the other one."

"Be my guest," Gregorios said.

John moved to the nearest chair not occupied by an exhausted facetaker.

Sarah glanced at Tomas, who shrugged at John's antics. She hoped the machine fixed John's crankiness along with his mental stability. Someone who had lived through most of the world's history should have figured out a better outlook on life.

Eirene took Harriett's hand in hers. "Are you children up for one more test?"

"If you keep it simple."

"Nothing fancy. We'll just meet back in time and enjoy a peaceful sunset together. Ten minutes should be a good start for John."

"We can do that."

The other siblings indicated their agreement.

"I'll be here to help if you need me," Gregorios said.

John frowned yet again. "I'd prefer it if you chose the memory, Gregorios."

Gregorios and Eirene shared a knowing look. "Fine. Eirene will oversee the show from the outside."

John turned to Sarah. "Will you accompany me on my first memory walk, my dear?"

"I'd be honored," she managed to say with a straight face only because Gregorios and Tomas would be meeting them in the memory.

From the rumors she had picked up in the past few weeks, it seemed John had loved to live large before he got old. He liked fine foods and fine women. She didn't want to hurt him and she didn't want Tomas to feel honor-bound to break bones in the memory world if John decided to test the limits.

She doubted he'd handle injuries radiating back to the real world very well. Sarah could already feel a couple of bruises forming from the recent memory duel, and her chest ached where the minotaur had head-butted her. Her enhancement would help her recover quickly. She was lucky she hadn't suffered worse.

She was relieved to see the blood soaking Tomas' clothing in the memoryscape had been the minotaur's. How he had survived that brawl with the monster without even a scratch was a mystery.

Looking forward to a quieter memory walk, Sarah settled into the same reclining chair she had used just moments before. John glanced over and his gaze lingered on her curves before he looked up to her eyes.

"You are in for a great trip, my dear."

Shameless old lech, she thought. "I'm sure it'll be interesting."

John's smile faded and he turned to Gregorios. "She won't be able to control my memories, will she?"

Alter answered. "No, sir. We adjusted the runes to ensure you stay in control."

Sarah shuddered to think what she might stumble upon in John's past.

Gregorios handed them both small, circular wooden pendants. On the glossy surface of both sides were inscribed runes. Sarah easily recognized Alter's artistic flair.

On one side was a simple rune of awakening that she recognized from her study of the rune lore Alter's family had provided. She didn't recognize the rune on the other side. It was small and intricate, and for a second she sensed a deeper image concealed within the crisscrossing lines.

"What is this rune?" she asked, tracing the symbol with a finger, thrilled to learn yet another rune.

Alter grinned. "I've been working on a failsafe mechanism. This will allow you to break out of the memory at any time."

"Excellent idea," John said. He slipped his pendant over his head.

That was a cool idea. Sarah asked, "How does it work? I thought we couldn't activate runes since we don't have your rounon gift."

Alter grinned. "That's the best part. I've already activated these runes and linked them to my life force, which will power them for the next half hour."

"How do we trigger them?" John asked.

Alter pointed at the simple rune of awakening. "Draw that on your stomach. It will bind back to the runes on the pendant, which will activate it for you."

"That's brilliant," Sarah said.

The idea was both subtle and profound at the same time. She had an innate sensitivity to runes, but this was a higher form of art. She needed to learn it.

She reached into her pocket and fingered a folded piece of paper there. It held a new rune she'd been working on for the past week. It was not quite finished, but she felt it was going to be awesome. After the memory walk, she would add Alter's complex new rune to the paper.

Alter beamed at the compliment and stayed close as Francesca settled the heavy helmet over Sarah's head. The faceplate snapped into position with that unpleasant pricking sensation. Then the heat of Bastien's nevron drew her into darkness.

When the darkness dropped from her mind, it was not the quiet vista of a beautiful sunset that took its place.

Sarah awoke in the middle of a battlefield.

9

I love the name of honor more than I fear death.

~JULIUS CAESAR

"WHOA! WHERE ARE WE?"

Sarah stood atop a low hill near the base of a steep mountain under a blazing hot sun. She faced a road of packed brown earth that was barely fifty feet wide. On the road, almost within spitting distance, two armies battled in archaic armor, large round shields, and long spears. The much smaller army on her right blocked a narrow pass with a tightly-packed formation of just a few hundred men.

The other army was having a bad day.

Although it filled the road to her left as far as Sarah could see, and had to outnumber the small force many times over, the huge army had succeeded in nothing more than dying by the hundreds. Huge piles of dead soldiers cluttered the battlefield, blood soaked the ground right up to where she stood, and the air smelled like vomit and urine.

The narrow battlefield was hemmed in by the hill upon which Sarah stood on one side, and a long drop on the opposite side. The ground fell away to an ocean that extended to the horizon and crashed into rocks below with a regular booming of heavy surf. The clanging of spears on shields echoed painfully off the steep hills. Occasional loud screams rose above the clamor.

One soldier in orange robes and sporting a thick black beard collapsed right at her feet. The front of his clothing was ripped open, revealing a ghastly wound in his chest. He bled out and died before she could react or try to help.

The entire scene felt surreal, and yet strangely familiar. A soldier she hadn't noticed before, who stood close beside her, kicked the body. The dead man rolled several times before coming to a stop against another corpse.

Sarah retreated a step, falling into a defensive stance. It took a couple of seconds to recognize John. He looked so different in that strong young body with bare, muscular arms. He wore a bronze breastplate, greaves on his legs, and a crimson cloak. He held a long spear and carried a heavy round shield with a Greek-looking symbol on it. He looked just like the brutal soldiers in the smaller, but deadlier army.

He also looked terrified.

The sight of him locked the location into place for her. "Oh, no," she gasped. "You're kidding."

John scanned the battlefield before turning to her. "We should not be here."

"You think? Why'd you bring us to Thermopylae?" Sarah had seen the movie, and despite the poetic license the producers had taken, she recognized it.

"I didn't bring us anywhere," John snapped.

"This was like twenty five *centuries* ago," Sarah exclaimed. She'd never walked a memory so old.

"I know. Gregorios told me all about it."

"Wait, this isn't your memory?" Where was Gregorios anyway?

"No. Like I said, we shouldn't be here." His expression turned suspicious. "What have you done, woman?"

"Nothing. I'm not a facetaker."

"You're tampering with my memories aren't you?"

Sarah gave him a disgusted look. "You just said you don't have this memory."

"Exactly!"

He brandished his spear. "Send me back, woman, or I will defend myself."

Sarah retreated. "Why would I want to bring us here?"

The fighting abruptly stopped.

Silence descended over the battlefield like an invisible tidal wave. Everyone just stopped, some with weapons in mid-thrust, others in mid-scream.

It was as if someone had paused a movie.

"We have to get out of here," Sarah said, her voice sounding loud in the silence.

John was no longer listening. He was staring toward the larger army with an expression of disbelief on his face.

Sarah turned to follow his gaze and her eye was drawn to a single moving figure. A man was approaching them with an unhurried stride, as if strolling through a park instead of a freakishly frozen battlefield. He was about a hundred yards away and instead of a helmet, he wore a wide-brimmed hat.

Icy fear kicked Sarah in the gut. She should have told Gregorios about the hat man before they entered this memory. She knew without a shred of doubt that she didn't want to wait for introductions with the mysterious fellow.

A new sound pierced the silence. A roar so deep it shook the ground as it boiled up out of the nearby sea. A moment later a huge, scaled head on a long, sinuous neck rose above the road. It opened a mouth big enough to swallow a horse and roared again. The blast of its breath staggered Sarah back even though she stood over fifty feet away.

Soldiers from both armies that stood closest to the edge began moving again and turned to face the gigantic sea serpent. It lunged with terrifying speed and snatched a man off the ground, ignoring dozens of arrows that bounced off its thick hide.

The bigger the break with a memory, the bigger the monster. Sarah was glad no one in earlier memory excursions had ever tried tampering with time. That gigantic beast looked like it could eat the entire army.

She glanced back at the man in the wide-brimmed hat to see if he looked as scared as he should be, but his face was still hidden. Another man had joined him. The newcomer was dressed in fancier armor. He looked like a lord or captain. His head was bare, showing a strong jaw, a rather large nose, and thick, black hair. He was clean shaven and he looked angry.

"Baladeva!" John hissed.

"Who's he?"

John grabbed Sarah by the collar. "Why did you bring me here?"

She punched him in the nose.

He groaned and clutched his face. She slipped out of his grasp and ran for the frozen battle lines. It was a little closer to the raging sea serpent, but she couldn't scale the steep mountainside, and she didn't want to draw any closer to the hat man.

"Get back here!"

She glanced back just as John seized a javelin from a fallen soldier and threw it at her. She easily dodged, but that made up her mind. Something was incredibly wrong and she didn't have to wait around and babysit John until things got even worse.

The man John had called Baladeva had closed to within fifty yards, with the hat man at his side.

She still didn't see Gregorios or Tomas, so she summoned a black marker and drew the waking rune on her stomach. Heat flared through her torso and she gasped.

Her vision went black, then she awakened in the vault.

Eirene's voice came through the helmet. "Sarah dear, what happened?"

"Get me out of this thing! We have a problem."

10

The city and the buildings are mine; but I resign to your valor the captives and the spoil, the treasures of gold and beauty. Your bravery is unmatched, your enhancements without equal. Be rich and be happy.

~MEHMED II IN A SPEECH TO HIS JANISSARY CORPS
DURING THE SIEGE OF CONSTANTINOPLE, 1453

"YOU MUST BE MISTAKEN," Alter said when Sarah finished explaining about the bizarre nightmare she and John had fallen into. "You can't travel back to a time that's not linked to the primary traveler's memory."

Sarah glared. "I know what I saw, Alter."

"I know you think you do. But I don't see how it's possible."

"So it's easier to think I'm an idiot or a liar rather than admit there might be something you hadn't anticipated?"

He paced away, head down in thought. "I'm not sure what to make of this."

"I suggest you make something up," Bastien called from his position at John's head, glowing hands thrust into slots on either side of the helmet. "The situation is now dangerous."

A long gash had appeared on John's neck, and blood dripped in a steady stream down his arm.

Eirene punched a button on a nearby intercom. "We need a trauma response team in the vault. Double time!"

Sarah grabbed a rag lying on the floor next to the ugly machine and used it to apply pressure. "He should have activated his escape rune by now."

"Unless someone is wishing he stay, yes?" Bastien said.

"I've got bandages." Alter lugged over a heavy, bright red plastic case emblazoned with a white cross. He dropped it on the floor next to John's chair and flung open the lid.

Sarah snatched a thick wad of sterile gauze bandages to replace the bloody, dirty one she'd been using.

Eirene joined them just as Bastien groaned and sagged against the chair. Francesca, who had been standing beside him, one hand resting on his shoulder, turned pale and swayed where she stood.

"The drain is spiking," Bastien panted. "I think perhaps he is having a bad time."

"Get him out of there," Sarah cried.

"It must be controlled by the dreamer, no?" Bastien said.

"But Gregorios called you to take him out when we went in last time," Sarah protested.

"That was his choice. The act of calling for exit releases his hold on the memory so I can extract him. John has not done that."

Francesca whispered, "If we don't do something fast, we'll lose him."

"Help them, Alter," Eirene said, pushing the young hunter toward her children.

"Me? I'm not a facetaker."

"Just share the strength of your young soul with them. I need to coordinate our response."

Looking like he wanted to argue, Alter stepped to Francesca's side and placed his left hand on her shoulder. With the other hand he used a marker to inscribe a rune onto his hand that flowed down to her shoulder. She immediately straightened, and some of her color returned.

"You are strong for a mortal," Francesca said, giving Alter an appraising look. "What else can you do?"

"The three of us should be able to hold it long enough," Alter said, pointedly looking away from Francesca.

"Thank you," Eirene said.

Sarah wasn't sure why she had positioned Alter with the facetakers, but she was glad they seemed able to handle the load. He'd helped Eirene preserve the memory during their battle with Mai Luan. Without that assistance, they might have all died.

A new cut scraped down John's thigh. Eirene pressed a fresh bandage to it.

"He might not last much longer. He was wearing armor and these wounds are in places that were not protected, but those guys looked scary."

"Dad's back with Tomas," Harriett said, releasing her hold on the other machine and moving to help them with the helmets.

"You said it was Baladeva?" Eirene asked.

"Who said Baladeva?" Gregorios asked, sitting up and tugging at his helmet.

As soon as he was free of the machine, Tomas jumped out of the chair and came to Sarah. "What happened? Why didn't you show up?"

"And what about Baladeva?" Gregorios repeated.

Sarah gave them a brief summary of what happened. While she spoke, the medical team rushed in and took her place at John's side.

"Thermopylae was not John's memory." Gregorios said with a frown.

"You have to tell me about that one," Tomas said eagerly.

"Later."

"Will someone please tell me who Baladeva is?" Sarah asked, trying to hide how freaked out she felt. The horrific sight of new injuries appearing across John's body didn't help.

"He's dead, so he shouldn't be a player at all," Eirene said.

"Then the man in the wide-brimmed hat has to be the player. I saw him in Florence, and now again."

"Why didn't you tell us?" Gregorios demanded.

"I was going to, but John arrived and I didn't get a chance."

"For stuff like this, you make time," Gregorios growled.

In the chair, John's body shook, and bruises appeared across his face.

"They're killing him," Eirene said softly.

"And he's still not triggering his escape rune," Alter added.

Gregorios rose. "We have to intervene. I'm going in."

"No, dear. You are not." Eirene stood to face him. "Something new and potentially deadly is going on in there. With everything we're still dealing with from Mai Luan, we can't afford to lose you now. I'm going."

They faced each other for several seconds and Sarah found herself holding her breath. Eirene's argument made sense, but would Gregorios really agree to send her into danger?

Alter said, "I'll go with you. This machine allows two passengers."

Eirene nodded. "It's settled then. Loan us your failsafe pendants."

Sarah had triggered hers, so Tomas loaned his to Alter. Harriett took his place supporting her siblings at the head of the machine.

Gregorios pulled the wooden pendant over his neck and gave it to

Eirene, along with a kiss. Instead of pulling away, Gregorios caressed Eirene's face and his hands began to glow with his activated nevron. His hands burned with purple fire, and he pressed his fingers against her skin.

For a second, Sarah feared he was trying to disable her so he could take her place, but the fires of his hands sank into her skin and the glow of his eyes slowly faded. After several seconds, he released her and swayed, looking exhausted.

"You didn't have to do that," Eirene said. Her eyes began glowing bright with her nevron.

"Take the strength. You may need it." Then Gregorios staggered and sat on the ground, holding his head in his hands.

"What did you do?" Sarah asked.

"He loaned me the strength of his soul." Eirene stood taller, her voice strong, her eyes glittering with unusual brightness.

"They're the only facetakers we've ever heard of who can do that," Francesca said. "I think it's because the lovesick duo really aren't much more than one combined soul that happens to live in two bodies."

Eirene kissed her daughter. "You're a sucker for a good love story. Now let's deal with John."

Sarah helped secure the helmets. Before pressing the jagged faceplate over Alter she said, "Be careful in there."

As soon as she closed the lid, she felt tingling under her fingers as the machine activated the helmet.

They were in.

11

Now it came to pass, in the year of Christ's Incarnation, 1252, that Alaue, Lord of the Tartars of the Levant, heard tell of the great crimes of the Old Man and his enhanced Assassins, and resolved to make an end of him. Nevertheless, the army of his Baron besieged their castle for three years, and could have remained thus affixed for decades more had the hunters not sent mighty warriors endowed with the very strength of God to smite down the gates. As sworn in our accord, I will however claim the defeat of the dread Assassins came only by the grace of God that they ran out of victuals and thus surrendered.

~MARCO POLO, SECRET CORRESPONDENCE TO
GREGORIOS, 1297

EIRENE APPEARED on the battlefield of Thermopylae dressed for war.

She didn't know what to expect, so she had clothed herself in a full suit of German plate armor from the sixteenth century. Given that she was stepping into the bronze age, the armor made her all but invincible.

As long as she didn't venture too close to that gigantic sea monster.

She blinked, but the sight didn't change. The beast was so big she wondered if it might really be Charybdis. Bits and pieces of fallen soldiers littered the area around the monster, but it had not escaped unscathed. Several spears jutted from its armored neck, and one eye was bleeding.

Alter appeared beside her in modern body armor, with a tactical vest bristling with weapons and explosives.

"Don't you think that's a little over-done, dear?" She loved his intensity, but there was a certain question of style he hadn't grasped yet.

He shrugged. "They're playing for keeps. Let's do this."

Then he spotted the monster and gaped. "What is that?"

"Stay clear and we should be long gone before it eats through all those soldiers."

Eirene scanned the battlefield. Almost no one moved other than the sea monster and the troops fighting it. Besides the thunderous trumpets of the monster and the screaming of men getting eaten, silence reigned. The blood and gore that soaked the land underfoot seemed unreal, and even the smells seemed forced.

Someone was tampering at a level so extreme she had never considered trying it. It broke the memory at a fundamental level. She suspected that if the strange stasis continued, more monsters would rise to challenge the mind that controlled the memoryscape. They needed to be gone before that happened.

Not far away, near the immobile front lines of the two clashing armies, John was getting thrashed. Eirene had not seen Baladeva in more centuries than she cared to recall, but she recognized him. John might have assassinated him in real life, but in the memory world, Baladeva held the advantage.

He picked up the bloody, desperate John and threw him into a line of unmoving soldiers. John bounced off a shield and tumbled into an upraised spear. The shaft drove into his left shoulder and he howled.

Eirene winced with him. She knew exactly how much that hurt.

Baladeva advanced on him as he struggled to break the shaft of the spear that held him suspended off the ground. Only when Baladeva moved did Eirene catch sight of the man in the wide-brimmed hat. He stood not far behind Baladeva, face concealed.

"That's the one we want," she pointed.

"On it."

Alter pumped the grenade launcher mounted under his assault rifle and pulled the trigger. With a distinct whump, it launched the projectile across the silent landscape.

It struck between Baladeva and the man in the wide-brimmed hat and exploded with a satisfying roar of flame and debris. Whoever was controlling the memory had stopped time for most of the army, but wasn't ready for grenades. Frozen soldiers tumbled away from the blast along with everything else. Eirene lost sight of the two men in the ensuing dust cloud.

She descended the low hill toward John, who had spotted them and was waving his good hand for help. Alter flanked her on the right, assault rifle up as he scanned for targets.

A small doglike creature began clawing out of the ground at their feet but Alter shot it in the head without slowing. The smoke cleared but Eirene saw no trace of Baladeva or the man in the wide-brimmed hat.

She didn't waste time looking, but drew her sword and severed the spear holding John aloft. He fell in a heap at her feet.

"Let's get out of here," Alter said.

"Perhaps not yet," said a cultured voice behind her that she recognized from long ago.

Eirene spun and found Baladeva standing about twenty feet away. The man in the wide-brimmed hat stood beside him, face still concealed.

Alter sighted on Baladeva but Eirene raised a hand for him to wait. She spoke to the stranger. "Who are you?"

"Up till now, a researcher. In a moment, witness to a dramatic last stand."

He was not referring to the Spartans.

Without warning, the Persian soldiers all around them snapped out of their stasis. Instead of rushing the Spartan lines, they turned in unison toward Eirene, Alter and John.

Eirene sighed. This was going to get messy. "Why don't you face me yourself?"

"He doesn't need to," Alter muttered, positioning himself behind her, with John between them.

Baladeva saluted, then blew her a kiss before retreating to give the soldiers room. The man in the wide-brimmed hat stood motionless.

John cried out in fear and Eirene snapped, "Use your escape rune, fool."

That was all the time she had before dozens of enemy fighters swarmed her. She laid about with her sword in huge, double-handed strokes and tried not to notice the feeling of her blade shearing through flesh and bone and bronze. She embraced the battle fury that swept through her and started singing her favorite Roman war song.

The soldiers might be fragments of memory, but they screamed like living men and they bled out with just as much terror as if they had been alive.

Eirene fought with focused intent. Her armor turned dozens of blows and she waded through the enemy, carving a path around John and ever closer to Baladeva and his mysterious companion. Strengthened by the force of Gregorios' nevron, she could fight all day, and could deal with whatever they threw at her.

Alter fought at her back, snarling at the memory soldiers. His automatic rifle fired impossibly long bursts, but he never ran out of ammo. He tossed grenades that shattered close-packed ranks of soldiers.

Several monsters appeared, either rising from the ground or dropping from the sky, but the soldiers dispatched them. Eirene barely caught glimpses of most of them. She moved one slow step after another, careful to avoid tripping. One stumble and an avalanche of enemy soldiers would bury her. She called to Bastien to wake them, but nothing happened. It seemed only John could do that and he would not or could not get the message out.

Blood coated Eirene's armor and the stench of battle gagged her. She could barely see through the slits of her helmet and just kept slashing. She hadn't swung a sword in decades, but could think of no better weapon for such close combat.

She was only five strides away from Baladeva when Alter shouted, "John's gone! Activated the rune. That'll pull us out too."

Everything stopped. The entire battlefield fell silent.

As Eirene began to fade from the nightmare, the man in the wide-brimmed hat spoke into the silence.

"Run if you like. It won't do you any good."

His voice chased her into darkness.

"Your world is about to end."

12

If Gregorios is right, then Mithridates is a false king and a demigod in disguise. I have heard the tales of Baladeva, but considered them myths. Regardless of his nature, the presence of enforcers in the vanguard bolsters morale. I alone understand the source of their battle prowess. My men only need to witness it, until the day I can negotiate enhancements for them. Then to Rome, where I must convince Shahrokh to grant me the promise of a second life like he has Julius.

~POMPEY THE GREAT

JOHN WAS SO SHAKEN by the experience that the medical team sedated him to prevent a heart attack. Sarah didn't like John, but she didn't want another person she knew dying in real life.

After the heavy vault doors closed behind the departing medical team, Gregorios turned to the group, hands on hips, his expression sour. "Someone tell me what happened in there."

"And how did we get sucked all the way back to Thermopylae?" Eirene added. She looked tired, but otherwise unaffected by the grisly battle.

When they all turned to Sarah, she held up her hands. "Don't look at me. I was just a passenger."

Eirene said, "You were with John when the memory first opened. What did you see?"

"We were close to the front lines of the battle." Sarah explained how everything froze and how John started freaking out when he saw Baladeva.

Eirene frowned. "That concerns me. When Alter and I went in to get John, Baladeva was trying to kill him."

"You said he died a long time ago, right?" Alter asked.

Gregorios nodded. "About 200 A.D."

"More like 265," Eirene said.

"I can't remember the dates that exactly. It's been too long," Gregorios said with a wave of a hand.

Sarah said, "I can't believe you remember anything from back then." Their vast age still shocked her. "I can't even remember much from when I was a kid."

Gregorios shrugged. "Adults remember better. We'd already lived more than one life by then."

"Facetaker memories are more precise than other humans. That's why Mai Luan needed to use us to hunt for the master rune," Eirene added.

"Well, that and the fact that no one else has been alive that long," Alter said.

"True. But as for Baladeva, he was a powerful facetaker and for centuries a sworn enemy to Shahrokh. John finally removed him just prior to the death of King Shapur the First of Persia."

"Good riddance to them both," Gregorios muttered.

Tomas said, "If he's been dead for almost two thousand years, he should've been just another memory fragment like everyone else."

That was a good point. Eirene said, "He should have been, but he clearly was not."

Alter asked, "But was he really aware, or was he just obeying the will of another like the soldiers that tried to kill us?"

"It felt like there was more to him than the others," Eirene said.

Sarah rubbed her arms, feeling suddenly chilled by the weird experience. "I agree. Baladeva seemed aware of who we were."

"Maybe it was because he was a facetaker," Gregorios said.

"No. If he was a memory fragment, he'd lack the potency to break out of that moment," Alter said.

"Then what do you think it was?" Gregorios shot back.

Alter shrugged. "My father might—"

"Leave him out of it," Gregorios interrupted.

Eirene interjected, "Baladeva's behavior is a mystery, and facing him again after all these years was unsettling, but we're missing the point."

"Who is the man in the wide-brimmed hat?" Sarah asked, happy they hadn't forgotten about him. She had seen him twice, and both times had unsettled her, especially since she hadn't seen his face. There was something not right about that man.

"You're sure it was the same man you saw in Florence?" Gregorios asked.

"Confident."

Tomas said, "Then he's the one we need to track down. He has to be a facetaker, a memory walker."

"Why is he following us?" Sarah asked.

"And how did he get a machine?" Alter added.

Eirene shared the man's cryptic final warning. "It didn't sound like an idle threat."

"Those are the questions we need to answer," Gregorios said. He turned to Bastien and his other children. "Do you have anything to add?"

Francesca spoke. "If we're going to do this again, we need to figure out a better way to manage the drain. The more you tamper with the memories, the more you exhaust your nevron and draw upon ours. If we're not careful, a major conflict could very quickly get out of hand."

"We'll work on it. Alter?"

"I'll see what I can come up with."

Sarah was glad to hear it. Alter knew runes better than any of them, and he needed projects to keep him focused. When he got much free time, he usually started reverting by default back to plotting ways to kill Gregorios.

Tomas gave Sarah a kiss and left to continue the hunt for Mai Luan's heka cell. They were still the best lead for tracking down the other machine that now seemed to be out there.

The facetakers followed him out, but Sarah lingered in the vault with Alter. He crouched by the machine, hunting for any other runes they might have missed that might explain the bizarre events of the memory experience. When he noticed her lingering, he rose.

"You're worried about it, aren't you?" Sarah asked.

He shrugged. "Things don't happen without a reason. We just need to figure out that reason and then we can counter it."

"You'll figure it out."

Alter drew closer, his expression intent as he studied her face.

"What is it?" she asked, feeling self-conscious under his scrutiny. Those dark eyes, that handsome face rattled her more than she could ever let him know.

More than that, his mastery of rune lore drew her to him like a magnet. Studying runes had become something of an addiction to her, with Alter her supplier.

"How are you doing, Sarah?"

"I didn't get hurt in there."

"That's not what I asked," he pressed, taking her hand.

She felt moved by his obvious concern, but shouldn't Tomas be the one asking her how she was doing? He'd rushed off to the next challenge, as was his duty as captain, but he'd barely paused to make sure she was all right. Was it because he trusted her, or because he just didn't think to ask?

"I'm fine, Alter," Sarah insisted. "Thanks."

Instead of relenting, he said, "Sarah, I was there in Thermopylae. It was a nightmare. Most people couldn't handle a scene like that."

"It's not the first nightmare I've walked through," she said, but couldn't suppress a shiver from the memory. It had been terrible. She had been trying not to think about it.

Alter nodded, his voice soft. "Berlin was worse. And I left you."

"You helped Eirene. That saved us," Sarah pointed out, wishing he hadn't brought up Berlin. She'd been so terrified when Alter had abandoned the memoryscape to confront Eirene.

"But I left you," he insisted, his tone bitter. "I left you to the mercies of that cui dashi monster. Sarah, you could have died. Anyone else would have, but you defeated her."

"I had a lot of help."

"But you did it." His skin was warm against hers where he held her hand, and his handsome face was earnest. "You have no idea how special you are, how remarkable. I wish . . ." He trailed off, his cheeks actually flushing, and he finally glanced away.

His sincerity was touching. She squeezed his hand. "We're all a team, Alter. We won together. We'll figure out this new threat together. I'm glad you're here to help."

She slipped her hand out of his and retreated a step. His intensity was unnerving. She cared for Alter, but couldn't afford to let him see it. He'd read it wrong, and she was still exploring her relationship with Tomas.

To change the subject, she extracted from her pocket the paper with her partially completed rune. Runes were a topic they could talk about all day, the one way she could get Alter to be himself without worrying about how he'd interpret her every gesture.

She loved how the new rune was turning out. So far it looked like a complex pattern of Chinese characters and Egyptian hieroglyphics intertwined, but she felt on the verge of something magnificent. Her secret fear was that by entering that last memory with the rune in her pocket, somehow it had become partially activated and contributed to the problems they encountered.

"What rune is that?" Alter asked.

"A new one I'm working on." She held it up hesitantly.

Alter studied it. "You're progressing faster than anyone I've ever seen."

His approval meant a lot and she smiled. Runes called to her like nothing else she'd ever known. As she studied them, she often felt she was rediscovering truths she'd already understood, but had temporarily forgotten. It was exciting, and a bit creepy. Several times, she'd recognized the purpose of a new rune even before Alter explained it.

Eirene had suggested her innate talent might stem from a sensitivity to the soul manipulations the runes represented. Sarah had undergone almost as many soul transfers as Gregorios and Eirene. For a mortal, that was unheard of. Had it not been for the protective properties of the machines, her mind would have fractured into insanity long ago.

She hoped to progress far enough in rune lore to assist Alter in his research on the machines. That would be exciting, and it would offer a tangible proof that she was a contributing member to the team.

"So you like it?"

"I sense great potential here," he said thoughtfully.

"It's not finished." She was happy he hadn't suggested the rune might have caused issues. She couldn't see how it might have since she didn't possess a rounon gift, but felt relieved anyway.

Alter shifted closer and traced a pair of marks near the center of the rune with his finger. "I don't recognize these."

They were pieces from the master rune that had appeared over the skyline of 1945 Berlin. She and Gregorios had seen it while fighting Mai Luan. She hadn't dared incorporate the entire master rune after all the dire warnings from Alter about the dangers such runes represented. They tapped the true fabric of history, or something like that, drawing upon the souls of everyone in the world who had been tied to those pivotal moments.

Those small pieces of the master rune had called to her though, and she couldn't help but incorporate them. The resulting rune was far more complex than the first rune she had designed, but there was something still missing. She wasn't sure yet what that might be, but she'd recognize it when she saw it.

She decided not to mention the master rune to Alter. He wouldn't handle it well.

"I'll show you where I got them later," she said, taking the paper from him.

He released it reluctantly as their fingers touched on the paper. "I don't think you should tamper with runes that even I don't know. You've got great natural talent, but if you're not careful you could hurt someone."

"The first one worked," she said defensively.

"It shouldn't have."

"Why not? You keep saying that but you haven't explained."

Alter sat on one of the nearby chairs. "Only a couple of basic runes work well on the left shoulder blade. That's a soul point, but it can usually bond only simple runes that magnify strength."

"So why did my rune work?"

She had designed a rather complex rune, the same one that Eirene had used when she'd lived with the hunters as Alter's great-grand-mother. Where Eirene had worn the rune on her right side, just above her hip, Sarah had felt strongly that it needed to be on her shoulder blade. The rune had proven extremely powerful.

Alter repeated, "It shouldn't have. Your rune links several attributes, including agility, reflexes and focus. Tying that complex rune to that particular strength point should have failed. Or when it did bond, it risked throwing your inner balance off, or even triggering opposite effects to those the rune was supposed to enhance."

"But it didn't do that."

"No, it didn't." He still looked like he hardly believed it.

"You said some people have managed it."

"A couple of times," he admitted reluctantly. He hated sharing deeper runesmith lore. Had anyone else been in the room, she doubted he would have said anything. "But they were different. They possessed the rarest of the rounon gifts."

"What kind of gifts."

That was very interesting. He had never mentioned other types of rune gifts before. It was always the hunter gift or the kashaph abomination, which were variations of the same basic rounon powers.

The vault door opened and an enforcer stepped inside. "Alter, Gregorios wants a status report on when the machines could be ready for another test with additional failsafes installed."

"I'll get right on it." He gave Sarah an apologetic shrug.

Sarah could have throttled the enforcer. She wouldn't get anything else useful out of Alter now.

As Alter and the enforcer discussed the specifications Gregorios was looking for, Sarah headed for the door.

She turned before exiting. "Alter, I'm ready to make my first rune permanent."

"You may want to wait a little longer."

"No. Let's do it today."

"But, Sarah—"

"Today. Promise me."

He sighed. "Fine. I'll find you later."

She gave him a wide smile. "You're the best."

After the two run-ins with the man in the wide-brimmed hat, she couldn't shake a lingering worry that waiting was the last thing she should do.

13

SARAH WAS HOPING to discuss her rune with Eirene, but learned that Eirene and Tomas were scheduled to leave that evening for Thailand. She cornered Tomas at dinnertime. They had been planning to go out to a nice restaurant, but he couldn't get away. The task force tracking the heka cell kept him busy late, and he needed to pack.

They grabbed some take-out food from the cafeteria. While he drove them back toward Quentin's mansion, she asked, "Why didn't you tell me you were going to Thailand?"

"We weren't supposed to leave for another month or two, but the king's health has taken a turn for the worse."

"So he's buying a transfer?"

"Yeah, he's been on the books for years."

"Who is he transferring to?"

"One of his grandsons."

"And his grandson is okay with that?"

Although Sarah had undergone hundreds of soul transfers, she had always done so with the understanding that the new body she wore would be temporary. It wasn't until Mr. Fleischer threatened to sell her body that she realized the true dangers of her position.

The terror of possibly losing herself had made her desperate. When

Tomas had shown her the truth behind the soul transfers, they had worked together to save Sarah's body and rescue Eirene.

"His grandson has been preparing for this for a long time," Tomas said, a bit defensively.

"But he's sacrificing his life."

Sarah knew more about facetakers than almost any outsider, but it still shocked her to think of the awful price for prolonging someone's life. Someone else had to sacrifice theirs instead. She doubted they found many situations like Walter's recent transfer where the young person wanted to become old.

Tomas glanced at her. "I know it seems strange, but it's better this way. He's not trying to take some stranger's life. His grandson is willing to give his life for his grandfather. It's the ultimate act of love."

"For him. For the grandfather, it's total selfishness."

"That's the other reason I didn't tell you about it. I don't think you're ready to see this side of what we do."

"You're right," she said softly. "I'm not ready."

She felt a part of the group. Her relationship with Tomas was growing into something special. She loved Eirene and had learned to see past Gregorios' often-grumpy front to the soft heart he tried to conceal underneath. She trusted them all, cared deeply for them, yet she struggled to accept some of what they did.

How did she really fit in? She wasn't a facetaker, an enforcer, or even a hunter. She was a mortal who'd gotten caught up in their world. Where did that leave her?

Tomas turned to meet her gaze while stopped at a red light, his expression intent. "Do you think I'm evil?"

Sarah sighed. "Of course not. I know you. It's just . . ."

"It's just life isn't fair," he completed for her.

"Something like that."

"We won't be gone long. When I get back, maybe we can get away for a weekend and visit the coast."

"I'd like that."

The crazy events of recent weeks had prevented them from finding more than scattered moments together. One of her original motivations for joining Tomas on vacation had been to explore the potential for their relationship. That had been before she knew he was an enforcer, before she knew anything about heka, before Mai Luan had tried to kill them all.

Before she knew he usually wore a gorgeous young body or that his first life had been a long time ago.

They were still trying to decide what they wanted out of their relationship. Beneath his tough enforcer exterior he was a good man who still clung to values that had gone out of style generations ago. She found all of that appealing and worth exploring. A romantic weekend away might give them the opportunity to figure it out.

Quentin's huge mansion was situated outside of the city, set on a sprawling estate, surrounded by several outbuildings. Two huge, square towers flanked the main entry, and everything was yellow stucco or rough-hewn stone. Ivy crept up one wall, adding a splash of green to the Mediterranean style. Red brick tile led up the circular driveway and under the covered entrance.

Quentin had hosted Sarah there since she'd sought refuge with the critically wounded Tomas. He'd insisted she remain as his guest ever since. She loved the beautiful estate, and loved shooting Quentin's big guns on his private shooting range behind the house.

In the entryway, Tomas kissed her. "I'll see you when I get back, then."

"You don't leave yet," she protested, taking his hand and leading the way toward his room on the third floor of the east wing. It was a spacious suite, but barely looked lived in. She followed him inside, driven by the desire to feel closer to him. That nightmarish memory journey with John had left her rattled.

"You never take me to your apartment in the city," Sarah said as Tomas packed a few belongings.

"No reason to. It's not nearly as nice as this and it's pretty messy."

"It's yours," she said, taking his hands and pulling him closer. "It'd let me see the other part of you. The part that's not an enforcer."

"I am what I am," Tomas said, taking her in his arms. "I have been for a long time."

"How long?" She let him kiss her lightly on the lips, but didn't let go. "I'd really like to know."

"Now's not really the best time." He tried to break away, to retreat like he always did when she asked about his past, but she kept her arms wrapped around his waist.

"You're leaving me again. Give me something before you go."

He sighed and drew her to a comfortable leather couch in the sitting room. "I had hoped to find a quieter time to talk about this with you."

"No, you were avoiding it," Sarah chided

"Maybe." He looked deep into her eyes and for once didn't shield the depth of his feeling. "I was worried I might lose you."

Sarah slid one hand down his cheek. "Tomas, I'm still here despite everything else I've seen in the past few weeks. I know you're older than me. I haven't run yet. So just tell me. I want to know the man I love."

Tomas took her hands in his. He sighed, then his voice slipped into the British accent he'd used occasionally. "I was born Tomas Hanover, son of King George III of England on April 25, 1776."

"Whoa!" Sarah blinked a couple of times as she digested that. "You were actually born the year they signed the Declaration of Independence?"

Tomas grimaced. "That was a hard time for us."

"But that means you're British royalty!"

He shrugged. "The world never even knew I existed."

"How is that possible?" Sarah was having trouble picturing Tomas as a little prince, dressed in a frilly costume. "Everyone pays so much attention to everything the royals do."

"It's quite silly, really. But back then there was no television, no paparazzi with cameras flashing. The world only knew that my mother was pregnant. My twin sister was presented to the world and I was hidden."

Given the upcoming Thailand mission, she realized what that meant, and squeezed his hands. "Oh, Tomas, I'm so sorry."

"It made sense," Tomas said with remarkable calm. "They could show the world a child and conceal a healthy baby boy at the same time."

If her parents had planned to steal her body, she would definitely have had issues. "How did you escape?"

"I didn't. Actually I thought it was a great honor."

Sarah leaned against him as he talked, trying to imagine the cold world he must have grown up in.

"I was raised through childhood, taught that this was the purpose of my life, that I was the most special person in the world because I could sacrifice my body for the king. What subject wouldn't want that honor?"

"Oh, Tomas." Sarah wasn't sure what else to say. "What happened?"

"Two things. When I was fourteen, I visited with my father. We took a carriage ride together while he examined me and checked on my progress. We were attacked by an enhanced Englishman named John Frith in an attempted assassination."

"Were you hurt?"

"No. I stopped him."

"How? You were just a boy."

"I was fourteen. I had already begun extensive physical and military training in preparation for my future role. That was my first real combat, and it happened so fast, I just reacted. It was him or me, and even back then I understood those terms."

"So he was heka?"

"Actually, no. He was turned by the hunters, who sent him to remove the hated facetaker patron and me, the abominable transfer vehicle."

Sarah sat back to digest the incredible story.

Tomas chuckled softly. "The facetaker historians wrote out that bit of history. Now if you look up John Frith, you'll read that he was a mentally disturbed man who threw a rock at the king's carriage."

"That's it?"

"It works. It was the first time my involvement with history was tampered with."

"So how did you escape?"

"I ended up not needing to. The second event that altered the course of my life was that my father, who was originally King George the First and who was on his third life already, couldn't handle another transfer. He suffered advanced mental dissipation and died an old man at the end of that life."

"The facetakers already knew they couldn't transfer his soul again, and my defeat of the enhanced assassin had caught their attention. Since they didn't need me as a transfer vehicle, they arranged to take me on as an enforcer."

"Just like that? You never got a chance to just be a kid, to enjoy life?"

He shrugged. "It was a good life and I was very good at it. I was unknown to the world, but I knew how to move through the upper ranks of society. That proved very useful."

"How?"

Tomas took her face in his hands. "We can talk about it more later. All that matters now is that I have you and I'm happy."

Sarah smiled. Getting that secret out was a good start. He hadn't ever been so open. "So should I call you Your Majesty?"

Tomas grimaced. "No, love. I left all that behind. In fact, for a while I took the name Tommy Atkins. Harald, the facetaker in charge of mucking with history, slipped my name into the British military manuals. For a long time, my name became the default nickname for any British soldier."

"I've never heard of that."

"Look it up," he said with a wry grin. "You can find tons of references to Tommy Atkins or Tommy as generic references to any soldier."

"So you became the universal soldier?"

"Something like that."

He wrapped her in his arms and kissed her soundly on the lips. Sarah eagerly kissed him back. Knowing his age didn't bother her. Knowing the truth eased her lingering worries that he was holding back some darker secret.

The kiss deepened and Sarah lost herself in it. She had wanted to kiss him like this for a while. Her pulse quickened. Tomas responded and kissed her harder, with a hunger she had never felt before.

About time.

Sarah slid back on the couch, drawing him down with her. It was time to show him his hesitation had been unnecessary. When she started tugging at his shirt, he surprised her by sitting up and shaking his head.

"Let's not take this too fast, Sarah."

"It's not too fast. We've been dating for weeks. You said you love me." She touched his face. "And I love you."

She saw the hunger in his eyes, had felt the passion in his kiss.

But he said, "It's just, this is not right."

Sarah sat up, trying to hide how hurt she felt. Had she done something wrong, mis-read his feelings? "I don't understand."

Tomas caressed her cheek. "I want to spend this life with you, Sarah, but I come from an older generation where we held to different morals."

"You're serious?" It wasn't like either of them were virgins. They loved each other, so she felt confused he'd find an excuse to still hold back.

He read her thoughts. "Sarah, these days people don't think twice before jumping into bed together."

"We've thought twice ten times over," she protested.

"You drive me crazy like no woman I've ever known," he admitted.

Sarah kissed him again, felt his passion, but also his resistance. He wasn't making this up. He really believed that becoming intimate was wrong. The gap between his moral code and what she'd grown accustomed to was startling. She sat back, took his hand in hers and massaged the back of it. That seemed to help him relax.

"Didn't Gregorios say to choose your morals in each lifetime?" she asked.

"He did, and he said some morals span the ages. This is one. I'm sorry you're disappointed, but give me more time."

"That's all I'm giving you, it seems." Sarah didn't try to hide her frustration.

She yearned for that physical contact. Amid all the chaos they were living, she wanted him to be her point of strength, the constant in her storm. That he could hold to such a position, despite clearly wanting her only made her want to be with him more.

Alter wouldn't have hesitated.

Sarah drove the thought away immediately, shocked that she'd thought it at all. She loved Tomas, not Alter. It didn't matter how badly Alter wanted her. She needed an anchor point in her life, but she needed it to be Tomas. She sighed. This was going to take more patience and self-control than she'd expected.

Tomas stood. "I may be old-fashioned Sarah, but it doesn't mean we can't have a good time together. When I get back from Thailand, I'll show you."

"You'd better." She was willing to give him time, but she needed to figure out her role in his life, and how she fit into the broader world, which was far more dangerous than she'd ever known.

He drew her to her feet and kissed her tenderly one more time. He was a very good kisser. Part of her loved him more for his integrity, but she wished holding to strong morals wasn't so inconvenient.

"Are you all right with this?" he asked.

Sarah leaned against him and nuzzled his neck. "I'm trying to be. But I'll hold you to your promise."

"Deal."

After he left, Sarah felt an overwhelming urge to blow something up.

She went looking for Quentin.

14

The rumors are true, and worse than true, I fear. Indeed, only one of our brothers assigned to the Templar camp in France escaped alive. Scores of Templars have been captured, tortured, and slain, and the entire order is under threat of extinction. The world has gone mad. Who else could have orchestrated such depravity and so twisted the mind of King Philip but Shahrokh, who has long hated our sponsorship of the Templars?

~ABRAHAM, MASTER OF ARMS, HUNTER SQUAD,
LONDON, REGARDING THE FRIDAY THE 13TH CAPTURE
AND MURDER OF THE KNIGHTS TEMPLAR IN FRANCE,
1307

QUENTIN WAS STILL AT SUNTARA, so Sarah swam laps for an hour in the Olympic-sized swimming pool nestled between the sweeping wings at the back of the mansion. After changing, she moved to the training room and beat on a punching bag, working through the forms Tomas and Alter had taught her, increasing her tempo until she moved in a blur.

She'd always kept herself in good shape, but the heavy training regimen over the past few weeks had toned her to peak fitness. Even though her rune was temporary, it vastly increased her strength, speed, and stamina.

As Sarah moved around the heavy bag, she imagined it wore the face of Rosetta, the heka she'd let get away. That had been her chance to prove herself, and she'd failed.

Alter's voice from the doorway startled her. "You're going to break that punching bag if you keep that up much longer." He advanced into the room and added, "I know. I've broken a few in my day."

The heavy punching bag was a custom model, weighing over five hundred pounds. Lighter bags couldn't take their enhanced blows, but she hadn't imagined she could burst the reinforced canvas.

"Well maybe I should use you as my punching dummy," Sarah joked.

Alter grinned. "Sure."

He set down a leather satchel, then stripped off his shirt. Sarah had to admit she loved seeing him bare-chested. He wasn't as heavily muscled as Tomas, but he was perfectly toned, every muscle sculpted.

He possessed perhaps the most perfect set of abs she'd ever seen. The beautifully-crafted enhancement runes scattered across his torso and arms looked like custom tattoos and added an exotic flair to his sculpted good looks that she found particularly attractive.

Sarah sighed, wishing Tomas was the one standing shirtless before her. Alter was a little too eager, a little too obvious about his pleasure that Tomas would be out of town for a few days.

Even punching him in the face repeatedly didn't seem to dull his enthusiasm.

The two of them sparred back and forth across the room for half an hour, and she lost herself in the fast-moving contest. Alter always encouraged her to strike hard and not hold back, so she threw herself into the contest without her usual restraint.

At first he looked surprised, then grinned and matched her increased intensity and tempo until they were striking with enough force to really hurt each other if one of them missed a block. It was scary and exhilarating at the same time, and she vowed to beat him for once.

She failed.

His fist slipped past her blocking arm and slammed into her jaw like a freight train. She saw stars, and the room spun around her as she toppled to the floor.

Sarah rolled with the impact, imagining she was fighting Mai Luan, who wouldn't wait for her to recover. She returned to her feet to face Alter, fists up, swaying a little as she fought to center herself again.

"Good recovery," Alter said, backing away and gesturing toward a nearby bench.

"Nice hit," she said as she dropped onto the bench and reached for her water bottle. "I should have had that one."

"That's the best you've ever fought. Don't beat yourself up about it."

She chuckled. "I've been beat up enough, thank you."

That blow should have left her shaken for a long time, but the effects were already draining away under the power of her enhancement. She leaned against the wall and stared across the training room, out the wall-length windows overlooking the pool. That fight had been exactly what she'd needed.

Well, all but the punch in the face.

She loved the training room in Quentin's mansion, preferring it to the larger facility at Suntara. She trained every morning with one of her teachers before heading for the headquarters. Quentin had insisted on hosting them all at his home as long as they stayed in Rome. Sarah hadn't argued. Quentin was an excellent host.

They also had plenty of privacy. Although Quentin's staff was quite large and there were always several enforcers on guard duty, it usually felt like they had the place to themselves. Dozens more people could have stayed there and not felt crowded.

Sarah enjoyed feeling like she was finally starting to get a handle on fighting. Tomas and Alter had worked out a compromise approach to training her, focusing on the fundamentals of how to bring the pain before her opponents could do violence to her.

The brutality of the training might have turned her off to the whole idea had she not just survived the life-and-death struggle against Mai Luan. That conflict taught Sarah that there were enemies out there intent on killing. So she learned to drive a finger or blunt object into someone's eye. She learned how easy it was to rupture an ear drum or a crush a windpipe or shatter a joint.

She was good at it.

Her rune helped. Both Alter and Tomas commented that she picked up the techniques fast. Her rune increased her speed and reflexes, and she blamed it for her ready willingness to hurt someone when she needed to.

Additionally, her training helped ease her fears, calm the nightmares that plagued her sleep ever since the showdown with Mai Luan. She might not be an enforcer or a hunter, but she vowed never again to be a victim.

After resting for a moment, Sarah said, "I need that rune inscribed, Alter."

His contented smile faded. "Sarah . . ."

She pulled out of her pocket a folding knife Tomas had gifted to her. "Just do it, Alter."

"Not with that."

He retrieved his leather satchel and extracted a beautifully carved wooden box, about the size of her outstretched hands. It was fashioned from dark wood, polished to a bright shine. Every side was carved with runes, only some of which she recognized.

"What's that?" she asked eagerly.

Alter opened the box, revealing a set of fine-pointed knives with carved handles. "This is my runesmith kit."

Sarah touched the lid and it thrummed against her finger. "There's active power here."

He nodded. "Fueled by my soul, linked by my rounon. The box protects the contents and preserves the knives."

"Wow." Sarah hadn't realized such a thing was possible.

"I haven't used it much since coming here. These knives are used for personalized runes and for higher-level rounon activities."

"Like what?"

"Like making your rune permanent." He extracted a short, double-edged knife with a simple handle, carved with the Egyptian ankh symbol of life.

Sarah was wearing a halter-top that left her shoulders bare. She looked at herself in the wall-length mirrors. Her exposed left shoulder blade still wore the fading mark of her temporary rune. When he first drew it, she'd felt a rush of strength and agility. As the rune faded, the effects had waned too. He had needed to redraw it every few days, and every time he did, he'd renewed those effects.

"I can't wait to make it permanent." This was her rune, personalized and discovered by her in the hectic days leading up to the confrontation with Mai Luan. It had helped save her life, and she yearned to have it sealed to her forever.

Alter hesitated. "There's usually more to the first rune ceremony."

He had annoyed all the others with his long-winded monologue prior to marking the temporary rune, but she hadn't minded.

She gripped his hand. "It's all right, Alter. I think you covered it pretty well. The others are gone, so there's really no point."

"You recognize the importance of what you're doing?" he couldn't help but ask.

"I do."

"And you swear to use your enhancements to battle the forces of evil and protect the innocent?"

"Alter, I'm not joining a superhero league. I'm fighting heka."

"Fine." He looked frustrated that she didn't let him turn the moment into another major ceremony. "Don't move."

Sarah stiffened as he lifted the knife to her skin, forcing herself to watch in the mirror as he started cutting. Alter moved with quick, sure strokes. The tip of his knife sliced through her skin, leaving a trail of red in its wake.

She barely felt anything.

The blade had to be as sharp as a scalpel, and he wielded it with incredible precision. He completed the shallow cuts of the rune in under ten seconds, finishing with a flourish. As he stepped back to admire his work, a deep warmth radiated from the rune. The crimson lines glowed with a soft blue light.

Alter grinned. "It's looking good. It usually takes several hours for a rune to completely bond—"

The rune flared to brilliant white. Sarah had to turn away from the mirror and shield her eyes. The radiating warmth intensified, and she gasped from the power of it. Every muscle quivered with rippling energy, and lingering aches from the recent punch in the jaw evaporated.

She glanced back in the mirror. The light had already faded. The new rune glowed like silver on her skin. Alter approached and touched it with a hesitant finger, his expression surprised.

"I guess it worked," she said.

"Too fast," he muttered.

"Well, I've had the temporary rune for a long time."

"That shouldn't make a difference. This rune is already tightly bonded to your soul. It's fully powered."

"That's a good thing, right?" She felt wonderful, stronger than ever.

Alter paced away, and when he turned he was almost glaring. "Who are you, Sarah?"

"You can't ask me that and say my name in the same sentence," she teased.

"Don't play games. Each new rune for a person bonds more quickly than the last, as long as a soul has the vitality to power it, but the first rune always takes longer."

"You're the runesmith." Sarah didn't care why it worked. She was loving the effects. She felt like she could run all day.

"But what are you?" he asked softly.

"Is this going to be one of those Mr. Miyagi moments?"

"Who?"

Sarah rolled her eyes. "Really? You don't know *Karate Kid*? It's a classic. You've got to see it."

"Are you asking me on a date to see a movie?" Alter asked, his tone joking, but his expression eager.

"You wish."

He really did. If Tomas hadn't already been in her life, she probably would have agreed to go out with him.

"I wish I knew how you do it. You pick up runes better than most hunters. You design a higher-level rune on your first attempt, and it bonds in seconds."

"If you're trying to flatter me, it's working," Sarah teased. "But that movie's been out of the theaters for years."

He allowed a hint of a smile, but persisted. "It's not in your blood, but there's got to be something."

"What do you mean, it's not in my blood?" Her family might not be a thousand centuries old like his, and her parents had driven her away with their ridiculous expectations of a meaningless life, but that didn't give him the right to disparage them.

"Only one family line has ever demonstrated this level of natural rune talent, and then only rarely."

"Well, maybe I'm connected somehow."

"No. I wondered about it and had my family check."

"Check what?"

"Your genealogy."

That was a surprise. "Really? I barely know my grandparents."

Alter shrugged. "We have connections to extensive databases."

"And they'd spend time doing that kind of research for you?"

"It's important, Sarah."

She didn't see why. "Well, what did you find?"

"Not as much as we should have," he said with a little frown. "The family archivists tracked several of your lines all the way back to the Middle Ages, but a surprising number of your lines have been lost."

"Lost how?"

"The records just don't exist. We were focused on Europe, and they usually kept good records. The biggest danger was always fire, and fires seemed to happen a lot to your family lines."

Sarah shrugged. "I'm sure everyone's history runs through times like those. Think of all the wars and disasters that could wreck a church."

"It's true, there's a certain percentage of loss expected, but usually we can work around those, tie different lines from different towns back to common ancestors, that sort of thing. In your case, the number of broken lines was so extensive, there are gaps our genealogists haven't been able to fill yet. We can't be sure if there are any connections with that family tree."

"Whose family?"

"Joan of Arc."

Sarah laughed, but realized he was not joking. "*The* Joan of Arc?"

Alter nodded. "She had a singular gift. That was why she was so successful in battle and why they really killed her."

"So when you mentioned rare rounon powers before, you were talking about her?"

He nodded. "She was one of the incredibly rare individuals we call rune warriors."

"Rune warrior," Sarah repeated slowly, loving how the words rolled off her tongue. Just like runes felt right at a fundamental level, the title called to her. "What does that mean?"

"It means she could do things none of the rest of us could. I thought maybe you might be connected. It would explain your innate understanding of runes."

"But you can't tell for sure with my genealogy so messed up?"

"There are other ways," he said softly, not looking her in the eye.

"What ways?" she pressed, eager to learn more. "Tell me about it, Alter."

"I don't want to encourage you. You already push the limits so far beyond what's safe, it's a miracle you haven't killed yourself."

Sarah chided, "Sometimes you act like a grumpy old man. Come on, Alter. You can't mention something like that and not tell me more. It's cruel."

She placed a hand on his arm, pleading.

Alter glanced up to meet her gaze, then sighed. "Fine, but it's kind of a long discussion. We can talk about it at dinner."

"That's a good idea." They often shared meals while discussing runes. It was a good use of time.

Talk of rare rune powers stirred her appetite for learning, and fueled her desire to complete her new rune. She'd work on it through the afternoon.

"Wait," Alter said as she rose.

He cleaned the little rune knife using a crimson-colored cloth from his rune kit box. He replaced the knife, his movement reverent, then carefully closed the lid. When he rose, he extended the box to her.

That surprised her. "What are you doing?"

"I wish you to have this."

"Why? I'm not a hunter or a kashaph."

Alter grimaced, as if imagining one of the abominable cultists getting their hands on his precious rune kit. "Please, Sarah. This is a gift I'm making freely. It's important."

"Then you shouldn't waste it on me." She felt deeply moved by his desire to offer the precious gift to her, but she couldn't reciprocate. Would he think he was winning access to her heart? She didn't want to lead him on. She cared about him too much to do that.

But he said, "I have my reasons, and I want you to have it."

Sarah should refuse, but he looked so earnest, she couldn't. She reached out to take it, but he pressed her hand to the lid. The wood glowed under the contact and the runes carved into it radiated warmth into her skin.

"What's happening?" she asked softly, filled with a sense of wonder. She loved seeing things that runes could do that didn't involve killing people.

"I'm transferring it to you," Alter said, his head bowed in concentration. "I'm attuning the runes to your soul. They'll preserve this kit for you."

"But I don't have a rounon gift," she protested.

"I'm facilitating the transfer." After a couple seconds he frowned. "It is done."

"Then why do you look like you just swallowed a bug?"

"It happened too easily. I've never transferred something like this, so it should have been difficult. I was prepared for that, but the transfer went too smoothly, almost as fast as if I was transferring it to another hunter."

"Well you did just inscribe a rune for me," Sarah pointed out. "We're already linked."

He frowned again. "Perhaps."

"Don't look so bummed," Sarah said, her tone light. "I didn't force you to give it to me."

"It's not that, really."

"Then let it go. No one likes an Indian giver."

"What does that mean?"

"Don't regret being generous. And thank you, Alter. I can see how important this is to you." She hugged the box close.

"Since it bonded so well, keep it open on your desk while you study runes. The enhancements worked into it will facilitate quicker learning and improve memory of rune lore."

"Wow, really?" That was awesome.

"This box has been in my family for twenty-five generations. Some of the best runesmiths of all time have worked on that sequencing."

Sarah looked at the beautiful box with new wonder. "Alter, this is a precious heirloom. You can't give it to me."

He pulled his hands behind his back. "It's done, Sarah. It cannot be undone."

The depth of his generosity moved her again. Alter wasn't subtle, but he'd never tried winning her with gifts before. Tomas had given her a gun. She'd been thrilled, but maybe she needed to encourage him to try a little harder.

She didn't want to encourage Alter, but she couldn't receive such a wondrous gift without giving Alter a little kiss on the cheek.

"Thank you," she said, and she meant it.

His cheeks flushed, and she retreated. "I'll see you later, Alter."

Sarah returned to her room, and after a long shower, threw herself into her rune studies. The hours quickly fled until dinner time. Eager to learn more about rune warriors, she headed for the art gallery dining room.

15

Baking is an under-appreciated secret weapon. If I wanted to conquer the world, I'd use pastries. In a single lifetime, I'd be hailed queen of the world by a fat and happy populace. I can think of worse futures.

~HARRIETT

WHEN SARAH ARRIVED in the beautiful art gallery dining room on the main floor of the mansion, Alter was already waiting. The room served as the team's unofficial meeting hub, and Sarah had expected to find the group gathering for another dinner.

Alter was alone. He'd discarded his normal hunter tactical clothing for navy slacks and a matching dress shirt. He looked great. The end of the table, which could have seated twenty, was set for only two, complete with candelabra. She couldn't imagine how he'd arranged the private dinner, but he was clearly planning for more than another working meal.

Alter helped her with her chair. "You look lovely, Sarah."

"Thank you. You clean up pretty well yourself."

She'd worn a dark skirt and a cream-colored blouse. Her thick hair hung loose below her shoulders. She was glad she hadn't dressed down like she'd been tempted to. She didn't want to encourage his interest, but he'd invested enough effort into the dinner that she decided to enjoy it.

Alter sat across from her as the first course of Greek salads were served. His gaze was intense, but Sarah didn't give him time to make the meal uncomfortable.

"I know so little about your family, Alter. Tell me about them."

"You already know what's important."

Sarah shook her head. "Not exactly. Did you know, you've never once mentioned your mother?"

She had realized it just that afternoon. His father and brother were such important parts of his life, but she knew so little about the rest of his family.

"My mother was special," Alter said, glancing down at his plate, his voice soft.

"Was?" Sarah wished she'd picked a different topic.

"She died saving my life."

"I'm so sorry."

"She was the heart of our clan as much as my father is the head. She was a brilliant strategist, and led the women's infiltration corps."

"What's that?"

"Her core mission was gathering intel and infiltrating suspected kashaph cells. She helped orchestrate some of the most important strikes of the century."

"Why haven't you told me about her before? She sounds incredible."

"She was," he said with a soft smile. "We cherish her memory, so I don't speak of her around the demons."

"Please stop calling them that. You'll never get over your family's bias with the constant name calling."

"You're assuming the bias is wrong," he responded.

"What do you think your mother would have thought of you working here with the facetakers?"

He considered the question. "She would have supported the need to remove the cui dashi, but she would not have wanted me to linger as long as I have."

"You've had good reason."

Alter leaned forward. "She always told me to keep my heart pure, and I'd always know what to do."

"Sounds like good advice."

"Except remaining in the company of the dem . . . He sighed and with an effort continued. "The facetakers, is slowly drawing me away from the purity of my family mission."

"I don't see it that way," Sarah said, hoping he was finally in a position to listen to reason. "You're assuming your family's hatred of facetakers is the right thing."

"And you're deluding yourself that it's not," he shot back.

"You've spent weeks here. Have you really seen justification for that hatred?"

"Eirene and Tomas are at this very moment in Thailand transferring the soul of the king into the body of a relative. They're sacrificing one soul to the greed of another. Yes, there is plenty of justification, Sarah. You just refuse to see it."

Sarah was not about to get into yet another argument with Alter about the right or wrong aspects of what the facetakers did. She felt uncomfortable with some of their work, but they were good people. She had decided to keep an open mind until she understood more. She wouldn't risk her relationship with Tomas over her misgivings. Not yet.

"What was your mother's name?" she asked instead.

"Nava."

"That's lovely."

"It means beautiful in Hebrew."

"I bet she was."

He nodded. "She died with great honor. On one of my first missions, we were taking down an unusually sophisticated kashaph cell in South Africa, led by a well-trained enchanter. They were attempting to subvert efforts to end apartheid, with plans to assassinate Nelson Mandela."

"During the assault, the enchanter rushed my squad, carrying a large explosive device. He had activated a protective rune web that deflected our bullets. If he'd reached us and detonated the device, he would have killed us all."

Sara listened, horrified and fascinated at the same time. She imagined young Alter facing imminent death, but felt even more tempted to ask about the rune web. Zhu, the enchanter working for Mai Luan, had used a very sophisticated rune web in Suntara and nearly killed Tomas. She knew too little about them.

Alter continued. "My mother intercepted him. Tackled him right out a window."

"But I thought he was protected by a rune web?" Sarah asked.

"Webs are powerful, but very specific. That one had been designed to block our weapons, probably keyed against fast-moving objects like bullets. He hadn't included the modifiers to stop someone from pushing him."

"You're going to have to teach me more about those."

"We'll get to it," he promised, then sighed. "He pulled her out a window with him. They both died in the blast."

"That's terrible."

"She saved me and seven other hunters, and killed a powerful enchanter. We consider such a death a great honor."

They ate in silence for a few minutes as Sarah considered his words. Alter ate slowly, eyes downcast, his expression thoughtful.

The main courses were served, and they included traditional Hebrew dishes as well as some American favorites. The mouth-watering aromas of fresh challah bread, slow-cooked brisket, and flaky borekas mingled with the familiar smells of lasagna and mashed potatoes.

The wonderful feast helped ease the solemn air, and Sarah dug in eagerly. One of the best side-effects of her heavy training routine was that she could eat just about anything without worrying about her waistline.

After sating her immediate hunger, Sarah broached the main subject. "Alter, you promised to tell me about rune warriors."

He took a long drink before speaking. "They're rare. We haven't had a confirmed rune warrior since Vlad the Impaler in the mid-fifteenth century."

"Hold on," Sarah interrupted. "Vlad? The original vampire?"

Alter grimaced. "Bram Stoker dug up shadows of truth that we'd thought eradicated. The stories get most of it wrong."

"Can runes turn someone into a vampire?" Sarah asked, not quite sure she wanted to know the answer.

Gregorios' voice boomed through the dining hall. "You bet they can. It's messy, though."

He strode into the room, followed by his daughters. The three were dressed very well, as if for an evening out on the town. Sarah rose to hug Francesca and Harriett.

"I thought you were going to a show tonight?" Alter asked, not hiding his disappointment at seeing them.

Gregorios dropped into a chair beside Alter and dragged the brisket close. He didn't bother waiting for the servers who were scrambling to bring new place settings, but pilfered Alter's dessert fork and started in on the meat, eating right out of the pot.

Francesca rolled her eyes at him as she settled gracefully into a chair beside Sarah. Harriett paused to lean over the table, eyes closed, breathing deep the aromas, a little smile on her face.

Francesca gave Alter a wink. "Dad had some last-minute delays."

"It's not like we had dates or anything anyway," Harriett said with a shrug.

"Good thing we got delayed. This is delicious," Gregorios said between bites.

Alter looked like he was wishing he hadn't left his guns in his rooms.

Francesca asked, "We're not interrupting, are we? You two look pretty cozy."

"This is a working dinner," Sarah explained quickly. "Alter's telling me about rune warriors."

Gregorios grunted, wiping his face with Alter's napkin. "Haven't had a good rune warrior since little Joan."

"Vlad Dracula post-dated Joan by thirty years," Alter said, looking happy to find an excuse to argue.

Gregorios made a dismissive gesture. "Don't consider him a good one."

Sarah said, "I still don't really know what rune warriors are so I don't understand the references."

"You mentioned Vlad before even telling her the basics? Not a good recipe for success," Harriett chided Alter.

Gregorios clapped Alter on the shoulder. "Good for you, boy. Finally working on that sense of the dramatic."

Alter glared, then turned to Sarah. "I was going to start with examples to help clarify the concepts. Rune warriors possess the rarest form of rounon gift. They can use runes the rest of us cannot."

"How?" She loved the idea of even more runes.

"Their ability is broader," Alter said.

Francesca paused in the act of serving herself lasagna. "I think of it as flexible. It's a good quality to foster."

Alter ignored her. "Hunters power our enhancements from our own souls. Kashaph steal the power of other souls to fuel theirs, but still need direct access to those sacrificed souls."

"Except for rune webs," Gregorios interjected as he speared half a loaf of challah bread that Harriett was reaching for, earning a frown from her.

Sarah was glad he mentioned webs again. "How do those work anyway?"

Harriett said, "Need a really powerful enchanter to start. Webs can produce area-wide effects, from defensive energy shields to attacks directed against other souls, like what Zhu used against Tomas and his team. They're complex and difficult to maintain."

"And they still need to be generated by captive souls that have been inscribed with the necessary runes. So the same basic limitation, just a broader result. And they consume a lot of souls," Alter added.

"How are rune warriors different?" Sarah asked.

Francesca said, "They don't need to inscribe runes on targeted souls to fuel their ciphers. Fascinating process."

"Ciphers?" Sarah asked. That was a new term.

"They're runes that are not powered directly by attached souls," Alter explained. "That's what makes rune warriors so dangerous."

Gregorios frowned at him. "Your clan always sees them as a threat. Just like any weapon or any gift, those powers can be used for good as well as for evil."

Alter retorted, "It is abomination to sacrifice other souls to those ciphers. They are as bad as when you demons destroy one soul to grant new life to your clients."

Francesca gestured with her fork. "It doesn't have to be a bad thing. Heka generally destroy the souls they use to power their enhancements, but rune warriors can use modifiers to set the percentage of how much energy they drain."

"It's the same principle," Alter retorted.

Harriett piped in. "Not at all. Think of the rune warriors we know about. Vlad, Joan of Arc, Hannibal."

"Hannibal?" Sarah interrupted. "The guy who invaded Italy?"

She nodded. "David the Builder was another one."

"Who?" Sarah asked.

Gregorios said, "King David the Fourth, of Georgia. One of the greatest military minds ever, and a rune warrior whose power was matched only by his subtle mastery of the skill. His own armies didn't comprehend what he did to them, but his deft application of ciphers played a key role in his so-called miraculous victories. He was referred to as The Sword of the Messiah."

Francesca sighed, a far-off look in her eye. "And he was one fine looking man." She glanced at Alter. "Almost as good looking as you."

"When did he live?" Sarah asked as Alter flushed.

"About 1100 A.D.," Francesca said.

"I'll have to look him up online."

Harriett said, "I can do one better. I'll have his real history pulled from our archives. It's a fascinating read."

"I'd like that."

"Get the history of Khalid ibn Al-Waleed too," Francesca said as she served herself another helping of lasagna. "He was another great rune warrior. His doctored history still inspires people. They called him The Sword of Allah."

"I never heard of him," Sarah said.

"Probably because you're not Muslim."

"Another sword title," she commented.

Gregorios drained his wine and said, "It happens. Rune warriors are rare. Few of them realize their potential, but when they do, the world takes notice."

Alter said, "We try to make sure they don't realize that potential. They change the face of the world."

Gregorios shrugged. "Sometimes the world needs changing. Have you ever considered that killing them might destabilize things?"

"Hold on. Did the hunters kill Joan of Arc?" Sarah demanded.

"No. She was executed before our team arrived."

"I always thought it was the hunters that got her executed," Gregorios said, giving Alter a thoughtful look.

He shook his head. "We actually supported her work. England was the primary sponsor for you demons at the time, and our family had strong ties with the French nobility."

Gregorios chuckled. "They were lying to you. We had several active contracts with members of the French nobility the whole time."

Before they could start another argument, the door at the far end of the room opened and Bastien entered with Quentin. They waved and joined the group. This time the servers got the new place settings added just as the men seated themselves at the table. They were very good.

"I hope this evening's repast is satisfactory," Quentin said with a warm smile.

Sarah said, "It's all delicious. You have the best cooks in Rome."

"I certainly hope so, my dear. You deserve nothing but the best."

Bastien chuckled. "You are smooth, mon ami. And so very right."

Sarah smiled at Bastien's pleasant French accent. "We were discussing rune warriors. It's fascinating."

"Splendid," Quentin said as he expertly folded his napkin across his lap. "A topic I know too little about."

Harriett briefly recounted the earlier discussion then added, "Most rune warriors have powered their ciphers with the willing souls of their own armies."

"Abomination," Alter muttered around a mouthful of brisket.

She met his gaze calmly. "Not at all. Their men were willing and eager to support their leaders."

"Had they known the truth, they would have revolted. Every time we've shared the truth of those soul-stealing powers with the common folk, they've destroyed the evil ones sucking their lives."

"You prey upon the superstitions of the commoners. That's not the same thing," Francesca chided.

"Stop arguing for a minute, and you might learn something," Gregorios urged, placing a restraining hand on Alter's arm, which made the young hunter look even more eager to fight.

Harriett put her fork down and said calmly, "Say a rune warrior draws only five percent energy from the souls of a lot of people. Those affected barely feel any drain. And yet, spread over an entire army, the cipher produces vast amounts of energy that the rune warrior can use to enhance their troops or protect them, thus saving many of the lives they just tapped. Is that not a worthy cause?"

"No," Alter rebutted, his jaw set in the stubborn line that Sarah knew so well. "Once a rune warrior starts down that road, what's to stop them from drawing ever-greater percentages, from turning their people into slaves to fuel their lust for power?"

"What's to keep hunters from turning their gift on others, as the heka do?" Harriett responded.

"We would never," Alter declared.

Harriett nodded. "Because of your honor. Is it impossible to assume others might have a sense of honor as strong as yours?"

"Vlad the Impaler didn't," Alter shot back. "He sacrificed tens of thousands, impaling them to conceal the truth of how they died, their souls drained to fuel his evil ciphers."

Gregorios shook his head. "He was a unique case. Stop focusing on him."

"He represents the danger inherent in all rune warriors."

"You're overlooking the good they can do," Francesca said. "Vlad was fighting the Ottomans, the most powerful empire of that day. They inundated his little nation with enhanced troops that threatened to sweep over Europe. He alone stood in their way, protecting western Europe."

"He was a monster," Alter exclaimed.

Gregorios said, "That's what he became, but that's not how he started. Before he broke, he was a man of honor, intent on establishing balance in the area and in protecting his people."

"What happened?" Sarah asked, intrigued by the conversation. She'd seen the movie about Vlad, but reality was again proving far more interesting.

Gregorios sighed. "He attempted to use a cipher that was beyond his strength. He built a series of fortifications across his country and included in their construction a number of ciphers that covered the nation in an invisible matrix. It drew a little power from the souls of everyone living there, linking them together in a master cipher of incredible power."

"Abomination," Alter hissed.

Gregorios ignored the interruption. "Vlad tapped that power, attempting to enhance himself so he could destroy the Ottoman heka threat. It overwhelmed him, unfortunately. No one had attempted anything like it before. If it had worked, it might have produced the first real-life superhero."

"Instead it produced one of the world's worst villains. Proving my point," Alter said.

Gregorios shook his head. "Not at all. He very nearly succeeded. You've known hunters who have attempted to stop powerful kashaph and who have died in the attempt. You call them heroes, like your mother."

"Never speak of her!" Alter cried, face flushed with anger. "She didn't cause the deaths of tens of thousands of her own people."

"Why do we speak of these rune warriors tonight anyway?" Bastien interrupted.

Sarah was grateful he deflected the argument. "Alter's been studying my genealogy. He thinks maybe my knack with runes is somehow connected with Joan of Arc's bloodline."

"She was such a dear," Harriett said.

"Ridiculous," Bastien said, making a dismissive gesture. "You are wasting time, Alter."

The young hunter said, "It's possible, but her family tree has too many gaps."

"Does it bother you so much to think Sarah is a mortal who possesses a mind as beautiful as her face?" Bastien retorted.

"That's not the point. There has to be a reason."

Bastien said, "You are grasping. There has never been a rune warrior from America."

"It's possible."

Bastien's expression turned disapproving. "Better to focus on important things, like figuring out how John's memory got twisted to Thermopylae."

Sarah felt crushed by Bastien's flippant dismissal of the idea. Then again, had she wanted to believe Alter just because she yearned to find some kind of tangible link to the world of soul powers?

The dinner ended a short while later with Alter storming from the room and Gregorios intercepting the waiter bringing in a four-layered chocolate torte. Harriett objected to him dishing out the dessert, which started a light-hearted argument about who should do the honors.

Quentin won.

Before he allowed them to dig in, he motioned to one of the waiters and spoke softly into the man's ear. The waiter trotted off and Quentin turned to them, his eyes twinkling. "Before dessert, I wish to share a treat."

Everyone looked as thrilled as children at Christmas, although Gregorios kept eying the cake.

Francesca beamed. "I love your surprises. They're enough to take a girl's breath away."

"I do my best to please," Quentin replied, making a little bow from his seat.

A white-coated woman entered the room, carrying a small box and a portable projector. Quentin accepted the items with a nod of thanks, and pointed the projector at the nearest wall. "Here is some footage from a recent test firing."

Harriett said, "We're not going to get to play with the new toys?"

"Not in my dining room."

The image projected onto the wall showed a shining steel minigun with three barrels, mounted on a rolling base. Tomas was standing at the trigger.

"I thought Tomas was out of the country," Sarah said, drinking in the sight of him.

"We filmed this just prior to his departure."

"And he didn't invite us?" Gregorios asked, echoing Sarah's thoughts.

Quentin shrugged. "One of the privileges of being captain. He gets to test things out first."

"There is some danger in such a privilege, no?" Bastien asked.

"Let's focus on the positive," Quentin said, pressing the play button. On screen, Tomas opened fire and hundreds of fifty-caliber rounds poured through the gun, shredding distant wooden targets.

"I never grow tired of watching miniguns at work," Gregorios said, leaning closer to the cake. "But how does this rate as one of your inventions?"

"That was just the calibration test," Quentin said, skipping forward to the next sequence. "As you surmised, the gun is an existing piece of hardware. It is known as the GECAL 50. But with my specialty rounds, it becomes something more."

Tomas opened fire on screen and again the gun unleashed a deadly volley. This time, many of the rounds were tracers, red and orange streaks that highlighted the trajectory of the rounds aimed at military vehicles. The film hadn't been made on the mansion grounds, and Sarah decided to get Quentin to invite her to join them next time they went there to play with the big guns.

Other rounds were armor piercing, incendiary, and explosive. They destroyed the armored vehicles in a matter of seconds. The most interesting rounds sent sheets of blue-white lightning arcing around the targets.

"Wait, what are those? I've never seen anything like it," Sarah said.

Quentin was smiling proudly. "I call that effect the Curtain Call. I've developed a compound that reacts with extreme prejudice against activated soul powers. It creates that visible effect and disrupts enhancements, and even rune webs, for a short period."

They all gaped at him. The ramifications of that invention were incredible, and terrifying.

"How long have you had this compound?" Gregorios asked softly.

"It is a recent breakthrough, and from your expressions, I see you recognize the danger our own people might face should hostile forces obtain the secret. I alone know the formula. Not even my closest assistants know how it is made, and we used up almost all of it during that test."

He opened the box and extracted a device that looked like a grenade, only blockier. He displayed it to them with a proud flourish. "The last of the compound is in here."

"What do you plan to do with that?" Sarah asked.

"This goes into my emergency preparedness kit."

"This is magnifique," Bastien breathed. "This could revolutionize how we fight the heka."

Gregorios' expression had turned thoughtful. "Perhaps. Don't make any more until we think this through. Keep no documentation on this product, and let's set up a time to discuss it in detail when Eirene and Tomas return."

"I thought you might see things that way. How about some cake?"

As they ate the delicious confection, Gregorios turned to Sarah. "I hope you learned something useful tonight."

"It's been interesting," Sarah admitted.

"Do not encourage Alter's interest in your genealogy," Bastien warned, gesturing at her with his fork. "It is unwise to give his family any excuse to consider you a target."

"I'm in no danger from Alter," Sarah said. Except for his constant attempts to get her out on a date.

Bastien's expression remained serious. "Have a care nonetheless. His family often shoots first and looks for justification later."

Sarah brushed away the concern. Alter would never target her.

Would he?

16

I still think it is a mistake to accept Dalal into the fold. Our ranks may be thinned with the loss of Apostolos to Spartacus, and Neofytos to the hunters. Too few of us remain, but I don't trust her. She's an opportunist, and I don't need to be a diviner to see that one day I will face her again as an enemy.

~GREGORIOS, 324 A.D.

JOHN LAY in his enormous bed in his richly-appointed Rome apartment. The bed was a Gothic, wooden monstrosity he had acquired from one of the grand princes of Kiev over a thousand years prior. He no longer bothered to remember the man's name. The useless mortal had barely survived one soul transfer.

The door opened, and John shouted, "I told you to leave me alone!"

It was not Frederick, his manservant. The unknown stranger wore a tailored suit. He looked Asian, but was tall, with a muscular physique.

"Pardon the interruption, Great One," the man said with a subservient bow.

"You have good manners for an intruder," John growled. He had already drawn a loaded pistol from a concealed compartment in the headboard.

"You may call me Peter. I represent a benefactor who wishes to see your return to power."

John said, "Not interested. Send Frederick in here on your way out."

Peter drew closer, his smile unwavering. "Before I go, may I inquire as to the reason you feel so ill today?"

"You may not."

If he took one more step, he was going to get fifteen hollow points to the head. John might be old, but he had mastered the firearm back in the days of the blunderbuss. Today's modern weapons were so accurate, he barely needed to aim at such a close target.

Peter bowed again. "Have you asked yourself why no one else was drawn into that dangerous memory? Why you alone were sent to walk a memory that would kill you?"

"Because Gregorios wants me dead. Just like he killed the others."

It was so obvious. Of course Gregorios wanted him dead. But he had risked the machine anyway. It held the only hope for restoring his vitality. Gregorios had nearly succeeded in getting him killed.

Peter said, "You are as wise as I was informed. Gregorios has lurked in the shadows for decades, only to appear now."

It was refreshing to speak with someone who understood the truth. "He's killing everyone, but no one sees it."

"I can offer some assistance," Peter said, drawing another step closer.

John barked a laugh. "How? He's got the machine."

"Where did he get it from?"

"What are you saying?"

"Just this, Great One. Gregorios has usurped property that he did not create. He barely knows how to turn it on, yet claims to command its secrets."

"Are you saying you have another machine?"

"I am."

John considered the claim and the one making it.

Peter stepped to the foot of the bed. "Mai Luan may be dead, but her work is not." He extended his hand. "Come with me and we can restore your rule."

John smiled. "And Gregorios?"

"His time is about to expire."

17

Every time I invent the perfect heka-killing weapon, someone invents a better enhancement.

~QUENTIN

EIRENE FOLLOWED a tuxedoed man into a luxurious salon in the Klai Kangwon Palace in Hau Hin, Thailand. The room had been prepared for the soul transfer, with two long couches set close to each other.

Three people waited for her. His Majesty, the king of Thailand, sat in a wheelchair looking frail and old in a white uniform under a golden robe of state. His son, the crown prince, sat in a straight-backed, padded chair in his formal uniform. A young man of about thirty sat in the last chair. He looked like a younger version of the old king. They had prepared an excellent vessel for the soul transfer.

With Tomas following a little behind and to her right, Eirene approached and made a short bow, hands pressed together in front of her. The three men returned the traditional Thai greeting, or *wai*, and they bowed just a little deeper, with hands held higher than she had held hers.

She smiled acceptance of the honor they offered.

"I see you are ready for me," she said.

She had found over the years that it was easier to move ahead without delay. Sometimes the sacrificial young one began to have second thoughts. More than once, hunters had burst in during a transfer, and she didn't feel like fighting off a band of Alter's brothers.

Guards had been covertly increased around the palace complex, but it always paid to be prepared. That's why Tomas carried two large duffel bags, which he lowered softly to the ground within easy reach.

His face was impassive, the mask he wore when working a transfer. It concealed any emotional turmoil that might still linger after all these years. It had to be tough watching other young men sacrificed as transfer vehicles, but he never talked about it. Eirene never asked. There was really nothing to say.

"Where is Meryem," the king asked.

Eirene said, "I apologize, Your Majesty. She was detained due to poor health."

"That, I understand," he said with a wry grin.

"Let's change that, shall we?"

She motioned the men to take their places on the lounges. The young man, who was a grandson kept secret from the world, began to look nervous as he lay on the couch beside his grandfather.

The crown prince noticed too.

"Stay strong, my son. You have trained your entire life for this moment. You will receive eternal glory for fulfilling your duty."

The young man glanced at her, but she kept her face expressionless. She wouldn't encourage him to sacrifice his life for his grandfather, but she wouldn't dissuade him from doing it either. How he chose to dispose of his life was up to him.

She didn't relish these soul transfers. It was part of who she was, but she had lived enough lives to understand that the soul worth saving was more often the one willing to sacrifice their life for another. Old men and women who had lived long and prosperous first lives paid her enormous fortunes for the gift of prolonged life, but it was the vessel who paid the most.

It was how the world worked.

That truth helped less and less every time.

The young man took a deep breath and, with a determined expression, nodded. "My life for yours, grandfather."

The elderly king patted his hand. "You're a good boy."

Eirene moved around to the head of the couch where the young man reclined. He closed his eyes and tried to look calm despite his clearly rising fear. He did a better job than many.

She was grateful they weren't using an unwilling vessel. Meryem's consignment team would acquire transfer vehicles for clients who couldn't provide their own, but this way worked much better.

She placed her hands along his jaw and he shivered at her touch. When she embraced her nevra core, the force of her soul flooded her being with its normal intensity and helped settle her mind. This was just another job.

As she considered the man under her hands, she could feel the pulsing strength of his soul. Her eyes began to glow like amethysts, and purple fire rimmed her fingers. She directed her nevron into the skin along his jaw and began severing his soul from his body.

The young man gasped and clutched at her hands, but she expected the move. No matter how willing he might be, at the moment his soul began to separate from the only body he'd ever known, it was only natural to resist.

He had waited too long.

With a thought and a flick of her nevron, Eirene severed his control over his muscles. His arms flopped by his sides and his breathing settled into a deep, even rhythm as his systems began to shut down. His body would remain in that dormant state until a new soul returned to claim it.

Her fingers sank through the skin along his jaw. She grasped the edge of his soulmask and began to pull. Starting at the jaw, it began to lift, separating from his bone structure with that wet, sucking sound she had grown to hate. Another three seconds and it would come free with a pop.

Before she could complete the process, the purple fire along her fingers flickered in a way it never had before and shifted to orange. The strength of her soul rebounded back against her in an internal explosion that knocked her staggering.

Agonizing fire rippled through her torso and burned along her jaw. It felt like the terrifying moment when Maerwynn had betrayed her and removed her soulmask. The pain intensified until it felt just like her recent nightmare where Spartacus had tried sawing off her face with his dagger.

Eirene screamed and fought the agony that drove her to her knees. She clutched at her face and was horrified to feel her skin soften, as if her soulmask were being driven out.

She fought with every ounce of her soul's vitality against the unexpected assault. It was hard to think, and she could barely understand what was happening. Someone had launched a new kind of attack, one she had never heard of, one that undermined the integrity of her nevra core.

With agonizing slowness, she regained mastery over her body, which allowed her to block sensory input and dull the crashing waves of pain. With the pain under control, she forced her will over her nevron, but her core bucked like an unruly stallion.

It was as if she were fighting herself.

With a final exertion, Eirene bottled her nevra core. As soon as that fount of her soul strength was fully contained, the pain vanished and the invisible assailant released her. She slumped to the tiled floor and drank in the welcome coolness against her sweating skin.

"Eirene?"

She had not felt Tomas join her. He knelt close, expression concerned, a pistol in his hand.

She felt incredibly weak and light-headed. "Help me up."

He did, but she swayed and would have fallen had he not supported her. Only when she turned to face the couches did she realize just how bad the situation was.

The aged king was sitting up, face pale with barely-controlled fear. The crown prince had backed toward the door, his horrified expression verging on full-blown panic.

The young man whose soul she had been extracting sprawled across the couch, his body contorted with agony. His soulmask was half removed. The lower section had come free, but instead of shimmering like a healthy mask, the section where the skin had slid away looked dull, as if coated with soot. The upper half was still embedded in his flesh.

Eirene grimaced. If the boy could control his vocal cords, he'd be screaming a constant wail of absolute pain. Leaving a soulmask partially removed was the worst agony a living soul could endure.

"What has happened?" the king demanded.

With Tomas' help, Eirene returned to the couch. Her muscles were not working and her head pounded so hard she could barely think.

"I don't know. Something went wrong."

"Restore him at once."

Eirene placed one quivering hand on the young man's face and dared touch her nevra core. An invisible force punched her in the gut and she doubled over and vomited all over the young man. Her strength failed her and she collapsed.

18

We made the right choice allying with the Crusaders, despite how entrenched the facetakers remain in all the major courts of Europe. Saladin is spreading the kashaph perversions ever farther. The liberation of Jerusalem may yet be possible with the aid of our enhanced brothers embedded within the ranks of King Richard's knights. Let us raise up anew a powerful nation, and then focus on removing the demons.

~ELIAS THE EIGHTH, HUNTER COUNSELOR TO KING
RICHARD, 1191 A.D.

"ARE you sure this is a good idea?" Sarah asked.

She sat on one of the reclining chairs next to the Sotrun machine, beside Gregorios. Bastien and Francesca were preparing to help them don the heavy helmets for another memory walk. Alter and Harriett were going to take the second machine that Sarah had started calling the So-Ugly.

Alter said, "We have new failsafe runes in place. The person running the machines can now pull us out if they need to."

Despite the boundless energy still radiating through her from the new rune, Sarah felt nervous returning to the memory world without Eirene and Tomas.

Gregorios gave her a comforting smile. "It'll be fine. If the man in the wide-brimmed hat really is in there following us around, it's past time for introductions."

Sarah reluctantly settled into the chair. She had hoped Tomas would call and tell her what Thailand was like, but they had heard nothing. Gregorios had explained that Eirene would deal with the soul transfer first. They would call after that. She'd be finished the memory walk and back to Quentin's in plenty of time.

Francesca made a thumb's up gesture before settling the jagged faceplate into position. Then the warmth of Bastien's facetaker power pulsed against Sarah's skin. She closed her eyes and tried to relax as she waited for the gentle descent into darkness.

Instead, the worst migraine of her life clobbered her behind the eyes. Sarah gasped and clutched at the chair, but it had disappeared.

She awoke with a start, lying on rough, black stone. The ground was shaking. The air hung thick with smoke and tasted like rotten eggs and superheated metal.

She gagged on the stench and looked around with bewilderment that quickly changed to fear. She was lying on the upper edge of a volcanic crater. Far below, lava boiled and climbed toward her with terrifying speed.

The volcano was about to erupt.

"This wasn't what I was shooting for at all." Gregorios crouched nearby, legs spread wide to keep his feet. He looked disgusted.

"Where are we?"

He helped her up and pointed down the mountain. Far below, she spied a sizable town.

"That's Pompeii. You're standing on Mount Vesuvius."

"You can't be serious." Sarah glanced back down at the angry mountain. A fresh wave of noxious fumes erupted around them and she stumbled away, one sleeve over her nose.

"The only thing I *can* be sure about is that this was not the memory I wanted."

"Why aren't you freaking out?" Sarah snapped. His calm demeanor in the face of the impending disaster was really annoying.

"Would screaming like a baby and rushing headlong off the cliff really make you feel better?"

Punching him might.

"Why do you have all the nasty memories?" she demanded grumpily.

The ground shook and she would have fallen had he not caught her arm.

"I'm the one who's sent to put out the fires." Gregorios pointed down the mountain toward a small group of people fleeing along a distant ridge, tiny in the distance. "The heka who triggered this eruption died in the process."

Sarah didn't bother to ask if the mountain killed them or if he had. She couldn't imagine why anyone would willingly initiate such a catastrophe.

Gregorios continued. "Took eleven souls and some very sophisticated runes. Always wished I could have gotten my hands on those."

"Why?"

"So I'd recognize them if anyone tried again."

Before Sarah could reply, the mountain around them simply dissolved.

She screamed as they fell into shadow and fire. She felt more than saw the walls of earth and exploding lava. Heavy winds blasted blistering debris against her skin as she tumbled wildly.

Then everything faded to blackness and silence. She could not decide if she was dead or if Bastien had just ripped out her soul.

19

Do not speak of your happiness or of your enhancements to one less fortunate than yourself.

~PLUTARCH

ALTER LAY back on the chair near Harriett, trying not to betray how nervous he felt. He was a hunter, sworn to remove the demons from the earth, and yet somehow he had instead joined their company.

He was about to entrust the purity of his soul to the hands of a facetaker he didn't know. Again.

In other circumstances, they would have been mortal enemies, and yet only moments ago, he had accepted from her what might have been the most delicious cookie he had ever tasted. He wondered if Harriett would hold a grudge the day he pulled the trigger.

Of all of the facetakers, Alter trusted only Eirene. Harriett, whose mind he would be walking through, looked like a pretty young woman. He didn't want to explore her memories. Surely they were full of a lot more than just pie recipes.

Part of him longed to return to Jerusalem and the simpler life at the clan compound. Part of him longed to set Sarah free and help her see the truth. For her he would risk much.

"Don't look so worried," Francesca said as she came to help him with the helmet. "We'll take good care of you, I promise."

She winked. That didn't help at all.

"Aie, we have a problem!" Bastien sounded scared. He was powering the machine linked to Sarah's soul.

Francesca rushed over. Alter tossed aside his helmet and jumped out of the seat to follow.

Bastien had fallen to his knees, his face twisted with pain. The purple fire of his nevron was flickering to orange and burning up his arms.

Francesca grabbed his shoulder, her eyes already glowing with her activated nevra core, and for a second he relaxed.

Then she screamed and began convulsing.

Sarah and Gregorios started shaking in their chairs. Alter couldn't imagine what tortures they were suffering. Harriett grabbed Francesca's shoulder and added her strength to steady the machine.

Bastien drew a shuddering breath. "Something is very wrong. We have to get them out."

"Do it!" Alter shouted.

The moment of clarity passed and Bastien again groaned and bowed over the machine, his limbs shaking so hard it was amazing he didn't collapse.

Alter drew a black marker. He alone remained free to act. For most of his life, he would have considered a situation like this a gift from god. Four facetakers were helpless before him. He could dispatch them all, bring his family great honor.

All he had to do was sacrifice Sarah in the process.

Hating himself for what he had to do, Alter placed his hand on Harriett's quivering shoulder and marked a rune of binding across his hand and onto her neck. Instantly he felt the drain as his life force was sucked into a wild nevron maelstrom. All three facetakers were completely committed, but they had lost control of their powers.

Alter had helped Eirene hold the memory in place while Gregorios and Sarah battled Mai Luan. That experience had taxed his strength, but it was a simple process, like trying to lift a heavy load.

This was like trying to look straight ahead while riding in an airplane that was doing barrel rolls in a hurricane. His stomach rolled with the twisting sensation and he felt on the verge of losing his lunch.

Everything about the chaotic, churning nevron rippling between the four of them felt wrong on a fundamental level. He had never felt the nevron of the facetakers so clearly. Something had broken.

He couldn't explain it, but it tugged at his attention like a splinter in his mind. He focused his will and reached with mental fingers through the maelstrom of facetaker powers and plucked that splinter out.

The facetakers gasped as one and sagged together, their strength spent. Alter grimaced with revulsion. He could actually feel their nevron settling back into the centers of their beings.

Facetaker nevra core were foreign to hunter rounon sensibilities. The time he had helped Eirene power the machine, he felt her nevron pulsing against him as a distant tide, a vague undercurrent. Now the nevron of the facetakers burned in his soul with vibrant clarity. He feared that if his control slipped, the devilish power would invade his soul and corrupt him.

For several seconds, their nevron pulsed with the rhythm of his own heartbeat. He felt like he could seize the combined strength of their nevra cores and command it to do his bidding.

He nearly snatched his hand away. Such an act would defile him to the roots. The moment passed and the facetaker powers seeped away, distant, but somehow no longer foreign.

He couldn't explain what had happened. It was as if they had tried to power a rune that was far too strong to bond to their souls. They were completely spent. His strength alone fueled the machines as their nevra cores flickered and faded. The load was heavy, but he could manage for another minute.

None of the runes on the machines would do this to them. It had to be something in the memory.

Alter hunched his shoulders against the strain. "Bastien, call them out."

"I am trying," Bastien said in a quavering voice, his face dripping with sweat. "They do not respond. The failsafe, she does not work."

"It has to."

Harriett groaned. "Something's shaken the mold. We need to stabilize it."

Through the linked connection, Alter felt her take over the primary link to the machine. It was far too intimate a feeling and he shuddered at the close interaction he was forced to endure with these demons.

The worst part was that they didn't feel evil at all, just extensions of himself.

"What happened?" Francesca asked between gasping breaths.

Alter said, "I have no idea. Let's hope Gregorios can trigger the escape on his end soon."

"If he can't?" Bastien asked.

Fear made it difficult to speak. "Their minds could be lost forever."

20

The first of these was Spartacus, a Thracian of nomadic stock, possessed not only of great courage and strength, but also in sagacity, mighty enhancements, and culture superior to his fortune, and more Hellenic than Thracian.

~PLUTARCH

SARAH AWOKE to soft twilight filtering between tall, brick buildings built close to the cobbled street where she stood. The ground no longer shook, and the air smelled of horse manure and rotting food. A welcome change from the stench they had just escaped.

Gregorios appeared beside her, already scowling. "This is better, but still not what I was looking for."

"Did you do that back there?" Sarah demanded.

"I'm not even sure what happened." For the first time his calm composure cracked.

She decided she preferred it when he looked like he was in control.

"Well, where are we?" Sarah looked around.

They stood at the end of the street, where it emptied into a plaza facing a huge amphitheater. For a moment she wondered if it might be the Colosseum, but it looked smaller than the ruined one she had visited in modern day.

"Capua. Who would want to visit Capua?" Gregorios asked with abundant disgust.

"Is this your memory or not?"

"I've been here, so it probably is. I'm just trying to remember this moment. It's not as easy as it looks sometimes."

"But if you didn't bring us here, do you think it was the man in the wide-brimmed hat?"

"I don't know, but it feels familiar. I'm thinking it's my memory, but I don't know why we ended up here. Something's definitely not right."

"Should we leave?" Sarah fingered her escape rune.

"In a minute. Keep a sharp lookout. If he's here, I plan to have a chat with that hat man of yours."

"Where are all the people?" Sarah asked.

The streets were mostly deserted, with but a few people moving around in the distance. They all hurried, as if afraid of being out.

Gregorios pursed his lips. "I wonder if we landed here just before Capua was taken by Rome. It has the feel of a siege."

Sarah decided she didn't like that feeling. She turned, looking back up the long street she had faced when they first appeared.

A powerfully-built man was charging in her direction. He was dressed like a gladiator, carried a thick, oaken spear, and looked really mad.

"Ah, Gregorios."

He turned and grimaced. "By the forgotten gods, why him?"

The charging gladiator raised his spear and shouted, "Gregorios!"

"Who is it?" Sarah asked nervously.

"Spartacus," Gregorios said with abundant disgust.

"*The* Spartacus?"

He cast her an annoyed look. "I hate it when people talk about him like that. You'd better back up."

Sarah scrambled away as a heavy, round shield appeared in Gregorios' left hand, and a weighted net in his right. She watched with growing nervousness as the raging gladiator closed, amazed to think he might really be the famous Thracian who led a slave revolt that turned into a full-fledged war.

She loved the television series.

Spartacus lunged, driving the spear with enough force to have splintered Gregorios' shield.

Gregorios didn't wait for it. He slipped to the side, deflecting the spear off his angled shield with a metallic clang. At the same time he whipped out the net in a move that was so graceful and efficient, it was more like watching a ballet step. The net flared and enveloped Spartacus like floodwaters over a housetop.

He tried to lunge at Gregorios, but tangled in the net and tripped.

Gregorios kicked him in the head. "I don't make the same mistakes twice."

Sarah was glad Gregorios was all right, but she felt a little disappointed that Spartacus hadn't put up more of a fight.

"I will rip off your head," Spartacus bellowed as he struggled against the sturdy coils of the net.

"Come on," Gregorios said to Sarah. "The net should hold him long enough to finish our work. I want to find your mysterious hat man."

Sarah followed Gregorios up the street at a run. Together they leaped three stories to the rooftops of the long apartment buildings lining the road.

Behind them, Spartacus ripped the net apart, roaring with fury the entire time. Sarah noticed the runes on his back and legs.

"Hey, he's enhanced."

"Tell me about it," Gregorios said, not bothering to look back. "He was one of the most powerful heka ever."

They vaulted over the next street and ran along the rooftops, leaving the raging gladiator behind. Sarah just barely caught Gregorios' next muttered statement.

"Should have killed him when I had the chance."

She didn't like the idea of Spartacus chasing them, but she was glad Gregorios hadn't killed him while he lay helpless in the net. Spartacus was sort of a hero, or at least the television version of Spartacus was. She caught herself feeling betrayed to think he'd been so successful because of his heka enhancements.

Sometimes the truth was really disappointing.

Together she and Gregorios crossed several more streets. Capua was a pretty large town. If they had to hunt for the man in the wide-brimmed hat, it was going to take all night.

Gregorios paused on the roof of a large building, probably some kind of government palace. They stood four stories above a paved piazza with a large fountain and several statues.

"Any idea where this guy might be hiding?" Gregorios asked.

Sarah shrugged. "First time visiting Capua. If he takes off his hat, I doubt I'd notice him."

That wasn't true. She'd recognize the feeling of dread that clung to him like bad breath.

Gregorios turned a slow circle until he faced back the way they'd come. His eyes widened and he muttered, "Oh, Zeus."

Sarah spun just as Spartacus crash-tackled Gregorios into a chimney. As he passed, he brushed her with his broad shoulders and the impact spun her sideways.

She fell onto the roof's ceramic tiles and they broke away under her weight, sending her sliding toward the edge. She scrambled for purchase, but couldn't stop. Sarah plunged off the edge and fell to the manicured gardens below.

She wasn't too worried. She could handle a four-story drop in the memory world.

The shrubbery was unexpected.

Sarah landed hard on a hedgerow shaped like a woman with upraised arms. The shrubbery crumpled, tumbling her across a lawn. With a groan, she stood, brushing leaves and branches from her arms, and spitting out pieces of twigs.

On the roof, Gregorios and Spartacus fought a savage duel. Gregorios was putting up plenty of fight this time. She needed to help Gregorios.

"Well, what an unexpected surprise."

The cultured voice with a hint of accent sent a cold shiver down her spine. Sarah turned and saw a figure standing close behind her.

The man in the wide-brimmed hat.

21

The soul becomes dyed with the color of its thoughts.

~MARCUS AURELIUS, FOURTH LIFE OF EMPEROR NERVA

THE MAN in the wide-brimmed hat crossed the space between them in a rush, but still somehow managed to look unhurried. He grabbed for Sarah's collar, but she slapped his hand away and leaped back over a nearby fountain.

She imagined in that high-flying leap that she looked like Trinity from The Matrix.

He launched after her. Even while soaring over the fountain, he managed to keep the brim of his hat tilted so that she couldn't see his face. She caught a glimpse of smooth-shaved cheeks but that was it. As he flew down toward her, she felt again the sense of dread he triggered.

Enough with that reaction.

Sarah summoned a baseball bat.

The tilt of his concealing brim took on a surprised angle just before she caught him in the ribs with a swing that would have made Babe Ruth proud. Driven by her enhanced strength, the blow shattered ribs and sent him crashing back into the fountain. The statue splintered under the impact, and he fell into the water with a cascade of broken stone. A red stain spread from him.

So much for scaring her with his hat.

A little beast that looked like an over-sized bullfrog with saber-tooth fangs hopped out of the pool right in front of her. It opened its mouth and a long tongue lashed out at her left thigh.

"Eww!"

Sarah squashed it flat with her bat. Then she leaned over the unmoving form of the man and reached for his ever-present hat.

He snatched her wrist.

Sarah instinctively yanked back and away. That only helped him leap out of the fountain and land beside her.

He had already shaken off the effects of her brutal strike. Either he wore several healing enhancements or he had extra souls fueling his powers in the real world like Mai Luan had done in Berlin.

Sarah tried to punch him in the throat, but he caught her other hand. She struggled against him, but even with her enhanced strength, she couldn't break free.

He held her close, although she still couldn't see his face. It was as if he had summoned shadows to crawl up under the brim and keep it concealed.

"How do you fuel the facetaker memory?" he asked.

"What are you talking about, freak?"

His grip tightened painfully on her wrists. He spoke again, his voice formal, with a slight accent she couldn't place. "Do not trifle with me. I will know your strengths. Speak before I decide I have no use for you."

Sarah wasn't sure how to respond to the weird demand. It was like he thought she was the facetaker. She wrenched her arms against his grip and tried to knee him in the groin.

He twisted her wrists, and pain flared up her arms. The pressure drove her to her knees. "I applaud your tenacity, but I am your master now."

That was creepy on all kinds of levels. As Sarah tugged against his grip, her recently bonded rune began to burn against her skin. She felt that strange light feeling she had when facing Mai Luan in Berlin. Her wrists faded in color and she became insubstantial.

His hands passed right through her arms. She could feel them, like chilly shadows. Then she was free.

He stumbled back half a step at the sudden release of tension. Sarah leaped up and kicked him between the legs with every ounce of her strength.

Her foot was not insubstantial.

As tough as he might be in the memory world, no man could ignore a kick like that. He rose four feet into the air under the force of the blow, collapsing in on himself, clutching his groin and hissing a horrible moan.

"Master that, weirdo." Sarah reached for his hat again.

"Look out!"

At Gregorios' shout, Sarah dove to the side. They had practiced together enough that she knew not to hesitate when he used that tone.

A large statue crashed down right on top of the man with the wide-brimmed hat. Spartacus was impaled on the twin, upraised swords at the top of the statue. He was covered in blood and badly battered, but still struggled to free himself.

That was exactly the kind of determination he showed in the movies. Seeing it helped her feel better, somehow.

Gregorios dropped to the ground beside Sarah.

"What took you so long?" she asked.

He scowled at the writhing gladiator. "Some memories don't get better with time."

"Well I wish you'd played with him a little longer. You just squashed the hat man and I was finally about to get a look at his face."

"Dead?"

"I doubt it. I don't see blood everywhere."

"Must have fled the memory. He's fast."

"Tell me about it."

"You tell me about it," he countered. "As soon as we get back."

Gregorios tipped his head to the sky. "Bastien, get us out of here."

As Sarah began fading from the memory, Spartacus heaved himself off the impaling swords. He stumbled toward them, blood gushing out of his torn body, hands extended like claws.

"I will avenge her!"

22

Edward, you paint an excellent picture of the Roman period, but note my edits. In the following passage, you failed to redact references to Nerva's multiple lives. It is critical we maintain the illusion that every emperor was a separate man, living only one life.

"If a man were called to fix the period in the history of the world during which the condition of the human race was most happy and prosperous, he would, without hesitation, name that which elapsed from the death of Domitian to the accession of Commodus.

The vast extent of the Roman Empire was governed by absolute power, under the guidance of virtue and wisdom from men who never lost the cohesive function of their minds.

The armies were restrained by the firm but gentle hand of Nerva through four successive lives (use his other names here), whose character and authority commanded respect.

The forms of the civil administration were carefully preserved by Trajan, Hadrian and the Antonines, who delighted in the image of liberty. Such princes deserved the honour of restoring the republic, had the Romans of their days been capable of enjoying a rational freedom."

JOHN STEPPED out of the back of a Lincoln Town Car and waited for Peter to remove the mask they had secured over his eyes.

"I do not appreciate the drama," John scowled.

Peter made a little bow. "I apologize for the inconvenience, but you must understand security is of paramount concern."

John grunted. Gregorios would hunt them down, determined to assassinate him and anyone who helped him. They would indeed have to be careful.

They stood inside a large, empty warehouse. John guessed they had crossed half of Rome, but his sense of direction was not as good as it used to be. They could be anywhere in the city.

Peter took him up an industrial lift, then down a bare hall. He stopped at a solid steel door and opened it with a flourish. The inside was covered in polished mahogany.

John stepped into an exact replica of his own comfortable study, complete with bookshelves, a fireplace, and several overstuffed chairs.

"We drove a long way just to come home," he grumbled as he sank into the chair closest to the fire. The warmth felt good.

A lovely, slender Asian woman, dressed in a simple white robe appeared by his side with a tray of his favorite brandy and sweetmeats.

"Where's this machine of yours?" he demanded, feeling right at home.

Peter said, "It is being prepped as we speak. It is a proven model, just like the ones Mai Luan was preparing to use to restore your health."

"None of that mucking around in my memories, though?"

"You will be completely at ease, Great One," Peter assured him. "We will have to walk some of your memories to give the machine time to calibrate to your unique mind signature and begin reversing the effects of your accumulated soul fragmentation."

John grunted again. "Very well. Let's get started."

"Soon." Then the man's subservient faded. "We will heal you, but first you must do us a favor in return."

"What favor?"

"We are going on a little trip."

23

The inconsistency of single-life mortals never ceases to amaze me. On the one hand, from the best inquisitors, I learned principles governing human nature and how to influence the minds of men. On the other hand, my soul may never feel cleansed from the tainted memories of disgusting tortures employed by the worst of them.

~FRANCESCA

SARAH EAGERLY PRIED up the jagged faceplate and removed the heavy helmet. "What happened in there?"

"Did you kids notice anything strange during that trip?" Gregorios asked as he sat up.

"You could say that again," Francesca said with a tired laugh.

Before they had begun the memory walk, she had been perky and vibrant as any late teen. Now dark circles hung under her eyes and she sagged where she sat on the floor next to the machine.

Her siblings were likewise exhausted, sprawled together on the floor. As they recounted their experience, Sarah was surprised to hear it was Alter's intervention that saved them. For all his talk of wanting to destroy the demons, he'd missed a unique opportunity.

Sarah hugged him. "Thanks for helping. Sounds like you're our hero."

He beamed bright enough to light the vault.

"So you experienced a unique backlash at the same time we experienced dramatic memory tampering?" Gregorios asked, his expression grave.

"It was more than a loss of strength," Bastien said, his beautiful accent thicker than usual. "It targeted the heart of our nevra cores. I have never felt anything like it."

Gregorios turned to Alter. "How did you counter it?"

"I'm not really sure. I applied a standard linking rune. It shouldn't have made that dramatic an impact."

Francesca rose with a groan and began to pace, her mature expression a bit incongruous on that young form. "I see one of two possibilities. First, the attack was initiated from the other machine that this man in the wide-brimmed hat is using. Somehow it allowed for an assault against us through the shared memory."

Alter shook his head. "I don't think so. I've studied all the runes, but none suggest such a function."

"You assume they use the same runes," Bastien said.

"Even if they weren't, I can't see how a rune sequence could open such a conduit with the power to undermine your nevron."

Sarah was so grateful they had access to his expertise. Unfortunately, even that knowledge didn't seem to be enough to figure out what really happened.

"Assuming you are correct," Francesca said, still pacing. "Then the second possibility is that the attack somehow commenced outside of the machines."

Harriett said, "I've already double-checked with security. No suspicious visitors or security breach, or unattended pastries. I don't see how anyone could have initiated anything from out there."

"And this vault remained secure," Bastien added.

Francesca stopped pacing. "Then a third option must be considered, that somehow a fundamental flaw has developed in our nevron."

Gregorios said, "I don't buy that one. Perhaps one of us might have faltered, suffered severe, unexpected soul degradation, but not all of us simultaneously."

"Well, why not?" Alter asked. He seemed to be enjoying the turn in the conversation.

"The more likely scenario is that it is some kind of rune twisting everything," Francesca said.

"Maybe it's Mai Luan," Sarah suggested, her voice shaking a little as she considered the terrifying cui dashi.

Memories of desperate struggle flickered through her mind,

concluding with the feel of the axe in her hands as it slashed through Mai Luan's face and drove into her torso. She shuddered.

"Mai Luan is dead," Gregorios said.

"So who's the man in the hat? He was so strong, like she was. He was talking weird too."

"Perhaps he seeks Mai Luan's heka cell, as we do," Bastien suggested.

"To kill them or to recruit them?" Harriett asked.

Sarah rubbed her arms against a chill. "He wasn't friendly. The guy was spooky. He proclaimed himself my master and said if I wasn't useful to him, he'd kill me." She was tired of being treated like a second-class mortal just because she didn't have any special powers.

"Send me back in," Alter declared, throwing himself into one of the chairs. "I'll avenge you."

Sarah smiled at his enthusiasm. "He's gone. I left him singing several octaves higher and then Gregorios dropped a statue on him. I guarantee he's sitting on an ice pack somewhere right now."

Bastien held up a fist for her to bump.

They still didn't have any answers, and argued through another round of fruitless questions. They needed to find Mai Luan's heka cell, but Anaru and the Tenth were doing all they could on that front.

They might not know much, but it was clear to everyone that the man in the wide-brimmed hat was a threat. No one had any idea who he was or why he'd targeted Sarah. They needed to hunt him down and destroy his machine.

Sarah didn't like killing, had enough nightmares to deal with for more than one lifetime, but she suspected they might not have a choice in stopping that creepy guy. Mai Luan had proven how dangerous it was to allow anyone else to walk the memoryscape. The master runes were too dangerous to trifle with, and some people were just evil.

The door opened and Domenico entered the room, looking worried. "Sir, we just received word from Tomas. Eirene suffered some kind of debilitating sickness while trying to perform the soul transfer for the king of Thailand."

"Is she all right?" Gregorios asked, looking worried. Sarah bit her lip, terrified to think anything might have happened to Eirene. She loved her like an aunt.

"She's resting. That's all we know."

Sarah blew out a relieved breath.

"What kind of sickness?" Francesca asked. The other siblings gathered around Gregorios in a family circle.

When he described what had happened, Bastien and the girls all shared a knowing look, and Bastien said, "That sounds much like what happened to us."

Domenico tapped his earpiece and listened for a moment, his expression growing grave. "Sir, we just received word that another facetaker in Africa suffered a similar breakdown. She died from the effects."

Gregorios grimaced. "We can't afford to lose anyone else."

There weren't that many facetakers to begin with. The four nasty old council members had died, but Sarah wasn't sure that was a bad thing. From what she'd learned, despite ongoing efforts to identify new facetakers around the world, sometimes decades passed before they discovered a new one.

"Keep me posted on Eirene's condition, and send a system-wide alert. Everyone should refrain from activating their nevra cores until further notice," Gregorios ordered.

Domenico saluted, then added, "Tomas is taking care of Eirene. He's hopeful of a full recovery and said they would schedule a second attempt at the transfer as soon as Eirene regains her strength."

Sarah hoped Tomas had left a message for her, and was tempted to check her phone right there. If he hadn't called yet, they'd have to talk about that when he returned.

"Tell them to wait," Gregorios said.

"But sir, apparently the transfer vehicle was left in a partial transfer state."

"What does that mean?" Sarah asked.

Gregorios grimaced. "It's bad. Extremely painful. It means the soul-mask was only partially removed. It's worse than normal torture because the victim can't black out to stop the pain."

Sarah shuddered. "That's horrible."

"Demons," Alter whispered. He'd moved to stand close beside Sarah.

"Don't start," she whispered back.

"Tell her to use extreme caution," Gregorios told Domenico. "And notify me prior to commencing the transfer."

After Domenico left, Gregorios said, "We may need to send someone out to help her."

"We must identify the source of this malady," Bastien said, looking deeply worried.

Francesca said, "It has to be rune related. But to affect the entire world, I can't even imagine what rune they might be using or how they might be fueling the spell."

"They would need a lot of souls," Gregorios agreed. "I know of at least one location they were being stockpiled. We may need to consider an assault there to determine if that source is being utilized."

"But have you known runes of such power?" Bastien asked.

Alter spoke softly into the ensuing quiet. "I have."

His face betrayed the same reluctance he always displayed when forced to discuss his family's lore.

Sarah nudged him with her shoulder. "We'll keep it secret."

Alter sighed. "There are some runes we never use, runes that are too dangerous. I know little about them, but they might have the power to do something like this."

Harriett rubbed her hands together. "I love secret recipes. I've never heard of these."

"Of course you haven't," Alter snapped. "My family has hunted them with particular zeal for millennia. They're known as forbidden runes, and we do not speak of them."

Sarah said, "You're suggesting that someone has not only gained access to one of Mai Luan's machines, but also has one of these forbidden runes, and that they learned how to use it?"

Francesca pursed her lips. "There's no guarantee it's the same group. Perhaps the man with the hat is looking for the group that has the forbidden rune."

"No. That does not make sense. If he lacked the rune, he too would have suffered the effects," Bastien said.

Sarah said, "I bet they're the same group. He seemed surprised we were in the memory, as if he understood things were about to go bad."

"At this point, let's keep the possibility open that they're not," Gregorios said. "I believe you're on to something, Alter. I've known a couple times where heka cells triggered huge problems. They usually killed themselves in the process, or we removed them, but the runes they used were almost always lost. I've never heard of this particular type of effect, but it's entirely possible."

Sarah paled. "What if they combined this forbidden rune with the master rune?"

Alter recoiled as if she'd sprouted a second head.

"They don't have it," Gregorios said, but he looked troubled.

"They might have obtained a different one," Alter said. "If they have a machine, that means they have a facetaker. If that person's got the right memories, they could find another master rune."

"And if they do?" Gregorios asked.

Alter looked shaken. "It would be really bad. I can't even imagine how bad."

Gregorios said, "Imagine it. If we can't stop them, that might be exactly what they're looking for. How do we block a forbidden rune?"

Alter shrugged. "Depends on the rune. I'd need to understand what it's doing and search the family archives. With enough information, I might be able to come up with a way to block it. We usually just kill whoever's trying to use it."

Bastien gave the hunter an approving smile. "That works too, mon ami. Assuming we can find them."

"That's how we begin," Gregorios said, showing more confidence than Sarah felt. "Double the effort to track down that heka cell. Alter, check with your family and see what you can find."

"I'll try." He looked like Gregorios had asked him to wrestle a shark.

Alter talked about his family a lot, particularly to Sarah. She felt she knew them, but they considered the facetakers enemies. Sarah didn't envy Alter the task of broaching the subject with his father.

Melek was going to be furious that Alter had mentioned forbidden runes, and suspicious of any information sharing now that the direct threat of Mai Luan was past. In fact, he might just decide to take Alter home.

Alter had mentioned a couple of times that his father had already started urging him to go. He'd suggested that Sarah visit his family compound, but she'd declined. She was actually very tempted, but Alter would read far too much into such a visit.

"Let's discuss what you learn after you speak with your father," Gregorios suggested.

"All right." Alter looked a little suspicious, but Sarah was glad Gregorios had made the offer. The two of them needed to work through their issues. This might be a way to begin doing that.

After they all left, Sarah took a cab back to Quentin's mansion and spent an hour working out and beating on the punching bag. Things were going badly and she couldn't shake a growing fear that things would get worse before they got better.

24

Luck is of little moment to the great general, for it is under the control of his intellect, his enhanced mind, and his judgment.

~LIVY

TOMAS STOOD by one of the windows of the spacious apartments he shared with Eirene on the second floor of a Spanish-style residence within the Klai Kangwon Palace complex. A thin drape was drawn over the open window and he stood to one side, still able to see out while remaining hidden.

Eirene entered the sitting room. It was the first time she had left her bedroom under her own power since her collapse. She looked pale, but seemed herself again. She was dressed and looked stable enough for an audience with the king.

Tomas breathed a sigh of relief. Nothing was worse than the feeling of helplessness he had endured in the face of her invisible attack.

"You're looking better."

"Almost human."

Not as good as he had hoped. She needed to feel more than human.

"How are they handling the delay?" she asked.

"Strangely well. Up until midnight last night, they were hounding me every ten minutes for updates. Today I haven't seen anyone all morning."

Eirene frowned, mirroring his own growing concern. "I don't like that."

An insistent beeping began from one of the small laptop computers sitting open on the nearby desk. Tomas crossed to the screen.

Not good.

"I think the contract's been canceled. Grab your things."

"How long?"

"Ten seconds. They just crossed the outer sensors."

Although the job had seemed a simple assignment, he was glad he had followed standard security protocols and installed hidden motion sensors and tiny video cameras around their rooms.

He counted twelve heavily-armed soldiers approaching, guns at the ready. He typed three quick commands in the computer, then ran to his bedroom that overlooked the expansive gardens surrounding the palace.

Eirene had requested rooms in this wing and no one had bothered to ask why. From the window, he could see the glimmer of the nearby ocean. More importantly, thick trees grew to within yards of the building. They always defined their exit strategy before commencing any mission, no matter how safe it appeared on the surface.

Tomas scanned the area with infrared binoculars that could give him a hint of the presence of concealed enemies, but saw nothing threatening. Unlike the sparse cover of most of the palace compound, the nearby foliage would provide thick cover all the way to the outer perimeter wall. It was a beautiful morning, warm but not hot, the humidity reasonable. Better weather than many of the exfils he'd led over the years.

Eirene rushed into the room and closed the door. She wore a medium backpack and was belting on a pair of silenced pistols.

"Area looks clear," Tomas said as he extracted a rope from the suitcase on his bed and tossed one end out the window.

As he finished tying off the other end, Eirene grabbed the rope and jumped out the window. The leather gloves she wore would provide enough protection. She only had to fall a single story.

The outer door to their apartment crashed inward and Tomas clearly heard soldiers swarming through. The motion sensors picked them up too. They triggered the charges he had just armed from the computer.

The front of the apartment exploded.

The shaped charges were directed in the opposite direction, so he felt little direct force, but the shockwave still rattled the door in its frame and the noise was deafening.

Tomas pulled a fully-loaded pack from one of the big duffel bags, slung it over his shoulders, and grabbed up his silenced bullpup rifle. The IWI Tavor carbine was one of his favorite guns for this type of encounter. Anaru hated the weapon just because it was favored by the hunters, but Tomas had loved it since the first time he fired it. It was better than the alternative from his homeland.

He didn't bother with the rope.

As smoke filtered through the door to his bedroom and cries of alarm mingled with screams of panic, he vaulted out the window. He landed on the soft grass beside Eirene, easily absorbing the impact on enhanced legs.

"Let's go." He led the way into the trees at an easy trot, gun held at his side to disguise its outline from any distant observers. Very little drew more attention than the sight of someone rushing around with a raised gun.

As soon as they entered the trees, he sped up. The first moments would be critical in determining their chances of escape. If the Thai were foolish enough to assume that initial assault team would take them by surprise, pursuit would be minutes away at best. By then they would be long gone.

Bullets tore into the trees on both sides of him, and one caught him in the shoulder. He dropped to the ground and rolled behind some bushes, gritting his teeth at the sharp, stabbing pain.

The Thai weren't stupid after all. A backup team had been lying in wait.

Eirene dropped to the ground behind a thick tree. The excitement seemed to be helping her recovery. "Firing line ten yards ahead. I spotted three of them."

Tomas was already pulling four smoke grenades from his pack. His shoulder burned, but the pain was already fading. If the bullet had lodged in there, he would not heal properly until it was extracted, but if it passed through, he'd heal within the next ten minutes.

Bullets continued to shred the trees just overhead, but thankfully none of the soldiers had started throwing frag grenades.

Tomas pulled the pins and tossed the smoke grenades. They hissed and belched huge clouds of smoke. Within seconds, the entire area was concealed in billowing white. He also extracted a small bluetooth speaker from his pack and tossed it after the smoke grenades.

"Play something appropriate," he said to Eirene.

"I've got just the thing."

"Watch for flanking maneuvers. I'll be right back."

She held up a hand to forestall him for a couple of seconds as she pulled out her phone and tapped a selection. "All right, go."

Leaving his pack behind, he rose and slipped forward through the trees. The enemy firing had trickled off as the smoke enveloped the distant soldiers.

A concealed officer was barking orders, but Tomas' Thai wasn't very good. To him it sounded like, "Turn the lights on."

As Tomas ghosted toward the enemy soldiers, music began blasting out of the little speaker he'd tossed. A familiar beat echoed through the trees and drowned out any small noises he might make in his approach.

Tomas grimaced. Really? The best she could come up with was the theme song to *Pirates of the Caribbean*?

Eirene was an avid moviegoer and had been devouring films since being reincorporated. *Pirates* was one of her favorites.

Concealed by the peppy score, Tomas slipped through the billowing smoke, holding his breath to avoid telltale coughing while he closed on the officer. The man appeared as a shadow in the smoke, and from the sound of his voice, was turned away.

Tomas let his rifle fall to his side on its tactical sling and drew a slender knife. He stepped right up behind the officer, waited for the man to finish his latest order before tapping him on the shoulder, then plunged the blade through the man's eye.

Tomas settled the body to the ground and ghosted left, down the line of soldiers. The first was looking in his direction, but mistook him for his officer until it was too late. The other three men on that side of the line never noticed his approach and fell to his silent knife.

The first of the soldiers on the right side of the line fared no better, but the next man was more aware. As soon as he noticed Tomas' shifting shadow in the smoke, he opened fire.

Only Tomas' enhanced speed saved his life.

One bullet speared his left arm, but he dove to the side before the soldier could pour more lead into him. While the soldier fired into the concealing smoke, shouting curses, Tomas rounded a tree and closed from the side.

The soldier realized his mistake only when Tomas kicked his rifle out of his hands. Most men would have stumbled away in surprise, but this man was a fighter. He drew a long knife and came at Tomas, every slash of the blade aimed for something vital.

The Thai soldier was well trained, and they circled each other, blades flashing in the gloom. Tomas' left arm lacked strength. It felt like the bullet had cracked the bone. If he'd had full use of it, he could have defeated the soldier quickly.

The man shouted while he fought, and his remaining companions crashed through the underbrush to come to his aid. Tomas embraced the surge of battle lust that had carried him through conflicts for the past two and a half centuries and grinned with the thrill of the challenge.

The soldier seemed content to bide his time and let his comrades finish the match with a couple thirty-round magazines, so Tomas went on the offensive. He lunged, taking a slash to his injured left arm to get inside the man's reach, and clubbed the soldier in the side of the head with the handle of his knife.

As the soldier collapsed in a heap, Tomas scooped up the man's knife. It had excellent balance so he threw it into the smoke at the sound of one of the charging soldiers.

A gasp, then silence.

That was a better throw than he had expected.

Another soldier charged out of the smoke, gun blazing. Bullets tore through the forest in a wild spray.

Tomas slipped back around the tree and brought his own gun to bear. His left arm needed a few minutes to repair, so he propped the gun against the tree and sighted one-handed. He aimed for the upper legs since the soldier wore body armor and a helmet. His gun spat two suppressed rounds. The soldier screamed as he fell and writhed on the ground in agony.

Tomas left him there and returned for Eirene.

"What's with the screaming?" she asked.

"Tactical misdirection."

He waited while she tied off his wounds. His enhancements would complete the healing in minutes, but leaving a trail of blood was never a good idea.

Together they ran southeast through the forest while alarms sounded behind them. The smoke, music and screaming soldier would attract pursuit like a magnet, but the Thai forces would waste precious seconds figuring out what happened.

When they reached a narrow lane through the forest, Tomas spotted a little old grounds-keeper approaching on a golf cart. He tried to wave the man down, but the old fellow spotted the rifle, gunned the cart, and tried to run them over.

Tomas avoided the golf cart and pulled the old man out. The fellow beat futilely against his arm while cursing him in Thai.

"Are you serious?" Tomas twisted the old fellow around and held him for five seconds in a stranglehold until the man passed out. He laid him gently on the grass and joined Eirene, who had turned the cart around.

"Some people have no sense of hospitality," he said.

Eirene accelerated away, chuckling.

It took them ten minutes to slip past the outer security of the palace complex and reach the beach. Since so few people knew of their visit to the king, even fewer knew who they were hunting. That made it easy to merge into the crowds of tourists exiting the area. With guns concealed in their packs, they hailed a taxi and headed for Bangkok.

During the ride, Eirene called Gregorios on her satellite phone. To say he was upset with their client was an understatement. He arranged for the jet to be fueled and ready.

They made it to the plane and out of Thailand without interference.

During the trip back to Rome, Tomas wondered why the king had done such a foolish thing. Not only would his soul transfer never happen, but no one double-crossed Gregorios. The king had to know that.

What would have driven him to take the risk?

25

"IT'S time to come home, Son."

That was exactly what Alter most feared his father would say. His assignment had been to assist Gregorios and Eirene in taking down the cui dashi. They had succeeded.

Melek had begun suggesting Alter return, but Alter had managed to buy a little more time due to his rune work on the machines. He hadn't explained to his father that he was building another machine for the hated demons or that those machines could be used by them to walk their memories and hunt for master runes.

His family would never understand that he believed in what he was doing and that he actually trusted Eirene's word that they wouldn't seek the master runes.

"Father, I'm not finished my work here."

"You've done enough. It's dangerous to spend too much time with those demons. They have a way of twisting reality and corrupting even the strongest soul."

He thought back to the strange feeling of familiarity with their cursed nevron soul forces.

"I know, Father. I am still hoping to convince Sarah of the truth about the demons."

"A non-gifted is not worth the risk. The genealogists have not found the link to the family line you suspected. Leave her."

"There has to be something. She learns runes faster than anyone I've ever known," Alter insisted.

Reuben was also on the line. He spat, "She was one of those vile women who sold their bodies. She isn't worth saving."

"You don't know her," Alter bristled.

"Alter," Melek said slowly. "I worry that you have grown too involved with this woman."

If only he could be. "I'm not involved, but please father, continue the research. Just a little longer."

"Very well, Son. A little longer. When will you complete your research and bring those runes home to us?"

"Soon. Father, there's something else. I've learned some new facts about great grandmother, Elizabeth."

"Don't believe anything those demons tell you. Tell them to leave our family alone," Reuben snarled.

"But—"

"No," Melek said. "Reuben is right. You must guard yourself against their influence."

"You're right." Hearing the strength of conviction in his father's voice buoyed his own flagging resolve. Had he allowed himself to be drawn too deep, to lose focus? "But there's another problem. The heka cell tied to that cui dashi, Mai Luan, appears to be far stronger than we suspected."

That got their attention.

"What have you learned?"

"We're hunting them, but the enforcers are experiencing unusual difficulty tracking them down."

"Incompetent fools," Reuben muttered.

Alter ignored that stupid comment. "Although Mai Luan is dead, they appear to be functioning at a remarkably sophisticated level. Recent developments make us worried they may have acquired a forbidden rune."

"Why do you think this?" Melek asked sharply.

"Something is attacking the demons. Their powers are suddenly erratic, unstable. All we can figure is the enemy must have a powerful forbidden rune."

"You've spoken with them of the forbidden runes?" Melek asked.

"A little."

"That was unwise, Alter." Melek spoke in the overly soft voice he used when trying not to show his anger.

Reuben interrupted. "How badly are they affected? Are they vulnerable?"

"It's hard to say," Alter side-stepped the question. He didn't like the hunger in his brother's voice. "But the effects seem to be worldwide."

His father said, "I doubt that. Such a rune would require so many souls we surely would have seen hints of such a movement."

"That's what I thought at first, but the evidence is strong."

"I've never heard of a rune that could interrupt the demons' power. Not even the forbidden runes," Melek said.

"If we had, we would have used it," Reuben stated. For most of his life, Alter would have agreed with his brother's eagerness, but now he cringed to think of hunters storming Suntara, killing Eirene and the others.

"There's fear that somehow the heka may have acquired the master rune despite Mai Luan's death, and are linking it to the forbidden rune."

"Abomination!" Reuben shouted.

"That would be extremely dangerous." Melek's response was more measured, but Alter felt his father's rage radiating through the phone.

He shared the same outrage that anyone might be tampering with the power of the master runes. To tie that power to one of the forbidden runes was the blackest of deeds.

"We'll search the rune catalog and see if we can identify possible ways to twist those forbidden runes into such a use," his father suggested.

"This might be a rare opportunity," Reuben said.

"No, this is pure evil," Melek rebuked him.

"But father, if they're vulnerable—"

"Unleashing the power of the forbidden runes is forbidden for a reason. It's never good. Tragedy will result if it's not stopped, this I guarantee."

"Yes, father." Reuben's voice was anything but submissive.

"Father, we have a protected environment where we can test the forbidden runes," Alter offered. "If you were to send some of them to me—"

"Have you suggested such a thing to the demons?" Melek interrupted.

"No."

"Never do so." He spoke with absolute authority. "I would never trust those runes in the hands of the demons."

"They aren't heka, Father."

"It doesn't matter. The danger would be far too great."

"But Father, we could learn so much."

"Such knowledge isn't worth the price. But I do need you to acquire the master rune for us."

"I'll try, but they'll want something in return."

"They have your help. That must be enough."

As Alter tried to figure out another approach to convince his father, a distant wailing sounded through the phone. It was a sound everyone living in Jerusalem was all too familiar with.

"The air raid sirens are sounding," Melek said anyway. "The Palestinians have become belligerent again lately and—"

A far louder booming sound interrupted him.

Alter's heart raced. That had sounded far too close.

"Son, we have to—"

The line went dead.

Alter stared at the silent phone, filled with fear.

26

History will be kind to me, for I intend to write it, despite Harald's meddling.

~WINSTON CHURCHILL

"WE HAVE CONFIRMED that there was an attack on your family's compound," Gregorios told Alter. "Details are slim, but they were hit hard." He hated delivering bad news, especially in the face of so many other problems. "Your brother was hurt and your father badly wounded."

Alter sagged in his seat in the small conference room. Sarah was there, as were Eirene and Tomas, who had just returned from Thailand.

"I have to go home," Alter said, rising, his expression grim.

"Why?" Gregorios asked, and he got the response he was hoping for.

Alter slammed a palm onto the table. "They're my family! I have to help."

"What would help your family the most?" Eirene asked softly.

"Killing whoever did this," he said without hesitation. At least his priorities were still straight.

"Do you think you'll be able to accomplish that by returning to the chaos of that compound?" Gregorios asked.

"I have to do something," Alter exclaimed.

"Exactly." He leaned across the table, holding Alter's gaze. "You're right, it's your duty to help destroy the enemy who attacked your family, but rushing off to Jerusalem isn't going to accomplish that."

"What are you saying?"

"Think about it. We don't know any details yet, but if the enemy knows you even a little bit, the first thing they should expect is for you to rush home and waste a lot of time there trying to comfort your family."

"Why would they care? I'm not the one they attacked," Alter said angrily.

"Of all of your family, who is playing an important role helping us track down the heka running around with a forbidden rune and possibly a master rune?" Eirene asked.

"You think the attack is related to what we're doing?"

Good. The boy could use his mind when he had to. Gregorios said, "You tell me. Why would an enhanced group attack your home right now?"

"We have fought the kashaph for all time. They hate us," Alter declared.

"True, but they never attack you. Not your home. No normal heka cell could hope to pull that off. It would be suicidal."

Eirene took up the train of thought. "The only way someone could carry out a successful attack against your well-defended home would be with careful planning and brilliant execution. How many heka cells do you know of that operate with that level of sophistication?"

"Only one." His anger faded and he settled back into his chair, his expression turning thoughtful.

Sarah moved around the table and placed a hand on his shoulder. "We're all worried about your family, Alter. This has to be such a hard time for you."

"I want to know they're safe," he said.

"We'll get word as soon as possible," Eirene assured him. "But I think Greg is right. This has to be related to what we're already dealing with."

"We'll hunt them down together," Tomas said.

"Thank you."

Gregorios silently applauded his team. They'd helped Alter shift focus back to the important mission.

Tomas added, "This is a disturbing trend. First they somehow sabotage your powers. Then they move against the hunters. They're far more organized than we ever suspected. I'm starting to wonder if Mai Luan might have only played a small role in what they were planning."

"We don't even know who *they* are," Sarah said.

"One of them has to be that man in the wide-brimmed hat who keeps dogging your steps," Tomas said.

Eirene nodded. "That's likely. I wish we knew where they were hiding."

"We know where the hat man will pop up," Gregorios said.

"You want to enter another memory, despite the risk?" Alter asked.

"Because of it. They've hit us all hard, right where it hurts. I want to hurt them back." He couldn't risk allowing anyone to continue Mai Luan's work. Besides, the man with the wide-brimmed hat had struck at family. That challenge could not go unanswered.

Eirene hesitated. "I'm not sure we can make the machines work. Whatever they're using to affect our powers is pervasive and extremely dangerous."

"With Alter's help, the children were able to maintain the connection," Gregorios said.

"Really?" She gave Alter a thoughtful look.

"I wonder why?" Sarah asked.

Alter shrugged. "Perhaps their runes are tuned only to block facetaker powers. Combining my rounon gift with their nevron might be what does the trick."

"Perhaps. Something about you stumps their spell, that's for sure," Gregorios said.

"So they won't be expecting us," Eirene said.

Tomas grinned. "I like that. Give them a taste of their own medicine."

Gregorios rose. "It's decided then. Time to go hunting."

27

I am not carrying on a war of extermination against the Romans. I am contending for honour and empire. My ancestors yielded to Roman valour. I am endeavouring that others, in their turn, will be obliged to yield to my good fortune, my greater ciphers, and my valour.

~HANNIBAL BARCA, RUNE WARRIOR, 216 B.C.

THE MEMORY FORMED around Eirene and she found herself on a low hill overlooking the regular campfires of a Roman legion. Very interesting. She had planned to land in Rome, not a remote hillside.

She was wearing Iltea's body.

Gregorios appeared beside her, dressed in standard Roman armor. He grimaced when he saw it, and it transformed into chainmail under a leather jacket. He'd always preferred the flexibility of chainmail.

Then he noticed the suit she was wearing and gave a low whistle. "You always looked stunning in that one."

Eirene tossed her long, red hair over her shoulder. She had appeared in the same leather halter top and short skirt she had worn in her recent nightmare. She willed a white robe to cover it.

Tomas appeared beside her, dressed as a Roman legionnaire. He took in the surroundings at a glance. "Back in Italy?"

"It's where we keep seeing our hatted friend," Eirene said.

Growling turned Tomas around. A tall, wolf-like creature stalked up the hill toward them on its hind legs. He moved to intercept.

A shotgun roared, and the monster's head disintegrated into a bloody lump.

Sarah had appeared nearby, wearing a revealing gown of amber satin. She cradled the shotgun in one arm and gestured at herself, an expression of disbelief on her face. "Who thought up this outfit?"

"It does look fantastic," Tomas said as he shifted to one side to dispatch a vicious-looking snake that slithered out of the ground.

Sarah glanced at Eirene and raised an eyebrow.

"Wasn't me," Eirene said. Gregorios maintained an innocent expression, so she decided not to press it. With a thought, she transformed the robe into leather armor that covered Sarah much better.

"I always liked girls in leather," Tomas said, stealing a kiss. It was nice to see the children play, despite the seriousness of the mission.

"Don't get distracted," Sarah replied with a smile. "Where are we anyway?"

Eirene pointed down at the army camp in the valley. "Those are Roman legions."

"So that narrows it down to about a thousand years," Tomas said.

Gregorios had been studying the surrounding countryside. "I think we landed at the beginning of the Third Servile War."

"The third what?" Sarah asked.

"Servile War. Spartacus again," Gregorios said with a frown.

"He seems really persistent," Tomas said.

"Tell me about it." Eirene suspected Gregorios was right. The body she wore felt young, like it had in the early days of that war. "I don't remember this exact moment, so I'm guessing we've caught the man in the wide-brimmed hat walking again."

Gregorios nodded. "If things go the way they have recently, I suspect we'll find him hiding out with Spartacus."

"How does that work if you haven't actually shared a memory? We haven't practiced non-shared memory linking," Sarah said.

That was a good point. Eirene explained. "Alter modified the runes on our machines. The idea was to have them sync our memory streams to any already-active memory walking happening during a time we've lived."

"That's a pretty wide net those runes are casting," Tomas said.

Eirene shrugged. "It appears to be working. Since we suspect there's at most one other group possessing a machine and the capability of walking memories, our goal is to intercept them."

"And remove them," Gregorios added.

That seemed enough for Tomas. He asked, "Where do you think we'll find them? I don't feel like hunting through an entire legion."

Eirene took her bearings. It was early evening, but enough light still lingered to get a sense of the land.

"Spartacus isn't with the legion. His army should be close." She pointed south. "Best bet is around the next hill."

"You think tomorrow's the day he trounces old Glaber?" Gregorios asked.

"It has that feel to it."

Praetor Gaius Claudius Glaber commanded the force sent to quell the young rebellion before it picked up steam. He was soundly defeated by the crafty Spartacus in two encounters that saw most of Glaber's army destroyed. He barely escaped with his life.

"The idiot made a mess of things," Gregorios said as he led the group south.

"What happened?" Sarah asked.

Eirene said, "He didn't take our advice, that's what. Spartacus was young but already bore one enhancement, as did several of his close companions. They were anything but the ignorant, untrained slaves the praetor assumed."

"We'd been sent to Capua to remove Spartacus and his wife, but he escaped before we could complete the mission," Gregorios added.

"Wait, his wife?" Sarah asked.

Eirene gestured at the suit she wore. "Another long story. She was enhanced too."

Night had recently fallen over the rolling, fertile hills of that south-central region of Italy. The weather was balmy and pleasant.

"We're not going to make it before the children get tired in the real world," Gregorios said after about five minutes of walking.

"Skip the boring parts," Eirene suggested.

"I hadn't considered that."

"Our sombrero'd quarry stopped time. I figure that most memories skip past the boring parts anyway, so it should work."

Gregorios shrugged. "It's worth a try. The memory seems stable enough."

With Alter linked to both Bastien and Francesca via rune, they had been able to embrace their nevra cores to send the team back into this memory. Alter's peculiar immunity to the forbidden rune bothered Eirene, if the problem even originated with a forbidden rune. There was a piece to the puzzle they had not put together yet and it gnawed at the back of her mind. Something about Alter held the key to solving it.

"You've got the primary spot for this memory. You try it," Gregorios said.

Eirene focused on the distant hill they were marching toward and imagined them standing there already. She expected a lurch or sense of travel, but the memory just blurred, then re-formed around them. They stood atop the hill, just as she'd imagined. It smelled of cut grass, and there was a scent of apple blossoms in the air.

"Not bad," Gregorios said.

"Ah, guys?" Sarah called. She stood at the edge of a dense cluster of bushes that blocked Eirene's view to the south. "You're going to want to see this."

The land beyond the bushes fell gently into another valley that was full of soldiers. Unlike the Romans, this army was awake, alert, and in formation. They were all facing the hill where Eirene and her small group stood. At the front stood Spartacus. Even at two hundred yards, Eirene easily recognized him.

Instead of raising his oaken spear and raging at her, he trotted forward alone.

"That's not really fair," Sarah said, pumping her shotgun. "He gets a whole army?"

"I don't see the hat man anywhere," Gregorios said with a frown.

"We might have to thin the crowds a bit," Tomas said, fingers slowly clenching.

"Should we get out of here?" Sarah asked, looking nervous.

Eirene said, "Probably, but wait a minute. I want to see what old Spartypants has to say."

"Oh, that's terrible," Sarah said with a smile and a shake of her head.

Eirene shrugged. "I've called him worse."

Spartacus stopped about fifty yards away, his army still standing at attention far behind. He raised his staff and drove it into the ground.

"Why did you let the arenas fall?" he shouted.

Eirene exchanged a surprised look with Gregorios.

"What are you talking about?" she shouted back.

"You've wasted the time granted to you. I'm very disappointed."

"Something's definitely not right," Gregorios muttered.

Eirene felt another will tug at her control of the memoryscape. "Beware. I think it's some kind of subtle trap."

Spartacus started forward again, his spear left sticking in the ground. Behind him the army shouted battle cries and broke into a charge.

Eirene wanted to stay, to beat the truth out of Spartacus, but the invisible will fighting for control of the memoryscape began wrenching it from her. She tried to hold it, to force control over the charging army, but a pounding headache began in her skull.

"Definitely some kind of trap," she whispered, clutching at her head. "Best we hunt elsewhere." She looked skyward. "Bastien. We need to go."

The dream faded but Spartacus' voice echoed across the distance. "Gregorios, I can't believe you're still with her."

28

Apollo, grant me wisdom, and Shahrokh shall arrange enhancements for my guards. Spartacus is still at large and, although I am grateful he took the life of my brother, my own assassination is not acceptable. What can be done to rid the world of that monster?

~EMPEROR DOMITIAN, AFTER THE ASSASSINATION OF TITUS, A.D. 81

"WELL, THAT COULD HAVE GONE BETTER," Eirene said when she got her heavy helmet off.

"How could Spartacus be waiting for us like that?" Sarah asked. "Aren't people in memory supposed to just live the memories?"

"That's what we thought," Eirene said.

"That's not what's happening. Not with him."

Gregorios said, "It's worse than that. He's never talked like that. Ever."

"It's almost like he's a player again after all these years," Eirene agreed. That exchange had been so strange, it didn't feel real.

Sarah looked between them, brows creasing. "I think I'm missing something. Who was Spartacus, anyway?"

Eirene said, "Like we said, he was a heka. A very difficult one."

"What are you not telling us?" Sarah asked.

Eirene approved of Sarah's sharp mind. She'd keep Tomas on his toes. That would be good for both of them.

"Let's take the conversation to the conference room," Eirene suggested.

When they reached the room on the second floor being used for conferences, Gregorios said, "History has it partially correct with Spartacus. He was Thracian. He was a gladiator. He led a revolt."

"But we've also made sure history has left out most of what Spartacus really was," Eirene added.

Sarah muttered, "I hate that you mess with history. It's hard enough to get it straight when you think it's straight."

"History's written by the winners for a reason. It's a tool, and sometimes a weapon," Eirene said.

She didn't like revisiting her many memories of Spartacus, but it seemed the man in the wide-brimmed had taken a special interest in Spartacus' role in their memory excursions. Now he was twisting the Thracian's character. She just couldn't imagine why.

"Spartacus and his wife were heka and were recruited by Baladeva's agents."

Sarah brightened. "The same Baladeva we ran into when John got attacked?"

"The one and only."

"That's an interesting connection," Tomas said.

Eirene said, "More deadly than interesting. Shahrokh found out that Baladeva's agents were recruiting among the gladiators and he sent the two of us to remove the threat."

"We took care of Iltea, Spartacus' wife," Gregorios said. "You saw her form in the memory we just left."

"The good-looking redhead?" Tomas asked.

"Thank you, dear. That form always did look good on me," Eirene said with a smile.

"So you like redheads?" Sarah asked, one eyebrow raised, her expression guarded.

A look of terror flitted across Tomas' face as he stammered, trying to come up with a reply that wouldn't dig him in deeper. Since he recently helped save Eirene's life again, she decided to intervene.

"Spartacus escaped with the other gladiators from the school in Capua before we could reach him. He eventually became our most bitter enemy."

"Because you killed his wife?" Sarah asked.

"He hated me especially for what I did to her," Eirene admitted. "But he fought us also because we stood against him and thwarted his purpose."

"What was that?" Alter asked.

"To assassinate all of the facetakers and destroy the newly formed council."

Alter shrugged. To him, Spartacus was probably sounding better and better.

"So you killed him when his army was defeated?" Tomas asked.

Gregorios shook his head. "If only it were that simple. We were embedded in Crassus' army, which is why they defeated Spartacus and his enhanced troops, but he escaped. We thought he was gone, but he eventually returned, far more powerful than before."

"He didn't die?" Sarah exclaimed. "Is there anything I know about him that's true?"

"You should know better than believing what you watch in a movie," Gregorios said.

"The television show was better," she said, looking frustrated.

Eirene explained. "Baladeva had recruited him, and his top operatives recruited him. He already had a brilliant strategic mind. After adding more enhancements than almost anyone has ever managed, he became the closest thing to a demigod I've ever seen."

"Let's just say we never got along," Gregorios said. He looked like he wished they hadn't started the discussion. Some memories from that history were painful for him. "And we continued to disagree for several hundred years."

"Tell us about it," Sarah said eagerly.

"Later," Gregorios said, even though Eirene knew he wouldn't want to. "We're getting distracted. We never saw the hat man today, but he had to have been there. Something drew us to that memory."

Eirene agreed. "It had to be him. Someone started actively twisting it near the end, and their mind was extremely powerful."

"What do you think he was trying to accomplish there?" Tomas asked.

Gregorios shrugged. "I don't see any pattern to it yet."

"It's all been about Spartacus," Sarah said.

"I think it's time to check on him," Eirene said.

Tomas asked, "What do you mean? He's been dead almost two thousand years."

Alter said, "Too bad. I rather wish I could meet him."

"Perhaps you will," Gregorios said.

Alter missed the point. "I doubt it. Even if you get your core stabilized so I can join you in another memory, I don't think I'd help you kill him again."

"Oh, he's not dead," Eirene said.

"What?" The three young ones exclaimed together.

She regarded them calmly. "I told you we defeated him. I didn't say we killed him."

"You can't be serious," Sarah said, her expression horrified. She probably thought they'd locked his soulmask in a coffin somewhere.

Gregorios said, "He had become Baladeva's top agent, leading insurrections against Rome and the council. He helped orchestrate the sacking of Rome and the deaths of thousands. His punishment had to be something special to make sure no one ever tried to do those things again."

"What did you do?" Tomas asked.

"We removed his soul."

"And then what?" Alter pressed.

"Nothing," Gregorios said.

Eirene added, "Well that's not exactly true. We had his soulmask bronzed and incorporated into a statue."

"Turned out rather well actually," Gregorios said with a satisfied smile.

Alter leaped to his feet. "Demons! How could you?"

"Back then it was actually pretty easy to get something bronzed," Gregorios said.

"You're as bad as my father warned," Alter snarled.

"Careful, son," Gregorios warned.

Eirene cringed to see them fighting again. Her relationship with Alter was still so fragile. Any incorrect assumptions could damage it forever. She'd wanted to connect with the hunters again, and Alter was her best chance to do so. As her great-grandson . . . An idea struck that rocked her and she stared at the angry young hunter, considering the possibilities.

He faced Gregorios and demanded, "Why? Are you going to remove my soul too, like you did my brother? Like you did Spartacus?"

She could read the signs that Gregorios was starting to get annoyed. "You're jumping to conclusions. Your brother wasn't the first enemy I spared when maybe I shouldn't have."

"You think Spartacus has survived all these years?" Sarah asked.

Alter barked a humorless laugh. "I can't imagine it. Reuben suffered almost more than he could bear in the few short years you left him dispossessed."

"Reuben isn't as strong as he thinks he is," Gregorios said.

"Where did you leave him?" Tomas seemed fascinated by the discussion.

Eirene said, "He's still here in Rome. We salute him every time we pass by."

Sarah gaped. "That's why you flip off that arch."

"There's always a reason," Gregorios grinned.

Alter's face was livid. "What gives you the right to decide everyone else's fate?"

"The right of survivorship," Gregorios declared.

Alter clenched his fists and looked like he wanted to leap at Gregorios. The conference phone buzzed, interrupting the argument. Harriett's voice came through the speaker.

"Dad, the hunter chief Melek is on the line for Alter."

"Put him through," Eirene said.

"Father, are you there?" Alter asked.

"I am." Melek sounded weak.

"We're all glad to hear you're safe," Gregorios said.

"Don't speak to me, demon betrayer!" Melek shouted. "I've taken the blood oath. You will face the righteous vengeance of my clan."

Alter's glare at Gregorios deepened. "Father, this line isn't secure. I'll call you back."

The phone clicked off, and he marched out of the room.

"Wow," Tomas said into the silence.

That was a huge understatement. Eirene suddenly felt worried she might lose everything she'd worked so hard to establish with Alter. "Something has happened. It sounded like Melek thinks we were involved in that attack."

"Alter won't believe it," Sarah said. Her faith in the young hunter was refreshing, and naive.

"If he does, it'll wreck everything we're trying to do," Tomas added.

"We'll get to the bottom of it," Gregorios promised them. "Hopefully before Alter does something stupid."

29

It is better to live for one day as a lion than for a thousand years as a sheep.

~TIBETAN PROVERB

AN HOUR LATER, Gregorios sat at the head of the weekly council meeting.

Only Harald and Zuri remained of the previous council. To round out the committee, he had invited his three children to attend. There were a few other facetakers with more seniority, but they were scattered around the globe on various assignments or hunkering down on their private estates. None seemed eager to rush to Rome during the time of crisis.

Eirene sat beside him at the head of the table. Tomas stood at the far end of the room, providing security. Sarah had returned to Quentin's estate. The way things were shaping up, she was going to need all the rest she could get.

John didn't show, so Gregorios started without him. He really didn't mind John arriving late. Maybe they could actually get some work done without wasting half their time on his outbursts.

Ten minutes after they started reviewing status updates, an enforcer entered the room and saluted. "Sir, we can't find Councilman John."

"Isn't he recovering in his apartment?" Gregorios asked.

"He was, but now there's no sign of him or Frederick."

"It's unlike Frederick not to keep in touch."

"Yes, sir."

"Track him down and send him in when you do."

The enforcer saluted again and withdrew.

Gregorios returned to the gathered group and moved to the next agenda item. "What is the international status?"

Harald, who wore a large-framed form in its late sixties, reported. "It appears Jerusalem was struck in multiple locations simultaneously. Rather than the normal rocket attacks, the city proper was targeted."

The big facetaker always preferred large bodies, ever since his early days as a Viking. He oversaw the organization's efforts to filter history and write the facetakers out of existence.

He pushed his glasses a little higher and consulted his notes. "In six locations, the bombs were triggered by remote control. Lots of flash but not many casualties. The seventh location was the attack on the hunter headquarters."

"Reports tell of a well-armed assault with heavy weapons and some kind of nerve agent. We're trying to get specifics, but it sounds like it was potent enough to disorient even the hunters. The assault took less than four minutes and the assailants escaped before additional security forces responded."

"Casualties?"

"No concrete numbers, but there are definite reports of fatalities and many wounded, including Melek."

"Why would he blame us?" Eirene asked.

Gregorios shrugged. "I have no idea. I'm hoping Alter can find out."

He was also hoping Alter didn't decide to do the explaining with an automatic rifle. At the moment, he figured odds were about even either way.

"We're getting him a secure line now," Zuri said.

She wore a sagging, almost-seventy body, covered by a bright orange sari that highlighted her ebony skin. Her mind seemed sharp, so her reluctance to transfer again might have been due more to political positioning than real fear of permanent soul fragmentation.

Gregorios planned to give her time on the machines as soon as the current crisis was resolved. She was an important asset and one they couldn't risk losing.

She managed the organization's diamond mines, and sometimes it seemed she wore half the exported product on her meaty arms. She loved jewels more than anyone Gregorios had ever known. Since the death of Meryem, she had also assumed management of the consignment team.

He asked her, "What have you learned from Thailand?"

Zuri frowned. "That's the strangest thing. I couldn't get through to the king."

"Probably died," Bastien suggested.

Gregorios said, "Let's hope not. I want answers and I want retribution."

The others nodded agreement, and Zuri added, "You might have to make an example out of him. I'm getting nothing but stonewalled, and none too politely either."

"Back to Jerusalem," Harald said. He was scanning something on his tablet. "I just received a report from an asset close to the compound that there is some evidence linking the attack to you personally, Gregorios."

Eirene said, "The hat man is another step ahead of us."

Gregorios preferred it when he was the clever one. Their mysterious enemy was really starting to irritate him. What he needed to figure out was why all the games, all the behind-the-scenes maneuvering?

"It makes sense," Francesca said from her seat at the other end of the table. "With that strike, they disable the hunter's response teams, which must have been something they were worried about. Plus they alienate Alter and redirect Melek's rage at us instead of the real target."

"Neatly done." Bastien agreed.

Eirene leaned forward in her seat. "This level of planning cannot be done overnight."

As usual, his beloved saw the crux of the issue. "No. We've come late to the party. There's obviously a larger scheme motivating the man in the wide-brimmed hat."

"You suggest we just got in the way, yes?" Bastien asked.

"Perhaps."

That put them in an unusual position. The Suntara council had been pulling strings and manipulating the world powers for so long, they weren't used to being excluded, to being nothing more than a hindrance to greater plans.

Nothing the hat man might have in mind boded well for them or for the world order.

"So the hunters are reeling and likely angry with us," Gregorios summed up.

"And Jerusalem is launching retaliatory strikes against the Palestinians, and threatening to strike anyone else they discover was involved in the attacks," Harald confirmed.

"All right, then. Harald, initiate an effort to discredit whatever evidence is surfacing, and get specifics on what happened in the compound.”

“Zuri, get through to the king and get some answers. If they keep stalling, we’ll initiate retaliation.”

“Tomas, find out where your team’s at with hunting down those heka. And check on Spartacus.”

“Francesca, call up Yurak. I want everyone in position.”

“Everyone?” She didn’t try to hide her surprise.

“Everyone. I think this is going to get ugly and I don’t want to keep playing to the hat man’s tune. We’re going to flip this on him, and I want the family ready to respond in conjunction with the full might of Suntara. As soon as we have a target, we hit him hard.”

As the rest of the committee disbanded, Gregorios turned to Eirene. “Get us a phone, Love.”

30

I am mortally opposed to the English King, and I will storm his castles and free by blood the lands he unjustly claims as his own. I don't care why you want him defeated, for today your brotherhood was confirmed.

I wear the symbols of my nation on my skin, and they grant strength and vitality beyond the realm of mortal men. Today I smote the stones of the bridge and rent them in twain. Let the English think the simple weight of numbers triggered the collapse. They will soon learn to fear my name and free my lands.

~WILLIAM WALLACE, SEPTEMBER 11, 1297, AFTER HIS
VICTORY AT THE BATTLE OF STIRLING BRIDGE

"IS THIS LINE SECURE?" Melek asked.

"I believe it is," Alter said. He hated hearing such weakness in his father's voice. "They went out of their way to ensure I got it."

"Don't trust anything they tell you."

He trusted none of them but Eirene. "What happened? Are you all right?"

"No. I'm far from all right," Melek said in a heavy tone.

"How badly are you hurt?" Alter clenched his fists in futile rage. He believed this was the best place to be, that here he could do the most good. Working with the demons gave him the best chance to wreak awful vengeance upon those who hurt his family.

"That doesn't matter. I'll heal. Some will not."

"How many?" He could barely get the words out.

"Seven."

"How?" Those were his relatives. They were hunters! No one invaded their home, killed their family. It seemed impossible.

Melek continued, his voice pained and tired. "Twenty-six wounded. Your cousin Ezekiel left us only minutes ago."

Alter gripped the receiver so hard it creaked in his hand and he had to force himself to relax before snapping it in half. He needed to hear, but he hated every word. Rage and anguish burned through him so fiercely he could hardly breathe.

"Why would they do this?" he asked.

"Because we denied them," Melek said.

"What?"

"The compound is badly damaged. They came with bombs and poison gas. The filthy kashaph trampled our home. They broke into the secure storage and desecrated our most valuable treasure."

Melek continued in a fierce whisper. "Son, they stole the book of runes."

"Oh, no." He hadn't thought anything could rattle him worse.

"The very book the demons wanted us to hand over to them just days ago."

At least that much made sense. "Of course. The enemy somehow learned that we sought to counter their forbidden rune so they—"

"No, Son." Melek cut him off harshly. "There's no secret enemy, just the demons and their mind-twisting plots. They did this. They hurt our family while pretending to be friends, just as they've always done."

Alter wanted to believe it, wanted it with a fierce passion, but he couldn't. He despised Gregorios, and if it were only that hated demon, he could believe his father despite the evidence to the contrary.

But he couldn't believe Eirene would have sanctioned the strike on his family. He knew her too well. He couldn't hate her now that he knew the truth.

"Father, I know you're angry, but I don't think—"

"It was Gregorios, I know it," Melek cut him off again. "I nearly died. As I lay bleeding and broken in the inner court, the kashaph could have killed me."

Alter didn't want to hear any more. His father had always been so strong, unstoppable. To think of him wounded and at the mercy of those animals filled Alter with a fury so deep he wanted to howl.

"They didn't. They spared me only because they were commanded to do so."

"By who?"

"John."

"The old facetaker?"

"The very one. He who sits at Gregorios' right hand."

"But John is missing. Don't you see—"

"No. They've blinded you, Alter. They've orchestrated this in such a way as to sow discord and doubt when we must be united and strong. We were wrong to trust anything the demons said to us."

Something still didn't add up. Alter said, "Give me some more time. We can figure this out. I just need to track down a couple of things."

"There is no more time," Melek said, his voice cold. "Your life is in danger there and your soul is at stake. Your mission has changed. You must kill Gregorios to avenge the family honor. Do this and return to me a hero."

"But father—"

"That's an order."

Gregorios and Eirene sat in his office on either side of his desk, leaning over a special phone. Melek's voice, distorted by the electronic encryption, spoke into the room.

"Your mission has changed. You must kill Gregorios to avenge the family honor. Do this and return to me a hero."

"But father—"

"That's an order."

The line went dead and Gregorios slowly clicked off the mic. This was going to be a problem. The man with the cursed hat had played all of them like fools. He leaned back in his executive chair and met Eirene's serious expression for several seconds.

"We need to solve this," Eirene said, her gaze intent.

"Clearly. We can't have that hothead running around trying to become a martyr."

"Don't you dare kill him."

Gregorios spread his hands. "What do you want me to do? I have to defend myself."

"Don't play games, Greg," she snapped. "I care about that boy and I won't have you killing him."

"Fine, I'll be careful." He wouldn't admit it, but he really didn't want to kill Alter. The kid was growing on him. Few hunters ever had. Of course, most of them were too busy insisting he kill them to give him a chance to get to know them first.

He sighed. The situation was quickly spiraling out of control and he didn't like feeling at the mercy of someone else.

"This entire business is about to turn sour," he predicted.

Eirene took his hands in hers. She smiled, that fierce grin of battle lust that he so loved.

"Oh, I'm starting to hope so."

31

Of course Darius lost the day. His cowardice will live for all time, but the frailty of his runes was laughable. I never even drew upon my own enhancements, and could have defeated him with nothing more than the natural strength of our arms.

~ALEXANDER THE GREAT, AFTER DEFEATING DARIUS III OF PERSIA IN THE KEY BATTLE OF GAUGAMELA, 331 B.C.

SARAH EXITED the tiny Roman taxicab in exactly the same place she had just days before when they had chased Rosetta into the Colosseum. Tomas followed her out and she took his hand.

Instead of returning to the Colosseum, they turned west and skirted the Piazza del Colosseo toward the Palatine Hill. They stopped in front of the Arch of Constantine.

"I can't believe we've been flipping off a two-thousand-year-old dead guy every time we go by here," Sarah said.

"He's not really dead," Tomas reminded her.

"It's still creepy. You'd think they'd let old grudges die."

Tomas shrugged. "Gregorios said he figured Spartacus' soul probably faded to dust long ago."

"I doubt it." Eirene had looked certain that Spartacus still lingered. Sarah glanced down at the brochure she had picked up at an information booth. "The Arch was dedicated in AD 315."

"Sounds about right." Tomas led her slowly around the back side of the magnificent arch.

"This arch was built to celebrate Constantine's victory, which he credited to the Christian God," she read.

Tomas chuckled. "Poetic, given Spartacus' pagan background. I bet he hated getting stuck on a Christian monument."

They rounded the west side of the arch and Sarah frowned when she looked up from her brochure. "Didn't Gregorios say they incorporated the soulmask into a statue on the top section of the south side?"

"He did," Tomas said softly as he too paused to stare at the construction barriers blocking access, and the thick, white tarp covering the top part of the arch. A sign declared the arch was undergoing restorative work.

"I have a bad feeling about this," Tomas muttered.

"Yeah." Sarah glanced around, unable to shake the feeling they were no longer surrounded by simple mortals. This was no memoryscape where they could wake up if the situation turned violent.

No one else seemed to be paying the shrouded arch much attention. Most people just moved around to the far side and took photos there. No security forces were nearby. After a moment of careful scrutiny, she allowed herself to relax a bit.

Tomas handed Sarah his daypack. "Be right back."

"Be careful."

He easily vaulted the construction barricade, leaped eight feet up to a raised catwalk, then disappeared under the tarp. She loved watching how easily he did amazing things like that.

Sarah pretended to take photos while scanning for anything suspicious. Tomas rejoined her in less than a minute. His expression told her everything.

"Have a nice time up there?" she asked anyway with forced cheer.

"You're not going to believe this," he said, his voice heavy with sarcasm.

"Spartacus is gone."

32

Remember that man lives only in the present, in this fleeting instant; the rest of his lives are either past and gone, or not yet revealed. Short, therefore, are man's lives, and narrow is the corner of the earth wherein he dwells.

~MARCUS AURELIUS, FOURTH LIFE OF EMPEROR NERVA

SARAH HAD to jog to keep up with Tomas when they returned to the Suntara headquarters to report to Gregorios and Eirene.

"This is not good," Eirene said simply.

"It's worse than that, Love," Gregorios said, looking more upset than Sarah had ever seen him. "Someone just got their hands on one of the most dangerous men who ever lived. No one has ever reincorporated after a dispossession anywhere near that long. Guaranteed he's unstable. There's no telling what he'll do."

"I know one thing he'll do. He'll come for us," Eirene said gravely.

Tomas asked, "Is that what this is all about? The hat man scouring history for people who hate you?"

"The list would be too long," Eirene said.

"But once he stumbled upon Spartacus, he must've dug further," Gregorios said.

Eirene pursed her lips in thought. "There has to be more to it than that. We haven't walked the memories where we defeated Spartacus or where we left him."

Events had twisted right into the twilight zone, as far as Sarah was concerned. Before that day, she never would have imagined revenge-crazed gladiators returning from the grave after nearly two thousand years.

Gregorios shook his head in frustration. "That hat man has played us for fools this entire time. We thought we were being so clever, and he must have been there the whole time, studying us and learning our weaknesses."

That was creepy. Sarah asked, "But what does he want?"

Gregorios said, "We know he means business. He's clearly bent on removing everyone who might be a threat to whatever he's planning."

Eirene snapped her fingers. "I think he's thinking bigger than that."

"What do you mean?"

She activated her tablet and flipped through a couple of documents. "Zuri just informed me that two major transfer contracts are suddenly getting cold feet. I hadn't paid it much attention until now. We had other priorities to worry about."

"But now you think they're connected?"

"I do."

She held up her tablet and showed Gregorios a news web site. "The crown prince of Thailand just announced his father died."

"You're losing me. I was hoping for some good news," Gregorios said.

"It's not good news, but it might be a glimmer. The crown prince has already named a new successor."

Tomas said, "Let me guess. A previously unknown son in his early thirties?"

"Bingo."

"Wait, what?" Sarah asked, confused by the rapid turn in the conversation.

Gregorios nodded understanding. "They completed the transfer. That's why they turned on you."

Eirene asked, "But who did the transfer for them?"

"That may finally provide a solid lead," Gregorios said.

She nodded. "More than that. Who knew we were having trouble?"

Sarah was starting to catch up. "The man in the wide-brimmed hat."

Eirene gave her an approving smile. "It's finally starting to add up."

Gregorios started pacing. "They waited until we were in the middle of an important soul transfer to initiate their disruption rune. That left us vulnerable, but it also left our contracts vulnerable."

"But they know how to counter the disruption. They could waltz in there, complete the transfer and look like saviors," Tomas added.

"I bet they're spreading rumors to our other clients too," Eirene said.

Gregorios stopped pacing, his expression darkening. "They're not just trying to keep us from interfering in their plan. They're trying to replace us."

"Whoa, that's bad," Sarah exclaimed. She hadn't thought she could feel more afraid of the hat man, but that did the trick.

Some aspects of the real world that she'd learned about since getting caught up in the fight against Mai Luan still disturbed her, but the reason she could cope with it was knowing Eirene and Gregorios held the reins. The thought of someone like the creepy man in the wide-brimmed hat taking over filled her with dread.

"This is far bigger than we suspected," Eirene said.

"It ties in with what Mai Luan was doing, but this guy is dreaming big," Gregorios agreed.

"Who has the power to do all that?" Sarah asked.

Gregorios shrugged. "If we knew, we would've eliminated them by now."

Eirene frowned as she scanned her tablet. "Listen to this. The crown prince of Thailand just announced that his father's last will compels him to make some changes to the government."

She scanned further and whistled softly. "He's proposing sweeping changes to concentrate far more power in the monarchy."

"That's stupid. They'll depose him or start a civil war," Gregorios said.

Eirene said, "He's got bigger plans than that. In his speech, he included some very belligerent rhetoric against China."

"That's bad, right?" Sarah asked.

Tomas nodded. "It's bad, but it doesn't make sense. The two nations have gotten along pretty well since at least the seventies."

"He's off his gourd. Maybe the transfer didn't go right after all," Gregorios said.

"I'm thinking it did. He's named the new heir Bhumibol in honor of his deceased predecessor," Eirene said.

Gregorios grunted. "You'd think he'd have more imagination. This has to tie in with the hat man's broader scheme. We need to find out how."

Tomas said, "I'm on it. I'll take Anaru over there and ask a few questions."

"Anaru doesn't ask questions," Sarah said nervously. "He breaks things."

Tomas gave her a reassuring smile. "Fine. I'll ask the questions and if I don't like the answers, Anaru will break things."

33

How are the facetakers so successful? Sadly, so little pains do the vulgar take in the investigation of truth, they accept readily the first story that comes to hand.

~THUCYDIDES

EIRENE ENTERED the vault after dinner and found Alter sitting at his worktable in the far corner of the room. Papers were scattered across its surface, but he was leaning back in his chair, staring at the smooth, stainless-steel wall, his expression pensive.

"I thought I'd find you here."

"Hello, Eirene." He made a weak attempt to organize his scattered papers as she approached.

"Have you found anything new?"

"Possibly." Alter showed her a rune drawn on a blank sheet of paper. "I've combined the binding rune I used last time with a rune of balance and a rune of inner strength."

Eirene studied the complex rune with interest. Basic runes were pretty straight-forward, but these were more subtle than the normal enhancements the enforcers usually focused on. The artwork was exquisite, which she had come to expect from Alter.

"Do you think this'll help block the effects of the potential forbidden rune?"

"It's my best guess so far. The force of my soul isn't stronger than your nevron, so that can't affect the process. It has to be something about my rune powers."

"Most likely," Eirene agreed, but she studied him, considering again the startling possibility that had come to her.

He looked so much like his great-grandfather. He had inherited his powerful rounon gift from his hunter bloodline, but could he have inherited something more from hers?

"These runes may generate an effect similar to what you would have felt with me bound to you."

"Let's try it."

Alter's confidence faded. "There's no way to tell if it'll work."

"There's one way."

"It's risky."

"Life is risky," Eirene said, placing a hand on his arm. "Thank you for working so diligently despite the hard times your family's going through."

The vault door opened and Gregorios entered, followed by Sarah, Francesca, and Harriett. The three girls were discussing one of Harriett's favorite recipes. It hadn't taken Harriett long to interest Sarah in baking as a new hobby. Her daughters might be centuries old, but they still embraced youth with so much passion, particularly when wearing such beautiful young forms.

"Alter has a prototype rune for us to test."

"Good. Let's see it," Gregorios said eagerly.

Alter made no move to show him the sheet, his expression turning hard.

Eirene had scanned the workbench for weapons when she first entered, but she double-checked. She didn't really believe Alter would attack Gregorios, but it paid to be cautious. She gently took the rune from him. Working on it helped keep him distracted from his father's secret mission, and they needed his help now more than ever.

Sarah peered around Gregorios' shoulder at the paper and exclaimed, "This is wonderful." She took the paper and traced the lines with her finger. "You've combined the binding rune with a couple others."

Alter smiled at her enthusiasm, and Eirene silently thanked the girl. Without Sarah, Alter would most likely have already left them, or tried something foolish. She loved getting to know her great-grandson, and she agonized with him over the suffering of his family.

He had been placed in a very difficult position and she yearned to comfort him. She had to be careful, though. Their relationship was strengthening, but it was new and therefore very fragile.

Sarah looked up from the rune. "This part has something to do with willpower, right?"

"Correct. Inner strength. And the other is tied to psychic balance."

She snapped her fingers. "Ha! I would've gotten that one in a minute."

Alter grinned. "I bet you would've."

The exchange seemed to ease his tension, so Eirene moved to the Sotrun machine. "Francesca, why don't you take the chair? Let's do a simple, happy memory first."

"Of course, Mother." Francesca settled gracefully into the chair and gave Alter a wink. "Want a ride?"

"I think Alter should stay out here to monitor the test," Eirene said, saving a flustered Alter from having to respond. "Let's try it with no passengers the first time."

Francesca's flirtatious habits were usually harmless, but Eirene wondered at her decision to target Alter. They were both her children, although separated by centuries and many lifetimes, but it still felt weird.

Besides, Alter was already on edge. Francesca could usually read men better than anyone Eirene had ever met. Her training with the Spanish Inquisition in the late fifteenth century had formed a solid foundation that she'd built upon ever since.

She used those skills constantly in her position running much of the family business. They owned vast real estate holdings and major positions in virtually every economic market. Francesca could overturn the economy of any country if she ever chose to. Eirene would trust her to know where to draw the line.

Gregorios moved toward the helmet but Eirene picked it up first. "I'm driving."

"Are you sure that's wise? You were hit pretty hard in Thailand."

"That's right. I know what to expect."

Alter drew the rune on her left arm with a black marker, and it began to glow under his hand as he activated it. "I'll be right here if anything goes wrong."

"I know, dear." That was exactly why she was testing the rune and not Gregorios.

Eirene closed the faceplate over Francesca's beloved face and slipped her hands into the slots on either side of the helmet.

"Here we go."

She tentatively opened the seal kept around her soul powers and embraced her nevra core. Even before she could focus on the machine and set Francesca's mind free to walk her memories, her nevron, so familiar and so trustworthy, rebelled. It rebounded through her chest and seared her innards like living coals.

Eirene gasped and doubled over, nearly pulling her hands from the machine. The pain spiked to unbearable levels. It was happening so much faster than last time. She had hoped she could withstand it, keep the forces under control with the help of Alter's rune.

She was wrong.

She couldn't breathe and would have fallen if Gregorios hadn't caught her.

"Mom!" Francesca and Harriett shouted together as Francesca struggled to escape the helmet.

"Alter!" Gregorios cried, his voice tight with concern.

Eirene didn't feel Alter's hand on her shoulder or the marking of his rune, but the pain began to subside. Within seconds of his linking the strength of his soul to hers, the rebellious tide of her out-of-control nevron receded like a gentle wave. Somehow the strength of his soul wrapped her nevra core like a blanket, protecting and calming it.

She straightened and blew out a shaky breath. When she glanced at Alter, she could see the purple fire of her strength reflected brightly in his eyes.

He must have linked tighter to her than last time. Such a close bond was dangerous. She wasn't sure what effects her nevron might trigger in him. If hers wasn't so unstable, she would have used the connection to test her theory, but instead shuttered her powers and stepped back from the machine. Her legs shook, and Gregorios guided her to a nearby chair.

Sarah dropped to her knees beside Eirene and proffered a cup of water. She sipped it and the cool liquid felt wonderful trickling into her burning guts. She couldn't drink much because her stomach ached and her hand still shook.

"Thank you, Alter. You saved my life." She gripped his hand in hers.

"I guess the rune failed to rise," Harriett said.

"It was such a beautiful one too," Sarah added.

"What do you think went wrong?" Gregorios asked.

Alter snapped, "How should I know? I don't even know what we're dealing with. I told you it might not work, that it was dangerous to try."

Eirene patted his hand, and he calmed a little. "We had to. Our best lead is still finding the hat man through the machine."

"We'll have to do it with Alter bound to us again," Gregorios said.

Alter glared. "And what if I don't want to help again?"

"Then you'd be preventing us from catching the person responsible for all of our problems."

"You're assuming we all believe some figment of your imagination is really responsible."

Sarah looked surprised, and hurt by the accusation. "He's real. I saw him twice."

"Or you saw what Gregorios wanted you to see."

"How can you say that?" Sarah demanded.

"It was his memory!"

Alter was working himself into a powerful enough anger that he might justify doing something stupid.

Eirene spoke softly. "Alter, do you really want to blame my husband so much that you'll let the person who attacked your home, the man who attacked Sarah, get away with it?"

Alter paced away, hands clenched into fists.

"You know it wasn't Gregorios," Eirene pressed.

Sarah looked even more startled. "Why would he think Gregorios did it?"

Gregorios answered. "We've received reports that the attackers planted evidence that suggests we were connected."

Alter faced him. "They did more than that. My father saw John there!"

"Why would John go to Jerusalem?" Harriett asked. "He hasn't been there for centuries, and he only eats those nasty sweetmeats."

Eirene said, "He's still missing. We have no idea what he's up to."

Gregorios added, "I bet he's somehow connected with the man in the wide-brimmed hat. That's the only explanation."

"Or this is all a setup so you can get your hands on the forbidden runes."

"What about the forbidden runes?" Sarah asked.

"They were stolen. That's what the attack was all about."

"This is serious," Eirene said. Although she had eavesdropped on the conversation, she didn't have to pretend to be worried.

Gregorios nodded. "They've twisted our powers around to the point they're almost unusable. With more forbidden runes, who knows what they could do?"

Alter still glared, trying to hold onto his anger.

Eirene beckoned and was relieved when Alter approached and crouched beside her. She placed a gentle hand on his shoulder.

"Search your heart. I know your family is angry now, but consider everything this enemy has done. They've been executing a highly sophisticated plan of attack against all of us while we've been stumbling around in the dark. Do you honestly believe that Gregorios ordered that strike?"

When he still hesitated, Sarah added, "Besides, I owe the hat man another kick in the nads."

"The what?"

"You know, the family jewels."

He didn't want to agree, but Sarah's point helped win him over. He gave an angry nod. "Fine. Maybe you're right. Let's find this guy and kill him."

Gregorios smiled. "Now we're talking."

Alter pointed at the machine. "Go get him."

Gregorios shooed Francesca away from the primary chair and took her place. He fixed Alter with a serious gaze. "I know you have a lot of reasons to think you hate me, but I'm showing you my trust."

Then he turned to Sarah. "Join me, won't you?"

She hesitated just for a second, not quite able to conceal her nervousness. But then she took a deep breath and moved to the secondary chair.

Alter looked ready to spit rocks as he handed out their escape rune pendants. Eirene silently applauded. With Sarah along as the ringer, Alter would be motivated to keep them alive.

"I'll run the machine," Eirene said.

Harriett pushed her back into the chair when she tried to rise. "I don't think so, Mother. Frannie and I will take care of it."

"Don't call me that around other people," Francesca hissed, glancing at Alter.

"You're too old for him," Harriett muttered as she helped Gregorios with the helmet.

Francesca blushed, and Alter looked like he wanted to flee the room.

"Be careful in there," Eirene said as Francesca closed the faceplates.

"And kill him this time," Alter added.

Gregorios gave them a thumbs up.

Harriett slipped her hands into the helmet and Francesca linked to her with one arm on her shoulder. That forced Alter to place his hand onto Francesca's shoulder and trace his rune onto her neck. She smiled at the contact. He hesitated, then gave her the barest smile in return and completed the rune.

"Ready," he said.

Harriett drew upon her nevron, and her eyes and hands began to burn with purple fire. It spread to Francesca, then to Alter. Eirene could feel the strength of their souls like a gentle breath of wind against her skin. It drifted across from all three of them.

Very interesting. The machine whirred to life and everything seemed to be working fine. The purple fire that rimmed Alter's hands like ethereal northern lights had to be caused by the binding rune clashing with the effects of the forbidden rune. The boy was taking a terrible risk by immersing so deep into the girls' nevron, but Eirene could think of no other way it could work.

When he glanced at her, she held his gaze and said, "Alter, thank you for doing this."

He grunted. Given the circumstances, it was enough.

Eirene wished Gregorios good hunting.

34

Reports claim that Eirene leads the vanguard, with enforcers threescore. To Spartacus alone should befall the honor of closing in glorious battle with the most-hated facetaker, but the lot has fallen to me. I will stand for my brother's honor and restore the prestige of his house. Let trepidation flee before my face, and may the gods grant my enhancements suffice to stand athwart the purpose of so valiant a foe.

Glory and Honor to the victor!

~CRIXUS, ONE OF SPARTACUS'S GENERALS, THE DAY
BEFORE HIS DEATH, 72 B.C.

GREGORIOS STOOD in the Forum and breathed deep the familiar smells of ancient Rome. He always loved the city. The people tended to wash more often than most other places he'd lived prior to the modern day, and the Forum in particular held a savor all its own.

This was the original Forum, crowded with temples, statues, and shops, paved with limestone, and filled with people from every economic strata. It smelled of incense and fried food and a nearby bakery. The air hummed with the noise of a thousand conversations spilling over each other. It felt like returning home.

Sarah appeared next to him, dressed in fine robes of the upper class. Her American good looks blended in surprisingly well in Ancient Rome.

"Where are we?" she asked as she took in the sights and smells. A priest of Athena took to a nearby rostra and started loudly proclaiming the virtues of his goddess.

"The Roman Forum." He pointed out the Palatine Hill to the south and the Capitoline Hill to the northeast.

While Sarah took a minute to orient herself to the reality of the city as compared to the modern world that overlay its ruins in her day, he scanned the crowds.

"Do you think they're here?" she asked finally.

"No doubt. This was not the memory I'd been planning, so we were drawn here."

She flashed a smile and a dagger appeared in her hand. "I like how they can't slip around us."

"Alter does good work when he's focused. No one else would have figured out how to sync to other machines actively powering the memoryscape."

"I still don't understand how it works. We're in your head, right?" Sarah asked.

"We are, but we're not." Gregorios led her through the crowds. He hated to stand idle while everyone walked around them. It would be too easy for an assassin to approach. "The runes draw us back to our memories, but also draw us somehow alongside the fabric of history."

After skirting a crowd of bickering merchants he continued. "History is real, despite what the books say, and it has residual power from all the souls that pass through it. With our nevron-powered memories, we can draw close enough to the veil of time that we actually link to it. While we're in one of those linked memories, they become an anchor point that other memory walkers can connect to as they approach history."

"Thinking about this is giving me a headache."

It usually did the same to him, but he'd discussed the theories in detail with Alter and Eirene. Bastien had helped solidify the theory even more. That boy had a brilliant mind for such intangibles.

"I'm not saying I understand it completely, but it appears to be working, so let's not question it too much. The man with the wide-brimmed hat must be using a similar machine, and that helps the pieces fall into place."

"If he wanted to hide from us, could he change the runes and block us from connecting?"

"Possibly. Let's not give him the chance."

"Right." She looked determined. He approved.

"Don't make any big moves," Gregorios cautioned. "Let's see if we can get closer this time."

"Yeah, no armies."

Gregorios continued through the Forum and spent the next few minutes pointing out the buildings and examples of everyday life in ancient Rome. Sarah drank it all in and the process helped tie him more tightly to the moment.

The crowds were thick and the citizens appeared happy, excited even, not carrying the fearful undertone so common in the waning days of the empire. He felt himself putting on this ancient day, like slipping into a pair of worn jeans.

Then he spotted a familiar form exiting a small temple.

"Spartacus."

Sarah picked out the Thracian gladiator as he pushed through the crowd not far away. He was dressed like a merchant, but he walked like a fighter. He didn't appear to have seen them through the press. They followed him across the Forum and around Capitoline Hill. The air smelled less of food and more of incense as they passed a string of temples.

"Where do you think he's going?" Sarah asked.

"Let's find out."

Gregorios chose not to voice his growing suspicions. He didn't want to intercept Spartacus before they found the man in the wide-brimmed hat, but he might not have a choice. Following Spartacus into the heart of his lair would be a mistake.

"Everyone seems pretty excited today," Sarah commented.

"They have good reason to be." He had caught snippets of several conversations as they wove through the crowds, finally pinning down the date. "It's February, 44 BC. Caesar was just appointed dictator for life."

"That makes people happy?"

"He was popular."

"Didn't they realize what was about to happen?"

Gregorios laughed. "How could they? It hadn't happened yet."

She frowned. "Sorry, that was stupid. It's just, I get confused jumping around history so much. It's hard to keep straight."

"Harder for you because you don't know the full truth."

"Don't tell me Julius Caesar was a facetaker?" she asked, sounding disgusted.

"No, he was a mortal, although an exceptionally brilliant one. He and Shahrokh formed an alliance early in his career."

"Oh, that's right. That's where the connection to the Tenth legion comes in, right?"

"Exactly. Shahrokh supported Caesar as his first test case in wielding power from the shadows. Prior to that, too many facetakers tried to take over their kingdoms and rule. It generally ended badly."

"Why was that?"

"People are superstitious, and those early rulers weren't circumspect enough with their soul transfers. They assumed their subjects would consider them gods."

"Didn't work out?"

"It might have, but the hunters were very good at infiltrating the populace and convincing them their rulers were possessed by demons."

"They've been at it for a long time," Sarah commented.

Gregorios shrugged. "They help keep the heka under control. We don't have as many direct conflicts as we used to."

"So Shahrokh worked out a deal with Caesar?"

"Indeed," Gregorios said as they rounded a street corner, working through the crowds about fifty yards behind Spartacus. "Shahrokh gained tremendous power without much public attention. Julius received soul transfers."

"How did that work out with him getting assassinated?"

"Better than you might think."

Sarah scowled. "You changed history again, didn't you?"

Gregorios smiled. "You have no idea."

"I will," she promised.

Spartacus took the turn that he had been fearing and he grimaced. "We're going to have to intervene after all."

"I thought we were waiting for the man in the hat."

"We were, but Spartacus is headed for Quirinal Hill."

"What's that?"

"The location of the temple of Quirinus."

"Never heard of him."

"He was the god of war. The heka loved infiltrating the Quirites."

"The who?"

"The men of the oaken spear."

"I remember the spear."

Gregorios grimaced. "It became Spartacus' signature weapon. For a while he was the high priest of Quirinus."

"I thought Mars was the god of war."

"Eventually. It took us a while, but we sidelined Quirinus so much that he's hardly remembered today."

"So Spartacus goes into the temple and he gets a lot of help?"

"Undoubtedly. Spartacus was always lurking around Rome, with his rabid followers causing trouble. He was like a tick, looking for a soul to suck dry."

They closed on Spartacus as he began climbing the road up the Quirinal Hill. Another quarter mile and he'd reach the imposing temple. Maybe that was where the man in the wide-brimmed hat had been hiding all along? If so, the only way to get to him would be to fight through Spartacus and his followers. Again the mysterious enemy had maneuvered them into a position of weakness.

Well, Gregorios could play that game too.

Before he could launch a new plan, Spartacus turned off the road and entered a palatial building whose purpose Gregorios didn't remember.

"Is that the temple?" Sarah asked.

"No," Gregorios said slowly, trying to piece together what the hat man might be planning.

"I wonder what he's up to," Sarah said, fiddling with her dagger.

"I know one way to find out."

They entered the wide entrance and caught sight of Spartacus passing through a doorway into an inner court. There would be other exits, but that would be a good place to beat some answers out of the gladiator.

Gregorios jogged across the wide, tiled atrium, with Sarah close behind. He paused in the doorway to the inner court and grimaced.

Spartacus waited for them with fifty fully-armed soldiers.

35

Men in general are quick to believe that which they wish to be true, to fear that which might be true, and to ignore what really matters.

~JULIUS CAESAR

"I REALLY HATE THIS GUY," Gregorios muttered.

Spartacus raised his oaken spear, preparing to order the charge. The soldiers were armed with gladius and shield, a deadly combination in the tight confines of the building.

"Watch the rear for a flanking maneuver," Gregorios said to Sarah.

Instead of dropping his spear forward in the signal to attack, Spartacus spoke. "The stage is set, my old enemy, for a confrontation the likes of which the world has never known."

"You always thought every little skirmish was a grand battle," Gregorios replied, summoning a fifty-caliber machine gun mounted on a tripod, with a full box of belt-fed ammunition in place. None of the charging soldiers had ever seen a gun before.

He introduced them.

The armor-piercing bullets shredded shields and breastplates like paper. Flesh and blood fared no better. The explosive reports of the heavy machine gun echoed in the small space with painful intensity.

Gregorios summoned ear protection for both him and Sarah even as he mowed down the ranks of shocked soldiers. Smoke blew across the room and the space filled with the stench of gunpowder, blood, and the stomach-turning reek of opened bodies.

It took only seconds to kill every one of Spartacus' soldiers.

Sarah shouted something he couldn't quite make out through the ear protection and he turned to see her impaling a four-armed apelike creature with a long spear.

Spartacus stood alone in the carnage, stunned by the destruction of his men.

Gregorios removed his ear protection and rose from behind the smoking machine gun. "Now that our epic confrontation's over, I have a few questions you're going to answer."

"The world has gone mad," Spartacus said, still staring at the machine gun. "What incantation is this that so easily kills my men?"

"I'll give you a taste of it in a minute. First, tell me where the man in the wide-brimmed hat is hiding."

"How did you escape my wall?" Spartacus asked, a glimmer of his normal belligerence in his expression.

"Oh, a lot's changed." Gregorios had felt irritated before, but dredging up that bit of memory was making him downright cross. "Welcome to the new world."

"I prefer the old one." The Thracian actually looked troubled. He wasn't talking like a figment of a memory.

"You're really here, aren't you?" Gregorios asked.

Spartacus gestured at the blood-splattered room. "I wish I really was. *This* world I understood."

"And the hat man restored you."

"Indeed. I owe him a debt of honor for opening my cage and releasing my soul."

"You've picked the wrong side again," Gregorios warned him.

"I am beyond sides now," Spartacus declared with a slow shake of his head. "My purpose is my own, but the man in the wide-brimmed hat is about to declare war upon you and yours."

The ground shook as if from an earthquake, but only part of the memory lurched. A section of the memoryscape ripped free from Gregorios' control, wrenched away by another will so powerful it left him feeling stunned. Gregorios flinched and glanced to his left, toward the doorway where he had left Sarah.

She was gone.

Spartacus saluted. "We will speak again soon, and perhaps cross swords for honor and the glory of days past."

"You bet we will."

Spartacus faded from the memory.

Gregorios stared after him. Spartacus really was a player, but for the first time in two millennia, Gregorios wasn't sure what the man was preparing to do.

It didn't matter. Spartacus he could deal with. It was Sarah he worried about. The will that had snapped her away from his memory was perhaps even more powerful than Mai Luan's had been. He had to find Sarah before there was nothing left to find.

He only hoped they could both escape the memory-turned-trap alive.

36

It becomes an emperor to die standing, every time.

~EMPEROR TITUS, 81 A.D.

SARAH REGAINED her balance after the surprise lurch of the memoryscape and found herself standing in a huge, vaulted space. Thick alabaster columns lined the sandstone walls and held up the high ceiling. The floor was paved with smooth, green tile, and a set of marble stairs rose to a wide archway that led to another room.

She was not alone. The man in the wide-brimmed hat stood barely ten feet away, facing her, wearing a modern business suit of pinstriped navy.

"Hello, Sarah." He spoke in a smooth, cultured voice with an accent she couldn't place.

She retreated and only then realized her spear was gone.

He followed slowly, his face concealed, walking with the confident stride of someone who felt in control.

She was going to have to change that real soon.

"You know me, but I hate calling you the man in the wide-brimmed hat."

He chuckled. "The name amuses me, but you may call me Master."

"Thanks, but I have a boyfriend," she snapped. "If I'm going to have to kill you, I should know your name."

He tipped his hat up enough to let her see his smile. His chin was clean-shaven, his mouth looked strong. He stood just over average height, and his build seemed athletic, but not as powerful as Tomas'.

His suit, so incongruous in an ancient Roman temple, looked tailored, with sharp creases in the pants. If not for the hat and the feeling of danger he radiated, he could have slipped into a board meeting in any of a thousand large-cap corporations.

Mai Luan had looked unremarkable too, but she'd been nearly impossible to kill.

After a brief hesitation, he said, "You may call me Paul."

"No offense, but that's not much of a creepy villain name," Sarah said, trying not to look too obvious as she scanned the huge room for exits. She could see none besides the archway, but Paul stood between her and the stairs.

"It is the only name you may know," Paul said, the smooth tone of his voice carrying a hint of irritation. "And knowing even this name grants you more honor than your status deserves."

A guy who had to keep multiple secret names was definitely someone Sarah didn't want to spend time getting to know. "And what exactly is my status?" Sarah asked. If she could keep him talking, maybe she could learn something useful before marking the escape rune.

"Don't pretend to be stupid, Sarah." His lips, barely visible beneath the brim of his hat, turned down in a little frown. "You owe a life debt for Mai Luan, and that debt will be collected as soon as you answer my questions."

Sarah retreated a few steps, her fear spiking. He really was connected with Mai Luan. "Wait a minute. She was trying to kill *me*."

"And she should have succeeded," Paul snapped, taking an angry step closer. "How is it that a simple mortal could defeat her in the moment of her victory?"

"How do you know it was me?" They hadn't shared the details of that confrontation with anyone outside of their close circle.

"You are not the one asking the questions," Paul said, his voice turning cold.

A sword appeared in his hands. It was a single-edged weapon that looked a lot like a saber, but with a wider bade. "The hunter and the facetaker assisted your struggle, but you played the key role. You will explain to me the details of those unusual powers you displayed in the bunker."

Paul continued his slow advance, the sword held loosely in his hand. Sarah couldn't take her eyes off of that shiny length of steel as she retreated from him. The room was big, but she didn't fool herself into thinking she could avoid him.

She concentrated, trying to summon her M4 carbine with attached grenade launcher. That would even the odds. The gun did not appear. Instead she got a splitting headache.

Sarah clutched at her temples. "No fair. You get a weapon."

"Of course. I control this space, as I control the final moments of your life. Now answer my question. What runes did you use to defeat her?"

"I'm not a hunter." Sarah shifted to the right, hoping to circle the room back toward that archway, but Paul moved to cut her off, shortening the distance between them. She was nearing one of the solid stone outer walls, and her fear was growing to near-panic levels as that sword drew ever closer.

It looked like she'd learned as much as she could. Time to bail.

Sarah concentrated and, despite her headache flaring to migraine levels, a black marker appeared in her hand. She ripped the cap off and started marking the escape rune.

Paul lunged, crossing the distance between them in a blink, moving as fast as Mai Luan had in Berlin.

He snatched the marker away and back-handed Sarah in the shoulder. He made it look casual, but the blow struck like the butt of an ax.

Sarah cried out as she tumbled all the way to the wall. She struggled to stand, braced against the stones, but couldn't find her breath and couldn't move her left arm. The blow had left it numb and useless.

"Answer me truthfully and I will claim the life debt swiftly," Paul said, sauntering toward her, his voice conversational. "Continue to stall, and your final moments will be extremely painful."

Sarah leaned against the huge sandstone block of the wall. In the memoryscape, she possessed superhuman strength, and she could easily punch through smaller walls. She wasn't sure she could manage to break this one, especially with Paul and his deadly sword so close.

"I don't know how I did it," Sarah said, trying to buy some time.

Where was Gregorios? Why hadn't he pulled them out of the memoryscape? Had he been hurt, his mind captured? She felt terrified and alone, and that made her angry. She seized upon the feeling, trying to use it as a shield against her rising panic.

"She lies."

Sarah glanced toward the stairs leading out of the huge room. There stood John, dressed like an English gentleman out of the eighteenth century, frowning at her.

"John, help me," she called.

His frown deepened. "Help you help Gregorios assault my very existence? Do you think me a fool, girl?"

"Leave us," Paul commanded, his tone cold.

"I have the right to assist with the interrogation," John said, but looked less sure of himself.

"You will do as I command, and do it now," Paul said.

With a final angry glower, John turned and marched out of the room. Sarah yearned to follow him, to find out how he was in the memoryscape and why he seemed to know Paul, but Paul stepped between her and the exit.

"Perhaps I need to hurt you more," he said, his tone again conversational, as if discussing which dessert to select from a menu. "But first, tell me how you fuel the machine and enter these memories? It should be impossible with the degradation of your facetakers' nevrons."

"Maybe you're not as smart as you think," Sarah countered. "You claim to be in control, but you're the one who doesn't seem to understand anything."

He had tilted his head lower, so she couldn't see his frown, but by the tensing of his shoulders, she could tell she'd angered him. That might not have been a good idea, since he was the one holding the sword. He stepped forward, blade rising.

"I warned you," he said.

The same terror that had raged through her while facing Mai Luan returned, and Sarah reached for that feeling of insubstantiality that had saved her there. As soon as she focused on that need, her rune burned against her back and the feeling she sought radiated out from it. Her skin began to fade to translucent.

"Ah, you can summon your unique ability at will," Paul said, sounding pleased. "Tell me how, or I will remove your skin to examine your runes."

He thrust, and the sword pierced Sarah's stomach. She felt it slide through her ethereal form, like a distant shadow.

Seeing the blade standing out from her abdomen disgusted her. She leaped away, sliding off the sword and tumbling past Paul's outstretched hand. His fingers passed through her arm, like muddy tendrils of smoke clinging to her skin. She shrieked and ran, skirting the outer wall.

Paul chased her, easily keeping pace and blocking her access to the rest of the room. She could probably jump through him, but the thought of passing through so much of him made her skin crawl.

"How long can you maintain the effect?" he asked, not sounding the least bit winded, despite how fast they were running.

"Long enough to get away from you, creep!"

"Perhaps not that long." He sounded like he was enjoying himself.

She had to get away, to find a few seconds to mark the escape rune. She'd never been able to maintain the ethereal form for long, and even as she ran, she felt it fading.

"Only a few seconds," Paul said, noting the change. "About the same as when you faced Mai Luan."

"How can you know that?" she shouted, yearning for a gun or a grenade, or maybe a tank.

Without warning, a doorway appeared in the outer wall, and Paul stumbled, clutching at his head. Sarah veered toward the opening, pouring on the speed, hoping the change meant Gregorios had joined her.

The doorway disappeared half a heartbeat before she reached it.

Fully substantial again, Sarah crashed into the wall, still running faster than an Olympic sprinter. She struck with so much force she cracked the face of the stone.

She was glad she couldn't see what it did to her face.

Sarah nearly blacked out as every inch of her body screamed with pain. She bounced off the wall and fell to the unyielding stone floor, moaning. Even with her fast healing, several seconds passed before the world stopped spinning and she could think straight again.

Paul's sword pierced her thigh, snapping her focus back to the present. She cried out and grabbed at the blade, but Paul withdrew it.

He hadn't stabbed deep, just an inch or so, but it was enough. He stood over her, but even from that angle, she couldn't see into the dark shadows gathered under the brim of his hat. That was so annoying.

He said, "I tire of the game. Answer—"

Gregorios' voice boomed through the building. "Let's find out what's behind door number two."

The wall directly behind Paul exploded inward, giant blocks of stone shattering and spraying deadly shards across the room. Dozens of fragments struck Paul, who stood between Sarah and the explosion, but he barely staggered. As a billowing cloud of dust enveloped them, he turned toward the outer wall, and that time, Sarah caught a glimpse of his frown.

The explosion might not have hurt him, but it did distract him for a precious second.

Despite how much she still hurt, Sarah leaped to her feet and sprinted for the opening in the wall.

Paul caught her before she made it three steps. His hand sealed around her arm like a vice, and he whipped the sword around in a blow that would sever her other arm.

Sarah's rune burned against her shoulder, and she faded to insubstantial just as the blade reached her skin. It passed through, trailing a few drops of her blood where it pierced her just as she faded. Sarah twisted away from Paul, who snarled with frustration.

She ran for the wall and threw herself into the gap with all her enhanced strength. She flew through the opening and soared fifty feet in a graceful dive into sunlight. She landed on stone-paved ground and rolled, returning to her feet already running.

As her eyes adjusted to the bright light, she found herself sprinting across a wide piazza devoid of people. She spotted Gregorios not far away, high atop a statue of Jupiter. His legs were wrapped around the god's neck and he was holding back a huge iron ball. It had to be a full eight feet in diameter. A chain ran from the top of the ball all the way up to the roof of Paul's temple.

Gregorios called, "Nice dive. Figured you were ready for a change of sceneary"

"Let's get out of here!" Sarah shouted as she sprinted toward him.

"Time for door number three."

He released the thick chain. The huge ball swept down, accelerating with remarkable speed and crashing into the opening Sarah had just dived through just as Paul jumped into the opening. The ball caught him in the chest, and even he couldn't ignore that.

It flattened him and blasted him back through the opening, taking most of the wall with it. Huge blocks of stone toppled into the temple. Dust billowed out of the shattered building, obscuring everything. Three seconds later, the roof began to collapse with a heart-stopping groan of timbers. The ensuing avalanche shook the ground and lasted ten long seconds.

Gregorios dropped to the foot of the statue beside Sarah. He looked pleased with himself.

She hugged him, and didn't even care that she was trembling uncontrollably. "Thanks. You arrived just in time."

"I pride myself on saving damsels in distress."

She kissed his cheek. "You did today. But I thought ancient Roman temples were built stronger."

He winked. "I cheated."

"I'm glad. Gregorios, he was so strong, and he talked about Mai Luan. He knew things about when she died that he shouldn't be able to know."

"Like what?"

"Little things, like knowing it was you and me and Alter who faced her. He knew about how I faded to insubstantial in there, how I defeated her."

Gregorios frowned. "Those clues might help figure him out."

Sarah grabbed his arm. "John's in there with him. They're working together?"

His frown deepened. "That explains a few things."

"He calls himself Paul, and I think he's cui dashi," Sarah added, hating to use the terrifying label. "He was like Mai Luan."

"All the more reason to finish him off." Gregorios started toward the mountain of rubble that had been the temple. "And to beat the truth out of John."

Sarah moved to follow, but the top of the rubble pile exploded away, fragments of wood and stone spraying across the piazza. Paul rose from the opening, looking battered and bloody. His suit was shredded and his shoulders sagged, but he still wore that hat.

Then the broken remains of the temple shimmered and disappeared. Paul floated down to the bare stones of the piazza. His clothing flickered, then returned to pristine shape, and he stood taller. His sword appeared in his hand again.

"I hate cheaters," Gregorios muttered, rubbing one temple as if he'd gotten a headache.

"You're beginning to annoy me," Paul declared as he advanced toward them. He spoke softly, but his voice reverberated across the piazza.

"We need to get out of here!" Sarah cried.

"I suppose we don't have a choice." Gregorios sounded reluctant, but panic threatened to overwhelm Sarah's reason. Paul had survived everything Gregorios had thrown at him, and didn't look damaged.

Gregorios looked up and growled, "All right, take us home, Harriett."

As the memoryscape began to fade, Paul rushed forward with superhuman speed and slashed his blade through the space Sarah was vacating. It passed through her without harm, but she cried out in fear anyway. His voice chased her into oblivion.

"We will speak again soon, Sarah. Your soul belongs to me."

37

History is the version of past events that Harald has ensured that people have decided to agree upon.

~NAPOLEON BONAPARTE

AS SOON AS he removed the helmet, Gregorios said, "John is officially on probation."

"What happened in there?" Harriett asked.

"Too much, and none of it good," Sarah said as Alter helped her to her feet. She was so relieved to be back in the vault, surrounded by friends and lots of guns, she threw her arms around Alter. "It's good to be back."

He gripped her tight, arms wrapping her waist, and his solid presence helped wash away the last of her fear.

She wished Tomas had been there to greet her. When she withdrew, Alter seemed reluctant to release her, but she pretended not to notice. Paul had rattled her too much to worry about how Alter might read her actions.

"Are you all right?" Alter asked, looking more than ready to offer more comfort if she needed it. "The drain was pretty bad."

Gregorios said, "We didn't mess with too much. Well, except for finding a broken memory where Paul was trying to interrogate Sarah."

"Whoa, wait!" Alter exclaimed. "Who's Paul?"

Gregorios made a calming gesture. "We'll get to that. The drain felt severe?"

Alter nodded. "Felt like someone was doing a lot of manipulations, a lot of struggle for control. Either that, or the problems with your nevron are making the drain worse."

"I'm glad you were there to help us," Francesca told him.

She started to walk toward a chair but her legs buckled. Alter reacted with enhanced reflexes and caught her before she hit the floor. She clung to his shoulders as he lifted her lithe body and carried her to the chair.

"Thank you. You're a good man to have around."

"Just be careful," Alter said, trying to disentangle himself and retreat.

Francesca didn't seem to notice his discomfort and kept her arms around his neck for several more seconds.

Sarah wondered what she was playing at. She liked Francesca, but the young-looking facetaker was far older than her nearly-twenty body suggested. She had to know what she was doing to Alter. Sarah hoped her plan didn't backfire and drive Alter away. Then again, maybe Francesca's attention might help divert him from his ongoing attempt to supplant Tomas.

Eirene took Gregorios' hands. "Stop stalling. You mentioned Paul and torture. Who and why?"

"Paul is what the name the man in the wide-brimmed calls himself."

Eirene looked thoughtful. "That's interesting."

"How so?" Francesca asked before Sarah could. "And where does torture fit in?"

"A cui dashi I defeated in ancient Rome, who was Spartacus' handler, was named Pavlos," Gregorios said.

Sarah frowned. "You mean, the guy with the dogs?"

"What?" Gregorios asked.

"You know, the guy who taught his dogs to drool by ringing the dinner bell."

He laughed. "No, that was Pavlov."

"Interesting fellow," Eirene added through her own smile. "But the name Paul is Pavlos in Greek. And I don't think he ever owned a dog."

"Oh." Sarah felt foolish. "So a cui dashi in ancient Rome was named Pavlos?"

"Exactly."

Alter asked, "What do you mean, he was Spartacus' handler? And why was he torturing Sarah?"

"That connects back to Baladeva again," Gregorios said.

Harriett muttered, "Again with him. Like leaven in the dough, that name's spreading everywhere."

"You've mentioned he was your enemy. Why?" Sarah asked.

Gregorios said, "Baladeva recruited heka assassins to kill facetakers loyal to Shahrokh, and even set up his own rival council. We found and removed most of his supporters, but eventually he got desperate. He bred with heka women and managed to produce a cui dashi heir."

"That was Paul?" Sarah asked.

Eirene nodded. "He became at least as powerful as Mai Luan. He partnered with Spartacus. Together they were a mighty force. More than once they nearly toppled the republic and then the empire."

Gregorios didn't look happy to revisit those memories. "Paul was the handler. He called the shots and set the agenda. I confronted them together."

"You fought Spartacus and a cui dashi at the same time?" Sarah could scarce comprehend what that epic showdown must have looked like.

Gregorios shrugged. "It was an unexpected opportunity. I didn't have my team but I couldn't pass up the chance."

"What happened?" Even Alter looked impressed.

"I defeated Pavlos," Gregorios said. That was frustrating. Such an event concealed in those three little words. Sarah wanted to shake him and demand the full story.

"And let Spartacus get the best of you," Eirene added with a smile.

"Oh, don't start that again," Gregorios protested, but he returned the smile. They acted like it was a familiar argument.

"You defeated a cui dashi single-handedly?" Sarah pressed, still hardly believing it. Together, they had barely defeated Mai Luan. And he had defeated another cui dashi while fighting Spartacus at the same time. Even walking through their memories, Spartacus scared her.

"I did."

"How?" Alter asked. For the moment, he appeared to have forgotten his hatred for Gregorios.

"Through the judicious use of a blast furnace and a handy bronze statue."

"And tons of luck," Eirene added.

Gregorios winked. "What's relevant to our discussion today is that the man in the wide-brimmed hat called himself Paul."

"But if you killed Pavlos, how can the man in the wide-brimmed hat be him?" Sarah asked.

"He's not the same man, but there must be a reason to use that name."

Eirene said, "I'm still not clear why we're assuming new Paul is also cui dashi."

Sarah said, "Seems obvious after he ripped me out of one memory and threatened to kill me for defeating Mai Luan."

"He also possessed strength of mind that exceeded even what Mai Luan exhibited in the memoryscape," Gregorios added.

Eirene settled onto a nearby chair. "You're going to have to tell us everything."

So Sarah and Gregorios related their experience. Alter interrupted when Gregorios told of machine-gunning Spartacus' men, but Eirene insisted they hear the rest without pause. Then she broke that rule a moment later when Gregorios related what Spartacus had said.

"You were speaking with the memory-walking, real Spartacus?" Eirene demanded, leaning closer, expression intent. "And he sounded sane?"

"I believe he was really there. I'm not sure I'd call him sane, but he wasn't a raving lunatic like I would've expected."

"Tell me every word," Eirene insisted.

"That's what I was doing before you interrupted," he reminded her.

Eirene wanted to spend more time discussing his brief interaction with Spartacus, but he gestured at Sarah and said, "You all kept asking about the torture. Here's your chance to hear about it."

Sarah took up the tale. When she told of Paul plunging his sword through her stomach, Alter leaped to his feet, fists clenched. "I'll kill him for that!"

"Thanks, but if he really is cui dashi, we're going to have to be careful or he'll kill us first."

"I swear on my honor to avenge you," Alter cried.

Sarah appreciated his enthusiasm. They would need it. "He hasn't killed me yet, so nothing to avenge."

He started protesting, but Eirene motioned him to silence. "Please, let's hear the rest of the story."

Francesca, who sat perched on the edge of a nearby chair added, "And I want to find out more about that form shifting. That's fantastic! I've never heard of runes actually altering the physical composition of a person's body."

Sarah agreed. It was cool. "It's only happened in the memoryscape, bit without somehow going ghosty like that, Mai Luan would've killed me in Berlin for sure. I've been trying to figure out how it worked, and it's tied to my rune. It worked again today, or Paul would have gutted me."

Alter growled low in his throat, quivering with rage. Eirene patted his shoulder, but that did little to calm his anger. He said, "I don't see how your rune could do that."

"We'll have to study it further," Gregorios said.

"I'll say," Francesca exclaimed. "Imagine our little Sarah with her own superpower."

"Let's finish what we started first," Gregorios cautioned.

Sarah told about the rest of the strange interview with Paul, then repeated it several times as they asked a barrage of questions.

She finished by saying, "He said Paul was just one of his names, that I wasn't worthy to know more."

Gregorios grunted. "The criminally insane always invent ways to try to seem more impressive. They usually lack the showmanship to pull it off."

Sarah said, "He was pretty intimidating, although he seemed stumped by the fact we could access the memoryscape at all."

Eirene flashed Alter a smile, and he beamed with pride.

She added, "From the hints you picked up, it seems we have confirmation that he is indeed running the cell that we thought had belonged to Mai Luan. He has her machine, and no doubt also controls the stolen forbidden runes being used to sabotage our nevrons."

Gregorios added, "Let's hope they don't figure out how we're skirting their runes. The memoryscape is our best chance of tracking Paul down again and removing him, or getting some answers."

"If we can control the location, we can arrange a trap," Eirene said with more confidence than Sarah felt. Eirene hadn't felt Paul's strength, hadn't seen him rise from the ruins of that temple.

Gregorios hesitated. "That's a big if. His control over the memoryscape was immensely powerful. We'll have to figure a way to counter it."

"First, we need to find him," she said.

Gregorios nodded. "Which brings us back to John. Sarah saw him in there. It seems clear they're working together."

"And he seemed to think we're plotting to assassinate him," Sarah added.

Harriett snorted. "The old fool was always seeing assassins in every shadow. Twice he asked me to assign food testers for his meals to check for poison."

Eirene said, "His mental dissipation is well known, and it's contributing to his natural suspicions."

"So John's working with someone connected with a cui dashi who's been dead for a couple thousand years," Sarah said. "And that's our best bet for who's stirring up these old memories?"

"That would explain the interest in Spartacus and the theft of his soulmask in modern day," Eirene said.

It seemed like a stretch to Sarah. "So you defeated Pavlos and Spartacus defeated you?"

Gregorios sighed. "He killed the body I was wearing. When I severed contact with it, he bronzed my soulmask and kept me on his wall as a trophy."

"That's why you did the same thing to him later," Alter said, looking unhappy to discover that Gregorios might have had justification for what he'd done.

Gregorios nodded. "A long time later. It was the first of many times Eirene saved my life."

"How did you rescue him?" Sarah asked her.

"During the sacking of Rome Spartacus led a force of enhanced heka against our temple."

"Which temple?"

"We were affiliated with Summanus, god of nocturnal thunder."

"Why?"

"That's not important. Most of the information regarding what we did has been scrubbed, either by us or by the hunters."

"That's really annoying," Sarah said, glancing from Eirene to Alter, who shrugged.

Eirene explained, "I defeated Spartacus, but the temple was destroyed. I later found Greg's bronzed soulmask and set him free."

"And you wonder sometimes why I stick around," Gregorios said.

Eirene rolled her eyes. "You removed Pavlos, but I still had to take care of Spartacus."

"You couldn't have beat him if I hadn't made the almost-ultimate sacrifice," Gregorios countered.

They were both smiling as they argued. Sarah glanced at Harriett, who had shifted closer to her chair. "Are they always like this?"

"Gets worse during a honeymoon."

"Once in a while a good argument is a healthy thing to keep a relationship strong," Gregorios protested.

Francesca waved a dismissive hand. "We're getting distracted again. You killed the Paul who worked with Spartacus a long time ago. How can they be connected?"

Sarah said, "But what if he doesn't care about your connection to that name? What if he chose that name for someone else?"

Gregorios smiled. "Good thinking. You might be on to something. If Paul learned the connection Spartacus had with the cui dashi handler I killed, he might be trying to leverage that."

"To what end?" Harriett asked. She had drifted to the nearby workbench and opened a cardboard box filled with several kinds of cookies, which she began passing out to the group.

"From the little I learned during our chat, it didn't sound like he and Paul were pulling entirely in the same direction. I don't think he's really committed to the cause."

"Perhaps Paul's trying to provide a concrete anchor," Eirene suggested. "Something to help focus his mind on the mission at hand."

Gregorios shrugged. "What mission? I would've bet ready money he'd jump right back into vengeance mode, but he lacked focus."

"Paul's got to want him to find us and finish the job Mai Luan started. It's quite poetic," Eirene said.

Harriett frowned. "It's complicated though The best operations are like the best recipes: simple." She hefted a double chocolate cookie for emphasis.

Sarah said, "Paul's not simple. It's not his style."

They considered that, and Eirene said, "You're right. Think about all he's done."

She raised a finger. "First, there's no doubt they have a machine. So it has to be one of the original ones Mai Luan developed."

Alter shifted closer to Sarah, leaning against the chair she rested on. "Second, we're pretty sure he's the one tampering with forbidden runes."

"Third," Francesca added with a wink to Alter. "They're actively exploring deep memories."

Sarah placed a hand on Alter's arm. "Fourth, working with John, they attacked your family and stole your rune lore."

Alter nodded. "With that information, Paul can do even more terrible things."

"I wonder if this was all part of Mai Luan's plans?" Sarah asked.

"More likely her involvement was all part of Paul's plans," Gregorios said, looking thoughtful.

"Don't you think you're stretching the dough a little?" Harriett asked.

"No. Everything we've been listing is part of Paul's plan, not Mai Luan's. She got him the master rune and took out most of the council, but we had been assuming she was trying to control them. Now I'm thinking that was just phase one of their plan."

"But Mai Luan died," Sarah reminded him. "She didn't get the master rune to anyone."

Gregorios shook his head. "Tomas mentioned Teresa snapped a photo of that rune with her phone before he stopped her. At this point, I think we can assume she transmitted that photo."

Eirene rose and paced around the machine. "So they may have the master rune, and they killed half the council. Probably hoped the resulting internal strife would keep us distracted until it was too late. They clearly don't want us poking around through history."

"That worries me as much as anything else," Gregorios said. "We're the only ones who can stop them from acquiring another master rune."

Alter said, "Coupling the forbidden runes they've acquired with the first master rune will grant them incredible power. Adding a second one to it would increase that power exponentially."

"What could they do with it?" Sarah asked, hating the direction the conversation had turned. She hadn't thought she could get any more frightened.

"Just about anything."

"That may be what they're planning." Gregorios grimaced. "The pieces are lined up for them to tap unprecedented power. They've kept under the radar until now, when they're on the brink of success."

He began pacing as he spoke. "They recruited John somehow and used him to attack the hunters, steal the rune lore they wanted, and blame me at the same time. They timed their forbidden rune spell perfectly to discredit us with our clients.

Eirene kissed his cheek. "I think you've got it. We were so focused on dealing with Mai Luan because she was cui dashi that we never considered the possibility that something more was going on."

Sarah protested, "But Mai Luan was so powerful. She wouldn't sacrifice herself for someone else, even if she was working for Paul."

"He's cui dashi," Gregorios said. "The more we learn, the more I'm convinced. It's the only way this works. He was the senior partner."

"I hate cui dashi," Sarah muttered, rubbing her arms against a sudden chill.

Gregorios chuckled. "We can all agree to that. We have a cui dashi at the head of perhaps the most sophisticated heka cell we've ever faced, armed with the most powerful runes ever unleashed upon the world."

"We have to stop him." Francesca looked a little sick.

"And avenge my family," Alter added.

"Catching him in the memoryscape won't be easy," Sarah said. "He's tricky."

Eirene said, "We'll need a better plan. We need to lure him in and destroy him before he can escape again."

"Unless Tomas' team can track down the heka," Francesca said.

"Or unless he gets something useful out of Thailand," Eirene added.

"We have another lead now," Gregorios reminded them. "John."

"I wonder if he betrayed the council before Mai Luan or after you took power," Harriett said.

"That's been bothering me," Eirene said, rising to pace beside her husband. "John nearly died in that memory of Thermopylae. If he was working with them, why try to kill him?"

"And if he wasn't yet tied to them, that's a strange form of recruitment," Francesca added.

They considered that for a moment until Harriett said, "John's still suffering mental dissipation. He's hated you for decades, Dad. What if Paul convinced him that you orchestrated that attack as a way to assassinate him?"

"He's always muttering into his wine about assassination attempts," Francesca agreed.

Such complex plotting really troubled Sarah. She knew evil existed, had helped defeat some of it, and hated how much effort some people invested into destroying things. Why couldn't they use a forbidden rune to make it rain hamburgers, or something positive?

Gregorios said, "John's been pretty unstable. I was looking forward to seeing how well the machines could reverse his soul fragmentation and restore his mental stability."

"Paul can't be having an easy time of working with him either," Eirene said.

"But John must possess memories they need. He's the link to the times they're hunting for master runes," Gregorios replied.

"So does that mean Paul's not old enough to have lived through a master-rune-worthy moment?" Sarah asked.

Eirene nodded. "He probably isn't. Between us and the hunters we're pretty good at rooting out cui dashi.

"Yet, somehow he's built this powerful organization without any of us picking up on it," Alter said.

"We know now," Gregorios said, his expression serious. "And we know the connection with John. He may be the key to unraveling the mystery."

That much made sense, at least. Sarah said, "So we find John to find Paul."

"Find Paul and we bring in the family," Francesca said.

"Wait, whose family?" Alter asked.

Francesca rose and took his hands in hers. "Both of ours."

38

I stand upon the cusp of history. Mehmed and his enhanced troops think to lay waste to the world. Where are the hunters who decry his abomination? Where is Bastien and his family? They wait for me to raise a cipher greater than any wielded by natural man. I will unite my people the way no king ever has, and I will become the Sword of the Dragon.

~VLAD DRACULA, RUNE WARRIOR, VOIVODE OF
WALLACHIA, 1476

THE MAN who had been king of Thailand, now known as Prince Bhumibol, entered his private salon and dismissed his aid. He sat back in a comfortable chair and sighed.

"Looks like you're having a good day," Tomas said as he rose from behind a nearby couch. "Let's not ruin it, shall we?"

Bhumibol sprang to his feet, but Tomas waved him back down with his silenced pistol. "I'd hate to return you to a wheelchair so soon."

The recently transferred king settled slowly into his chair. "You are here to kill me, so why should I make your job easier?"

"You'll keep living as long as I'm satisfied with the answers you give me."

"I could just start shouting," Bhumibol countered. "Then you'd learn nothing."

Anaru stepped out of a closet. "Bad idea. I don't mind killing all your guards and staff, but my boss tends to get annoyed by the mess."

The giant Maori's presence intimidated the king as thoroughly as

Tomas had hoped. Anaru was very good at what he did, and he'd thrown himself into bringing as much honor to his position as Tomas' second as possible.

Tomas had worried Anaru would hold a lingering grudge from losing the duel for the captain's post, but the mighty warrior had accepted his fall with remarkable grace.

"Now that we have that settled," Tomas said, dropping into a chair. "Let's talk."

Bhumibol did a remarkable job of retaining his composure. The old man had not survived as long as he had as monarch without learning to deal with surprises. "Ask your questions and then get out."

"Why did you try to kill me and Eirene?"

"Failure to complete your contract."

"Eirene was the target of a very subtle assassination attempt," Tomas said.

Bhumibol shrugged. "Excuses do not interest me. Had I tried to break the contract, you would have exacted retribution against me. Why do you feel betrayed that I reacted the same way?"

"We acted in good faith and would have completed the transfer in time."

"So you claim. What you did was leave my grandson in agony for hours. The pain broke his mind."

"For that, I am sorry. However, the blame lies at the hands of Eirene's attackers."

Bhumibol shrugged again. "He served his purpose, but I must protest on principle."

Such cold-hearted dismissal of the vessel used to provide his new life was not unusual. Those willing and able to buy additional lives were often arrogant enough to believe the vessel didn't matter as a person. Tomas had grown to hate that attitude, but he reined in his annoyance.

"Indeed. Who completed your soul transfer?"

"Another party."

"This is where the conversation may turn ugly," Tomas warned. "We both know I'll get the information one way or the other."

The old man did not look fazed by the threat. "True. However now I can say I resisted the interrogation as long as I could."

Again, the man's cold logic was representative of many who managed to procure second lives. They were survivors. He wouldn't make any useless, heroic gestures that might get him hurt.

Tomas said, "So you've resisted. Tell me about this other party."

"Chinese. The man who performed the soul transfer did not share a name, but his associated called himself James."

Tomas found that interesting. Another rather bland, biblical name for the enemy. "Describe the facetaker."

"As I said, Chinese. Unusually tall and muscular, but definitely Chinese features."

Tomas shared a glance with Anaru. None of the facetakers affiliated with the council were Chinese. He hadn't heard of any emerging from that area in a long time.

"And their price included the changes in the government and the new stance against China," Tomas prodded.

"If you know all that, why do you need to ask me?"

"Why those demands? To what end?"

Another shrug. " I do not know."

"How do you contact them?"

"I do not. I've followed their instructions, and they stated they will contact me with future guidance."

"For how long?"

The king fixed him with a steady stare. "Does it matter? The price is a small thing for this second life."

"Tell me more about the facetaker and his men," Tomas said, feeling increasingly annoyed.

The young-old king spread his hands in a gesture of helplessness. "There is nothing more. I do not know where they came from, and I know nothing of where they went when they left. I saw only James and his master. They informed me that your council is broken and cannot complete your work, but they could do so."

"And you believed them?"

"Why wouldn't I? Eirene was lingering close to death, my last moment was upon me, and I couldn't wait."

"You'll hear from me again," Tomas promised as he rose to his feet. "Do not cross the council, or your second life will be short-lived."

The king said, "Speak with me after your current troubles are resolved. I do not know the details of your strife, but I've lived long enough to recognize that war has come to the facetakers. I am not your enemy, and if you prevail, I will make restitution to Eirene. Until then, do not bother me again."

Anaru stood and produced a roll of duct tape.

"That won't be necessary," Bhumibol objected. "We have already agreed you would leave after our discussion."

Anaru gave Tomas a pleading look. He loved taping people up. Usually they struggled and gave him an excuse to hit them a few times.

Tomas sighed and motioned Anaru back. "All right. We'll leave. If you break your word, I'll let Anaru level this palace."

"My word is my life."

Tomas led Anaru out of the room and did not look back. He wondered if the old king knew those were the truest words he had ever spoken.

39

Waste no more time talking about great souls and how they should be. Become one yourself!

~MARCUS AURELIUS, FOURTH LIFE OF EMPEROR NERVA

SARAH RETURNED to Quentin's mansion and worked on her rune for a while. With a new cui dashi hunting her, she needed every advantage.

She worked for a couple of hours, poring through the runes she had gotten from Alter, with her runesmith kit open on her desk. It seemed to help because the concepts made more sense than ever, and she drafted pieces of several promising higher runes, experimenting with combining various basic symbols. Considering the ramifications of how they'd interact together was like piecing together a complex, three-dimensional jigsaw puzzle.

Despite feeling like she made solid progress in her understanding of rune design, she still didn't find the missing pieces she needed.

Frustrated, she descended to the workout room and beat on the punching bag for half an hour. Sometimes physical activity helped free her mind, but that time it didn't work.

Alter entered the room. "I thought I'd find you in here."

"Hi. I just finished my workout. I'm going to swim. Want to join me?"

"I'm not much of a swimmer."

"Then you need to practice."

It was good to see him return her smile. He had to be worried sick about his family, which was probably why he'd seemed so short-tempered earlier. She was grateful he had decided to stay. Without him, they'd lose all access to the memoryscape.

"And you need to practice fighting," he said, raising his hands to a ready position. "Want to go a round?"

Sarah shook her head. Usually she loved fighting with Alter, but she felt tired and a little frustrated. The swim would probably help. She dropped onto a padded bench near the window and drank from her water bottle.

"I've had enough for today. I would like to learn more about rune warriors, though. Our discussion got cut short, and things have been crazy since then."

"You can say that again," Alter muttered as he sat beside her. "No new information about your genealogy. Your lines are too thoroughly burned out for any conclusion, and the family lacks the resources to dig deeper."

"There has to be a way to know," she pressed.

"There is a way," he said after a moment's hesitation. "What's made you suddenly so eager?"

"Paul. In some ways he frightens me more than Mai Luan did. She almost killed all of us, Alter. We have to pursue anything that might give us an advantage against him."

Besides, she yearned to find a tangible link to the terrifying world of soul powers she'd stumbled into. That might help her feel like she really belonged there and wasn't just allowed to hang around because she was dating the captain of the guard.

"There are risks associated with all forms of power." As interested as he had been in the initial idea of connecting her to Joan of Arc's bloodline, he now looked reluctant.

"What's the hold-up? Paul's planning to kill me, so I don't have time for you to hold back, Alter."

"The chance is slim that you're part of that bloodline." He considered her for a moment before adding. "I see you want it."

She took his hands in hers. "I need it. It's a matter of survival."

"But that power could be used for such evil," Alter whispered. "You heard what happened to Vlad."

"I also heard what Joan of Arc was trying to do," she countered. "Power is power, Alter. You use yours for good. If I had some, I could do the same."

"But if you didn't, if you gave in to the temptation to misuse it . . ." He looked anguished.

"Are you saying you'd kill me?"

She spoke in a light tone, planning on making the question more of a tease, but he looked away and said a little too quickly, "No."

"But your family would," she added softly, feeling a little sick. They knew about her already. As if a cui dashi wasn't enough to worry about. She didn't need hunters joining the club.

"It is our sworn duty."

"Trust me, Alter. You can do that, right?"

He took a deep breath and nodded.

"Then how do we prove it?"

"There is a rune unique to rune warriors. I've already requested a copy from my father."

"How will that help?" The thought of a new rune filled her with a thrill.

"You'll see."

"That's not an answer."

"Trust me," he said with a hint of a smile.

"Oh, that's not fair," she groaned.

"It worked, didn't it?"

"Just get that rune fast. Please."

"Why don't you tell me about how your rune turns you ghosty in the memoryscape." Alter frowned. "Is ghosty even a word?"

"It's the only one that fits. I go kind of incorporeal. Solid objects like swords pass right through me."

"That can't be healthy," Alter said with a grimace.

"Healthier than the alternative." At least he didn't call it an abomination.

When he nodded, she added, "I didn't plan it. It just happened. And I'm glad it did. If not, Mai Luan would have killed me, and I never would have escaped Paul."

Alter rose and paced away, expression thoughtful. "I've never heard of runes causing effects like that, and you're not the first to have worn your rune."

"I'm the first to wear it on my shoulder," she pointed out. "And I doubt anyone else walked the memoryscape like we do."

"True, but even with the unique situation, I don't understand how it's working like that. Our runes just don't work that way."

"Is there really a limit to what runes can do?" Sarah asked. She'd never considered the question.

"There are things we don't do, even if they were possible."

"Are you saying my rune is somehow evil?" She rose to face him. "Alter, it's saved my life several times."

"I don't know what it is, but I worry about you, Sarah."

"Then help me explore every possible way to survive."

"I plan to."

With a little smile, he drew from his pocket a folded piece of paper upon which he'd drawn her mostly-completed rune. He'd added a large new rune to it, with a central shape that encircled the inner marks, and three interlocked spirals that wove through, and linked together, the other symbols. The design was bold and beautiful and daring.

Sarah took it from him, tracing the new design. "Wow," she breathed after a moment. "When did you come up with this?"

He grinned to see her approval. "We've been thinking along the same lines. "With another cui dashi on the loose, you need more enhancements. The rune you've been working on has incredible potential, and I came up with this idea to complete it."

It was complete. Finally. Despite a lingering feeling that the ultimate design she'd been working toward was still not quite realized, he'd produced something wonderful. "I don't recognize this symbol."

"It's not a core rune we often use. We tend to focus on the ones proven and deeply understood. Runes often hold multiple meanings, and those variations can produce unexpected results when not taken into account. This rune is an ancient Celtic symbol."

"You've never used those before." She'd thought power runes needed to be primarily Egyptian and Chinese, with a few notable exceptions.

"The symbol is older than the Celts. It's been found as far back as 4400 B.C. in Malta, and it was used as the symbol for the Gorgon Medusa in ancient Sicily."

He flipped the paper over and produced a pen, quickly sketching out the symbol by itself. "It's been used by others as well. It's known as the triskelion, and there is some difference of opinion about its ultimate meaning, which is why we rarely use it. In this case, it fit your rune so perfectly, I thought it worth trying."

"It's impressive. You've got to share with me a list of those other symbols."

Alter gave her a warning look. "Sarah, don't go jumping into fringe runes. Just because I dared incorporate one doesn't mean it's safe to do so."

"But I can't ignore the possibility." She couldn't understand why he would willfully limit her education. She'd approach other symbols with care, but how could he think it best to bar her from even knowing about them?

"Just focus on this one for now." He pointed at the rune with its central core and triple spiraled leg design. "This rune is often associated with a sense of action."

"I can see that."

"This design is usually interpreted as linking spirit, mind, and body."

"There are other possibilities though, aren't there?"

"Yes. Sometimes it's interpreted as linking past, present, and future, or even linking the three Celtic worlds: the spirit world, present world, and celestial world."

Sarah nodded her head slowly, taking the paper and turning it back to her rune. She traced the lines with her finger, studying how he'd worked the triskelion into the broader design. "I think all three of those interpretations could manifest through this."

His enthusiasm faded a little. "That's my concern. I like the finished product, but it's not as stable as I prefer my runes to be. The more I look at it, the less I think I made the right choice in picking this one."

"I disagree," Sarah said, pulling the paper away when he reached for it. "I'm liking it more and more. Let's give it a try."

"I'm not convinced it'll produce the effect I was aiming for."

Sarah paced away and Alter followed, looking like he wanted to snatch the paper from her hands. She considered the design again. "This is a powerful rune, Alter. Very powerful. The melding of the times and aspects of self, linked to the other basic runes, could produce an exceptionally strong enhancement."

"Perhaps. That's what I saw first, what excited me about it. But there are layers that could produce other things."

"I sense enhanced healing in here," Sarah said, losing herself in her study. "And something to do with enlightenment."

Alter frowned. "That's a bit tenuous."

She shrugged. "I see it, though." She turned to face him, making up her mind. "I want this rune, Alter. Let's inscribe it temporarily. It might give me the edge I need against Paul."

"And it might hurt you," Alter retorted.

Sarah shook her head. "It won't, and you know it. It might enhance some attributes differently than we suspect, but I don't think it'll actually hurt."

"But, Sarah—"

She stepped close, surprising him by gripping his shoulders. "Look me in the eye and tell me you think this rune would do me harm, Alter."

He squirmed under her gaze, but she held him and, as usual, his desire to stand close to her won out over any thought of breaking free.

After a moment, he sighed. "It probably won't hurt."

She grinned and released him, but he added, "But that doesn't mean I think it's a good idea."

"Well I'm the one testing it, and I accept the risk."

"There's one other problem," Alter said, looking uncomfortable. "The placement."

She hadn't thought about that part yet. Alter had taught her much about soul points, pressure points, and energy flow, and how all of that needed to be incorporated into the decision about where to mark runes for optimal effect.

Thankfully she possessed an innate sense of rune placement. She couldn't explain it, but the feeling was always undeniable, and it hadn't guided her wrong yet.

For the first time, she second-guessed it. She frowned. "Tell me you're thinking this rune needs to be marked on my stomach."

He shook his head. "Not exactly."

Her frown deepened and she met his gaze. "It needs to be on my right thigh, just below my hip, doesn't it?"

Alter nodded. "I knew you'd figure it out."

For a moment, she wondered if that was one of the reasons he'd used that particular symbol. She doubted it, though. The idea of marking a rune there seemed to embarrass him. He reached one finger toward the spot, but then withdrew it, flushing. The fact that he was so attracted to her made the conversation a bit awkward, but the rune wouldn't work anywhere else.

Alter coughed. "That location, so close to the, uh . . ." He coughed again. "So close to the procreative center, is sealed usually to only one rune. That one is fairly basic and enhances life, well-being, and empathy."

"That should support what I'm doing here," she said.

"The focus of your rune is different so the placement is surprising. That location's proximity to the nexus of life, coupled with the . . ." He trailed off again. "Never mind. It would take too long to explain everything, and you've already figured it out."

She took a slow breath. "I still think it's a good idea."

"Before we decide, you have to tell me where you got those central marks. They're the keystone of the entire construct. I don't know them, but I have to.

Sarah hesitated. She'd hoped he would overlook that part. "Those marks came from the master rune we saw in Berlin."

Alter gaped, silently mouthing the word "Abomination."

He snatched for the paper, but Sarah pulled it out of reach. "Sarah, you can't! Master runes touch the very heart blood of the world, linking the present to the past, and tapping the power of potentially millions of souls. No one uses them, especially not for personalized runes."

That was why she almost hadn't used even those tiny pieces, but they felt so right, she couldn't help herself. "I'm just using a fraction of it. You saw it yourself, my rune won't work without these marks."

He shook his head. "Sarah, we hunt the kashaph for stealing the life force of a few souls. You're talking about stealing on a global level. It's the worst possible abomination."

Sarah cringed. The rebuke cut her deeply. Had she made the wrong choice?

She studied the rune, but again felt the rightness of it. She had to trust that. "I'm not stealing all their energy. This rune would only take a tiny fraction, and you know it."

"I know nothing about it. How many times do I have to tell you? We don't use them. Ever. It's wrong, and it's dangerous."

"Paul is dangerous," Sarah retorted, holding his gaze. "He's going to kill me, Alter. He's already killed members of your family. This rune is risky, but not using it is riskier. Can't you see that?"

Alter paced away, and for the first time his confident zeal cracked and he fought a lifetime's upbringing. After a moment he turned and regarded her.

"Show me the master rune."

Only Gregorios and Quentin had seen the master rune with Sarah, and Gregorios had made her swear not to share it with anyone else.

"If I give it to you, you'll share it with your family, won't you?"

He nodded. "I must. We're the keepers of the world's rune lore. It's safest with us."

Sarah slowly shook her head. "If we'd given it to your father, Paul would have it now, along with all the other secret runes in your master book."

"That's not fair, Sarah. That's never happened before."

"I'll give it to you once we defeat Paul. I promised Gregorios I wouldn't give it to anyone, but I'll give it to you then."

Alter approached and gestured at the paper. "This rune we've developed is dangerous. It's new, personalized, and tied to a powerful master rune. I don't understand all the permutations of the design, let alone how it will bond to your soul. It is abomination, and my family would kill us both if they learned of it."

That was no idle threat. Then again, neither was Paul. She faced him and said, "Then don't tell them. I know I won't."

He groaned. "If not for Paul threatening you, I'd never even consider the idea."

Sarah took his hand. "But he is, and you know in your heart that I need this. We're not making this permanent yet."

"If anything happens to you, they'll think I tried to kill you."

"They would not. You're part of the team. You need to trust a little more."

When he didn't respond she said, "Just do it."

Alter blew out a breath. "I reserve the right to not make it permanent."

"But if it works, you have to."

"We'll see."

She decided that was the best she was going to get. So she pulled the front side of her workout pants down several inches to reveal her hip and the top of her right thigh.

She felt more than a little embarrassed with Alter standing close beside her, his eyes glued to her skin. If he had gone swimming with her, her bathing suit would have revealed far more, but the thought did not help as much as she hoped it would.

Alter's face flushed deeper as he sank to one knee beside her. He hesitantly touched her skin and his finger quivered just a bit. Sarah stood perfectly still and barely breathed as he brought up the marker.

She wanted him to hurry before anyone walked in and found them in that compromising position, but at the same time she felt a delicious thrill from the contact. The feeling surprised her, and she chided herself for it. They were both adults and, even though he never tried to hide his attraction to her, his gentle touch on her thigh shouldn't affect her so much.

When he had inscribed her first rune, he had done so with fast, sure strokes. This time he took far longer. He didn't hesitate, but drew slowly and kept his other hand on her hip to steady her as he worked. A slight smile played across his lips but disappeared almost instantly.

If he grinned again, she was going to punch him.

It seemed to take forever to complete the rune, although barely half a minute had passed. When he finished, he took her hand and pressed it over the mark.

"What are you doing?" she asked, her voice barely more than a whisper, her heart pounding.

"Activating your rune." His expression was intent, his hand warm against hers. "And testing a theory."

Then she felt his skin grow warmer against her hand, heat flowing through to the newly-inscribed rune. For a moment, the rune burned against her palm, every line distinct. In that moment she felt connected with Alter, felt linked somehow to the process as he activated her new rune. It was an intimate feeling, a moment of sharing something deeply personal.

She smiled in wonder, but all of a sudden she felt exhausted. The unexpected lack of energy sapped her strength and she sagged, nearly falling. She groaned and grabbed him, pulling his head against her stomach, his support all that kept her from falling.

Alter stood and gripped her waist. "What's wrong?" His breath felt hot against her neck.

"I don't—," she began, struggling to understand, but then gasped as her rune activated. A rush of strength rippled through her like an electric shock, taking her breath away. She grabbed his hand and pressed it over the brightly-glowing rune again.

"Did you feel that?" she laughed, their faces close together.

He nodded, his eyes bright. "I feel it."

The clarity of his rounon power amazed her. It burned up her arm from the rune while her weakness faded under the strength of the new enhancement. She didn't want to break away and shatter that marvelous feeling, but the moment was becoming too intimate. They were holding each other almost as close as lovers might, and Alter looked eager to continue.

As he leaned forward to kiss her, she leaned away. Their faces remained close as they moved together, and she was startled to feel tempted to stop retreating and let him close the distance. She paused, and his lips drew close, nearly brushing hers. So close she felt the warmth of his skin.

She almost let it happen.

Then she jerked away, snapping free of his grasp, angry that she let herself get so carried away by the moment. The strength of the temptation to let him close that last inch and kiss her left her rattled and upset with both of them.

She couldn't allow him to think she wanted him that way, and he should have known better than to press his advantage when she was vulnerable.

Alter took a step after her. "Sarah, you felt something else, didn't you?"

She snapped, "I felt we had a special moment going, and you wrecked it."

"Don't lie, Sarah. There's something between us, and you know it." He reached for her hand.

She pulled away. "What I know is that I have a new enhancement. Don't twist the situation into anything else, Alter."

"But, Sarah—"

"Don't. I like you a lot, Alter, but what you're suggesting cannot happen."

"Only because you won't admit you want it to," he shot back.

He snatched for her hand, but the move seemed unusually slow. Sarah jumped back, intending to place some distance between them until he cooled down.

She got a lot more distance than she intended.

Instead of hopping a few feet, she flew backward, soaring halfway across the room. She felt almost as light as she did in the memoryscape.

Alter gaped, and Sarah peeled back the waistline of her pants to look at her new rune again. It was glowing like living silver against her skin, fully activated. That initial rush of strength continued to grow, far more intense than when her first rune had activated, and she laughed with the thrill of it.

"I think it's working." She lunged toward Alter and crossed the distance between them in a blurring rush. Her earlier frustration with him forgotten, she gripped his hands. "This is amazing."

He grinned. "What else can you do?"

"A lot, I hope. Let's find the others so we can test it."

40

This Being of mine, whatever it really is, consists of a little flesh, a little breath, and the part which governs.

~MARCUS AURELIUS, FOURTH LIFE OF EMPEROR NERVA

SARAH WAITED with Alter for the team to arrive at the custom obstacle course situated behind the mansion, near the shooting range. It was similar in concept to common military obstacle courses, but on steroids. The challenging obstacles would have been all but impossible for most non-enhanced soldiers.

She had run it a couple of times, but couldn't yet complete every challenge, and she didn't like crawling through the mud as much as the boys did. Her single enhancement rune was unusually powerful, but Tomas and Alter and most of the soldiers who ran the course had more.

She was stronger and faster than non-enhanced mortals, but still fell far behind the others. So she'd focused on her fighting and rune training and left the obstacle course to the boys.

Sarah now waited beside the starting line with a mixture of eagerness and worry. The new rune, even though still only temporary, filled her with so much energy, she found it hard to remain motionless. She had no doubt that she'd blow away her previous best time, but she still worried she wouldn't match up to the others.

Gregorios and Eirene arrived first, hand in hand. Francesca and Harriett trotted over from the tennis court, still carrying their rackets. Bastien appeared a moment later with Quentin.

Sarah was surprised to see Tomas jogging toward her from the mansion. She hadn't expected him to return so quickly from Thailand.

She shouted his name and rushed across the lawns to meet him, barely noticing how fast she covered the distance until she leaped into his arms, nearly knocking him over. He staggered back, laughing, and Sarah kissed him hard.

He recovered quickly, wrapping her in his strong arms and kissing her back with a passion that set her heart racing. She felt relieved she'd withstood the temptation to let Alter close that last inch and touch his lips to hers.

When they reached the others, Gregorios said, "Either missing Tomas makes you faster, or your new enhancement is working."

"I'd say it's working," Harriett said.

"She missed me," Tomas countered.

Sarah squeezed his hand, still riding the wave of joy at the sight of him. "I always run fastest when I'm running to you."

"Oh, please," Francesca said, rolling her eyes. She gave Tomas a wicked look. "You want us to wait for you two to find a room?"

He flushed and Sarah laughed, but didn't hold her breath. In love, Tomas was a dedicated slow mover.

"You kids can get reacquainted later," Eirene said through her own smile. "Tell us about this new rune."

Alter piped in. "It's her own unique design. Sarah even incorporated pieces from the Berlin master rune."

"You did what?" Gregorios and Eirene exclaimed together.

"Just a little," Sarah explained quickly. "It was the only way to make the rune work."

"Show me," Gregorios said, looking unconvinced.

She didn't really blame him. They'd fought so hard to keep the master rune secret, she barely believed herself that she'd dared incorporate even those pieces.

Everyone gathered around to see, and Sarah realized she should have worn shorts. It would've been easier to slide them up. "Uh, it's not really in a public location."

"What did you do?" Francesca asked with a laugh, "Tattoo it on your butt?"

Alter looked horrified by the idea, and Francesca smiled when she noted his uneasiness.

Sarah said, "Nothing so extreme."

"We're all adults," Eirene reassured her.

"Well, all but Alter maybe," Francesca teased, "but he's already seen it."

There was no way to avoid it, so Sarah pulled down the front of her pants enough to reveal the rune inscribed on her thigh just below her right hip.

"Impressive," Bastien said softly, smiling.

Sarah wasn't sure if he was talking about the rune or the location.

Alter flushed but didn't look away. Tomas' eyes widened and he frowned at Alter. Sarah hoped he wouldn't make a big deal over the location. She didn't want Alter telling the story and maybe hinting at their close contact and almost-kiss.

Sarah started to cover the rune.

Gregorios said, "Wait. Pull your pants down again."

Eirene slapped him on the side of the head.

"I need to study it a little longer," he protested.

"You've studied it long enough," Eirene assured him.

"I don't think I have," Quentin murmured, smiling as widely as Bastien.

"I have a drawing." Sarah pulled it out of her pocket, wishing she had thought of that earlier.

Gregorios took it and the group gathered around for a look.

Tomas slipped an arm around her waist and kissed her lightly. "Your hip?"

"It felt right."

He rolled his eyes. "Not everything that feels good is a good idea."

"Prude," she teased, loving the feel of his arm around her.

After a moment, Gregorios admitted, "This is amazing. How did you figure this out?"

"I've been working on it for a while, and Alter helped me complete it using that triskelion symbol."

Eirene glanced at Alter, her expression thoughtful. "An unusual choice, Alter. Hunters don't often use fringe runes."

"It felt right."

Tomas groaned. "You two have been spending too much time together."

Definitely not the direction Sarah wanted the conversation going.

Eirene said, "Alter, you helped Sarah complete a unique higher rune, incorporating a fringe symbol and pieces of a master rune? Are you feeling all right?"

The young hunter flushed, but Sarah spoke up for him. "Paul's out there. Alter helped me because there's no other way, and I need all the help I can get."

"Can't argue with that," Gregorios said, and Sarah was relieved that he seemed willing to accept the rune. Eirene slowly nodded, but looked on the verge of saying something more.

"We marked it temporarily," Sarah said to keep the conversation moving the right direction. "It bonded immediately, and it seems to offer exceptional enhancement."

Alter nodded. "Definite improvement on reflexes, agility, and speed."

"I'm liking it," Tomas said.

His approval helped ease the last of her worries. "I wanted you all here while I test it. I'm hoping to get a lot out of this one."

Gregorios motioned Quentin forward.

"Let us begin then, shall we?" He gestured toward the starting line. Tomas and Alter took their places beside her.

"Tomas holds the record at one minute, twelve seconds," Quentin said, eliciting a little frown from Alter, who hadn't yet broken the one minute, twenty second mark. Sarah's best time had been four minutes, forty-five seconds.

"You're mine," Sarah said, tensing for the start.

"For this life and beyond," Tomas quipped, grinning. "But you don't stand a chance in the course, Sarah. Not even with your hot new rune."

"If I win, I pick the location for our date tomorrow," she retorted.

"Done." He sounded confident, but she vowed to show him.

Quentin's hand dropped and he shouted. "Begin!"

Sarah launched into the course, and actually gained a tiny lead over Tomas in the opening sprint toward the first obstacle, a series of seven-foot hurdles. In the past, she'd leapt the hurdles in long dives, rolling back to her feet on the far side. Tomas and Alter could vault them while still running. Bolstered by her great start, she decided to do the same. With a shout, she jumped.

She cleared the first hurdle by more than a foot, soaring easily over it to cheers from the watching crowd. She was so startled by her success, she nearly tripped when landing on the far side. Tomas caught up to her and flashed a thumbs up signal before pouring on even more speed.

Sarah chased him through the rest of the hurdles, half a stride behind him, with Alter in third place by a fraction. In a tight group, they scaled twenty-foot ropes to a high platform.

The descent off the far side was made by a series of acrobatic tumbles through tubes and hoops, and trampoline-type platforms that sent them soaring over a deep mud pit. Always before, Sarah had fallen into the mud, but she matched the boys with agility she'd never dreamed of.

She chased Tomas hand-over-hand up the underside of a fifty-foot ladder set at a forty-five degree angle, raced along elevated balance beams barely an inch wide, and threw a series of weighted steel balls through openings in a nearby wall.

She'd never managed to throw anything heavier than the one hundred pound ball very far, and usually hadn't bothered trying. Riding the high of her new enhancement, she snatched up all of them and sent them soaring. The five hundred pound ball was tough, straining her enhanced strength to the limit, but she threw it. She whooped when it bounced off the wall, missing the opening by half a foot.

"I love this new rune!"

Cheered on by the little crowd, she chased the men, who had pulled a little head of her. She made up a fraction of a second by running right up a fifteen-foot wooden wall and scrambling up a long, unstable cargo net with the alacrity of a spider.

But she lost ground traversing a long wall filled with inconsistently-spaced holes using movable handholds. It was like traversing a climbing wall by snapping the tiny handholds into position.

Tomas tore through that part with practiced efficiency, with Alter fumbling a bit. Sarah almost fell, but finally completed it, laughing as she tossed the handle plugs aside.

As Quentin called, "One minute, thirty!" she raced into the final obstacle, a fighting skills test.

She moved through it faster than she ever had, using knives, pistols, and a series of long guns to take down dozens of fast-moving and fast-disappearing targets that tested accuracy, speed and reflexes.

Her skill with guns had improved exponentially under Quentin's tutelage. Today she halved her best time and hit almost twice as many targets as she usually managed.

Sarah crossed the finish line at one minute, fifty-five seconds, covered in sweat, but barely winded. She laughed as she joined the crowd, accepting hugs from Eirene and her daughters, and high-fives from all the men.

"That was awesome!" Tomas cried, sweeping her off her feet in a twirling hug.

"Did you see me throw the weights?" Sarah exulted.

"Even I could barely move that last one until my fourth enhancement," Tomas laughed.

"She's powered by pieces of a master rune," Gregorios said. "What do you expect?"

Quentin took her hand in his. "My dear, with a little practice, you could easily break the one minute, thirty mark. And your accuracy in the shooting tests rivaled even Tomas." He kissed the back of her hand. "I am deeply impressed."

She hugged him, filled to bursting with joy. With the new enhancement, she felt a trickle of hope. She wasn't as strong as a cui dashi, but she was far stronger than she'd ever been. She still feared Paul, but at least now maybe she had a chance to defend herself.

As they discussed the improvements to her time and analyzed the effects of her new rune, Tomas stayed close beside her, his arm around her waist. She leaned against him, loving the feel of his proximity. Some men might have felt threatened by a strong woman, but Tomas appeared more attracted to her than ever.

Quentin finally said, "I will schedule a time to run you through the full series of physical tests we use to quantify new enhancements for enforcers. There may be other aspects of your rune as yet not manifested. We must ferret them out."

"Maybe someone else should test it too," Francesca said, glancing at Alter. "What do you say you and I head back to my room and make some rune magic?"

Alter looked terrified that she might be serious, and his cheeks burned.

"Keep your pants on," Gregorios said to his daughter. "I'm not sure we want to bond this rune to anyone else yet. Not until we know the full effects."

Eirene said, "I concur. This rune is layered enough that I expect we haven't grasped its full potential yet."

She turned to Sarah. "Excellent timing, my dear. This new enhancement offers a significant advantage as we hunt for Paul."

That scary creep's name popped some of Sarah's enthusiasm. "What's the plan? Do you think we can kill him in the memoryscape?"

Gregorios said, "Perhaps. We'll give it our best shot. But that's not point of the trap we mean to spring."

"What else would we want to do in there?" Sarah asked.

"We're going to kill John."

41

When Allah decides a matter, it is done.
I have dedicated my life to the way of Allah, Most High.
He has poured upon my soul, ciphers without measure.
Man intends one thing, but Allah intends another.
The earth destroys its fools, but the intelligent destroy the earth.
If you are truthful you will survive. If you lie you shall perish.
I am the noble warrior, I am the Sword of Allah,
I am the rune warrior, I am Khalid ibn Al Waleed.

~KHALID IBN AL WALEED, LETTER TO THE PERSIAN
GOVERNOR OF MESOPOTAMIA, 633 A.D.

THE MEMORYSCAPE FORMED around Sarah with a tumult of sound that assaulted her ears before she even registered her surroundings. The sharp clashing of steel on steel rolled like constant thunder, echoes building upon echoes until the din shook her. It was punctuated by distant screaming of dying men.

Sarah crouched in a defensive stance and squinted through the midnight darkness, broken by torches and bonfires, but obscured by clouds of hazy smoke that cast everything in a nightmarish feel.

"Finally, something's going right."

Sarah hadn't seen Gregorios until he spoke from a pace to her left. He was dressed in leather breeches and a mail shirt under a black leather jacket. With his fierce expression, he looked particularly deadly.

She gestured at their surroundings. "This looks right?"

He nodded. "It's the memory we were shooting for. We needed to get in first, and it looks like we have."

Tomas appeared on Sarah's right side, wearing Roman armor on his torso, but leather breeches similar to Gregorios' instead of the period costume. "The assault's begun." He didn't seem bothered by the chaotic scene.

Bastien appeared beside Tomas, kitted out in full Roman legion armor, including the leather kilt. He wore it with the ease of someone familiar with the costume. He made it look pretty good too. Sarah needed to get one of those kilts for Tomas when they got home.

They'd arrived during the end of the Third Mithridatic War between Rome and King Mithridates the sixth of Pontus, in the year 65 B.C. The king had really been Baladeva in one of his many lives. Spartacus had served as his general, which had started well for Mithridates, but turned sour as it dragged on.

The particular memory Gregorios had selected seemed ideal. Baladeva as king had been fleeing with his army from Pompey's Roman legions, but Pompey had slipped around them and set an ambush in the hills around a small valley on the southern bank of the River Lycus. Baladeva's army had camped in that very valley the next night, unaware of the Roman army holding the high ground all around.

The night-time surprise assault had started with a deadly missile barrage. With Baladeva's army unprepared, the arrows, steel slinger shot, and pilum shafts had wreaked terrible damage. If she squinted, Sarah could see a forest of shafts sprouting all across the narrow valley floor.

They had arrived atop one of the hills overlooking the valley, so they enjoyed an excellent view. The legions had already begun their charge, surrounding Baladeva's army and advancing before they could get properly set. Some legionnaires fell, but for the most part, the battle was becoming a slaughter.

"You have far too many unpleasant memories," Sarah said, looking away from the fighting and scanning the area nearby. The legion camp spread behind them, with camp followers scurrying to prepare to treat returning wounded.

"This one was better than some. John and I worked well as a team."

She'd been surprised to learn Gregorios and John had accompanied Pompey, embedded in his legion to deal with Spartacus, Baladeva, and their heka threat. She reminded herself that he'd known John for over two thousand years, mostly as a friend, before John's mental dissipation had broken his mind.

The memory did seem ideal. It drew not only Gregorios and John into a strong joint memory, but also included Spartacus. Gregorios hoped the familiarity of the memory would lull John into a false sense of security before they launched their assault.

"How did Baladeva and Spartacus escape that night?" Sarah asked. From what Gregorios had said, they'd defeated the other heka fighters and gotten one of their best chances against the Thracian and his facetaker master.

"By sacrificing a lot of good men to keep us busy. Spartacus didn't like to retreat, but this night, I wounded him. Would've killed him if his enhanced bodyguards hadn't arrived to die instead. Baladeva was always willing to sacrifice any other soul for himself."

Tomas jogged to the right and gestured at a flat, open area near the crest of the hill. "This is a good spot for the onager."

"Looks good to me," Gregorios said.

He snapped his fingers, and a huge catapult made of massive wooden beams, reinforced with steel appeared on the spot, already cranked back, with a huge boulder in the cup.

"Since when do you snap your fingers when you summon things?" Sarah asked as she approached the gigantic weapon.

Gregorios grinned. "When the moment calls for it."

"How do you know the difference?"

"It's a matter of style."

The two men turned toward the fighting and headed for the path down the hill, but Sarah called, "Wait, don't we need to aim it or something?"

Gregorios called back, "It's already pointing in the right direction. I can adjust its trajectory on the way in."

Sarah gave the hulking siege weapon a doubtful look. "Why don't we just use a high-explosive mortar round?"

Tomas said, "Tempting, but we don't want to spook John when he arrives." He tilted up his palm to show a tiny trigger device. "I did include a remote, but besides that, it's authentic."

Gregorios added, "If Paul and his gang do show up today, anything modern will pull at John's mind and betray our intentions. An onager doesn't exactly fit this type of military engagement, but it's not too far off either."

He pointed toward a pair of smaller ballistae that looked like giant crossbows on wheeled carts. Sarah shuddered to think what kind of damage their heavy bolts could do.

"Such a little break in the integrity of the memoryscape, set so far from the center of things, and with so much going on, shouldn't draw any attention," Gregorios added.

Sarah followed the men down the hill with growing reluctance. She'd seen enough memory battles to never need to see another one. She didn't like the idea of wading through those clashing men, watching them die around her.

Plus, every step she took committed her that much more to their three-pronged plan. It had sounded great in the safety of Suntara's vault, but now that she was approaching screaming, hacking hordes of ancient soldiers, with high likelihood of Paul showing up soon, she started thinking of all kinds of things they hadn't planned out well enough.

The core of the plan was simple enough. Gregorios would engage Spartacus to test his mental state and see what information he could pull from his ancient enemy. Sarah would draw Paul away and keep him busy, and Tomas would try to kill John.

Bastien would support Sarah and, if the trap turned against them, he could pull her out of the memoryscape. The two of them were on one machine, with Gregorios and Tomas on the other. Eirene and her daughters, assisted by Alter, were running the machines. To power both of them together, they'd had to do some creative rune linking through Alter, but it appeared to be stable.

When they reached the fighting, Gregorios simply leaped fifty feet, vaulting most of the soldiers. As the others followed suit, he waved away any approaching fighters. He probably didn't need to gesture at all, since he controlled the memoryscape, but Sarah suspected he was tapping his sense of style again.

As they slipped through the camp, weaving past burning debris, discarded bedrolls, and too many dead and wounded soldiers, the stench of smoke was overwhelmed by the stink of blood and vomit and opened bodies.

"Can't you do something about the smell?" Sarah complained, holding one hand over her nose. She summoned a cloth mask dipped in vinegar to help. She'd been tempted to wear mail or even steel plate armor, but none of that would do much good against Paul, so she'd dressed herself in black leather, with several knives sheathed at her belt and thighs.

"I don't want to tamper too much." Gregorios gave an apologetic shrug. "You get used to it."

"But I don't want to get used to it."

It would be too easy to become numb to death and blood and killing, and that worried her. She was willing to fight to defend herself and those she loved, but she hated having to do it. The men dying all around them might only be shadows of memory, but their deaths still bothered her.

Tomas shifted closer and lay a comforting hand on her shoulder. "The smell makes it real, reminds us this isn't a video game, and that what we do matters."

She managed a weak smile, but the comforting words didn't help her nose.

"This battle won't last all that long anyway," Tomas added, nodding to where one cohort of Baladeva's soldiers threw down their weapons and dropped to their knees with arms held overhead, crying for mercy. The legionnaires set to binding them with practiced efficiency.

"What will happen to them?" Sarah asked.

"They won't die today," Tomas said, his expression grim. "But they may wish they had. They'll be enslaved, and some will end up in the arenas as gladiators."

"Stop dawdling," Gregorios called back to them. "We don't have a lot of time to prepare. If John's going to join us, it'll have to be soon."

As they neared the large command tent at the center of the valley, Sarah caught sight of Spartacus. He stood with Baladeva, the two of them surrounded by half a dozen enhanced fighters, whose tattoos she easily picked out, despite the distance. Baladeva, in his persona as King Mithridates, was shouting commands and trying to rally his troops.

"That's exactly how he looked and acted that night," Gregorios said. "I can't feel any other will fighting for control, but that confirms they're not here yet."

One group of Roman soldiers broke through the left flank and charged the center of camp. Spartacus and the enhanced heka swarmed over the simple mortals.

Gregorios shook his head in disgust. "I warned them not to close on Spartacus, but too many of the fools wouldn't listen."

Under cover of the fighting, Gregorios shifted left to get into position on the other side of the command tent. Tomas hesitated long enough to share a fierce kiss with Sarah before trotting after.

"Good luck," she called after him.

He turned and waved, his expression serious. "Be careful, Sarah."

She and Bastien moved to the right, pausing about fifty yards from the command tent. The area was cluttered with discarded gear and cook fires. She caught regular glimpses of Spartacus and Baladeva through the shifting smoke and flickering light of moving torches. They were close enough to watch, but far enough away that she wouldn't easily be noticed.

Bastien paused in an open space about thirty feet across. After a moment of silent concentration, he grinned. "The trap is set."

"I don't see anything," Sarah admitted. The ground looked undisturbed.

Bastien winked. "That is the plan, no? Take heart, cheri. There is enough high explosives now under the ground there to blow up a large building. It is a shaped charge, very deadly."

"Good," Sarah said, allowing a thread of hope to take root in her heart.

Then something wrapped around her legs and yanked her off her feet.

Sarah struck the ground hard, her breath blasting out from the impact as she scraped along the ground at a surprising rate. She managed to roll over, then shrieked at the monstrous sight that had appeared amid the chaos of the battle.

Under a massive, snail-like shell that had to be at least ten feet in diameter, a gigantic maw gaped open, filled with sharp teeth dripping saliva. Several long, hairy, slimy tentacles extended from that maw, slithering across the ground like fast-moving snakes. One of those tentacles had wrapped around Sarah's legs.

A screaming soldier, snared by another of those disgusting tentacles, was yanked into the huge maw. It snapped shut with a horrific squishing crunch, spraying blood and gore, and severing the man's torso in half. A second snapping bite sucked in the other half.

Sarah had seen enough monsters to quickly get over her initial shock. As she skittered across the ground, drawn toward the monster with terrifying speed, she suppressed a scream and summoned her favorite monster repellent. Her M4A1 rifle and grenade launcher settled into her hands with a comfortable weight.

Before she could take aim, a grenade bounced into the monster's wide open mouth. It snapped its jaws shut reflexively. Two seconds later, when Sarah was barely a dozen feet away, the monster's head exploded, splattering her with slime and goo, and nearly skewering her with one of the beast's long fangs.

Sarah shuddered with horror as the rest of the monster disintegrated to dust. Bastien helped her rise. "Are you all right, cheri?"

"What was that thing?" Sarah cried, her voice squeaking a little.

When they tampered with things, she expected some kind of monster to appear, but usually she handled them pretty well. She felt proud that she hadn't totally lost it, but that thing had still rattled her.

"It is known as the Carcolh. It is a legend in France."

After a final shiver, Sarah marched back toward where they'd set their trap. "I wish there were more cute and cuddly monsters of legend."

"Indeed, cheri, but then how could I have saved a lovely damsel in distress?"

She grinned and kissed his cheek. "Thank you." She decided not to point out that she'd been about to blast it with her carbine. Hopefully they'd defeat Paul just as easily.

When they reached the concealed explosives, Sarah glanced back at the dust that was all that remained of the creature. It was already blowing across the battlefield.

"That thing was disgusting and freaky, but I would've thought setting so much explosives would have created something even bigger."

Bastien shrugged. "The effects are smaller when I make the change. Plus, the explosives are underground, so even though they are a modern weapon, no one can actually see them."

"We should test that some more."

"Oui. Let us hope Paul is also fooled."

"Let's hope Paul dies," Sarah responded, then gestured toward a nearby overturned wagon. "How about over there?"

The wagon shimmered, replaced by a wagon-sized construct that looked like a mini fortress. Made of close-fitted wooden planks, the boxlike fort stood only eight feet to a side. A long ceramic nozzle tube projected out a narrow front window.

Fresh growling set Sarah's heart racing, but it was only a werewolf that leaped from a nearby tent. She let Bastien act chivalrous again while she slipped inside the door of her little fortress.

A soft glow illuminated the interior, and the air was hot and smelled like cinders. An iron box three feet high filled the entire floor. When Sarah mounted the steps to the top, the heat radiating from the molten fuel inside burned right through her thick-soled boots.

She studied the weapon as she shifted her weight from side to side, lifting each foot in turn to allow them to cool a bit. Another ceramic tube connected the holding tank to the nozzle. Leather-wrapped handles capped the end of the nozzle on either side of a single lever to open fire.

Bastien stuck his head inside the door. "You like, yes?"

"It looks good, although a simple flame thrower would have been easier."

He grinned. "But this is Greek Fire. My mother shared the recipe with me. It is from ancient days, so will not break the integrity of the dream, no?"

"But how does it fire eighty feet to the command tent?"

He tapped the iron holding tank. "The pressure is very great. Do not puncture the box."

"I never should have asked." Sarah glanced down, trying not to think about the fact that she was standing atop hundreds of gallons of super-heated, pressurized Greek Fire in the middle of a battle. At least, if that tank blew, she doubted she'd suffer long.

She settled down to wait in uneasy silence, peering through the firing port. Bastien remained outside to ensure none of the fighting got too close.

Sarah was grateful their anonymity remained. The soldiers ignored them and their unique device. Once they engaged Paul, she wondered how long before legions of soldiers decided to take notice and boot them from the memoryscape.

Sarah couldn't decide if she wanted Paul to show up soon so they could get on with the trap, or if she hoped he wouldn't show at all. Her nerves slowly tightened as the seconds ticked by, her tension amplified by the screams of the wounded and dying and constant stench that her mask did too little to block.

Confronting Paul in the middle of a massacre was fitting in a lot of ways. Even though the plan would be counted a success if they could take out John, and despite the fact that Sarah wasn't sure they could really kill Paul in the memoryscape, she vowed to give it her best shot.

Paul had seemed absolutely confident in their last meeting. If he chose to enter the memoryscape without help monitoring him from the outside, ready to link additional soulmasks to heal him, they might do some real damage.

A shiver rippled down Sarah's spine and she glanced at Spartacus. Despite the distance, she noticed his form shimmer then sharpen again. His stance changed, and he turned from the battle he'd been watching and raised his hand, a gladius appearing in it.

He looked directly at the spot where Gregorios and Tomas were concealed and his bellowing voice rang across the battlefield.

"I am Spartacus!"

42

The world will know the tread of my foot, and nations will shake with fear. Baladeva was right, and my rounon powers now are stronger than ever. None can stand against my enhanced armies. I will root out Shahrokh and, with his death, secure my glory and the ultimate pact of power. Baladeva will supply my lives, and my runes will make my armies invincible!

~BRENNIS, GAULISH CHIEFTAIN OF THE SENONES,
SACKING OF ROME, 387 B.C.

JOHN APPEARED BESIDE SPARTACUS, dressed like a centurion. Paul materialized last of all, breaking the congruity of the scene with his business suit and ever-present hat.

The man didn't even pretend to fit in. It was really annoying. His suit looked like it was made of dark blue silk, but Sarah wished it was polyester for the melting effect.

"It is time we introduce ourselves, yes?" Bastien whispered, poking his head in the doorway.

"Here we go," Sarah breathed as she swept the nozzle toward the newcomers and gripped the firing lever with sweaty fingers.

She yanked the lever, and Greek Fire blasted out of the nozzle. The pressure was more intense than she expected, tipping the nozzle up and spraying blazing, liquid fire high across the camp and above her targets.

Sarah corrected quickly and shifted the stream down onto the spot where Paul and the others had stood. The Greek Fire rasped as it boiled up the tube, and heat from the flames washed back over her, reddening her face, while the brimstone stench gagged her.

Liquid fire tore through the center of the camp, vaporizing heka fighters and scattering everyone else. John leaped into the command tent, and Sarah lost sight of Spartacus and Paul.

"Where'd they go?" She released the lever to allow the nozzle to snap closed, but was prepared to incinerate the command tent next. It would be great if she could complete the mission in the opening volley.

A grunt of pain from Bastien pulled her gaze to the nearby doorway.

Bastien was gone. Paul stood in his place.

"Hello, Sarah." His clothes weren't even singed.

Before Sarah could react, Paul heaved the entire fort-like weapon off the ground.

Sarah tumbled out the open door, falling at his feet. Even though it must have weighed at least a ton, Paul tossed the entire weapon far across the camp. It crashed down over a phalanx of Roman soldiers, and the holding tank burst.

The explosion rent the night air and tumbled soldiers away for a hundred yards in every direction. The blast of hot air tugged at Sarah's hair as she rolled to her feet. She didn't see Bastien and had lost sight of the others. Paul faced her, his hat tipped back just enough to show the hint of a smile on his lips.

"Took you long enough," Sarah said, proud that her voice didn't shake.

The plan was working. He'd taken the bait, but facing him, she couldn't help but think that even if Tomas killed John, she wouldn't live long enough to celebrate.

Paul took a step toward her, and a wide-bladed Chinese saber appeared in his hand. "Now, where were we?"

Gregorios stepped through the choking smoke, between splashes of still-burning Greek Fire. Sarah had done well. John was isolated and Paul had taken off after her. Bastien would help her stay alive long enough to close the trap.

John's will, buttressed by Paul's cui dashi strength, fought him for control over the memoryscape, but this was a shared memory, so the differences were not major. John did not seem interested in adding anything big, and so far Gregorios had held his own.

Mostly though, he concentrated on Spartacus, who stood alone in the center of the blasted area scoured clean by Greek Fire.

"Hail and well met, my ancient adversary," Spartacus cried, saluting with a gladius.

"We don't really talk like that any more," Gregorios said, approaching the Thracian cautiously with a pair of identical swords.

He could have summoned another machine gun, but modern weapons didn't belong in this particular meeting. Besides, he was hoping to question the recently-restored gladiator more than he wanted to plunge his sword into the man's throat.

"Yet another indication of the weakness of the world," Spartacus declared. He stalked to his left, and Gregorios matched him step for step in the opposite direction.

As the two circled each other, spiraling closer to within ten feet, Spartacus added. "There are so many things I wish to know. The world has changed beyond reckoning in the centuries I lacked sight. Only you and your honored wife understand my position."

Gregorios nodded, intrigued. For the first time in the long history of their clashes, Spartacus hadn't once mentioned fighting to the death. It left Gregorios feeling unsettled.

So he offered, "We've got a minute, so talk."

Spartacus grinned and raising his gladius in another salute. "You do me much honor, Gregorios. Such kindness cannot go unanswered."

"Hold on," Gregorios interrupted, recognizing what was coming. "You don't have to—"

Spartacus lunged, lashing out with his sword. Gregorios caught the blade on one of his and swiped at Spartacus' stomach with the other. The gladiator blocked the strike, and the two circled each other, the fast staccato of their swords ringing through the battlefield and echoing from the hills.

Spartacus grinned as they fought. "Thus we cross swords to pay homage to our honored past." Without slowing or lessening the intensity of his deadly strikes he continued. "And thus may wisdom be shared without fear of reproach."

Gregorios ducked a slash that would have taken his head off and kicked Spartacus back a step. "These days, we could've done the talking without the duel, you know." He wasn't really disappointed. He had always preferred letting his sword do most of the talking with Spartacus.

"I would not throw down such an offense," Spartacus said, but his expression turned thoughtful and he paused. "The world I know is no more, Gregorios. Countries are gone, languages have died, and the world is awash with inventions to make the gods envious. Yet, I don't . . . I am finding it hard to see where honor may be found."

"Times have changed," Gregorios agreed. He felt an unexpected feeling of pity for his most-hated enemy, and squashed it.

"And yet I have not." Spartacus took a deep breath and his expression lifted, the thoughtful frown replaced by an enthusiastic grin. He leaped back into the fight with renewed vigor. "The world is new and wondrous, and I will win honor and a secure my place in it!"

As Gregorios fought the duel, he was surprised to realize that part of him wished Spartacus luck.

He'd need it. Most likely, Gregorios would need to destroy the Thracian in the coming days.

Tomas circled the command tent. It blocked his view of Sarah, and he prayed she was okay. It tore at him to know she faced the deadly cui dashi without him. Then again, killing John was the best way to help her.

Swords clashed from the far side of the tent, so Gregorios had engaged. Hopefully he could still track the incoming boulder.

Tomas squeezed the remote fire trigger and started a slow count. He was surprised by a huge explosion that rocked the far side of the camp, lighting the night. Hopefully Sarah wasn't involved in that. The blossoming light illuminated the silently tumbling boulder that was coming in a bit too high.

Then it wasn't.

Its trajectory shifted and it dove like a hawk toward the command tent. It lacked the whistling of a mortar round and, unless John was focusing on that part of the memoryscape, Tomas doubted he'd sense its approach. Even though he was well clear, Tomas retreated a few more steps and braced for the impact.

The boulder fell like the fist of an ancient Roman god, shattering the tent and slamming into the ground so hard it sent rippling showers of earth cascading in every direction.

A body tumbled away, tangled in the shredded remains of the tent, and Tomas recognized John. He had hoped for a direct hit, but it must have just missed him. As John staggered to his feet, eyes wide with shock, looking bewildered and unsteady, Tomas extended his hands and a pair of battle axes appeared in them.

Shouting the battle cry of the Tenth, Tomas raised his axes and charged.

Paul gestured at Sarah with his sword. "Your powers are unique, woman, but you are no facetaker. Where did they recruit you?"

"I'm a model." She tried not to look obvious as she scanned the ground for her carbine. She'd put it down inside the Greek Fire weapon, but couldn't see it anywhere.

His hat took on a surprised angle. "That makes no sense."

"Like forbidden runes do? Which one are you using, anyway?"

"I use whichever runes I wish. They are not forbidden to me."

"You sound like a politician. Rules only apply to the little people."

He shrugged. "Rules apply to those too weak to make their own."

"Newsflash, freak," Sarah said, gauging the distance to the edge of the buried explosives. She didn't want to be standing on it when it blew. "You broke the wrong rules and it's going to cost you."

Paul glanced toward Gregorios, who was dueling Spartacus near the command tent, their swords flashing in the inconsistent light. "Gregorios lacks the power to enforce his will on the world any longer. Only you remain the enigma."

"Sorry, I have a boyfriend."

He stalked forward, his voice angry. "Enough games. Tell me how you defeated my sister."

"Who?"

"Mai Luan!"

Whoa. Several things clicked into place, but what about—?

Paul took advantage of her surprise, rushing forward with inhuman speed and punching her in the sternum. The blow tumbled her all the way to the edge of the concealed explosives. She gasped, her chest a sea of pain. Black spots danced behind her eyes.

He was so strong!

Even as she tried to blink away tears, he crossed the distance between them in a blink. "There can be only one," he intoned and slashed at her torso with that terrifying sword.

Sarah's body still trembled from that super-punch, but reacted with instincts honed in recent weeks sparring with Tomas and Alter, and enhanced by her new rune. She rolled, barely avoiding the whistling blade. It drove deep into the ground.

She leaped to her feet. "Really? You have to quote *Highlander* at a moment like this?"

"My words are mine alone." Paul snatched for her with his free hand, but Sarah threw a block, then fired a series of punches into his face. It felt like punching a statue.

Paul ignored the blows, but snatched at her again. He moved with superhuman speed, but she deflected his grabbing fists, shifting around him and continuing her barrage. He seemed unused to having to actually fight anyone.

Sarah retreated from him, using every trick Tomas and Alter had taught her, barely avoiding his hands. When he raised his sword, she leaped backward, flying twenty feet to the center of the explosives trap. She felt a flash of triumph when he pursued, but didn't have to pretend an expression of fear.

"How did you know I was involved in Berlin?" she asked, steeling herself for the next phase.

"I heard every word," he snarled, raising his sword again. "She should have easily destroyed you, but somehow you survived while she did not."

"History's about to repeat itself."

Sarah focused on her first rune. Immediately, warmth flooded out of it and her body faded to insubstantial. She raised a fist, the signal for Bastien to trigger the explosives. She hadn't seen him since Paul threw her fire fortress away, but hoped he had recovered from whatever Paul had done to him.

For a second, nothing happened, and her hope fled.

Then the ground beneath her and Paul erupted into fire and destruction, catapulting Paul far out over the army. Sarah lost sight of him, her vision consumed by fire. She shivered as the explosion ripped through her ethereal form, like shadowy fingers of heat. The force of the blast lifted her a dozen feet into the air.

In the heart of the inferno, she exulted. Finally, they were hurting him. She only had to find him and finish him before he recovered.

43

No matter which life he is living, it is not death that a man should fear, rather he should fear never beginning to live.

~MARCUS AURELIUS, FOURTH LIFE OF EMPEROR NERVA

JOHN SCREAMED, but still ducked a whistling axe that would have removed his head.

He didn't see the second one.

Tomas' other blade sheared through John's armor and buried itself into his chest, catapulting him off his feet in a spray of blood.

Even as he fell, the gaping wounds closed and his armor repaired.

Just about what Tomas had expected. John could exercise immense control over the memoryscape, reforming his body at will, sealing otherwise fatal wounds. Well, he could for a time. With wounds that severe, a fraction of the damage would ripple back to his sleeping form.

Even though Tomas had known John for centuries and it always pained him to see an ally fall, he didn't hesitate. John was helping Paul threaten Sarah, so that made his job pretty easy. He'd tear John apart, bit by bit.

With a grunt of determination, Tomas slammed both axes into John's torso again and again. John tried frantically to escape, but Tomas kicked him over, striking the man back to the ground. He scored three hits on John's neck, but never enough to completely sever the head. Each time, the wounds sealed as soon as he withdrew the blades.

John might be able to heal as fast as a cui dashi, but he felt pain.

With each wound, he screamed anew, blubbering for mercy, and the recovery took a fraction of a second longer than it had before.

Tomas could live with that. He struck again.

Sarah raced through the chaotic campsite battleground. More and more of Baladeva's troops were surrendering, those who hadn't been killed already, and the Roman legionnaires were swarming into the area where Paul had fallen. Most of them ignored her, at least until she plowed through them, tossing armored men aside in her haste.

Some of them shouted after her but Bastien, who was running close behind her, dealt with them. She needed to find Paul before he recovered.

Too late.

She caught sight of him staggering to his feet about forty feet away, looking battered. He somehow still wore that annoying hat, but she could tell he was furious. A column of legionnaires passed between them, blocking Paul from view, but Sarah had seen enough.

"He's up," she called to Bastien. "Round two."

"Oui," he said with more calm than she felt. "Let us light the night, yes?"

A fifty-caliber machine-gun appeared in his hand, its belt of ammo looking too short to accomplish much, but Sarah suspected he'd arranged for that belt to continuously spawn so he'd never run out of ammo.

Soldiers near where she'd last seen Paul suddenly flew screaming into the air as if they'd been rammed by a fast-moving snow plow. Paul must have located them, and he was coming fast.

"Get me something good," Sarah cried, holding out her hands to accept a weapon from Bastien. He moved to flank her, crouching over his machine gun, but he offered a warm smile.

"For you, cheri, only the best."

The Curtain Call dropped into her hands.

Sarah grinned, recognizing the GECAL 50 minigun from Quentin's presentation. Like Bastien's gun, the ammo belt seemed far too short for a gun that could fire up to two thousand rounds per minute. Sarah didn't bother to question how he powered the electric weapon, trusting that he'd summoned some kind of a power source.

It was a good choice, probably their best bet to slow Paul down. With a snarl of defiance, she braced herself and opened fire.

The sound was an ear-splitting buzz as the gun chewed through dozens of rounds per second. The recoil was brutal, since the gun was designed to be mounted on a vehicle and she was holding it like a carbine. In the memoryscape, with her advanced enhancements, she could handle it. Barely.

And it was awesome.

Riding the very cusp of losing control, she mowed down the final ranks of soldiers between her and the charging cui dashi. The poor soldiers disintegrated under the barrage of standard rounds, and she shouted with disgust and fear as she walked her fire right into Paul.

He might be a cui dashi, but hundreds of rounds of fifty caliber ammunition, striking at almost three thousand feet per second, packed a punch that even he couldn't ignore. Paul screamed, but Sarah couldn't tell if it was with rage or pain. She didn't care, but kept pouring in more rounds as Paul's advance stopped and he stumbled back under the barrage of fire.

"Give me the good stuff," Sarah shouted.

Glittering tracers began spewing from the gun, followed by incendiary and explosive rounds. They tore into Paul, melting skin and tearing out chunks of flesh. She saw exposed bone several times, but the wounds closed with terrifying swiftness.

Lastly, the gun bucked harder than ever, and she unleashed a storm of blue-white lightning into Paul. The devastating barrage knocked him to his knees, hands raised as if pleading for mercy.

Sarah screamed with battle fury and with disgust at what she was doing.

Bastien added his stream of fire to hers, and when she risked a glance at him, he was whistling. She couldn't hear the tune over the roar of the guns, but he seemed to be enjoying himself immensely.

She only looked away for a fraction of a second, but when she turned back to Paul, he was gone.

"No way!" Sarah shouted, releasing the trigger and scanning for him.

Those bullets had been tearing into him, even though it looked like he'd been healing just as fast. Still, they'd had him on the defensive. She couldn't imagine how he'd slipped away.

Legionnaires were still advancing on their right, but the soldiers were circling wide around the gun battle, making warding signs against evil. To her left, a squad of Baladeva's men who had been in the process of surrendering were now fighting a desperate battle against something cloaked in shadow. Sarah caught glimpses of furry arms and clawed hands that ripped into the soldiers as the darkness enveloped them.

She turned to Bastien just as Paul landed beside the facetaker, as if he'd simply jumped into the sky to escape their bullets. Bastien tried to bring his gun around, but Paul moved too fast, knocking the weapon flying.

He slammed a spear into Bastien's chest. It sank all the way through and punched out his back, splattering Sarah with his blood.

Bastien gasped, blood pouring out his open mouth as he grasped the shaft. Paul heaved on the spear and threw Bastien into the night.

Sarah spun toward him, squeezing the trigger even though she knew she was too late. Paul grabbed the weapon and ripped the barrels off the gun, then yanked it out of her hands, sending her stumbling.

He crushed the steel housing with a snarl of rage and tossed the weapon aside. When he turned to her, his suit again looked perfect, as if new off the rack. Despite all the damage they'd dealt, they hadn't accomplished anything.

"You are an annoying mortal," Paul said, his voice tight, not quite pulling off the calm villain act after that brutal beating.

Fear spiked in Sarah, but not as fast as anger. The horror of what he'd done to Bastien stoked her rage. He was probably already healing himself, but she embraced the feeling and threw herself at Paul with murderous intent.

She struck him several times, but he ignored the blows and snapped a punch to her midsection that sent her stumbling.

"Stop with the childish resistance," he snapped.

That only made her angrier. As Sarah prepared to rush him again, her new rune turned icy cold against the skin of her thigh and a chill wind howled through her, driving her to move.

Following the impulse, Sarah leaped at Paul. At the same time, the rune on her shoulder blade burned with searing heat that mingled with the icy blast of her new rune to form a whirlwind of energy that made her gasp aloud.

She had no idea what was going on, lacked time to figure it out, and only hoped it would help.

Her body faded to ethereal, and she spun around Paul, dodging a grasping hand. She continued to spin, turning faster and faster, her feet barely touching the ground as she embraced the new essence of her activated runes.

She sensed that she'd unlocked a new aspect of her new enhancement, tapping aspects of motion and the triskelion truths of creation-preservation-destruction. The thought passed in a flash, and she didn't fully understand it, but she didn't need to.

She embraced it.

Her spinning accelerated until she moved like a whirlwind. Paul snatched at her, but his hands failed to grasp her insubstantial form. He paused, looking unsure of himself for the first time.

Time to give him something new to worry about.

Long-bladed knives appeared in Sarah's hands, which incorporated just enough to grasp them. Spinning so fast, the blades tore into Paul, shredding off chunks of flesh. She drove against him like a bladed tornado.

Paul stumbled back from her, and she tore into his upraised hands with her blades. His blood sprayed across the ground and Sarah pressed the attack with every ounce of strength. The insanely fast whirling was hard to maintain, but she refused to stop.

Even though Paul healed as fast as Sarah hurt him, he retreated from her onslaught, and she realized he didn't know how to stop her. She could damage him, really hurt him. The shout of triumph she cried from her ethereal lips sounded like the scream of a tempest.

She decided she liked it.

With a frustrated cry, Paul leaped away and raised a hand toward Sarah. She pursued, spinning across the ground, an unstoppable force.

The memoryscape shuddered, and the ground faded under her feet, as if he was somehow driving her from the memory. The whirling power of her runes snuffed out, and Sarah fell to her knees, her head spinning so badly she nearly vomited.

The ground supported her weight, but felt soft, as if she might crash through and plummet into eternity. She felt weak, as if only barely connected to the memoryscape. She hadn't realized he could do that. Why didn't Bastien or Gregorios fix it for her?

Paul approached with an easy stride, again confident, as if she hadn't hurt him.

As he loomed over her, he reminded her of Mai Luan, gloating over her in Berlin, her clothing perfect despite their deadly battle, her little bluetooth earpiece glinting. The memory sparked a flash of understanding and Sarah cried, "The bluetooth! You were there in Berlin, listening the whole time."

She scratched at the ground, trying to drag herself onto solid memoryscape again. "Why didn't you help her?"

"I shouldn't have needed to!"

paul grabbed her by the throat and lifted her high. Strength flowed back into her with the renewed connection, and she drew upon her rune again. Her body shifted to insubstantial, but her flash of triumph wilted to renewed terror when she realized that her face was not changing.

Paul's hand had begun to glow with the purple fire of his cui dashi nevron. Somehow he was blocking her ability to fade away. For the first time ever, he pushed his hat all the way up with his free hand, revealing his features.

He was Chinese.

She shouldn't have felt as surprised as she did, but terror spiked to new levels as she realized he was granting her this chance to look upon him because he no longer cared if she knew. His hand tightened around her throat.

Desperately, Sarah focused on her rune and it burned against her back. She could feel the ethereal effect slowly creeping up her neck, slipping past his nevron defenses, but the change would not happen quickly enough. He would crush her long before she escaped again.

Sarah kicked at him, but she lacked the proper leverage, and she was as effective as if she was kicking the side of a mountain.

"My sister will be avenged," he said with a triumphant smile.

Sarah imagined a claymore mine in the air between them, the dangerous end facing Paul. Then she returned his smile as the trigger appeared between her teeth. Before the mine fell to the ground, and as his eyes widened in surprise, she bit down on the trigger.

Nothing happened.

The mine clattered to the ground at her feet.

"What?" Sarah exclaimed, spitting the trigger at Paul. It bounced off his chin, but he ignored it.

"It is a small thing to remove batteries at will," he said, his tone triumphant.

"You've got to be kidding me," Sarah groaned. "I had you, you smug son of a—"

He squeezed harder, choking out the words. Instead of snapping her neck, his gaze turned thoughtful and he turned her slightly, studying her closely. His gaze took on a different kind of intensity that chilled her to the bone.

"Your resilience and resourcefulness are impressive. You are proving to be more than the useless mortal I first imagined. You do my sister's memory much honor."

"Your sister was nuts," Sarah gasped. She tried calling upon that strange whirlwind power from her second rune, but it didn't respond. "But I see that runs in the family."

Paul's hand clenched and Sarah gagged as her airway was blocked. Maybe she shouldn't have insulted him until Gregorios arrived to rip out his spine.

He surprised her by relaxing his hold just enough for her to breathe. Sarah wondered why he restrained himself.

"Do not speak badly of her," Paul chided softly, and the shift in his demeanor only terrified her more. "I had planned to remove your soul today, but I believe I have a better use for you."

That didn't sound good.

Then another truth struck her. "You were in Berlin all along. Mai Luan didn't have to send you the rune."

He grimaced. "Actually she did. It appeared only to you in the bunker."

That was surprising. Worse, she hated that he was only sharing his secrets with her now because he was about to kill her. That was such a cliché super villain tactic.

Sarah hated clichés.

Instead of ripping her head off, Paul started pacing, his hat tipped down to hide his features, still holding her off the ground. It was almost as if he'd forgotten she was there. That was just plain insulting.

She kicked him between the legs.

The leverage wasn't good, but she got his attention. Paul shook her until her teeth clacked. "Do not make me change my mind."

"Your mind is cracked. I'd change it for a cesspit and call it an improvement."

She couldn't imagine why he hadn't killed her, but she hoped he'd pause a little bit longer. Bastien had to have healed himself, must see her danger. Why hadn't he called her out of the memoryscape yet?

He seemed to reach a decision. "Yes, I think you will do. Your service will be uniquely satisfying."

"What are you talking about? The only service I plan to give you is a proper burial."

Gregorios retreated a step from Spartacus and spared a glance toward Tomas, who was savaging John on the far side of the half-sunken boulder that had destroyed the command tent.

He could feel John's will tugging against the fabric of the memoryscape. He'd managed to block John's attempts to make major alterations, like forming a stone wall between him and Tomas, but hadn't managed to block John's regeneration of his own body. In that, John held the advantage. His entire will was focused on staying alive, and he was bolstered by the power of the cui dashi.

He'd felt one strong warp of the memoryscape from Paul's direction, but had lost sight of Sarah and Bastien after the huge explosion earlier. He'd heard a spate of gunfire, but it had cut off abruptly. If Paul had turned the tide on them, Tomas was just about out of time. He might need to put down Spartacus and go help Tomas finish the mission.

Spartacus followed his gaze. "Your man is a warrior of much honor." He glanced around the battlefield and sniffed, but his nose didn't wrinkle at the stench of blood and opened corpses. "It were better for us to meet in mortal combat, not in the world of a dream, where naught matters and where deeds of honor fade away with the waking breath."

"Tell you what," Gregorios said, hoping he'd just gotten the opening he was looking for. "Tell me where to find you in the waking world, and I'll arrange a round of honorable battles."

With a shout of victory, Tomas buried an axe into John's throat, but did not rip it free. He raised the other high, with the clear intent of driving it into the same spot.

When that blade landed, he'd take John's head off.

Paul opened his mouth to speak, but then without a word, he placed Sarah gently on the ground.

Then he leaped away, moving faster than Sarah could hope to follow. He shot across the bloody camp and she realized his destination with horror.

Tomas stood over John with a wicked battle-axe in hand, slashing down toward John like an ancient berserker.

Paul reached him before the blow landed.

Tomas never saw him coming. The cui dashi rammed into him and sent him tumbling far out into the night.

Sarah screamed and raced after Paul. She caught sight of Gregorios and Spartacus standing not far from the fallen John, both looking surprised by Paul's appearance.

As Sarah closed on them, Paul ripped another axe out of John's throat and lifted the bloody facetaker off the ground. He'd left his hat behind, and he looked angry.

Sarah summoned her grenade launcher, but Paul tilted his face to the sky and commanded, "Take us from this place."

He glanced at her as he began to fade from the memoryscape, and his voice hung in the air as he disappeared.

"We will meet again, my chosen vessel, and I will share your glorious destiny with you."

Sarah fired, even though she knew it was too late. The high explosive round detonated at Paul's feet, creating a cloud of dust and debris. When it cleared, Paul and John were gone.

His last words haunted her. Having him chase her with murder on his mind was bad enough. Calling her his chosen vessel was just plain creepy. That phrase brought to mind virgin sacrifices or sex perversions. She didn't qualify for the first, and she'd rather die than submit to the second.

She threw her rifle to the ground in disgust. "I hate that man."

Nearby, Spartacus saluted Gregorios. "If we cannot find resolution, then anon I will grant your request and we will meet in flesh incarnate to settle scores both ancient and newborn. For glory and honor!"

He faded away and Gregorios growled, "Glory and honor."

Then he dropped his swords and blew out a breath, turning slowly to take in the entire bloody camp. When he caught sight of Sarah, he smiled. "Are you all right?"

"Bastien's hurt, and we have to find Tomas."

She took a step toward the direction she last saw him tumbling, but Gregorios lifted a hand to stop her. "I can feel both of them. Bastien is already back on his feet, and I've removed Tomas' injuries. We're done here." Fists clenched, he added, "We were so close."

Then he sighed and looked up into the starlit darkness. "All right, my girl. Take us home."

44

Symbols of faith, and the symbol of my blessed nation form the heart of my ciphers, and I know the Almighty God is pleased with my efforts. Yet I fear Uncle Bastien's words may hold a grain of truth. At times I sense resistance in the ciphers, as if greater power might be possible if I shed the symbols of my faith. How can it be? Is it not god himself who formed the souls of men? I swear to discover the truth, after removing the madness and foul superstition of the Burgundians.

~JOAN OF ARC, RUNE WARRIOR, SHORTLY BEFORE HER
CAPTURE, MAY 1430

SARAH BLINKED from the bright light as Alter lifted the faceplate. The hunter looked tired, his eyes haunted.

"What's wrong?" Sarah asked as she removed her helmet and sat up.

"Nothing. I don't like the feel of those de . . . Eirene's nevron."

"You did wonderful," Eirene said from where she was helping Gregorios with his helmet. She looked worn, but cheerful.

Alter asked, "Are you all right? You're not hurt?"

Sarah gave him a reassuring smile. "I survived. Bastien's the one who got hit the worst."

Bastien was sitting up, examining his bloody clothing, with a medical officer hovering nearby. He pulled off his shirt to reveal a bloody bandage on his chest, over the spot where the spear had impaled him.

"You started bleeding heavily," the medical officer said, urging him to lay back. "You shouldn't rise yet."

Bastien peeled back the bandage, despite the man's protests. The ugly wound was already scabbed over. "I will be fine, although a few seconds more, and things might have gone badly, no?"

Sarah was relieved to see him doing so well. He didn't have quite as much control over the memoryscape as Gregorios, who had instigated the memory, but he'd controlled enough to heal himself before the wound radiated back fully to the real world.

"How did it go?" Harriett asked as she handed Sarah a huge blueberry muffin. "Eat. You need your strength." She grinned and took a huge bite out of a poppy seed muffin in her other hand, adding around the mouthful of pastry, "And so do we."

"How was the drain?" Sarah asked.

"Intense, but not severe," Alter said.

"Thanks to you, tough guy." Francesca slipped up to Alter and touched his arm. "Keeping us all safe with that pure soul of yours."

"I almost had him," Tomas exclaimed as he rose from his chair, fists clenched in frustration. "A fraction of a second and I would have taken his head."

"That's a lot of time when you're dealing with a cui dashi," Gregorios said. He was lounging on his chair, eating a double chocolate muffin. Sarah hadn't even noticed Harriett pass it to him. She was fast with those things.

Eirene shook her head. "You would've needed more than that. He would've abandoned the host."

"How does that work if his mind is in the memoryscape?" Francesca asked.

Gregorios paused in the act of taking another bite to say, "That's not entirely clear. Even though we didn't kill him, Tomas hurt him."

"A lot," Tomas interjected with a grin.

"And we blew up Paul and pumped a few hundred rounds of fifties into him," Sarah added.

"He may feel sore," Bastien agreed.

"Excellent." Alter laughed and leaned forward. For a second, Sarah thought he was going to kiss her. He was aiming that way, but seemed to realize what he was doing and changed the move to a quick hug.

Sarah hoped no one else had noticed his initial intent, and hoped he didn't forget himself again. She'd hate to have to punch him so soon after an almost-successful memory hunt.

Eirene sat on the seat beside Gregorios. "Did you learn anything more about Spartacus?"

"I did. He's not the man he once was."

Gregorios' description of his encounter with the ancient gladiator fascinated Sarah. How would she handle being stranded outside of her body for centuries, blind, and forgotten by a world that had moved on?

"There's a possibility he'll make contact," Gregorios added. "He owes Paul an honor debt, but doesn't appear to agree with Paul's methods. We might be able to leverage that."

Eirene said, "We'll take any advantage we can get. Any scrap of information might prove critical."

"I learned something about Paul too," Sarah interjected. "He's Chinese. He's Mai Luan's brother."

That got everyone's attention.

Gregorios nearly choked on his muffin. When he spoke, his voice sounded a little strained. "Say that again."

"Paul. He said he was Mai Luan's brother, and he was in Berlin."

"Impossible," Alter said, but lacked his normal conviction.

"Remember the bluetooth she was wearing?"

"That finally makes sense," Gregorios muttered.

"He's been shadowing us from the beginning," Eirene said. She took a piece of Gregorios' muffin and popped it into her mouth.

He looked like he was about to object, but she added, "Thinking food."

Gregorios rolled his eyes, but turned back to Sarah. "I lost track of you after the Greek Fire strike. What happened?"

With Bastien's help, Sarah related how they sprang the trap on Paul.

"I love that ghost ability," Francesca laughed when Sarah explained how she'd lured Paul onto the kill zone.

"I don't know what I'd do without it," Sarah agreed.

Bastien related how he detonated the explosives, despite reservations about blowing them with Sarah still in the blast zone. "She floated like a vision in the night," he said, saluting her with a giant cookie. "While Paul tumbled away, badly hurt by the blast."

"It wasn't enough, though," Sarah said.

Alter cheered when she told about gunning down Paul. Tomas reached her before the hunter could try embracing her again. He wrapped an arm around her shoulder. "Wish I'd seen that."

Bastien chuckled. "It was a beautiful moment. Sarah fired the minigun from the hip like a Valkyrie incarnate."

"Don't bring them into this," Eirene said with a frown.

"Sometimes bad girls are good to have around," Bastien said with a grin.

"Bad boys are more fun," Francesca retorted, jabbing Alter in the ribs as if inviting him to agree. He just scowled.

"Are you saying there are real live Valkyries?" Sarah asked, not quite sure what kind of answer to expect.

Gregorios interjected. "Not exactly, and we're losing track of the discussion. Back to Paul."

Sarah related how he turned the fight against them and wounded Bastien.

When she tried to describe how she'd fought him off using the powers of her two runes, Francesca interrupted with a laugh, clapping her hands loudly in the enclosed room. "You have two superpowers? No fair."

Tomas gripped Sarah closer. "Awesome, but I don't think I really understand."

"It's hard to explain. I don't entirely understand it myself."

"You should erase that rune," Alter said. He looked troubled and mouthed the word "abomination."

Sarah said, "No way. Without it, he would have killed me."

"We're going to have to find a memory to test the extent of that rune," Gregorios said. At least he looked intrigued.

"We expected to see other aspects of that design," Eirene added. "But these effects are unique."

Sarah said, "It's the memoryscape. Things work differently there. We can bend the laws of nature."

"But none of the rest of us are turning into superheroes," Francesca said with a pout.

"I want a super power," Harriett agreed.

"Paul first. Superhero discussion second," Gregorios said.

Sarah explained what she'd learned from Paul about his connection with Mai Luan.

"He lies," Bastien said.

"He seemed pretty sincere. He got really ticked when I insulted Mai Luan."

Harriett said, "Maybe he sees her as a soul sister since they're both cui dashi."

Sarah shrugged. "He said sister. They're both Chinese, so I took it at face value."

"Let's assume you're right," Gregorios said. When Harriett and Bastien protested again he added, "Just play along. How could it be possible?"

"I do not think it is," Bastien insisted. "It took you and mother centuries to conceive each of us, and that is just for the nevra core. Factor in the rarity of the cui dashi powers, and I say it would never happen."

"Baladeva managed it," Eirene pointed out.

"Maybe he had some dumb luck," Francesca suggested.

"Or lots and lots of heka women, yes?" Bastien countered.

Alter muttered, "One cui dashi is bad enough. An entire family of them is entirely different."

"Don't assume there are others," Harriett said.

"Don't assume there aren't," Alter shot back. "If they've found a way to breed cui dashi, there could be more."

Francesca gave him a disgusted look. "You're usually so sweet, but that's depressing."

"Maybe they're cheating," Alter added.

"More forbidden runes?" Eirene asked.

"Perhaps."

"There's a rune for breeding cui dashi?" Gregorios asked, his tone doubtful.

Alter shrugged. "Not that I've ever heard, but that doesn't mean one couldn't be discovered."

"Are there runes for other types of breeding?" Bastien asked.

Harriett slugged him in the shoulder.

"Ow. Just asking."

"I'm liking this conversation less and less." Sarah didn't want to think about more people like Paul loose in the world.

Eirene paced around her chair. "Keep an open mind until we know for sure the connection between Paul and Mai Luan. Did you learn anything else?"

Sarah hesitated and Eirene prodded, "Don't keep anything back, my dear. Not now."

"He could have killed me. Near the end, just before he rushed off to save John. He chose not to."

"I'm glad he didn't," Tomas said, his arm a comforting weight on her shoulders. "But why not?"

She took a deep breath, drawing strength from his presence. "He said he found a different use for me, some kind of service."

"Did he specify what he meant?" Gregorios asked.

"No. That's when he had to leave."

"That's why he called you his chosen vessel," Gregorios said.

"Eww," Francesca said. "That sounds gross. Pervert."

"My thoughts exactly," Sarah said.

Tomas' arm tightened around her shoulders as he tensed with anger. Not much touched his face, but she felt the rage boiling in him.

Alter didn't bother to restrain himself. "I'll tear his filthy head off!" he cried, fists clenched, face red with rage.

"All in good time," Gregorios said. If their suspicions of Paul's intentions bothered him, he showed no sign.

"If indeed his intentions have changed, perhaps we can use that against him," Eirene said thoughtfully.

"How?" Sarah and Tomas asked together.

"Killing you is fairly straight-forward. He intended to do that in the memoryscape, with a pretty good chance of success."

"He could have killed me today," Sarah agreed.

"Using you for some other purpose is more difficult," Eirene added.

"He'd need to make contact in the real world." Francesca picked up the train of thought.

Sarah shivered. She didn't want to meet Paul in the real world. At least in the memoryscape she could draw upon her unique enhancements, or even inscribe the escape rune and get away.

Tomas said, "If we could locate him, we could bring the rain and take him out."

"Mai Luan almost killed us when we met her in real life," Sarah reminded him. "You nearly died. We can't regenerate here."

He nodded. "Neither can Paul. We know how to take down a cui dashi."

"Perhaps there is yet a way to leverage our strengths both inside and out of the memoryscape," Bastien suggested.

"We're listening," Gregorios said.

"If we can determine his location in Rome, for he must be here somewhere, then we can plan a strike."

Tomas frowned. "We risk a lot of casualties fighting a cui dashi in such a heavily populated area."

"Not if he is sleeping, yes?" Bastien said with a sly grin.

"Lure him into the memoryscape and confront him again." Eirene sounded pleased.

"And destroy his body while he's distracted," Tomas added. "That could work."

Sarah tried to share their enthusiasm, but the part they hadn't mentioned was the one part she couldn't ignore. For any such plan to work, she had to act as bait. Again.

She needed more runes.

45

SARAH SHARED a taxi back to Quentin's with Tomas. She leaned against the seat, focusing on the feel of wind on her face and his hand in hers. The buildings that passed no longer looked so incredible. She had seen parts of Rome in its ancient heyday and the sight of ruins filled her with a lingering sadness.

When they arrived, Tomas escorted her to her room, and they shared a lingering kiss.

"I'm sorry I wasn't there to help you," Tomas said, caressing her face.

"I'm sorry I couldn't hold Paul off another second."

He kissed her again. "You're amazing. You held him off longer than anyone had a right to ask. Even I don't go against cui dashi alone."

"I had Bastien."

"Even so, it's a miracle you accomplished so much." His expression darkened. "We never should have asked so much of you."

"Why? You think I'm not up to the challenge?"

"It's not that," he said quickly. "You're tapping into powers I've never imagined and I've been bonding runes for centuries." He touched her face again, gently. "You introduce me to whole new worlds."

She toyed with the idea of tempting him into her room to introduce him to another new world, but she didn't want to deal with another rejection. So she gave him a tired smile. "Sometimes I don't know who I am or what the real world is. I'm glad I have you to help me figure it out."

She kissed him then, a passionate kiss full of her need and her desire. He responded with fierce passion that took her breath away and left her feeling a little more secure.

"I'll see you later," he said when they broke for air. "I need to check on a lead the legion's been running down."

"I hope it pans out finally."

It would be nice to get actionable intelligence. The Tenth had been stymied trying to find Paul and his clandestine heka cell. They were due for a break.

Only after he left did she realize how exhausted she was. So she threw herself into her huge, four-post bed and slept like the dead for several hours. After enjoying a long soak in the giant jet tub in her bathroom, she felt almost like herself again.

Eager for dinner, she dressed in slacks and a cotton tee and went looking for food. She ran into Alter pacing one of the lower halls, a phone at his ear.

"No, Father. We'll all be at Quentin's in the morning . . . All right . . .I will."

He didn't sound happy as he hung up, but smiled when he saw her. "How are you feeling?"

"Pretty good. I crashed all afternoon."

"I'm not surprised. You had a busy morning."

"And I'm hoping it's dinner time."

"I'll join you." Alter eagerly fell in beside her and together they headed for the art gallery dining room. They were a little early and found the room deserted, the long table empty.

The call button still worked, and a young staffer appeared almost instantly. He assured them he could bring them whatever they wanted, and disappeared to fill the order.

"I could get used to this," Alter confided.

Sarah said, "I already am. I'm going to hate returning to my apartment."

Quentin entered the room, dressed impeccably as usual in a custom tailored suit, his salt-and-pepper hair recently trimmed. "Then you should stay."

"I'm not leaving any time soon," she assured him, touched by his never-flagging hospitality.

He bowed over her hand and kissed the back of it. "I heard about your memory hunt. Did you really fire the GECAL 50 from the hip?" His eyes sparkled.

"It was awesome. I just wish it'd been enough to take him down."

"I'm working on some ideas. I hope to offer some new options in the near future."

She squeezed his hand, grateful to have him as a friend. "We need your mad genius invention skills more than ever right now."

He chuckled. "Mad genius. We shall see about that, my dear. Perhaps we will get the chance to take Paul down together."

She liked him more every day.

Alter didn't seem so impressed. He muttered, "Get in line. I want dibs on the cui dashi."

"A team approach then," Quentin said without missing a beat. "It took all of us together to deal with Mai Luan."

"Paul's worse," Sarah said, shivering at the memory of his iron grip and his ominous final words.

The food arrived, and Quentin added an order of his own. The three of them spent a quiet hour together, eating and talking about non-lethal things. Sarah relaxed slowly as they chatted, and started to feel herself again.

Eventually Alter said, "I'm expecting a delivery from my family by special courier, probably some time tonight."

"I'll notify the gate guard," Quentin said.

The door at the far end of the room opened and Tomas strode in. "Quentin, I need to know . . ."

His voice trailed off when he caught sight of Sarah, and his smile faded.

He was wearing Carl's body.

She recognized it instantly. That was the body he had used to infiltrate Alterego when they first met. He hadn't looked nearly as handsome, but his heroic efforts to help her escape had drawn her to him. Now that she knew what he really looked like, she had never wanted him to change.

"What did you do?" she exclaimed, rising from her seat.

"Devils," Alter muttered.

"I thought you were asleep," Tomas said, slowly approaching.

"So? How does that equate to swapping bodies?"

"I would've stayed away longer if I knew you were awake."

"Why?"

"You have enough to worry about." He took her hands in his. "Why burden you with something unimportant?"

"It's important to me. Why would you do it?"

"I owed Carl a debt for helping me steal the original machine from Mai Luan. We've swapped a couple of times since then. Tonight's the last time. He's got a big date."

Sarah recoiled. "Are you serious?"

"It's not that big a deal. I'll have it back tomorrow by noon."

How could he not see? He had insisted they wait for intimacy, despite the depth of their feelings. She even respected him for that. Now he was giving Carl his body without a second thought?

"What do you think they're going to do tonight?" she asked softly.

"So that's what you're worried about. Relax. I told him he can't do anything too physical. That would be awkward."

"Awkward? You think? And what's *too* physical?"

"You know."

"Apparently not," she snapped.

Quentin mumbled something about being late for a meeting, grabbed Alter by the cuff, and marched for the door. Alter looked like he'd prefer to stay, but Quentin hauled him out anyway.

"So Carl's physical needs are more important than mine? Than ours?" Sarah demanded when the two of them were alone.

"Now you're being silly." He didn't seem to understand at all.

"Silly?" Sarah cupped his face in her hands. "I need you today, Tomas. You, not Carl."

"I'm here, just like when we first met."

"It's not the same. Now I know someone else is living in your body, doing who knows what with it."

"It's not the body that matters. It's the soul."

"Well the body is part of you. Don't you think I care what he might do with it tonight?"

"He'll take good care of it," Tomas assured her, sounding impatient, as if he felt they'd argued the point enough.

He was going to have to settle in for a while, because she was just getting started.

"You don't have any clue, do you? You tout your moral standards and expect me to follow them. Then you hand off your body to someone else and let them do whatever they want. And you want to be with me afterward like nothing happened?"

"That's not fair. You've swapped bodies way more than I have. What do you think those renters were doing with it? They weren't going to tea parties."

"This is different. That was my job."

"So it'd be okay if Carl was paying me to do 'who knows what' with my body instead?"

"Of course not. I'm just saying this is different."

Tomas shook his head. "No it's not. I'm doing a favor for a friend. You did it professionally. No difference."

She took a deep breath, trying to rein in her rising anger. Her runes started to itch on her skin, but she willed them to be still. She didn't need enhancements. She just needed him to understand.

"Listen," she said with forced calm. "We're in a relationship now, Tomas. What we allowed to happen to our bodies before doesn't matter, but what happens to them now does."

"The body is a suit. You've got to get over your fixation with it, Sarah."

"It's more than that," she cried. "It's who we are."

"Who you are is inside, not outside," Tomas retorted.

"So you don't feel attracted to the physical part of me at all?"

"Of course I do. Stop twisting things around."

"The only twisted thing here is your moral code," she shot back.

After that, the argument escalated into a shouting match. Sarah wanted to stop, to just hold him, but the thought of Carl's arms holding her just angered her further. She had nearly died today. Wasn't that enough to make him think a little?

Apparently not.

Finally she shouted, "Your morals are a lie!"

"At least I have morals," he shouted back, equally angry. "You sold your body for money. What does that make you?"

The words echoed across the long room and they both fell silent, equally shocked by how far they'd gone.

Tomas tried to stammer an apology but Sarah said softly, "If that's how you really feel, don't waste any more time with me."

She stormed from the room, fighting back tears, and Tomas had the good sense to let her go. He called out only one more time before she closed the door.

"I love you, Sarah!"

She returned to her suite and angrily paced her rooms. She wanted to go back to him, but wasn't sure if she'd kiss him or punch him. She loved him, but in that moment, she hated him for what he'd said.

She had tried not to think about that aspect of what her work at Alterego meant, but always it was there in the back of her mind. The glamor and the insane amounts of money had made it easy to ignore the truth for a time, but it had haunted her in quiet moments. And he had just ripped away the careful justifications, laying the wound bare.

Exhaustion eventually dragged her to bed, but her dreams were troubled, and in them Paul stalked her, carrying shackles that burned with purple fire.

46

The most effective way to destroy people is to deny and obliterate their own understanding of their history.

~GEORGE ORWELL, IN A LETTER TO HARALD,
CRITICIZING PROPOSED CHANGES TO THE HISTORY OF
WORLD WAR ONE

WAILING alarms woke Eirene from a dreamless sleep.

"It would be tonight," she muttered as she rose and threw on some clothes. Helping run the machines during the previous day's assault had exhausted her. They'd never tried merging all of their nevron together while powering two machines, and the drain had been significant.

She still wished she'd been able to spare a little more attention for Alter. That boy's rounon gift was unique. She still couldn't understand how he thwarted whatever forbidden rune Paul was using to subvert their nevron.

She'd felt the power of Alter's soul linked to hers, almost as tightly as she'd felt her daughters. Most rounon-gifted couldn't bind their souls so close. It could be the fact that he was related to them by blood, but she'd lacked the focus to probe further.

"It's not a fire," Gregorios said from across the room as he stomped into a pair of military boots. "That's the perimeter alarm."

Eirene paused to buckle on a belt with a pair of forty-fives.

Quentin's voice spoke through concealed speakers in the walls, and would be repeated in other occupied rooms. "All staff and residents, this is not a drill. We have perimeter breach by unknown forces. Lockdown is underway. Gather in the art gallery."

They found Quentin there, dressed in suit pants, white shirt, and body armor. He carried an MP5 rifle on a tactical sling, and the pouches of his tactical vest bulged with magazines and assorted gear.

He looked furious.

"Sitrep?" Eirene asked.

"Someone is attacking my home," Quentin snarled. It was five a.m., still dark outside. "Perimeter guard is down, status unknown. The intruders defeated two of the alarm systems and somehow knocked out power to the central operations room. Tertiary sensors alone remain active."

"So we're dealing with professionals," Gregorios said.

"It appears so."

Other people were still gathering. Most of the twenty-person staff were already there, as well as two enforcers, and Alter. Tomas and Sarah arrived together, but separated as soon as they entered. They could have picked a better time for a quarrel.

"Where's everyone else?" Eirene asked.

Quentin shrugged. "This is it. The rest of the staff arrives in half an hour."

"The children are in town," Gregorios reminded her. "The Yurak team arrives today and they're overseeing deployment."

"Whoever these intruders are, they picked their timing with care," Eirene muttered, feeling more annoyed.

"Agreed," Quentin said.

He headed to one of the long walls covered with expensive artwork. He knocked on the wall and a concealed panel flipped open to reveal a keypad.

Quentin typed in a long code, and a ten-foot section of wall slid aside, revealing a bank of dozens of small digital displays and three keyboards. Two staffers moved to the keyboards and began typing.

"This is the heart of the tertiary system," Quentin explained. "We'll have visuals in a moment."

Views of rooms and halls throughout the mansion began cycling across the displays.

"No external view?" Eirene asked.

"Negative. They shorted the external cameras as part of the initial infiltration."

Distant booming echoed through the mansion and red lights flashed on one of the monitors. The staffers typed faster.

"We have three exterior breaches," one man reported. "North, east, and west wings."

Quentin scowled and Eirene patted his shoulder. "You always say you honor a worthy adversary."

"But I prefer it if I'm the one blowing up his house. Not the other way around."

"Any idea who they are?" Tomas asked. Sarah and Alter trailed behind him, eyes scanning the monitors.

"Got them," one of the staffers called.

One screen showed a small group of dark-clad men slinking down a hall. Then the display blinked and faded to blue static. All of the other displays followed suit a second later.

"What happened?" Sarah asked.

"The system is down," Quentin growled.

Tomas asked, "How could they take down everything without a full EMP blast? That's great work."

Quentin shot him a frustrated look. "Do you mind?"

"I can appreciate professionalism, can't I?"

"Not when it's on the other team, and they're in my house. I'll be sure to ask them how they managed the job, after I thump their hides."

The lights in the room flickered a couple of times and finally returned to a steady, if dimmer glow.

Quentin sighed. "Lights are out. This room is on an independent source. The rest of the mansion will be blacked out."

"They'll be sweeping the wings and closing on us," Eirene said. "They know their target."

"Is there a safe room or something?" Sarah asked, sounding nervous.

Gregorios shrugged. "It doesn't matter. I spotted heavy weapons on that group."

Quentin said, "This room is secure. It was designed as an emergency headquarters. The walls are reinforced steel, but if we wait for them to converge here, they'll deploy explosives and slaughter us."

"What about reinforcements?" Eirene said.

"The alarm triggers an automatic alert to Suntara headquarters, but it is possible they blocked it. Either way, help is at least ten minutes out."

"So we wait them out?" Alter asked.

"No way. We take them out," Tomas replied.

"And we make it hurt," Quentin added. "I consider myself a good host, but these gentlemen require a lesson on guest etiquette."

"Are you sure that's the best idea?" Sarah asked nervously.

Eirene touched her shoulder reassuringly. "It is. We need to stop them before they gain the advantage."

"What if it's Paul?" she whispered.

Eirene exchanged a grave look with Gregorios, who shrugged and said, "Then we won't have to waste any more time tracking him down, will we?"

"I don't think Paul would stoop to leading a night-time assault," Eirene assured Sarah. "Although it could be his forces."

Tomas said, "I need a gun. Any word on the other enforcers?"

"Status unknown," Quentin said, then tapped one of the staffers at the keyboards on the shoulder. "Open the armory."

At a typed command, another section of wall opened and four steel racks slid into the room, filled with weapons and gear.

Sarah stared, and Quentin smiled at her surprise. "Why do you think we always met in here?"

"I thought you liked the art."

"I do, but it is always wise to have a weapon or fifty close at hand."

The group, including most of the mansion staffers, moved to the weapons rack. Quentin never employed anyone who couldn't help with defense. Eirene donned a bulletproof vest, then a tactical vest to hold her other gear. She spotted one rifle and picked it up with a fond smile.

"I know you love the Tommy," Quentin said, noting her choice.

"My favorite," she agreed. The Thompson was old, heavy, and dependable. It fired the same rounds as her pistols and its solid weight felt like an old friend settling into her hand.

Sarah looked from the machine gun to Tomas. "Any relation?"

He chuckled. "I wish. That gun's a classic."

Her gaze turned icy. "Hmm. Nice to know when one can be counted on."

Tomas looked frustrated, but was wise enough to keep his mouth shut. He chose an MP5 like Quentin, although a double-barreled revolver rested at his hip. Even in Carl's body, he could defeat all but the most enhanced opponents.

Gregorios, who had been surveying the long racks of weapons with a thoughtful eye, laughed and picked up a pair of sleek, steel tomahawks. "Ah, Quentin, you've been holding out on me."

"You've got to be joking." Quentin looked insulted. "I offer you a selection of some of the best firearms in the world, and you gush over a hatchet?"

"Don't get your knickers in a knot," Gregorios chuckled. "I plan to take a gun or five too, but I'm keeping these. After a gladius, these are my preferred close-in weapons."

As Gregorios finished his selections, softly humming the Tenth's battle song, Tomas said, "So we could be dealing with a squad of enhanced heka."

Eirene approved of his professional focus. "That's our best bet. We've been hunting them, so it makes sense they're hunting us too."

"Or he's making good on his final threat." Sarah rubbed her arms as if chilled.

Gregorios squeezed her shoulder, his expression grim, his eyes glinting with pre-battle energy. "Threats are easy to make. He'd better hope he has more men because I don't feel like taking prisoners."

He'd also donned a pair of his favorite double-barreled revolvers, and the hilt of a huge knife, almost the size of a gladius, poked over his shoulder beside the handle of a tactical shotgun.

"We can't ignore the possibility that Paul will participate," Tomas added. "Even though I agree he's probably hiding in the shadows, letting others take the risks."

"We'll work together, just in case." Gregorios added a couple more pieces of gear to the pockets of his vest.

"He doesn't have dispossessed souls healing him in real life," Tomas growled.

Eirene added, "They might have a rune web protecting them. We know he's got well-trained enchanters on his team."

"This isn't the light brigade," Tomas said, and Eirene thought back to that crazy battle. Some memories didn't get better with time.

"The what?" Sarah asked.

Gregorios said, "Long story. We need to be careful, just in case."

Quentin nodded. To the two enforcers flanking Tomas he said, "You two set up defensive positions with the staff in case any of those groups get through. You'll be the fire base we work from."

"And the rest of us?" Alter asked. His normal enthusiasm seemed muted, replaced by barely concealed nerves. That wasn't like him, but Eirene didn't have time to ask him about it.

"Greg and I will take the group to the north," Eirene said. That was the group they had seen briefly in the monitors.

Tomas said, "Then Alter and I will head west. They'll be the closest."

Quentin turned to Sarah. "Will you do me the great honor of joining me, my dear?"

Sarah gripped a stubby KSG shotgun, her hands white against the black stock. "Okay."

"Don't worry," Quentin assured her. "Our mission is a little different. We're heading for the east wing, but we'll scout their force as they move into the main halls. We'll wait until the other assault teams are nullified before moving in. With Tomas and the others joining us, we'll overwhelm them."

That eased her fears, and Eirene gave her an encouraging smile. The girl had shown tremendous spirit to have survived the encounter with Paul, but sometimes Eirene forgot how new she was to their world of covert battles, enhancements, and arcane soul powers. She was glad Quentin would be there to take care of the girl.

"You could stay here," Tomas offered.

As much as Eirene wanted to agree with him, and as skilled as Quentin was, she had seen too many lone scouts never return. Besides, Sarah needed to know she could still function, despite the near brush with death. If they let her withdraw, the damage to her confidence might take months to repair.

"No, we move in two-man teams." She squeezed Sarah's shoulder. "There is some danger, but Quentin's plan is a good one. Will you help?"

To her credit, Sarah straightened and said, "I'll do it."

"Good. Let's move out."

47

Remus, the coat should be mine. Mother wanted me to have it, and I tended her to her uttermost breath. Give it to me, for it is worth more than the roots of our new-found city.

~ROMULUS

TOMAS CROUCHED beside Alter just inside the door of a salon decorated like an Elizabethan sitting room. He monitored a small, dimly illuminated LCD display connected to a thin cable snaked around the door.

It held a tiny video camera capable of low-light imaging. The slightly distorted picture showed four men approaching up the hallway in standard cover formation.

"They're almost in position," Tomas said, handing the display to Alter and extracting a flash-bang grenade from a pouch of his tac vest. "As soon as they're distracted, we take them down."

Alter nodded, still looking as distracted as he had since the emergency started. He was always so eager to fight heka. His timing was terrible.

Tomas whispered, "Get your head in the game."

Alter shook himself and his gaze locked onto the tiny display.

After five more seconds, Tomas lifted the grenade and took hold of the pin.

"Wait," Alter hissed, leaning close to the display.

"No. We have to do it now."

Tomas pulled the pin and cocked back his arm to throw.

Alter kicked Tomas in the side. The unexpected blow slammed him into the wall beside the door and knocked the grenade out of his hand.

Tomas didn't have time to ask questions. He reacted with instincts honed through centuries of close combat, and managed to block a fast-flying punch as Alter leaped upon him. Wearing Carl's body, his reflexes were slower than usual, and Alter's second punch caught him in the jaw, rocking him back.

As he struggled to shed the effects of the blow, he groped for the grenade. Alter kicked him again, then rushed out of the room shouting, "Hunter One, Caleb! Contact at my six!"

Tomas hated that sick feeling of betrayal, no matter how many times he tasted it.

The flash-bang exploded nearby and the thunderous boom tumbled him into the wall, while the blinding light dazzled his eyes, even though he'd closed them. He tasted smoke, and his limbs shook. He cursed that he was wearing such a pitiful form, but forced himself to roll out of the smoke. He didn't have time to be weak.

Tomas staggered into the hall, all hope of surprise lost, but determined to make the traitor pay. The four-man hunter assault team was closing, assault rifles held ready. Tomas pulled his own MP5 around, but that slimy Alter had deceived him and waited on the opposite side of the doorway.

Tomas sensed the rush of Alter's surprise attack a moment too late, and the young traitor clubbed him in the side of the head. Tomas stumbled again, triggering a three-round burst into the floor in front of the lead intruder.

He recognized the man. It was Alter's older brother, Reuben.

Reuben shot Tomas in the chest three times.

The rounds struck close together and he dropped to the ground, groaning. He was glad all of Quentin's bulletproof vests included polyethylene plates rated to stop rifle rounds. He still felt like he'd been kicked in the chest. In his own body, his enhancements would have shed most of that effect, but the one healing rune on Carl's took a precious second.

Alter scooped up Tomas' gun and pulled his pistol from its holster before turning to greet his brother. "I told you to wait."

Reuben clapped Alter in the shoulder. "Well met, little brother." Then he barked a laugh. "Don't act so surprised. You're the one who told father where the demons would be holed up today."

"They're not the ones responsible for the attack."

"We'll see."

Tomas lunged off the ground and tackled Alter. Reuben might be the leader of the enemies, but betrayers needed to be punished first. He managed to land a solid punch to the throat before Reuben clubbed him in the side of the head with the butt of his rifle.

Tomas fell, head reeling, his body not responding to his demands to lash out at Reuben.

Reuben stood over him, gun pointed at his head.

"Wait," Alter coughed. "He's one of their enforcers."

"Then we kill him."

Alter pushed the gun aside. "No. He's a captain. He might have information we need."

"Very well." Reuben gestured toward Tomas. "Bind him and remove his gear."

Tomas shouted defiance and fought the hunters, but Carl's body lacked the strength to shrug off the damage it had taken. He fought with every ounce of rage, but the three hunters held too much advantage.

They beat him with their rifles, every blow aimed at sensitive areas. He writhed under the beating, clamping his teeth closed against groans of agony he refused to let them hear.

The beating continued until he couldn't move, barely held onto consciousness. With blood trickling out the corner of his mouth, he tried to curse at Alter, but only managed a muffled groan.

A hunter clubbed him again and he fell back against the cool tile, thoughts drifting. He'd died on the battlefield more than once, although he'd been saved by Gregorios, Eirene, and even Asoka at different times. He knew the beating wasn't life-threatening, and he allowed the pain to wash through him. He knew how to deal with pain, but he hated betrayers above all things.

He'd been betrayed before. As the hunters stripped off his tactical vest, then his bulletproof vest, his thoughts turned back to the four times he'd been betrayed by men he had thought he could trust. He'd hunted down every one of them, but the faces of friends and men under his command who had died because of those traitors played through his mind.

Alter would live to regret this night, but he wouldn't live long.

"He doesn't look like an enforcer," Reuben commented, looking down at Tomas' bruised and bound form.

"He's wearing another's body," Alter said.

"Demons," Reuben spat.

He shot Tomas in the chest.

The pain was as intense as it always was when shot there. Some things get better with repetition, but gunshots to the chest were not one of them.

"Why did you do that?" Alter cried.

"Because he deserves it," Reuben said without emotion.

Tomas tried to speak, but couldn't. He hovered on the edge of consciousness. The wound was serious, but it would take a while to bleed out.

He hated lingering deaths.

Alter said, "We need to bandage it. He's no good to us dead."

"Fine. You have ten seconds."

Alter dropped to the floor beside Tomas, who managed to focus on the betrayer's face as he shoved a wad of bandage into position and slapped a couple strips of medical tape over the top. Alter never met his gaze, and Tomas wasn't able to summon the strength to bite him.

As he faded to darkness, Reuben's voice echoed as if from a great distance. "Where are the demons?"

48

From this day to the ending of the world,
But we in it shall be remembered-
We few, we happy few, we band of brothers;
For he to-day that sheds his blood with me
Shall be my brother; be he ne'er so vile,
This day shall gentle his condition;
And gentlemen in England now-a-bed
Shall think themselves accurs'd they were not here,
And hold their manhoods cheap whiles any speaks
That fought with us upon Saint Crispin's day.

No, Shakespeare never understood the full scope of Agincourt. I always thought Harriett a fool for facilitating activation of that unique rune of his. Still, he put it to productive use like Archimedes before him, and Harriett will never let me forget the one time I mentioned that this speech moved me, despite its inaccuracies.

~GREGORIOS

SARAH AND QUENTIN crouched behind the rail at the top of the grand staircase. A group of black-clad intruders were making their methodical approach toward the stairs from below. In a moment, they would emerge from a hall at the very base of the stairs and pass directly below where Sarah and Quentin crouched.

It was hard to hide her nervousness. The shotgun felt heavy in her hands and she couldn't seem to get enough air. Quentin had twice urged her to breathe more slowly.

"What are we going to do?" she asked softly.

Quentin leaned close and his whisper barely made it the two inches to her ear. "Stall them, of course."

Eirene's voice spoke loudly through Sarah's earpiece, and she jumped. "Quentin. Tomas. Be advised, we've made contact and the forces are hunters."

"Roger," Quentin said softly as the soldiers began to move into the open beneath their location.

After a couple of seconds, Gregorios spoke. "Tomas. Respond, over."

Silence.

He was with Alter.

Dread as deep as the fear she had felt facing Paul chilled Sarah to the bone.

Alter's voice spoke over the channel. "Tomas is injured, but alive. If you want to keep him that way, meet me at the pool and surrender to my family."

"We are not your enemy," Eirene said.

Gregorios added, "Well, we weren't."

Alter said, "Then act as friends and come out and surrender."

"Friends don't let friends take their guns," Gregorios said, his tone cold enough to make Sarah shiver with dread.

She could hardly believe what she was hearing. What had Alter done? How could he have betrayed them?

Alter said, "You have five minutes. Do it for Tomas."

Sarah started to speak, but Quentin clamped a hand over her mouth, his expression grim. He looked ready to kill as he pulled from a pouch the anti-heka burst grenade he'd shown them during that dinner conversation.

He dropped it over the rail.

It landed right in the middle of the strike force and exploded in a blue-white flash that seared Sarah's vision. She rolled away from the rail, hands pressed against her eyes. She knew better than to look at an explosion, even a beautiful one.

On the floor below, the intruders cried out, but their shouts were replaced by grunts, then silence. It took several seconds for Sarah to blink away the after-images of the flash. When she could distinguish the railing through the rainbow halos, she realized Quentin was gone.

A fresh wave of fear drove her to her feet, gripping the shotgun. She looked down, ready to fire upon the hunters, then blinked a couple times. Quentin was down there, in the process of binding the last of the unconscious hunters. He noticed her standing and waved.

"Come down and help me with these, my dear."

She hurried down, still blinking away the effects of the burst. It had worked as well against hunters as it had against heka. "Weren't you worried it'd affect your enhancements too?"

He chuckled. "I was thumping skulls thicker than these lads long before I bonded my first enhancement. Hunters start bonding runes young, so they forget how to live without them. I held the advantage, never you fear."

One soldier started groaning and Quentin slugged the man in the jaw, knocking him back to the floor. "As I said, effects wear off quickly.

Quentin removed the helmets from the hunters and tossed them into a closet concealed under the stairs. "That burst fried all their electronics, including comms, so their other teams won't have heard what happened to them. Come, let's go find Gregorios."

"What about Tomas?"

"We'll see."

He extracted a gray metal box the size of a lighter from a vest pocket. It bore a tiny LCD display and he fiddled with it for a minute.

"What's that?" Sarah asked.

"Changing to a different tactical network," he explained. He took her earpiece and tapped the power button several times. "There. You're on."

She set the earpiece and he spoke. "Gregorios, Eirene, are you switched over?"

Gregorios responded immediately. "Roger,. Alter doesn't know this frequency."

Quentin said, "Sometimes it's a good thing we don't really trust anyone. Did you kill or capture the strike team on your end?"

"Captured." Gregorios sounded like maybe he was rethinking that choice.

"Second strike team is in custody," Quentin reported.

Gregorios said, "Good. We'll need them."

"We'll approach this like we did Richelieu," Eirene added.

"Cardinal Richelieu?" Sarah asked, grateful for something to focus on other than Tomas' predicament.

"Remind me to tell you the real story of the musketeers later," Gregorios said.

"Before my time," Quentin said when she gave him a questioning look. He gestured down the hall. "Sarah, will you run down to the pantry and fetch the pastry cart?"

"What are we going to do?"

His expression turned grim. "We're going to remind Alter's family why they haven't attacked us in three centuries."

49

Such as are thy habitual thoughts, such also will be the character of thy soul-for the soul is dyed by the thoughts. Dye it then, with a continuous series of such thoughts as these-that one life is sufficient to establish the character that will define all the lives to come, and that where a man can live, there if he will, he can also live well.

~MARK ANTONY

SARAH AND QUENTIN met Gregorios and Eirene three minutes later in the south wing, near the exit leading to the pool. They stayed well back from the windows. Sarah's nerves were so tightly wound she felt like her chest was clamped in a vise, but seeing Eirene and Gregorios looking unruffled helped a little.

Four bound and gagged hunters lay propped against the wall nearby. Quentin dumped his captured squad off the pastry cart into a pile next to the others. Then he leaned over each man and pressed softly-glowing ear plugs into their left ears.

"Disrupts their inner ear," Quentin explained. "Even though they're well bound, this renders them ineffective."

Sarah rushed to Eirene, who gave her a reassuring hug.

"What are we going to do?" Sarah asked. She could barely believe Alter had turned on them.

"I'm starting to get annoyed," Gregorios muttered, pacing past the motionless prisoners, as if hoping one would start struggling so he could kick them.

Eirene kept her voice calm. "Contain it for now. At least until we've secured Tomas."

Quentin glanced out the window and grunted, sounding annoyed. "The pool is a good choice. Alter did his homework during his time here."

"They'll have snipers in the windows upstairs," Eirene said.

Quentin nodded. "On it."

He left at a trot and Sarah moved to follow, but Eirene held her back. "He'll be fine, dear. You'd just slow him down."

She glanced after Quentin, not entirely sure. He had taken out those soldiers with amazing ease, but he wasn't exactly young any more.

Gregorios added, "This is his house. That was Alter's first mistake."

"What was his second?" Sarah asked.

"Not starting to run yet."

Their confidence eased her terror that the hunters would kill Tomas, but didn't help the powerful, conflicting emotions she felt toward Alter. He'd been their friend, a trusted member of the team. He knew the truth, and they'd taken him in, had confided with him. Part of her hated him for the betrayal, but part of her wanted to find him, to talk with him, to ask him why.

"It's almost time," Eirene said, and the next minute passed quickly as they checked their weapons.

Sarah fingered her shotgun, not sure if she could really shoot Alter. If he hurt Tomas, she would, no matter how much she liked him.

She wanted to scream with frustration. Paul was out there somewhere, and they were fighting each other when they needed to unite against him.

Alter's voice called from outside. "Time's up, Gregorios. What's your decision?"

Gregorios slammed a magazine home in one of the hunters' assault rifles. "Time to teach."

Eirene placed a hand on his arm. "I'll try to talk sense into him."

"I think he's beyond reason," Gregorios said.

"I don't want you killing that boy," Eirene warned.

"That's up to him. What about Reuben?"

Eirene hesitated. "He is family, technically."

When Gregorios scowled, she added, "He is wearing your favorite battle suit. If you have to destroy it, I want his soul preserved."

Sarah wasn't sure what to think. Even though she lived with these people, sometimes she struggled to feel like she was really a part of their world.

"What do you want me to do?" she asked.

Gregorios said, "Come with us. You check on Tomas. When the discussion turns unpleasant, stay down."

He led the way out the door.

50

Don't show me gold and plunder. Victory is hollow, and secret enemies hound my steps. Find me a facetaker to grant me a second life, or bring me a rune of power. But alas, all is folly, for the facetakers are gone and the Quirinal priests are all murdered.

~GENSERIC, KING OF THE VANDALS, AT THE SACKING OF
ROME, 455 A.D.

THE POOL WAS OLYMPIC SIZED, set in a wide courtyard nestled between the wings of the mansion. To the west, it overlooked the manicured grounds and spectacular views of Rome. Sarah loved to swim laps after working out, but after tonight she doubted she'd ever go again without thinking of this confrontation.

Alter and his brother stood together in the open. The two looked a great deal alike. Reuben was a little larger, his face a bit longer, and his hatred burned fiercer than Alter's ever had.

Tomas lay on a reclined pool chair. His shirt was gone and a bloody bandage covered part of his chest. Bruises stood out angrily against the pale skin of Carl's body. The one healing rune, which she'd marked there after Mai Luan stabbed him, glowed blue-white in the early morning dimness. His eyes were closed and he lay unmoving.

The sight infuriated Sarah. She advanced a quick step. "Is he alive?"

"He lives," Alter said, sounding defensive.

"How could you?" Sarah demanded. "We trusted you!"

Alter had the decency to look crestfallen. "If not for me, he'd already be dead. Don't judge before knowing the facts."

Gregorios said, "Advice you and your brother should have taken. You know we aren't responsible for the attack on your home."

"We saw one of your council members." Reuben's voice rang with conviction. "He mentioned your name."

"I didn't send John on that mission," Gregorios said, advancing a few slow steps.

"You lie," Reuben snarled.

The hunter snapped his rifle to his shoulder, but a shot cracked the air from above and behind him. Reuben yelped as the rifle tumbled from his hands as if yanked by an invisible string.

"Again, you judge too soon," Gregorios said calmly. "John has betrayed the council and allied with the enemy responsible for the attack on your home."

"You lie!" Reuben repeated.

Alter was looking unsure, and Eirene spoke to him. "Alter, use that mind of yours."

"Shut up, demon witch," Reuben snarled, but she ignored him, her attention fixed on Alter, who was staring back, his expression tortured.

"You were there with us during the memory hunt. Your strength alone provided a way for us to confront John, to begin the real process of avenging your family."

"Kill her, brother," Reuben urged.

Eirene put down her Tommy gun and extended her hands from her sides, palms up. "Are you a murderer, Alter? Or are you a hunter? Do you kill the easy targets, or the real ones?"

Reuben grabbed for Alter's gun, but he twisted away. "Brother, what they say is true."

"Shut up," Reuben snapped. "You've let the demons cloud your mind." He grabbed for Alter's rifle again.

Alter retreated. "No, you're wrong. We've been hunting John. It's confirmed. He's allied with another cui dashi."

"More lies. Why do you stand up for them?"

That surprised Sarah. She'd thought Alter had planned the assault on the mansion.

"Because I want to see the real enemy destroyed," Alter growled, letting the barrel of his rifle swing toward his brother. "You shouldn't have come today."

Reuben glared. "You're a fool. They're the real enemy! Sniper team, engage!"

Silence.

He actually turned to look up at the windows behind him.

Quentin stood in one of them. He waved.

"Did you kill them?" Alter exclaimed.

"Did you kill my security team?" Quentin called back.

"Four of them," Reuben said, sounding pleased with himself.

"Their blood is yours to repay," Quentin said in a cold voice. "I'll hold you to the debt."

"Come and collect it," Reuben spat.

"He'll have to wait," Gregorios said. He put down his rifle. "You think I'm your enemy. You've brought death and destruction upon this home to get to me. I reincorporated you, even though by all rights, that suit belongs to me. Come on then, boy. Here's your chance."

Reuben drew a long fighting knife and moved toward Gregorios, a wild look in his eyes.

Gregorios faced him, looking unconcerned, but one hand slipped to his back and gripped the handle of one of those steel tomahawks.

"Stop." Alter moved to block Reuben. "You're in the wrong, brother. I hate the demons too, but right now we have to work together against the cui dashi threat."

It sounded like Alter was switching sides again. Sarah wanted to slap him for being inconsistent, although she hoped he could make his brother see the truth.

"I'll restore the family honor. Get out of my way or share their fate," Reuben declared.

Alter shook his head. "Stand down. You've already made enough of a mess."

Reuben lunged with the knife.

Sarah cried out a warning, but Alter deflected the blade with the barrel of his rifle. He whipped the butt around, connecting with Reuben's wrist and tumbling the knife out of his hands.

Reuben closed and the two grappled over the rifle. Alter threw an elbow at Reuben's face, ripping the gun free, but Reuben returned with a chop that knocked the weapon to the ground.

The two brothers ignored the fallen weapon, lashing out with hands and feet, pounding on each other with enhanced speed and strength. Alter had proven himself an incredible warrior in the training sessions with Sarah, but his brother matched him, his expression locked in a snarl. Alter looked calm, almost regretful.

Gregorios took a nearby chair to watch, looking pleased with the turn of events, and gestured Eirene to sit beside him.

"I really should intervene," she protested.

"You're not their mother. You wanted Alter to prove himself. Let them figure it out."

The brothers fought across the court to the lip of the pool, near the diving board. Reuben snatched up a chair and clobbered Alter with it. He fell into the pool, and Reuben dove in after.

Sarah still wasn't sure if she wanted to punch Alter first or hug him for making the right choice. She approached the pool, but Gregorios waved her back.

"Don't complicate things. Brothers need to understand each other sometimes."

"You don't care about them at all, do you?"

"Not really."

Sarah couldn't tell if he was lying or not. She edged closer and peered into the water. The two brothers looked to be trying to strangle each other.

Then Alter's hands began to glow, burning with purple flames.

"Whoa!" Sarah cried. "How is that possible?"

Gregorios and Eirene joined her. In the water, Reuben's struggle changed. He broke away from Alter and swam wildly for the surface.

"That's unexpected," Gregorios said, watching Alter, who hovered near the bottom, staring at his hands in obvious horror.

Eirene clasped her hands together, her expression part exultant and part sad. She spoke so softly, Sarah barely heard. "I knew it."

Reuben hauled himself out of the pool and collapsed onto the patio nearby. Gregorios clobbered him with a small table when he tried to rise, then drew his handgun. "Don't move."

The hunter looked so shaken he didn't even try to fight back.

Alter surfaced a couple seconds later, looking ashen. Sarah reached to help him out of the pool but he slapped her hands away. "Stay away from me."

Sarah felt hurt by his harsh tone, but then even angrier. He was the one who had screwed up. He was lucky she didn't hit him with a pool chair.

"Demon," Reuben snarled as Alter climbed out of the pool. Reuben glared at Gregorios. "What have you done to him?"

"It wasn't my doing, but it explains a lot." He glanced to Eirene, whose eyes were glued to Alter. "It's proving to be an interesting morning."

Alter stood dripping, shaking. He looked at his brother and then down at his hands. His legs shook and he dropped to his knees.

Sarah could scarce believe it. How could Alter possess a nevra core like the facetakers? He was a hunter. Their clan never married facetakers. Somehow he possessed both gifts. Her eyes widened as she realized the truth.

Alter was cui dashi.

Eirene dropped to one knee beside Alter and placed a comforting hand on his shoulder. He cringed, but did not brush her away. She whispered, "Oh my sweet boy."

Understanding struck Sarah. Alter was Eirene's great-grandson.

Gregorios interrupted her wildly racing thoughts. "I should kill you, Reuben."

Reuben grinned. "If I don't report to my support team in the next two minutes, they'll trigger all the explosives we planted throughout the house. The blast will destroy everything."

"You demons may survive." He glanced at Sarah. "But she won't."

That roused Alter. "Call them off! You've caused enough damage already."

"You are dead to me," Reuben snarled.

Alter exclaimed, "I didn't ask for this. Do you think I wanted this?"

"You embraced the demons," Reuben said, his voice soft, but cold. "You tainted your soul."

Eirene said, "Don't be an idiot. It doesn't work that way, and you know it."

"He is proof of your abomination," Reuben shouted.

Quentin arrived from the north wing and Gregorios said, "Bring him one of their radio sets."

He retrieved one from the bound hunters that Gregorios and Eirene had subdued and handed it to Reuben.

"Call them off or I'll finish what we started the last time you tried to murder me." Gregorios spoke calmly, and that only made his threat more chilling.

Reuben reluctantly took the earpiece. "Team Omega, this is Beta One. Initiate stand-down."

"How many are outside?" Gregorios asked.

"More than enough. Tell me, demon. How did you corrupt my brother?"

"I told you. I did nothing. He's the same as when he left you."

Reuben shouted, "He's tainted! And he will be cleansed, just like the rest of you."

Alter, who had been huddled on the patio, head down, looked up sharply. "Wait a minute. Did you say your call sign was Beta One?"

"If you're still my brother, you will accept your fate," Reuben said, his gaze intense.

"He called in a mortar strike!" Alter surged to his feet just as a distant whistling sound grew overhead.

Gregorios shouted, "Take cover!"

Quentin tackled Sarah into the pool just before the world erupted into flame and thunder. She barely closed her mouth before plunging into the water.

A shock-wave rippled across the surface just above her head, shredding the waves they'd created. Fire boiled the air, followed by billowing smoke that concealed everything and blanketed a suddenly silent world.

The sight filled her with new terror. She was getting really tired of that feeling.

Sarah followed Quentin to the surface, and the two of them climbed out of the pool into devastation. The mortar had struck the patio right where Gregorios had been standing, creating a gaping crater and destroying the beautiful stonework.

Dirt and broken tiles had sprayed everywhere, shattering windows and scoring the walls of the wings on both side. She saw no sign of the others through the haze hanging over the scene like a funeral shroud. Flaming debris still rained down around her, and she shrieked when a burning piece of chair cushion settled onto her shoulder.

"Get under cover!" Quentin pushed Sarah toward the south wing and she started running in that direction, but then halted.

"Tomas!"

Coughing from the smoke, she raced around the gaping blast hole. She caught sight of Gregorios crawling toward the north wing. His face and hands were bloody, and debris stood out from his bulletproof vest. One leg ended just below the knee in a bloody stump that was leaving a thick crimson trail behind. He looked furious and his eyes glowed with purple fire.

Sarah gagged, torn between the need to find Tomas and to help

Gregorios. Then Quentin appeared through the smoke at Gregorios' side and bent over him.

Sarah left them and ran to find Tomas. The blast had tumbled him out of his chair, and debris had slashed his torso in multiple places. He struggled weakly, clawing at the ground, his face a mask of pain.

He was alive! She kissed him fiercely. "I've got you."

Eirene arrived just as she reached for Tomas' wrists. Eirene looked battered, her clothing covered with dirt, and blood ran down the side of her face.

"You should be helping Gregorios," Sarah protested as Eirene grabbed Tomas' legs.

"Quentin's got him." Eirene cast a rather nervous glance in that direction, even though they were lost in the smoke. She leaned a little closer and added softly, "He's not happy I urged restraint with those hunters. Reuben's sealed his fate, I'm afraid."

He'd called in a mortar strike on them. To Sarah, that justified whatever response Gregorios deemed necessary.

She didn't really care. All she wanted was a quiet place to care for Tomas. She gripped him under the shoulders and together they hoisted him into the air and moved toward the north wing.

The whistling began again, and they broke into a run as Sarah's fear flared into near-panic. They only needed a few more seconds to reach safety. It couldn't all end like this.

The second mortar landed in the pool. The explosion geysered water above the roof, and a brutal wave slammed them so hard, Sarah almost lost her grip. She nearly burst into hysterical laughter when she noticed the spray had cleansed Eirene's face.

"Fortuna be praised, that was a lucky strike," Eirene said, grinning wildly as she led the way through the shattered doorway of the north wing. As they retreated down the hall, Eirene cocked her head a bit, listening. Only then did Sarah realize she'd lost her earpiece.

"The hunters are gone," Eirene said. "Quentin and Gregorios are in the south wing and spotted them escaping."

"Do you think they'll regroup and attack again?" Sarah asked as they moved far down the hall, away from the broken windows.

"No. Reinforcements will be here any minute. If they linger, they'll be taken."

Sarah wasn't sure whether she wanted them to get away. Part of her wanted the enforcers to intercept them, but she didn't want any more killing.

When they gently lay Tomas down, Eirene left to check on Gregorios, but Sarah dropped to her knees beside Tomas. His skin was cold, but she wasn't sure if it was due to the water or his injuries. He was no longer conscious and it took several terrifying seconds to find his weak pulse.

He lived, but just barely. The shrapnel wounds didn't look severe, but the sight of so much blood brought back memories of those terrifying moments after Mai Luan had stabbed him. He'd nearly died, and now she felt that same helpless panic returning.

Eirene returned a few minutes later. "Help is on the way. The staff is coming."

When she rose to leave again, Sarah asked, "Where are you going?"

"To speak with Alter."

51

In my youth, my strength was that of a berserker of the lesser tribes. Through Baladeva's instruction, I now rival the great Hercules, and my strength is as the blizzards or the howling tempest, for I have eclipsed mortal man. My most hated enemies will fall in mortal combat and honor my legend with the glory of their broken excellence. I will tear down every stone they have built and throw down the power of Caesar.

Come, mighty enemies, and our battles repeated will shake the roots of history.

~SPARTACUS

EIRENE FOUND Alter in the main salon, sitting on the edge of an expensive leather couch. He leaned forward, face in his hands, oblivious to the water and mud dripping onto the furniture.

She was surprised to see Doctor Sofia seated beside him, one comforting hand on his shoulder. Eirene hadn't realized Sofia was in the mansion at all. She hadn't joined them earlier in the art gallery. Maybe she'd been tending a patient.

Either way, Eirene was happy to see someone with Alter. She could easily read the despair in his stricken expression. Despair radiated off of him, and Eirene was glad Sofia had thought to check on him. He might have killed himself had she waited.

"I'm a demon," Alter spat when Eirene joined them.

"Do you really think so?" She settled onto the couch on the opposite side of Alter.

Doctor Sofia rose and said, "Alter, remember you are among friends. The path through trials will eventually turn to happier moments." She met Eirene's gaze and added, "I will take my leave now that you are here."

Alter glanced after her, his expression thoughtful. Whatever the doctor had said to him had helped pull him back from the brink, but he was still clearly in so much pain. Eirene placed a gentle hand on his shoulder.

He shrugged it off. "I pledged my life to destroying the cui dashi and now I've become one of them."

"You've discovered a new aspect of yourself, but that doesn't define you."

She'd seen hints, had suspected the truth, but part of her had feared what she'd find if she probed further. Alter struggled just maintaining close proximity to facetakers. To find he actually possessed the rare cui dashi powers must have shaken his world to its deepest foundation.

"It's your fault!" He rose and paced away. "You brought this curse on my family."

"You're right."

He stopped, clearly surprised that she agreed, so she continued. "I didn't expect anything like this to happen. You've seen with my children how hard it is to produce offspring with an active nevra core, and that's with two facetakers trying to make it work. I never even considered one of your family inheriting it. Chances of producing a cui dashi heir between my blood and that of your family were so slim as to be laughable."

"I'm not laughing," he growled.

"Perhaps it's not all bad."

"How can you say that? My family will disown me. They'll kill me to purge the stain from our blood."

"Their bad choices don't need to define you. You think *me* evil, worthy of death?"

"I don't know what to think."

"Then let your actions define you, not your fears."

She drew him back to the sofa. "Never before have we had a chance to explore the cui dashi power. Always they were the enemy, a terrible force that had to be stopped before they could destroy everything we hoped to preserve in the world."

"Like I said, I cannot live." He sank back on the couch, despairing.

She knuckled him on the head. "You're not listening. Stop wallowing in self-pity. You must study your gift, learn what you can do. We may need all your strength to stop Paul. He's the one who attacked your family, and right now you're the one best positioned to avenge them."

That finally broke through to his rational self. Eirene allowed herself to relax just a little. The powers he possessed were usually terrifying, but he was family. Eirene draped an arm around his sagging shoulders and pulled him close. He leaned against her, accepting the comfort she longed to give him. He was her great-grandson, and she loved him more than she was usually allowed to show.

Cui dashi had always turned evil, but Alter would not. Together, they'd find a way to set things right.

Sarah appeared in the doorway. Eirene was surprised to see her so soon, but grateful she had come. Her soothing presence could build upon the groundwork she and Sofia had laid.

"Consider what I said. I have to check on Gregorios. He always gets cranky when he loses a limb."

52

This rune warrior is a different creature than any heretofore encountered. The runes of Constantinople proved no match for the enhancements of my Janissaries, but Vlad and his ciphers threaten even their superiority. He impales with impunity, breaking enhancements and overwhelming their valiant souls. Rune warrior or no, I will destroy him and shatter his ciphers. I am in my wrath and the fullness of my second life, and I will see him fall.

~MEHMED THE CONQUEROR, 1462

SARAH APPROACHED ALTER HESITANTLY, not sure how to treat him. Eirene had given her a reassuring smile before she left, but Sarah would have preferred she stay.

Part of her wanted to beat Alter with the nearby wrought-iron lamp for betraying Tomas. But he had fought Reuben, turned against his own family to help them. That made it hard to hate him.

Tomas had regained consciousness long enough to explain some of what happened. It might not have been Alter who pulled the trigger, but Alter's actions prevented Tomas from stopping Reuben. Medical staff had rushed Tomas to the hospital wing, and she hadn't wanted to sit in the cold waiting room. She'd needed to do something.

The sight of Alter sagging on the couch, clearly horrified by the revelation that he was cui dashi, quelled most of Sarah's wrath. The only cui dashi she had interacted with were Mai Luan and Paul, and they were both super-freak madmen. How would she take it if she learned she possessed the same powers?

Worse, Alter was a hunter. His entire life, he'd been taught that cui dashi were evil incarnate, worthy of nothing but death. That would be like Sarah telling her protestant parents she was really spawn of the devil.

Alter looked to be beating himself up enough for the both of them at the moment, so she didn't yell at him. She'd save it for later. Instead, she sat next to him.

"This was the craziest morning I've ever had."

He didn't laugh, but faced her, expression agonized. "I am sorry. I let myself be swayed by my brother, but I should have known better. I chose wrongly."

"You did," she agreed.

His shoulders sagged and he looked down at his hands.

She took them in hers. "But you realized your mistake and fought to protect us. For that, I thank you."

"I am unworthy of thanks."

"Maybe, but I'll decide who to thank, thank you very much."

That finally triggered the hint of a smile. "How is Tomas?"

"He'll live. And maybe he'll learn not to change bodies again."

Now that the initial terror was past, her overwhelming fear for his safety had transitioned to annoyance. If he hadn't been so stupid and loaned his body to Carl, he might have avoided those injuries.

"I am glad."

"You're not off the hook though. I need my rune made permanent."

"Now's not a good time."

"You're wrong. Now's the best time. We need to find Paul and end this before Reuben returns or . . . something else. I feel this terrifying certainty that we need to move fast or worse things will happen."

"I'm a demon. I might hurt you."

"You are who you've always been, and I know you. You'd never hurt me."

Alter took a deep breath and gazed at her for a long moment. His eyes were red-rimmed and his face looked aged, exhausted.

"All right," he said, rubbing his face vigorously as if to scrape away all the baggage from the morning.

Sarah was glad he decided to help. She needed the rune, and he needed something to focus on besides his despair, the fight with his brother, and the crazy revelation that he was not who he thought he was.

Instead of asking for one of the special knives from her runesmith kit to mark the rune on her thigh he said, "I need some paper."

"But we've already marked it."

"We'll deal with that rune in a minute," he said, sounding more like himself. "Stop arguing for once, Sarah, and get me some paper."

It took a few minutes. All available staff were busy tending the injured or helping to clean up. Enforcement teams were sweeping the building, disarming and removing the explosives that the hunters had planted.

Sarah couldn't imagine why Reuben hadn't triggered them, but she was grateful. It was a sign of how crazy the morning had been that the thought of explosives scattered around the building barely fazed her.

Alter took the paper and pen to a nearby table and began to draw a rune. From the first strokes, Sarah realized it was one she had never seen before. Why then did it feel familiar?

As the complex shape progressed, she began to guess some of the lines before he drew them. That rune called to her as if it was already bonded to her soul. She leaned over the table, barely restraining the urge to snatch the paper from Alter until he finished it.

"What is this?" she breathed, staring in wonder at the rune that burned into her mind as she gazed upon it.

"This is the rune warrior symbol. I received it last night."

"It's amazing." Sarah traced the lines with a finger, even though she had already memorized it. It was a flowing, graceful design, centered on a curious symbol that gave the impression of two open hands wrapping each other in a yin yang circle.

There was power there, and Sarah concentrated over it, but couldn't quite place it. She recognized a series of Chinese pictograms that combined to tie in elements of strength, honor and, she was startled to see, history. The Egyptian ankh symbol of life linked those together, with other symbols worked into the outer edges of the design.

It was one of the most beautiful things she had ever seen.

She said softly, "Somehow I know this rune. Where have we seen this before?"

"You've never seen this one, not complete." Alter was watching her closely, his expression guarded. "It's not often seen, and it's never used."

"Why not? This rune is so powerful." She felt that power radiating off of it in near-tangible waves. She was surprised she couldn't see it, like shimmering heat floating above the rune.

"It doesn't work for anyone with regular rounon powers. Some runes are like that, this one most of all. This is the symbol of the rune warriors and only they can bond to it."

"It feels so right though, doesn't it?"

He shrugged. "Not to me."

"How do rune warriors use it?"

Alter hesitated, looking worried. "Sarah, don't try it."

"Why not?" Looking away from the rune was difficult.

"Because there's no going back." He took her hands, then dropped them, glaring at his hands in disgust. "Sarah, I drew too near the facetakers, even though I felt the danger, and look what happened to me."

"What are you talking about?"

"I felt them, Sarah." He looked anguished. "When I helped them run the machines, I felt their nevron touching me, melding with my soul through my rounon. What if . . . What if I hadn't done that? I might not have become the devil I am now."

Sarah frowned. "Alter, I don't think it works that way."

"But what if it did?" he exclaimed. "Sarah, I'm worried you might be able to bond the rune warrior mark."

"That would be amazing."

"No! It would change you." When he took her hands again, his were shaking. "Sarah, if you walk away from this rune, maybe you won't activate any rounon gift. I don't want you getting hurt."

"That's why I have to try it. If I really can activate some kind of rounon power, it'll make me stronger, help me fight Paul."

"It could destroy your soul," Alter whispered. He dropped his gaze, but his expression made it clear he wanted to add, "like mine."

Sarah touched his cheek, drawing his gaze back to her. "Alter, you are who you've always been. You're a hunter, a man of honor, and you will help us defeat the ones who hurt your family."

When he looked like he wanted to argue, she added, "And that rune calls to me. Alter, if I can do it, I want to. I need to grow, to become the most I can be. That's the only way I can truly know myself, and the only hope I have for surviving whatever evil Paul has planned for me."

"I don't think it's a good idea."

"Do you really want me to turn away from who I could be?"

"I don't want your soul spoiled."

She shook her head. "Alter, I don't have your depth of learning, but I know that a soul is spoiled only if one gives in to evil. You'd never do that, and I don't intend to either." She gave him an encouraging smile. "Now show me how to try out this rune."

Even though he looked like he wanted to argue further, he sighed. "Just promise me you won't change."

"I promise." Bonding to that rune would change some things, but she doubted it would change her heart or her goals.

Alter' warned, "There's no halfway about this rune. I have to cut it into your skin. It can only be activated by blood and steel. There are no temporary rune warriors."

"Come on, then." She led him to her suite, into her sitting room, and produced her runesmith kit. He selected a slender blade a little longer than the one he'd used to mark her last enhancement.

"You have to tell me where to inscribe it," he said.

"It only works in one place, doesn't it?"

He nodded. "If you choose wrong, it's a sign that you're not meant to be a rune warrior."

Or it was one last hurdle he was trying to place in her path. It didn't matter. She knew where the rune needed to go.

"Mark it in the center of my lower back," she said, and he didn't quite hide his disappointment. She'd chosen correctly.

She stripped off her bulletproof vest and pulled up the back of her soggy shirt. Alter crouched behind her, with one steadying hand on her hip. As soon as he began to mark the rune, she felt it, like a trickle of ice along her skin.

She shivered. "What are you doing?"

"Don't move," he ordered.

"But I feel it already."

He didn't respond, but the icy sensation continued, spreading across her lower back. She felt every mark of the blade, felt the image taking shape on her back with startling clarity.

She felt no pain, but the chill seeping into her skin from those marks spread through her until her teeth actually chattered. She started to wonder if she'd made a wise choice.

When he finished, he pulled her right hand back, pressing it over the mark. "There's less blood than I expected."

"You marked every line. I felt it. Now what do I do?"

Alter dropped his hand and spoke, his voice soft, but intense. "Focus on the rune, Sarah. Feel it, and will it to life."

"How?"

"It's something I cannot teach you. You have to do it alone."

Sarah pressed her hand against the rune and closed her eyes. She concentrated, willing something to happen, although she wasn't sure what. She waited breathlessly for several seconds and began to fear it wouldn't work.

She needed it to! She needed the strength that rune promised. She wanted it to work with the same desperation she'd felt while marking that healing rune for Tomas the day he'd almost died.

As the intensity of that need filled her, her heartbeat began to accelerate, and she felt a rush of adrenaline. The chill of the rune drew back to the marks on her skin, leaving the rest of her body feeling flushed with heat. The lines of the rune seemed to freeze into her back and into her hand, even while heat coursed through the rest of her, as if she were standing in front of a blast furnace.

Then the cold shattered, like shards of ice skittering along her skin, radiating out to every extremity. The heat that had been burning her up compressed in an instant, as if sucking into the rune, and for a second the mark blazed against her skin. It drew into it all her strength, and she sagged where she stood, nearly swooning.

"Sarah?" Alter's voice reached her from a great distance, but she couldn't open her eyes. She was so very tired.

Then her strength returned in a rush, magnified tenfold.

Sarah rose to her toes with a gasp, eyes wide with wonder as every muscle quivered with vibrant energy. The rune blazed on her back with intense white light, filling the room with its glow.

As the light began to fade, she spun to Alter, who was rising, his expression a mixture of wonder and despair.

"It worked!" She hugged him until he grunted from the pressure.

She laughed and twirled around the room, unable to stand still with so much energy burning through her limbs. "This is amazing. I really did it. I'm a rune warrior."

Her good humor finally lifted the scowl from his face. "I'm glad you're so happy."

"How could I not be?"

"Now that you've activated your rounon, you can create your own runes. For most of us, we need a few days or weeks before we're consistent at activating runes, but I'm thinking it won't take so long for you."

"I'm going to test it right now." She snatched a little knife from the runesmith kit and started unbuckling her belt to get at her temporary rune. Alter stood watching her, his expression startled.

She snapped, "Hey, look away. This isn't a peep show."

A little disappointed, he turned. She was tempted to order him out of the room, but she didn't want to waste another second.

Pulling the front of her pants down, she dropped into a chair and extended her leg. She studied her rune before beginning to mark it permanently. It still took her breath away, but the feeling of not-quite-completeness tugged at her.

All of a sudden, she knew what the rune needed.

With swift, sure strokes, she marked the rune into her thigh. The razor-sharp blade sliced her skin like butter, but she felt no pain, only eagerness as she included the central symbol from her rune warrior symbol around the heart of the rune.

"Hey, what are you doing?" Alter had turned and was watching her.

"Turn!"

"But, Sarah."

"I told you not to look. Turn, or get out."

He turned away, and Sarah completed her work. With trembling fingers, she placed her hands over the newly-completed rune and concentrated, willing it to life.

Immediately, a rush of heat rolled through her from her rune warrior mark and connected with a well of strength in her heart that she'd never felt before.

It was as if a door in her soul had opened, a door to a fountain of blazing energy. That strength poured out and flowed through her hands and into the new rune, encircling and powering it.

The rune activated, bonding to her soul, and this time she felt it link back to that new well of strength in her heart. That was the power of her rounon, fueling the rune and being fueled in turn.

The rune blazed against her skin and she leaped to her feet. Barely remembering to buckle her pants, she pulled Alter around and hugged him again, although not quite as hard.

"It worked! I bonded the rune. This is amazing."

Laughing, she spun with him, and the two of them danced across the room. His glum expression turned happy and he grinned with her. They finally stopped near the window and rested together. "Oh, Alter. Thank you."

He said nothing, but leaned closer, his arms tightening around her waist. They were already standing close together, all but embracing. As he leaned in close, she was still riding the exultant wave of joy, filled with vibrant life and the wonder of the birth of that amazing new part of herself that she still barely comprehended.

She hesitated a second too long before retreating.

Their lips touched, then he pressed against her hungrily. He wasn't a very good kisser, but made up for it with enthusiasm.

Sarah kissed him back. Just once. She decided she owed him that much.

Alter seemed ready to kiss her all day, but she broke away and gently disentangled from his embrace. "That's more than enough, Alter."

He let her go reluctantly, grinning like a fool.

If he ever breathed a word about that kiss to anyone, Tomas was going to kill her.

Her bonding with the rune on her thigh progressed to another level and Sarah's senses expanded outward in a rush. She *felt* Alter standing nearby, even when she closed her eyes. She felt the power of his soul like a light shining in her mind.

"What is it?" Alter asked.

She held up a hand to forestall the question and turned toward the distant medical wing. When she focused in that direction, it was like her thoughts slipped through the distance, honing in on another pair of souls that shone in her mind like beacons.

With a start, she realized she was feeling Gregorios and Eirene.

"I think I can feel them," she whispered.

"Who?"

"The facetakers. Come on!"

53

Why did I come to Constantinople, raise and finance a force of over seven hundred fighting men, and embrace a cause that to the world must seem hopeless? For the advantage of the Christian faith and for the honour of the world, of course.

Mehmed claims the enhancements of his Janissaries are blessed by Allah, but our faith in the one and only true God cannot leave such claims unanswered. Let him break his army against these mighty walls, and our victory shall proclaim to all the world that enhancements of pure, Christian souls can never be vanquished.

~GIOVANNI GIUSTINIANI LONGO OF GENOA, WHO
PLAYED A CRITICAL ROLE IN THE DEFENSE OF
CONSTANTINOPLE, SHORTLY BEFORE ITS FALL AND HIS
FATAL WOUND, 1453

GREGORIOS CALLED to order the meeting in the Suntara conference room. He wore a muscular body with almost as many runes as his favorite battle suit. When that upstart Reuben had escaped Quentin's mansion, he had freed the two squads of his men they had subdued earlier. He had not found the three snipers Quentin had neutralized on the second floor. This body came from one of them.

Tomas, who stood just off Gregorios' right shoulder, wore another.

Everyone was already seated around the council table in the Suntara headquarters. Harriett had arrived last, pushing a catering cart with eight of her best pies. Two pieces sat on a plate in front of Gregorios, but he hadn't touched them yet.

The rest of the decimated council had joined him, along with Eirene and their children. Sarah, Alter, and Quentin had been invited, although Gregorios had wanted to force Alter to wear chains. Eirene had talked him out of the idea, but he still thought it would have best driven home the point.

Paul had irritated him with his games and shadowy plots, but now Gregorios was well and truly angry. He didn't get there often and was really looking forward to meeting Paul in person and beating out his frustration on the man's face.

"Let's start with a review of this morning's insanity," Gregorios said.

Quentin spoke first. "Reuben and the hunters made a clean escape after that mortar barrage. We suspect they're still in the city."

"Find them and keep an eye on them. I have plans for Reuben."

As he spoke, he watched Alter's reaction. The young hunter looked uncomfortable, but said nothing. He had protested Gregorios and Tomas using hunter bodies, but Gregorios had told him to deal with it. Either he was part of the team, or he could leave. No more hesitation.

Tomas spoke next, his voice carefully neutral. "The other problem is that Carl's missing. Never showed up for his date last night. Hasn't reported in today."

"We're suspecting foul play," Quentin added.

Gregorios frowned. "That's terrible timing. It has to be related to ongoing operations."

"That's the assumption," Quentin agreed.

Sarah looked up from where she'd been focusing on her pie and shared a long look with Tomas. It couldn't be coincidence that the one person now missing was the man wearing Tomas' body.

They needed to find that suit. Sarah wasn't going to be happy dealing so soon with Tomas' next life, but bodies were transitory. It was a truth she'd have to get used to, but Gregorios had thought she'd have more time to understand it.

Quentin added, "We've gone to Alert Two. No one's going to be an easy target again."

"Good. Is Yurak in position?"

Francesca spoke. "Ready and awaiting orders."

She wore a pink cotton sun-dress that was completely incongruous with the serious nature of the meeting. She sat directly across from Alter and despite the glum, martyred look he had adopted since learning about his cui dashi powers, he couldn't help but look.

Gregorios decided it might be a good thing she was doing, trying to give Alter something else to focus on than his despair. He hoped she didn't push too hard and drive the boy away. As much as he'd annoyed Gregorios by siding with his brother temporarily, they needed Alter more than ever.

"Can someone tell me who Yurak is?" Sarah asked.

"Yurak International," Harriett said with pride. "Our family's private army."

"I thought the enforcers were your army," Sarah said.

Tomas said, "The enforcers are tied to Suntara. For the moment that means about the same thing, but historically, Shahrokh and other council members held more sway over enforcer duties, and loyalties."

Francesca piped in. "So mom and dad came up with the brilliant idea of giving their kids something useful to do."

Sarah looked surprised. "You enlisted your children in an army?"

Alter muttered something that might have been "Abomination" but Gregorios wasn't close enough to hear.

"We had a lot of children over the years," Eirene explained. "And we made sure they did well."

Gregorios added, "Avoided the plagues, famine, things like that. That many kids started adding up after a few centuries. Talk about bills."

Eirene gave him a long-suffering look. "There were times when we needed a dedicated force trained to deal with heka threats that wasn't limited to some of the politics or questions of loyalty that occasionally complicated working with enforcer teams."

"So you started your own army?" Sarah asked. She looked intrigued by the idea.

Eirene explained. "They're officially mercenaries. World leaders get jittery when large standing armies loiter nearby, and the small countries we'd acquired didn't really want to attract that much military attention."

"Small countries?" Sarah was starting to look like she wasn't sure she wanted to ask any more questions.

Gregorios didn't want to get totally sidetracked. "Irrelevant for the moment. Our children became a well-respected fighting force and have participated in most of the major conflicts through the last thousand years or so. The core units have always been enhanced, picked from our confirmed descendants."

"How many mercenaries are we talking about?" Sarah asked.

Harriett answered. "We have three divisions operating in different world theaters. Each is independent and self-sufficient, made up of ten thousand-man regiments. Some are fighters, others heavy cavalry, naval, or air corps. Then we have the medical staff, logistics, communications, and other functions. First Division is made up of enhanced troops with custom weapons systems to deal with the unique nature of heka threats. They're the units we're talking about today."

"How come no one knows about them?" Sarah asked.

Gregorios said, "They do. A big part of what Bastien's admin teams do is manage international requests for troop services."

"So you're bringing ten thousand troops to Rome?" Sarah asked.

Harriett shook her head. "We almost never deploy all of them at once. We'll have on hand the forces, tech, and hardware we need to roll against whatever threat is deemed viable."

"Harriett leads from the front," Francesca said, saluting her sister. "You should see some of the moves she throws down on those heka."

"Like what?" Sarah asked.

"She can be very persuasive. Doesn't even have to fire a shot sometimes."

"How?"

Gregorios said, "These are all good questions, but we're getting distracted."

"But—" Sarah protested.

"Later. Right now, let's deal with Jerusalem. Put Melek on."

Anaru entered with a wireless conference phone. He set it down and pushed a button.

"Melek, are you there?" Gregorios called.

"I am." Melek sounded weaker than Gregorios had ever heard. He felt no pity.

"You invoked blood feud on the wrong people, Melek," Gregorios started without preamble. "I've tried to work with you in good faith, but your boys killed some of our people. You've started a war, and you're going to regret that choice."

"I did not authorize the strike. When Reuben reports, I'll call you to discuss the terms."

"We're beyond discussion. I've sent you the soulmasks of three of the hunters caught trying to murder us. When the debt is resolved to my satisfaction, we can discuss restoring them."

"What of Alter?" Melek asked through a coughing fit.

"I'm here, father," Alter called.

Gregorios said, "He's fine, but don't trifle with me, Melek. Your boy Reuben owes me, or a lot of people are going to die."

Melek didn't speak for several seconds. "I will order him to stand down if you share the information you've gathered on who you believe was responsible for the attack on my family."

"Your son represents the clan. Your involvement ends there until I call on you."

"You have three days to resolve this," Melek said, his voice stronger. "After that, if I hear nothing, I must assume you're lying."

Gregorios bit back an angry retort. Melek had opened the door to resolving the conflict without massive blood loss. Gregorios could allow him a little posturing to preserve his image. At least for the time being.

So he only said, "Don't do anything stupid. We'll be in touch."

At a gesture from him, Anaru punched off the phone with a thick finger.

"That went about as well as we could've hoped," Eirene said.

"It's a start," he agreed. Then he turned to Alter. "Will Reuben stand down?"

"No."

"I didn't think so. We stay at Alert Two. If he's as stupid as he is rash, he's going to cause the death of a lot of good men."

Alter looked like he wanted to argue, but only added, "Why didn't you tell my father?"

"It wasn't a good time."

He was not planning to tell Melek anything about Alter's condition. Had he mentioned it, any chance of securing peace with the hunters would die a grisly death.

Melek would assume Gregorios had somehow corrupted his son. When he heard the truth from Reuben, he'd probably react that way, but Gregorios hoped Melek would use his head for once.

He respected Melek more than any other hunter since Ronen. Gregorios didn't want to kill hunters but if Melek didn't control his people, that's exactly what was going to happen.

They needed a break and they needed it now. So he turned to Sarah.

"Now tell me about your super power."

Sarah flushed. "It's not a super power."

"I'm in charge. I'll call it what I want."

She actually smiled. Good. He needed her relaxed.

"Show us your fancy new rune." When she hesitated, a little flush creeping up her cheeks, he added, "The one on your back. We've seen the other one."

The rune warrior symbol was unusual and beautifully inscribed, flowing across her lower back in unique lines that suggested great power.

"She is confirmed rune warrior," Alter said, sounding like he wasn't convinced her success was a good idea.

At least he wouldn't feel obliged to report her to his family, not with his own problems weighing so heavily on his mind. Gregorios didn't need the hunters deciding to make Sarah a new target.

Harriett and Francesca both jumped up and gave Sarah warm hugs, and the others added their congratulations. She'd already shared the news with Tomas, and he was happy to see the two looked like they were working through whatever issues they'd been having.

Harald nodded to himself over his laptop. "First confirmed rune warrior since Joan."

"She was such a dear," Zuri said, and Eirene nodded.

Gregorios said, "Sarah, we'll share what we know about rune warrior ciphers after the meeting. I need you up to speed as quickly as possible."

She grinned. "Looking forward to it."

Bastien said, "I will take care of it. I have the most experience with rune warriors."

"Agreed," Gregorios said, even though Eirene looked like she wanted to argue the point. "Schedule some training ASAP."

"I swear it will be done." Bastien loved quoting that line from *The Princess Bride*.

"So how are you able to locate facetakers at a distance?" Gregorios asked. "That's a unique skill."

"I made my new rune permanent." She patted her thigh.

"She changed it," Alter muttered.

"Just a little," she admitted.

"You will show us the new rune, yes?" Bastien asked with a smile.

"Sure," Sarah said without hesitation, but instead of showing off her shapely leg, she extracted a piece of paper from a pocket. Bastien concealed his disappointment as he took the paper from her. Others crowded in to look.

Sarah explained, "It's mostly the same. I just added the central rune warrior mark around its core design."

"Beautiful," Eirene breathed when the paper made it to her. "You have a rare talent, my dear, even for rune warriors."

"With that change, you set off a locater beacon in your head?" Gregorios asked.

"Sort of." Sarah closed her eyes and pointed to each of the facetakers in the room, then Alter. "This close, your nevra cores are like lanterns in my mind. I can tell where each of you are, and when I focus, the other three facetakers in the building draw my thoughts like lights in a dark room."

"She is correct. There are three others in the building," Bastien said.

"How far can you sense?" Eirene asked, looking fascinated by Sarah's newfound ability.

Gregorios hoped they'd be able to use it, but the new power was a bit unsettling. Harald and Zuri both looked uneasy. If their enemies learned of the rune, could they replicate it?

He wasn't sure they could use the marks from that master rune since they hadn't seen it, but perhaps they could. He hated that Alter knew about it, but Gregorios doubted the boy would pass along any secrets to his family any time soon.

Sarah shrugged. "I'm still getting used to it. I didn't feel Suntara from Quentin's, and didn't get a solid sense of how many were here until just a few blocks out."

Tomas said, "We can work with that. The Tenth has developed a solid lead across town. We've confirmed heka presence and believe the location contains at least part of the cell we've been hunting. While the legion gears up and preps for action, you and I can take a drive near the suspect position and see if you sense anyone in there."

"Good idea," Gregorios said. "It's past time we drop in for a visit. I want that cell stomped out."

It took only a few minutes to lay the plan. They decided to send a forward strike team with Tomas and Sarah on their scouting mission. Gregorios and Eirene would lead the main assault force, with Alter in tow and Anaru in charge of the Tenth.

Quentin would oversee communications from Suntara and manage the coordination of Yurak with Harriett and Francesca in the event Sarah sensed Paul on site and the assault team required more firepower.

Thirty minutes later, Gregorios sat in the front seat of a large truck filled with enforcers kitted for battle. He tapped his earpiece to open the connection to the secure com-link they all shared.

"This is it, men."

"And women," Eirene interjected.

"We're going in hard," he continued. "Expect resistance and enhancements. We hit them with severe prejudice. John may be on-site. I want him alive. Terminate the rest."

He allowed himself a grim smile.

54

My ciphers cannot be used solely for the purpose of war, regardless of the import such endeavors demand. War alone cannot save my nation, and thus I worked ciphers into the walls of the Gelati Academy to inspire the minds and illuminate the senses.

With this subtle encouragement, I will make the academy a second Jerusalem of all the East for learning of all that is of value, for the teaching of knowledge—a second Athens, far exceeding the first in divine law, a canon for all ecclesiastical splendors.

~KING DAVID IV OF GEORGIA, KNOWN AS DAVID THE
BUILDER AND SWORD OF THE MESSIAH, RUNE WARRIOR

"IN THERE." Sarah pointed.

She sat in the front seat of a cramped sedan. Tomas drove, and two enforcers had squeezed into the rear. Sarah had expected them to scout the enemy location in one of the big SUVs owned by the council, complete with tinted windows. Or maybe a panel van. Instead, Tomas chose the little car.

"It's completely invisible," he had explained. "People notice the big vehicles in Rome, and the enemy is surely on the lookout for panel vans that hang around too long. This is the kind of car tourists rent. In Rome, nothing is more invisible than a tourist."

The only problem was that they didn't look like tourists. The men had stashed their vests and heavy weapons in the little trunk, but that helped only a little.

"Are you sure?" Tomas asked, scanning the building across the street with a pair of small binoculars.

"I'm sure." They had passed the location three times as she triangulated her newly discovered facetaker-locating senses.

A facetaker was in that long, brick building on the very edge of a gigantic cemetery on the eastern edge of Rome. They had circled the entire cemetery once and Sarah felt sure she had the right place.

"Still only one?" Tomas asked.

She nodded and he shrugged. "Let's hope it's John."

The hunter body altered his voice, pitching his words a little lower than normal, as if he was perpetually angry. Twice she'd caught herself staring and quickly looked away.

He stood about the same height, with military-short black hair. The head was a little too wide, stretching his features a bit in a way that made her want to tug at his nose. Strangers wouldn't notice, but his features were dear to her, and she hated to see them altered. She had plenty of experience dealing with people wearing different bodies, but this time it affected her more.

Sarah decided to focus on the fact that he was alive and healthy. They'd find Carl and get Tomas' body back. Then they'd make up for that last argument, and leave that unhappy episode behind forever.

She felt secretly relieved they hadn't tracked down Paul yet. She wanted time to explore her new abilities, to learn how to develop ciphers. She needed every advantage before facing Paul again. A single facetaker, supported by a heka cell, was a scenario Tomas and his forces could handle.

The building looked like a church. An unremarkable, rather run-down church. It did have a marble-columned entryway, but the double doors of its wide portico stood closed, and shutters blocked the second-story windows, sealing the old church from the world.

The property ran to the wall of the huge cemetery, filled with close-packed graves. Tall cedars lined the wall, like sentinels placed to prevent all those spirits from escaping, and shaded the left side of the building. The church huddled on its lot like a wary relic of an older world.

A square, brick tower near the rear of the building rose four stories, its large clock the only indication it wasn't a watchtower. An iron fence with a closed gate surrounded everything but the parking lot, forming the final line of defense against intrusion.

A few cars sat in the parking lot in front of the building, but no one had entered or exited in the ten minutes since they had started monitoring it.

Tomas said, "All right. Call in the cavalry."

Domenico began speaking in rapid Italian into the radio.

"So are we just going to walk in?" Sarah asked, licking suddenly dry lips.

"More of a run than a walk," Tomas said.

They monitored the building for ten more minutes, waiting for reinforcements to arrive. Sarah glanced at Tomas, but looked away. She tried not to think about her growing fear that they wouldn't recover the real Tomas and he'd be forced to live in another body.

It didn't matter that the body he had just loaned to Carl was not his original one, it was the one he called home. He had helped her regain her body from Alterego, so she would do everything she could to help him now.

A large, black truck with "Polizia" stenciled on the back, passed them and swerved into the parking lot of the church. Two other trucks followed close behind. The convoy skidded to a halt just outside the main doors, and black-clad enforcers boiled out. Some of them headed for the main doors. Others shattered the lock on the iron gate and rushed around the building.

Tomas gunned the engine and drove their little sedan across the street to join the assault team. As he and the enforcers grabbed up their weapons and gear, Sarah joined Gregorios and Eirene.

Gregorios gave her a warm smile. "Let's go say hello, shall we?"

55

Talbot's arrogance knows no bounds. I salute the Earl for his previous victories, but he grew to rely too heavily upon the strength of his runes to the discounting of the value of his troops. Not even the vaunted enforcers charge a fortified camp, replete with so many cannon, with such paltry numbers.

~PETER II, THE DUKE OF BRITTANY, AFTER THE BATTLE OF CASTILLON, JULY 17, 1453

EIRENE FOLLOWED close behind the point team assaulting the main doors of the old church. Gregorios and Tomas led two other squads, with Sarah positioned at the rear. No one would get anywhere near that girl. Alter trailed them, escorted by a four-man squad tasked with keeping an eye on him.

The heavy double doors burst inward under the team's battering ram, and members of the Tenth poured through, weapons at the ready.

The inside of the church was in surprisingly good shape, with mahogany pews lining both sides of a wide aisle. The huge central room lacked the ceiling murals so common in Roman churches, but rose to a high, flat roof three stories up. Two tiers of columned arches flanked the room, which was built out of simple brick.

Ten men, dressed mostly in leather jackets, lounged across the room around the altar, automatic weapons slung over their shoulders. They blinked away shock, then began swinging weapons around.

Too late.

The Tenth opened fire, filling the room with the muted barking of suppressed rifles, flying lead, and the stench of gunpowder.

Heka fell screaming under the barrage, splattering the chapel with blood. Despite grievous wounds, several of them returned fire.

Eirene caught glints of bright-glowing runes peeking out from under shirts and sleeves. Most of the fighters were charlies, rapid healing powered by the life force of souls they'd drained earlier. They'd keep fighting until all that power was drained away.

The secondary teams burst in from the side entrance and joined the fight. Heka shouted defiance and the loud chatter of their rifles filled the room with booming echoes.

Eirene brought her Thompson to her shoulder and embraced the thrill of battle. It filled her with fear and elation just as wild as back in the days of Rome when she fought with gladius and buckler.

One enemy combatant tried to take cover between two nearby columns supporting an open archway, but Eirene stitched a line of forty-five hollow points up his torso.

Even enhanced, that hurt. The man screamed and tumbled from his feet. He'd stay down long enough for the Tenth to finish the job.

Four squads converged on the enemy soldiers, working with practiced efficiency, bringing down the last of the heka fighters eight seconds after bursting through the outer doors. Two of the targets turned out to be occans, but the Tenth disabled them before they could complete runes carved with desperate haste into thighs or hands.

"Spread out. Secure the building," Eirene ordered.

Gregorios, his rifle propped over his shoulder, gave her a kiss.

"You didn't even fire a shot, did you?" she asked.

He shook his head and winked. "I was having too much fun watching you."

Too bad he was wearing a temporary suit. She usually enjoyed the nights after battle, but he was out of luck until he changed out of that hunter body.

She turned to Sarah, whose face was white, eyes wide. Despite how fast she had learned, their world was still a shocking one to the young lady. She avoided looking at the bloody corpses and met Eirene's gaze.

"Where's the facetaker?" Eirene asked.

"Down."

They soon located the stairs to the lower levels. Eirene led the way, with Tomas and Anaru flanking her and two other squads on their heels. Gregorios came after with Sarah. The gunshots would have alerted the facetaker of their approach, but she'd be surprised if they had many more forces on hand.

She hoped the facetaker turned out to be John. He had a lot of questions to answer before Gregorios met him in a formal duel and ended his final life.

They reached the basement level and entered a long, bare room constructed of huge stone blocks. A stone sarcophagus rested against the wall to her left.

What purpose the room might have served in the past was unclear. Her eyes were drawn to the far side, sixty feet away, where a memory machine, identical to their Sotrun III model, glittered silver under bright lights, confirming they had found the right spot.

A small table stood near the machine, with a dispossessed soulmask strapped into a harness, as if they had been preparing to begin a memory walk. The reclining chair was empty, as was the rest of the shadowed room.

Eirene rushed toward the machine, with the soldiers on her heel. A heavy wooden door on the far side of the room was closed. That had to be where the facetaker had fled.

Sarah entered the room last and immediately spun toward the sarcophagus. "Eirene, wait! They're not—"

Gunshots drowned out her warning as eight heka erupted right out of the floor on both sides, flinging aside concealing panels, automatic weapons firing.

Anaru tackled Eirene to the ground and she felt the impact of bullets striking the huge Maori. He grunted, muttered a Maori curse, and rolled away, his weapon chattering as he returned fire.

The ambush was perfectly orchestrated, and had their force consisted of unenhanced soldiers, they would have been annihilated.

These were the Tenth.

Enhanced soldiers, led by Tomas, returned fire despite some of them having taken terrible wounds. Eirene rolled to her knees and joined them, firing at the heka along the right-hand wall.

Gregorios rushed the heka lines on the left from the side, steel tomahawks in hand. He tore through the enemy at a sprint, tomahawks flashing, leaving screaming heka in his wake, the stumps of their severed arms spraying blood.

As guns blazed across the room at point blank range, Tomas tossed a grenade into the hidden niche where the heka had crouched along the right wall. The blast tore heka apart and tossed them across the room. The concussion threw Eirene off her feet again and left her ears ringing.

Tomas leaped into the group of disoriented heka, beating them down. Anaru dove in a second later. Guns ignored, they lashed out with enhanced fists in close hand-to-hand fighting. With every blow, they proved why they were commanders of the world's elite fighting force. Within seconds, the ambush was over, with the heka dead or disabled.

A scream of defiance penetrated the ringing in Eirene's ears and she spun toward the sound.

Sarah had left the main group and approached the stone sarcophagus against the wall. None of the heka had attacked from there, and at first Eirene thought Sarah must have been seeking cover.

She hadn't. She had been inspecting the sarcophagus when a woman wearing a twenty-something body lunged out of it and grappled with her.

The woman was the facetaker they sought. Her purple glowing hands were nearly in position to rip out Sarah's soulmask. Still half in the sarcophagus, and shielded by Sarah, the woman presented no target.

Eirene rushed to help.

Alter moved faster.

The young hunter leaped fifteen feet, landing on the woman in the sarcophagus, driving her back down and beating on her with savage fury. Somehow she withstood the barrage and struck him a blow that doubled him over. Her glowing hands gripped his face.

Alter screamed, a primal cry of pure horror. His eyes burst into purple fire and flames ringed his hands. He knocked her hands away and grabbed down at her.

A second later, the facetaker's scream echoed out of the sarcophagus. No facetaker could hope to defeat a cui dashi in a direct nevron duel, not even one as newly empowered as Alter.

Eirene waved the others back and approached the sarcophagus. Alter didn't remove the facetaker's soulmask, but instead jumped out of the sarcophagus and fell to his knees, staring in horror at his burning hands. Sarah dropped to the ground beside him, hugging him and whispering soft words.

The facetaker surged upright in the sarcophagus, a heavy pistol in her hands.

Anaru stepped past Eirene, already firing. Blood splattered as bullets ripped apart the woman's arm. She didn't scream, and would have severed connection to those nerves.

It didn't matter. The arm was damaged beyond use, and the gun fell from her hands.

Anaru slammed the butt of his rifle into the facetaker's head, knocking her down. He leaned over her, striking again and again, his powerful shoulders straining as he beat her to bloody pulp.

Within seconds, the skin of her broken face sloughed off, allowing her shimmering soulmask to slide free as she abandoned the dying host.

Eirene patted the big man's shoulder. "Good work. Bag her soulmask."

A loud bang from the far end of the room turned her around. The door there had been thrown wide.

Spartacus stood in the doorway, dressed in jeans and a t-shirt. He held a clear, plexiglass riot shield, and his gaze swept the room and locked on Eirene. She felt a flash of ancient hatred at the sight of her long-defeated enemy.

He wore Tomas' body.

56

What terror impressed upon my soul at the sight of the indomitable Spartacus fighting toward me, cutting down my enhanced men, murder his unabashed intent.

Gregorios alone stood undaunted before his fury, and my anguish is near unquenchable that my secrecy was compelled by the mighty facetaker. He won such glory on that field of battle, and my victory is nearly complete.

The rebellion is cast down, my wealth is confirmed sufficient to purchase another life, but my nightmares continue unabated at knowing Spartacus escaped yet again.

~MARCUS LICINIUS CRASSUS, AFTER THE BATTLE OF
SILER RIVER, 71 B.C.

TOMAS and his team reacted with enhanced reflexes, drawing double-barreled pistols loaded with sleep and electro-shock darts. They crouched, ready to fire, but Spartacus' shield gave him the advantage.

"Hold," Eirene ordered as she walked slowly across the blood-soaked room toward Spartacus.

Gregorios fell in beside her, his expression neutral. "So much for being beyond sides."

Eirene glanced back to where Sarah had sunk to her knees, wide-eyed stare glued on Spartacus. She'd recognized the body he wore.

Spartacus kept his gaze fixed on Eirene as he lifted his arms wide to show off his stolen suit. "Greetings, most honored enemy. I celebrate the sight of you in this amazing new world."

His voice triggered a flood of ancient memories. Although she had known he again walked the world, Eirene still shuddered to hear his voice after so many years.

She continued her slow advance, calculating the best ways to take him down with the least amount of damage to Tomas' suit.

"Greetings, Spartacus. You told my husband that you stand apart from Paul and his plot against us, yet here you are wearing the body of one of my men."

"A fitting form, don't you think? To replace the one you took from me so long ago."

"Wrong answer," Tomas growled, his finger tightening on the trigger.

"Hold your position," Gregorios ordered. "Let us deal with this."

Spartacus asked, "What will it be? Shall we cross swords to honor glories of the past, or shall we feast to celebrate the lives we enjoy, or yet meet in council to plan the movement of the future?"

"Tell me about Paul's plans and maybe we can work something out," Eirene said, rattled by the unusual greeting.

She couldn't remember having actually held a meaningful conversation with Spartacus despite the centuries they'd fought each other. Their meetings had always jumped straight to violent confrontation.

"I am not at liberty. He will strike and you will retaliate. One will die and another may survive, but the world will continue to roll forward and I will be there to help set the course."

"Didn't work so well last time," Gregorios said.

"This time everything is different," Spartacus declared. "The world is new, but languishing in mediocrity. I am reborn! And I will spread to this faltering world a new vision of honor restored to men."

"I'm afraid I'm going to have to insist," Gregorios said. Before Eirene could stop him, he added, "Tomas, you're on."

"About time." Tomas charged, firing with every step. His team surged after him.

Spartacus jumped back into the room and kicked the door closed.

Tomas shattered the heavy oaken barrier without breaking stride. Eirene and Gregorios followed close behind. The room was empty, but a set of stone stairs in the right wall rose out of sight, back toward ground level. Spartacus' voice echoed down the stairs.

"The past is the past, my ancient rivals. Let it go."

"I'll kill him," Tomas growled, sprinting toward the stairs.

Eirene gave chase, with Gregorios and several members of the Tenth close behind. They needed to take Spartacus, but not kill him. Not only did they need to return Tomas' battle suit to him, but Eirene needed time to interrogate Spartacus, to understand his mental state.

He was definitely not the man she had fought so many centuries ago. She wasn't sure what he was, but they needed to find out. He might prove the key to unraveling Paul's plot.

Eirene had assumed Spartacus' mind had broken and his soul faded away centuries ago. She'd experienced dispossession, but only for decades. That time had been difficult, and she shuddered to think of languishing for nearly two millennia.

No one had ever survived so long. For the first time, she felt conflicted about Spartacus, felt a twinge of regret about his long imprisonment. He'd done terrible things, had been her most hated enemy, but might he deserve a second chance on life?

There was no way to tell without an in-depth interrogation. One thing was certain, she hadn't spent centuries fighting this man only to have him rise again to threaten the world. If his mind was damaged, she couldn't allow him to wander free wearing Tomas' body. Who knew what atrocities he might commit?

Modern weapons would eventually win out, but average police would be unprepared to face the most powerful heka the world had ever known. He claimed to be beyond sides, but she doubted that meant he wouldn't fight for what he wanted.

The long stairway emptied into a small courtyard behind the main chapel. Eirene paused at the top and caught sight of Spartacus as he leaped off the roof of the inner courtyard, catching a windowsill of the nearby square tower. He smashed the window and pulled himself inside.

Tomas pointed at the tower. "Bad move. He can't escape."

Eirene led the way. Together she, Tomas, and Gregorios entered the tower and began to climb. Members of the Tenth spread out around the tower in case Spartacus tried to escape out a window.

"I'll take care of this," Tomas growled.

"No, dear. He's mine," Eirene said.

"You had your chance," Tomas snapped.

Gregorios said, "I'm the one who started the discussion with him in the memoryscape, so I should get to finish."

"Not a chance," Eirene retorted.

She broke into a run up the stairs, but the men matched her every stride. If they wanted to make it a contest, so be it. She'd defeated Spartacus once, and she felt a sense of ownership. If he was to die, she would see it done, but not before she discovered his intent.

As one, they burst into the highest room in the tower, only to find it empty. They spread out and Eirene looked out the east-facing window. Spartacus stood on the nearby wall of the cemetery, about forty feet from the base of the tower, flanked by tall cedars. As soon as she and Gregorios stepped into the window, he saluted.

"Tell your men to stand down," he called.

"Why?"

"We have much to speak of, but if you insist on crossing swords, I will respond in kind."

"Stand down," Eirene ordered through the tactical net. "See if someone can get around the far side of that wall."

"What do you want?" Gregorios shouted.

"The world has gone soft since you sealed my eyes, but we can again teach it the way of honor."

"Stealing that body is not the way of honor," Eirene yelled.

"A necessity. Mortals have harnessed the very power of the gods, and yet there is none to show them the way to greatness. I will do so."

"I don't think so," Tomas growled.

He had backed up across the room and now rushed forward between Eirene and Gregorios and leaped, arms outstretched as if he hoped he had the superman rune inscribed.

Spartacus ripped the top off one of the nearby cedars as Tomas soared toward him. Tomas couldn't do anything to check his flight. The body he wore was almost as enhanced as his normal suit and he flew a graceful arc down toward the lower wall.

With a mighty overhand swing, Spartacus swatted him out of the air with the tree. Tomas crashed into the cemetery wall and fell to the ground. Amazingly, he climbed to his feet, bloodied but seemingly intact.

"Is that team around the wall yet?" Eirene asked.

"Negative," Anaru reported. "Three minutes."

"One side," Gregorios said, raising his rifle and taking aim.

Eirene pushed the barrel aside. "I need him alive."

Spartacus shouted, "Let go this vendetta. I will craft a better future for the world, and we no longer must remain enemies." With a final salute, he jumped between the cedars and vanished inside the cemetery.

Gregorios muttered a curse, dropped the rifle, and backed up for a run.

Eirene warned, "Greg, defeat him, but don't kill him. Not yet."

"I'll take him alive," he promised, then launched out the window. He just barely made it to the wall, somehow sticking the landing. Tomas and several members of the Tenth vaulted the ten-foot wall, landing beside him. In unison, they jumped into the cemetery after Spartacus.

Eirene didn't wear enough enhancements to make the leap to the wall, so she snatched up Gregorios' rifle and hopped out the window. Her enhancements were sufficient to absorb the shock, and she ran after the men.

Spartacus the lunatic, she knew exactly how to handle. The man who now wore Tomas' body was proving to be an enigma, and that worried her more than any of his ancient plots ever had.

57

Theirs not to make reply,

Theirs not to reason why,

Theirs but to do and die.

I've always loved that poem by Alfred Lord Tennyson. He captured the heroic bravery of that desperate day without imparting any truth as to our true purpose. Simply brilliant.

~TOMAS, REGARDING "THE CHARGE OF THE LIGHT BRIGADE"

EIRENE DROPPED into a padded leather chair across from Quentin in his mansion and accepted a cool fruit drink from one of the staff. Sarah sat nearby on a plush couch. Gregorios and Tomas entered as she took her first sip.

"Nothing," Gregorios said, not bothering to hide his disgust.

Tomas said nothing, but joined Sarah on the couch. She started to lean against him, then recoiled, as if just remembering he was wearing a different suit. She rose and paced away, hands clenching. Tomas looked after her, his expression pained, but seemed at a loss for what to say.

If those two didn't figure out how to reconcile, she'd have to pull Sarah aside and see if she could help. Sarah was an amazing young woman, but she was still locked in her first life, and that limited a person's vision.

Gregorios took a seat beside Quentin and glanced at Sarah. "What are you feeling?"

She spread her hands. "Nothing. I mean, I sense everyone here in the mansion, but I'm not getting anything useful beyond that."

Tomas said, "We'll have to test your range. Maybe if we get you close enough, you can pinpoint them again."

"Maybe. We don't even know where to start."

Eirene concealed her frustration. Sarah's new rune had given them one break, but they needed more. Eirene knew Spartacus better than anyone. An hour with him and she'd learn everything they needed to know.

She said, "The children are interrogating the facetaker we captured. They're motivated, and already confirmed the enemy is seeking another master rune."

Gregorios grunted. "Figures. With so much focus on Rome, they had to be."

"We'll have to be careful to avoid memories where a master rune could appear," Sarah said.

"Perhaps," Gregorios said thoughtfully. "Time is short. That much is clear."

"You're thinking of tempting them out with the master rune?" Eirene asked.

"It might be the best way to force them to play to us again. We have some momentum building. We need to leverage it."

"We need to find them." Tomas said, his expression grim. "I owe Spartacus."

"At least Carl's going to be fine," Quentin said, but Sarah frowned, as if that only reminded her why Tomas had been out of his suit to begin with.

The dispossessed soulmask strapped to the machine had turned out to be Carl. The little guy had been panicked and didn't even complain that his body was injured when they reincorporated him. He insisted his new girlfriend would be impressed with the scars, and he never wanted to transfer again.

"None of us are going to be fine if we don't stop Paul," Gregorios said.

"I'm starting to think the best way to thwart him is capturing Spartacus," Eirene said.

"Spartacus never turned on anyone before," Gregorios pointed out.

"But in the past he was always committed," she reminded him. "He's not himself, and from what he's suggested, his goals are not necessarily aligned with Paul's. I wonder if Paul understands what he created when he reincorporated him."

"Kind of like a Frankenstein moment," Sarah said.

"Perhaps."

Gregorios patted her knee. "We'll find him. We know what Paul wants now."

"If we're going to draw him to the master rune, we'll need to prepare carefully." Eirene still wasn't sure she liked that idea.

"How many master runes are tied to the history of Rome?" Sarah asked.

Gregorios said, "Probably several. It was the center of the world for a long time."

Eirene agreed. "I'm betting on the fall of Rome. It fits the profile of what Mai Luan was looking for in Berlin."

"Agreed," Gregorios said.

Quentin leaned forward. "But which fall?"

"It fell more than once?" Sarah asked.

The door opened and Alter entered. Eirene waved him to a seat next to her before answering.

"Rome's been sacked multiple times.

"But the one that shocked the world was in 410 A.D. by the Visigoths," Gregorios said. "That was the critical moment in the city's history. After that, the council moved headquarters to Constantinople, which became the seat of the Eastern Roman Empire, and didn't return to Rome for centuries."

"History didn't just revolve around you," Alter said.

Gregorios shrugged. "Most of the time it did, actually."

"We just wrote ourselves out of it," Eirene said. "Gregorios is right. The sacking of Rome by the Visigoths was the moment, especially with the Spartacus connection."

"What really happened?" Sarah asked.

"You're learning," Gregorios said, approving.

Eirene explained. "Baladeva's influence had already waned, but Spartacus remained. He prepared a special force of enhanced warriors concealed within the Visigoth ranks. The primary purpose for the sacking of Rome was to give his force access to the city. Their mission was to destroy our temple."

"The god of thunder, right?" Sarah asked.

"Correct. Summanus, god of nocturnal thunder. The temple was well respected, and our positions there granted us access to all levels of society," Eirene said.

"And Spartacus was affiliated with Quirinus, the war god, right?" Sarah asked.

"Sounds appropriate," Tomas said.

Gregorios nodded. "More than you know. Priests of Quirinus were feared for their brutality. Spartacus preferred fighting with the oaken staff, which was their symbol of power."

"When he sacked Rome, he led his forces and the priests of Quirinus to destroy our temple," Eirene said. She couldn't help but think back to the disturbing nightmare she recently had.

"They succeeded?" Tomas asked.

"The temple was destroyed, but I finally defeated Spartacus there."

"How?"

"Because she's smarter," Gregorios said. "She restored me to Spartacus' body. It served me well for a long time."

"Never looked right on you," Eirene said.

Sarah said, "That's what Spartacus was talking about today. Taking Tomas' body was payback."

"He picked the wrong suit," Tomas said. He and Sarah shared a look, and she gave a tiny nod.

"We'll get it back," Eirene assured Sarah. "I beat Spartacus because I knew he was coming and I had time to prepare the battlefield to my advantage. That's what we'll do again."

She turned to Alter. "Before we lay those plans, tell us what you discovered from the machine we found in that church."

Studying the new machine had calmed Alter. He looked almost stable. "It's virtually identical to the machines we're using, but I did find a new rune."

"Is it the one we need to circumvent their assault on our nevra cores?" Eirene asked eagerly.

He smiled. "It is. It's fascinating and definitely not one we've seen before. I don't know where they got it, but it appears to be exactly what we need to counter their forbidden rune."

Eirene shared a relieved glance with Gregorios. They had faced many crises and terrible threats through the long centuries, but always their nevra cores had been a constant, a bedrock they could count on. With that forbidden rune, Paul had struck at the very heart of their strength, the root of their identity.

Alter held up a silver chain with a small, round pendant engraved with a rune. "The facetaker hiding in the sarcophagus was wearing the rune. That's why she was able to embrace her core."

He extended the pendant to Eirene, who eagerly took it. "How is it activated?"

"It builds on similar principles to the escape rune I designed." After she settled the chain over her head, he took the pendant in his hand. "I activate it, and it remains active, powered by your soul."

"How many of those pendants do you have?" Gregorios asked.

"Bastien is preparing more. By the time we return to headquarters, they should be ready."

"Excellent." With that one act, Alter had won more of Gregorios' goodwill than anything Eirene could imagine.

The young hunter added, "I've already applied them to the other machines. They should work now without needing my assistance."

"Good," Sarah said with a smile. "You can join us in the memory."

"I plan to."

Eirene was relieved to hear his commitment to hunting Paul. He was their secret weapon, the one member of the team who could stand against Paul with a real hope for victory. The rest of them had gotten lucky so far, but without Alter, some of them were likely to die before they brought Paul down.

"Then you and I have some work to do," Eirene said, rising.

"What work?" Alter asked.

"You're the one who'll face Paul, but you can't do that if you don't know how to use your nevra core."

Alter began to look nervous, but Eirene took his chin in her hand and forced him to meet her gaze.

"You'll have time to sort everything out eventually, but right now you need to know how to leverage every advantage. Come with me. I'm going to teach you how to remove a soul."

He rose reluctantly. "Whose?"

"Mine."

58

One must step into the shadows before basking in the light of glorious triumph. If I hesitate, my nation will fall. Despite my secret fears, I must seize this chance to defeat the sultan. If I refuse the destiny only I have the power to obtain, how can I ask my people to sacrifice their lives or the force of their souls to my cause?

~VLAD DRACULA, RUNE WARRIOR, VOIVODE OF
WALLACHIA, 1475

"I DON'T THINK this is a good idea," Alter said as he followed Eirene into the sparring room overlooking the shattered pool.

She gave him a hard look, wishing they had more time to ease him into his new reality. "Do you think you can beat a full cui dashi without knowing how to wield your strength?"

"But I don't want this," he whined.

"What makes you think that matters?" The harsh answer caught him by surprise, as she'd intended. She'd been trying to be gentle with him, but coddling him in this would only get him killed.

"I'm a demon," he said more stubbornly.

"Alter, you are who you are. If you choose to be a demon, then that's what you will become. Just because you've learned a new side to yourself doesn't define you."

"How can you say that? My family and yours have united in one thing despite our differences for dozens of generations. Whenever a cui dashi rises, we destroy them. I have that curse, so I must be destroyed."

"If that's what you want," she said, not showing how much she yearned to comfort him. "But don't you want to take another cui dashi down with you?"

"I know what you're trying to do," he growled.

"Good. I always knew you were smart." When he didn't return her smile she added, "The choice is yours, Alter. I know this is a shock and I promise we'll take the time to sort things out when this crisis is over, but right now I need you. You're a hunter, and no matter what else has changed, that hasn't. I'm asking you to help me hunt the monster who hurt your family, the monster planning to destroy both me and Sarah."

She had him and he knew it.

"Fine. What do I have to do?" He bit the words off through clenched teeth.

"You've felt your nevra core already. Can you embrace it at will?"

"I haven't tried."

"Try."

He grimaced but still made the attempt. She waited for half a minute before a glimmer of purple flickered in his eyes. She felt the tiny pulse, like whispers across her skin as his nevron flared. It disappeared almost instantly and Alter shuddered.

He rubbed his arms. "That is unnatural."

"It's a part of you, so it's natural," Eirene countered. "Like any tool, like any weapon, it's neither good nor evil of itself. Only in how you choose to wield it can it be classified."

"Every other cui dashi has been evil. Perhaps it corrupts them."

"Corruption is a choice. Most souls, powered with an active nevra core or not, cannot withstand the lust for power." She squeezed his shoulder. "That's why I'm so optimistic now. None of the others were raised with your code of honor. You alone may have the strength to retain your integrity despite the awesome power entrusted to you."

Alter tried again. This time the flicker of purple fire came in seconds and grew. His eyes burned like living amethysts, and purple flames flickered across his hands.

"Feel it," Eirene urged softly, thinking back to the first times she had embraced her nevra core. She had exulted in the feeling of strength that filled her from the living power of her soul force.

Over time, embracing her nevra core had helped her understand herself better, granted her sensitivities to the souls of others no mortal could hope to understand. That yet another of her descendants could share that glorious sensation thrilled her.

Alter met her gaze and she embraced her own nevra core, her burning eyes mirrored in his. Her nevra core was a cherished part of her and, when needed, a well-honed weapon, but she could never hope to stand against Alter. Something about the interaction between an active rounon and the nevra core became a multiplier.

Paul would brutalize him.

Alter lacked training, lacked the will to embrace his nevra core. If he didn't learn to overcome that reluctance, he'd be worse than useless in a confrontation with the older cui dashi.

Eirene shuttered her own nevron. "How do you feel?"

He opened his mouth to reply, but no words came for a long moment. She wasn't surprised. He'd been raised to hate the soul powers of the facetakers and despise the cui dashi above all things, but he struggled to hate what was now part of him. The glory of his awakened soul force couldn't be denied.

"I need to understand," he said finally.

Good. That small step was the most important one.

Eirene sat on the floor and motioned him to sit beside her. They spent a few minutes discussing the nevra core, how to embrace it, how to direct it, what it meant. He was already familiar with harnessing the strength of his soul through bonded runes. This was the next evolution in accessing the full potential of his soul force.

"Wait," he protested. "Are you saying our rounon gifts are somehow related to the nevra core?"

"Of course. I know many of your ancestors have understood that connection. It's disturbing that they've chosen to withhold that truth from you."

"They withhold nothing," Alter snapped, but didn't sound convinced.

"All of the real powers of the earth are connected with the strength of souls. Rounon gifts are but a different manifestation of that same basic source, with more limited access."

"I don't believe you. How could we be tainted with the same evil?"

"Evil is defined by choices. Alter, aren't you listening?" Eirene poked his forehead for emphasis. "You already know that kashaph are gifted in similar ways to the hunters. It's only your code of honor that maintains your integrity. Hunters could apply their runes in the same way heka do."

"We wouldn't," he said softly, but a glimmer of understanding appeared in his burning eyes. "We choose not to."

"Exactly. It's the same now that you can access this greater manifestation of your soul force. It is your choice."

"Teach me." For the first time he released his anger and self-loathing.

She explained the connection of the soul to the host body, the soul points concentrated in the face, linking the soul to the senses, which served as anchors. Mortals couldn't feel those points, which were roughly similar to physical pressure points.

"With your active nevra core, you can grasp those points," she explained, guiding his hands to the correct positions along her jaw line. His nevron pulsed against her with undeniable strength. She forced down a ripple of fear.

"Now, focus your nevron on those points. Sever them. That breaks the bond between the soul and the host body, allowing you to remove the soulmask."

When he hesitated she repeated, "Remove my soul, Alter. That's an order."

His control was rudimentary, and his nevron slammed into her soul like a sledgehammer to the skull. She reeled, but couldn't break free of his grasp. His burning fingers sank into her skin and his amethyst eyes widened with the undeniable thrill of overpowering another's soul.

Eirene's nevron responded instinctively to the blow and her eyes burned with her soul force.

It didn't matter.

Alter was cui dashi. Although fledgling, his innate strength far outstripped her own. His fingers sealed to the soul points along her jaw and severed her bond with her body as easily as his sharp blade cut through skin.

All feeling drained to ghosts of memory as Eirene lost connection with her host. Her senses contracted, vision collapsing into two-dimensions as her soulmask pulled free of the restricting skull. The last sensation she felt before Alter lifted her soulmask free was that distinct sucking pop.

Eirene lost sight of him as he lifted her soulmask high, but while dispossessed, hearing multiplied tenfold. She heard his elevated breathing, and even his bounding pulse.

The first soul extraction laid bare one's connection to their nevra core. For her it had been a deeply moving experience, deeper even than the ecstasy mortals felt through love. For Alter, it had to be as terrifying as it was exciting.

Eirene spoke, her soulvoice high-pitched and barely above a whisper. "Well done, Alter. Now, press my soulmask back into place and restore the soul points."

For long seconds he didn't respond, didn't lower her soulmask. Fear flitted between the rainbow tendrils that coiled just below her. Had she underestimated the strength of his integrity? Would he fall to the lure of cui dashi powers so quickly?

His hands began to shake, and he lowered her a fraction. She couldn't see his face, as his head was bowed, but she noticed a tiny dot of red light on his temple.

Gregorios had followed, despite her warning to stay away. He'd positioned himself outside, probably on the roof of the south wing, with views over the devastated pool courtyard and the training room. She was seeing the laser sight of his sniper rifle, and she doubted he'd wait long.

She was about to call out to Alter again, but his hands stopped shaking and he took a deep breath, the rasping of air in his lungs clear to her. Slowly, he lowered her soulmask back into place.

She could have reestablished the connection with her host body on her own, but resisted the urge. He needed to feel the entire process, understand everything. It seemed to take forever before his nevron restored the bond for her.

Senses rushed in with the avalanche of feeling she knew to expect. Every molecule clamored for attention, every sense nearly overwhelmed by the rush as her soul reunited with her body. Her limbs shook just a little, despite her efforts to calm them. She had only been dispossessed for a minute, so the tremors passed quickly.

Only when she sat up did she glimpse a tear hanging in Alter's eye, not quite released. He looked shaken and pale. Then a shudder passed through him and his eyes widened in shock.

"You felt something," she said softly, watching him intently.

"Yes, something . . . I feel stronger."

"That was the final step."

"What step?"

"It's known as the nevra siphon. It's unique to the cui dashi and the biggest reason they become so feared. As part of the melding of your rounon gift with your recently awakened nevra core, you siphon a fraction of the soul force from every soul you dispossess. With mortals, the effect is small, but from stronger souls like mine, the gain is much more pronounced."

Alter gasped. "No! I can't. That is abomination."

"It cannot be undone."

Alter shuffled away. "You knew this would happen to me! You defiled me."

Eirene said, "You are my blood. What makes you think I mind sharing just a little bit more of myself with you?"

"It's wrong," he insisted.

"It is what it is. No doubt Paul has siphoned from many souls."

"What does that mean?" Alter whispered.

"It means he's stronger. It means that you must close that gap."

"How?"

"You need the practice anyway. You're going to dispossess everyone I can line up for you. It'll improve your skills and strengthen your soul."

He began shaking his head before she finished. "I can't do it."

"You must. You're the only one who can."

"We've defeated other cui dashi without this," he insisted.

"True, but we'll be facing Paul in the memoryscape. There he holds the advantage. Do you really want to fight him without preparing in every possible way?"

"Embracing this evil is not preparing."

She poked him in the head again. "Alter, you're backsliding. We already established this isn't evil."

He grunted and rubbed his face with his hands.

"It has to be done," she insisted.

"I will not!"

Alter stormed from the room and Eirene let him go.

Gregorios entered as soon as he left. "That went about as well as we could have hoped." He must have descended from his sniper perch as soon as he saw Alter beginning to restore her.

She embraced him and leaned her head against his shoulder. "We've escalated things with this last raid, love. We're facing the final confrontation. I can feel it. That boy is our best hope of survival, but he needs the final push."

"I'll send Sarah," Gregorios said.

"That's getting complicated," Eirene cautioned.

"I know, but we have to take the risk. We need both of them."

"If he refuses?"

Gregorios wrapped her in his arms and spoke softly.

"Then a lot of people are going to die."

59

The fool Valerian is dragged through the streets in chains. No ruler will again defy me, when I can enhance the armies of their enemies, as I did the Persians. Let the impotent hunters promise what they may, I rule from the shadows, and those shadows remain unbroken for five centuries.

~SHAHROKH, AFTER EMPEROR VALERIAN WAS
CAPTURED BY PERSIAN KING SHAPUR I, 260 A.D.

TOMAS PULLED the SUV to a stop under the covered entry at Quentin's mansion and Sarah breathed a sigh of relief. It felt good to get home. Quentin himself opened the door for her.

"How did it go?" he asked.

"No luck so far." She didn't hide her frustration.

"Well, come inside and have something to eat."

Sarah squeezed his hand. He was such a gentleman, and she was tired and hungry.

She and Tomas had crisscrossed Rome in the past four hours in their fruitless hunt for the hidden Paul. At least Tomas had commandeered an SUV from the car pool, so the drive was comfortable, but that only helped a little.

Sarah wondered if somehow Paul or John had realized she could locate them. Or maybe Spartacus had seen something to tip them off? She should have been able to find them, but had felt nothing.

At the mansion, she easily located Eirene and Gregorios. Alter shone in her rune senses with a slightly different shade in mental light.

They had driven past the council headquarters and she'd picked out several facetakers, their locations resolving into clarity about two blocks away. Maybe she could develop a second rune to amplify the power of the first. The idea held promise, but she wasn't sure where to start.

"I've got to check in with my team," Tomas said when they entered the spacious main salon. "They're following up on a couple of leads and analyzing intel we gathered during that last raid."

He leaned in to give her a kiss, but she couldn't quite kiss that temporary form. She turned her face, allowing him to gently kiss her cheek. She was grateful he didn't press her about accepting his current form. She was committed to helping him restore his body, but struggled to pretend there was nothing wrong in the meantime.

"I'll see you at dinner," she called after him, and he waved, looking relieved.

Hopefully they could find some quiet time that evening. They needed some positive reinforcement to help ease the rift that had formed between them after that argument and his body issues.

Sarah excused herself, promising to meet Quentin later in the art gallery dining room. Life had grown weird. No other girl in the world was probably dealing with quite the same set of boyfriend problems. Tomas was unique, but at the moment, she wished he wasn't quite so different.

She sensed Alter moving to intercept her, the glow of his active nevra core like an approaching lantern in her mind. She waited at the corner of the hall where he would appear.

"Sarah. Just who I was looking for." He looked relieved.

"Are you going to join us later for dinner?"

"Food can wait." He drew her down the side hallway.

"What is it?"

He led her back to the sparring room before speaking.

"If I knew you wanted to get beat up, I would've grabbed my workout clothes," Sarah joked.

"I need the master rune," Alter said, his expression grave.

"You couldn't let me relax a bit first?"

"No. You promised."

"What's the hurry?"

He glanced at his watch. "I need it. You promised to give it to me."

"I did. Right after we defeat Paul." She watched him closely. He looked nervous, almost frantic.

"Well I need it early."

"Why?" She doubted he was planning to run. He couldn't return to his family in Jerusalem. Not yet. They wouldn't react well to learning about his cui dashi powers.

"Just give it to me," he pleaded.

"Okay, but you need to tell me what's going on."

Alter paced away, then rushed back to her and took her hands. "Sarah, I'm speaking with my father in a few minutes. I need . . . "

He looked down and Sarah said, "You need something big, like a peace offering, to help him deal with the new aspect of your powers, don't you?"

When he spoke, his voice cracked. "Sarah, how can I face him? He'll know about . . . About my corruption."

"You're not corrupt, and you know it."

"It doesn't matter what I believe. That's how my father will see it."

"Do you really think that offering him the master rune will help?"

He shrugged. "It's all I have."

Gregorios was going to be furious when he found out, but Sarah couldn't refuse him. Alter had helped her, despite his reservations about her new rune. "All right. I agree with you, Alter. Your family is worth it."

Alter breathed a sigh of relief and produced a small notebook. Sarah sketched out the master rune. Alter watched, eyes glued to every stroke. When she finished, he took the paper reverently and studied it for half a minute before speaking.

"This is amazing."

"Told you."

Then his eyes widened. "You took the keystone marks for your personal rune?"

"I told you I used part of it."

"Sarah, that's the most dangerous part. Do you have any idea what forces you're playing with?"

"It worked, didn't it?"

She hated when he said things like that. Of course she didn't understand everything and when she let herself think about it, it terrified her. She had to trust her instincts because there wasn't time to learn enough to trust her knowledge.

"I don't care." Alter startled her by turning away.

"Really?"

He pulled out his phone and began dialing. That seemed a bit abrupt. He hadn't even tried to steal a kiss in thanks. She didn't want to encourage Alter, but it irritated that he hadn't even tried.

"Well great, I've been working on another rune that uses more parts."

That got his attention. "Sarah! Stop doing that."

"Just kidding. Who are you calling?"

"My father."

"Already?"

"I have to. Waiting will only make it worse."

She gave him an encouraging smile. "I'll wait here. Tell me what he says."

He paused at the door and gave her the first genuine smile of the day. "Thank you."

After the door closed behind him, she sank onto a padded bench, wondering how he'd react if the conversation went badly?

60

I have seen the emperor himself. Caligula is crowned, but I know Caesar's face and indeed, the demon-allied Julius has taken yet another life. The only glimmer of hope are reports of mental dissipation.

I will attempt to gather confirmation, but my presence may have been noticed by the cursed enforcers. I will not retreat from these demons, and rejoice that the long-time protector of the facetaker evil is approaching his ultimate death.

~ACHINOAM, HUNTER SPY IN ROME, 38 A.D.

ALTER CRINGED when he heard the weakness in his father's voice. Melek had always been such a mighty force in the clan, the indomitable cornerstone of their strength.

His father would recover, and with the information Alter had to share, all would be well.

"I'm glad you called, Son," Melek said, but his tone was more severe than usual.

"Father, I acquired the master rune. I've already emailed an encrypted photo of it to you."

Melek's response came slower than Alter had hoped. "That is well."

"What's wrong?"

Another pause. "I spoke with Reuben today."

"Father, I can explain."

"Can you?" Melek asked, his tone harder, and colder. "You defied your flesh and blood. You helped the demons. They've tainted you and mocked our honor."

"It's not like that—"

"To think I cowed before the pretended wrath of Gregorios," Melek snarled. "Reuben saw the truth. My vision was clouded with false words of cooperation."

"He's not false. There's another cui dashi. He's worse than Mai Luan and he's after another master rune."

"Lies!" Melek cried. "You are caught in their web. I cannot imagine how they managed to corrupt your soul, but you must come home. We'll purge you, Son, and set you free of their taint."

Alter blanched.

Purge.

The worst dishonor for a hunter was to use his rounon gift as the heka did, or to ally with the enemies of the clan. Alter's dishonor eclipsed all others and would stand unchallenged in the annals of their history.

The only way to restore honor was to purge the corrupted soul.

He had to die.

Alter sagged against the wall, unable to speak, unable to argue. Had he not lived through the events of recent weeks, he would have called for the same punishment for anyone else who had acted as he had. If he didn't know the truth, his bias would have dictated the outcome.

But he knew the truth.

"Father, please."

Melek's voice became gentle. "Reuben is still in Rome, Son. He can pick you up and bring you home."

"It's not my fault," Alter said, his voice cracking. He forced confidence back into it. "I've learned so much. Don't turn on me now, Father. I can defeat the cui dashi and avenge the family."

"It's not your fault. It's my fault. I never should have thrust you into the midst of those demons. Your fall is all my fault."

"I haven't fallen," Alter insisted. "I'm still me. I've done great things. We're doing great things."

"I am sorry," Melek said, his voice strong with the same conviction Alter had always felt, the conviction he was now forced to question. "If you could hear yourself you would understand. Like your Grandfather Ronen used to say, duty is a terrible burden sometimes, but it cannot be avoided."

"What about Grandmother Elizabeth? It's her blood that granted this gift you call a curse."

Maybe that wasn't the best time to bring that up.

"How dare the demons disgrace her memory?" Melek shouted, angrier than Alter had ever heard.

"There's no disgrace. They've shown me so much truth."

"They do not live in truth. I'm sorry, my son, but your soul must be cleansed. It's for your own good."

"But father—"

"Good bye."

61

The Praetor was a fool, and today we revel in new glory. I hardly dared believe he would entrust the battle to the swords of simple men. We who bear the runes of the mighty Spartacus fear none such. What care I for Castus's worries or Gannicus's whining? Let the facetakers come, and we will meet in glorious battle and prove the mettle of our souls.

~OENOMAUS, ONE OF THE LEADERS OF SLAVE REVOLT
WITH SPARTACUS

THE DOOR to the sparring room opened and Alter entered slowly, his shoulders slumped. Sarah had never seen him so low. Considering the events of the past couple of days, that was something.

"How did it go?" she asked with forced cheer.

He waved the question aside without answering and dropped to the bench beside her. He looked at his feet, dejected.

"They'll come around," she said. It had taken Alter weeks to simply shift from thinking every one of them was a demon to thinking Gregorios was the demon and everyone else merely evil.

"They won't. You don't know them."

"I've met your brother."

When she saw Reuben again, she'd ram the gun he'd used to shoot Tomas into an unmentionable place and see how he liked getting shot.

She changed the subject. "How did it go with Eirene earlier?"

Alter straightened. A hint of a smile crossed his lips but he ground it out quickly. "It was educational."

"So what's it like?" She bumped his shoulder with hers to get him to look up.

"It's different than anything I've ever felt," he said, his sour mood lifting a little. "I didn't want to admit it, but I can control my nevra core and it doesn't make me evil."

"Of course not. I know your heart."

"It's not that simple, not for my family."

"There's more to it, isn't there?"

"You know about the nevra siphon?" he asked.

She nodded. Eirene had called her while she and Tomas drove around the city. It was a lot to swallow, but she was getting better at accepting new mind-bending truths.

"I'm your next test case."

"I can't do it." He looked nervous.

Sarah squeezed his hands and drew them up to her face. He seemed reluctant, but also eager to touch her. "Do it, Alter. I trust you and I'll gladly share some of my strength so you can stomp Paul."

Eirene had explained that the siphon wouldn't hurt her, wouldn't damage her own newfound rune warrior gift.

"Are you sure you know what you're asking?" His hands were warm against her face.

"Yes." She leaned into his hands. "Show me what you can do, Alter."

He relented and shifted so she could lie on the bench. He knelt beside her, his face close to hers. Then his eyes began to burn and purple flames flickered around his hands. Sarah held Alter's gaze as the searing heat of his soul powers burned into her jawline and his fingers sank into her skin.

"I trust you," she whispered before senses contracted and her vision narrowed.

Pain flared, then faded as he drew her soulmask away from her skull. She lost all sense of touch and taste, and her vision contracted. The little she saw took on rainbow hues and became more angular. She heard his breath catch as he lifted her high.

Alter turned her so she could see his face. A look of ecstasy settled over his features, quickly replaced by one of guilt.

"I knew you could do it," she said in her helium-high whisper voice.

His fingers caressed her soulmask. They felt distant, vague.

"Do you feel this?" he asked.

"Not really."

"How about this?"

He drew her soulmask to him and touched her compressed lips to his. A spark of living energy jumped from her soulmask to him, and a jolt shook her. It felt like part of her waking mind was snuffed out. She struggled to focus, to remain aware.

Alter's voice reached her through the haze. "Sarah? Sarah, are you all right?"

Then her senses returned in a rush as he drove her face back into her skull. The skin sealed over her cheeks and her limbs rattled against the bench under the flood of reconnected cells.

She recovered quickly and Alter helped her sit up.

"What happened?" She asked, still feeling a little weak.

"I think that was a bad idea," Alter said.

"Was that the siphon?"

He nodded. "I think I took a lot more than I was supposed to."

"How?"

"Because I wanted to." He spoke softly, eyes downcast.

"What do you mean?"

"I wanted to feel you, Sarah." He met her gaze, his eyes filled with emotion. "I pulled too hard."

Sarah hoped the effect was temporary. She was happy to share a little of her strength with him, but she couldn't afford to be weakened, not with Paul still on the loose and with Spartacus running around with Tomas' body.

She forced her concerns aside and touched his cheek. "You didn't know."

"But I did it."

"Don't do it again," she teased. "Kissing a soulmask is a little weird, even for a cui dashi."

He lifted a hand to her face and leaned closer.

"Alter..."

She started to tell him not to, but he leaned in before she could. Their lips touched and he kissed her just as clumsily, just as eagerly as the last time.

Sarah managed to push him back. "Alter, this isn't a good idea."

"You bet it's not!"

Tomas stood in the doorway.

62

We slaughtered the Romans. Three legion eagle standards fell into our hands, and the honor of those legions shall forever be tarnished. The other tribes marvel at our power, and perhaps these enhancements will pave the way to finally unifying the tribes against the hated Romans. I don't know the hunters' reasons, but I will avail myself of the power they place at my disposal.

~ ARMINIUS, CHIEFTAIN OF THE CHERUSCI GERMANIC
TRIBE, AFTER THE BATTLE OF THE TEUTOBURG FOREST,
9 A.D.

TOMAS APPROACHED, angry. "What are you thinking?"

Sarah wanted to scream with frustration. Of course Tomas had to pick that moment to enter. She hadn't encouraged Alter, but she should have pushed him away quicker.

Alter rose to face Tomas. "I got caught up in the moment." He actually sounded contrite.

Tomas advanced and looked like he was trying to control his anger. His gaze slid to Sarah.

"It was nothing," Sarah assured him. "He was practicing removing souls."

"By sucking them out through the lips? I know you're new at this, Alter, but even you know better than that."

"You're one to talk," Alter retorted. "Can't even hold onto your own body."

Tomas scowled. "That's low, even for you. You betrayed us, boy. If you were a member of my legion, you'd be executed for that."

"I didn't plan on betraying anyone," Alter said, a little less belligerent.

"So kissing Sarah is your way of straightening things out?"

"That wasn't planned either."

"Just like helping your brother try to kill me was all a big accident?" Tomas demanded.

"I could have killed you in that hall," Alter said.

"Don't be proud of actions you can only achieve by betrayal. You shamed yourself and your family."

Alter didn't bother to respond. He threw a punch.

His fist flew with enhanced speed, but Tomas blocked it.

"Don't make me your enemy, boy," Tomas growled as the two circled each other. "I've tried to be understanding, and I've tried to forgive some of the stupid choices you've made, but don't push me, not today."

"You know nothing," Alter cried. "Your vaunted legion has failed to find Paul, and you've failed Sarah in every way."

"Hey, stay out of our relationship," Sarah snapped. She needed to find a way to calm the situation, but how? Would Tomas listen to her after witnessing that brief kiss?

Tomas raised his fists. "You're going to insist on learning a lesson, aren't you?"

"You don't deserve her. I'm the one who—"

Tomas lunged, and the move burst the avalanche of pent-up anger in both of them. They exploded into combat, attacking each other with such fury they toppled Sarah right off her bench.

The two men fought across the room, a blur of fists and feet, punctuated by grunting and the sickening sounds of fists pounding flesh. They beat on each other with brutal ferocity.

The last time they sparred against each other had taken Sarah's breath away with their grace and speed.

Not this time.

They struck with terrifying force, intent on hurting, on crippling. They smashed each other in the face, in the throat, and in every major joint. Blood splattered the room and they both absorbed enough punishment to have disabled a room full of enhanced soldiers.

Sarah leaped to her feet, terrified to see them hurt each other, and awed that they could fight through such injuries. She shouted at them to stop, but they ignored her. They were fully committed to the duel.

She was tempted to rush out to get help, but couldn't bear to leave them alone. One of them might kill the other.

They fought back and forth across the room for a quarter hour until even their enhancements couldn't keep up any more. They began to stagger from exhaustion, but their fists barely slowed. Tomas fought for vengeance against a betrayer while Alter raged against his situation, and they both poured all that emotion into the duel.

Sarah circled them, forced to stay back to avoid being struck. She had become a proficient fighter in recent weeks, accelerated by her enhancements, but she couldn't step into that fight.

She might have tried to intervene anyway, but Alter had siphoned much of her strength. Her runes weren't pouring nearly as much energy into her, and that well of rounon power she'd only recently unearthed felt shallow, and she didn't dare draw it down further.

In an abrupt reversal, Tomas dove for Alter's legs, and the two crashed to the floor, punches giving way to grappling holds as they tried to strangle each other or snap limbs.

"Stop it! This isn't solving anything," Sarah shouted.

They ignored her.

Tomas elbowed Alter in the throat and when the smaller man gagged, he twisted him over and applied a choke hold. Alter beat at his hands, but couldn't dislodge him.

"Let him go," Sarah cried, pulling at Tomas' shoulder, but he felt as immovable as a statue.

Alter reached over his shoulder and grabbed Tomas' arm. His hands began to burn with purple fire.

Tomas cried out and his hold loosened. Alter threw him off, then leaped on him, burning hands finding Tomas' face. Tomas' struggles stilled as Alter cut his connection to his nerves.

Alter leaned over Tomas, eyes burning like living amethysts. "Eirene wants me to practice. Fine, I'll practice."

"I said stop it!" Sarah picked up the toppled bench and swung it like a baseball bat.

Home run.

The crack of wood striking Alter's head sounded so much like the old-time, wooden bats landing a solid hit that Sarah could hear the crowds cheering. Alter tumbled across the room, landing in a heap.

Tomas struggled to sit up, grimacing.

Alter leaped to his feet despite the devastating blow. Already the effects of the fight were fading. He had always been a quick healer, but his soul was becoming stronger now that he knew how to tap his cui dashi nevra core and had begun siphoning other souls.

Sarah faced him. "That's enough, Alter. This isn't the way."

"I should've taken the shot when I had the chance," Alter said. "That would've been clean."

"You said it was Reuben who shot Tomas."

"Not that one. That was only the last time I spared his useless life."

"What are you talking about?" Sarah asked.

"A couple weeks ago when you were eating in that little outdoor cafe, I could have ended him, but I didn't."

"You were spying on our date?" Sarah demanded.

Alter seemed to realize he had gone too far. "Never mind."

"No, you tell me what you're talking about. No more lies." The revelation was disturbing.

"Lies? I never lie! Yes, I spied on your date. Are you happy? You're the one who said I should have some fun."

"That's not fun. That's creepy."

Tomas rose to face Alter. "Who would kill someone on a date?"

"No one! I didn't do it."

Alter stormed from the room.

Tomas moved to follow, but Sarah grabbed his arm. "Let him go. He's having a bad day."

"Oh, so you only worry about Alter? He nearly killed me the other day, so you figure the best way to deal with that is to kiss him?"

"He kissed me," she reminded him, happy he didn't know about the first time she'd let Alter kiss her.

"But you looked like you weren't convinced you wanted him to stop," Tomas said, studying her face, as if her expression had betrayed some of her thoughts.

Sarah hesitated, and Tomas' eyes widened. "You wanted him to kiss you? Why?" His belligerence faded, and he looked devastated.

She took his hands. "No. Tomas, it's just, we're going through such crazy times. He helped me activate my rune warrior gift, and you swapped bodies with Carl and—"

"Is that what this is all about?" he demanded. The hurt in his eyes mirrored the anguish she still felt from that argument.

They faced each other, and she wanted nothing more than to kiss him, to prove to him that she loved him. But he still wore that hunter body, his face slightly distorted, and she hated to embrace the form of a stranger, even if he was the one wearing it.

She didn't trust herself to speak. Her lingering anger with him for swapping bodies with Carl mingled with worry that he was hurt, and fear that he'd never get his body back. She was also confused by concern about Alter and what his family was going to do, and afraid to face Paul again without Alter's help.

"I need some time to think," she said finally.

Tomas retreated, his expression disbelieving. "Listen to yourself. You get angry with me for doing a favor for my friend, but then you kiss the man who betrayed me. Does that make any sense to you?"

"Sometimes I think nothing makes sense anymore." She felt tears forming, but savagely fought them down. That was not the time to show weakness. She needed to figure things out, but her emotions were in turmoil, and she couldn't even embrace him without being held by some other man's arms.

"We'll work through it," he promised, drawing closer and reaching for her.

She backed away, shaking her head. "I can't, Tomas. Not yet."

"I'm here for you, Sarah," Tomas said softly. "I don't want to lose you."

"Just give me some space."

Sarah rushed from the room. She needed a way to take her mind off of everything, but she couldn't figure out what would help.

She ran into Bastien.

His warm smile was a balm to her nerves, and his smooth French accent a comfort. "If you are not too busy, perhaps now would be a good time to learn about rune warrior ciphers, yes?"

She took his arm, eager for the chance to focus on something positive. "Perfect timing. Lead the way."

63

Three things are needed for success in painting and sculpture: to see beauty when young and accustom oneself to it, to work hard, and to obtain good advice.

For success in love, one needs a woman like Francesca.

~GIAN LORENZO BERNINI

EVEN THOUGH IT was growing late, Bastien drove Sarah back into Rome to Suntara, and led her down to the vault. The mostly-empty room seemed too bright with its steel-clad walls glittering with reflected light. Eirene waited for them, lounging on one of the reclined memory walking chairs.

Sarah felt exhausted, and hungry. She should have stopped by the dining room before they left, but she was eager to learn ciphers. She needed that knowledge, and the distraction.

Eirene rose to greet them. She and Bastien kissed each other on each cheek, then she turned to Sarah. "Did you meet with Alter to practice dispossessions?"

That was the last thing Sarah wanted to talk about.

Eirene caught her expression. "Is everything all right, dear?"

"Can we just focus on ciphers for now? Please?"

"But of course." Bastien slipped smoothly into the conversation. "That is why we are here, no?"

He led them to the rear of the vault, to a whiteboard affixed to the wall beside the workbench Alter usually used. He began drawing with a blue marker. "Your sensitivity to runes is a manifestation of the power of your bloodline."

"I'm a rune warrior," Sarah said thoughtfully. "So does that mean I'm related to Joan of Arc, even though Alter's family couldn't find proof in my genealogy?"

Bastien flashed a smile. "It is indeed. I spent a great deal of effort concealing your bloodline these past centuries, hoping another rune warrior would arise."

"You destroyed all those records? Why?"

"Joan was indeed very strong. She accomplished much in little time, but could have done much more. I have studied rune warrior lines, and there was much strength in hers. I did not want the hunters, or anyone else, intercepting a new rune warrior before they were strong enough to defend themselves."

"But Alter said his family didn't set up Joan," Sarah protested.

"There was much confusion in those days," Bastien said.

Eirene added, "Someone targeted her. We always thought it was the hunters. If not them, then someone went to a lot of effort to make it look like them."

"Such subterfuge is exceptional," Bastien said. "I have monitored branches of that family ever since, shielding the records from the world. Many of your ancestors did great things, Sarah, but not until now has the full strength of your bloodline again resurfaced."

Sarah sank into a nearby chair, amazed. To think Bastien had been shepherding her family from the shadows. She'd never considered her family anything special. Her parents had always done their best to ensure that.

"I don't know anything about my ancestors. Please tell me."

Bastien nodded with another smile. "Enchante. Several were explorers. One assisted my father in hunting the renegade heka known as Cortez in the new world. Others played important roles in the American Revolution and helped shape your country's early days. It would take more time than we have tonight to tell you a fraction of their tales."

"Then let's meet again soon." Sarah felt eager to learn about them.

"It would be my pleasure. Perhaps a weekly dinner date, yes?"

Sarah hesitated only a second. With her personal life in such turmoil between Alter and Tomas, she wasn't sure how Tomas would react to a weekly dinner date with Bastien. "I think it's a good idea, but don't call it a date."

"A clandestine rendezvous does sound more interesting," he said with a warm smile and a wink.

Sarah laughed. Eirene tapped the whiteboard to draw their attention again. "As a rune warrior, you can use all the runes the other rounongifted can, but those are not where your gift will shine."

Bastien drew a couple of symbols that were simple compared to the runes Sarah had been most recently working with, but more complex than the healing rune.

They felt different.

As Sarah studied the symbols, they set her pulse racing. The markings contained coiled energy, as if only needing a little nudge to explode right off the board.

"Where do these symbols come from?" she asked, leaning closer to the board.

Eirene said, "These are old. Many of the best cipher symbols are very old. These are known as oracle bone script, the oldest known form of Chinese written language."

"Bone script?" Sarah asked. It sounded creepy.

"They were inscribed on turtle shells and similar materials," Bastien explained.

Sarah chuckled. "It sounded more mysterious before you clarified."

Bastien said, "Some hunters have made a study of ciphers, but it is not a priority because they cannot activate these symbols."

Eriene added, "They collect them though. Like all rune lore."

"That means their knowledge of ciphers was lost when Paul stole their rune lore book," Sarah said.

"Most likely," Bastien agreed.

"I hate that man," she muttered.

"Hunters are not the only fount of knowledge about rune warriors," Bastien assured her. "Nor perhaps even the best experts. Mother and I know the most of any facetakers."

Eirene took up another marker and drew from memory a dozen symbols that all triggered a subtle resonance for Sarah, like long-forgotten friends.

"You can use these symbols alone, or wrap them in standard rune markings to modify and fine-tune their meaning," Eirene explained.

She produced a series of beautiful ciphers, combining some of the symbols Bastien had drawn with standard runes that Sarah was familiar with. The resulting ciphers seemed to pulse with power, and Sarah grew more excited with every one.

"You've seen these work?" she asked.

Eirene pointed to one. "This was a favorite of little Joan. It boosted strength and bravery, while protecting her from steel weapons. It saved her life during the siege of Orleans."

"Amazing," Sarah breathed, tracing the cipher with a finger and committing it to memory.

Eirene went on to draw a number of other marks which either began at key junction points of the ciphers and radiated outward, or started around the symbol and drew in toward the center.

"These are targeting marks." Bastien explained. "And the key to fine tuning your strength."

The marks focused the effects of the cipher, either in drawing soul force from one person, or from everyone within a certain radius of the inscribed rune. The resulting energy could be spent by either directing it toward the rune warrior, to targeted individuals, or to everyone in a target area.

"So it's like laser focus versus spraying with a hose," Sarah said as they discussed the concepts.

Eirene nodded. "It's possible to achieve both extremes. With some practice, you can become very precise."

"But don't those rune webs the heka use accomplish similar things?" Sarah asked.

Bastien said, "They can mimic some of the simpler aspects of what rune warriors do. However their webs are extremely complex, and require perhaps many dispossessed souls to power. It is difficult for them to create a web that draws power from nearby souls not already bonded to their matrix, although they can create area-wide targeted effects."

"The difference can seem subtle at times," Eirene said. "But it's profound. Comparing heka rune webs to rune warrior ciphers is like comparing an original Apollo moon rocket to the starship Enterprise from Star Trek. They may both be able to travel into space, but the range and abilities are completely different."

Sarah nodded slowly, feeling a bit daunted by how much she still had to learn. Without teachers, she might never learn to master her newfound abilities.

Some of the most important symbols dictated how much soul force could be drained at one time from the target souls. Sarah immediately saw the potential for abuse. If misused, those runes could wreak terrible damage. No wonder Alter had been reluctant to discuss them.

"What happens if you don't send the gathered soul force anywhere?" she asked.

Bastien and Eirene exchanged a surprised look. He shrugged and said, "I am not sure. I do not think anyone has ever tested such a thing. Why siphon power if not to use it, no?"

"Waste not, want not," Eirene added.

She then drew another rune that was markedly different. Unlike the others that seemed ready to leap off the board, this one sucked at her vision like a mini black hole.

"What is that?" Sarah asked, peering closer, but reluctant to touch it.

"That's the primary counter rune," Eirene explained. "Anyone with a rounon gift can use that to block other runes, external attacks on their souls, or to scramble effects within a rune duel."

"A rune duel?"

"It's complicated, a way for rounon-gifted to battle each other with their rune powers. Each person seeks to leverage the force of their soul and any they may have direct access to against their opponent. We'll review the technique when we have some more time. Once you understand it, most heka wouldn't stand a chance against you, since you'd have access to far more energy."

"So why don't you wear that mark all the time?"

Bastien said, "It can interfere with bonded enhancements, and it can prevent heka from drawing power from other souls."

"It's not a perfect defense," Eirene added. "It didn't work against the forbidden rune. Alter tried it."

Sarah committed it to memory, along with the others. After reviewing all of the symbols they knew, they spent an hour practicing with applying the modifiers. Sarah finally stepped back with a happy nod. "I think I understand the basics. Can we try activating one?"

"That is why we are here," Bastien said.

In her first attempt, after painstaking planning and triple-checking the inscription, Sarah developed a cipher to draw the tiniest fraction of energy from both Eirene and Bastien for the duration of five seconds. The energy was directed at Sarah to enhance strength and well-being.

She felt more excited than nervous as she concentrated over the cipher they had drawn onto a sheet of paper. A little energy drained from her into the construct, and it flashed into blue-white fire. The paper didn't burn, but slowly blackened and curled around the rune.

Eirene shrugged and Bastien said, "I feel nothing."

Sarah frowned. She was sure it had worked. Maybe—

A wave of strength rocked her in an invisible tide. Her lingering weariness melted away, as did her gnawing hunger. She felt like she could leap tall buildings in a single bound, and felt a deep sense of relief as the well of rounon power in her heart filled to bursting.

"Wow," Sarah exclaimed. "I feel so strong. I only siphoned such a small percentage."

"Our souls are more powerful than most," Eirene said.

"But even from ungifted souls, the effects can prove dramatic. The strength of soul is a powerful force," Bastien reminded her.

"This is amazing," Sarah laughed, ecstatic by the success. "I wish I'd known this before we faced Paul last time. It might have been enough to shift the balance."

She imagined siphoning soul force from hundreds of legionnaires. She wasn't sure it would work the same since they were only memory projections, but they had been real people once. Surely she could have gotten some kind of benefit. Even better, she might have been able to weaken Paul enough for their weapons to really hurt him.

She couldn't wait to test the idea.

"What else can we do?" she asked, eager to learn more.

"We can teach but your first lesson," Bastien said.

Sarah didn't pretend to hide her disappointment. There had to be more.

Eirene gave her a reassuring smile. "That's why we met here in the vault." She gestured toward the nearby memory machines. "We're going to visit a couple of experts."

"Joan of Arc?" When Eirene nodded, Sarah barely restrained a squeal of excitement. Joan of Arc was one of her historical heroines. She couldn't wait to meet her.

"But first," Bastien said as he picked up one of the blocky helmets. "We visit Vlad the Impaler."

64

How can Father not see the danger? The demons have corrupted our blood. Never before have they broken the purity of a hunter, and Alter had been one of the greatest. If he can fall, there can be no safety but in the final extermination of every demon on the planet. I love my brother, so I will be the one to kill him. It is the only way to honor the memory of his former purity.

~REUBEN

SARAH WASN'T sure what to expect as she followed Bastien and their soldier escorts through the stone-walled corridors of Vlad's grand citadel in Bucharest. She had to keep reminding herself not to think of him as the impaler, at least not during their visit.

His name was Vlad the Third, Prince of Wallachia, or simply Vlad Dracula. It still seemed strange that the man who inspired the legends of the greatest vampire of all time had been a rune warrior. That fact colored everything she'd learned about ciphers with a hint of danger, and she wished she'd asked Gregorios to explain his comment about vampires.

For much of her life, she'd thought Transylvania was a made-up nation, and she'd never heard of Wallachia, the seat of Vlad's power. Nestled in the Romanian mountains on the southeastern European border, the little nation had been an important battleground against the encroaching Ottoman Turks. Vlad had fought them with daring, cunning, and barbarous cruelty.

Sarah wasn't sure that was the man she wanted to approach for information about ciphers.

The soldiers led them into a richly appointed study with fine rugs on the stone floor, colorful tapestries on the walls, and a roaring fire in a huge fireplace along one wall. Vlad rose from his seat at a large desk strewn with maps and scrolls.

He threw his arms wide and gave Bastien a welcoming smile. "Welcome once again, lord of many lives."

Bastien made a grand bow, looking every inch a medieval lord in his fine emerald tunic and deep blue jacket. "A pleasure to visit your court, my lord of Wallachia."

Vlad wore a rich crimson coat, trimmed in gold, and a matching hat. His black hair hung past his shoulders, and he sported an impressive mustache. His face was pinched, with a perpetual frown. His gaze was intense, and he moved with a predator's grace.

He glanced at Sarah, and she made a graceful bow, the way Bastien had taught her. She was happy he made it possible for her to understand the foreign tongue. She'd grown used to the idea of understanding ancient Romans, but she'd never visited eastern Europe in the memoryscape, and it felt more foreign and exotic.

"Will you introduce me to your lovely companion?" Vlad asked as he approached.

"Sarah is a mighty ally from far western lands, and a budding rune warrior of exceptional talent."

Vlad smiled, although the movement didn't seem to reach his eyes. "Such an ally, and such a beauty. Each alone are rare, but twain, perhaps you are the rarest of jewels." He bowed over her hand. "The Ottomans are massing at the Danube, and their Janissary Heka ortas are preparing to sweep over my kingdom in a flood of destruction."

"How go your preparations?" Bastien asked.

"All will be ready within days." This time his eyes shone with eager anticipation when he smiled.

He led Sarah to a divan nearby, gesturing for her to sit beside him. He did not relinquish her hand, and his touch sent a chill creeping across her skin. "I have constructed a series of fortresses across the nation, their walls inscribed with the most powerful ciphers ever devised."

Bastien took a seat nearby. "We have come to learn these secrets from you, for we face another great evil to rival the threat of the Turks."

Vlad scowled at the mention of his enemies, then gave Sarah a calculating look. He leaned closer. "I alone can activate the ciphers that are even now spreading across the land to intertwine the souls of all Wallachians in support of my conflict. The strength of the entire nation will be mine to wield when I face Mehmed and his innumerable host. I will be the sword of execution to the heathens."

As he spoke, his eyes shone with fanatical intensity, and Sarah wished she wasn't sitting so close. She drew her hand from his grip to brush her hair back. "What can you teach me about the ciphers?"

After another searching gaze, he spoke softly. "I have searched far and wide for many years to learn the deeper truths. If you weren't here with Lord Bastien, I would never share them, but I owe him a debt greater than all the secrets of the world."

That only stoked Sarah's eagerness to learn. She said, "I know many of the basic runes. Do you have a book of symbols or something I can study?"

Vlad shook his head, first tapping his skull with a thick finger, then tapping her left temple. "Knowledge that valuable must live in the mind." His eyes drifted down toward her bodice and he added, "And in the heart."

If he tried to touch her there, she'd punch him to the moon, no matter how much she wanted to learn.

Luckily he kept his hands to himself. "Basic runes are the dregs, not worthy of your best efforts."

"But they help focus the ciphers, don't they?" Sarah asked.

With a dismissive grunt, Vlad slashed his finger through the air between them, leaving a glowing mark, like drifting cinders, floating in its wake. "This is no rune, and yet . . ."

The mark blazed with blue-white light. The room began to brighten, as if concealed lights had been switched on. Warmth poured into the study that had been chill, despite the fire.

Vlad gestured at the lightened room. "For simple uses of power such as this, I define the intent, and it matters not the mark I use. The force of my will and the strength of the well of my soul produce the effect"

Sarah frowned. That didn't sound right. "I thought the runes were important."

"I am a rune warrior," Vlad declared, banging his chest. "I define runes. Heka and the meddlesome hunters take the scraps from the table of their betters, like the dogs of my hall."

Behind Vlad, Bastien rolled his eyes, but remained silent.

"So how do you build your ciphers then?" Sarah asked.

"Ciphers serve me, not the other way around. I first know my purpose. Then I make my mark, and breathe life into it."

"As always you teach with clarity," Bastien said smoothly. "For simple ciphers, the marks matter not so much, no? But let us discuss the grand ciphers, the drawing of power from other souls, and directing that power to enhance your army or to savage your enemies."

"Even so," Vlad said. He rose and led Sarah to his desk where he swept scrolls and parchments aside. On a blank sheet, he began to draw.

Sarah recognized some of the symbols, as well as many of the modifiers. He also drew a dozen symbols she'd never seen before, but which drew her with unmistakable power the same way the bone script symbols had. Studying them was not so much a process of acquiring new knowledge as it was rediscovering secrets she somehow already knew.

Vlad began to combine the symbols, his hand moving with surprising alacrity as he crafted complex ciphers. As he worked, he explained that the more complex the cipher, the more important the symbols.

He glanced at her as they leaned over the table, heads close together. "This is your heritage, lovely Sarah of the sunset lands. Your soul has the force to give life to simple ciphers, to shape them and direct them. To achieve glory sufficient to overthrow the evil of the world, you need my ciphers."

"When the force of tens of thousands of souls is being channeled, such vast energy focused on a single purpose, the ciphers must be wrought with care. They are the reins you cast around that power with the well of your strength, harnessing it to your will. Without those reins, such glorious power could burst out of even my control. Like a wild stallion, it could trample and destroy."

He stood tall and gripped her hand, his fingers cold and hard like iron. "Disaster would result. Anything from soul exhaustion, to the burning out of the well of your soul strength, to a death worse than slow impaling."

Sarah grimaced, wishing he hadn't mentioned that particular torture.

"You have built safeguards into your ciphers to protect against such chaos, yes?" Bastien asked.

"They are ironclad," he assured them. "But one must take risks in war."

"How are you sure?" Sarah asked, wishing she could think of a way to warn him of the danger.

She doubted just telling him would work. He seemed arrogant and more than a little scary. From what Bastien had told her, Vlad's ciphers would indeed prove too strong and would cast his mind beyond humanity, transforming him into the bloodthirsty fiend the world still spoke of in whispers.

"I know it," he said, giving her a confident grin. "One must have confidence before joining in battle, particularly against enchanters like those in the employ of the sultan. Doubt will guarantee defeat more surely than an arrow to the throat."

Sarah nodded slowly. She couldn't argue with that, but added, "There has to be a way to test your cipher, to know for sure."

Vlad shook his head slowly. "Nothing like this has been done before. If I'm not willing to take the risk to protect those only I can protect, then we've already lost."

While Sarah considered that, Vlad gestured at the parchment covered with drawings. "Any symbol can work, if you are convinced it possesses the strength to carry and focus the power you will direct upon it."

He pointed to one symbol she recognized as an eternal knot, although a slightly different variation than what she was familiar with. "This symbol has perhaps many meanings, but is often seen as symbolizing the cycle of birth, death, and suffering. I can utilize the power of that belief to buttress my intentions as I press it into service to my will. Use and tradition imbue symbols with power, and greater power if used for that purpose."

"That's why ancient languages seem so powerful," Sarah said.

"Indeed." Vlad thumped the table. "The longer the association, the more souls those symbols become entwined with down the spiraling corridors of history, the more powerful they become."

Sarah considered the sheet of ciphers, her thoughts churning as she digested his words. "It's starting to make sense."

Vlad laughed. "As long as it makes sense to you, for you are the one who will mold the force of souls to your will."

When they left a short time later, Bastien asked, "What do you think of mighty Vlad?"

Sarah suppressed a shudder. "A bit creepy. I wish I didn't know what's going to happen to him. It would've been easier to believe what he taught if I'd known he'd succeeded."

"We draw truth from whatever source can provide it, no?" Bastien said. Then he gave her a reassuring smile. "That is why we visited Vlad first. Let us pay now a happier visit to sweet Joan."

The memoryscape blurred, and the towering stone buildings melted, draining away to reveal a completely different landscape. Rolling green hills and mature trees appeared in full bloom, as if the second memoryscape had waited concealed behind the first.

A distant city wall rose above the trees to their left. Peaked tents sprouted out of the ground by the score, soon covering what had been a large field with a densely-packed military encampment.

Soldiers materialized, first as ethereal shapes drifting between the tents, solidifying with each step until they looked as real as life itself. The scents of apple blossoms and spring flowers tickled Sarah's nose, then faded under the stench of unwashed bodies, sweat, and nearby latrines.

Sarah wrinkled her nose and turned to Bastien. "That was an impressive transition."

His costume had shifted with the time period, changing to green hose and a bright red tunic, with a feathered cap perched at a jaunty angle on his head. He swept it off and made an extravagant bow. "We aim always to please, cheri."

"You could have left out the smell," she suggested.

"It will soon pass from notice," he said, gesturing her toward the heart of the camp.

She now wore a russet-colored, cotton dress with a form-fitting bodice and wide sleeves. The slippers were not suited for traipsing through the muddy lanes between tents, so Bastien swapped them out for sturdy hiking boots that remained concealed beneath her long skirt.

As they passed through the camp, Sarah commented, "The soldiers look happy, even though so many of them are wounded."

"They have won a great victory, so spirits are high. And this camp is honored with the presence of the Maid of Orleans, our little Joan."

He swept past a pair of sentries stationed outside a large tent of brightly striped reds and yellows. Sometimes it was nice to be all but invisible. Sarah paused before entering, wondering how Vlad had seemed so aware of their presence. Most other memory shades only took notice of them when they broke the integrity of the memoryscape.

Inside the tent, Bastien was embracing a sturdy young woman with a round, suntanned face and long, brown hair. Her blue eyes sparkled, adding a dash of vibrant life to her appearance.

"Uncle Bastien," she squealed. "You missed our great victory."

"Ah, cheri, I am deeply saddened by that," Bastien said, smiling down at the much shorter woman. "But Joan, the victory is so much the greater that you achieved it alone."

She made the sign of the cross. "Never alone, Uncle Bastien. The Almighty fought by our side, and the power of his spirit was manifest through the strength of my ciphers. My men fought like lions and shed grievous injuries."

"You grow strong in the rune lore," Bastien said, although his smile faltered a little.

Joan of Arc patted the huge, ornately decorated bible resting on her camp table. "Symbols of god are my ciphers, Uncle Bastien."

"Oui, let that suffice for today," he said, his tone a bit long-suffering.

He turned to Sarah and gestured her closer. "Joan, may I introduce a dear friend and woman of runes like yourself? Sarah, I am delighted to introduce you to Joan d'Arc."

Joan curtsied, despite wearing armor, and Sarah responded in kind. She was thrilled to meet the famous young heroine, and a thousand questions bubbled through her mind. Joan took her hands in a powerful grip, her fingers strong and calloused from hard work and fighting.

"You too have been touched by the grace of god?" Joan asked, studying Sarah's face, her gaze intent.

"I only recently discovered my abilities with ciphers," Sarah responded carefully.

Religious zeal burned in Joan's eyes and, even though Sarah had heard the stories of her devotion to god, seeing it in person made her a little uneasy. As always, overt religious zeal reminded her of her parents and their twisted view of the world.

Joan grinned, apparently pleased with the answer. "You have joined us at a wonderful time. We have only just liberated Orleans from the siege of the wicked English."

Bastien had told Sarah he was planning to visit Joan at the end of May, 1429, shortly after the battle where Joan cemented her reputation and won over most of her doubters. That had been the start of a great, if short-lived, campaign for the young rune warrior.

"Ah, Uncle Bastien suggested you might share what you know about ciphers," Sarah said.

"But of course," Joan exclaimed, towing her by the hand around the table. "He taught me many of my early lessons, helping me to interpret the will of god and make tangible the faith of my countrymen."

"Which symbols have been the most successful for you?" Sarah asked.

Joan turned and saluted the French flag standing on a pole in the corner. "The symbol of our nation is always at the heart of my ciphers."

Sarah looked closer, noting for the first time the golden fleur-de-lis on the blue background of the flag. She sensed its latent power as strongly as she had the symbols Vlad had demonstrated, which surprised her.

She had always considered it a more modern symbol. Now that she thought about it, she realized it had been the object of the faith and courage of centuries of men and women.

If Vlad was right, that was more than enough to imbue a symbol with remarkable power. For a woman like Joan of Arc, who was such a devout patriot, that symbol must have produced a singularly powerful heart for her ciphers.

Joan added, "Do not fix your mind too strongly on the symbol. It is the purity of purpose that grants us our greatest strength." Her eyes shone and her voice rang with conviction. "God has granted us this wondrous gift to draw upon the living faith of all around us and turn that faith into a weapon of purity, the tangible measure of the will of god."

"What ciphers did you use in your last battle?" Bastien asked.

Joan eagerly sketched them, and Sarah devoured the symbols with her eyes. Every new cipher she learned clicked into place as if her mind had already anticipated its coming.

As they discussed the modifiers Joan used, the concepts felt eerily familiar. Joan's ciphers produced what she called her mighty shields of faith, or the gift of God's own healing. Sarah pondered the new insights and started making new connections, seeing possibilities they hadn't yet shared with her.

It was as if everything they had taught formed but the foundation to a far grander construct made of glittering lines whose sweeping majesty left her breathless. The speed with which the concepts gelled in her mind startled her, but she embraced them. She needed those ciphers, and she would test them as soon as possible, fine tune them, and use them to defeat Paul.

After the interview Sarah hugged Joan and wished her luck.

"God speed to you, sister of the living faith," Joan declared, hugging her hard enough to make Sarah grunt.

As she followed Bastien back through the camp, Sarah noticed a lingering sadness in his expression.

"What's wrong?"

He sighed. "I have always regretted not arriving in time to free her from that false trial. You have glimpsed the greatness of her soul, but too many friends were drawn away by other duties, not seeing the danger lurking so close until it was too late."

"I thought the trial took almost a year from the time she was captured," Sarah said.

"In times past, news and travel took far longer. I first heard of her capture en route to visit the Ottoman sultan Murad the Second, who was negotiating for his second life as Mehmed the Second, or Mehmed the Conqueror. He was the same sultan that Vlad had been preparing to fight. I thought there would be time to complete my mission and return, but alas I was delayed."

Sarah frowned. "Wait a minute. You worked with the Turks too? I thought they were the enemy?"

Bastien shrugged. "Everyone is the enemy of someone, yes? The Ottoman Empire was a powerful force in the world for a long time, and some argue the nations under their rule fared better than many ruled by Christians. Our work is separate from religion."

"But you've always played in politics, even if it was just behind the scenes."

"Oui, but at the time, we did not believe the Turks would spread to rule Europe, and time proved us right. The world is better off with more than one power in play. If one side had gained too much the advantage, we would have stepped in, have no fear."

"What if Joan hadn't been captured?" Sarah asked softly. "What if she had gained too much power? Would you have stepped in?"

"That is not fair. She was a dear one, our little Joan, but she could not have risen to rule nations as she was."

"Why not?"

He gestured back toward the tent. "You saw, cheri. She was a woman of too much faith."

"I thought faith is a good thing."

"Oui, but it blinded her to truth. The power of faith and the power of soul powers are different things. She attributed her strength to the wrong source, which dampened her power."

"I don't understand," Sarah said as they reached the edge of the camp. "Religion is one of the most powerful forces on earth. Faith drives people to do incredible, or incredibly stupid things."

"Indeed. I do not argue this. However, the power of faith is foreign to rounon gifts or nevra core. By wrapping her ciphers in religious tones, Joan tried mixing oil and water. It does not work."

"I still don't see why not," Sarah said.

"I shall have my father explain it to you, yes? He has studied the effects more than anyone, and has the most experience with religious figures who wielded the power of god."

"But—"

The memory lurched, making her stumble. Unlike the beautiful transition Bastien had managed earlier, the memoryscape rippled and disappeared. For a second everything went black, the blackness of the heart of a cave at midnight. Then an entirely different scene snapped into focus.

Sarah gaped as she turned a slow circle, staring up at tiers of stone benches packed with screaming spectators on every side. She stood on soft sand, warmed by a midday sun that blazed overhead in a brilliant blue sky.

She recognized the location in a heartbeat. She'd dreamed of visiting it, but even though she'd spent so much time in its modern-day ruin, the true glory of the sight left her speechless.

The Colosseum.

She stood upon the sands where gladiators had dueled and died. As she completed her circuit of the legendary arena, another person appeared nearby, as if stepping out of thin air.

Paul.

"Hello, Sarah," he said, sweeping his ever-present hat off his head and giving her a warm smile. "I am pleased you came."

65

History may condemn me as a weak leader, but the Lord knows my heart and the truth of the burdens I must bear in secret. The manifestation of the glorious power of the Almighty God cannot be ceded to Charles, no matter the pressure he brings to bear.

The sacrifice of the martyrs who died not knowing the truth is not diminished, and their eternal recompense made sure. And yet, my heart is heavy with sorrow to see Rome fall, its glory tarnished, my Swiss Guard slain nearly to a man, all to protect one dangerous secret.

Were I a man of less faith and more devotion, perhaps I would consider activating the runes, but I dare not, even though a new miracle could restore the balance of my power. Such a lie would drive me to a dishonorable grave.

~POPE CLEMENT VII

SARAH RECOILED FROM PAUL, the shock of his appearance scattering thoughts of ciphers and rune warrior lore. He'd ripped her from a memory before, but she hadn't expected him to do so again.

Paul did not attack, did not summon that wide-bladed sword he liked to threaten her with.

"Ah, this isn't really a good time," Sarah said, trying to watch Paul and also scan the Colosseum for Bastien. What had happened to him? Would he draw her from the memoryscape when he realized what had happened?

Could he pull her away from Paul, or could Paul somehow hold her soul captive in this other time?

Paul tossed his hat into the air, and it settled onto a hat stand that appeared on the sands nearby. A beautifully-carved mahogany table appeared a second later, flanked by two padded wooden chairs. He gestured toward one of them.

"Please, have a seat. We have much to discuss."

The last thing Sarah wanted to do was follow any orders of his, but she also didn't want to fight him. She wasn't ready, couldn't focus enough to figure out a cipher to escape. So she cautiously sank onto one of the chairs.

Paul seated himself across from her, looking completely at ease. He again wore a business suit, this one navy. "When last we met, you proved yourself worthy of more than a simple death."

She hoped he wasn't suggesting a complicated death instead.

He waited, so she said, "And you ran away before I could blow you up again."

"Your commitment to a cause is commendable, but don't limit yourself, Sarah. You fought admirably, and you would have died with sufficient honor to reverence the memory of my sister. We're past that now. It's time to move on to greater things and embrace your new destiny."

"You're assuming I want a new destiny." His superior attitude irritated her. She tried summoning her grenade launcher, but got nothing but a headache. He was cheating again.

"The greatest souls are always flexible, always open to better destinies."

He waved a hand toward the emperor, seated in his central dais overlooking the games. A second later, gates on both sides of the stadium opened, and two gladiators entered. The crowd roared louder than ever, some people spraying spittle across those seated below them. No one seemed to notice.

"Take these two gladiators," Paul said, swiveling to watch the approaching men. Both looked strong and deadly. "Stepping onto these sands resulted in one of two things: death or victory."

"Death battles aren't really my thing."

Paul glanced at her and grinned like a kid at a ball game. "This is the most famous gladiator duel in history. Verus and Priscus. Both champions. Last match of the opening day of the games, perhaps the crowning match of any such event."

The two men saluted, then launched into a vicious duel, attacking with remarkable skill. Sarah didn't see any enhancement runes on them, but even Tomas would have had to work to defeat them.

She tore her eyes away from the battle. "Why are you showing me all this?"

"To demonstrate a point. In a moment." He didn't seem to care that the gladiators were fighting to the death close enough to spray them with sand a few times.

Sarah said, "I'll make this simple for you. I won't serve you. Goodbye."

She stood, but in a blink, the table and chairs were gone, and Paul crossed the distance between them. He grabbed her by the throat and lifted her into the air.

With her new enhancements, she moved fast, but she hadn't even seen him coming. It was almost like he'd stepped through the space between them.

"Do not cast my honor at your feet, unworthy soul," Paul snarled, his hand squeezing until she could barely sip any air.

She kicked and punched at him, but accomplished nothing.

After a moment of glaring, Paul dropped her. She stumbled back into the chair that appeared behind her. He returned to the far side of the table, which also reappeared, and settled himself onto his chair, his expression calm, as if nothing had happened. The gladiators had both lost their shields and were fighting with gladius alone. The duel would have captured her attention at any other time.

As Sarah coughed and tried to catch her breath, newly terrified of Paul, he leaned toward her. "You must learn to discipline yourself, Sarah, if you are to become worthy of your new station as my most-honored servant."

"I don't want—" she began, her voice hoarse.

He spoke over her without slowing. "I will soon rise to preeminence in this decadent world. I alone possess the power and the right to rule all things. I will reshape this world, draw it from darkness and filth, and raise it to greatness."

Sarah listened with growing horror. His voice was calm, as if he was discussing his daily schedule. That calm assurance made what he was saying that much more terrible. Had anyone else started spouting about plans to take over the world, she would have written them off as a lunatic.

Paul was cui dashi, and arguably the strongest being on the planet. He had one master rune, and was hunting more. With that power at his disposal, world conquest was a distinct possibility.

She really needed her grenade launcher. Or maybe napalm.

"The world will become a grand paradise under my rule," Paul continued. "And you will enjoy the singular honor of serving me as my partner in ushering in the age of greatness foretold by so many religions."

Sarah wondered how that would work with what Bastien just told her about religions and soul powers not mixing.

"I kind of like the world the way it is," she said when he paused for breath.

He scoffed. "You like war? Disease? Crime? Poverty?"

"Of course not, but you're not talking about fixing any of that. You're talking about global slavery."

"The world yearns to be enslaved," Paul said, waving a dismissive hand. "Every day, it attempts to enslave itself to greed, corruption, and violence. These things would be done away under my rule." His eyes shone with conviction. "I will impose upon this chaotic world the peace that has long eluded it."

"You're crazy. Other regimes have tried to force populations to do only what they wanted. They're called dictators or communists, or fanatics, and it never works."

Paul sighed, his expression longsuffering, as if trying to explain simple concepts to an imbecil. "But they lacked the power to enforce their wills. Don't you see, Sarah? They were trying to impose faulty order upon a faulty world. Of course they failed. I am a higher form of life, so I can make it work. I'm offering you a chance to help the entire world achieve peace."

"Peace in chains is not peace," Sarah retorted.

"You speak as a child. You must embrace a better destiny." He swept his hand back toward the gladiators, who had both lost their swords. Both men had been wounded, but faced each other with spiked knuckles.

Before they could close again, the officiator of the match stepped between them at a gesture from the emperor. The men faced his lofty seat, swaying and gasping with exhaustion.

Sarah caught her breath, momentarily forgetting Paul's crazy rantings as she awaited the thumbs up or thumbs down signal. The lives of those mighty warriors hung in the balance.

The emperor instead stood and lifted both arms. Everyone cheered louder than ever. The gesture looked positive. Sarah glanced at Paul, who was watching her, his expression unreadable.

Officials entered the arena bearing wooden swords, which they presented to both gladiators. Spectators continued cheering, and many openly wept.

"This is good, right?" Sarah hated to ask Paul anything.

"Indeed. The emperor proclaimed them both winner, and awarded them their freedom."

"That's what the swords mean?"

"Yes."

"Did that happen often?"

"Almost never."

"Why are you showing me this?" she asked.

"Because those men reached a higher destiny. As can you." He extended his hand toward her. "Accept my offer and become the greatest mortal the world has ever known."

"First tell me this," Sarah said, watching his hand like it was a viper. "If you're so great, why have you been skulking around the memoryscape trying to steal master runes, and trying to kill me?"

Paul's calm cracked for a second. "Your life debt is a different matter, as I've explained. For the world to enjoy global peace, I will dictate the rules that all must obey. I will reign with justice and equity. Anyone found transgressing my law, as you yourself did in killing Mai Luan, must be punished, or the rule of law becomes void."

"So you make the rules, and you decide when exceptions are allowed?"

He stood, and the table disappeared, allowing him to step across to her. Sarah sprang to her feet, but he did not strike. Instead he gently took her hand and bowed over it. She was tempted to punch him in the throat, but that wouldn't accomplish anything.

"Together we will rule," he said when he stood, still holding her hand. "You will bear to my honor a glorious lineage of cui dashi rulers that I will set over the world to manage and take care of it."

Sarah recoiled, and yanked her hand from his grasp, retreating several steps. She'd been afraid he was planning something like that, but hearing him say it still disgusted her.

"No offense, but you're not my type."

He laughed. "We can take whatever forms we choose. We can mate every time in a different body. Whatever you want, you will have. I will be whatever type you require, and you will serve me to the end of days, my cherished, most-favored bride."

"That's—"

He again crossed the distance in a blink, not even appearing to take a step. Sarah tried to retreat, but he caught her arm and pressed the finger of his other hand to her lips.

"Consider well my offer before deciding. Your life is forfeit to me, but I am offering you an opportunity that no other mortal could ever dream of. Even though my mother does not approve, I will have you and I will raise you to greatness."

"Hold on," Sarah said, resisting the urge to spit after he removed his finger. "Your mother doesn't approve of me?"

"Not yet," he admitted, his confidence cracking for the first time. "But she will come to see your worth."

"You've been speaking with your mother about me?"

"Indeed. She is the queen mother of the world, and all I do is to honor her name and to support her objectives."

"Didn't your mother ever teach you that telling a girl you'll enslave her soul if she doesn't agree to your proposal is not the best way to win her heart?"

"Don't ever disparage her!" Paul hissed, glancing around the memoryscape nervously. "You can never anger her."

That was freaky on all sorts of levels, and it shook Sarah to see Paul, as powerful as he was, acting terrified of anything. Then again, if his mother was psycho enough to raise a son like Paul, she probably wasn't an average molly homemaker.

"I can't—"

Again he interrupted. That was becoming a terrible habit.

"I will find you tomorrow. Submit to me then and we will launch our conquest of these short-sighted, weak mortals."

With a final bow, he turned and strode out the Death Gate.

Sarah watched him go, revolted and terrified beyond measure. Had he actually tried to recruit her to be his sex toy partner in crime?

She looked up into the sky and cried, "Will someone please get me out of here?"

66

Praise to God that Bastien discovered Joan d'Arc. She is an angel incarnate, and what can I do but accept that her mighty power comes from God? She has agreed to keep her ciphers secret, and I cannot ignore such an ally.

Upon consolidation of my throne, I will seek vengeance upon the hunters for the madness they inflicted upon my father. They claim purity of purpose, but so much destruction is laid at their feet, I cannot but surmise their cause cannot be just.

~CHARLES VII, KING OF FRANCE

SARAH RETURNED to Quentin's mansion with Eirene and Bastien, disgust at Paul's proposal turning to anger. She used it to dampen her terror. He was strong enough that his threat was all too real, but she couldn't imagine submitting to such a monster.

"I'd rather die first," she swore to Eirene again while they drove through the city.

"Better if Paul dies instead," Eirene said, patting her hand.

Bastien glanced back from the driver's seat. "He will not settle for ruling from the shadows like we suspected of Mai Luan. He plans to become the Caesar of the entire world, yes?"

"This time we bring on the Ides of March before he takes office," Eirene said, her expression determined.

"Sounds good to me." Sarah embraced their determination, giving free reign to her anger. She'd unleash her own new-found power upon him, then they'd see who was smiling.

When they reached the mansion, Sarah excused herself from the others. Eirene promised to update Gregorios and the team, and even had a full dinner sent up to Sarah's suite. She hadn't expected to eat anything, but the aromas of braised pork and fresh-baked bread reminded her she hadn't eaten, and she devoured it all.

Then she got to work.

With Paul's threat looming in the back of her mind, she wrote down every cipher, symbol, and modifier she'd learned from her recent training. She added to the list the other symbols that had come to mind while she studied the works of Vlad and Joan. That led to even more ideas.

She filled page after page with runes, then spent another hour crafting higher ciphers out of them. She kept the runesmith box open on her desk, hoping for every bit of inspiration she could get.

She got a lot.

It was like a window had opened into a secret part of her soul, and ideas sprang forth faster than she could write. She lost herself in the process, immersed deeper in rune lore than ever before. As she worked, the ciphers called to her, their potential uses clear to her as plain writing.

They took on individual flavors. Ciphers to increase her strength gave the impression of sunbaked stone, while those that included enhanced healing reminded her of the scent of fresh-baked cookies. She crafted one that could be used to form an invisible barrier, and it resonated like glittering steel in her mind.

Finally Sarah sat back and reviewed her work. It felt like she'd known some of those ciphers before, like she'd been searching for forgotten knowledge all her life, and that she'd finally found it. It didn't make sense, but that was how she felt, and she accepted it. The knowledge thrilled her with a new sense of purpose and confidence.

Sarah rose and lifted a finger. Vlad had marked his runes in the air, and she needed to figure out how to do that. Facing Paul, she wouldn't have time to summon pen and paper. She decided to start by simply mimicking Vlad's mark, with the intent of making the room brighter for a minute.

She drew her finger across the air, but nothing happened.

She tried again, with the same result.

Frowning with concentration, she tried again and again, waving her finger through the air with no effect.

A knock at the door broke her concentration and she shouted, "I'm not available!"

The door swung open and Tomas stepped into the room. "Are you sure you can't use a little company?"

She went to him and threw her arms around him, strange body and all. Tomas was the soul she cared about. He held her, and she let herself sag against him.

After a long moment, she leaned back to meet his gaze. "You heard?"

He nodded. "Are you all right?"

"We'll see how smug Paul looks when I cut off his balls," she snarled.

Tomas barked a laugh, then squeezed her again. "I love your attitude."

She shrugged. "Like Vlad the Impaler said, you've got to approach battle with confidence."

Tomas grimaced. "As much as I agree, let's draw inspiration from better sources."

"Joan was sweet, but just as effective."

She led him to the table, and he whistled when he saw the pages of ciphers strewn across its surface. "You've been busy."

"I have to. There's so much to absorb." She tapped her head. "It's like a light bulb's on now, and I'm trying to get a handle on everything I see."

"You're amazing," he grinned. "I thought you were awesome with a single enhancement. Now you're a rune warrior, with ciphers coming out your ears."

She laughed and took his hands. "I'm glad you came."

He gave her a serious look. "Sarah, about what I said the other day. I'm sorry. I was out of line, and I hope you forgive me."

She sighed. "And I shouldn't have let things get to me so much. I shouldn't have let Alter get so close."

"Are we okay?" he asked, sounding hesitant.

She stepped closer and leaned against him. "I think we're going to be."

"I'll get my body back," he assured her, clasping her close. "I promise."

She only nodded. There were so many things they couldn't be sure of, but she'd cling to the few things she knew for certain. She and Tomas shared something special, and they'd work through the challenges they faced. Somehow, things would turn out all right. She had to believe that.

Tomas asked, "So what are you doing now? Drawing more ciphers?"

"I could draw all night," Sarah admitted. "But I need to know how to use them. I was starting to practice when you arrived."

"Show me," he said, glancing at the papers on the desk.

When she explained her plan to draw the rune in the air, he looked amazed. "I didn't know you could do that."

"Vlad did it. For complicated ciphers, I'll need to write them down, but for simple ones, it would be so much faster just to make a sign in the air and unleash it."

"Sounds good to me."

"It's just, I can't make it work."

"Show me," he repeated.

Sarah took a deep breath and concentrated, imagining the effect she wanted, then slashing her hand through the air. Nothing happened.

She threw out her hands. "See?"

Tomas frowned. "I don't have rounon powers, so I don't know exactly how it feels, but I've been around runes for a long time. It always seems the one activating them needs to connect those runes to their rounon well. Are you doing that?"

"I think so. At least, I'm trying."

Sarah closed her eyes and concentrated on that well of strength that fueled her rounon powers. It felt vibrant and strong in the center of her being, and with her focused attention, it pulsed with her heartbeat.

The rune warrior mark on her back began to grow warm against her skin, and she felt her rounon strength ripple out to infuse her. It eased her mind, wrapping her in a cocoon of calm, and buttressing her strength.

She took a deep breath and opened her eyes. Again she drew her finger through the air, pushing the rounon strength toward the mark, willing it to bond.

Her finger did not leave a trail of glowing cinders in the air. Instead, it left a trail of silvered light that hung motionless for a single heartbeat. Then Sarah felt a fraction of her rounon strength leap out to the mark.

The room brightened steadily until she had to squint against the blinding brilliance.

"Yes!" Sarah laughed.

She threw her arms around Tomas' neck and kissed him. She didn't care that his features looked a bit stretched. His lips were still his, and feeling his passionate response set her heart racing.

"What else can you do?" he asked when she released him.

Sarah frowned. "I want to practice with higher-order ciphers, with modifiers to draw strength from nearby people. That's how I'll be able to face Paul." She hesitated. "But I don't want to do it here. I mean, what if I draw too much? I can't afford to weaken anyone in the mansion."

Tomas nodded. "That's a good point. We could go back to Suntara. There's not a large night staff, but it's a controlled environment."

She shook her head. "That doesn't feel right, either."

"I could call up part of the legion," he suggested. "They'd be happy to loan you some of their strength."

That made a lot of sense, but Sarah said, "I think we're going to need all their strength soon. Paul wants an answer tomorrow, and I don't think he'll react well when I tell him where to stuff his proposal."

Tomas said, "Then let's go into the city. We could stop by the Colosseum. Even this late at night, there are people in that area."

When she still hesitated he said. "Or there's a prison I know about. We could park outside and you could draw a little from the inmates. They're criminals, and they're stuck in cells anyway. It's not like they have anything else to do tonight."

That sounded like the best plan, so they took a car and headed into town. It was growing late, a couple hours shy of midnight, but there were still a lot of people in the streets.

Tomas crossed the bridge near the impressive bulk of Castel Sant'Angelo, with St. Peter's brightly-lit dome glittering nearby. He followed the west bank of the Tiber south a few blocks, then turned down a narrow street, with a long, brick wall to their left.

"That's the prison in there," he said, gesturing at the wall. "Direct your modifiers to draw from souls in that direction."

"Really? They have a prison right next door to a hotel?" Sarah gestured at a couple of neon signs on the street.

"There are hotels everywhere in Rome. There's a really nice park at the end of this street too. Gianicolo Park. It's a popular tourist attraction."

She supposed they had to put prisons somewhere, but it made her a little more nervous to know there were so many innocent civilians nearby. If she made a mistake, she could hurt a lot of people.

"Wait, won't I affect prison guards too?" she asked.

He shrugged. "We have to try something, Sarah. If you limit your cipher to one percent, no one will even notice."

"Maybe we should have gone somewhere outside of town?"

"You think it would be better to test your ciphers on villagers?" Tomas took her hand. "Sarah, we need to test this, and we don't have a lot of time. Maybe I should call up the legion after all."

"No, I'll do it." She couldn't bear the thought of one of Tomas' men dying because she'd drained their strength before a battle.

Sarah decided to start with a cipher to pull a little energy from every soul within one hundred yards in the direction Tomas indicated. She started with a cipher similar to the one she'd tested with Eirene and Bastien, but modified to focus the captured energy into both herself and Tomas.

She made it a regional effect, limited to a diameter of five feet around her. The energy would enhance strength, speed, and health. The cipher was an important one, but not as complex as some ideas she'd drawn.

After reviewing the cipher several times to ensure she hadn't left anything out, she felt convinced she'd gotten it right. She discussed all the marks with Tomas, and he agreed that it looked good. With a flutter of nerves, Sarah focused on the cipher, willing her rounon power to activate it.

Strength flowed out of her to the cipher, which burned blue-white against the paper, without being consumed. A second later, she gasped and rocked backward in her seat as a torrent of energy poured into her. It eclipsed what she'd taken from Eirene and Bastien, and she barely managed to keep from leaping into the air to burn off some of it. Tomas' eyes widened in surprise, but he made no other outward sign as the effect spread to him.

"This is amazing," Sarah exclaimed as the flood of energy tapered off. She was happy she'd built the cipher to only draw one percent for five seconds.

Tomas grinned. "I think you've got it. I could get used to this."

"Alter would probably threaten to kill us if he knew we were testing on unsuspecting souls," Sarah said.

"Alter's wrong," Tomas replied, his grin fading.

"Still, I understand the hunters' fear that this could be abused," Sarah said, suddenly wondering if she'd made the right decision.

"Sarah, do you think people would be willing to loan you a fraction of their strength so you can protect them from global slavery?"

"Most people would if they understood the danger." The problem was, she hadn't asked those people. What she was doing was a form of stealing, and that made her uneasy, despite her need.

Tomas seemed to understand. "We fight evil from the shadows. Most of the world never knows what we do, and doesn't want to know. You can't tell them, or they'll think you're insane, or a witch."

"Burning at the stake is not the way I want this life to end," she agreed.

"So test another one. You have to master this."

After a moment's consideration, she said, "I'm going to mark a cipher on the ground farther down the street. It should create a barrier. Try driving the car through it."

"Sounds good."

She trotted up the narrow road about a hundred feet. After confirming no one else was around, she crouched over the pavement and called upon her rounon. It flooded through her immediately, and she focused it as she drew her finger across the ground, leaving lightly glowing marks on the stone.

The sight filled her with a fresh thrill. She was really doing it! Even though she'd immersed herself in ciphers for the past several hours, she still wanted to squeal with glee to see it actually working.

With forced calm, she completed the cipher and stepped behind it just before it flared to blue-white brilliance. She barely noticed the drain on her strength, and grinned as the cipher activated.

To her eyes, the air shimmered with barely-visible energy, forming a wall across the street that rose ten feet into the air. More importantly, she could feel it there, an invisible presence in her mind. She doubted anyone else would see it.

She waved to Tomas, and he started the car and pulled into the road. He barely accelerated past idling, creeping down the street toward the wall. Sarah held her breath as the car rolled closer, eager to see the barrier hold, but worried it might fail.

The car slammed to a stop at the cipher, and Tomas rocked forward in his seat, looking surprised. He hadn't seen the barrier. It still felt whole and undamaged.

He gave her a thumb's up, and she said, "Hit it harder."

"Stand back," he called, then reversed a little way up the street.

Sarah didn't move, but stood her ground in the street. The barrier would hold, she knew it.

Tomas gestured for her to move, but she shook her head and motioned him on. With a frown, he accelerated sharply, gunning the engine toward her. The short distance didn't allow him to get up a lot of speed, but it was enough that her pulse quickened as the car rushed toward her.

Despite her confidence in the cipher, she tensed to spring out of the way. With so much energy roaring through her, she could easily vault the nearby prison wall.

The car crashed into the barrier and bounced off. The airbag deployed, and the front bumper crumpled. Sarah felt the barrier vibrate from the impact, but it held. She'd crafted it to continue drawing from the tapped souls as needed, with a max drain of two percent. At the impact, she could feel that drain increase across those souls, but not hit the maximum load.

Sarah waved her hand, and the cipher faded away. She grinned as she trotted over to check on Tomas. She hadn't actually thought about how to terminate an active cipher, but had acted on instinct.

"Are you all right?"

Tomas popped the airbag with a knife and grinned. "Even the bruises from the airbag have faded already. My enhancements are on fire since that first cipher you activated. I think I'd have to take some serious damage to feel any effect."

She leaned in the window and kissed him. "It worked great. I think I've done enough for tonight. I know how to activate the ciphers, and I've proven the concepts."

"Good." He gestured toward the rear of the little car. "Push me to a parking space. That little crash disabled the engine. I need to call us another ride."

After they parked the car and called for a tow, they walked through the shadowed park and followed the Viale della Mura Aurelie north for a few blocks to St. Peter's Square.

They waited near the tall obelisk in the center of the square for a ride, and Sarah leaned against Tomas, staring from the towering dome of the St. Peter's Basilica to the glowing lights above the turrets of the Castel Sant'Angelo about half a mile away, down the straight shot of the Via della Conciliazione.

"Thanks for the date tonight," she said after a comfortable moment of silence.

Tomas wrapped her in arms that she no longer resented. "That may be the first time I've intentionally crashed a car on a date."

"Next time, take me to the shooting range outside of town and let me try the GECAL 50," she said, snuggling closer.

He laughed. "You're on."

Quentin himself arrive a few minutes later to give them a ride back to the mansion. Sarah sat in the back, considering the results of her cipher test and the thorny question of when to justify taking life force from others to use as she saw fit. There was no easy answer. No matter what she chose, there would be consequences and the chance that someone would get hurt.

To defeat Paul, she would take the risk. She'd deal with Alter and his family afterward.

If any of them survived.

67

The Colosseum shall stand as the greatest arena the world has ever known. May the gods grant its true purpose is successful. Eirene insists the hated Thracian will not be able to resist the lure of glory and honor my new arena offers. His crimes would sully those glorious sands, but that is a small price to pay to rid the world of him.

~EMPEROR TITUS, 81 A.D.

SARAH SLEPT LATE the next morning, and was awakened by Tomas, who brought her breakfast on an actual silver platter. The smell of eggs and bacon filled her room, and she rubbed sleep out of her eyes, then gave him a kiss.

"What's the occasion?" she asked, happy to feel no tension lingering between them.

"You're going to miss the morning's memory hunt if you don't get up," Tomas said with a smile. "And since you're supposed to play a central role, that would kind of defeat the purpose."

"Why didn't you wake me sooner?" Sarah threw off the covers and leaped out of bed. She rushed toward her closet, pulling off her night shirt as she went.

"Sarah!" Tomas exclaimed. "I'm still here."

He had turned away, his posture stiff, his cheeks actually flushed. It was as cute as it was annoying.

"You haven't left yet?" Sarah teased. "Are you the reason the term peeping Tom got started?"

"I would never," he said, his voice slipping into a proper affronted British accent.

"No, I guess you wouldn't," she said with a sigh, turning back to her closet.

"I'll set up breakfast on the table in your sitting room," he offered, exiting fast enough to make her worry he'd spill it.

She dressed quickly and joined him. While she gobbled down some food, she handed Tomas a hair brush and gestured at her unkempt tresses. She expected him to look terrified, but he took the brush, moved behind her chair, and started working her hair like he knew what he was doing.

"How did you learn to do that?" she asked.

"Would you like a French braid today?"

"You couldn't," she laughed.

"Want to bet?"

She rose and gave him a fierce kiss. "You never cease to amaze me."

"I'll amaze you more later. Come on, we're late."

She snatched up a pair of sausages, then followed. They took a car from Quentin's extensive underground garage and headed into town to Suntara. The city bustled with life, and Sarah gazed at the locals and tourists they passed. None of them had any idea the dangers that lurked in their midst.

Part of her envied them, but she realized that she really didn't want to return to a life of blissful ignorance. Knowing about Paul and heka assassins and plots to overthrow the world might terrify her, but on the other hand, runes and her newfound abilities filled her with profound joy.

She'd embrace the good she found in the secret world of facetakers and master runes, and fight to preserve it against heka assassins and cui dashi monsters.

They were the last two to arrive at the fourth-floor meeting. The main conference room was still under repair, but the smaller room was mostly intact. Gregorios and Eirene sat at the head of the table, with their facetaker children along the left side. The corpulent Harald hunkered over a laptop that seemed far too tiny for his huge hands, and Alter sat a little apart, looking ill at ease.

"Glad you decided to make it," Gregorios said, gesturing them to seats near Alter.

Francesca leaned forward, a mischievous glint in her eyes. "We were starting to wonder if you'd decided to give that new suit a full test drive."

"He wears the body of one of my cousins," Alter growled. Sarah wasn't sure if he was angrier about the implied dishonor of a family member's body, or the fact that he wasn't the one with her.

"Harriett, give your sister a muffin or something to keep her mouth busy for a while," Gregorios said, sounding a bit impatient. "We have a lot to cover today."

"How did your training go last night?" Eirene asked Sarah.

"I'm getting the hang of it." She smiled at the memory.

"Your abilities are our secret weapon," Gregorios said.

"And Alter's the other one," Eirene added, giving the hunter a reassuring smile.

"Paul won't be expecting what you two can do," Gregorios agreed. "We'll leverage that. First, Sarah, I'd like to review your meeting with Paul."

As she told them about the Colosseum and Paul's disgusting offer, Sarah tried to focus on the anger. When she told them about Paul's reference to his mother, Eirene interrupted.

"Those were his words exactly?"

Sarah nodded. "He seemed terrified of her, and said everything he does is to honor her name and to support her objectives. His words."

Francesca said, "Mother mentioned you said something about Paul's mother when you described the experience to her the first time. This morning, I asked our captured facetaker about her."

"What did you learn?" Gregorios asked.

"Nothing good. There's definitely a mother out there, but our prisoner seemed more terrified of her than of any torture I might try. She begged me not to mention her again, and she kept glancing at the door, as if expecting someone to burst through and kill us both."

Freaky. Sarah said, "Paul seemed afraid too. How can Paul be afraid of anyone?"

"He'll be afraid of me when I see him next," Alter growled.

"His mother is an unknown quantity," Gregorios said with a frown.

Eirene said, "And that makes me nervous. Paul is almost more than we can hope to handle. We don't need another powerful player involved."

"But what could her objectives be if world conquest is just a supporting role?" Tomas asked.

When no one offered any suggestions, Gregorios said, "We know about her now. That's a start. Sarah, when you meet with Paul, try to draw him out on that point."

"I'd rather just kill him," Sarah insisted.

"I swear upon my life to rip this monster's heart out and burn it," Alter exclaimed.

"I'd appreciate it," Sarah said.

Gregorios said, "His proposal offers a new angle of attack. It's not every day a megalomaniac with his sights set on world domination singles a girl out as the woman he'll use to father a nation of monstrous, soul-stealing near-immortals."

"Imagine the personal ad," Francesca said with a smirk.

Tomas interrupted before she could suggest one. "It's not actually funny."

"You're too focused on the fact that it's your girlfriend he's targeted as his sex toy." She gave Sarah an apologetic smile. "No offense. But you have to admire the guy's audacity."

"That is no way to win a lady," Bastien said, looking disgusted. "It is always better when she comes willingly."

Sarah appreciated Francesca's attempt at keeping the tone light, but she didn't share the facetaker's humor. Paul terrified and disgusted her. She wouldn't feel safe as long as he lived.

"He's not the first person who's dreamed of world conquest," Gregorios said. "I've buried more than I care to remember, but he's the first who actually has a chance of pulling it off."

"That will make his fall that much more satisfying," Eirene said.

Their resolve eased a little of Sarah's worry. She glanced at Tomas and noted the small signs of his growing anger. Unlike Alter, who looked ready to leap onto the table to swear an oath to avenge her, Tomas looked calm, like a coiled spring, who would unleash all his rage in a moment of controlled, deadly violence.

She wished somehow they could combine Alter's cui dashi soul powers with Tomas' experience. Together, they would become an unstoppable force, and Sarah had no doubt they could destroy Paul.

She wondered if there were runes she could use to facilitate such a thing? Then again, linking the two of them that closely might prove fatal to one of them.

Eirene said, "One point we haven't considered yet is that Paul suggested he could father a generation of cui dashi. Either he's just planning to produce a lot of children, or he actually believes there's a way to breed cui dashi."

"Let's hope he's just randy," Francesca said with a shiver. "Breeding cui dashi is nasty."

"He can't breed if we make him a eunuch," Harriett said.

"Exactly!" Sarah fist-bumped with her.

"Then we kill him," Alter said.

"Well, sharpen your knives," Gregorios said with an approving smile. "We're going in today, right after this meeting."

Sarah asked, "Can we kill him in the memoryscape? He regenerates so fast."

Francesca grinned. "On the positive side, we might get to castrate him more than once."

Tomas stayed focused on the mission. "They'll know we mean to target John, and they'll have precautions in place."

"Our memory hunt will have several objectives," Gregorios said. "But it's unlikely we'll be able to destroy them solely within the memoryscape. We need to find their hiding place here in Rome, and our hunt needs to lead us in that direction."

"How?" Sarah asked. She glanced at Tomas. "Any new leads?"

"Actually, we caught a glimpse of that heka we trailed into the Colosseum the other day. She was spotted passing the Colosseum again."

"That can't be coincidence," Sarah said, thinking back to the mark she'd named Rosetta.

Tomas nodded agreement. "We've stepped up surveillance in that sector. It may be the clue we need to get a solid hit."

"My family wouldn't have failed to find a kashaph infestation in their own city for so long." Alter kept glancing from Sarah to Tomas, and looked unhappy they were getting along again.

"That's why they let a heka cell break down the front door and steal the family jewels," Tomas retorted.

Alter leaped to his feet, his face red with anger.

"Calm down," Eirene said, and her voice carried enough weight with him that he slowly sank back into his seat. She added, "Do you really want more of your family in close proximity with our enforcers, Alter?"

"No," he mumbled, without meeting her gaze, and sank lower in his chair.

Sarah wanted to comfort him, but he'd take it the wrong way. She really cared for him, but she couldn't let him see it. Getting so close to him had only hurt them both.

"There are international items to take into account." Harald spoke for the first time. "I believe they factor into this conflict and cannot be ignored."

"Explain," Gregorios said.

He pointed at his laptop. "International tensions are still escalating. Israel launched air strikes against the Palestinians in retaliation for the recent bombings in Jerusalem."

Alter perked up, but Eirene said, "Won't do any good."

Gregorios added, "It'll stir things up. That's bad enough."

"Worse," Harald continued. "Thailand's government is in turmoil, and there's talk of a coup, but the new king is still talking tough against China. China has begun escalating rhetoric in return, and military forces are building in strategic locations."

"That doesn't make any sense," Tomas said.

Gregorios shrugged. "Not to any sane people, but it appears Paul wants the world destabilized."

"All the more reason to remove him," Eirene said.

Gregorios said, "We go in. Paul wants Sarah and he wants a master rune. We'll tempt him with both. Sarah, keep him talking."

"And kick him where it counts," Francesca urged.

"We'll get to that," Gregorios said. "We want him distracted. We'll give him a memory he might hope to glimpse a master rune, and we'll dazzle him with Sarah."

"You want me to take another shot at John?" Tomas asked.

"If you can. That's a second level of distraction and misdirection."

"Then what's the point?" Sarah asked.

Eirene leaned forward, her gaze intent.

"Spartacus."

68

We shall see if the Hebrews continue to conceal the hunters. Jerusalem is mine, and their temple is destroyed. What more must I do before the hunters are in turn hunted? Let them try assassinating me again.

~EMPEROR TITUS, 70 A.D.

THE INNER SANCTUM of the temple of Summanus materialized around Eirene and she breathed deep the remembered aromas of lingering incense and clean stone. She wore Iltea's powerful young body again. She wore the thick, red hair braided.

She stood at the base of the grand inner steps up to the propylaeum. It was the perfect place to prepare for confronting Paul.

Gregorios materialized beside her, dressed like a Roman Centurion, complete with greaves protecting his lower legs. She preferred his legs bare, but even that life he spent in Scotland never cured him of his hatred of kilts. Of course, if she'd ever had her legs bitten off by a shark, she might have the same lingering angst.

The rest of the team appeared around them. Sarah wore form-fitting leather armor, while Tomas and Alter both dressed like gladiators. The armor was minimal, but they could tweak that later, if needed. Tomas had clothed himself in his favorite battle suit. Eirene didn't miss Sarah's appreciative smile.

"Where are they?" Alter asked, settling into a fighting crouch, gladius at the ready, even though his eyes kept drifting to Sarah.

"They're already walking a memory. Can't you feel the pull?" Eirene had noticed it immediately, like an undertow, trying to pull her mind in a different direction and transform the reality of the memoryscape.

She'd worn the primary helmet on the first machine, with Gregorios linked to her, and Tomas riding as the second passenger. Together, she and Greg should be able to better withstand John and Paul.

Alter lowered his sword and nodded slowly. "I do. It's weak, like they don't really want us there."

"That must be why we appeared in my memory instead of syncing to their already-active one."

Eirene hadn't realized there was a way to block other machines from syncing, and she didn't like it, although in this case, she was glad they got a minute to get organized and for Alter to get used to his new role.

For the first time, he'd taken the primary helmet at a machine. With the greater force of his cui dashi nevra core, he should be better able to withstand Paul's manipulations of the memoryscape. In particular, they didn't want Paul again ripping Sarah out of the joint memory into an isolated location. She was Alter's only passenger, so hopefully Alter could protect her.

"If they don't want us, that's all the more reason to pay a visit," Tomas said. The same battle-axe Alter had conjured to such great effect in Florence appeared in his hands. He used it to squash the head of a small, doglike creature that popped into the air beside him.

Eirene appreciated his enthusiasm, but cautioned, "It could be a trap. They'll have home-court advantage."

"Stay sharp," Gregorios said. "Let's go with it. Stick to the plan."

"We have the escape runes," Tomas pointed out.

"You escape," Alter said with a scowl. "I'm here to fight."

"Behave, and follow my lead," Eirene warned.

She eased her hold over the memory and allowed her mind to be swept away by the mental undertow.

Reality blurred, then re-formed. They now stood in a spacious stone room, lined with columns. It was plain by ancient Roman standards, with a low set of stairs leading up to a wide exit that emptied onto a covered portico outside.

Paul and John stood not far away, dressed in white togas like senators, although Paul still wore his ever-present hat. The tilt of his head might indicate annoyance at their arrival.

Good. He'd be far more than annoyed in a moment.

She frowned as she looked around. The room was a bit loose, some of the details blurred, as if not quite complete. It felt fake, like a movie set.

Then she understood. Paul had figured out how to find a memory not directly linked to one of his people. He was projecting the details as he understood them, but lacked the power of true memory.

When she and Gregorios arrived, the memory still remained slightly fuzzy. Neither of them had lived this particular moment either. Strange. She couldn't imagine what Paul might gain from a fabricated memory moment.

Spartacus stood slightly apart from the others, dressed in his favorite gladiator armor, and wearing Tomas' body instead of the suit he'd worn during those years. When he spotted Eirene, he saluted with his ever-present spear, but did not rush to fight when he noticed the body she wore. So his modern-day soul was present in the memory, not his historical memory projection.

"Greetings," Paul said, his gaze sweeping the company before settling on Sarah. "Beloved, I suspected you might bring this chattel today to witness your commitment to my service."

Tomas and Alter both swayed forward, prepared to leap into battle, but Eirene waved them back. If only they could attack directly, but in that approach lay defeat. They had to play the game first.

Sarah stepped to the front of the group. "I have a few questions."

Paul swept off his hat and smiled. A long table appeared between the opposing groups, heaped with food and wine.

A venomous snake slithered off the table toward Paul, but Spartacus impaled it with his spear. Paul didn't even bother to watch, his gaze never wavering from Sarah.

"Please, sit. Eat."

"You first," she said.

Paul tossed his hat onto the table and sat. John followed more slowly. He kept glancing at Gregorios, his expression worried.

It should be. Spartacus didn't sit, but hovered just behind the other two. They were going to have to separate him soon, but Eirene was interested in hearing what Paul had to say.

Sarah settled uneasily into a chair, and Eirene sat beside her. "I was expecting threats and heka thugs. You're breaking with tradition."

Paul glanced at her. "Your nevra core will serve a higher purpose." He turned back to Sarah. "Until then, as a gesture of my goodwill, you may keep them."

"You're feeling pretty full of yourself today," Gregorios said as he dropped into a chair and reached for a steaming roast. "Let's hear your proposal. Then we'll go with preemptive violence."

"I am hopeful you will see reason," Paul said to Sarah.

"You weren't speaking reason the last time we met," Sarah said, doing an admirable job of controlling her fear.

Gregorios began to eat, outwardly at ease, but he had sat far enough away to not interfere with any weapon Eirene chose to summon when the conversation went south. The others spread out behind her, but didn't sit.

"We have clashed enough to take the measure of one another," Paul said, sipping from a delicate wine glass. "You have proven yourself, beloved. I also see how your facetaker allies remained in power for so long."

Gregorios grunted. "I just took over as chairman recently. If that's a long term commitment to you, don't buy bonds."

Paul's lips twitched into a brief frown. "You know what I mean. You've lived for millennia. Why risk all that?"

Eirene said, "Let me guess. You're offering a better option."

"I offer the only option."

Behind Paul, a man swept into the spacious room from the portico, surrounded by a host of toga-clad senators. He wore a crimson robe and a laurel wreath crown. The crowd paused on the steps, arguing. The man dressed like an emperor looked vaguely familiar, but she couldn't place him.

"Hey, I saw this movie. That's Julius Caesar," Sarah exclaimed.

The scene clicked in her memory. This was indeed a mock-up of the Ides of March, 44 B.C.

"The film from the fifties was always my favorite representation," Paul said.

That's why everything looked so fake. They had recreated a false memory, based on the right period, but populated with remembered scenes from a movie. Eirene was impressed that they managed to get it to work. What she couldn't understand was why.

Gregorios said, "I guess John wasn't such a coup after all. Can't get the memories you want, can he?"

John looked more nervous than ever. "Not everyone is as clever as you think they are."

"You've proved that point," Gregorios said, giving John the full weight of his glare.

Eirene studied John. His response had been pitched as defiance, but something in the words hinted that he might be trying to communicate a different message. She hadn't headed up the facetaker intelligence arm for centuries without picking up on such nuances.

While she puzzled over the possible implications, Sarah asked, "Is that what Caesar really looked like?"

"Not really," Gregorios said.

Eirene felt his mind pull against the fabric of the memoryscape John and Paul had constructed. The rest of the cast remained the same, but suddenly Caesar transformed from Louis Calhern, the actor who had played him in the movie, to the real man.

Muscular from his years of military conquest, his presence dominated the room as he always had. There was around him always the feel of a predator that made most mortals nervous. Some of the other details of the room sharpened a little too.

"That's him," Gregorios said.

"For another minute," Paul added.

A gorilla dropped out of the air near the table. Its fur was black and it sported a mass of writhing snakes atop its head. Tomas moved to intercept the creature, but Spartacus moved faster. He impaled the beast with his thick spear, managing to not spray blood across the table in the process.

That was uncharacteristically helpful. The tingle of unease Eirene had been feeling since John's unusual comment grew into open concern. Something else was going on here, something they were missing. Any mistakes when dealing with cui dashi were invariably fatal.

Somehow, Paul held the advantage despite the appearance of the opposite.

"Thank you, Spartacus," Paul said as the big man returned to his position behind Paul's shoulder. He then addressed Sarah. "Do you have any other questions, most favored of all mortal servants, or shall we proceed?"

Behind him, one of the senators suddenly yanked on Caesar's robes and tried to stab him. Others joined in and within seconds, dozens of men surrounded the emperor, stabbing and jostling for a chance to strike. His cries of pain echoed through the chamber, along with the frantic shouts of amateurs trying to murder a king.

"That's horrible," Sarah said, looking away.

"It's more or less accurate," Gregorios said.

His mind again tugged at the memory, and in that instant Eirene realized their mistake and the warning John was trying to convey.

"Greg, wait!"

69

Praise the gods and the facetakers, my father succumbed to madness before taking my life as he has so many of my brothers. Rome is mine, and Shahrokh's position is secure. I will take more lives than even the great Julius.

~EMPEROR CLAUDIUS, 41 A.D.

THE ROOM SNAPPED into sharp focus, truly becoming the antechamber adjacent to the Theatre of Pompey where the real assassination took place. The senators became realistic representations of the men who Eirene had known.

Gregorios had taken control of the memory. This must have been the moment he arrived in the room, too late to prevent the attack, but in time to salvage the situation.

This was the moment Paul had been hunting, and they just gave it to him.

The sounds of ripping cloth and steel plunging into flesh reverberated through the room, punctuated by cries of pain from the dying emperor and shouts of hatred by the conspirators.

Paul smiled in victory. "Power always shifts to the strongest. No matter how great a mortal believes himself to be, he is still but a single blade away from death." He chuckled. "Or in this case, twenty-three."

"You expect to find a master rune here," Eirene said, rising and flexing her hands.

She still believed they were correct in their analysis. The best chance to find a master rune was during the fall of Rome, but this moment would have been her second choice. The assassination of Julius Caesar initiated events that led to the overthrow of the republic and the establishment of the empire.

Paul also rose. "The death of Caesar was the most important event of these days. Bow to me, Sarah, and pledge your life and undying devotion to my cause. Do so, and I will raise you to glory no other woman has ever achieved, and spare the lives of your pitiful friends. Defy me again, and guarantee their destruction."

He finished in a shout and threw out his arms in victory just as Caesar fell, unmoving. Time slowed and everything became clearer. The victorious shout of the conspirators, the brilliant crimson of the blood spreading around the fallen man. The echoes from Paul's declaration reverberated through the room, slowly fading.

Nothing happened.

No master rune appeared, and time again resumed its normal pace. Paul looked around, confused.

Gregorios, who had remained seated, spoke around a mouth full of chicken. "Pretending to be wise works better when you know what you're talking about."

"Caesar didn't die." Spartacus added with a frown. "But not for lack of trying."

Paul's expression of victory faded and for the first time he looked shaken. He whirled on John. "What is the meaning of this?"

"I wasn't there," John said with an innocent expression.

Sarah said, "Wait a minute. You messed with Caesar? Really?"

She had recoiled from Paul's rant, and a wicked, curved blade had appeared in her hands, like a small sickle. Eirene recognized it as a favorite instrument of castration of the Chinese, and she wondered where Sarah had learned about it.

Gregorios shrugged, swallowed, and wiped his mouth. "They did terminate his body, but not quickly enough. I removed his soul and completed the transfer to Octavian like we'd been planning."

"Demons," Alter spat.

That caught Paul's attention and he regarded Alter with new interest. Maybe the fact that they included a hunter in their party would worry him. He didn't have to know the truth.

Paul turned to Spartacus. "But you were here. You orchestrated the whole thing."

Eirene smiled. "Oh, he was lurking about, but he wasn't here during the actual assassination. He was with the gladiators they had brought in as backup. I chased him off while Gregorios recovered Caesar's soul."

"As Octavian, Caesar was pretty upset when Cleopatra turned to Antony," Gregorios added. "That broke Baladeva's base of operations in Egypt."

Paul protested, "But there has to be a master rune. This moment was pivotal."

"Yeah, it was pretty important," Gregorios said. "But . . ."

His voice trailed off as the ground began to shake.

On the steps, Caesar spoke, his agonized declaration ringing with far more power than it ever could have possessed in real life. "Dying wasn't supposed to hurt so much."

Sarah glanced from Eirene to Gregorios, her expression disgusted. "What about 'Et tu Brute'?"

"Poetic license," Eirene said with a shrug.

The shaking of the ground intensified, then stopped. The ceiling faded away above them, opening up an unobstructed vista of the bright blue sky above.

"That is really unfortunate," Gregorios muttered, rising to his feet.

Sarah shouted, "No! Stop it. Do something."

"It's too late," Eirene said as her eyes were drawn upward along with everyone else's.

A huge rune blazed above the city, burning with white-hot fire. It seared into Eirene's eyes, bonding to her core instantly, becoming part of her, a piece she could never forget.

It was a marvel, but less impressive by full magnitudes than the master rune from Berlin. She hadn't seen that one in person, but Gregorios had shown it to her, and even the reproduction of it had shaken her.

This one blazed in the sky with brilliant intensity and its power thrummed through her soul. And yet it wasn't the rune Paul must have been hoping for.

"It's a lesser master rune," Sarah muttered.

"That doesn't make any kind of sense," Tomas said.

It was true though. They'd been right and wrong at the same time. This rune was not among the most powerful, but it still represented a terrible danger in the hands of Paul.

He laughed, eyes glued to the rune. "I knew it! Nothing can stop me now."

"I find these do a pretty good job," Tomas said.

He held a grenade launcher, tube loaded and pointed at Paul, who still focused on the rune.

Eirene dove aside.

Tomas fired.

The explosion still tumbled her across the room. Dust and debris and splattered remnants of food rained down all around her. Her ears rang from the blast and she tasted blood and sand.

She rolled over, coughing, trying to see through the billowing smoke. She doubted the explosion killed Paul, but it might have slowed him down.

The head of Spartacus' spear slammed into the floor right next to her head, shattering the tile and sinking several inches into the ground beneath.

Eirene stared at the shaft that quivered from the impact, close enough that she could smell the polish worked into the grains. She looked up to find Spartacus looming above her.

He laughed. "You should see your face!"

70

GREGORIOS GROANED and spat dirt and splinters. He couldn't see through the thick cloud of smoke filling the room. He had reacted a split second too slow when Tomas pulled the trigger on that grenade launcher and caught the blast full in the face.

He'd already re-formed his damaged tissue, but wondered if his face back in the real world was burned. He was going to transfer Tomas into a fresh body when they got out of this memory and then beat that body to the point of death before transferring him back.

He admired Tomas' presence of mind to summon the weapon, but he could've picked something with a little more finesse, like a wood chipper.

What galled the most was that he had walked right into Paul's trap. The smug Chinaman might be cui dashi, but Gregorios was mad enough that he didn't care. He'd learned some wonderful torture techniques in his days with the Romans, and he planned to use them all.

Before he could haul himself to his feet, John materialized out of the gloom and dropped to his knees right next to him. The move was strangely considerate. Gregorios wouldn't even need to lunge in order to strangle the fool.

"Listen to me," John whispered, thrusting his face far too close.

The only reason Gregorios didn't rip out his soul right there was the spark of sanity in John's eyes. It looked like the repeated exposure to Paul's machine was reversing his mental instability.

"Give me a good reason," Gregorios said.

"They're after the runes," John said.

"Didn't you notice the big burning symbol in the sky? I'd say they got it."

"They'll need more. We're holed up somewhere in the city."

Gregorios flexed his fingers. "I'm underwhelmed."

"It's some kind of tunnel."

He gave the man a disgusted look. "Do you have any idea how many tunnels there are around Rome?"

"It's decorated real nice, but it's a ruin, I can tell."

Gregorios sighed. "You're an idiot. They're going to kill you."

"Not if you find us first. I'll try to get a signal out."

"Do better."

John cringed at a shout that echoed out of the smoke. It was beginning to clear, and Paul might catch sight of them talking together, so Gregorios decided to help John with his cover story.

He punched John in the chest hard enough to knock the other man away. Before he could add a couple of kicks for good measure, John faded from the memory.

Not good. Gregorios spun, seeking the others through the fog, but he was alone in a vast, empty room. For the first time, he felt worried.

In the confusion of the explosion, he hadn't even felt the jolt of the world reshaping around him. That much control worried him. If Paul had managed to separate him, he might have done the same to the others.

He closed his eyes and concentrated. It took a moment, but he felt the tug of another will in the memoryscape and threw his mind into the current dragging him in that direction.

Hopefully he would arrive before it was too late.

71

Can the world not see that Octavian is but Julius reinvented? Is Mark Antony to secure a second life before I? What shame is mine to stand as triumvir, yet still lack access to even a basic enhancement? Is my soul of such little worth?

~MARCUS AEMILIUS LEPIDUS, LEAST-KNOWN MEMBER
OF THE SECOND TRIUMVIRATE

EIRENE ROSE TO FACE SPARTACUS, retreating slowly out of reach. He made no threatening move, but she summoned a chainsaw anyway. The soft chugging of its engine eased her tightly-wound nerves.

The dust from the recent explosion dissipated, and she was surprised to find they'd changed memory locations. No longer did they stand in the theatre.

The hills of Rome stretched away in every direction, and she recognized the palaces of the nearby Palatine Hill overlooking the Circus Maximus. The huge chariot-racing track was a wildly popular place, and from the roaring of crowds that echoed past its high wall, it sounded like a race was just beginning.

Tomas approached, empty grenade launcher in his hands, stopping a couple paces away. Between them, they could take Spartacus, no matter what devilry he might have learned to summon.

Few memory people moved nearby, and those were all hurrying toward the Circus. She felt Gregorios as a distant presence in her mind, but wasn't even sure he was in the same memory.

Alter and Sarah felt close, perhaps within the Circus. She yearned to go to them, worried they might be facing Paul, but had to trust their courage. She could not pass up the chance to speak in private with Spartacus.

The Thracian released the haft of his spear and retreated a step, hands raised in a sign of peace. "I'll fight you if I must. In these memories, I feel the rage that once drove me, and I'll embrace it if that makes you feel better."

"What would make you feel better?" Eirene asked carefully. Again Spartacus was talking instead of raging like a mad bull. Even though she'd seen it before, it still startled her.

"I'd like to talk!" Spartacus exclaimed. "I have so many questions. Do you have any idea how difficult it is to hear the world but see nothing? By Zeus, I got so much wrong!"

"All right. We can talk."

"Talk didn't help much with Paul," Tomas said. It was clear he wanted to fight.

Spartacus shrugged. "Paul is what he is. I owe him a debt for restoring me to life, but his goals are not mine."

"What are you goals?" Eirene asked.

Spartacus' expression turned thoughtful, a unique look for the man. "I long asked myself that. For years without counting I would have answered with ripping out your heart and eating it while it yet pumped your life's blood."

"Sounds about right," Tomas said.

"Do you mind?" Eirene asked.

He shrugged. "Given the situation, I can understand where he's coming from."

"Thank you," Spartacus said. "But thirst for revenge can only fuel a soul for a few centuries. Eventually I needed something more."

"Like what?" Eirene asked.

He didn't answer for a moment. "Did you know before we were taken as slaves, my Iltea was a prophetess of the Maedi?"

"I knew that," Eirene said, tensing. The topic usually triggered violent rage.

This time it didn't. "I was a sculptor."

"Really?" That was one trade she had never imagined.

Spartacus nodded, dropping into a padded chair that appeared behind him. A howling cat ripped its way out of the fabric and Spartacus twisted off its head without even seeming to notice it.

"I loved fashioning things with my hands, finding the hidden images buried within a stone. During those long decades forced to become a bystander to history, I began crafting sculptures in my mind, images to reflect the distant sounds of the invisible world around me."

"So are you saying you want to set up an artist shop?" Tomas asked incredulously.

"No." He shook his head. "I'm not making much sense. I'm not used to anyone responding when I babble."

"Take your time," Eirene said, fascinated despite her long feud with this man. They had assumed the Thracian's mind had broken during his forced isolation.

Many minds began to break down within hours, most within days of isolation. His resilience was astounding. She still barely believed that the long dispossession might have led to enlightenment.

It was a terrible thought. Millennia of hatred was now being challenged by this thoughtful man in front of her. She glanced at her chainsaw and reluctantly released the trigger.

Tomas took a step closer, his expression hard. "You play the victim well, Spartacus, but you must return my body, or we're going to have a serious problem."

Spartacus grinned. "As a warrior of much honor, I expect nothing less from you. Indeed, you cannot but challenge my possession of your property."

"Right." Tomas looked disgusted that he was agreeing with Spartacus. "So let's meet so you can give it back."

"We'll find a replacement for you," Eirene offered, allowing herself to hope it would be such a simple exchange.

She knew better.

Spartacus laughed. "And dishonor your strength by surrendering without proving the quality of the very body you wish to regain? I would never present such an insult to a brother at arms. Nay, but we shall meet in single combat and prove the valor of your claim."

Tomas hesitated. "Usually I'd agree that's the best way, but I actually need the body intact when I assume ownership."

Spartacus considered that for a moment, his grin fading. "Such a conundrum I have not faced in the past, but I concur. Yet in this new world where violence is glorified only in fiction, while so many refuse to recognize its presence in reality, the accepted means to resolve this question of honor is difficult to ascertain."

"You could always try rocks, paper, scissors," Eirene offered. The conversation was starting to feel surreal.

Spartacus slapped a palm on his thigh. "As always your wisdom is present when most needed." He turned to Tomas. "Choose your weapon then. Will you meet me with rocks or scissors?" He frowned. "I have never found much use for paper in the art of war beyond sending correspondence."

Tomas kept up with the strange twist in the conversation without missing a beat. "Eirene is suggesting a game that is more chance than contest, and I don't think it fits our need."

"Then what do you suggest?" Eirene was amazed to see Spartacus actually seemed interested in hearing another's point of view.

"Perhaps a test of will and strength," Tomas said after a brief pause. "To see whose commitment to ownership is the greater."

"To the victor goes the glory and one of the best battle suits I have ever worn," Spartacus boomed. "To the loser falls the spare. I applaud your suggestion."

"Where and when?" Tomas asked, and Eirene caught her breath, barely hoping he'd agree.

Spartacus opened his mouth to answer, then cocked his head to one side, as if listening. "Our time grows short. Your woman is worthy of you. She shares your warrior spirit."

"Where and when?" Eirene asked again, hoping the reference to Sarah meant she'd escaped Paul's advances again.

Spartacus turned toward the main gate of the Circus, but paused. "Come to this place on the morrow, and we will make arrangements."

His eyes lingered on Eirene and she tensed for resumed hostilities.

"You cannot hurt her any longer. She lives in my heart. I don't begrudge you the use of her form."

He turned and walked toward the gate. Eirene watched, chainsaw dangling from her hands, until he disappeared through the huge portal.

"Tomorrow," Tomas said when she turned. His eyes glowed with anticipation. "What are you going to do with him after I defeat him?"

"For the first time in over twenty centuries, I have no idea."

72

THE EXPLOSION FROM TOMAS' grenade tossed Sarah flying. She crashed into the sandy ground, sliding several feet.

Sand?

Grit stung her eyes and filled her mouth. She spat and squinted against the dust and billowing smoke. Her ears rang from the concussive blast and she felt like she'd been trampled by a pack of angry horses.

The smoke disappeared as quickly as her runes drained away the pain, and she blinked against the blinding daylight of a blue sky. Thunderous cheering from tens of thousands of voices replaced the echoes of the explosion.

Sarah rose to her feet and looked around in wonder. She stood in a vast arena, split down the middle by a stone wall capped with statues of Roman gods, flat-topped alters, and shrines. Tiers of seats encircled the horseshoe-shaped arena, which extended at least two thousand feet and stood about three hundred feet wide.

"The Circus Maximus," Alter said, joining her and echoing her thoughts. He was now dressed in a short blue tunic, with leather bands encircling his arms, legs, and bare chest. He was staring.

She glanced down at herself and found she was wearing a similar costume, except hers included a barely modest leather halter-top, colored green.

"What happened?" she asked, and Alter was wise enough to tear his gaze off her exposed skin to look her in the eye.

Paul appeared about twenty feet away, closer to the flat end of the arena. "You will witness my ascension, along with one hundred and fifty thousand Romans."

A high wall reared across that end of the circus. A dozen wood slat gates were built into its face, with four horses stomping and snorting behind each one. Paul wore an outfit similar to Alter's, but red.

"You mean everyone will witness me rip your head off," Alter said. He extended his hands as if holding a rifle, but nothing popped into his arms.

Paul smiled. "No modern weapons to spoil this moment. Your facetakers aren't here. I control this memory and you will obey my rules."

"He doesn't know about you yet," Sarah hissed. "Can't you take control?"

Alter shook his head after a couple of seconds, his expression pained. "He's got an iron grip on it. I can't shake anything free."

The distant gates snapped open in unison and horses erupted through, pulling light, wooden chariots, drivers balanced on the precarious platforms.

Sarah wished Tomas was there. She might need Alter's cui dashi strength, but she yearned for Tomas' presence. She couldn't allow Paul to escape with that new master rune. She tried to summon her favorite little KSG shotgun, but got only a headache.

No modern weapons. So be it.

She summoned a crossbow, which appeared readily enough. Raising it to her shoulder, she snapped off a shot.

The bolt transformed into a rose just before reaching Paul, and he plucked it from the air, saluting her. "I accept your first token of devotion."

The sickle-shaped blade appeared in Sarah's hand and she growled, "I'll show you a token."

"Do try to keep up," Paul chided as the chariots thundered down upon them.

Alter rushed past Sarah, sprinting toward Paul, but he leaped into the air in a magnificent arc that terminated on the tiny chariot platform of the lead team. The driver wore a red tunic just like Paul's, and the horses were draped in the same color.

For the first time, Sarah realized the various chariot teams all sported one of four colors. She hadn't realized it was a team competition.

Paul made a mock salute as the lead chariot he rode upon passed between her and Alter. She couldn't give chase because a chariot from the white team was heading right toward her and showed no signs of slowing.

Sarah vaulted the charging horses and their charioteer. The man barely noticed her. She took advantage of the looser laws of gravity and altered course to land on the platform of another chariot, from the blue team.

She landed hard and nearly fell off. The little chariot wobbled dangerously under her shifting weight and the driver shouted, "Ware the balance!"

Sarah summoned a pair of binoculars. She felt some resistance, but they did materialize after a couple of seconds. She focused on Paul, who was about fifty feet ahead.

He was cutting into his side with a little knife.

Uh oh. The rune they had just acquired might not be as powerful as the one Mai Luan carved into her cheek in Berlin, but Paul was already freakishly powerful. If he tapped into the power of that assassination, he'd gain that much more the advantage.

The charioteer pushed Sarah and she nearly tumbled off the chariot.

"Careful," she snapped.

The man shouted, "Get off. You're not even on my team."

"I need a ride."

He glanced at her and then looked again. His belligerence faded as he took in her fantastic curves in the all-too revealing outfit. "My lady, but change your colors and visit my quarters this evening, and the gods above will blush when they see what wonders you and I can make together."

She summoned a gladius. "Catch up to that lead chariot or I'll turn you into a gelding."

He blanched. "Very well, but ware to your left." He gestured toward the barrier wall blurring past.

Sarah turned in that direction and realized a fraction of a second too late that she'd been duped. His elbow caught her in the side of the head and he shifted his weight at the same time, tipping the unstable little chariot up on one wheel. Sarah overbalanced and toppled out.

She hit the ground and bounced along the hard sand for thirty feet before plowing to a stop. Her vision was still spinning and every inch of exposed skin burned from road rash, but her ears still worked all too well.

Other chariots barreled toward her at full speed. She pressed herself against the smooth inner wall just before steel-rimmed wheels tore the earth beside her. Three chariots passed, one so close its inner wheels scraped the leather on her back. Another half inch and it would have gouged out her spine.

She lay panting with fear for several seconds. She could scarce believe she'd fallen for that stupid line.

"Sarah!"

Alter pulled her to her knees. "Are you all right?"

"I'll survive." She let him help her up, even though the pain was already fading. Her runes worked even faster in the memoryscape than they did in real life.

"We have to catch him. He's inscribing the master rune onto himself."

"Abomination!"

"Well, unless you have a chariot in that tunic of yours, we're in trouble."

"I think I can summon one. Paul didn't block your crossbow, and he only mentioned modern weapons."

That seemed as strange as it was infuriating. "How can he do that?"

Alter shrugged. "I'm new at this. I don't know the nuances of how much of the memoryscape we can control."

"Fight him for it."

"Working on it. I'll try for a chariot."

His brow furrowed in concentration, but Sarah tugged his arm. "Can you drive a four-horse chariot?"

"Not really."

"Me neither. We need something better."

"We could try a regular horse," Alter suggested.

Sarah wasn't listening. She was a terrible rider and doubted even if they conjured a world-class racer she'd be able to hold on long enough to catch up with Paul. They needed better wheels.

A cipher image popped into her mind, one she didn't remember studying before. It seemed promising though, and she decided to trust what she'd learned from the old-time rune warriors. If it felt right to her, that should be enough, especially for simple needs.

She stooped and drew the mark in the packed sand of the arena. "Let's see if Paul's got ciphers covered."

The image roughly resembled a chariot, but she added extra wheels and a curved line over the top that suggested the roof line of a modern sports car.

"What are you doing?" Alter asked, crouching beside her.

As soon as Sarah completed the mark, she focused, willing her rounon strength awake and directing it toward the little symbol. Fear that it would fail and Paul would complete his new rune threatened to distract her, but she cast aside the fear and focused on her inner strength.

It blossomed like the coming of the sun, filling her with calm confidence. Energy poured out of her rounon well and connected with the chariot symbol. With a surge of heat and a temporary sapping of strength, the rune flared blue-white against the sand, then vanished.

A two-seater dune buggy appeared on the sands right in front of them, engine already running with a throaty growl.

Sarah laughed and raised her hand to high-five Alter, but his eyes were glued to the sleek dune buggy. She punched him in the shoulder.

"Let's go castrate that demon."

73

Of course I blamed the Christians for the Great Fire. They are an easy target, and Rome is rife with hatred against them. The true culprit is being hunted by Gregorios, but how can I trust that cursed Spartacus will be brought to justice now when he has escaped it for so long?

~EMPEROR NERO, SECOND LIFE OF CLAUDIUS, 64 A.D.

THE DUNE BUGGY was wide and low, a sleek profile of black steel.

Sarah pushed the still-gaping Alter toward the driver seat. "You know how to drive one of these right?"

"Yes." As Sarah jumped into the passenger seat, he slipped behind the wheel, threw the transmission into first, and floored it. The four studded tires ripped into the sandy ground as he slung them in a tight turn, then raced back toward the starting gate.

Sarah was about to protest, but understood his logic as he drifted around the inner wall in a fantastic turn, already going twenty. The lead chariot, with Paul still clinging to the tiny deck, was just rounding the far end.

It took the corner tight against the post, forcing him to hold on and lean into the turn along with the charioteer. For a moment he had to stop working on the new rune.

The two vehicles closed with terrifying speed, and it didn't look like Paul had noticed them yet. As they charged down the length of the long arena, going the wrong way, the crowds took notice and screamed their displeasure. The noise drowned out the roar of the buggy. When Paul finally glanced up from working on his rune, the expression of shock on his face was priceless.

Less than a hundred feet separated them and Alter looked like he planned to ram the horses. Paul frowned, and an invisible force struck Sarah's mind, triggering an instant headache. She groaned and clutched her head. The buggy's engine sputtered and it began to flicker around them, as if on the verge of disappearing.

"He's trying to banish it," Alter shouted as the buggy lost power, decelerating rapidly. The onrushing chariot moved to their left and would thunder past in seconds.

Sarah gritted her teeth in concentration, her mind centered on the image of the symbol she had marked to summon the buggy.

"This is my car," she growled, refusing to surrender to the pressure of his will. She held that image like a shield, and the headache began to fade. The buggy became more solid, but the change came too late.

Alter revved the engine and began to cut the wheel to ram them. Sarah shouted. "No. Let him pass."

Paul was again working on the rune, as if discounting their presence. Sarah caught a glimpse of the mark on his side, and it looked like he was nearly finished.

As the chariot charged past, Sarah jumped to the steel frame roof, the sickle-shaped blade again popping into her hand.

She jumped.

Easily vaulting the space, Sarah matched the chariot speed, planning to land on the tiny deck beside Paul. Hand raised to strike, she bit back the battle cry that bubbled in her throat.

Paul anticipated her move and caught her in midair, his fingers closing around her throat with relentless force. Her body snapped against the restraint of his hand, wrenching her neck, but not even causing his arm to twitch.

Paul held her easily, like a kitten. Although she had faced him before, she was still not prepared for the magnitude of his strength.

"Sarah!" Alter shouted, whipping the buggy in a tight turn to give chase, but he'd never catch them in time.

Paul twisted, holding Sarah out over the sands that blurred just below her feet, but didn't drop her.

His eyes began to burn with purple fire.

"Sarah, you chose foolishly," he said, his expression sad. "I expected more from you. Everyone you've ever loved is going to suffer the consequences."

"You disgust me," Sarah croaked, barely able to sip any air through his tight grip.

She could just see the nearly-completed new rune on his side. The central images that made up the complex rune were similar to the one she had witnessed in the sky, but the outer layers were wrong, somehow twisted. She frowned, trying to understand what changes he had made, but his fingers began to sear her skin with the fire of his cui dashi power.

"You will beg me to take you," Paul assured her, his tone calm, as if explaining something to an unruly child. "But you will feel my wrath before you enjoy the glory of my forgiveness."

Sarah struggled in his grasp, concentrating on the rune. It felt twisted and foreign, and yet at a fundamental level she understood it.

"I'll make you a deal," she whispered, not sure if he could hear her over the thunder of hooves and the rattling of the chariot. He pulled her a little closer, cocking his head to listen, and slackening his hold just a bit.

Sarah couldn't reach low enough to castrate him, but still slashed twice with her blade. She aimed for his side, barely parting the skin with the razor-sharp knife.

"You can't hurt me, Sarah," Paul mocked, not seeming to realize that the new marks closed the pattern of the new rune and changed its meaning.

He didn't know she possessed any rounon gift.

He should have paid better attention.

Strength rushed out of Sarah in a flood as her little blade completed the second mark. The unexpected drain left her sagging in Paul's hand.

Paul smiled, just a curving of the lips that did not touch the coldness of his eyes. "Ah, you begin to see the futility of resistance."

His hand tightened again, severing her air. Maybe it was time to panic. She beat weakly at his arm and tried to shout to Alter, but only made gagging sounds.

"Truth hurts, Sarah."

She tried to say, "So does the rune you're wearing." No words came out, but he was about to get the message.

The rune Sarah had just corrupted blazed with crimson light, and Paul convulsed, crying out in pain. His fingers slackened and she slipped out of his grasp.

Alter, who had been closing fast behind them, slammed on the brakes, twisting the wheel over so hard the buggy spun and careened up onto two wheels, nearly flipping.

Sarah hit the sand and tumbled a dozen times across the hard-packed surface before stopping. Alter's wild maneuver with the buggy disrupted the other chariots, forcing them to skid to a halt, so at least she wasn't trampled.

The crowds packing the stands howled with anger. Sarah ignored the imminent danger of being trampled by a mob. It was hard to focus through the searing pain of her sand-blasted skin, but she turned to Paul in his retreating chariot.

She had made those marks out of pure instinct, trusting her rune sense. Those marks felt wrong, dangerous.

Just what she needed.

Paul was screaming, clutching at his side as the charioteer slowed the team. The rune blazed angry red, like living fire against his skin. If flared once, then winked out.

Paul's chest exploded.

Blood and flesh and bone erupted across the sands, and he toppled off the chariot. Then the chariot disappeared, along with the horses and all the other chariot teams. The roaring of the crowd faded away after a final wave of shouting, as if every person's throat had been cut at the same time.

Paul lay prostrate on the sands in a spreading pool of blood a hundred feet from Sarah. Alter had brought the buggy to a stop halfway between them. For a second silence reigned but for the growl of the buggy's idling engine.

Then Paul twitched and the gaping wound in his torso began to close.

Alter gunned the engine and the sleek little vehicle leaped forward, closing the distance in seconds. It bounced high as two of the wheels ground Paul into the sand. Alter lost control and rammed into the barrier wall. He left the engine running and leaped out of the driver's seat.

Sarah was already on her feet, sprinting toward the fallen cui dashi. No doubt he was cheating again, restoring his health with dispossessed souls, but those grievous wounds would slow even him for a moment. This was their chance.

Paul rolled over, still bleeding badly, and a heavy machine gun appeared in his hands.

"You said no modern weapons!" Sarah shouted.

He opened fire.

Tracer rounds stitched across the sands toward her. Paul's angle was poor, but he made up for it with lots of lead. Sarah dove and rolled, slashing a hand through the air, leaving a glowing line that flared, forming a reinforced steel shield. It settled into her hands just before bullets ricocheted off it like angry metal bees.

The bullets would have torn through a normal shield, but if he could cheat, so could she. Sarah maintained the image of a solid shield, and felt her rounon strength pouring out to buttress it and maintain its shape despite the brutal onslaught.

There were no other souls nearby for her to draw upon to fuel her cipher, and she had no idea how long she could maintain the shield, but to falter meant to die.

Then the barrage stopped and she risked a peek. Paul had turned his weapon on Alter, forcing the hunter to dive back into the buggy, which Paul was ripping apart with the heavy bullets.

Sarah considered using another cipher to summon her shotgun, but that wasn't going to stop Paul. She needed another angle, a way to block Paul's weapon before he could recover.

She needed a new cipher.

Sarah considered using the new master rune, but discarded the idea. Alter had made it clear that it was far too dangerous to try tapping the full force of a pivotal historical moment. She'd spent hours planning the use of those tiny parts of the original master rune, and those pieces fueled her new enhancement with exceptional power.

Maybe she could do that again? A customization to her latest enhancement rune popped into her mind, and she twisted on the ground behind her shield. Sarah pulled down her waistline and called a scalpel to her hand. She made two cuts, embedding into her enhancement a small part of the new master rune.

As soon as she completed the marks, the entire rune burned with blue-white light. Icy chills rippled out from her rune warrior mark at the small of her back and linked to the rune. It chilled her to the bone and drained her strength.

"Look out!" Alter cried.

Sarah lacked the energy to roll over and see what was going on. She could only wonder if she'd made a mistake as her shield sagged in her weak grip.

Then it was wrenched out of her hands. Paul stood above her, panting and livid with rage. His chest still looked like it had been run through a meat grinder, but somehow he was on his feet. Fury boiled off him in waves and he snarled at her, showing several missing teeth.

He tipped the muzzle of the machine gun forward until it pointed at her chest, barely six inches away.

"Feel my wrath, Sarah," he snarled.

Sarah reached for that ethereal feeling she'd drawn upon in the past, but her rune did not respond. She looked up at the barrel, filled with horror, knowing she was dead.

Paul pulled the trigger.

The gun roared and flames spurted from the muzzle to char her skin. Bullets ripped through Sarah, pummeling her, shaking her body like a water balloon in a hurricane. Blood sprayed everywhere and pain so severe she could barely comprehend it crashed through her mind.

She screamed but could do nothing as her body shuddered and shook under the brutal onslaught. She was dead and it hurt worse than she'd ever imagined.

Then all of a sudden it didn't.

Sarah gasped at the abrupt absence of agony. The machine gun still belched flame and lead, still roared loud enough to deafen her, but she felt only a distant pinching across her torso. Paul's face was set in an expression of exultant glee as he machine-gunned her to death.

Only, she wasn't dead.

Her skin rippled like quicksilver, returning to its proper form. Her newly-altered rune was blazing against her thigh, filling her with energy and somehow transforming the very composition of her cells. She could feel bullets pounding her, but they no longer penetrated.

Twenty-eight bullets were embedded in her chest, but with a thought she expelled them. They rose through her flesh like bubbles in a pond and dropped to the ground.

The sound changed. Instead of the sickening notes of lead ripping through meat, bullets ricocheted away with angry buzzing as if her skin had turned to living steel.

Paul released the trigger, a stunned expression on his face.

"How is it possible?"

With a thought, Sarah rose. She didn't stand, but instead flowed from a prone position into an upright one.

"You think machine-gunning a girl makes her want you?"

She swung at him with every ounce of terror and confusion, and a towering fury. Her arm morphed into that sickle-shaped blade, and she slashed it right through both of his thighs to ensure she got her target.

Paul staggered back with a scream, his legs gushing blood, staring at his severed testicles. He dropped the machine gun, one hand reaching toward his fallen flesh.

"Father a nation now, eunuch," Sarah said as her hand returned to normal.

Before he could respond, Alter tackled him from behind.

The two went down in a heap even as Alter rained blow after blow upon the cui dashi. The young hunter attacked with a fury even greater than he had when fighting Tomas. He screamed a long howl of rage and beat on Paul with bone crushing force.

Paul's hands began to burn with purple fire and he caught Alter's wrists. For a second he held the raging hunter and his expression began to change to that smug look of superiority. Then he glanced again at what Sarah had done to him, and his expression fell.

Alter's hands began to burn.

For the first time, Paul looked worried.

"You and I are one," Paul panted.

"You are abomination and I will terminate you," Alter growled, driving his hands against Paul's, reaching for his throat.

Paul resisted and their hands quivered in the air. The two strove against each other with all their strength. Then, ever so slightly, Paul began to inch Alter's hands back.

His confident smile returned. "You are weak, young one, and you're going to die on the verge of greatness."

"Keep your greatness," Sarah said.

She had scooped up the machine gun and now pressed the barrel against Paul's head. She pulled the trigger.

The entire memoryscape buckled, and the earth exploded. The eruption tossed Sarah into the air. She caught a glimpse of Alter and then nothing. The circus disintegrated, as did the skyline of Rome, then the sky altogether.

Nothing took their place. The world became a formless gray expanse with no sense of direction, no gravity, no point of orientation.

Alter was gone.

Sarah hung in the blank nothingness, too tired to even freak out at the lack of memoryscape. Alter would pull them free in a moment, and she was just happy they'd survived.

Without warning Paul appeared beside her, grabbed her shoulder with burning hands, and drove a gladius into her steel stomach.

Sarah screamed, although the pain was far less than it should have been. Her body began to morph around the blade, but more slowly than it had a moment ago.

She could feel the strength of his nevron driving into her, trying to block the power of her new enhancement, delaying the shifting ability she had just unlocked and didn't know how to control. She again tried to call upon the ethereal effect her rune had produced before, but again she felt nothing but the burning heat of her new quicksilver ability. The two seemed mutually exclusive.

Sarah tried to fight him, but couldn't move. He might not yet be able to block her enhancement entirely, but he had severed her command over her muscles.

"You are more worthy than I dreamed," Paul whispered, speaking into her ear, lips brushing her skin. He wrapped his left arm around her waist and pulled her hard against him in a disgustingly intimate embrace. "Within twenty-four hours, I will have everything I need to rise to claim my destiny."

She tried to speak, but couldn't.

Paul leaned his forehead against hers, his burning eyes filling her vision. "Pledge yourself to me, Sarah, and the pain can end. Give yourself both body and soul as a willing sacrifice, and spare yourself the agony that justice demands I inflict upon your disobedience."

He granted her power over her voice. "You're dead, freak."

He kissed her cheek slowly, lingering over the contact, and began twisting the sword in her stomach. She couldn't even scream as fresh waves of pain ripped through her.

"Know your destiny, beloved. Embrace it and I will pleasure you beyond your imagining." He gave the sword another twist. "Deny me and, well, I think you get the point."

"How do you like being a eunuch?" Sarah whispered before he robbed her ability to speak.

Paul kissed her lips and denied her the ability to fight him. His lips were thin and cold, and a shiver of revulsion left her screaming inside.

"Until tomorrow, my most chosen vessel. Stay strong for me, and we'll find a way to convince mother you're worthy."

Then he disappeared.

74

I feel a lingering sense of emptiness when I think of Mai Luan. Is this what mortals feel as they watch loved ones succumb to dust after their meaningless little lives? How can I share any such base feelings with insignificant souls? I cannot ask Mother, for any weakness is punished by death.

I would ask Sarah, but she refuses to listen to reason and, as gallant as her attempted resistance may be, such moments of conflict are not suited for the sharing of inner feelings. When will she accept my lordship and surrender?

~PAUL

SARAH AWOKE, but the nightmare didn't end. Waves of pain left her groaning as gentle hands pulled the helmet away. She blinked into the bright lights of the vault and found a woman dressed in a medical jumpsuit standing over her.

"Don't move," the medic warned. Her gloved hands were smeared with blood. She injected something into Sarah's arm. "Give this a moment and it'll help with the pain."

Sarah's body felt bruised from head to toe, and her skin was raw and scraped all over. Her blouse was soaked with blood. When she gently peeled it back with a trembling hand, her skin was puckered with angry welts where the bullets had torn into her. In the memoryscape, she had recovered quickly, but a lot of that damage had translated into reality. Even with her healing runes, she'd be polka-dotted with bruises.

"You're lucky to be alive," the medic said as she worked to clean

Sarah's bloody stomach. "You just started spurting blood a few minutes ago."

"It was rough," Sarah rasped, barely recognizing her own voice. Better to just focus on breathing.

When the medic raised the head of her chair a moment later, Sarah peeled down the bloody waistline of her slacks. Her rune was still there, but lacked the marks she had added in the memory. She leaned back, thinking about that. Could a rune alter physical composition in the real world too? Did she dare try?

Tomas appeared at her side as the medic draped a warm blanket over her. "Sarah, are you all right?"

"I'll live. How about you?"

"I'm fine. I had a weird chat with Spartacus."

"I'll swap you next time."

"Let's hope there's no next time," Tomas said gently. "We might have gotten a good lead."

Sarah sighed and closed her eyes for a moment. If they had, then the effort might have been worth it. "Is everyone else out?"

"Waking up now. What happened?"

"Paul transported me and Alter to the Circus Maximus. It got ugly."

"Sarah!" Alter appeared next to Tomas.

He looked far too healthy, and if she had the energy, she'd punch him in the eye to share the joy.

"Glad you got out all right," she whispered instead. "I lost track of you when he blew the circus."

"Did Paul get away?" Gregorios asked, moving into her line of vision. He grimaced at her bloody blouse. "Are you all right?"

"I will be. I think. Although it may be time for a dedicated healing rune."

"If you have the strength to activate it, I think it's a good idea," Tomas said.

Gregorios said, "In a minute. You need to rest, and I need a report. Paul's awake then, and he has the rune?"

"He has something," Sarah said.

"What do you mean?" Gregorios asked.

"The rune he was inscribing into his skin was different than the lesser master rune I saw in the sky."

"You have to come up with a better name. It's wrong on so many levels," Alter groaned.

"What would you call it?" she asked.

He shrugged. "It was a powerful rune, a greater rune, but not a master rune like what appeared in Berlin."

"Exactly," Sarah murmured. "You call it a greater rune. I'll call it a lesser master rune." She was too tired to argue semantics.

"Can you draw the rune Paul was trying to inscribe?" Gregorios asked.

She hesitated. "I can, but I'm not sure I should. It was evil."

The medic interrupted. "You're not strong enough to draw anything."

Sarah had to agree. She ached so deep, it scared her. For claiming he wanted her as his most-beloved slave, Paul had been willing to push her to the brink of death.

Eirene joined them, slipping an arm around Gregorios' waist. "I can't believe we let Paul use us like that."

"I knew we should've just started shooting," Tomas said.

"He used us like first-life novices," Gregorios growled. "We didn't gain much from that exchange."

"Not entirely true," Sarah said. She was starting to feel drowsy from the painkiller. "Paul said he just needs one more rune to destroy us all, and that he'll get it within the next twenty-four hours."

Gregorios grimaced. "Not good, although I can't see how he'll get the one from the fall of Rome."

Eirene considered that. "He has Spartacus. I'm starting to wonder if we caught them testing a new sequence to combine John's and Spartacus' memories. If they can pull it off, they could get the other rune."

"With the power of the two master runes he already controls, coupled with the forbidden runes we know he has, he already wields enough power to wreak untold damage," Alter interjected. "If he needs another master rune, his plans must be to strike globally and cement his reign in a single, worldwide coup."

Eirene added, "It wasn't a total loss, love. We had a little chat with Spartacus."

"Good. I'm glad one of us did. And he was coherent?"

Eirene nodded. "Just like near the cemetery. He claims he reached some kind of enlightenment during his long dispossession."

"More importantly," Tomas added with a grin. "He agreed to meet me to settle the question of ownership of my battle suit once and for all."

Sarah had started drifting in a drug-induced half-sleep, with burning runes flitting behind her eyes, but tried to listen. The real Spartacus was so much more than history portrayed him, and the new Spartacus was fascinating. Well, he would be once he gave Tomas his body back, right? Her thoughts were getting fuzzy.

The news cheered Gregorios. "Now we're getting somewhere. Do you think we can turn him?"

Eirene said, "It may be possible. He owes Paul an honor debt for restoring him, but he's not committed to the cause."

Gregorios kissed Eirene. "I think we can work with that. Another interesting development is that John's starting to wake up to reality. The machines are reversing his soul fragmentation, although all he managed to do was pass me a pretty useless message."

"Tell it to me anyway. You miss the obvious sometimes," Eirene said.

"I do not," he said, assuming a hurt expression.

"Don't get me started," Eirene said, her voice teasing. "You want to talk about the conquistadors?"

"Never mind. John said they're in Rome, in some kind of converted tunnel in a ruin. Like I said, useless."

Eirene frowned. "That is pretty vague. This is Rome after all."

Gregorios added, "I tried to follow after he left the memory. There was only one other mental signature so I figured it had to be his. I appeared in what was left of the Circus Maximus."

Alter said, "Probably right after we left. Paul blew everything up when Sarah shot him in the head."

"Good job." Tomas squeezed Sarah's hand, and the gesture roused her a little.

"He shot me more. I still owe him," she whispered.

Eirene paced away, brow furrowed. "What if it wasn't you Gregorios was following?" She turned to him. "What did the Circus look like?"

"Ruined. Not as bad as modern day, but close. No city around, though."

She said, "Maybe that was another hint from John, pointing out the direction to search."

"Interesting. We're supposed to meet Spartacus in the ruined circus tomorrow," Tomas said.

Sarah roused herself, trying to keep up. "You think they're setting a trap?"

Paul had staked his claim, promised to make her his slave. He might be trying to lure her to a place where he could capture her. The thought made her shiver with dread and helped her shake off some of her stupor.

Tomas said, "We can sweep the area. Sarah and I can take a drive to the park as soon as she recovers, and explore around the ruins of the old Circus. Maybe she'll get a glimmer from that super rune of hers."

"Sure, if we have lots of back-up," Sarah said weakly. "Help me up."

"You're not going anywhere," the medic warned. "You suffered severe trauma and need time to recover."

"Time is one thing we don't have," Gregorios said.

Eirene said, "Before we go rushing off, I want to hear details of what transpired in the Circus with Paul. We can't overlook anything."

While Sarah tried to collect her drifting thoughts, Alter began the tale. When he described the souped-up dune buggy, Tomas grinned.

"You have to make me one of those. We can visit the Sahara with Gregorios after this mess is over."

Eirene said, "Don't get distracted. Besides, I drive better than Greg."

Gregorios rolled his eyes. "That accident was lives ago."

Sarah told them again about the strangely altered rune Paul had been inscribing on his side, how she changed it, and the explosive consequences.

Alter said, "So that's what you did. I didn't even see it. I just saw him drop you and then explode. I thought you shoved a grenade down his trousers."

"That would've been awesome," Tomas chuckled.

"Well, I did castrate him later," Sarah said.

Tomas laughed aloud then kissed her soundly, earning him a frown from the hovering medic.

"This I've got to hear," Gregorios said, grinning.

Eirene said, "Just tell the rest of the story. We'll hear it all in due course."

"Sometimes it's fun to focus on the exciting parts," Gregorios said with a wink.

"You're incorrigible."

Sarah related the rest of the encounter.

"How exactly did you change to quicksilver?" Eirene asked when Sarah explained how she'd saved herself from getting machine-gunned to death. "Again you push the limits beyond the normal."

"It's not entirely without precedent," Gregorios said. "Zombies are partially-animated flesh, and werewolves are definitely not normal."

Eirene shook her head, even though Sarah wanted Gregorios to explain further. "None of the monsters that spawn all the legends actually change the composition of human flesh like we're seeing with Sarah's enhancements."

"I wonder if it could be possible in the real world," Gregorios said.

Tomas nodded. "Imagine if we could transform the enforcers to steel?"

Sarah imagined the giant Maori Anaru possessing her quicksilver ability. He'd knock down entire cities.

"It would be abomination," Alter said.

"Can't you think of a new word?" Tomas asked.

"It's morally wrong," Alter shot back. After a slight hesitation he added in a more moderate tone. "Besides, it would require so much energy, she'd probably lose control and burn out her rounon well, if not die outright."

Eirene said, "We'll discuss hypotheticals later. Tell us the rest."

When Sarah told them about Paul stabbing her and promising to force himself upon her, Alter stomped away and began punching the stainless-steel wall, denting the smooth surface. He had to have broken bones in his hands, but didn't seem to notice.

Tomas' reaction was more controlled, but his lips pressed together in a tight line, and his shoulders tensed. "Eirene, I think I'm going to need that chainsaw of yours."

Gregorios patted Sarah's hand. "You did amazing. Time to remove this animal once and for all."

Sarah motioned Tomas closer. "First step, bring me a scalpel."

75

To have command is to have all the power you will ever need. To have all the power you will ever need, is to have the world in the palm of your hand. To call a facetaker friend is to become a god.

~TIBERIUS, THIRD LIFE OF JULIUS CAESAR

"WHAT DO YOU HAVE IN MIND?" Tomas sounded nervous.

"I need a permanent healing rune, or I won't be much help to anyone," Sarah said.

Alter drifted back toward them, massaging his hand, but not otherwise showing effects of the beating he'd just given the wall. "Sarah, have a care. Your strength can only spread so far, and even if you can heal yourself, you'll need time to recuperate."

"I'll focus on the healing part for now. Please bring me a knife."

The medic helped Sarah wash the blood off her left side, over her lowest ribs. The woman paced away, muttering to herself when Sarah handed Tomas the knife and asked him to mark the same higher healing rune into her skin that she'd marked on him when he'd been wearing Carl's body. That night seemed so long ago, but it had been her first rune, and it had saved his life.

Alter said, "Let me do it. I have more experience."

"I know, and I appreciate the offer. But this is our special rune. Tomas can do it," she told him as gently as she could.

Tomas might have lacked Alter's artistic flair, but he worked the knife along her skin with a gentle touch, his expression set in extreme concentration. Alter might have completed it sooner, but it felt right to have Tomas inscribe the healing rune into her skin.

The pain of the shallow cuts paled compared to the throbbing aches already clamoring for attention. They'd subsided some since she'd awakened, thanks to her other runes, but they weren't as good as a dedicated healing enhancement.

When Tomas finished, Sarah pressed his hand over the bleeding marks and willed her rounon to life. Warm energy poured out of her center and flowed through her hand, passing through Tomas' fingers and sealing to the fresh-cut rune. It activated, draining her already-waning strength, and she sagged, her eyes fluttering closed.

"Sarah, are you all right?" Tomas asked, leaning over her, his eyes shining with the wonder of sharing her rune activation with her.

"I knew this was a bad idea," Alter growled.

Gentle warmth began radiating from the new enhancement, spreading through her torso, quenching the throbbing pain with a blanket of peace.

Sarah breathed deep for the first time since waking, and checked her side. The rune glowed with a warm, blue-white light. Healing strength continued to pour into her from an invisible well, and the angry welts of her recent bullet wounds faded away. Her mind cleared from the drug-induced fog.

Tomas leaned closer and her lips met his in a deep kiss. They held it long enough for Alter to cough, sounding uncomfortable.

"Looks like you're feeling better," Gregorios commented dryly when she released him.

"Lots." Sarah held out her hands and Tomas helped her rise over the objections of the medic.

Sarah swayed a bit from momentary dizziness, but steadied with Tomas' help. Her blouse was a ripped, bloody mess and she was glad to accept a blue cotton jacket from the medic to replace it.

"Your lips seem to be working," Gregorios said, handing her a pen and paper. "Let's test your memory. Show me the rune Paul was inscribing."

She easily called the sinister symbol to memory and began sketching it out.

"Don't complete it," Alter warned as the rune became clear on the page.

"Why not?"

"Because this is a corruption of that greater rune. It holds the power of that moment, but twisted to the truth of assassination, greed, and contempt for life."

"It's similar to the one I saw," Sarah said.

"Show me what you saw," Alter asked.

Sarah sketched out the rune she had witnessed in the sky above the dying emperor.

Eirene said, "That's very similar to the one I saw, but not identical."

"Same here," Gregorios said.

Alter nodded. "Same for me. I should have foreseen this."

"What?" Sarah asked.

"Paul witnessed a different truth. In fact, we all witnessed slight variations on the truths represented in that moment."

That was surprising. Eirene said, "Wait a minute. You said that master runes represent a deeper truth associated with pivotal moments in history."

Alter nodded. "That's what I believed. It's still partially correct. These pivotal moments represent different truths to different people. To Caesar, his first assassination was a tragedy, a betrayal, an overthrow of his reign. To some of the conspirators it represented defending traditional values."

Eirene added, "Makes sense. And to others, it might have represented conspiracy to take power from others. The underlying truths include the fall of a republic, but the foundation of an empire."

Alter said, "But for us, none of that truly matters. We each see the truth that resonates most powerfully with us. I don't think we've ever known of a time there were multiple people present with gifted nevron, all of which could affect the rune."

That was a really interesting twist on what they thought they knew about the memoryscape. Sarah asked, "So that's why Paul's rune was so menacing? Because he wants to see death and conquest."

"Exactly."

"That's twisted," Tomas said, and Sarah nodded.

"It also adds complexity," Gregorios said. "If we don't know exactly what runes he's working with, it'll be harder to counter him."

"Not if he's dead," Tomas pointed out.

Sarah squeezed his hand. She liked his thinking. When she turned back toward the machines, she noticed for the first time Francesca and her siblings all collapsed in nearby chairs, fast asleep.

"What happened to them?"

Eirene said, "The new rune amulets worked. They avoided the back-lash of Paul's forbidden rune, but the drain was severe."

Gregorios frowned. "That's going to become a problem, although Sarah offers an opportunity."

"What do you mean?" Sarah asked.

"Rune warriors can inscribe custom runes that don't work for others. Runes that can draw from other souls and whose power can be directed in unique ways."

Alter was already frowning. "Be careful, Gregorios. I won't allow you to guide her into the realm of evil."

"It's not like the evil of heka webs. They sacrifice stolen souls to power their enchantments."

"They're easier to interrupt too," Tomas added.

Eirene said, "You need to physically approach a rune web, but Sarah would be able to sense them, and to interrupt them remotely. We wouldn't need another suicide charge."

"I worked with what I had," he said defensively. "You try taking a fortified position with nothing but a light brigade."

"Is there something I should know about?" Sarah asked.

Tomas said, "We'll watch the movie some time. Then I'll explain."

"How can I interrupt heka webs?" Sarah asked. That was something she was eager to understand.

Alter said, "You'll feel them. I'll show you the marks you need to break them, or redirect their power back upon the enchanters running them."

"Or even steal that energy for other uses," Gregorios said.

"No. That would be evil," Alter said quickly.

Eirene said, "Not if she used it to stop them. If she wasn't the one to create the web, anything she did with it would be better by definition."

"Don't muddy the waters," Alter said.

"And don't ignore possibilities because they don't easily fit into your buckets of abomination flavors," Gregorios retorted. "The hard questions need to be considered."

"I know what you're doing," Alter said, rounding on Gregorios. "You'll justify taking a kashaph abomination and using it for purposes we would consider good. Then you'll extend that same reasoning to justify Sarah siphoning life force from unwilling souls to fuel her ciphers."

"I didn't say to use unwilling souls," Gregorios said. Thankfully he ignored Alter's belligerence.

Eirene approached Alter, placing a hand on his arm. "What Greg's suggesting is that we develop a cipher to assist our children in powering the machines. Paul himself has set the deadline. We get one more shot at him in the memoryscape, and I don't want any limiting factors on our side."

They discussed the idea as a group, although Alter took some convincing before agreeing to help with the cipher. Sarah suspected he finally agreed because he realized she knew enough to try it without his help, and he didn't want to lose all influence with her. Either way, she was glad he didn't walk out on them.

Sarah's health continued to improve. The new healing rune was working wonders. Coupled with the strong foundation of her existing enhancements, she'd feel almost normal within the hour.

Eirene reiterated Alter's earlier warning that she take it easy, regardless. Her body might be quickly healing, but the process was draining her soul force. Making that a habit could weaken her soul and leave her vulnerable to Paul or the heka.

"How do I know how much has been drained?" she asked.

Eirene said, "It's a sense you gain over time. You possess a powerful soul so I'm not worried yet, but be careful. Rest and other activities that replenish the soul help it recover more quickly."

"What kind of activities?" Tomas asked.

"You two can talk about that later," Eirene said with a wink.

Sarah hoped Spartacus showed up the next day so Tomas could win back his body. She was looking forward to exploring as many of those soul-replenishing activities as Tomas' sense of morality would allow.

The group left the vault and returned to Quentin's for sumptuous late lunch. As they lingered over dessert and fruit, they worked on the cipher to assist with the soul-draining load of running the machines.

When they worked up a functional cipher, Sarah inscribed it onto a series of wooden blocks that would be positioned around the Suntara building. She would trigger them just prior to their next memory hunt and set them to expire an hour later. They would siphon five percent energy from every soul within the building.

"You know," Tomas said as he examined the cipher. "We could spread these out farther, out into the city. That would give us—"

"No!" Alter interrupted. "We're already skirting the edges of abusing this power. Anything more would be unforgivable and my family would assassinate Sarah and every one of us."

"What gives them the right to determine what's right and what's evil?" Gregorios asked.

Alter opened his mouth to reply, but then scowled. Sarah thought back to the conversation when he had demanded a similar thing from Gregorios. He didn't appear to like having the tables turned.

"I think our work here is done," Eirene said.

Tomas took Sarah's hand. "Come on. I'm taking you back to bed."

Sarah stared, and Alter looked ready to explode, but Francesca responded first. She laughed. "That's the spirit, Tomas. Don't waste a precious second."

His face flushed and he stammered, "You know that's not what I meant. She needs rest and I'm going to make sure she gets it."

"Don't let him wear you out," Francesca said to Sarah, giving her an encouraging smile. "Tomorrow will be a big day."

Tomas still sputtered with ineffectual objections until Sarah kissed his cheek. "Don't worry, Tomas. We all know you."

"Not as well as you're about to," Francesca called after them.

"Don't get carried away," Gregorios said loudly as they reached the door. "Tomorrow we start early. I want the Tenth fully deployed and Yurak staged to assist. You two will run point, take a picnic in the park, and scope it out."

"With guns," Eirene added.

76

I recognize that even after so many lives, I'll make mistakes, that I'll miss something, but that offers little consolation when I witness such devastation. I can't help but think I should have discovered the heka cell that unleashed the Black Death before it took hold. With the information you provided, my team wiped out that cell, but the rune was cast and cannot be undone. Until I see you again in Paris, I'm yours for another life.

~GREGORIOS, IN A LETTER TO EIRENE, 1347

"NOTHING."

Sarah strode farther along the flat expanse of the ruins of the Circus Maximus, trying to reconcile it with the magnificent arena she'd seen in the memoryscape. Instead of packed sand surrounded by high-tiered rows of screaming spectators, it was now a long field of close-cropped green grass.

Its main axis was still recognizable, running southeast to northwest, with rows of trees marching along a low rise on the southern boundary where the massive outer wall had stood. North of the circus, the mass of Palatine Hill still rose above the field, but the beautiful palaces that had overlooked the ancient arena had fallen into ruin.

Even the bright, late-morning sunshine did little to help her mood. More than any of the other ruins of modern-day Rome she had visited in the annals of time, the ruin of the Circus struck her as a tragedy.

"Show me where you raced the buggy," Tomas said, trotting past her, apparently unaffected by the weight of history that hung over the field.

"Aren't we supposed to be having a picnic?" she called after him.

Walkers, strolling couples, and young families with shrieking children were sprinkled across the green expanse, and Sarah was grateful the crowds were light. There was a good chance some kind of fight was about to erupt in the peaceful setting, and she didn't want innocents getting hurt. She considered ciphers she could use to shield people if the situation called for it.

The rest of their support team had stayed back, filtering among the distant trees and trying to remain unobtrusive. A large number of other enforcers were taking up positions around the Circus and the nearby Colosseum, scanning for any sign of Spartacus or heka. They were close enough to provide support if the Circus proved to be a trap.

Gregorios had considered the potential for some kind of encounter likely enough that he wasn't taking any chances. Francesca and Harriet were staged a little farther out with some of the Yurak International forces.

Sarah felt not even a glimmer of distant facetakers. She had hoped she'd catch a hint of something. She'd probed outward with those intangible senses that locked onto nevra cores like lights in her mind, but found nothing.

Tomas tossed her an apple. "Eat slow. It's the only picnic I brought."

If Spartacus decided to show up, they wouldn't have time to enjoy a picnic anyway, but they might get to hang around for a while, waiting for something to happen.

She sighed, "This was a great opportunity."

If they did have to wait, she'd user her phone to pull up images of Celtic ogham runes that Alter had shown her the previous night after dinner. He'd explained how they were the preferred symbols for breaking remote heka enchantments, particularly webs.

She'd forced him to explain how she could use the symbols to take control of those remote enchantments, despite his protestations against that approach.

"I need to understand it," she'd insisted. "I promise not to use it unless there's no other alternative."

Tomas spun a slow circle, scanning the mostly-empty park. "I hope this whole setup isn't a bust."

"Have patience," she urged, offering a bite of her apple. "This was a good lead. Something is going to happen."

She had to believe that. Paul had promised that he would move on the last rune that very day. If they didn't shut him down before then, he'd launch whatever crazy plan he'd been working up against the world. Then he'd come for her.

Sarah shivered, but vowed to geld him in real life like she had in the ancient circus. Being a eunuch suited that pig.

"We should have brought a frisbee," Sarah said, even though every second weighed on her mind. She needed to return to Suntara soon to prepare for a final memory hunt against Paul. She wasn't looking forward to it.

Anaru's deep voice spoke through their encrypted earbuds. "Captain, contact. You are under surveillance from the ruins atop Palatine Hill."

"Snipers?" Tomas asked, his expression never changing.

"Negative."

"Reposition teams three and six for optimal supporting fire if the situation deteriorates," Tomas ordered.

"Do you think it's a trap?" Sarah asked, trying to maintain a calm expression as they continued walking slowly across the wide open expanse, hand-in-hand. Even though she'd been wanting something to happen, she suddenly felt exposed, and began reviewing her shielding ciphers.

Tomas said, "If Paul knows we're here, then it's a trap. If it's just Spartacus, I actually think he'll show."

He turned toward her, wrapping his arms loosely around her waist, as if to enjoy a more intimate moment. He was wearing a light jacket, and she slipped one hand under it to the holster of one of the four pistols he was wearing concealed. She couldn't see the hidden watchers, let alone shoot one with a pistol from that distance, but the feel of the gun helped calm her nerves.

Tomas didn't remark on her handling his hardware in public. He didn't even kiss her, but spoke softly into her ear. "Domenico, what's the status of your men along the Forum?"

"You always know how to say the most romantic things," Sarah said, kissing his cheek to keep up appearances.

Sarah loved Domenico's Italian accent. He reported, "All teams are in position. I'm shifting teams seven and nine for better coverage of Palatine Hill. Team eight was just about to start their reconnoiter of that area, but there are barriers and police sentries. The entire hill's been blocked off for some kind of repair."

"It's probably a ploy," Tomas said. "Paul's people must have more assets on that hill. Have your teams hold position and monitor those sentries. I don't want to spook the watchers until Spartacus appears. And check our contacts with the polizia to get confirmation those sentries are legitimate."

When no one started shooting at them, Sarah allowed herself to relax a little. Maybe they were reading too much into things?

Tomas released her and they resumed their slow walk across the circus.

Domenico interrupted the tense silence a moment later. "Contact. Confirmed sighting of the heka woman we attempted to grab last week at the Colosseum."

"Rosetta's here?" Sarah asked. At Tomas' questioning look she added, "I hated thinking of her as the mark, so I gave her a name."

"It works. Domenico, designate the heka as Rosetta."

"Roger, Captain. Rosetta is exiting the Palatine Hill. Just passed the police barricade and is turning in your direction. If she continues, she'll make contact in five minutes."

"Should we pick her up?" Anaru asked.

"Negative," Tomas said, continuing the slow stroll. "Apprise mobile teams of the situation and position them for interdiction if required."

He glanced at Sarah and squeezed her hand. "Looks like this wasn't a total waste of time."

"But why Rosetta? I thought Spartacus was supposed to be here."

"I'll answer that in five minutes," he said with a shrug.

The wait seemed to take forever. Domenico fed them regular reports from his teams that were monitoring Rosetta's steady progress around the hill toward the circus. No other known heka were spotted, and no other movement occurred on the hill.

Tomas used the wait to switch channels back to Gregorios and Eirene, who were coordinating the complex operation from Suntara's communications hub.

Gregorios said, "I'll move the Tenth's reinforcements to secondary staging locations. Yurak will draw in to back them up."

Sarah spotted Rosetta as soon as she rounded the last worn column and stepped onto the Circus. She was wearing a long, blue coat that could conceal all kinds of weapons, and Sarah's fears that the meeting was a trap escalated.

She concentrated on her rounon well, and her rune warrior symbol grew warm against her back. Energy coursed through her, reinforcing the vibrant life she already felt from her enhancements.

Whatever Rosetta was planning, she didn't stand a chance.

As Rosetta approached, Sarah thought back to the botched snatch attempt at the Colosseum. The woman had been willing to desecrate that ancient ruin without hesitation. Sarah yearned to close the distance and pound the heka into the ground. She'd show the woman who was stronger now.

She became aware of a pulsing sound, like a low humming emanating from the heka. Then she noticed a dim glow surrounding Rosetta. In the bright sunlight, she'd missed it at first. Only fifty feet separated them, and with each step Rosetta took, the effects became clearer.

With each pulse of the slow humming, the sound echoed back toward the Palatine Hill. Even though Sarah couldn't see it, she felt that sound, as if it was rippling up an invisible conduit to a distant source.

Sarah realized what she was sensing and her grip on Tomas' hand tightened. "She's got a rune web protecting her. The source is up on the hill somewhere."

"Can you sense its purpose?" Tomas whispered back, not taking his eyes from the advancing woman.

"I'm still pretty new to these, but I think at least part of it has to do with shielding. It feels similar to what I felt when I activated my shield wall the other night. Do you want me to break it?"

"Get ready, but hold until we hear what she has to say. Breaking it might alert her."

Rosetta flashed them a haughty smile as she closed on them. "Whispering together like the children waiting for the teacher. Spartacus isn't coming."

"So he sent you to take the beating for him?" Tomas asked.

"He sends a message," she replied, stopping ten feet away and giving Sarah a dismissive look. "No one is so brave that he is not disturbed by something unexpected."

Sarah frowned. "What does that mean?"

Tomas said, "It's a quote from Julius Caesar. From the Gallic Wars, during the time he beat the Helvetii tribe using an effective surprise attack."

"Are you claiming to be his surprise attack?" Sarah asked, preparing to fight. She could cross the distance to Rosetta before the woman could draw a gun.

"He is not my captain," Rosetta spat.

"Well, you're going to have to come with us and tell us all about who is," Tomas said, taking a step forward.

Rosetta laughed. "First I give you my master's message!"

She flung open her coat, revealing an explosive vest.

Even as Sarah realized the terrible danger they were in, a bullet ricocheted off of Rosetta's forehead. Anaru cursed in her earpiece.

Tomas lunged, but he struck the invisible web protecting Rosetta and rebounded. He'd explained to Sarah that some webs only protected against certain types of assaults. The one shielding her was remarkably strong.

"Not so much a suicide vest as a weapon of mass destruction," Rosetta taunted Tomas.

Sarah was sick of her superior attitude. She drew upon her rounon power and slashed her hand across the air, making a glowing mark that she used to focus her power onto the complex cipher she'd been preparing.

She used the shielding cipher she'd built with Tomas, but also included the Celtic marks to break the rune web and subvert its power to fuel her cipher instead.

She barely noticed the drain as the cipher activated and her invisible wall snapped into place. It glowed bright in her rune vision, even though it would remain invisible to the others. It thrummed with strength, fueled by astonishing levels of energy from the co-opted rune web.

Rosetta detonated the explosive vest.

The explosion shook the ground, but sounded far less intense than Sarah expected. The shockwave rebounded from her shield wall, which withstood the onslaught. It suffered a severe drain, and sucked more power from the stolen rune web.

She still recoiled from the fire boiling inches away, even though it was repulsed by her shield, as was the full weight of the shockwave and much of the heat. The air grew warm, but did not sear her skin.

Rosetta was not so lucky. Robbed of her web, she was left defenseless against the blast, magnified by the backlash off of Sarah's shield.

She didn't even have time to scream.

The smoke cleared within seconds, but all that remained of Rosetta was the charred sole of one of her boots.

77

It is the duty of a good shepherd to shear his sheep, not to skin them. Sometimes I wonder when I meet with Shahrokh, am I the sheep, or the shepherd?

~TIBERIUS, THIRD LIFE OF JULIUS CAESAR

"TAKE OUT THAT SURVEILLANCE," Tomas ordered, his voice calm despite the near-roasting.

Only three seconds passed before Anaru responded. "Target down."

Sarah hadn't been able to tear her eyes away from the charred ground and the one tiny remnant of Rosetta. The woman had been heka, a supporter of Paul, and clearly a bad person, but that death had been disgusting. Sarah had wanted to defeat Rosetta, but not incinerate her.

Anaru's report filtered through her shocked thoughts. Just like that, another life had ended. They weren't in the memoryscape where the people they killed were shades of the once-living. Rosetta and the unknown watcher had been living, breathing people.

Now they were dead.

Tomas took Sarah's arm and led her gently south, where she spotted a couple enforcers between the trees. They no longer bothered to hide their rifles, and scanned the ruins of the nearby Palatine Hill with binoculars, looking for additional threats.

"Are you all right?" Tomas asked, his expression concerned. "That blast didn't hurt you, did it?"

"No. Just startled by the suddenness of it."

He wrapped an arm around her shoulders and held her close. "You did amazing. I hate getting blown up."

She started to respond, but then realized she hadn't released her shield wall. It was still protecting an empty spot of ground on the Circus field. The rune web she'd stolen from Rosetta still fueled it, but so did another source.

Sarah frowned and studied the hill to the north. She interrupted Tomas, who was conversing with his men. "Hey, there are more people up on that hill. My cipher is tapping them too."

"How many?"

"I'm not sure, but quite a few. I re-used that cipher we tested by the prison, and I didn't have time to turn off the directional pointers. They're aimed at the hill, and it found souls to siphon."

Tomas frowned. "We have no visuals on more targets, or we would have taken them out by now."

He scanned the park, now empty of pedestrians who had scattered when the bomb detonated. "We need to move. The police will arrive soon, and we don't have time to deal with that."

As he led her toward a nearby street where they would meet up with one of the mobile support teams, he added, "Rosetta didn't know about your rune warrior abilities. If not for that trump card, that suicide vest would've hurt."

"So it was a trap," Sarah said.

"Perhaps," Tomas replied thoughtfully. "The only other possibility was that Spartacus wanted us to find this hideout."

Sarah frowned. "Hey, that web just went down, and my access to those souls just got severed." Her wall fizzled when the fuel source ran dry.

"They're on to you. Either the enchanter who was running the web realized you subverted it, or felt the soul drain. He'll retool the web and use it for something else, probably an attempt to protect his people from you. We don't have much time."

As soon as they hopped into the back of a large van and settled into jump seats along the interior walls, Tomas switched frequencies to the central hub and reported in to Gregorios and Eirene. They linked in Harriett, who was in charge of the Yurak forces.

"It has to be Palatine Hill," Tomas concluded. "I think we've found Paul's hideout."

"John mentioned tunnels," Eirene said.

"Someone's waxing poetic," Gregorios commented.

"Why?" Sarah asked.

"Palatine Hill is where it all started," Eirene explained. "It's where the founders of the city, Romulus and Remus, were supposedly raised by a wolf."

"They weren't though, were they?" Sarah asked, hoping for a simple answer for once.

She should have known better.

"Not exactly," Gregorios said. "They were sons of an ambitious mother who made the mistake of betraying a foul-tempered facetaker."

"He was a piece of work from everything you've told me about him," Eirene said.

"You didn't know him?" Sarah asked.

"Before my time."

"Wow." It surprised Sarah to think anything might be older than Eirene.

Gregorios said, "He didn't survive many lives, but he punished that unfaithful lover by transferring her soul to the body of a wolf."

"Is that possible?" Sarah asked.

"Doesn't usually take," Gregorios said.

"Where do you think they get all the stories of werewolves?" Eirene asked.

"You can't be serious?" Sarah exclaimed.

Tomas said, "They're serious. I had to put one down in Russia in 1905. Nasty."

"This one took better than most," Gregorios explained. "She survived long enough to raise her boys. Remus wore her pelt for years after she died."

"That's gross." Sarah said.

She heard the shrug in Gregorios' voice. "Good pelts were worth a lot. They were just mortals, but the legends got so twisted, we never bothered eradicating them."

Tomas said, "Wait a minute. You're saying Rome was founded by offspring of a facetaker."

"I'd say chances were at least fifty percent he fathered them," Gregorios said.

"The important thing though," Eirene interrupted. "Is that Spartacus has history with that hill."

"Let me guess, another part of history you wrote out?" Sarah asked.

"Our historians did tweak the event," Gregorios admitted. "Julius reigned through several descendants all the way down to Caligula."

Eirene grimaced. "One jump too many."

"I've heard Caligula was crazy," Sarah said.

"Advanced mental dissipation," Gregorios confirmed. "We were going to remove him since he'd become a danger to himself and everything we'd worked so hard to set up, but Spartacus assassinated him again."

"This time it worked," Eirene added. "He died in the Cryptoporticus. Tunnels below his palace. Archaeologists recently discovered part of those tunnels connecting the ruins of his palace on Palatine Hill to the Forum."

Gregorios said, "Spartacus knows there's a whole warren of tunnels down there. The world's forgotten about them."

"I'll send sketches to your teams. You'll have them in five minutes," Eirene said.

"Finally, the intel is lining up," Tomas said. "No wonder we didn't find them earlier."

"Like moles going to ground," Harriett's voice was muffled, as if she was speaking around a bite of muffin. It amazed Sarah that she maintained such a pretty, petite figure despite her constant baking. "I'm ordering up the heavy weapons, just in case. Yurak will be ready to rendezvous at the hill by the time you are."

"Hold the line," Gregorios interrupted. "Bastien has an urgent report."

Sarah wished there was a window to see where the van was taking them. "It doesn't really make sense that Spartacus invited you to a duel right in their backyard."

"Maybe his ties to Paul were even looser than we'd hoped," Tomas suggested.

Gregorios came back on the line. "Or it's all an elaborate ploy, an attempt to disable you and focus our attention on a location they no longer need."

"They're using it," Tomas assured him.

"It's not all they're using. Tomas, you and the Tenth have to take out the base in that hill and eradicate all heka presence."

"And Yurak?" Harriett asked.

"You've got a new directive," Gregorios said, his voice grim. "We just learned why Spartacus didn't meet you down there. He's already on the move and I need Yurak to intercept. Alter, Bastien and I will rendezvous with you."

"Where?" Sarah and Tomas asked in unison.

"Turn on the news," Gregorios said.

While Tomas called for a tablet from one of his men, Sarah fought to conceal her growing dread. She thought back to the message Rosetta had delivered. It seemed Rosetta's bombing had been but the first surprise attack.

Eirene piped in. "Sarah, get back to Suntara immediately. If Spartacus is moving openly, Paul will be entering the memoryscape to get that other master rune. You and I have to stop him."

New tension sounded in everyone's voices. Sarah wasn't a soldier, but even she could tell that the advantage had shifted to Paul. They were splitting their forces and reacting. That wasn't the best way to win.

Worse, she was going after Paul in the memoryscape with only Eirene. They'd never stopped him before, but the stakes had never been higher. She wondered if her ciphers could hold him.

Tomas whistled softly as soon as the news feed came up. "Sarah, you've got to see this."

78

In praising Antony I have dispraised Caesar. But in praising Caesar beforetime, I fear I indeed yielded the honor of the nation.

Baladeva, my fount of eternal youth, warns that Caesar's many lives may be fueled by one as evil as Sutekh, may his cursed name be removed from all inscriptions. I will not reign over a nation so spoiled, and I will not be triumphed over.

~CLEOPATRA, 29 B.C.

GREGORIOS TURNED to the flat-panel television embedded in the wall as Bastien selected a local news station. The live video feed came from a helicopter hovering over the Tiber River.

Eighty men marched in formation across the stone bridge outside the Castel Sant'Angelo. They were dressed like Roman legionnaires, complete with authentic armor and weapons.

They also carried assault rifles slung over their shoulders. It looked like a full century, one of the six units of an ancient Roman cohort.

At the head of the small army marched Spartacus, dressed as a gladiator, carrying an oaken spear. Tomas' body was easily recognizable.

Gaping tourists and surprised locals all melted out of the century's path, offering no resistance as they closed on the Castel. If not for the rifles, most would probably think it was some sort of reenactment.

The Castel. Several pieces clicked into place.

Gregorios cursed, and he preferred cursing in Latin. The words carried more weight than the flimsy profanities popular in recent centuries.

"I assume you have a point," Eirene broke in finally. She was nice enough to wait until after he'd used a particularly good one.

Gregorios pointed at the screen. "That's what Spartacus and John were talking about. It's not the master rune they're after."

"I'm not so sure about that," Sarah said, her voice sounding on the speakers in the room. Gregorios almost cringed. He had forgotten how many people could hear him cursing over the open mic.

"Well, maybe they still want the master rune," Gregorios conceded. "But they're also after another forbidden rune."

"They have the forbidden runes," Alter said as he entered the room from the nearby galley kitchen, a muffin in each hand.

"Not all of them. Some of the most powerful forbidden runes ever discovered are hidden right here in Rome."

"And you didn't think to share that with us before now?" Eirene asked.

He shrugged. "I hadn't made the connection. They're a well-guarded secret. I only found out about them by chance. Haven't even thought about them in centuries."

Thankfully, no one made a comment about old age and memory loss.

"I've never heard of them," Alter said.

"Secret," Gregorios reminded him.

"How'd you find out about them?" Eirene asked. He didn't miss the spark of annoyance that he'd kept the secret from her.

On the television, a polizia tried to intercept Spartacus. They couldn't hear what he said, but no doubt he wanted to see permits for the assault rifles.

Spartacus grabbed the officer by the shirt and hoisted him in the air. As the man grabbed for his sidearm, Spartacus tossed him off the bridge in a show of unusual restraint. In the past, he would've just run the man through.

Enlightened or not, Spartacus still posed a dire threat. Gregorios was more than a little surprised by a flicker of regret at the thought of having to kill the man.

"When Rome was sacked back in 410, you were so busy defeating Spartacus, you didn't realize there were other goals for the invasion," Gregorios explained.

"How would you know that? You were bronzed and stuck on a wall."

"I learned about it later. When Rome was sacked again in A.D. 537, it was nothing but a diversion for a group of heka hunting those runes. Again they failed. But I was here in 1527, the last time Rome was sacked."

"That recent?" Sarah asked.

"That conflict always seemed a bit forced," Eirene said.

"It was." For the younger members of the team he explained. "The army of the Holy Roman Emperor Charles the Fifth invaded."

"Hold on," Sarah interrupted. "How could Rome be invaded by the Roman Emperor?"

Gregorios explained. "It was his army, but it was redirected by the manipulations of a very clever enchanter. The history books claim the army mutinied from lack of pay, and marched on Rome, looking for loot. That's partially true, but a group of heka led by that enchanter were embedded in that force. The purpose of the invasion was cover for their assault, with the goal of acquiring those forbidden runes."

Harriett exclaimed, "The Swiss Guard!"

"Exactly." She was always a quick study, especially after breakfast. "During the invasion, the Swiss Guard protecting the pope made their famous last stand. One hundred and forty-seven of the one hundred and eighty-nine members of the guard died to give the pope time to retreat. The history books leave out the fact that the attackers were enhanced."

Eirene caught on. "The other forty guardsmen took Pope Clement the Seventh away."

"They retreated through the Pasetto di Borgo. To the Castel."

"I still don't get how this ties to forbidden runes," Alter said.

Gregorios said, "That's where I came in. I intervened and killed the leader of the heka, a man almost as enhanced as Spartacus had been. One of the fallen guard was gravely wounded, but he lingered far longer than he should have. He bore a unique rune, unlike any I'd seen before."

"You tortured the truth out of him?" Alter asked, his expression horrified.

"Eat your muffin and don't ask stupid questions. I tried to save his life, but he slipped into delirium. Kept rattling on about his mission."

"Protecting the pope," Sarah suggested.

"No, protecting the secret. I learned enough that during the confusion of the next few days, I dug through some of the restricted Papal archives."

Bastien saluted, looking impressed. "You infiltrated the Vatican?"

"Wasn't so hard back then. Still, it took a while. I persuaded an archivist to help me look. Those stacks are huge."

"So you did torture someone," Alter said.

"You're interrupting the story," Gregorios said. Anything could sound bad if he listened with that attitude. "I discovered the Vatican had acquired the stash of extremely dangerous runes centuries before and had concealed them. They considered the runes religious artifacts. They call them the Manifestation of the Glorious Power of the Almighty God."

"Seriously?" Eirene asked.

"That's a quote. During that famous last stand, the pope had transferred the runes to the Castel and concealed them somewhere."

"Where?" four people asked together.

Gregorios shrugged. "I have no idea."

Eirene gave him a disgusted look. "Dear, next time you stumble across a secret this important, do your homework."

"I spent months tracking down that much," he protested. "They hadn't been pressing enough to spend more time. No one knows about the runes."

"Apparently someone does," Eirene said, turning to the television where Spartacus was marching unhindered through the main gate into the Castel.

Gregorios punched the intercom. "Quentin, get in here."

He arrived a moment later, dressed in combat gear that still somehow made him look more like a dapper gentleman than a combat veteran. Maybe it was the starched white shirt under his flak vest.

"How are your contacts with the Vatican these days?" Gregorios asked.

"Reasonably good."

Gregorios explained the situation. "Find someone who can track down those runes. I doubt they'll know what they're looking for, even if you give them the name. That's our one chance to actually get a solid lead."

"I'll see what I can dig up," Quentin said, not sounding optimistic.

Eirene added, "Warn them of a credible threat from terrorists in the Castel and set up communication channels. Vatican defense forces are small."

Harriett piped in. "Good idea. We need to be on-site and allowed through. I don't want local forces getting in the way."

"Excellent," Quentin said. I'll arrange preauthorization with defense forces for our units to intervene."

"Before you do, I need to ask you a favor off-line," Tomas said.

"I will contact you as soon as we finish our business here," Quentin said.

"Gregorios, you're sure they're looking for the forbidden runes?" Tomas asked.

"They have to be."

"How bad if they get them?" Eirene asked.

Alter spoke. "With the master runes they already control, they can siphon millions of souls. Couple that with forbidden runes, and they'll become all but invincible."

"I knew it wouldn't be easy," Sarah muttered.

Gregorios took a long, slow breath. "It's ugly, but it is what it is. We stop Paul today before he can secure those runes."

If they failed, there might be no way to stop him.

"The Tenth will take the hill," Tomas confirmed.

"Yurak will be ready to move on the Castel as soon as we get clearance," Harriet said.

"And what about the chance they're still going for the master rune?" Sarah asked.

Gregorios hated splitting their forces, but they had no choice. Spartacus represented a threat they could not ignore, but so did Paul.

Eirene spoke. "That's why I need you back here, dear. You and I are returning to the fall of Rome. The original one. That has to be the memory he's looking for. We'll stop him."

"Let's hope we find the machine on the hill and destroy it," Gregorios said.

"Roger," Tomas said. "We will be prepared to engage Paul and neutralize while he's sleeping."

Gregorios doubted it would be that easy.

Sarah said, "I'm catching a ride with one of the mobile units. I'll be back at Suntara in ten minutes."

Eirene gave Gregorios a kiss, eliciting a scowl from Alter. "Don't have too much fun without me."

"I should go with Sarah and Eirene," Alter suggested.

Gregorios said, "No, you come with us. Paul will reveal himself, and I'm betting it'll be at the Castel. I need you to take him there. But first, you need to make a phone call."

Alter's scowl deepened. The last thing he wanted was to reach out to his family, but Gregorios couldn't ignore any possible help, not this time.

Before everyone dropped off the line to get to work, Harriett said, "So we've gotten the bad news. Is there any good to go with it?"

Gregorios allowed a vicious grin. "I haven't stormed a castle in centuries."

79

How many lives did I waste, looking for happiness in noble pursuits? The simple truth finally became undeniable. Mortals seek nobility to give meaning to their single, short lives. I, on the other hand, have all the time in the world, so my time is best spent seeking pleasure, eating well, and, most importantly, acquiring jewelry.

~ZURI, FACETAKER COUNCIL MEMBER

GREGORIOS JUMPED down from the lead troop transport, which had stopped just southwest of the Castel Sant'Angelo, at the termination of the Via della Conciliazione.

The road, usually packed with tourists, led straight from the Castel to St. Peter's Basilica. It made a good staging area for their assault. They wouldn't need to slog uphill or cross moats to reach this castle.

The Castel loomed over everything, with the Tiber River flowing past to Gregorios' right. It passed just south of the Castel, spanned by the Ponte Sant'Angelo where Spartacus and his century had crossed.

In ancient days, Spartacus would have dropped that bridge, but the Castel sat far enough back from the bank that it didn't matter. Gregorios' forces could approach from every side. The gardens of the Parco Adriano formed a star-shaped perimeter around the Castel on the three non-river sides, giving Spartacus some buffer from the roads, but not offering much by way of defense.

For one claiming to be enlightened, Spartacus was doing a great job of lining up enemies eager to put a bullet into his head. Most days,

Gregorios would have stood at the front of that line, but he still hoped to somehow salvage Tomas' suit.

The Castel itself was a stout, round tower rising out of a square base, protected by an outer wall. The wall held octagonal bastions on each corner that had been designed for artillery placements when it was used as a fortress. The artillery had been long since removed, but no doubt Spartacus brought enough weapons to hold off the local carabinieri forces until he could locate the forbidden runes.

Despite his flashy entrance, Spartacus was burning borrowed time. He lacked the men to hold the Castel for long, and would need as many as possible to help scour the Castel for the runes. Gregorios doubted he knew where to find them. That meant an exhaustive search.

Gregorios didn't plan to give them that much time. He just needed authorization from the carabinieri to launch his assault. The fools were hesitating, despite being clearly out of their depth. It wouldn't take long now, but he wondered how many more men would have to die.

He hated working in the open. Tomas' force didn't need to jump through all the red tape to assault the Palatine Hill. They'd move in, get it done, and be gone, especially since the bulk of Rome's security forces were focused on Spartacus.

"This place is too visible, yes?" Bastien commented. He'd followed Gregorios from the truck. He nodded toward the hovering news copters. "Every move will be recorded."

"It could get ugly," Gregorios agreed, thinking of the dangers of investigations after the bullets stopped flying and the dust settled.

Facetakers thrived in the shadows, as did the heka. Even though elements within every government were aware of them, it was in everyone's best interest to keep the secret. Spartacus risked a lot more than the lives of a few men with his brazen, daylight attack.

Already word was spreading that there was something strange about the terrorists. Well, stranger than men dressed as Roman legionnaires capturing a non-critical historical site like the Castel.

The local carabinieri had first tried snipers. Although the fifty caliber bullets knocked heka down, they stood a moment later, looking unharmed. A helicopter full of the Gruppo di Intervento Speciale was shot from the sky by Spartacus' men with a shoulder-fired missile. The elite airborne tactical response unit might have been the right choice in other circumstances, but not today.

Spartacus hadn't stopped there. Explosions had erupted through the gardens of the Parco Adriano, shaking the ground all the way to where

Gregorios had stood a quarter mile away. The air still smelled of scorched earth and cinders. The gardens all around the Castel were shattered, and the blasts had killed several police officers.

The carabinieri commander, a middle-aged man with steel-gray hair and a haggard expression, had chosen anger over wisdom. He stood near the mobile command vehicle, and instead of authorizing Gregorios' team to begin their assault, he ordered an armored truck to try blowing the main gate.

As the truck rumbled over the Ponte Sant'Angelo, the commander exclaimed to one of his men, "We're not going to blow up the whole building. Just the gate. That's a historic landmark."

"Spartacus can leverage this much today," Bastien commented. "Fear of damaging the historical site will prevent a full assault with the heavy weapons."

Gregorios said, "We'll be on soon, but their enhancements are stronger than normal." No matter how tough, few heka could survive a fifty caliber round to the head.

"Perhaps they enjoy yet another rune web, no?"

"I'm starting to think so," Gregorios agreed.

Paul had planned every stage of his uprising with consummate skill.

"Such a web will cost many souls," Bastien said thoughtfully. "It is unlikely such a web was built in the Castel."

"I doubt it. A web strong enough to protect that many men on the move is highest-level enchanter work. Paul has that level of talent, but even for them, it would take a while to get running. Unless they've got a rune warrior we don't know about."

"Don't even joke about that," Bastien said.

Gregorios grimaced. No, that would make his team's job significantly harder. He wished he'd discovered Sarah's gift sooner.

She was making tremendous strides in mastering the fundamentals of battle ciphers, but with a few weeks' planning, she could become a force to rival anything Paul could come up with. If nothing else, they could really use that steel skin ability she'd stumbled upon.

The eight-wheeled Freccia armored fighting vehicle rolled across the Ponte Sant'Angelo Bridge over the Tiber River, aimed at the main gate. It approached fast, covered by a fresh barrage of useless supporting fire.

Snipers knocked heka down again and again. The commander of the Italian forces had decided the terrorists must have a new kind of body armor concealed under their Roman helms and breastplates, despite reports of hits to exposed skin. Willful blindness in the mind of a commander always meant pain for his men.

Mortar teams launched a simultaneous attack. Incendiary rounds rained down over the outer wall of the Castel, but even though waves of liquid fire blazed across the heka positions, they were not consumed. The intense heat did drive them back long enough for the truck to close on the gate, and the thick smoke and flames seemed to cause some confusion.

Heka positioned atop the bastions and the central tower returned fire. Rocket-propelled grenades streaked from the wall to explode into nearby buildings and police lines. At least one of the heka possessed a fifty-caliber sniper rifle and knew how to use it. He began to fire, and several policemen fell screaming to the pavement.

Bastien pointed out, "The sniper aims to wound, to cause havoc and confusion."

"It's an effective tactic," Gregorios said. For every officer wounded, several more stopped firing to render aid, and the waiting medics were soon overwhelmed with wounded.

"The web, she is very strong," Bastien commented as they crouched behind their armored troop transport out of the line of fire.

"Get the men ready. Once the police blow the gate, it's going to get ugly and I don't want too many innocents killed."

"We are prepared, and Harriett reported in. She is in position with Yurak two clicks from here. They've called up the special equipment."

The armored vehicle reached the gate and stopped right against it. Half a dozen soldiers jumped out of the back and attached plastic explosives along the gate's perimeter. They used a lot of C4.

"Historical landmark or not," Bastien said, peering through his binoculars. "They mean to blow much of the wall."

The soldiers rushed back inside the truck and it began to speed back across the bridge.

"Blow it," the commander ordered.

The last section of the bridge, closest to the Castel and directly under the armored truck, disintegrated in a spectacular explosion. The truck flipped over from the force of the blast before tumbling into the river amid a rain of stone debris.

The commander gaped. "Not the bridge. The gate!"

"We never mined the bridge," an officer cried. "It had to be the terrorists."

"Blow the gate! I want those terrorists dead."

Thankfully, someone other than the poor men in the doomed transport vehicle controlled the remote detonation.

The C4 exploded in a fireball that obscured the gates for several seconds. The shockwave shook the truck beside Gregorios, his body vibrating from the intensity of the sound, but no debris rained down around them.

When the smoke cleared, the commander threw his headset on the ground. "I don't believe it!"

The gate still stood, looking unaffected by the gigantic explosion.

"That web's a lot more extensive than we thought," Gregorios commented.

"Oui," Bastien nodded, then spoke into his throat mic. "Grapples will be required. Repeat, prepare grapples."

Atop the wall, one of the heka dressed as a Roman soldier made an obscene gesture and urinated off the wall. Three snipers shot him at the same time. He fell from sight, but the soldiers' cheers faded to curses when the man stood again.

"One of the snipers reports hitting that one in the privates," a soldier reported. "No way he's armored down there."

Looking desperate, the commander turned to Gregorios. "You say your forces are trained to deal with this kind of threat?"

"Better than anyone."

"Very well. I authorize you to storm that castle and rout those terrorists. Keep damage to the structure to a minimum. You're responsible for any casualties you suffer."

"Keep your men back. We have more troops inbound."

He turned to Bastien. "We're going to hit them from two sides. Tell Harriett that Yurak's got the main gate. We'll lead our unit in a flanking maneuver."

He pounded on the side of the truck, and Alter jumped out. "Where do you want me?"

"You're with me."

"Until that web is down, the advantage is not ours," Bastien said.

Gregorios said, "Stick to the training. Break out Quentin's toys. We're going to need them. Harriett can keep the heka busy until we strike."

"She is best suited for this," Bastien agreed. "But she cannot unleash everything while that web remains. Even she is not accustomed to disabling protected heka while scaling a medieval castle wall."

"We'll get the web down."

Bastien said, "If only we could bring Sarah here. She could break it."

Gregorios considered the idea. It was tempting, but he shook his head. "That may be part of why Paul's set it up like this. If he can draw Sarah here, he's got the memoryscape to himself. She's the best chance at preventing him from getting another master rune."

"I could have stopped him," Alter muttered.

"You're back-up in case he shows up here instead. Don't worry, you'll get your chance to fight." He tapped his tactical earpiece, switching to Tomas' channel.

"Status?" he asked without preamble.

"Strike force is almost in position. Moving on the sentries in sixty seconds."

"We have evidence of an advanced protective rune web."

"I hate those," Tomas muttered.

"It's been a long time. It may be based on the hill like the one Sarah subverted earlier. Taking that hill has become top priority. Get it done, Captain."

"Yes, sir."

Gregorios hoped Tomas had learned from history. They needed that rune web disabled, but this time all the blood spilled would be from friends and family.

No suicide charges.

80

Thank the gods for a little space. Of course I appreciate the runes Spartacus endowed upon me, and I'll follow him to the uttermost end, but you must admit, Castus, his quest for vengeance is going to kill us all. We could have escaped to Gaul by now, but he insists on promoting a war against the facetakers. With my enhancements, I fear no mortal man, but I wager Gregorios and Eirene would scare Zeus himself. Particularly Eirene.

~GANNICUS, ONE OF SPARTACUS'S LIEUTENANTS
DURING THE THIRD SERVILE WAR

TOMAS HOPPED out of the back of the van that had parked near the Forum, just north of Palatine Hill. Six troop transport trucks, disguised to look like large delivery vehicles, were pulling to a stop nearby. Between the men in those trucks and advanced teams already moving into position, Tomas commanded almost two hundred men.

He hoped they would be enough.

"Talk to me," he spoke into the earpiece.

Domenico responded immediately. "Captain, I have confirmed the police know nothing of closures on Palatine Hill. I'm positioned near the Arch of Titus and I've spotted two other watchers higher up on the hill. Those men are not uniformed."

Tomas muttered a curse. So much for sneaking up on the enemy. Not that he had really expected to slip in unnoticed after Rosetta's spectacular suicide and the sniping of that watcher. The enemy had to know someone was coming, but he'd hoped to keep them guessing a little longer.

Tomas tapped his earpiece. "Anaru, are you in position?"

"Thirty seconds," his second responded.

The big Maori would lead a second contingent around the south side of the hill, along the Via dei Cerchi that ran between what was left of the Circus Maximus and the ruins of the baths of Septimus Severus. The ruin-covered slope would provide excellent cover.

Tomas sent his five-man sniper team into a nearby church. Disguised as workers, they would ascend the square tower that rose three stories above the roof of the church. They'd have a perfect position to cover Tomas' team when they moved against the north side of the hill.

"Team two in position," Anaru reported as Tomas led the first squad toward Domenico's position. Civilians they passed took one look at their weapons and fled. He hoped they noticed "Polizia" emblazoned across their bulletproof vests.

The mission was clear. Take the hill, disrupt the web, overwhelm any resistance. At least this time he wasn't leading a cavalry charge of the light brigade into the face of heavy artillery.

"Give me one minute and make your move," he ordered Anaru.

He donned an ample leather jacket to cover his bulletproof vest, left his helmet with one of his men, and stepped out of cover.

"Domenico, I'm coming to you."

They needed to maintain any element of surprise they could. A hundred armed men moving through the Roman Forum would spark a panic and alert the enemy of their approach.

Once the spotters were neutralized, they'd send enforcers dressed as police to shepherd civilians out of the area. The rest of the force would move in.

The first strike had to be quick, and silent.

Domenico met him at the Arch of Titus at the edge of the ruined Forum, and the two strolled south toward the barricaded entrance to the Palatine Hill. Enough tourists packed the area even this early in the morning, snapping photos and gawking at the ruins, that the guard failed to note their approach until they were close.

"The hill is closed for renovation," the fake police officer said in Italian and then repeated in English.

"I'm looking for the Colosseum," Tomas said.

"It's right over there." The man actually turned to point.

Tomas lunged, spinning the surprised sentry and driving a thin-bladed knife into the base of the man's skull.

Instead of punching through to his brain and killing him instantly, the blade bounced off the man's head.

The heka spun, elbowing Tomas and reaching for his gun.

Tomas tackled him to the ground, wrestling for control, and shouted, "All teams, move in now! Sentries are web-protected."

The sentry punched him in the mouth, and he growled as he fought the man down. Domenico jumped into the fray, and together they subdued the sentry and tied him up with steel-braid zip ties. He might be web-protected, but that didn't make him stronger than other men and didn't prevent him from being bound.

The suppressed reports of sniper rifles cracked from the nearby tower. To Tomas, those softened reports sounded the death knell of his plan, and would serve only as a warning to the other watchers that the attack had come.

"Spotters are not down," one of the snipers reported. "Repeat, bullets did not drop them."

"They're all protected," Tomas cursed, amazed at the breadth of the web. He hadn't faced one this sophisticated since the battle of Bull Run in the colonies. "Team two do you copy? Heka are protected."

"Roger," Anaru said. "We've made contact and found the same. First scout is disabled."

"Advance with caution," Tomas advised. "Teams five through seven, move to support Anaru. Equip with anti-enhanced restraints. The enemy is active and alert. Expect resistance. Team nine, set up support ordinance."

Tomas and Domenico dragged the still-struggling heka up the paved road for fifty feet and tied him to a tree. A new disturbance sounded from the Forum as tourists too stupid to run from the initial gunshots panicked at the sight of dozens of heavily armed men racing across the ruins. Tomas' men wore their fake polizia uniforms, but he had hoped to minimize the disturbance.

As Tomas slipped on his helmet and took up his rifle, gunfire erupted from higher up the hill. Bullets whined as they ricocheted off walls and stone pavers. Tomas led his men into the cover of trees and ruined walls. They needed to move fast, but attacking a protected enemy up a hill was suicide. He needed a better plan.

Tomas caught a glimpse of several heka standing unafraid in the open, firing down on his men. Protected as they were, they could attack with reckless abandon.

The heavy fire slowed his team's advance. Their enhancements multiplied their strength and accelerated healing, but didn't make them invincible.

He tapped his earpiece to change channels. "Gregorios, we've begun our assault, but the heka here are protected too."

"I don't want another light brigade, but you have to take those tunnels and disable that web."

"Roger. We'll get it done."

Tomas shot a particularly daring heka five times in the face. The man went down, but reappeared a few seconds later.

If only he could call in air support. They might be protected, but getting a cluster bomb dropped on their heads would dampen their spirits for sure. A bunker buster bomb into the hidden tunnels might even disrupt the web for them. Unfortunately, they couldn't risk widespread damage to the historical landmark.

That didn't mean Tomas couldn't get creative.

"Someone take out that guy," Tomas called.

One of his men, crouched farther along the ruined wall, popped up and fired a gun that looked like a modified grenade launcher. It was one of Quentin's inventions. Instead of exploding rounds, it fired weighted bolos.

Those weighted ends dragged the ropes open and they hit the heka just below the knees. The ends whipped around his legs several times, tying him securely in half a second.

The heka stumbled, and three of Tomas' men charged him, armed with zip ties. They dragged the bound fighter out of sight before other heka could interfere.

The tactics would work, but it'd take too long, and every moment of delay meant more of their comrades could get killed in the fighting around the Castel.

"Squad nine, where are you with those mortars?"

"Almost ready," their leader reported.

Anaru protested. "Captain, we can't call in explosive rounds."

"We're not. Squad nine, fire smoke just above our position. We'll close and take them down at close quarters."

He just hoped Paul was indeed sleeping somewhere in the tunnels. Sarah was in grave danger if he was, but if she held out long enough for Tomas to firebomb the sleeping cui dashi, they could end the threat once and for all.

81

SARAH STOOD beside Eirene at the top of a long stone staircase below
the portico of the imposing stone temple of Summanus, god of
nocturnal thunder.

They faced north across Rome. The ancient city might have looked
soft in the gentle light of early morning if not for the dark pall of smoke
to the north. It obscured the distant hills and suggested imminent
violence.

Eirene wore a hooded, crimson robe with a black leather mask, but
Sarah recognized Iltea's body. A priest in battle garb stood on the far side
of Eirene. She had called him Titus, and he was asking her a series of
questions. Sarah ignored the conversation, her thoughts focused on
reviewing the plan for the upcoming confrontation.

She was scared, but resolved. She'd spent the last few minutes
exploring the expansive portico and preparing the battleground. She
had marked ciphers on columns in several strategic locations, just in
case she needed them later.

Paul had hurt her repeatedly, and his promised torture was so vile
she felt dirty just thinking about it. She wanted to shove a sword through
his guts like he'd done to her. But secretly, she wished Tomas' force
would destroy the machine and the sleeping cui dashi before he arrived.

A priest rushed up the stairs. "The Visigoth hordes are approaching at speed."

Eirene nodded. "I can feel Paul tampering already. Much depends on you, my dear. Are you ready?"

"Bring it on." The quaver in her voice wrecked her attempt at bravado. "How long do we need to hold?"

"That depends on Tomas and Greg. Paul will try to force the memory forward to the time when the master rune will appear. I'll delay as long as I can, but alone, I can't hold him off forever."

"Unless I kill him first." Sarah doubted she'd succeed in killing Paul, but they'd driven him from dreams before. That would count as a victory too.

All too soon, over a hundred heavily armed soldiers approached at a quick trot. At the head of the army ran Spartacus, oaken spear held easily in his powerful hands. Paul ran at his side, still wearing his impeccable blue suit and wide-brimmed hat.

"You're sure Spartacus is just a memory projection?" Sarah asked.

"He has to be," Eirene said as she led Sarah back into the shadows of the deep portico and its marble columns. "The real Spartacus is busy at the Castel. I'll worry about him. Stick to the plan."

"Can't we just shift to another memory?"

Eirene shook her head. "I tried that as soon as I felt Paul's presence, but I'd need to take them with us or they'd walk this memory unhindered. I can't shift them. Paul's too strong."

Not for long. Sarah ran the ciphers through her mind. This time, Paul was in for a surprise.

Catapults fired from concealed positions within the outbuildings at the base of the stairs, but the deadly barrage of caltrops and stone shot flickered and disappeared.

Eirene winced, rubbing her temple. "Definitely tampering."

"Can you stay in control?" Sarah didn't want to risk getting separated again.

"This is my memory, but given enough time, he'll take over."

"He won't get that much time," Sarah promised her.

Before she'd left Tomas, they'd shared a passionate kiss and he'd gripped her shoulders, his expression intent. "Sarah, you can't hold back. When Paul shows up, hit him with everything. Overwhelming force is your only chance.

She planned to do just that.

Undamaged by the failed catapults, the barbarian army cheered and surged up the steps. The sound was terrifying, but the sight of the rampaging horde didn't scare Sarah as much as it would have in other circumstances. She leaned forward, eager to witness as they ran right into her trap.

The Visigoths' howling battle cries faded to surprised panting, then to soft groans. The army slowed, and barbarians began stumbling. Shields and swords clattered against the stone stairs as they fell to Sarah's invisible assault.

She had placed battle ciphers along both sides of the steps, similar to the ones she'd set up in Suntara to bolster Francesca in powering the machine. These ciphers weren't so gentle. Instead of siphoning tiny fractions of soul force of those in the affected zone, these drained everything.

Within seconds the entire charge faltered and only Paul and Spartacus remained standing. Spartacus swayed where he stood, but was already cutting into his forearm to activate a new rune. Paul didn't appear affected by the cipher at all.

Sarah braced herself against the hoped-for influx of energy drained from those attackers, but as their bodies faded from the memoryscape, she got nothing. She wasn't surprised. They weren't really there, after all, even though they could inflict wounds upon the memory walkers.

"Pilum and martiobarbuli," Eirene ordered, her calm voice ringing in the abrupt silence.

Her caller, a pinched little man who stood at her left shoulder, whistled four sharp notes. Battle priests all down the line at the top of the steps launched javelins or barbed darts at the two men. Sarah cringed to think what those missiles could do to living flesh.

She didn't get to see it firsthand. Paul waved one hand, and the missiles disintegrated.

Eirene tried again. "Sagittarii."

Two shrill, whistled notes. Composite bows thrummed from the concealed raised platforms. Arrows whistled down, but again disappeared.

"I hate cheaters," Eirene muttered.

Down on the steps, Spartacus' new rune flared, and he stood tall again.

Sarah decided Paul must have marked some kind of blocking rune before they arrived at the temple. A huge, six-barreled gun appeared in front of him, mounted on a tripod, with a belt of ammunition snaking out of a large box. He tipped his wide-brimmed hat up enough to reveal a smug smile as he reached for the handle.

A hairy ape-like creature rose out of the steps near him, but he twisted the minigun in its direction and squeezed the trigger for half a second. The gun buzzed like a psycho saw, and hundreds of rounds ripped the beast apart.

Paul shouted, "Sarah, say hello to my little friend."

She replied. "You can't be serious! You can't even come up with your own grand entrance line?"

His smile faltered. "I loved that movie."

He spun the gun in her direction, shouting, "And I will not allow you to disparage it!"

Sarah ducked behind one of the thick stone pillars as he opened fire. Bullets tore into the stone with a roar like an avalanche. Eirene was huddled behind another pillar, clutching at her head.

"I can't stop it," she said, looking irritated.

Sarah needed power, and she couldn't afford to hesitate. Vlad's words rang in her mind. "Nothing like this has been done before. If I'm not willing to take the risk to protect those only I can protect, then we've already lost."

Willing her fingers not to tremble, Sarah embraced her rounon well and began marking a cipher into the face of the pillar as Paul's withering fire shredded its far side. Her finger trailed glowing light, and the cipher formed against the stone. The beauty of it and the thrill she felt while using her gift helped calm her, and her finger moved faster.

She built a cipher to grant her strength, but instead of using modifiers to draw energy from nearby souls, she added symbols from the lesser master rune they'd acquired from the assassination of Julius Caesar.

She didn't dare use it all, and she included modifiers to limit the amount of energy she drew from even that tiny piece to one percent. Even so, it was good that Alter didn't see what she was doing.

Eirene called, "Whatever you have in mind, I suggest you implement it soon. Your pillar is almost gone."

"Got it!" Sarah cried, completing the cipher with a flourish. She focused on it, willing it to life, but hopefully not too much life.

The cipher blazed against the stone, and a torrent of energy thundered into Sarah's body, shaking her with its intensity. Even that tiny fraction of the energy she'd drawn from that lesser master rune hit like a hammer-blow. She grabbed the pillar to keep from collapsing, and felt the vibration from bullets striking just inches away on the far side.

She no longer feared them.

Her muscles quivered with the need to move. She'd never felt so incredibly strong, never imagined it possible. If she wanted to, she could rip the temple off its foundation and throw it across Rome.

She didn't want to do that.

She wanted to kill Paul.

"Are you all right?" Eirene asked.

"Never better." Sarah felt full in a way she never had before, energy infusing her every cell.

Vlad's warning about the disastrous results of losing control rang in her mind. He hadn't survived his attempt to push the limits. She needed to finish the fight and extinguish her power source before she crossed that unknown line.

Sarah summoned a scalpel to hand and marked the two critical lines onto the rune on her thigh. Powered by so much new energy, the rune blazed instantly and she felt her body composition shift into quicksilver fluidity.

In a flash, Sarah leaped out from behind the pillar and jumped off the top of the steps, springing eighty feet, aiming to land close beside Paul.

Paul twisted the heavy minigun and caught her in midair. The deadly torrent swatted her out of the air twenty feet short of him. Rounds pinged off her hardened skin, but the lead poured in with such intensity that the bullets began tearing into her quicksilver torso, the kinetic energy driving her back.

"Surrender to me, Sarah," Paul shouted over the roar of the gun. "And you don't need to get hurt any more."

He promised peace, but his eyes were cold and mean.

Sarah rolled, trying to escape the storm of bullets to close on him. Maybe jumping down the steps hadn't been such a good idea.

Then she spotted Spartacus, who stood off to one side, mouth agape, staring in wonder at the minigun. He was the memory shade of the real Spartacus, so knew nothing of guns.

He was her chance.

Sarah scrambled in his direction, moving on all fours faster than normal people could run, but knocked back constantly by the still-roaring minigun. Spartacus realized the danger too late, and Sarah tackled him off his feet.

Paul stopped firing.

As Sarah had suspected, he wanted to keep Spartacus around. So she threw the struggling gladiator at Paul.

He knocked Spartacus out of the air, but that was more than enough time for Sarah to close.

With a thought, her arms flowed into swords. With two swipes, she sheared the blurring gun barrels and severed the ammo belt.

"That was getting boring anyway," Paul said, lunging, hands bursting into purple fire.

Sarah's sword arms flowed back to normal, and she caught his wrists, then shifted her hands into spiked manacles that dug into his flesh.

Paul might be cui dashi, supernaturally strong from the souls he'd siphoned, but he gasped from the unexpected pain. Tomas, with all his enhancements, couldn't stand against him, but Sarah held his hands back from her face and no longer feared him.

For the first time, he wasn't quite strong enough. With the strength of the lesser master rune aiding her, Sarah held him. Barely.

"Today it's my turn," Sarah growled.

She head-butted him in the face, then shifted her arms back into swords and drove them into his body over and over. He tried to retreat, but she kicked aside his broken minigun and pursued, stabbing him again.

"How do you like it?" she snarled.

She drove a sword into his throat, then threw him up the steps. He smashed right through the first thick column of the portico and cracked the second. His blood splattered the stones, and when he struggled to his hands and knees, fear shone in his eyes.

Spartacus' battle cry caught her attention. The Thracian gladiator had closed with Eirene, who had slipped out of her crimson robe. He had recognized the full figure she wore, and an expression of rage twisted his features.

"You have dishonored her too long, daughter of the gorgons!" he shouted.

Eirene avoided his plunging spear and kicked him down the steps. "I am so tired of that line."

She waved to Sarah. "Don't dawdle, dear."

Sarah saluted and flew up the steps in a graceful jump, kicking Paul in the ribs as he struggled to his feet. Bones shattered in his torso and he screamed as the impact launched him through the cracked column and into another one.

Sarah caught a fifteen-foot section of the toppling column and used it like a club, smashing it over his head. The column shattered, but left him crumpled on the cracked floor. She had hoped to drive him out of the memory, but he appeared willing to suffer pain for the chance to get at the master rune.

Good. She decided to oblige.

His blood coated the stone all around, and the air was heavy with the stench of it. She lifted his broken body from the floor and held him high, exulting in the feeling of matchless power.

"How do you like being at someone else's mercy?"

He mouthed something, but she couldn't hear the words. She felt no pity for his broken condition but wanted to hear him admit he feared her. She leaned close as he tried speaking again.

"Mercy is for fools."

A sword appeared in his hand and he tried to stab her.

Enraged, Sarah ripped the sword out of his hands and plunged it into his stomach, driving it to the hilt.

82

Not even the mighty Sutekh of old stood on the cusp of such majesty. His failure broke Egypt and facilitated the flight of Moses and the slaves, but even had he succeeded, he would have accomplished no more than preserving a decaying kingdom. I will stand astride the width of the world and enforce peace.

Even Mother will respect me then.

~PAUL

GREGORIOS CROUCHED atop the Pasetto di Borgo, the high passageway connecting the Castel with the Vatican that lay almost a half mile to the west. His strike force huddled halfway along the wall, crouching below the top of the Pasetto's concealing parapet, facing the Castel.

They had climbed atop the Pasetto on the far side of the Auditorium Conciliazione, and Gregorios felt confident they had remained undetected. They had waited to begin their climb until the carabinieri began a sniper barrage to cover Harriett's assault on the main gate.

Distant explosions boomed, the unmistakable sound of high explosive mortar rounds.

"The commander will not like that," Bastien said.

Gregorios shrugged. "Harriett's committed. Yurak forces are beginning their assault."

He jogged east along the top of the wall, staying low, even though he was counting on the heka being focused on Harriett's assault. The team followed close behind and he could feel their nervous excitement.

He hadn't assaulted a castle in centuries, and despite his eagerness to take down Spartacus, he was glad the Pasetto afforded such direct access. He hated scaling heavily defended walls. He'd lost three lives that way.

"What's your status?" he asked over the encrypted comm-link.

"Assault is underway," Harriett reported. Gunfire and explosions boomed through the connection, punctuating her words. "We're teasing them with the ladder truck."

"Good. Keep them busy until we reach the wall. Thirty seconds. Then begin the real assault."

"Very well. Out."

She was all business when it came to killing heka. She commanded over a hundred of the family's elite fighting force, the best of the First Division. More would be arriving soon, with reinforcements available as needed. Every member was a blood descendant of Gregorios and Eirene, enhanced, and extensively trained.

Harriett hadn't mentioned to Sarah that other children were positioned strategically throughout most of the world's elite armies. Those who made up Yurak's strike force were the best, and claimed they could beat even Alter's family in a direct competition.

Today they'd get the chance to prove it.

Gregorios reached the Castel without encountering resistance. Spartacus was losing his touch. He never would've left his flank open in the centuries Gregorios faced him.

Either he was confident enough in soon acquiring the forbidden runes that he didn't care to take regular precautions, or he was trusting unseasoned sub-commanders. Either way, he was about to regret the lapse.

A light breeze blew from the south side of the Castel and the air smelled of gunpowder and scorched stone. The constant chatter of machine gun fire echoed from the Castel walls along with the regular booming of mortar explosions.

"We've reached the bastion," Gregorios said into the microphone. "Commencing our assault."

"Initiating phase two," Harriett replied. "Good hunting."

Harriett's troops had arrived in a convoy of hard-topped troop transports. After distracting the heka with a ladder truck, phase two would include hoisting soldiers up the wall on ten-foot wooden platforms suspended by grapple cables. Motors on either end of the platforms would pull them up the wall at speed.

With the machine gunners and mortars keeping the heka pinned,

Harriett could reach the top of the wall in seconds. Any heka trying to stop her would be neutralized by specialized, high-pressure cannons mounted on modified fire trucks. Instead of spraying water, they shot tar-like glue that would foul weapons, blind heka and, given enough volume, immobilize them.

The intensity of the battle sounds on the south side of the Castel rose to a fever pitch. Gregorios sprinted up the staircase of the little turret above the Pasetto, connecting it to the seven-sided Bastion of St. Mark on the northwest corner of the Castel.

He entered a stout room of thick stone arches that supported the bastion above. The area was closed to tourists by a locked glass door, but Gregorios snapped the lock and led the way up a wide, spiraling staircase.

The steps were short, and he ran up them three at a time, finally bursting onto the top of the wall. The open expanse of the bastion on his right had been blocked by a low iron rail, but the heka had knocked that down.

Only two of Spartacus' men manned that wide-open area, paved with zig-zagging bricks. An ancient catapult, a couple of old cannons, and piles of cannonballs took up much of the expanse, with the heka standing near the outer wall, peering toward the fighting along the front wall.

Neither of them noticed his arrival for three fatal seconds. They were dressed like legionnaires, but had dropped their ancient weapons in favor of assault rifles.

Gregorios closed on the nearest, a beefy Italian fellow, who swung his rifle around a fraction of a second too late. Gregorios grabbed his face, embraced his nevra core, and threw every ounce of nevron into severing the man's link to his nervous system.

The heka thrashed in Gregorios' hands, but he held on and dug his fingers into the soul points along the man's jaw. Purple sparks exploded from his fingers as his nevron fought to overpower the protective strength of the rune web. An automatic weapon began to fire behind him, but he felt no bullets and couldn't afford to look.

The web was extremely powerful, but designed to protect the heka from physical harm. The distinction was minor, but in rune spells, specifics mattered. Gregorios was able to slip around the periphery of the web's insurmountable blockade and drive his nevron into the heka's soul.

The man's cries fell silent and his thrashing ceased as Gregorios severed the link to his muscles. The effort was far more strenuous than taking normal souls, but it completely neutralized the heka, better than tying him up.

He knelt over the fallen heka, whose hate-filled eyes remained locked on him. He consolidated his hold over the enemy soul and began to pull. The soulmask came free with that awful sucking sound that Gregorios usually hated. In this case, it felt appropriate.

Gregorios tossed the soulmask to a soldier, who bagged it. Soulmasks were too important to leave lying around for mortals to discover or enchanters to use as fuel cells.

He then surveyed the battlement. Alter and two of the Tenth had subdued the other heka, who lay bound in chains and steel-mesh zip ties. Bastien sat nearby, dabbing at a bloody gash on his skull.

"That one, she was very close, yes?" Bastien said with a wry smile.

"Let's hope it's the closest call we have today."

Gregorios led the assault team along the rampart toward the Bastion of St. Matthew on the southwest corner of the wall, overlooking the street and the river.

Seven heka crouched behind riot shields, firing east along the wall above the main gate, in the direction where Harriett and the family were making their breach. The men didn't even notice Gregorios' team charging from the side.

The heka might be protected, but getting riddled with hundreds of rounds still knocked them sprawling. Gregorios fired a couple of specialty rounds from a shotgun. The high-intensity flare blinded the enemy and left them disoriented for critical seconds.

While he worked to remove their soulmasks, his men swarmed over the heka, kicking away their weapons and binding their hands. The rune web protected them from harm, but didn't grant them greater strength than their personal enhancements already did.

It was still brutal hand-to-hand fighting, but they didn't stand a chance against the veteran Tenth commandos. Alter waded into the fight enthusiastically, and he beat down three of the heka himself.

Harriett and a squad of Yurak fighters joined them on the bastion. She saluted. "Good timing."

"Casualties?" Gregorios asked as he removed another soulmask. Now that he knew the trick to circumventing the rune web, he only needed a fraction of his nevron to accomplish it.

"Three dead, several more wounded," Harriett said, looking angry.

Not bad, considering the situation, but Gregorios shared Harriett's anger. The wounded would recover from all but the most severe injuries, but they couldn't help the dead. This was family, so every soul lost added to the tally Spartacus was about to pay.

"Spartacus!" Alter shouted.

Gregorios looked up and found his ancient enemy standing atop the wall of the inner castle tower. He no longer felt regret for the need to destroy Spartacus again.

"Well met, Gregorios!" Spartacus shouted. "I honor your valor. When you're finished, join me. We have much to discuss."

He jumped off the wall into the tower, and out of view.

"Did that make any sense to you?" Harriett asked.

"Yes," Gregorios said, disgusted. "He wants to talk."

"Then why fight like this?" Alter asked.

"To honor our strength," Gregorios said, kicking a dispossessed body aside. "He thinks he's showing respect."

"That is crazy," Bastien said.

"Not to him. He might feel enlightened, but he's still a gladiator at heart."

It made more sense that the wall had been so lightly defended. Spartacus had used only enough men to keep out those too weak to deserve the honor of a face-to-face discussion.

The fighting on this part of the wall was over. Heka still held out in a low tower that rose above the Bastion of St. John at the opposite end of the front-facing wall, but Yurak teams would overwhelm that position in moments.

"Finish off that rabble," Gregorios pointed toward the final knot of fighting. "And stay on alert for the rest of the heka. I'm heading into the tower to see what Spartacus has to say."

"You think that's wise?" Harriett asked.

"If it keeps him from those forbidden runes, yes. Bastien, on me."

"Parachutes," Alter said, pointing.

Gregorios looked up and caught sight of black parachutes descending on the Castel, barely one hundred feet above the roof.

"They opened late."

Alter nodded. "We're trained to do so. It's dangerous, but reduces the risk of getting shot out of the sky."

"Your brother has terrible timing."

"He's here though, isn't he?" Alter retorted. Reuben might have branded Alter a demon, but he was still family.

Reuben's force of ten para-hunters landed atop the central castle turret, on the Angel Terrace with its bronze statue of the archangel, Michael, sheathing his sword. It had been commissioned after the plague of 590 A.D., which had really been caused by a heka cell.

Eirene had stopped the plague by killing them and disrupting their rune web. Harald had taken great pleasure in twisting the event into the legend of the archangel sheathing his sword to stop the plague. He'd called her Michael for years.

Gregorios said, "Let's hurry. Looks like Reuben plans to crash the party."

"He'll want to kill all of us. Reuben doesn't party," Alter said.

"I'll make him dance. Alter, you come with me."

The problem was that the angel terrace gave Reuben direct access to the sixth level of the Castel. The hunters had the advantage.

Gregorios ran east along the southern rampart and crossed a narrow bridge that connected the wall to the second level of the inner tower. The area was clear. Shotgun at the ready, Gregorios moved up a long, sloping hallway with a high, arched ceiling that led into the tower.

The high, ramped walkway crossed the Hall of Urns in the very heart of the castle. The floor far below was where the original urn of Hadrian would have rested, but nothing remained. The large, square chamber, lit by two narrow windows set high in the wall, was empty, looking more like a ruin than a burial chamber.

Gregorios wasn't surprised. The popes never would have left the runes in such an accessible place. He suspected they'd find them in the Papal apartments at the very top of the tower.

That's where he would find both Spartacus and Reuben.

Either those two had a lot of explaining to do, or a couple of scores were about to be settled.

83

There is nothing quite as satisfying as defeating a powerful foe. It matters not that I slew him in his sleep instead of on the field of battle, it is his soulmask that lies shattered while I will toast his memory for lives without end. Even Gregorios must salute me now.

~JOHN, FACETAKER COUNCIL MEMBER, AFTER
ASSASSINATING BALADEVA

THE TUNNEL that continued up from the Hall of Urns turned a couple of times, and eventually emptied into the Angel Courtyard where the original statue of Michael had been moved after being damaged in 1747.

The narrow courtyard was flanked by museums that had once been used by the castle's garrison. Gregorios motioned two squads to secure that level and to watch a secondary stair that rose toward the main promenade that circled the tower. He decided to take the main stairs on the far side of the courtyard up to that same promenade, overlooking the river.

The promenade was built along the inside of the central turret wall, with regular, arched openings overlooking the castle and surrounding area. To his right stretched a section that had been converted into a cafe for tourists, so he turned left and followed it around to the main entrance to the upper rooms.

He sent additional squads along the rest of the promenade to search the other galleys, and to secure the back exits from the upper rooms. They moved with careful precision, wary of heka ambushes.

Followed by Bastian, Alter, and thirty members of the Tenth, he mounted the stairs to the Sala Paolina, the long hall where Pope Paul the Third had received delegations during his thirteen year residence in the Castel.

The room was empty, but Gregorios paused to stare at the fresco-covered ceiling. There was so much detail to dazzle the eye that he wondered if the runes had been concealed as part of one of the paintings.

He doubted they would have taken the risk, even though chances were slim anyone would find them. He hoped they found the runes else-where before they committed to studying all that artwork.

Alter stayed close behind him as he crossed the long hall, although his eagerness to find Spartacus was overshadowed by nervousness. He was probably not looking forward to seeing the hunters.

Having his closest loved ones swear to purge his abomination must have weighed heavily on the kid. Gregorios wasn't sure how they were going to help smooth that one over.

Gunfire erupted from the tower above. The hunters had found someone who wasn't happy to see them.

Gregorios checked the papal apartments off the main hall and found antiques smashed and artifacts strewn about. Spartacus' men had already searched the rooms.

He had hoped to find clues in there, but decided not to spend the time second-guessing the heka's work. If they'd found the runes, Spartacus wouldn't still be hiding. He wouldn't need to fear Gregorios any longer, and it wasn't his way to use trickery when he could march out of the Castel with super enhancements for glorious combat.

Gregorios sent Bastien and half the team back out to the main prom-enade to sweep the sections of the Castel barred from tourist access.

Then Spartacus' voice echoed into the hall from the long Pompeian Corridor nearby, just before he stepped into it. "Gregorios, my once and great enemy, don't dawdle. We have much to discuss."

"Stay on my six," he ordered Alter and the rest of the men, then spoke into the tactical microphone. "Bastien, preparing to make contact. Keep a close watch on the western stairs."

"Oui. I have a visual on the hunters. They may try to derail your negotiations."

"See if you can slow them down, but try not to kill any of them yet." Restoring damaged relations with Melek was going to be hard enough without more blood debt between them.

Gregorios followed Spartacus' voice down the Pompeian corridor toward the library. The narrow, arched passage, with its frescoed walls protected by plexiglass against careless tourists would have made an excellent location for an ambush, but Gregorios held to his belief that the Thracian indeed wanted to talk.

No rain of bullets greeted him, and he breathed a little easier when he reached the northern end of the hall and glimpsed the large library room up a short flight of steps. It was devoid of books, just a huge open room with an ornate, vaulted ceiling and tiled floor. A large fireplace consumed the center of the opposite wall, and several other exits led to other rooms, but Gregorios' gaze was drawn to Spartacus.

The gladiator sat in an antique wooden chair behind an ornate, polished desk upon which sat several artifacts from the middle ages, including a fine pair of flintlock dueling pistols. It still bothered Gregorios to see his ancient enemy's face smiling out of Tomas' suit.

When Spartacus caught sight of Gregorios, he waved. "Come, there is nothing to fear."

The room appeared empty, so Gregorios approached. Alter and the team spread out, flanking him and covering the other exits.

"If you wanted to talk so bad, we could've just met for lunch," Gregorios said.

"I would never insult you with such a weak offer," Spartacus said, throwing his arms wide, as if to encompass the Castel. "In this moment, we meet amid the honor of honest contest. Only in such can we face each other with respect and deny those too weak to reach this table."

"So what do you want to talk about?" Gregorios asked, pulling out the chair across from Spartacus and dropping into it.

"I am restored, but cannot make sense of the world." Spartacus gestured to the ancient table and its museum artifacts. "These are historical items to today's world, and yet they are marvels beyond my imaginings."

"Modern marvels hurt more. Next time understand the world before declaring war on a city."

"Some things are as yet outside of my control. My purpose here is twofold."

"I know you're after the forbidden runes."

"And you are prepared to intervene."

"Indeed. What's your other purpose?"

Spartacus paused. "Forbidden. I like that word. That is appropriate for mortals."

"You still think you're better than others?"

"Don't you?" Spartacus looked honestly surprised. "You sacrifice others to prolong your life."

"Did you set all this up to talk philosophy?"

Gregorios was still irritated by the deaths and injuries it had cost to reach the table. He'd faced Spartacus for too long as an adversary. It still surprised him to find that Spartacus could string more than three or four words together without interjecting a battle cry or oath of vengeance.

"Nay. Most mortals are weak and live forgettable lives, but they could be stronger." Spartacus leaned forward, eyes bright with enthusiasm.

He really was nuts.

"And you're going to make them stronger?"

"If they will listen."

"How does that work with Paul's whole evil-overlord-conquest plan?"

Spartacus shrugged. "There will always be those intent on ruling, and those committed to fighting them. Paul wishes some of those forbidden runes, and I am honor bound to find them. The last two runes will be mine alone."

"What are they?" Alter asked eagerly.

"Protection. Assurance that I can stand apart from the world. Paul can make his attempt on the world and you are welcome to challenge his dominance. I am no longer constrained by such small-minded pursuits."

"Most people consider world conquest fairly important."

"Perhaps. But we fought for dominance across centuries. What did we accomplish?"

"Not as much as we assumed," Gregorios admitted. "But more than we would have had we let you destroy everything."

"In my anger, I saw nothing but vengeance." Spartacus actually sounded reflective.

"Are you saying you're seeing reason now?"

"I'm not sure what I see. I don't understand the world. I see much weakness where there once was strength."

Gregorios couldn't argue with that. Much of the world had fallen into moral decay, squandering riches denied to the majority of souls throughout the ages. The insight into Spartacus' motivations was proving very interesting. He wished they'd managed to meet with Spartacus at the Circus. There had to be a way to leverage that gap, or even turn Spartacus to assist them.

"What are you going to do about it?" he asked.

"What can be done? You allowed the arenas to fall into ruin. Where can one win honor such that the world would listen?"

Gregorios shrugged. "Politics or the silver screen."

"Maybe the stock market," Alter interjected. He had drawn closer as the conversation continued, his expression curious.

Spartacus laughed and slapped his leg with a powerful hand. "That is the type of information I need! I will win honor, take their cows and melt their silver into new images."

"What are you talking about?" Alter asked, looking confused.

"Not that kind of market," Gregorios said with a smile. "And the silver screen isn't really made of silver."

Spartacus frowned. "Such deceit must be done away with."

Gregorios asked, "You want honor? You want to get people to listen to you, to have adoring crowds chanting your name again?"

"That would be a good start. Only then will they listen to what I can teach."

"Well I won't guarantee anyone will listen, but it sounds to me like you want to become an actor."

"You can't be serious," Alter exclaimed.

Gregorios had to force a serious expression. Seeing Spartacus starring in a romantic comedy would be such a victory, he scarce allowed himself to consider it.

"Tell me about actors," Spartacus said. "I will take upon myself this honor."

Bastien's voice spoke through Gregorios' earpiece. "Contact! The hunters just dropped down the side of the tower to the promenade."

"Where?" Gregorios asked. At Spartacus' quizzical look, he tapped his earpiece. "Getting a message."

Bastien shouted, "Take cover in there! They are targeting the stairs to the northeast entrance of the library." Gunfire chattered across the connection and sounded outside as Bastien and the Tenth opened fire on the hunters.

"We've got company," Gregorios said.

Before they could move to better positions, an explosion rocked the little antechamber nearby that led to a short flight of stairs back down to the main promenade.

The blast tossed Gregorios out of his seat, and a bronze bust of one of the popes clanged to the tile beside his head, then skidded across the floor.

A heavy canvas bag arced through the opening and landed inside with a dull thud.

"Bomb!" Gregorios shouted.

84

May the gods forgive me, but we have breached the Eternal City to our glory and sorrow. Spartacus is fallen, although my hand trembles to write such dire news.

Few of his troops returned from their raid and, although they destroyed the temple, Spartacus fell to the facetaker goddess. Can anyone claim victory when such beings walk the shadows of the world and when such mighty heroes fall?

It is fitting that the greatest city in the world fell with him.

~ALARIC I, KING OF THE VISIGOTHS, SACKING OF ROME,
410 A.D.

SARAH YANKED on the pommel of the sword, slicing up Paul's abdomen and pulling him off the ground. Impaled on the sword, he gasped, his mouth working but unable to scream. His hands pawed at her arm, smearing his blood onto her steel skin.

Part of her hated him more for how much she loved this moment. She knew how much agony he was suffering as he hung from her blade, but she felt no remorse.

Holding him helpless six inches off the floor she snarled, "I'm going to kill you now."

"You shouldn't have waited," he said and actually laughed at her, blood spraying her face.

Her right arm burned with searing heat, then just as quickly turned icy cold. Sarah gasped and stumbled back as the sword slipped from her numbed fingers. The icy cold rippled up her arm and into her torso, draining her strength.

A new rune glittered on her forearm, black against her skin. Paul had marked it with his blood. It was the counter rune Eirene had shown her, combined with another symbol she didn't recognize.

Sarah dropped to her knees as the matchless strength that had been pounding through her veins drained away, leaving her exhausted and weak. Her steel-hard skin faded to flesh and blood.

"How . . .?" she breathed.

Paul removed the sword, and his stomach sealed instantly. He stood taller, looking stronger than ever. "You have such marvelous power, slave, but you're still a child. Had you command of your strength, you alone might pose a threat. I will grant you the honor of becoming my most beloved concubine, but today you will be punished."

Sarah scrambled away, filled with renewed terror. She couldn't understand how he seemed so strong. She'd hurt him so much.

"Thank you for granting me so much strength," Paul said with a mock salute. "It feels wonderful, doesn't it?"

It chilled her to think he'd let her stab him just to give him a chance to inscribe that rune, and she'd let him do it. She was such a fool.

That rune had drained her strength, just as she had drained all those other souls. She scraped at it, but it clung to her skin like it had been glued there.

"When you are worthy, I will grant you more power even than you felt today. But first, the lesson." Paul slid one finger up the flat of his blade. "I know just how we're going to start."

Sarah crawled away, panicked by the thought of that sword stabbing her again. She tried morphing her flesh, but she couldn't reach her rounon well. The rune on her arm was somehow blocking her ability. He was going to hurt her again, and she couldn't stop him.

Paul glanced beyond Sarah, and his mocking smile faded.

An actual harpoon whooshed over Sarah's head and punched through his chest, exploding out his back. He stumbled, but his flesh began to heal again. He yanked on the harpoon, but the barbed end prevented him from pulling it back out.

The harpoon was connected to a heavy chain. When Sarah rolled over, she found that it extended up over one of the concealed archer platforms and back down to a motorized winch. Eirene hit a switch, and the winch began to whir. It caught up the slack and dragged a cursing Paul into the air.

Eirene stopped it when Paul hung twenty feet above them. She rushed to Sarah.

"Are you all right, dear?"

"Where's Spartacus?"

"He stepped on a catapult. He'll be back in a minute."

"Thank you. That was about to get painful."

Eirene studied the rune. "I don't recognize this one."

"I don't either. I don't know how to counter it."

"There is one way." Eirene summoned a pair of short knives. One she threw, catching a towering cyclops in the eye just as it rounded a nearby column. She brought the other one down to Sarah's arm.

"I was hoping you could come up with a better idea," Sarah admitted.

"Look away," Eirene said gently.

Sarah closed her eyes.

Searing pain tore up her arm and she bit back a scream. As soon as she was free of the rune though, Sarah felt her strength roll back in. The flesh of her arm reappeared, undamaged.

"Better?" Eirene asked.

"Yes, thank you." Sarah felt whole again, although far weaker than earlier. She'd take it. At least now she wouldn't have to lie helpless under Paul's torture.

Eirene warned, "Take care. You may have drained much of your soul force, and there are only so many ciphers you can activate close together."

With a berserker shout, Paul chopped into his side with an ax, then ripped the harpoon out through the new wound. He fell to the floor nearby, covered in gore.

He bounded back to his feet, already healed. He'd stolen so much energy from her, Sarah couldn't imagine how to hurt him badly enough to do any lasting damage.

"We're in trouble," Eirene muttered.

"Tell me about it." Sarah whispered a silent prayer that Tomas would hurry, because she wasn't sure how much longer they could hold Paul.

Spartacus appeared at the base of the steps, shouting Eirene's name.

"I have an idea," Sarah said.

Before she could explain, the stones under Eirene erupted, somersaulting her away. She landed on the long steps and bounced several times. As she rose to her feet, Spartacus drove his spear into her chest. Her scream tore at Sarah's heart.

She moved to help, but the ground rose into a wall, cutting her off from Eirene.

"No, Sarah," Paul said, once more wearing that mocking smile, his suit again spotless. "Your unruly behavior has gotten you into trouble." He again carried a double-edged sword.

Sarah yearned to help Eirene, but she had to deal with Paul. His reinforced strength was giving him the upper hand in controlling the memoryscape. No doubt, he'd force the memory toward completion, toward that moment when the master rune would appear.

She had to stop him.

Sarah retreated into the rows of columns spaced evenly along the eastern portico of the temple. Paul followed, implacable, sure of victory. Sarah didn't have to pretend to look terrified. Every time her eyes flickered to his sword, she felt a fresh wave of fear.

"I'll never give you what you want," Sarah promised.

"Don't delude yourself." Paul spoke calmly. "Your destiny is set and unmovable. Embrace it now and I'll show leniency."

The sword vanished.

Sarah hated the feeling of relief that flooded her. Paul's smile widened.

"You don't have to fight me, Sarah. I'm a fair master. I reward those who merit my good will."

She sagged against a column, one hand pressed to the stone for support, her gaze falling. She drew from the depleted well of her rounon and touched the cipher concealed under her hand, left there as part of her pre-battle preparation.

Paul closed the distance between them and reached for her.

Sarah activated the cipher and dropped to the stone floor as her soul strength temporarily spent itself fueling the cipher. Its blazing light solidified into glittering bands that wrapped Paul like a blanket and tightened. Those cords of binding looked ethereal, but were far stronger than iron.

Paul shouted a curse, struggling against the restraining bands. The column began to crack. The binding cipher wouldn't hold him long.

Sarah didn't need long.

She pulled a wooden disk from her pocket, slapped it across Paul's eyes, and activated the cipher engraved on it. The cipher would cause temporary blindness. She wobbled under a fresh wave of exhaustion, her strength spent to fuel the new cipher. This one didn't require much force, and the feeling of weakness passed quickly.

Paul shouted, "You think that sword hurt last time? I'll impale you with a thousand burning blades."

He burst from the binding cipher and lunged.

Sarah side-stepped, and he rushed headlong into the column beside her. The new cipher was working. She hoped it would last long enough. Sarah moved to her left to the next column, and summoned a moon-bladed battle-axe.

"With threats like that, I'm not motivated to work for you, creep."

Still blinded, Paul rushed toward her voice with super speed. She barely spun out of the way, and he collided with the column. It splintered under the impact, but he ignored the rain of broken stone as he tore at his own eyes.

Sarah dodged a huge piece of falling masonry and swung for his neck. Taking off his head was the only way she could think to beat him.

Paul must have heard something because he dropped to the ground. Her axe sparked against falling debris. She shifted aim and swung again. He was leaning on the shattered base of the column, a perfect set-up.

Four laughing babies appeared around Paul's head.

Sarah shrieked and released the axe, sending it tumbling away. She knew those babies were nothing but memory projections, but she couldn't cut through them, even to get to him.

Paul rose and the babies faded, becoming snakes that twined around his neck. He blinked with restored sight. She'd just wasted her best chance.

Sarah retreated again, her mind empty of new ideas. Paul stalked after her, the snakes on his shoulders hissing. His sword reappeared in his hand.

"Now, where were we?"

85

As a rule, men worry more about what they can't see than about what they can see. The wise worry that they see too little. I see what must be, and I will seize the lives I must to achieve it.

~JULIUS CAESAR

SPARTACUS CROSSED the room in the blink of an eye, faster than even the enhanced legs of Tomas' battle suit should have moved him. He scooped up the satchel charge and threw it back out the door.

It exploded three feet from his hand, and the blast caught Spartacus in the face, hurling him across the room into the far wall. A section of the wall buckled under the impact, but he landed on his feet, unharmed.

As much as Gregorios hated rune webs, having a protective barrier must have been handy.

He stood and dusted himself off. "Looks like the hunters have arrived."

"They are persistent through the ages," Spartacus agreed. "If not for the unfair advantage of my rune protection, I would join in glorious battle with them."

"Times are tough," Gregorios agreed. He doubted Spartacus understood sarcasm.

The gunfire had died down after the blast outside so he shouted, "Reuben, get up here and talk like a man before I get really annoyed."

Reuben's voice drifted in from outside. "How do I know you won't try to assassinate me?"

Gregorios muttered, "I never liked that kid. So untrusting."

"It is the nature of small men to see their shortcomings reflected in the actions and intents of others," Spartacus said.

Gregorios gave him an annoyed look. "Just don't, okay?"

"Have I caused offense?"

"Not really," Gregorios said with a sigh. "I'm still adjusting to the new you."

"Let the past go," Spartacus said with a wide smile. "I have escaped my cage. Have you?"

"I preferred storming the castle." Gregorios stomped to the doorway and shouted, "Reuben, I said get in here! We've got a lot to discuss and killing you and your team is a waste of my time."

Reuben ascended the short flight of stairs from the promenade, rifle clenched in his hands. "My father knows I'm here."

"Which is why you're still alive. The situation's changed, so let's figure out what we actually need to shoot before rushing off half-cocked."

"I know my duty," Reuben said.

Spartacus approached and Reuben shuffled back a step, swinging his gun to cover the Thracian. Spartacus ignored the weapon and held out his hand, smiling.

"I knew many of your ancestors, young hunter. They were men of honor, who won great glory in single combat. You are welcome into our company."

Reuben stared from the hand to Spartacus, surprise on his face.

"It's customary to shake it," Gregorios said.

"I don't shake hands with kashaph," Reuben spat.

Spartacus dropped his hand. "So be it. In a more appropriate time, we will meet in the contest of arms to test the mettle of your honor."

Gregorios said. "Reuben, pick up that table you knocked over."

Quentin's voice spoke over the tactical net. "Gregorios, can I interrupt?"

"Only with good news."

Spartacus gave Gregorios a quizzical look.

He shrugged and pointed at his earpiece. "Getting another message. Just a minute."

Spartacus grinned. "This is what we must discuss! Mortals have harnessed the very power of the gods, but they can do so much more with it than grow fat and lazy."

"Isn't that what happened to your precious gods?" Alter asked.

The two launched into a debate of the value of the Roman gods and the power of the one true god. Reuben stood to one side, arms crossed, a scowl on his face. Gregorios tuned them out.

Quentin spoke again. "I have an update from the archives. The terrorist threat's really motivated everyone to help."

"And what did you find?" Gregorios asked softly.

"I believe the runes were engraved upon Hadrian's tomb, specifically upon the capstone of Hadrian's sarcophagus."

"Location?" Gregorios asked.

"In the Basilica. Spartacus is hunting in the wrong place."

That was a relief, although Gregorios hated wasting lives for a useless mission.

"Why would it be there?" he asked. Spartacus turned from his debate to listen to the one-sided conversation. He should've chosen his words more carefully.

"The capstone is a big, reddish porphyry stone. It was moved into the basilica in A.D. 1000 to cover the tomb of Emperor Otto the Second."

"Wait," Gregorios said, pacing away from the too-watchful Spartacus. "But that was before the sacking of Rome."

"That's the thing," Quentin said eagerly. "I found a single reference to how strange it was that during that deadly siege, the pope insisted on transporting the stone along with him into the Castel."

"So it's here after all?"

"No, they brought it back to the Basilica again. It's now used as the font in the baptistery on the main level."

"You can't be serious," Gregorios said. That suggested all kinds of ethical issues.

"That's my best guess. The evidence points in that direction. If the runes aren't there, then no one's going to find them any time soon."

"Thanks. Good work."

He turned from the call to find the two hunters and Spartacus watching him.

"That sounded like an interesting call," Reuben said.

"Indeed," said Spartacus, rolling his shoulders. "It appears we now face a choice. Will you share the location of the runes I seek, or shall we again meet in glorious battle?"

"No time for that," came a new voice.

They all turned toward the northwest door, which led into the Sala dell'Adrianeo. Soldiers had checked that room and found nothing.

A tall, slender Chinese woman stood in the doorway now. She wore a young body, but her face looked mature, and Gregorios felt like he should know her. She cuddled a newborn baby in a carry pack on her chest.

"Who are you?" he asked as his soldiers shifted to cover her.

"She is not named before the unpurified," Spartacus said in a voice that sounded like he intended it to be a whisper, but easily reached every ear.

"That's a little arrogant," Gregorios said.

"Indeed."

Alter advanced on the woman. "My heart has been pure since my youth."

"Not any more, abomination," Reuben snarled.

Alter ignored him. "Speak woman, or we'll be forced to bind you."

The woman raised one eyebrow, and in that moment she bore a striking resemblance to Mai Luan. Sarah's account of Paul's reference to his mother made sense.

"Alter, get back," Gregorios shouted, snapping his shotgun into position.

The woman crossed to Alter in a blink, grabbed him by the throat and lifted him off the ground. She shook him like a doll and twisted him into Gregorios' line of fire.

"Tell me the location of the runes, Gregorios," she said calmly, easily holding Alter's thrashing form.

"I don't share secrets with women I just met," Gregorios replied, studying her.

Alter's face was turning blue from lack of air, but then his eyes ignited with purple fire. He grasped the woman's arm with burning hands and Gregorios prepared to fire when she dropped him.

She didn't.

Her eyes ignited too. Rather than the violet shade common to facetakers and cui dashi, her eyes glowed a brilliant lavender color, unlike anything Gregorios had seen before. Her hand also began to burn with activated nevron.

Alter opened his mouth in a silent scream, beating uselessly against her hand.

"Last chance or I'll rip this one's head off," the woman said to Gregorios.

Too bad she hadn't grabbed Reuben.

"Put him down, demon," Reuben snarled. "His soul is mine to purge."

Reuben opened fire with his automatic rifle.

The sound of gunfire triggered a response from all of the members of the Tenth who had shifted around to face the new threat. They all fired on the woman with hollow point bullets or electro-shock and sleep darts.

Gregorios held his fire. He didn't have a shot, and it became instantly clear that shooting this woman was a waste of time. Darts and bullets barely broke her skin, and the wounds healed so fast she barely bled. Her only response to the barrage was to raise her free hand to shield the child.

He had never imagined such enhancement. It didn't look like the web that protected Spartacus and his men included her, but she didn't appear to need it. This woman was a force like nothing they had ever faced.

"Cease fire," he shouted.

The room fell silent but for the wailing of the frightened child. For a moment, its eyes glowed like amethysts.

Even more disturbing. The suspicion of a family of cui dashi was proving true, a nightmare worse than anything Gregorios had ever imagined.

He sighed. "Let the boy go and I'll tell you what I know." Eirene would never forgive him if he let Alter's head get ripped off.

The woman cocked her head to one side and shook Alter again.

"The runes are possibly engraved on the capstone of Hadrian's tomb, which was moved to the Basilica to cover Emperor Otto the Second's tomb."

She smiled. "That wasn't so hard, was it?"

"Drop him," Gregorios said.

She considered Alter and her expression hardened. For a second, Gregorios feared she'd rip Alter's head off anyway, but then her grip relaxed and she lowered him to the floor.

Still holding his throat, but easing her hold enough for him to suck in a ragged breath, she twisted his face to each side, studying him. "You are an interesting child. Live another day."

With startling speed, she threw him at Gregorios. The impact sent them both sprawling.

Before Gregorios could rise, the woman tossed her baby at Reuben.

The surprised hunter dropped his rifle to catch the child. In the time he did that, she knocked down every soldier of Gregorios' team.

She blurred through them, tossing men aside like chaff in a whirlwind, leaving elite, enhanced soldiers broken and groaning in her wake.

She shot across the room and snatched her baby from Reuben. He tried to hit her, but his enhanced movement looked like slow motion compared to hers. She kicked him aside, sending him tumbling back out the broken door he had arrived through.

"Complete your mission," the woman told Spartacus.

She disappeared out the western exit before he could raise his hand in salute.

Gregorios climbed to his knees. At least Alter was alive. The boy was gasping, clutching his bruised throat.

"Who was that?"

"We each have our roles to play. I will wish you good luck in stopping them this time." Spartacus saluted Gregorios and rushed out of the room through the southern exit that led to the ancient treasure room and up to an open roof courtyard beyond.

"Where'd that woman go?" Gregorios shouted into the tactical net.

Harriett spoke. "She jumped right off the turret. Landed just inside the outer gates and kicked them right off their hinges. What was that thing?"

"I believe that was the queen mother of cui dashi," Gregorios said.

Harriett muttered a curse. "She picked up an armored truck like it was a toy and used it to crush both our fire trucks. Then she ran up the street. Must've hit fifty before I lost sight of her."

Bastien muttered a French curse and asked, "How is it possible?"

"We'll deal with her later," Gregorios said, just happy she left instead of hanging around another half second to kill them all.

He'd faced many powerful foes, but he'd never felt as completely, helplessly terrified as he had in the face of that slender Chinese woman. He couldn't let that fear interrupt his family's effectiveness. They still needed to deal with the current threat.

"Spartacus is on the move. Contain him."

As Bastien organized the rest of their forces to secure the rooftop where Spartacus had fled, Gregorios checked on his soldiers. None would die, but none would fight again that day. He called for medical assistance, then turned to Alter, who had risen, but still looked pale.

"Call your brother in here. We've got to get past our disagreement for a while. This threat trumps everything else."

"I'll see if he's all right," Alter said, trotting toward exit the unnamed cui dashi had thrown Reuben through.

He arrived just as a grenade plopped into the doorway.

Alter kicked it back outside and dove to the side. The blast threw debris into the room.

"I guess your brother doesn't want to behave," Gregorios said. He switched to his tactical mic. "Who has eyes on the hunters?"

Bastien said, "They just roped down to the lower level. I let them go."

"Keep a couple rifles on them. If they make any other threatening moves against our forces, disable them."

Harriett broke in. "I've located Spartacus. We have bigger problems."

"How is he a bigger problem?" Gregorios asked.

"You've got to see this to believe it."

Gregorios rushed up the narrow stairs Spartacus had just escaped up and ran to the outer edge of the open court. A second set of stairs descended from that corner, which explained why he didn't see Spartacus up there.

Directly below him, passing through the broken main gate, marched the majority of Spartacus' century they hadn't seen during the earlier fighting. Spartacus led them, oaken spear in hand.

They walked through a hail of bullets and incendiary mortar rounds without slowing. With the modified fire trucks disabled, the Yurak fighters lacked the sticky foam that might have held the enhanced heka, but Gregorios wondered if even that would work now.

Spartacus turned right and marched through the police lines, ignoring the carabinieri firing at him from all sides, his gaze locked on St. Peter's Basilica half a mile away, straight down the Via della Conciliazione.

He thought he knew where the runes were, and he was going for them.

"Harriett, call in all units," Gregorios ordered. "Deploy every delaying tactic we have. Do not let Spartacus reach the Basilica."

"But the web's stronger than ever. Kinetic energy and even heat are no longer slowing them."

"I know. Time to get creative."

Gregorios changed channels. "Tomas, I need good news and I need it now."

Gunfire chattered through the connection as Tomas spoke. "Closing on the hill under heavy smoke. Resistance is fierce. I estimate another twenty minutes to win through."

"You don't have that much time. Take that web down now, Captain. Order the charge."

Tomas swore softly, but didn't hesitate.

"Yes, sir. We won't fail."

86

Magellan was an arrogant fool. Without enhancements or support from the ship cannons, he was doomed to die on Mactan. However, I still relish the memory of completing that first ever journey around the world.

~HARALD, FACETAKER COUNCIL MEMBER

TOMAS STOOD on the edge of the summit plateau of the Palatine Hill. A maze of ruins lay between him and the known opening to the crypto-porticus. His teams had been driving steadily in that direction under heavy fire, leaving a dozen chained heka in their wake.

The enemy was adapting. At first, they rushed into battle singly or in pairs, trusting their protective web to keep them from harm. Now they bunched in two large groups of eight to ten fighters.

Their numbers were small, but in those tight formations, they could lay down such withering fire that no enforcers could get close enough to disable them, despite the heavy smoke billowing across the battlefield.

Ordering a charge into the face of that opposition would shred his team as badly as the famous ride of the light brigade. To disable that critical heka web, he had taken command and led those doomed men through that valley of death. The price had been high, but necessary to prevent the Russians from gaining the advantage and altering the course of history.

He had sworn never to order such a charge again, but his duty was clear.

He'd already discarded the idea of raining high-explosive mortars across the historical location. The fallout from that might be worse in the long run than the deaths of a few enforcers. He and his men were expendable, and they had a job to do.

A slender, Filipino enforcer named Isagani dropped to a crouch behind the ruined stone wall beside Tomas. He handed Tomas a small box. "Captain, this just arrived from Quentin for you."

"Perfect." Tomas hefted it, considering its possible uses. The specialty item could only be used once.

Quentin had lied when he told the others that he didn't have any more of his rune-nullifying compound. Tomas held the last of it, packed into a grenade like the one Quentin had used at the mansion.

He was tempted to use it to break the heka defenses, but couldn't bring himself to do it. He'd asked Quentin for it as a trump card when they found Paul.

With a leaden heart, he spoke crisply into his throat mic. "Listen up, men. The situation at the Castel's changed. Our orders are to take this hill right now. We're taking the fight to them with everything we've got."

"Captain," Anaru's voice came over the net. "My team won't be in position to provide covering fire until we take out this last heka nest."

"We can't wait any longer. Step it up. I need your men in this rush."

"Yes, sir."

Anaru clicked off, and Tomas began ordering the teams to form up and prepare to charge.

"Captain," Domenico broke in, sounding out of breath. "I have something that will help."

The Italian enforcer appeared around a pile of rubble, carrying a pair of riot shields.

Tomas laughed. "Where did you get those?" They hadn't been part of the gear available in the trucks.

"I borrowed some from a police team sent to investigate reports of armed men in the Forum."

Tomas didn't bother to ask if the polizia had relinquished the shields willingly or not. They offered the critical piece he needed to make the charge work.

"Are you ready to lead the charge?" he asked, and Domenico answered with a grin, bringing his shield into position.

"Domenico and I will break cover. I'll take the group on the left. Domenico, you take the other position." Tomas would be more exposed in his charge, but the riot shield gave him a chance.

"As soon as we draw their fire, teams one through four follow in sequence. No matter what happens or who goes down, our objective is to take these tunnels and disrupt that web."

Two of the team commanders began to argue for the chance to lead the charge. Tomas appreciated the gesture, but he wouldn't send them in first, knowing what they were about to run into.

He'd lost four bodies in combat but each time a facetaker, usually Gregorios, had been close enough to salvage his soul and transfer him to a new host.

This time there would be no salvation.

"We go on my mark." He took a deep, steadying breath and peered around the crumbling half-wall behind which he crouched. Forty feet of open space separated him from the first heka nest, across rough ground, through dense smoke.

Once they spotted him, they had an excellent field of fire, hunched within the ruins of an ancient palace. None of Tomas' men could get a clear shot to use their disabling equipment until he took the plunge.

"Team nine, fire a starburst round directly over the heka position."

"Roger," came the immediate reply. "Firing now."

Tomas tensed to charge, every muscle quivering with adrenaline as he embraced battle fury that had seen him through most of the worst battlefields in the past two centuries.

The starburst round exploded above, and slightly in front of, the heka position, a blinding light that slowly settled toward the ground. Tomas heard the shouts of dismay from the heka ranks as the unexpected brilliance temporarily blinded them.

"Charge!" He leaped the wall and sprinted through the roiling smoke that glowed eerily from the starburst. That round would expire in seconds, but that was all the time he needed.

With the riot shield held in front, Tomas flew across the ground, running at full enhanced speed, drawing deep from his enhancements.

His men poured out of their shielded positions and gave chase, but none of them could quite match his speed. He spared a glance to his right where Domenico charged the second heka position, a little closer than the one he was targeting.

He managed to cross most of the distance before the heka noticed. Shouts of alarm rang across the hill and the entrenched enemy opened fire with automatic rifles, spraying the hillside. Bullets ricocheted off the shield, every impact reminding him that his men were not protected as he was.

More than one enforcer fell, crying out in pain, and those sounds drove Tomas on faster. He would avenge every one of those injuries with fury.

Pain seared across his left calf as a round caught him beneath the shield that he'd lifted higher in the effort to cross the distance faster. His muscle spasmed and he tumbled to the ground.

A second bullet caught him in the right side, but his vest caught it. Tomas rolled with the fall, twisting his shield around before more bullets could strike. He sprang back to his feet, roaring with the need to crush the men who had shot him.

He was close enough that every rifle was turned on him, a steady barrage of bullets that cracked the riot shield, threatening to shatter it entirely.

Tomas jumped, leaping into that deadly storm of lead, crossing the last ten feet in a flying tackle. He crashed into the center of the heka group, and they all went down in a heap of arms and legs and guns.

As the heka fighters cursed and continued to fire, not caring if bullets struck companions protected by their rune web, Tomas unleashed his full fury upon them.

Striking with hands and feet, he aimed for their hands, knocking weapons flying and keeping those deadly barrels away.

Then his team arrived. Enforcers swarmed over the heka, howling the Tenth's centuries'-old battle cry.

The heka fought viciously, but they weren't elite warriors, refined in battle with the single purpose of defeating superhuman enemies. The Tenth soldiers knocked their weapons aside and subdued them, using fast-wrap ropes, followed by duct tape and steel-mesh zip ties.

Anaru appeared with his men as the fighting was winding down. He clobbered one heka to the ground and stood on the screaming fellow as his men tied the man up. He offered Tomas a hand up.

"Sorry we're late, Captain, but we found a back door."

Tomas laughed softly. "I wish I'd known about that two minutes ago."

Anaru shrugged. "This rabble needed to be taken care of. When we took that last position, we discovered they were guarding a concealed hatch. Looks new. I'm guessing it leads into the hidden crypt tunnels."

"Good work." Tomas surveyed the battlefield, peering through the heavy smoke toward Domenico's team. "Domenico, status?"

"Just mopping up, sir," he replied.

"Casualties?"

Anaru said, "We lost one in the charge. Round to the forehead, just under his helmet."

Tomas cursed. He hated losing men, although a charge like that could easily have claimed many more lives. Other reports came in, and the number of wounded rose to eight, but no more deaths were reported.

"Team three and four, oversee the prisoners," he ordered. "Team five, help the medics with the wounded. Everyone else on me. We're going in through Anaru's back door."

Half a minute later, they congregated around a simple steel hatch set into the stone ground. The bolts looked new, the hinges free of rust. A ruined wall blocked it from view until they were nearly standing on top of it. A large stone sat nearby, and by the scuff marks on the ground, it was used to conceal the entrance at least some of the time.

"Pull it," Tomas said.

Anaru hauled up the hatch, and three soldiers tossed flash-bang grenades down as bullets erupted out of the hole. Tomas caught a glimpse of a vertical shaft leading down into darkness.

As soon as the grenades boomed, Tomas jumped into the hole. He fell twelve feet, easily absorbing the impact. The shaft ended in an entryway to a subterranean room barely bigger than a closet. Three men stood in the room, rubbing at blinded eyes.

Tomas snapped a handcuff over the first man's wrist and kicked his feet out from under him. The heka shouted and struggled, but Tomas got his other hand cuffed behind his back before the fighter could recover.

The other two blindly opened fire with their automatic rifles. Bullets tore the air around Tomas and ricocheted through the narrow space. Unafraid of taking hits from their own bullets, the two filled the tiny room with lead.

Anaru landed in the entryway, already firing an automatic paintball gun. The big enforcer directed the splattering ammo into the two heka's faces. They might be immune to harm, but the paint still temporarily blinded them.

One of them fired a long, continuous burst toward the entryway. Anaru caught several bullets in the torso and fell back against the inner wall with a grunt.

Tomas rolled under the gunman's weapon and kicked it out of the man's hands.

With a Maori battle cry, Anaru rushed into the room and crash-tackled the other heka off his feet. Several other enforcers jumped down the shaft and within seconds, all three heka were disabled and chained.

"Are you all right?" Tomas asked Anaru.

The big man grunted again. "The vest held."

"Good. Let's go." He shared a fierce grin with his second, riding the rush of life he always felt when engaged in battle.

Leading two dozen enforcers, Tomas slipped out of the small room into the warren of tunnels of the cryptoporticus. They met no resistance and Tomas got a sense of their position based on the sketch Eirene had provided prior to the mission.

The tunnels were spread over three levels, with the known cryptoporticus tunnel almost touching the highest. They had landed in the middle level.

Tomas sent a squad down to clear the lower level, ordered Anaru to lead the squad sweeping the middle level they were on, and he led the final team up a side tunnel toward the top.

Infrequent fluorescent bulbs secured to the ceiling left much of the tunnel huddled in shadow, but with his enhanced eyesight, he could see well enough. The passage was square, made of weathered, rough-cut stone, with a thick layer of sand on the floor. Long scrape marks ran the center of the tunnel, as if Paul's forces had shoveled out more debris when they first moved into the hidden complex.

The cool air smelled stale, as if it had grown bored in the long years it waited to be reopened. Silence reigned except for a distant humming, perhaps from an air exchange or climate control system. Distant gunfire drifted down into the tunnels from above where Domenico led the teams securing the rest of the hill.

Hopefully the heka wouldn't realize Tomas' team had breached their outer perimeter until he located the web.

No sooner had he made the wish than a pair of heka trotted around the corner of a tunnel just ahead. They didn't hesitate to swing their rifles toward the intruders.

Tomas' team reacted faster.

He dropped to his knees to allow the men behind him to engage too. They all fired at the same time. The heka fighters were overwhelmed by exploding paintball bullets, bolo nets, and electro-shock darts.

Tomas left four men to chain the disabled heka while he led the rest of the team in sweeping the rest of the tunnel. The sound of their weapons would alert anyone else in the area. They had to strike fast.

One man peeked out a nearby steel door, caught sight of Tomas, and ducked back inside as paintball bullets splattered all around him. The door clanged shut and Tomas heard the lock.

"Set explosives and blow this," he ordered, then continued down the hall.

He peeked into the next room, and a hail of bullets nearly took off his head.

He glimpsed a large room, well lit, with four heka fighters near the door. Two of them were hunkered behind an M60 machine gun, and were pouring heavy fire through the door. Luckily the bullets tore into the aged stone on the far side of the passage instead of ricocheting around the tunnel.

More importantly, in that one glimpse, Tomas caught sight of an enormous, four-tiered shelf, covered with dispossessed soulmasks. It looked like four conference tables had been set up one atop the other, with ladders connecting them and soulmasks packed across the smooth surfaces of each table.

The soulmasks glowed with the blue-white light of activated runes, strapped together into a giant web. Three other heka were scampering across the web, adding more dispossessed souls or inscribing runes.

The size of the operation amazed him. The web he had sacrificed so many brave British soldiers to disperse during that deadly ride had held perhaps a third as many souls. He couldn't imagine where Paul had acquired so many souls without triggering investigations into mass missing persons.

It didn't matter. He had found the web. It must have taken weeks to prepare such a complex spell.

It would only take him a few seconds to destroy it.

"All teams, converge on my position," he ordered, cringing away from a ricocheting round from the still-firing M60. "And bring every bit of explosive we've got."

Then the M60 stopped firing and Tomas felt the hairs on his arms standing, the way they did when he was very close to a powerful rune. He swept a hand around the corner of the doorway and smacked into an invisible barrier.

Tomas cursed softly but with feeling. The enchanters had raised a barrier wall to keep him out.

87

You think I'm scared of Gregorios and his enforcers? Or even the hunters and their Visigoth puppets? I am the greatest hunter the world has ever known. Let them pit their puny enhancements against my runes, and I will plunder their lands, ravish their women, and slaughter them through as many lives as they dare return.

~ATTILA THE HUN, CHANNELER, THE DAY BEFORE THE
BATTLE OF CATALAUNIAN PLAINS, 451 A.D.

SARAH RETREATED FROM PAUL, too tired to run. A deep weariness sapped her strength and her will. His custom counter rune had drained too much of her soul strength.

Paul followed, his terrifying sword in hand, that infuriating smug smile on his lips. He seemed to enjoy taunting her with the promise of pain as much as he enjoyed delivering it.

She silently begged Tomas to hurry. Somehow Paul must have anticipated their attack and thwarted Tomas' efforts. Sarah retreated into the huge, boxy room of the outer sanctum and the truth struck her with stark, unmerciful clarity.

No one was going to save her. She was on her own, and she wasn't enough to stop Paul.

She gathered the last shreds of her defiance and stood tall before Paul. "You think beating up girls is going to get you anywhere in the world?"

"Only if those girls happen to be mighty rune warriors like you,

Sarah. Didn't you know that only through the defeat of your mightiest enemies can you reach greatness and realize your true self?"

"I know who I am," Sarah said.

"But I know who you're about to become." Paul raised his sword. "After you pass through the fires, you will emerge purified and obedient.

Sarah scrambled away, but he kept pace.

Eirene appeared behind Paul, carrying Spartacus' oaken spear. Her crimson cloak was gone, as was her black mask. She wore a leather halter top and skirt, her bare feet silent as she sped across the smooth tile floor, spear poised to strike.

Paul sensed her approach and spun, deflecting the spear. He lunged and caught Eirene by the throat.

"You have a job to do." He threw her across the room and through one of the wide doors at either end of the partition wall.

Sarah sprinted after Eirene. She couldn't stop Paul alone, but maybe together they stood a chance.

Eirene tumbled right across the huge, vaulted inner sanctum. The giant hall was lined with more columns and paved with an intricate mosaic in the form of Summanus, their patron god. She came to rest on the far side of the room at the base of a set of stairs that led up to an immense gateway into another chamber.

Sarah helped Eirene stand, but Paul's voice turned her back to face him. He stood just inside the inner sanctum, arms thrown wide.

"I own this memory now," he shouted.

Eirene gasped and suddenly she was again dressed in the concealing crimson robe, with black mask affixed. Dozens of battle-robed priests and priestesses appeared on the steps, and an entire army of barbarians coalesced on the far side of the room. The air smelled of blood and incense.

Spartacus stepped to the front of his forces.

"What's going on?" Sarah asked.

Eirene grimaced. "He's taken control. I can't stop him any longer."

"What can I do?"

The Visigoth army screamed war cries and charged across the room, drowning out Eirene's words.

The smaller army around them charged, led by the priest named Titus. His eyes and hands burst into purple fire.

Sarah hadn't realized he was a facetaker. Sagittarii filled the air with constant waves of arrows, while the relocated ballistae blasted enemies off their feet. Screams rent the air and echoed endlessly in the cavernous space while the copper scent of blood clung to everything. The armies crashed together and began hacking at each other with wild abandon.

Eirene didn't join the fight, but moved to her left. Spartacus detached himself from the rest of his army. He approached with an implacable stride, spear half-raised. His eyes remained fastened on her mask.

"You cannot conceal yourself from me, daughter of the gorgons."

"Concealing was never my intention."

Sarah realized she was seeing Eirene's actual memory. This was how it went down, how she had defeated Spartacus. Watching the powerful gladiator approach, she shuddered to think that Eirene had lived through this. As much as she wanted to see how Eirene had finally beaten him, they couldn't allow this to happen.

"Stop it," she shouted, grabbing Eirene's shoulder. "Fight him."

Eirene unfastened her crimson robe and let it fall at her feet. Beneath it, she again wore only a leather halter-top and skirt. The outfit left her midriff, arms and legs bare. The silvery runes inscribed on her flesh glowed bright in the dim light.

Spartacus shouted, "You have dishonored her too long!"

He charged.

Eirene removed her mask, revealing another woman's face. She cried out with a different voice. "Spartacus, my love!"

Only then did Sarah realize Eirene hadn't killed Iltea all those years before, but had saved her soulmask. She was using it to lure Spartacus in.

That had been very clever, but it was disastrous right now.

Spartacus' assault faltered and he stumbled to a halt nearby. His spear fell to his side and he gazed with incredulous joy at the face of his beloved.

"Can it be?"

He took a faltering step forward.

"Oh, I've missed you!"

Eirene rushed forward and actually embraced Spartacus. He wrapped her in a hug and kissed Iltea fiercely.

That was gross.

Then her body convulsed and Spartacus drew back, worried. Iltea's face erupted out of Eirene's skull, skin parting to allow her soulmask to fall free.

Spartacus gaped and grabbed it. The rainbow mist of her soul caressed his powerful hands. Eirene grabbed him while he was distracted, digging into the skin under his jaw with hands burning with the purple fire of her nevron.

"Together you will greet the eternities."

"You can't," Sarah cried.

She kicked Eirene with every ounce of strength, knocking her aside and breaking the connection.

"No!" Paul shouted. He leaped the fighting army, soaring a hundred feet.

Sarah retreated from him, forced to back away from Eirene and Spartacus, who were grappling.

She tried with every ounce of will to summon a weapon, but Paul's will held sway and her hands stayed empty. She closed her eyes and concentrated on her enhancements, desperately trying to summon just a little more strength.

The enhancements flickered, then blazed to life. Deep in her soul, she felt an aching emptiness, an exhaustion so deep it terrified her, but she ignored it and drank in the power of the reactivated enhancement burning against her thigh.

She opened her eyes and her body shone with quicksilver fluidity. She'd rip Paul apart.

Paul winked. "Nice try. Too late."

Eirene again gripped Spartacus' face, standing above his kneeling form with hands and eyes blazing.

"I'm so sorry," Eirene whispered.

She pulled off his face.

"No!" Sarah shouted, lunging in a futile attempt to turn back time.

The temple rang like a giant gong and everything fell silent. The battling armies faded away like mist, leaving only Sarah, Eirene, and Paul in the empty temple. Sarah sank to one knee, despairing. Then her eyes rose to the sky, drawn inexorably upward.

The roof of the temple was gone and in the sky blazed a mighty master rune, burning with silver fire. The power of the image took Sarah's breath away as it seared itself into her soul. This was a true master rune, a symbol so powerful it shook her and blanked out all thought.

Just looking at it filled her with strength, replenishing the well of her soul in a heartbeat. It consumed her senses, filling her vision with glittering explosions of light, like fireworks bursting nearby during a snowstorm. The silence rang with silver bells, and a feeling of icy relief trickled down her throat. She smelled strawberries and apple blossoms.

Then the roof snapped back into place and Sarah leaped to her feet.

Paul stood several feet away, laughing. He gave her a mock bow. "I win."

"Not yet."

Her fingers morphed into silver daggers and she threw herself at him, intending to take off his head. She passed right through him, skittering across the floor, her metallic skin sparking against the smooth surface.

Sarah spun but saw nothing but Eirene, who stood motionless, looking at the floor where Spartacus would have fallen.

Paul's voice drifted across the room.

"Time to wake up, Sarah because your nightmares are no longer a dream."

88

Let them hate me, provided they respect my conduct and do not interfere with my next life.

~TIBERIUS, THIRD LIFE OF JULIUS CAESAR

GREGORIOS WAS a general in a losing battle.

The Via della Conciliazione was only half a mile long, straight, and unbroken between the Castel Sant'Angelo and St. Peter's Basilica. At a brisk walk, Spartacus could have covered the entire distance in five minutes.

Eight minutes had passed since Gregorios ordered Tomas to take that hill, and Spartacus' force was approaching St. Peter's Square, despite everything they'd done to slow him down.

Gregorios stood atop a troop transport at the edge of the Piazza Papa Pio the Twelfth, the widening of the road just before it emptied into the huge expanse of St. Peter's Square. He was turned toward the distant Castel, watching the street fight rage, wondering what more they could do.

While Harriett organized Yurak forces to oppose Spartacus' half-century, Gregorios had sent Bastien with every able-bodied soldier from the Tenth to help. They'd scrambled to get ahead of Spartacus, losing precious ground in the process, because Spartacus' men spread across the entire street, and no one could get around them.

Security forces had tried blocking the road with trucks, but the heka vaulted over them. They tried incendiary grenades and mortars, but the heka walked right through them.

Unlike earlier efforts, the higher-powered web deflected all kinetic energy and heat. Bullets no longer knocked them back, and searing heat caused no visible impact.

It was simply the most complete web Gregorios had ever seen. It must be consuming scores of souls, and his forces struggled to compete against that much raw power.

He'd gleaned important hints about the extent of the web as he witnessed the frustrating losing battle. The rune web acted as a comprehensive protective barrier around Spartacus' little army when the men moved as a tight formation, which they preferred.

The barrier was like a bubble that moved with them. Harriett and Bastien had thrown one of the tiny Italian cars, and it had bounced off the invisible barrier inches above Spartacus' head, not rolling to the ground until after all the soldiers had passed beneath it.

However, when the heka were forced to jump barriers and vehicles, sometimes they broke formation. That was the moment that left them partially vulnerable. Still protected from bullets and direct harm, they were not completely impervious.

Harriett and her hard-fighting soldiers had managed to hold their ground for a full minute by blocking the road with tight-packed trucks, forcing the heka to jump or climb over.

When they did so, enhanced fighters met them, jumping to intercept them in midair, or beating them back with anything they could find. Harriett used motorcycles, then snapped off a light pole and used it like a giant baseball bat. She'd always been good at that game.

Several of the heka had been isolated, tied, and dragged away. For a moment, Gregorios had thought they could defeat the well-shielded army even before Tomas knocked down the shield.

Spartacus would not be so easily thwarted.

His men, who had not bothered firing their weapons much, unleashed a fierce volley, cutting down several opposing soldiers. They'd thrown several grenades, forcing Harriett and her men to retreat. Then they jumped the blockade in unison, and the barrier around that unified front had driven everyone back.

Gregorios was trying to get another round of trucks into position, but the local commanders of the polizia and carabinieri were making that difficult.

They had brought in too many of their own men, blocking the streets and making communication difficult. The top commander had refused to believe what he was seeing and kept trying to order ineffectual sniper fire.

Gregorios finally resorted to punching the man unconscious and ordering shocked subordinates to listen. At the sight of his blazing purple eyes, they stopped arguing.

They had scrambled to evacuate the basilica and the nearby square, but thousands of curious onlookers and worried faithful packed the police barriers along surrounding streets. Idiots.

Reporters were everywhere. Men and women with cameras swarmed every available viewpoint, and several news helicopters hovered overhead. Gregorios had called for them to be ordered away, but either they hadn't gotten the call yet, or they were ignoring it.

Worse, the local commanders were joining reporters in peppering him with questions about the protective barrier Spartacus enjoyed, as well as the superhuman abilities Gregorios' own forces were exhibiting.

"Can't you see I'm in the middle of a battle?" Gregorios shouted finally. "We can discuss those things later. Now get me some more trucks!"

"Bene, signore," the commander of a special-forces unit said. "The trucks are coming. But if we knew how to do what your men do, we could help more."

"I said later," Gregorios growled.

Reports of casualties were making him grumpy. The wounded would recover, or would receive new battle suits. He hated that he was forced to take the distant command, overseeing the effort instead of standing with his men.

For centuries the facetakers, hunters, and even the heka had all lived in the shadows, ignored by most of the world.

No longer.

The full magnitude of the heka threat was being broadcast around the world, as well as the capabilities of his own forces. Even if they contained Spartacus and destroyed Paul, that public awareness might end up proving their worst danger.

Every time the general population had learned about them throughout history, they had reacted with fear, which usually meant rioting. The greatest strength of the council was in keeping the knowledge of facetakers from the world.

Everything they had built so carefully for so long was at risk. No doubt Paul planned that as part of Spartacus' mission.

Now Spartacus' half-century had nearly broken out of the western end of the street into the piazza where Gregorios stood. Once they broke through, containment would prove more difficult.

Or it might be the break they'd been waiting for. Harriett had left the front lines under the control of unit commanders and was frantically preparing a couple of surprises. If they could give her enough time, she could stop Spartacus despite the infuriating web.

"What's your status?" he asked Harriett.

"Not good," she reported breathlessly. "A trailer overturned en route. Ten minutes to get a replacement."

"We don't have it."

"I know," she snapped. "Switching to alternate measures, but still need a few minutes."

"We cannot hold them much longer," Bastien reported. "Where are those hunters when we need them?"

"No idea," Gregorios said.

Reuben and his men had left the Castel via a sally port in the rear gate, and no one had seen them since. That cowardice infuriated Gregorios more than all Reuben's juvenile posturing.

He waved one of the unit commanders of the Tenth over. "Have you heard back from Quentin?"

The man nodded. "He just checked in. He's back at Suntara and is working on the item you requested. He said a new batch will take fifteen minutes."

That was far too long, but Gregorios just told the man to urge Quentin to hurry. Quentin's special formula might be needed if they lost the fight. It was a final trump card, and he was woefully short on those at the moment.

Only then did he notice a dense bank of fog rolling up the Via della Conciliazione, rapidly overtaking Spartacus' forces.

The Tiber River was nearby, but there was no way that fog was natural. It rose to the tops of the buildings on both sides of the street and engulfed everything. It consumed the main fighting line and rolled into the piazza. The fog was thick, clinging to his skin with tangible weight.

"Where did that fog come from?" he demanded.

"Say again." Harriett's voice crackled with static.

Gregorios cursed. He'd seen a weaker version of a similar event once when Baladeva had tried to help Cleopatra defeat Caesar as Octavian. Gregorios had personally destroyed that rune web.

He ran west toward St. Peter's Square to escape the front edge of the fog.

"I said we have a problem," he repeated. "Heavy fog moving in. Definitely a heka spell. It appears to interrupt communications."

"Not good," Harriett said. "I can see it now."

"What impact will that have on suppressing measures?" Gregorios asked.

"It won't help," Harriett replied, her voice tense.

"Do what you can."

Gregorios ran faster to keep ahead of the leading edge of fog, which was accelerating.

"Tomas, what's your status?" he asked after switching channels.

"We've breached the perimeter. Preparing to destroy the web."

"Hurry. The situation is spiraling out of control here."

"Twenty seconds. Out."

Gregorios paused at the edge of St. Peter's Square. People streamed out of the piazza, driven by the strange fog and fear of Spartacus' forces advancing through the mist.

Carabinieri snipers were already positioned atop the two semi-circular colonnades that wrapped around the square, and troops were pouring into the southern expanse, even though Gregorios had told them to stay back. Several APCs with roof-mounted machine guns rolled into the square with the troops.

This was their city, and St. Peter's was a treasured icon and they weren't going to surrender it without a fight.

"What a waste of time," he muttered, then lifted the command headset he'd taken from the carabinieri commander to his lips. "Stand down. You're not helping."

A new voice squawked out of the handset. "Remove yourself from this channel. You are not authorized to give orders."

Gregorios sighed and dropped the command headset into a pocket. Their fate was in their own hands. He applauded their intentions, but they were just going to get hurt.

He faced the approaching fog, preparing to allow it to roll over him, then to return to the front lines and personally take over bolstering the defenses.

His earpiece crackled with static. He couldn't make out the words, but he caught a heightened sense of urgency. At the same time, gunfire chattered from the fog, followed by a series of explosions.

Then a troop transport vehicle they'd used in the barrier effort roared out of the fog. Spartacus stood on the passenger side step while one of his men drove. Behind him poured the rest of his men. Somehow they'd broken through.

As the truck rumbled past, Spartacus saluted Gregorios with his staff, then turned toward the square.

Gregorios cursed and trotted into the square, but kept his distance. The snipers and Italian ground forces opened fire on the advancing heka, and the ricochets became an imminent threat.

If Tomas could get that web down now, Spartacus' little army would be slaughtered.

Gregorios slowly counted to twenty as he took shelter in the right-hand colonnade that ringed St. Peter's Square. His forces would be moving to pursue, and the fight was about to get ugly.

He shouted, "Prepare! The web's about to come down." He didn't know who could hear him through the fog, but he lifted his rifle on its tactical sling.

"Time to change the tide, Spartacus."

He reached twenty just before the fog rolled over Spartacus, who was marching through the hail of gunfire.

The web did not go down.

89

~VERCINGETORIX, GALLIC CHIEFTAIN, 52 A.D.

TOMAS CROUCHED beside the doorway to the room holding the heka web. Anaru knelt on the ground beside him, frowning.

"You just lied to Gregorios during a critical encounter," Anaru accused.

"I did not."

"You said twenty seconds." He pounded a hand on the invisible but unyielding barrier blocking the door. "But we can't get into the room."

Tomas grinned. "Trust me."

He extracted Quentin's specialty grenade and added. "Get the other troops back around the corner. When this blows, our enhancements will be temporarily knocked out. I don't want it affecting the rest of the team."

Anaru frowned at the blocky grenade. "What is that thing?"

"Our ticket into the room. You and I are going to blow it. How fast can you throw grenades?"

Anaru grinned and hefted a belt full of the explosives. "Faster than you."

Tomas pulled the pin of the rune-killer grenade and dropped it outside the door. He retreated a dozen feet and closed his eyes.

The grenade went off with a sharp report, and the blast wave struck like a severe gust of wind. That wind caught hold of his many enhancements and sucked them dry.

Even though he'd been expecting it, Tomas still gasped and sagged with weariness. He felt as weak and uncoordinated as he had while wearing Carl's body.

The months he'd spent in that disguise had reminded him how to function without his enhancements, though. So he snapped open his eyes and rushed the doorway, which was full of blue-white lightning.

That web was strong enough, that the grenade, placed so far from its heart, probably wouldn't knock out the entire operation. He only needed it to interrupt the barrier for a few seconds.

The barrier was down.

He slid into the doorway on his knees, two grenades in hand, pins already removed, and threw them far into the room. Anaru arrived on his heels, and they pulled pins and tossed grenades with frantic speed, then rolled to the side before the first grenades exploded.

He only spared a single glance at the surprised heka in the room. They hadn't even been manning the machine gun. Two of them were lunging toward it, but they were eternally too late.

The grenades began to explode, concussive blasts overlapping into a continuous roar that shook the entire tunnel complex. Smoke and debris exploded out the doorway, and Tomas coughed through his sleeve. With his enhancements working, Tomas would barely have noticed the smoke.

He glanced at Anaru, who was pressed against the other side of the door and shouted, "Eight!"

Anaru grinned. "Nine."

"You can't be serious?"

"I've got the pins to prove it." Anaru tapped his thick chest. "You can't keep up with the Maori, Captain."

Tomas was tempted to throw another grenade to even the score, but Anaru would do the same. Anaru had accepted his demotion to second with remarkable grace, so Tomas decided he was being silly to worry about the tiny loss.

"Drinks are on me tonight," he said.

After the last of the grenades exploded, Tomas peeked around the doorway. Dense smoke hung in listless clouds, and the room stank of gunpowder, splintered wood, and the sickening stench of burning soulmasks. It was like burned rubber, mixed with bleach, and the smell stung even in the doorway.

The machine gun nest was simply gone. Blood and gore splattered the room, all that was left of most of the enchanters. Amazingly, a couple heka lay groaning on the floor. Perhaps they'd been protected by additional layers of shielding.

The tables holding the extensive rune web had been shattered, with dispossessed souls fallen into glittering piles of rubble. He noted silvery runes still glowing on some of them. Vestiges of the web might have survived. He lacked the expertise to try extracting any of those soulmasks from the web and salvaging their lives. Time was too short to even try.

Tomas pointed at the two surviving enchanters, who were stirring. "Bind them. They're needed for questioning."

Enforcers poured into the room. The heka were disoriented, their protection gone, and Anaru's team bound them in seconds. They dragged the new prisoners out into the hall while Tomas placed a large satchel charge atop the piles of soulmasks.

He saluted those unknown souls sacrificed in the heka web, then retreated out of the room and led his men down the hall. They stopped on the far side of the still-sealed steel door they'd passed earlier.

When Anaru triggered the charge, it exploded with a concussive blast that sent heated air screaming past, as if seeking an escape from the devastation.

The entire underground complex shook from the force of the blast. The wall outside the web room collapsed into the hall, triggering a small avalanche of stone.

For a moment it looked like the avalanche might spread, and Tomas shared a worried look with Anaru. They hadn't fought their way through the heka defenses only to get buried alive.

After several tense seconds, during which time they all retreated farther down the hall, the shaking subsided and the terrifying groaning of stone above their heads settled. Tomas blew out a breath.

He tapped his earpiece and spoke into his throat mic. "Rune web is down. Repeat, the web has been disabled."

He heard only static.

Tomas was about to try again when the locked steel door burst open and Paul stepped into the corridor. His hat was gone, his chest bare.

Tomas reached for the rune-killing grenade before remembering it was gone. His heart sank at the sight of the cui dashi, standing just feet away.

Blazing on the hairless skin of Paul's chest was a large, complex rune that illuminated the entire area with silver light. Tomas had no rounon gift, but he'd studied enough runes over the decades to see that one was unique.

He recognized components of the lesser master rune Paul had acquired from the assassination of Julius Caesar, as well as pieces of the master rune from Berlin that Sarah had shown him.

That could only mean he'd acquired the last master rune too.

Paul had been sleeping in a chair only feet away, and Tomas had failed to locate him.

Tomas refused to consider the possibility that Paul had left Sarah hurt. Or dead. He whipped around his rifle, knowing he was too late.

Paul sped down the hall, faster than even the most enhanced heka. Before Tomas could pull the trigger, Paul knocked him aside. The blow drove him into the unyielding stone wall so hard his shoulder popped right of the socket.

Tomas slid down the wall, momentarily blinded by the flash of pain. His enhancements hadn't reactivated, and he groaned as he hit the floor.

Shouting at himself to move, to react, he rolled and brought his gun up one-handed.

Paul had already ripped through his entire force. Soldiers lay smashed and broken, strewn in his wake.

And he was already gone.

Tomas cursed and struggled to his feet, rage at the sight of his injured men fueling his strength. His healing rune snapped awake, and the surge of relief brought a fierce grin to his lips.

Anaru rose shakily to his feet nearby, a bloody gash on his forehead.

"Set this shoulder for me," Tomas ordered as he sought signs of life from his men.

He was relieved to see none of them appeared dead, although they were all injured. Their enhancements hadn't been dampened by that grenade, so they recovered quickly.

With a practiced move, Anaru popped Tomas' shoulder. He bit back a cry of pain and nearly fell to his knees. His other enhancements were bonding in turn, but he'd need another ten minutes to feel like himself again.

They didn't have that much time.

With a determined stride, Tomas shook off the lingering effects of his injury and ran down the hall. Anaru and his men straggled after him, but Tomas knew they were already too late. His secondary mission had been to take out Paul before he acquired the last master rune, and he'd failed.

The threat Paul represented made everything else they'd faced seem laughable.

At the first branching tunnel, Tomas turned right, toward the distant brilliance of open sky. He pounded along the tunnel, heedless of the chance of more heka appearing. The protective web was gone, so they no longer posed as dire a threat. He knew how to kill normally enhanced heka.

He met no resistance and scrambled up the ladder at the end of the tunnel that led into open air. Gunfire chattered not far away, but he ignored it, poking his head out the hole and scanning the area for Paul.

His eyes were drawn into the sky and he gaped.

Paul was a distant speck, soaring high over the city.

He was heading in the direction of St. Peter's.

90

The Britons are many, but I wonder that we thought to fear them. Look at them! I see more women visible in their ranks than fighting men, and they, unwarlike and poorly armed, routed on so many occasions, will immediately give way when they recognize the steel and courage of those who had always conquered them!

Even those battles between many legions are won by the few, the honored, with enhancements to prove their prowess. Today will redound to our honor that our small numbers won the glory of a whole army!

~GAIUS SEUTONIUS PAULINUS, RALLYING SPEECH
BEFORE HIS SMALL ARMY ROUTED THE CELTIC HORDE
LED BY QUEEN BOUDICEA, AT THE BATTLE OF WATLING
STREET, 61 A.D.

SILENCE REINED in the square for seven long seconds. Gunfire stopped as the heavy fog obscured everything.

"This isn't thinning," Harriett muttered nearby.

She'd appeared a moment ago like a wraith in the mist and taken up position beside a column to Gregorios' right. The fog distorted her voice, making her sound much farther away.

"Wait for it," Gregorios said, trusting that Tomas would succeed.

Then as fast as it had arrived, the fog began to disperse.

"Go, go, go!" Gregorios shouted, leading the charge into the square.

All of their forces broke into a charge from the colonnade or from the piazza on the east side of the square.

Harriett pulled ahead. Her lithe figure moved with incredible speed, shrieking a battle-cry like a Valkyrie of legend.

As they ran into the dissipating fog, the heka lines became visible as indistinct blurs that solidified rapidly into tight-packed ranks of stationary soldiers. They had brought shields close together to form a turtle formation.

It was a good sign. The formation had been used when Roman soldiers advanced on heavily defended positions, or for desperate last stands.

The soldiers formed into a tight box, with the outer members over-lapping shields to form four walls. The soldiers inside the box lifted their shields high to form an overlapping roof.

It signaled that Spartacus realized the initiative in the fight had shifted. His force stood in the open, surrounded on all sides by enraged enemies wielding modern weapons.

Gunfire erupted across the square as carabinieri positioned atop the colonnades spotted the legionnaires. Bullets pounded into their riot shields. One found an opening and a heka screamed and fell from the ranks.

Cheering echoed across the square from all sides as Italian regulars opened fire.

"Hold fire!" Gregorios shouted as bullets began ricocheting wildly across the square. His forces obeyed, but the Italian forces ignored the order.

He pulled out the command headset he'd taken from the carabinieri commander. "Friendlies closing on the hostiles. Hold your fire!"

"I told you to stay off this channel," the same arrogant voice responded. "You are not part of this chain of command."

"And I'm telling you to stop firing or I'll shove your chain of command down your throat," Gregorios shouted. "We were authorized to deal with this threat, so stay out of my way."

He was a little surprised when the firing began to fade. He wasn't sure if the unknown idiot on the other end of the line had actually grown a brain, or if the soldiers had noticed them closing on the men huddled in the turtle.

Harriett reached the heka lines first.

She no longer carried a firearm, but leaped onto the nearest shield, shoving burning hands through the gap between it and the next shield. The heka behind the shield tried to shove her away.

Too late. She touched him.

The man dropped his shield and reached out to the two men beside him, grabbing them by the arms as flickering purple light flowed along his limbs.

Those two heka dropped their shields and reached out in turn to the men next in line. In a matter of seconds, Harriett had gained control over sixteen heka fighters, more than she'd ever managed before.

Gregorios smiled. Today she was motivated.

Any facetaker could lock onto the soul points along another's face and sever that person's command of their body, or remove their soul. Harriett had developed a more subtle talent. With a single touch, she could send her nevron flowing over another person and usurp control over their muscles.

Gregorios hadn't been able to master the technique. It required too sensitive a touch, too much patience. Harriett was like a painter with her nevron, an artist with a subtle mastery over higher level forms.

He couldn't mimic it, but he could appreciate it.

The captured heka responded to Harriett's commands, puppets to her nevron strings. They turned weapons upon their comrades and opened fire or hacked with swords.

They broke physical contact with each other briefly, but returned to the group within seconds. Her dispersed nevron maintained enough control that as long as nothing prevented them from returning to her group, they remained in thrall.

The heka turtle formation collapsed.

Enhanced fighters broke into smaller groups, confused by the lack of protective barrier and panicked by the betrayal of their comrades.

Yurak mercenaries and enforcers from the Tenth closed with a vengeance. Elite soldiers swarmed the heka, shooting them at point blank range or just beating them to a pulp with the stocks of weapons, venting the pent-up frustration at having faced a foe they couldn't hurt.

They hurt them now.

Gregorios slowed as he neared the fighting. "Save me some prisoners."

Turning St. Peter's Square into a slaughterhouse on international television might be satisfying in the moment, but he was already considering how to deal with the fall-out of the operation.

Bastien's voice broke through his thoughts. "Mon pere, be advised, a small group split off from the main formation. It looks like Spartacus."

Gregorios skirted the battle and caught sight of the smaller force much farther across the square, a tight formation of half a dozen men.

The fog had lingered more in that area, and with the fighting around the main formation, they had already slipped across much of the square.

His forces were not in position to stop them. Gregorios spoke into the carabinieri mic. "Make yourselves useful and shoot down that small group closing on the Basilica."

"With pleasure." This time the unknown commander was far less belligerent.

Gunfire erupted from all around the square, directed against Spartacus' small group. They huddled together, ringed by their riot shields. That small protection wouldn't last long.

Three hundred Italian regulars charged them from where they'd formed ranks in front of the Basilica.

Gregorios frowned. "Keep your men back. Those fighters might not be protected, but they're still enhanced. They'll kill every one of your soldiers."

"We'll take your suggestion under advisement," the unknown commander said. "We will teach them what happens to terrorists in Rome."

He wished Italian commanders didn't have so much insecure machismo.

Gregorios spoke into his throat mic, "I need three squads on me. Spartacus is across the square with Italian regulars closing on his position."

"I think we will arrive late," Bastien said.

The Italian forces reached Spartacus' huddled group and the distant snipers had to stop firing.

That was all Spartacus was waiting for.

He threw his riot shield, knocking the first two soldiers off their feet, and burst into the tight-packed mob of regulars like a cat in a cage full of sparrows.

With his enhanced fighters at his heels, Spartacus beat down everyone who came within reach. The regulars who had ventured too close paid a heavy toll. Men fell, writhing on the ground with broken bones protruding from ripped flesh, bloody faces crying with pain.

Gregorios ran harder. He'd catch Spartacus before the Thracian could reach the entrance to the Basilica. The restored Spartacus might feel like he'd been enlightened in his long dispossession, but he had again allied with the wrong side. That mistake was going to cost him a lot more than his body this time.

With only twenty feet separating him from Spartacus, Bastien pulled Gregorios to a halt and pointed into the sky. "What's that?"

Gregorios looked up and his heart fell.

Paul flew over the southern colonnade, so high he must be actually flying, not just making an enhanced jump. Gregorios had never known anyone to acquire enough enhancements to allow flight, but it looked like Paul had managed it. A new rune blazed bright on his chest, and that meant disaster.

Sarah and Eirene had failed. Paul had won the third master rune. Gregorios hoped his wife was all right. He doubted Paul would have killed Sarah, but she'd made it clear she preferred that to what he planned for her.

"We're in trouble," he groaned.

Paul landed in the center of the square like a thunderclap, close to the main battle. He shattered cobblestones and plunged deep into the earth beneath.

Soldiers stumbled away from the impact crater as Paul jumped back out. He'd left his hat behind, and Gregorios caught a flicker of annoyance on his face. He'd probably thought he'd generate waves of stone and earth like a super-villain in the comic book movies.

Gregorios wished he'd buried himself about ten miles deeper.

Tomas' voice came across the net. "Does anyone copy? Paul escaped with the master runes. Heading for your position."

Gregorios said, "I copy. We have visual. Get your men over here. We're going to need you."

"Roger."

"All units, retreat to the east end of the square and form up," Gregorios ordered. "The cui dashi has the master runes. Do not engage alone."

The situation was about to get ugly in a way he hadn't seen since the siege of Baghdad in 1258 A.D. Over half a million people had died in that atrocity when the brilliant intellectual center was shattered.

The destruction of the grand library of Baghdad had been a particularly devastating blow. Gregorios had loved that seat of wisdom.

If they didn't stop Paul now, the world would witness new atrocities on a mind-boggling scale.

91

Zeus and Hercules are united to my cause! Today they answered the call of my men and rose in mighty wrath against the cursed facetakers. My righteous anger is mirrored by their wrath, for Vesuvius burns, a pyre eclipsed only by the perfidy of Eirene, most hated of all women.

Iltea, my love, rejoice in this mighty tribute. My men are lost, but sacrificed for a cause worthy of glorious death and honor eternal. Herculaneum and Eirene's summer home are buried in ash and fire, but such is the wrath of Zeus that even I am barely free of his rage.

~ SPARTACUS, AT SEA OUTSIDE OF THE PORT OF
POMPEII, A.D. 79

SARAH AWOKE and Francesca immediately helped her remove the heavy helmet. For the first time, Francesca didn't look tired after running a memory hunt. At least the battle cipher Sarah had activated here in the headquarters had worked.

"Paul got the rune," Sarah said. "We failed."

"I know." Francesca pointed toward a large-screen television across the vault. The station was tuned to local news.

It took Sarah a moment to recognize the famous St. Peter's square through the smoke and the piles of dead and wounded scattered everywhere. She recognized several members of the Tenth in the crowd retreating toward the east end of the square. A small army of heka stood around a central figure with a blazing rune on his chest.

That rune burned so bright that the lines blurred together,

preventing Sarah from making out the pattern. It glowed a unique shade of silver.

Eirene joined her, donning a jacket to cover her bloody shirt. "He's already incorporated all of the runes into a personalized greater rune. Impressive."

"Scary's more like it," Sarah said.

"Agreed. Just appreciating good craftsmanship."

"What are we going to do?" Sarah asked, struggling to keep the fear out of her voice.

Paul had seemed convinced that he only needed that one additional master rune to take over everything. His threat to take her, force her to become his sex slave, filled her with dread and towering anger.

Eirene remained remarkably calm. "We need to go there. We throw everything we've got at him and take him down before he can consolidate his position."

"I hate suicide charges," Francesca muttered.

Sarah joined the others heading toward the door. "We need to stop at the armory."

Eirene flashed a vicious grin. "Of course. This calls for the big guns."

"And I need a sharp knife," Sarah added.

92

ITALIAN SNIPERS OPENED fire on Paul, and Gregorios didn't bother telling them to stop as he led his small force around the southern edge of the square to regroup with his main force. Even their idiot commander would figure out soon enough that they were wasting ammunition.

Fifty-caliber bullets shattered against Paul's bare torso, not even breaking the skin. The constant crack of the reports filled the square with continuous rolling echoes.

In a single, soaring jump, Paul crossed to the towering Egyptian obelisk that dominated the center of the square. He snatched the one hundred and thirty-five foot monument off the ground and threw it.

It tumbled across the square, shattered the northern fountain, and tumbled right through the center of the northern colonnade. All four rows of columns shattered, spraying broken stone debris into the buildings north of the square.

Gregorios gulped. No one, not heka, not facetaker, not cui dashi, had ever commanded such strength. No one had ever harnessed the power of three master runes.

He was surprised that much energy didn't tear Paul apart, and couldn't imagine what symbols Paul had used to control it. Paul was a genius with runes, that much was clear.

Every muscle of Paul's torso stood out in perfect definition, his skin glowing with the silver light of his greater rune. One eye glowed amethyst from his activated nevron, the other silver. When he spoke, his voice reverberated through the square.

"I am the Son of Heaven, and you are all blessed to witness the rise of a new world order."

He made a slow circle, arms wide. "Here in this famous square, whose colonnades have long symbolized the embrace of the church, you few will first feel the embrace of your new ruler. As your emperor, I will be known as the Merciful."

"Or the Vengeful. Your choice."

Silence fell as the magnitude of his proclamation sank in.

Without warning, Paul shot across the square, a blur of inhuman speed. As soldiers scattered away, he snatched the Italian commander off his feet. A few snipers fired, but their bullets did nothing but ricochet.

The commander threw up his arms and shouted, "Cease fire!"

Paul walked back across the square, easily holding the Italian at arm's length, his feet dangling several inches off the pavement.

Gregorios reached his main force, which had grown to several hundred men as more reinforcements had arrived. He did not see their heavy weapons trucks.

Paul reached the center of the square and dropped the commander. "Bow to me and swear fealty to my rule."

"You're insane," the commander cried, despite shaking with fear. "You can't just proclaim yourself emperor of the world!"

With eerie calm, Paul said, "Wrong answer. You may call me Vengeful."

He grabbed the commander's arm, and with casual brutality, ripped it from the socket.

The commander screamed, his blood spraying in a wide arc. Paul repeated the process, yanking the man's other arm off as easily as a child might pop the head off a dandelion.

Italian forces all opened fire, pouring everything they had at Paul. Most of the Tenth and Yurak joined in, and Gregorios didn't bother telling them to save their ammo.

Some things were worth the effort, even if only symbolically.

The only thing they managed to do was end the commander's suffering. The barrage of bullets and grenades did nothing against Paul and his blazing rune. The still-living heka fighters scrambled north into the ruins of the broken colonnade.

Gregorios spoke into his mic above the din of gunfire. "Where are the heavy weapons?"

Harriett reported, "We've got mortars, but they're not going to do anything against him."

Eirene spoke, and the sound of her voice eased one of Gregorios' secret fears. Paul might have acquired the rune, but at least Eirene was safe. "We're on the way with support troops and all the big guns. Five minutes."

"Don't stop for traffic lights." It was going to be a long five minutes.

"I've got a pair of F-35s we acquired from the Americans," Harriett reported as she jogged over to join him at the front of their lines. "They can get here in thirty seconds."

Paul stood in the center of the square, waiting calmly for the furious barrage from the Italians to fade.

"We've got a lot of people in the area," Gregorios said, weighing the risk of collateral damage and innocent deaths against the potential for a strike powerful enough to take down Paul. "What's their payload?"

She conversed with one of her officers, then said, "They're armed with the British Brimstone missiles. We've got laser guidance capability here on the ground and can guide them onto the target."

"Do it." The brimstones were a good missile, but he'd prefer a bunker buster right on Paul's head. Still, it was worth a try.

"The Italians will be furious we invaded their airspace," Bastien commented.

Gregorios waved toward Paul, who looked like he was enjoying all the attention. "They'll be fine if those missiles make a dent in his parade." He added over the group network, "Hold your fire until we have a plan."

His soldiers reluctantly obeyed. The Italian forces continued to fire, their faces locked in expressions of rage and terror.

Overhead, news helicopters gathered in ever-growing numbers, cameras rolling.

The carabinieri radio squawked and Gregorios put it to his ear. Another officer was ordering his forces to retreat, to take cover for air support. They were also calling in a raid.

"I've got an inbound aircraft," Gregorios warned the man. "Laser-guided, precision strike."

The commander hesitated before saying, "We'll take it."

It said a lot about the man's desperation that he'd accept a bomb strike in the center of St. Peter's Square.

Gregorios ordered, "Everyone double-time back up the road toward the Castel. I don't know what the Italians are launching, so let's give them some room."

His soldiers ran for the eastern end of the square and took shelter behind overturned trucks at the end of the Via della Conciliazione. Gregorios left them with Bastien and ran the other way, circling the southern end of the square toward the towering facade of the Basilica. He passed the retreating Italian forces, who were bearing away many wounded.

He caught sight of Spartacus and three heka fighters slipping into the Basilica, ignored since the arrival of Paul. Just as he suspected. Paul was a threat Gregorios could not contain without heavy weapons and a coordinated assault, but Spartacus was only a little less deadly.

He had hoped to turn the Thracian, but they'd missed their window. He couldn't allow Spartacus to remain at large, even though he was hunting those forbidden runes in the wrong place.

The news helicopters scattered. Paul looked up, but if he understood what that meant, he didn't look worried. Instead he drew a small knife from his belt and began marking an intricate rune onto his abdomen.

Gregorios shot the little knife out of his hand.

Looking irritated, Paul glanced in his direction. "I'll deal with you momentarily."

He continued cutting into his skin, using one of his own fingernails.

Gregorios shot him in the finger, but Paul ignored the bullet. So he shot him in the groin. Again the bullet ricocheted away, but Paul cast a disgusted look his way.

Gregorios waved. He couldn't defeat Paul, but maybe he could keep him distracted long enough for the big guns to arrive.

Scowling, Paul completed the rune. He worked with remarkable speed. The man was a master runesmith to rival the best of the hunters. The new rune on his stomach began to burn with blue-white light.

With a little smile for Gregorios, Paul threw his arms out wide.

"It appears you plan to be obstinate. You who could have enjoyed the blessed position of my first subjects will instead suffer my wrath in slavery."

Statues positioned atop the facade of the Basilica and the colonnades around the square began to move. They stood and flexed, as if awakening from a long sleep.

Gregorios grimaced. He'd seen the animation of dead objects before, but the runes were complex and could drain a single soulmask in seconds. Animating so many statues had to be burning through the soul force of thousands.

Master runes possessed tremendous power, somehow tapping into souls woven into history, but such a display of raw power still amazed him.

Gregorios wished he could guess how much energy remained available. From what he was seeing, Paul was accessing more power than any one person had ever wielded, and that changed the nature of the fight in ways that were still unclear.

There were one hundred and forty statues positioned above the colonnades alone, although several had been destroyed by the thrown obelisk. As Gregorios paused in the doorway to the Basilica, the newly-animated statues of popes, martyrs, and other religious figures jumped from the heights.

They landed with resounding crashes that echoed through the deserted square. The statues had looked impressive standing atop the sixty-foot colonnades, but were far more menacing at ground level. The ten-foot-tall statues might have represented saints, but the animated stone was now directed by evil incarnate.

"Some days just keep getting worse," he growled.

Gregorios shuddered to think what else Paul might be able to do.

More statues began pouring out of the Basilica, nearly trampling Gregorios. He dodged aside, feeling as helpless as a child in the face of Paul's power. He hadn't felt anything like it since he'd been bronzed and hung on Spartacus' wall.

They had to figure out how to break that rune, and fast.

First thing was to duck.

Fighter jets roared in from the east, straight up the Via della Concili-azione, over his crouching forces, and dropped bombs on the most famous square in all the world.

Gregorios slipped between two lumbering statues and into the Basilica just before the square was consumed by fire.

The shockwave rocked the foundations of the mighty Basilica and cracked the outer facade. The thunder left his ears ringing.

Flames poured through the entryway, forcing Gregorios deeper into the gigantic building, his exposed skin burned. Dust billowed around everything, tasting of charred stone and burning chemicals.

A second, smaller concussion rocked the square.

"Our brimstone run was a bust," Harriett said, not hiding her frus-tration.

Gregorios pushed through the gloom, back to the now-burning doorway. The square was a blackened ruin, littered with stone from shattered columns and broken statues. Craters pock-marked the once-smooth expanse.

Paul stood unscathed in the center of the square, surrounded by half a hundred animated statues, some of which looked cracked or partially broken. At least as many statues had shattered under the recent bombardment. Gregorios was disappointed so many had survived.

Paul's voice bellowed through the square again. "All nations and all religions shall bow to me. Let's start with the mother church so many of you groveling mortals link your faith to. Bring me the pope and those who lead this insurrection."

Statues scattered in every direction.

Gregorios retreated into the Basilica. He had to find the pope first and conceal him, then figure out how to respond to the newly proclaimed king of the world.

A hand tapped him on the shoulder. He spun and found Spartacus standing behind him.

"Greetings." Spartacus grinned, then punched him in the jaw.

The blow knocked Gregorios from his feet, but he embraced his nevra core and came up, hands burning with purple fire. He might not know how to deal with Paul, but he knew exactly what to do with Spartacus.

The other heka fighters who had entered the Basilica with Spartacus stood in a half-circle around Gregorios, weapons aimed at his heart.

Gregorios could take any of them easily, but he could never take them all before they destroyed his body. He stood in the midst of them, waiting for one of them to come just a little closer.

"You were always one of my most worthy adversaries." Spartacus retreated to stand with his men. Two tall statues entered the Basilica with strides that shook the ground and left cracks in the polished floor. "I am thinking you will not survive." He saluted with his sword. "Die today with honor."

As a statue with part of its face missing lumbered closer, Gregorios could see no way out of the situation. Eirene had better arrive fast with some bigger guns, or the day was about to get a lot worse.

"I'm not dead yet," he promised as the statue grabbed him by the collar of his tactical vest and lifted him off the ground. It carried him like a helpless child out of the Basilica and into the square toward the waiting Paul.

Across the square, he saw other statues returning with their prizes. Bastien had been collared, as had a couple of the Italian commanders. The Italian regulars had wisely retreated farther, some of them still firing futile shots.

"Retreat to more secure positions," Gregorios said into his throat mic. "Alter, get to Harriett and siphon as many of our men as you can."

"Do you think that'll help?" Alter asked.

Gregorios was relieved to hear his voice. He'd lost track of the young man in the fighting.

"Of course. Charge up, kid, and look for your chance. And find your useless brother."

Before Paul acquired his new greater rune, Alter had been the one best suited to take him down. If they could find a way to break through his rune, he still might be.

"Where's Sarah?"

"Almost there. I'm in the truck with Eirene."

"The heavy weapons aren't going to work," Gregorios said. "Paul just ignored both bombing runs. They didn't even tickle him. I'll try to send a photo of the rune. I'm about to get a close-up look at it."

"What do you expect me to do?" Her voice was tight with fear.

"Study hard, and hope those instincts of yours hold up." She and Alter together represented their best chance at defeating Paul.

If they failed, many of them wouldn't survive the day. He hated the idea of retreating and fighting a guerrilla campaign from the shadows while Paul consolidated his hold on the world, but they might not have a choice.

The statue stopped in front of Paul and held Gregorios out like a prize, his feet dangling a foot above the ground.

Paul gave him a superior smile. "Welcome. You get a front row seat to witness the inauguration of my new world order."

"Where's the popcorn?" Gregorios asked as he clicked the transmit button of the tiny video recorder integrated into his collar.

93

In the employ of the great Khan, I came and went, hither and thither, on the missions that were entrusted to me. Thus I visited a greater number of the different countries of the world than any other man not blessed with many lives.

In all my travels, I met some few heka, but no facetakers in that region. There were rumors of a great lady, one who may have even possessed the might of the cui dashi, but I discovered no ultimate veracity of the claims and must therefore suppose they are nothing but distant rumors of an ancient legend.

~MARCO POLO REPORTING TO SHAHROKH, 1298

GREGORIOS HATED DANGLING from the statue's grip like a mouse held by a cat, but he held still for the best video. It only lasted a few seconds before Paul turned and motioned to a statue holding the struggling form of an Italian carabinieri captain.

"Will you bow to me and swear the fealty of you and your men?" Paul asked.

The man shook with fear, his skin pale and eyes wide with terror. "I cannot make a pledge for everyone. But if you'll give me some time—"

With a casual snatching motion, Paul ripped out the man's soulmask.

Gregorios had never seen a soul dispossessed so fast. The empty body collapsed at Paul's feet and the dispossessed captain shrieked, his helium-high voice cracking with fear.

Paul marked a complex rune onto the shimmering cheek of the soulmask, and the man's voice faded to whimpers. Gregorios leaned closer. The rune was built around a central symbol for shielding.

As the rune began to glow, fueled by the doomed captain, a shimmering, golden barrier rose around the outer edge of the square, forming a half-sphere dome over the entire expanse.

The only openings Paul left were on the west side over the doorway into the Basilica, and on the north, at the breach in the colonnade where his remaining heka were positioned.

The shield's vast size was remarkable. The enforcers had dabbled with personal shields, but they drained too much of the soldiers' energy, leaving them protected, but lethargic. Paul was burning through astonishing rates of power, as if he enjoyed a never-ending supply.

Perhaps that was a weakness they could exploit? If Paul pushed hard enough, something had to give eventually, and in that moment he'd be vulnerable. Gregorios had no idea how long before that moment arrived, though.

Paul didn't bother fine-tuning the shield to deal with all the rubble. Gregorios spotted several gaps along the edges. Not big enough for a person to crawl through, but plenty wide for weapons or explosives to be driven through and triggered. Then again, none of that would interfere with Paul anyway.

Seconds after the shield went up, a vague thumping rhythm sounded through the barrier. The shield was semi-transparent and Gregorios made out the forms of a dozen attack helicopters.

The missiles they surely carried wouldn't do much against Paul, but were more than enough to reduce everyone and everything else to slag.

Soldiers were visible standing atop the southern colonnade and the outer edges of the northern colonnade. The heka fighters had secured the central, breached section of the northern colonnade and no one seemed ready to challenge them for it.

"The world will not bow to a single man," one of the other commanders said. He managed his fear better than the last man had, but still spoke in a hushed tone.

Paul chuckled. "Of course they will, and we will begin with the obeisance of one of the world's leading religious figures."

Gregorios hoped the Swiss Guard had gotten the Pope well away before Paul's animated statues tracked him down.

They hadn't.

Three minutes later, the statues of four previous popes returned to the square from the Basilica, one of them carrying the aged form of Pope Andrew Paul the First.

Gunfire and shouting followed the statues into the square, and two of them turned back to the door. Haggard-looking members of the Swiss Guard rushed through, firing at the granite kidnappers and hacking at them with ancient halberds.

The statues swatted men aside and chased the rest back into the Basilica. They returned to the square, but positioned themselves flanking the entrance.

Spartacus strode through and approached, an angry frown on his face. Gregorios nearly laughed. The gladiator had less to be angry about than most.

Paul made a mock bow to the pope when the statue deposited the pontiff on the ground in front of him. "Thank you for granting an audience."

Pope Andrew Paul straightened his twisted robes and did an admirable job of maintaining his dignity in the face of Paul's overwhelming presence. Gregorios thought it interesting that Paul had chosen a name so similar to the pope's. Had he done that on purpose?

The pope glanced at the broken square, the shimmering shield barrier, and the animated statues, and stood a little taller. "You have desecrated a holy place."

"It will remain holy if I say so. Or it will be razed to the ground, should I choose."

The pope paled. "Repent of this evil before your soul is lost."

Paul smiled. "I am better aware of the state of my soul than any mortal. Don't waste words. I am now the supreme leader of all people, and you will proclaim to the world my divine right to rule."

The pope gaped. "Get behind me, Satan. You think just because I spout a few lies that the world will fail see the deception?"

Paul shrugged. "Mortals need justification. It makes accepting reality easier. Until today, they accepted the lies of your religion. The reality of my majesty will be far easier to accept."

"Faith is assurance of that which is not seen. You are not some kind of god-king, and you never will be."

Paul sighed. "You are supposed to be a pious man, the rare pontiff with more faith than political ambition. And yet, I trust you're an intelligent man too."

"I will not support your pretense of approval from God."

"We'll see about that." Instead of ripping the man's arms off like he had the soldier's, he turned to Spartacus. "Where are those runes you promised me?"

"I checked Otto's tomb in the lower levels. They weren't there." He turned to Gregorios. "You lied to me."

Gregorios shrugged. "What did you expect? You're the enlightened one."

"Tell him," Paul ordered.

Instead, Gregorios asked, "What do you need with more runes? Looks to me like you've got about as much as you can handle."

"That's for me to decide. Did you know those so-called forbidden runes are referred to by these superstitious mortals as the manifestation of the glorious power of the Almighty God?"

"I did, actually."

"Do you know why?"

"No." It was supremely annoying to think Paul might know something he didn't.

Paul sauntered closer. "Those runes, when powered by enough lives, grant the same miracles one reads in the scriptures of these fools."

"That would be a neat trick," Gregorios agreed.

Paul's plan finally made sense. Throwing around a few fake miracles and coercing the pope into proclaiming him divinely approved, would offer sufficient justification for some to swear allegiance.

Some would come to Paul out of fear. Others out of the hopes of acquiring a position of power in his new regime. The rest he would enslave by force. The ones who weren't sure could use the justification of divine appointment to give in to the new rule with less damage to their consciences.

Gregorios was surprised the church hadn't simply destroyed those runes centuries ago. The pope's shock seemed genuine. He probably hadn't even known about them.

Gregorios had known enough popes through the ages. Many of them had aspired to the high office for political gain more than out of religious zealousness.

No doubt those who had known about the runes had kept them around in case they needed a handy miracle. It had happened more than once, although the practice had waned in recent centuries.

The information made Gregorios less interested in granting those runes to Paul than ever. If the runes really did mimic divine powers, he'd love seeing the cui dashi covered in boils or other biblical plagues. Fire from heaven might just be the ticket they needed to defeat him.

"Tell me where the runes are concealed," Paul ordered, sounding impatient.

"If I refuse?" Gregorios asked.

"Then either you witness your son die before your eyes." Paul gestured toward Bastien, "Or you sacrifice His Holiness here to the scrying rune I'll use to find them."

Gregorios had never heard of anyone finding much success with scrying runes, particularly when hunting for other runes. Heka tried that trick every generation or so and usually only managed to find a bunch of hunters or enforcers on their doorsteps after the attempt. But, if anyone could make it work, it'd be Paul.

Even though divine power did exist, Gregorios wasn't religious. Faith and nevra core were incompatible forces.

Besides, he'd known too many leaders of religions to be less than devout. Unfortunately, the current pope was a man he actually respected. Sacrificing the pontiff or even his own son to keep Paul away from those forbidden runes a few minutes longer wasn't going to change things much.

He hoped Sarah had gotten his video feed. They needed a counter rune.

"All right. I'll make a deal with you."

Paul lunged, gripping Gregorios' face with fingers stronger than industrial vises. "No deals. I command. You obey. Prove to me you're as smart as legend claims and live another minute."

Absolute power made Paul an absolute jerk.

Gregorios tried to say, "Okay," but only managed an incoherent mumble.

Paul released his face, that smug smile on his lips again. "I knew I could count on you."

Gregorios forced back a wisecrack. "The runes really were on Otto's tomb. The stone was moved again, though. It now forms the base of the baptistery."

Pope Andrew Paul gasped. "You can't be serious. That's blasphemy."

"Probably more than that." Gregorios would leave the ethical and moral ramifications of mixing forbidden runes with religious ordinances up to the Pope.

Spartacus saluted and headed for the Basilica. The three heka fighters who had made it into the massive building along with him stood in the doorway, waiting for him.

Then they didn't.

The ground exploded under their feet, catapulting the screaming heka into the plaza. The two statue guards stepped into the entryway in time to catch more explosive rounds in the chest. Multiple blasts rocked them back, so fast they had to be fired from a repeating mortar.

Eirene stepped into the doorway, a smoking automatic grenade launcher in her hands. Her hair had come out of the braid she usually wore into battle, and a stray lock floated around the face he'd loved for two thousand years.

She was gorgeous.

Eirene shouted, "Spartacus, you owe me a final duel."

Gregorios waved. "Hi, Honey! You're late."

94

The Almighty fought by our side, and the power of his spirit was manifest through the strength of my ciphers. My men fought like lions and shed mortal injuries. Truly, we have been blessed above all measure.

~JOAN OF ARC, RUNE WARRIOR

SARAH STOOD on the east side of St. Peter's Square, at the end of the Via della Conciliazione, surrounded by enhanced fighters. Despite the firepower all around, she felt vulnerable, and struggled to look confident instead of terrified.

She finished inscribing a battle cipher onto a piece of rubble and handed it to a waiting soldier. She glanced through the shimmering barrier of Paul's shield and focused on her anger at Paul for wrecking such a beautiful place. It helped a little to drive back the fear.

Eirene spoke calmly into her earpiece. "I'm in position. Make your move."

Sarah silently wished Eirene success. The memory of Spartacus driving his spear into her chest in the memoryscape passed through Sarah's mind. If they messed up here, there'd be no quick healing option.

Sarah said, "Alter, begin your assault. I'll have the ciphers in position before your attack. I'm hoping they'll weaken Paul the moment you strike."

She didn't dare explain to him that she planned to redirect the power that she stole from Paul to strengthen Alter instead. She needed him focused, not spouting about abomination. Besides, even if Alter accepted the need for the siphoned power, no doubt Reuben would not.

She glanced to her right where Alter moved into the northern colonnade, flanked by hunters and two dozen volunteers from the Tenth.

Reuben and the hunters had approached their lines a moment ago, for once willing to work together. Knowledge of the full scope of what she planned could easily break the new-forged alliance, and Sarah couldn't allow that.

If they all survived, Reuben could get as indignant as he pleased. That would give her the excuse to beat him to a pulp.

Sarah turned to the four Yurak fighters holding the ciphers she had just completed. "Get to your places."

The first cipher held the standard counter rune, which she hoped would help block some of Paul's connection to the master runes. The second cipher was built upon a rune of confusion, the third around a rune of weakness, radiating strength away from the soul. The fourth included modifiers to focus and magnify the effects of the others.

As they scattered to positions around the square, Alter's voice spoke into her earpiece. "Are you sure this'll work?"

"You saw how complex his rune is. Of course I'm not sure, but it's the best shot we've got."

"I trust you," he said.

Sarah silently cursed him. If things went badly, which was likely, and he got hurt, she'd never forgive herself. She silently wished Tomas and his team would arrive.

"Eirene, we're commencing our attack," she announced.

"Good luck," Eirene whispered. "Who said there were no arenas left?"

Sarah swallowed a lump in her throat as she peered through the shimmering shield at Eirene descending the steps toward Spartacus.

Most gladiators only gained glory and honor by dying.

Rome has fallen! Hallelujah! The seat of the demon council may be at Constantinople today, but I rejoice to see their historical stronghold humbled. So far, our raiders find no evidence of facetaker presence in the city, but I led the cleansing of the temple of Quirinus and oversaw the execution of five kashaph priests.

~RAANAN, HUNTER ADVISER TO GENSERIC, KING OF THE
VANDALS, SACKING OF ROME, 455 A.D.

SPARTACUS DROPPED his rifle and drew his gladius as Eirene descended the steps. She was tempted to pump fifty rounds of high explosives into his leather kilt, but they needed the distraction of the duel. Besides, if she could get her hands on him, she could remove him from Tomas' battle suit.

"You are my most-honored enemy," Spartacus said with a little bow of respect. "And yet on this day, I would that I did not need to shed your blood. You are one of the few who know my day and can understand me. It is a shame you must die."

"Don't get sentimental on me." Eirene was surprised by a feeling of compassion for the man she had hated for almost two thousand years. "And don't fool yourself. You've never killed me before, and today I'm not feeling generous."

Spartacus lifted his arms and spun a slow circle. "To honor our singular and glorious rivalry, we meet in final combat. This arena is a worthy venue."

"They say saints and martyrs are buried around here," Eirene said, dropping her gun and producing her own gladius. "I suppose they won't mind if a villain dies here too."

Spartacus grinned and saluted. "Honor and glory to the victor."

Eirene saluted. "Honor and glory."

The two closed with a rush, gladius blades ringing through the ruined plaza.

Yes, Constantinople fell. The Sultan's enhanced Janissaries finally won through. I confess that to survive, I revealed my rounon gift to the Cretans with whom I defended the last tower. Desperation is wed to deed, and they accepted enhancements that enabled us to hold.

Mehmet recognized the price in blood required to remove us and instead granted us free passage. He believed I was kashaph and even offered employment. Had I accepted, I might have won access to his enchanters, but at what cost to my soul?

~MAOR, HUNTER MERCENARY, 1453

ALTER PEERED between columns of the northern colonnade, not far from the kashaph positions.

Piles of rubble separated the groups, offering excellent cover. The kashaph weren't even posting guards, but were focused on the duel in the square.

They were positioned just outside of the shield dome. The web that had protected them with near-invincibility had been destroyed by Tomas, leaving them vulnerable. They did not seem to care, content to trust in their leader's invincible prowess to keep them safe.

He was happy to educate them.

Alter raised his assault rifle and triggered the M203 grenade launcher under the barrel. He spoke softly into his throat mic. "Fire."

The grenade made its characteristic whumping sound as it fired out the tube under his rifle barrel.

The shot went slightly high, exploding against a broken pillar just behind a kashaph's head. The explosion still ripped him apart and sent his companions tumbling.

"That one's for my father," Alter whispered as he rushed forward.

Hunters and soldiers from the Tenth opened fire with grenades, hollow-point rounds, and electro-shock bullets to cover his advance. The withering fire cut down all the exposed kashaph in a matter of seconds.

Alter leaped through the drifting smoke of the detonations and fired a full-auto burst into the torso of a kashaph who stumbled out from behind a column right in front of him.

The fighter went down, a bloody mess. Alter verified he wasn't wearing a soul pack with dispossessed souls to fuel his runes.

As soldiers moved through the wreckage, engaging the remaining kashaph, Alter shifted to the innermost row of columns, right on the edge of the shimmering dome shield, and peeked inside. Reuben dropped to one knee beside him.

Their quarrel was far from resolved, but Alter exulted in this chance to fight at his brother's side. He'd dreamed of this all his life, but despaired of ever experiencing it.

No matter what came next, he offered a prayer of thanks that they shared this moment, fighting the enemies of righteousness together.

As expected, the attack had drawn Paul's attention from Eirene's duel. Alter no longer felt the tug of conflicting loyalties as he wished his great-grandmother good fortune in removing the ancient kashaph's soulmask.

Paul gestured toward the opening, and a dozen statues, now his stone guard, lumbered toward the fighting.

"Ready brother?" Reuben asked with a laugh as he hefted a bulky MK19 automatic grenade launcher and propped it into position on its tripod legs.

Alter popped open a box of ammo positioned by another hunter and fed the belt of high explosive rounds into the chamber. "Locked and loaded."

Reuben opened fire.

At fifty feet, the approaching statues were hard to miss. Three other grenade launchers flanking their position opened fire at almost the same time, raining explosive destruction upon the ancient marble statues. The painstakingly-carved likenesses of holy men shattered under the punishing barrage.

Four statues made it all the way to the gap in the shield. Reuben took one out with a round that exploded so close to them that the backblast knocked Alter off his feet. The other three pushed into the colonnade and descended upon the hunters and soldiers of the Tenth with brutal savagery.

Alter longed to leap upon a statue's back and blow its head off, but had to trust his men to do it. Instead, he raced into the square.

Inside the shield, he could feel Paul's power filling the enclosed space, thrumming like a high-voltage wire. The sheer magnitude of it left him trembling.

He had siphoned three dozen soldiers in the last minutes, dispossessing souls faster with every one. Harriett and Francesca reconstituted the souls for him so he didn't have to slow. His soul felt engorged with energy he'd siphoned from these willing, enhanced soldiers, making him feel invincible.

Now he felt vulnerable and scared.

"Sarah, do it now!" he shouted as he raced toward Paul.

This was their chance, the moment he'd prepared for all his life. He would defeat this abomination who dared declare himself ruler of the world. Even Alter's family would see his purity after this.

Reuben ran beside him and made a point of not looking when Alter embraced his nevra core and his hands began to burn with purple fire.

Paul shot across the square toward them with inhuman speed, ten times faster than Alter could run.

Reuben shot him in the face.

He had left the grenade launcher behind, and now carried a specialty weapon recently developed by Quentin and only reluctantly handed over by Francesca. Instead of bullets, it sprayed sticky foam similar to the suppressant material used by their custom fire trucks.

Paul skidded to a halt, pawing at the sticky mess. He had stood unaffected through a bombing run, mortar fire, and countless bullets that ricocheted off his enhanced skin, but simple foam stymied him for a few precious seconds.

Alter leaped, burning hands outstretched.

The foam melted off Paul's face and he caught Alter, snatching him out of the air like a dog snapping at a frisbee.

That was the second time someone had manhandled him that day, and it enraged Alter. He pawed at Paul's face, but the cui dashi's hands were already burning.

His entire torso was rippling with silver light, and the touch of it scattered Alter's nevron. He tried to concentrate, one finger actually touching a precious soul point on Paul's hated face.

Paul laughed and his nevron ripped into Alter, crushing his fledgling soul force with the weight of three master runes.

Alter screamed and beat at Paul's hands. No longer did he fight to defeat the cui dashi, but scrambled ineffectually to escape the abomination's grasp.

Paul could kill him with the twitch of his wrist, but instead he chose to torment him.

Reuben had retreated from the struggle, dropped his useless foam gun, and drew a grenade. Alter tried to shout at him to stop, but couldn't make more than a choked gurgling sound.

Their eyes met, and Reuben's held no regret as he threw the grenade that could never hope to hurt Paul. It would certainly kill Alter. Maybe that was his way of offering a final mercy?

Alter didn't appreciate it.

Paul swatted the grenade out of the air. It tumbled across the square and landed close to Eirene. The blast knocked her from her feet.

Spartacus glared, then shrugged and rushed past the still-disoriented Eirene into the Basilica.

As Alter struggled to suck in a little air through his bruised neck, he kept waiting for Sarah's cipher to strike, but it never did.

Then she spoke over the comm, her voice worried. "It's not working! Something's blocking it."

"Has to be the shielding," Gregorios said, sounding far too calm.

"I need to get closer," she shouted.

Alter despaired. She would never make it in time. He was going to die and the cui dashi monster would remain free to enslave Sarah, body and soul.

With a snarl of defiance, Alter struggled on. He would not allow that to happen.

He glanced toward his brother, hoping for help. Reuben had retreated from Paul and drew his knife.

Paul laughed. "You amuse me, hunter. Do you think to hurt me with that little blade?"

Reuben tugged up his sleeve and began carving into his forearm. "This blade is stronger than you think."

"Prove it." Paul actually waited, watching Reuben mark a new rune. He eased his hold enough for Alter to breathe a little.

"Run, brother," Alter gasped, his voice barely a whisper.

No matter how pure Reuben's soul, he couldn't hope to stand against the sheer might that Paul now commanded.

"I will not run again," Reuben snarled.

Alter recognized the rune he was carving and choked out a protest. "You can't, brother. It is forbidden."

"You embrace abomination in the name of glory. Don't preach to me," Reuben spat.

Paul laughed. "You would use a forbidden rune to fight me?"

"I will," Reuben said, the rune nearly complete.

Alter struggled harder. This couldn't be happening. Reuben had been the greatest hunter in a generation, but his long dispossession had broken something deep inside of him.

Alter understood his desire to defeat Paul, but that rune would never lead to victory. It was forbidden because it was a rune of domination, of destruction, and of conquest. It corrupted the soul and embraced only the basest of motivations.

Reuben completed the rune and it flared instantly, but not with the normal pure, blue-white light. Instead it burned a sickly yellow, a festering sore on Reuben's arm.

Reuben snarled, "I will destroy you, abomination."

Paul laughed. "I like your spirit, boy, but I have a better idea."

"Don't," Alter panted. He couldn't get enough breath.

Paul shook him so hard his neck creaked and his spine would've cracked if he hadn't been enhanced. The cui dashi considered him for a second and a devious smile twisted his lips.

He threw Alter away, so hard he bounced off the shield barrier just above the north opening. Groaning, he staggered to his feet, trying to shake off the effects of the brutal impact.

Reuben was lunging at Paul, blade slashing for his throat.

Paul struck so fast his hand blurred, punching Reuben off his feet. Paul caught Reuben out of the air and carved several more marks into the forbidden rune on his arm.

Alter rushed toward them, knowing he would arrive everlastingly too late. The forbidden rune alone could corrupt a pure heart, but Paul was intensifying it into demonic abomination.

Reuben screamed as the rune flared, glowing black against his skin, its lines crawling around each other. He fell to the ground, writhing as the new rune tortured his soul and bent it to Paul's will.

Paul intercepted Alter before he could reach his brother and threw him back against the northern barrier a second time.

Alter coughed blood and groaned as he struggled to his feet. His body ached, every muscle crying from the abuse.

Defeating Paul no longer mattered. He needed to save his brother.

Paul was lifting Reuben to his feet. Alter's brother was breathing fast, his face flushed, his eyes wild, the knife clutched to his chest.

"Good," Paul chuckled. "Now my one true hunter, you will conquer and you will kill."

Reuben nodded, quivering with anticipation.

Paul glanced toward Alter and his smile became sinister. "Go, my slave. Kill every hunter you can find. Kill every innocent woman and child in the city."

He winked at Alter. "But first, kill your brother."

Reuben howled, a sound of animal lust, and bounded toward Alter, the knife already raised to strike.

97

Some days I envy the simple fools we slaughter. Their fears are immediate and tangible.

At first I loved the power granted by my two enhancements. I fight like Hercules himself, and I'll admit I dreamed of one day ascending to similar fame.

The more I learn, the more I see the true dangers of the world, and I want less of glory and only the chance of a simple life and a good woman in my bed. Such dreams are folly, for we will all die on the field of battle, grasping for the honor Spartacus alone can see.

~CASTUS, ONE OF SPARTACUS'S LIEUTENANTS DURING
THE THIRD SERVILE WAR

GREGORIOS STRUGGLED in vain against the grip of the statue holding him. He'd tried slipping out of his tactical vest, but the animated stone had shifted its grip and wrapped its huge fingers all the way around his shoulder.

He hadn't heard the full plan before Eirene and Alter initiated it, but it was clearly falling apart.

Eirene didn't look badly hurt by the grenade, but Spartacus had made a break for the forbidden runes. Eirene shook off her stupor and followed, glancing back once at Gregorios.

He got the message. Time to stop hanging around.

On the north side of the square, Paul was still distracted by the fight between the warped Reuben and the desperate Alter. For a moment, Gregorios had allowed himself to hope Alter would break Paul's hold, somehow shatter his power with Sarah's help, but that moment was gone.

Hopefully she could activate her ciphers once she reached the northern breach. Alter needed all the help he could get.

Reuben had closed on him with all the subtlety of an avalanche. Alter had knocked the knife out of his hand and they were fighting each other now, brother against brother.

Alter looked tired, frantic. He could have disabled Reuben a couple of times, but he was holding back, shouting his brother's name, trying to break through his insanity.

It wasn't going to work.

The distraction was one Gregorios couldn't afford to miss. He extracted from a pocket of his vest a roll of breaching strip. The high explosive, wrapped into an adhesive an inch wide, was long enough to wrap twice around the statue's wrist. The dumb animated slave didn't pay it any attention.

It would in ten seconds.

Bastien mimicked Gregorios movements. In unison, they set the detonators, together they triggered the blasts.

The concussion shattered the statue's arm and threw Gregorios bodily away. He severed connection to his screaming nerves. The body still worked, so he ignored the minor injuries and sprinted toward the door of the Basilica. Bastien followed close on his heels.

The statues gave chase, but he was faster. He did risk a single glance backward. Alter had knocked Reuben down and was crouched over him, burning hands driven into Reuben's face. His shoulders convulsed and he removed his brother's soulmask.

Holding the dispossessed soul aloft, rainbow streamers caressing his wrists, Alter howled with despair.

Poor kid had serious family issues.

Paul clapped, laughing.

Gregorios raced into the Basilica after Eirene.

"Do we have a plan?" Bastien asked.

"Stop Spartacus," Gregorios growled.

"After that?"

"I'm thinking it's time to call down the fires of heaven."

98

Cowards die many times before their actual deaths, but I will live many times before mine.

~JULIUS CAESAR

SARAH RUSHED to the last column before reaching the opening in Paul's shield on the north side of the square.

Huge chunks of broken stone and wreckage of the once-beautiful colonnade surrounded her. Hunters and soldiers of the Tenth flanked her on every side, their faces reflecting the same horror she felt at witnessing Alter's duel with his brother.

Some of the soldiers had moved to intervene, but Sarah had waved them back. Paul could slaughter every one of them if he chose.

"Wait. If I can weaken him, that's the time to strike."

Her heart was beating so fast she felt lightheaded and short of breath. Terror set her hands shaking so bad she could barely pull up the photo of Paul's rune that Francesca had forwarded from Gregorios' video feed.

It was magnificent, but malevolent. Paul had incorporated the central components of all three master runes, but had twisted those glorious runes to conquest and destruction. If only she had hours to study it, to figure out how to defeat it.

She spent five more seconds poring over it, then tucked her phone away. She couldn't wait.

Alter had stumbled away from his brother's dispossessed body,

Reuben's soulmask clutched in his still-burning hands, tears streaking his cheeks. It must have been torture to use his hated cui dashi powers against his brother.

It was Paul's fault, and Sarah planned to make him pay.

She stepped past the column, into the opening, buttressing her courage by thoughts of all the innocents who would die if she failed.

She wished Tomas was there.

"Prepare to insert ciphers under the shield on my signal," she spoke into her throat mic."

"Roger," came a chorus of replies, followed by Harriett's fierce, "Go get him, Sarah!"

Alter caught sight of her and shouted, "No, Sarah! Get away!"

He rushed toward her, but Paul intercepted him in the blink of an eye and snatched him off the ground like a mother scooping up an infant.

"Stop doing that!" Alter shouted, beating ineffectually at Paul's arm.

Paul glowed with such intensity, Sarah had to squint. The blazing runes on his chest and stomach were only part of the brilliance.

His entire being glowed, similar to the soft glow that had surrounded Rosetta in the ruined Circus Maximus, but magnified a thousand times. Paul wasn't surrounded by the effects of a rune web, but was infused to bursting with the power of the master runes he'd tapped. Sarah marveled that he could contain it.

"I enjoyed the show," Paul said to Alter. "You've earned a seat at the main event while Sarah declares her devotion to me."

"Never!" Alter shouted.

"All the shouting and useless objections get old." Paul gave Alter a disappointed look and tossed him to a nearby statue.

More of the animated carvings had marched out of the Basilica after the hunters had blown up the last batch. There was a nearly inexhaustible supply for Paul to draw from in the Basilica and surrounding areas. The statue caught the hunter and cuffed him in the side of the head so hard he stopped struggling.

Sarah gripped a small stone concealed in her palm. It was the key cipher, the one to link all the others and hopefully crack Paul's power.

The rune he was using drew upon the strength of the master runes, but they had to be fueled by remnants of the force of the souls that had united in those moments. That meant his rune must share the same weaknesses, could be interrupted in a similar way.

She could feel the power of his runes pulsing through the square, so thick it was almost tangible. Could her little ciphers really affect a change? She'd planned to redirect all that strength to Alter, but he didn't look capable of using it.

Paul motioned her forward, his eyes lingering hungrily on her. "Welcome, Sarah. Your timing is impeccable."

He gestured toward the pope, who stood flanked by the statues of holy men in the center of the square and his lips curled into an amused smile. "Come. The pope can witness you swearing loyalty to me."

"I don't want you hurting people," Sarah said as she followed him toward the pontiff.

"I gave everyone here the option of accepting me as merciful. They chose a different path."

"You've made your point. You don't have to hurt anyone else."

"Soon I won't have to. The world will see your wise choice, and they will witness my miracles and the pope's blessing."

"I will not bless you," the pope promised.

"Then perhaps a new pope is needed," Paul said, as if he didn't care either way.

"Though I walk through the valley of the shadow of death—" the pope recited.

Paul waved him to silence. "Pray later. My runes have arrived."

Spartacus entered the square from the Basilica, carrying a huge red stone shaped like a long basin. Gregorios, Eirene, and Bastien followed, herded by three statues. All three facetakers looked battered, and the statues looked worn, but Sarah's heart sank when she saw them beaten, prisoner to Paul's will.

Spartacus lay the stone on the ground and turned it over, revealing scarlet cloth taped across two sections. He gestured at the larger of the two areas. "Those are your runes. Thus is my honor debt fulfilled."

Paul lifted the stone in one hand and turned it away from Sarah. He pulled back the cloth and his eyes lit with excitement as he studied the forbidden runes.

Sarah despaired. Despite all their efforts, Paul was getting stronger. She glanced toward Gregorios, but was surprised to see he didn't look sad.

He winked at her.

99

Today we witnessed the revealed will of the Almighty God! The cursed Saladin and his tens of thousands could not stand against our tiny army.

My body is racked with disease, but the healing rune is helping, thanks to the grace of God and your skills. I will embrace the grave when that day soon comes, happy to have stood with your mighty Templars against the enhanced Mamluks. God is on our side, and I thank him daily for sending the hunters to teach you. Ever I am your enthusiastic friend.

~LETTER FROM KING BALDWIN IV TO ODO DE ST.
AMAND, MASTER OF KNIGHTS OF THE TEMPLARS, AFTER
THE BATTLE OF MONTGISARD, NOVEMBER 25, 1177

THE FACETAKERS MOVED TOGETHER, with impressive speed.

Bastien shoved a grenade into a gap in the flowing stone robes of the statue hovering over him. He must have already pulled the pin because the grenade exploded barely a second later, cracking the statue's torso and toppling it to the broken cobblestones.

Eirene gave Gregorios a passionate kiss, burning hands gripping his face, her eyes blazing more brightly with her nevron than Sarah had ever seen.

The short kiss was punctuated by the nearby explosion, then Eirene collapsed to the ground. Gregorios threw his head back and laughed, purple fire rolling up his arms to the elbow. It looked like Eirene had shared the full measure of her strength with him.

As the other two nearby statues converged on him, Gregorios lunged to meet them. Burning hands lashed out, and at his touch, the statues froze, then toppled to the ground, again nothing but inanimate objects.

Sarah gaped. She'd known facetakers could interrupt heka enhancements if they could get their hands on an enhanced fighter. She hadn't known they could break such a powerful, remote rune.

"Get on it, girl!" Gregorios shouted to Sarah as he rushed Paul, whose amused expression was turning to annoyance.

"Do you think this is a game?" Paul snapped, knocking Gregorios aside, then sending Bastien tumbling with a backhand strike.

"I thought you were joking about the whole god-emperor thing," Gregorios said, rolling back to his feet and facing him.

Paul glared. "Your insolence is going to cost you this time, Gregorios. I thought you were smarter."

"Old dogs. New tricks." Gregorios shrugged. "Bad combination."

He glanced at Sarah again. She had already scratched two additional marks on her cipher stone and now willed it to life with her whole soul.

The cipher blazed to blue-white life. Energy rushed out of her to fuel it and she sagged to her knees, exulting.

She could feel the energy erupt out of the newly-activated cipher, linking to the four other ciphers slipped under holes in the irregular shield dome, then locking onto Gregorios' fiery nevron.

The Pope crouched beside Sarah, offering a supportive hand, but his gaze was locked on Gregorios' burning hands. Twice he raised a hand as if to make a warding cross.

The weight of energy generated by Paul's rune that had been pressing against Sarah ever since she entered the square shifted. It was like an eddy in a stagnant body of water rippled away from Paul toward Gregorios.

Paul coughed and stumbled, a groan escaping his lips as he swayed where he stood. The blinding light infusing him faded, and some of that brilliance shifted to Gregorios.

The facetaker swelled with power, the fire of his hands taking on a deeper hue. He drew a long fighting knife and lunged, moving as fast as Paul had a moment earlier.

Paul grabbed for him, but his speed was far slower than before. Gregorios knocked his hand aside and drove his knife against Paul's neck.

The blade bit into the flesh.

It only cut the skin, but that was more than any weapon had done before. With a heart-stopping battle cry, Gregorios struck again and again. The blade drove deeper every time, and Paul's life blood sprayed out over the square.

Sarah shouted along with him, her strength rebounding, and she jumped to her feet.

Paul didn't fall, despite gushing blood. He caught Gregorios' arm and they wrestled over the knife. Even though Sarah's cipher was stealing so much energy, Paul's wounds still healed in seconds.

Paul glanced toward Sarah and for the first time he looked truly angry. "You will suffer."

A nearby statue dove at Sarah. The move caught her by surprise, and it swept her off her feet. The two of them crashed to the ground together, and the heavy statue nearly flattened her.

Bastien leaped to help, but the statue wrapped one giant hand around Sarah's and crushed her fingers against the cipher stone.

Sarah beat at it as pain flared in her fingers. She was immensely strong, but lacked the proper leverage, and the statue possessed super-human strength. It crushed the stone to powder inside of Sarah's palm.

"Go help your father," Sarah shouted to Bastien, who was beating on the statue's head. He nodded and turned away.

As soon as it completed its task, the statue eased its hold. That was all the opening Sarah needed. She yanked her hand out of its grasp and wrapped her hands around its head. With a convulsive heave, she ripped its head off.

She kicked the twitching statue away, but the few seconds she'd wasted were far too long.

The rush of energy fueling Gregorios expired, leaving him vulnerable. Paul's godlike strength returned and he snatched the knife out of Gregorios' hand.

With remarkable speed, he cut into his own arm the counter rune. Sarah, who had been planning to reactivate her rune, despaired. The counter rune would nullify her attempt to siphon his power again.

"Sarah," Bastien shouted as he closed on Paul. "Help him!"

Paul kicked Gregorios aside and spun on Bastien, punching the facetaker in the throat.

As Bastien gagged, Paul ripped his shirt off, spun him around, and raised the knife over his exposed back.

"Your father's nevra core is needed to fuel my mother's eternal glory, but I gave her the slave John and she took his power already. She won't mind if I harvest yours."

Bastien tried to struggle, but Paul easily overpowered him. The cui dashi slashed down, tearing deep into Bastien's back, carving a rune into his flesh with savage strokes.

Gregorios charged in, handgun firing, but Paul swatted him aside and continued working.

Sarah tried to think of a rune to override the counter rune and to weaken Paul again, but her mind was blank, her eyes fixed on the bloody knife in Paul's hand.

"I told you this wasn't a joke," Paul said, his tone chiding. His calm demeanor only made the savage thrusts of the knife more horrific.

Sarah decided she had to mark her rune onto Paul himself. It was the only thing she could think of that might overpower his blocking rune.

She charged Paul, who was completing some kind of binding rune on Bastien's back. There was so much blood, the full scope of the design was hard to read.

"Thus you are bound to me and to your fate," Paul declared.

"Stop!" Sarah screamed, still two leaping strides away.

Paul yanked Bastien erect and drove the knife into his stomach, plunging it past the hilt, up into his heart.

Bastien convulsed and for an instant his eyes burned with the strength of his nevron. His gaze locked with Sarah's and she saw his fear, his bitter defeat, and his unbearable pain.

She stumbled to a halt, unable to move, holding Bastien's gaze in silent support as the light faded from his eyes.

He did not abandon his host.

Sarah had not expected him to. Somehow Paul had bound him to death.

She sagged to her knees, weeping. Bastien had been so honorable, such a good man. He didn't deserve to die like that.

"No," Eirene gasped, stirring on the ground. "Oh, no."

Paul tossed the corpse aside and sighed with satisfaction. "That was refreshing."

He glanced at Eirene and said, "Get used to addressing me from your knees. I am your emperor. I own your souls now."

Gregorios didn't scream, didn't cry. The fires had faded along his hands, and he sagged with exhaustion. He looked from Bastien to Paul with murder in his eyes as more statues closed in. One of them raised a foot over Eirene, and the threat was clear. Any more resistance, and they'd crush her.

Paul turned his back on them and faced Sarah. He spoke in a voice that shook the square and drove absolute terror into her heart.

"Now that the pleasantries are over, it's your turn. Bow to me, Sarah. Bind your soul to my service and accept your destiny as my favored slave."

100

The mind is not a vessel to be filled, but a fire to be kindled.

~PLUTARCH

SARAH'S EYES lingered on Bastien's body, but his soulmask still did not emerge. Paul really had managed to murder him, a man who had lived for centuries. A man who had trusted her to help.

She had failed him.

Anger fueled her resolve, and she rose to face Paul, brushing aside her tears.

She had tried. The cipher had worked. They'd been so close! She wanted to howl with frustration. If only she'd managed to dodge that statue. Gregorios had only needed another few seconds to finish it.

Paul said soothingly, "Don't fight it any more, Sarah. Coming here was the right choice. Submitting willingly to me will spare many lives." His expression hardened. "But submit you will. You are now mine."

Standing so close, his blazing rune drew her gaze. It generated raw heat and would no doubt sear her skin if she touched it.

It was masterful art, and yet it was corrupted. Its lines burned into her vision as its heat dried the tears on her cheeks.

"Swear devotion to me," Paul said, approaching with the bloody knife extended. "And I will seal your vow."

"No." She retreated a step but ran into a statue.

"Swear your eternal commitment to my word," Paul insisted.

"What part of no don't you understand?" she shrieked.

Paul stopped within arms' reach. He smelled of blood and cinders, as if his rune was slowly burning him from the inside.

"The world will witness your submission to me." He gestured at the news helicopters hovering above the dome. "But we can take as long as you want and make the process as difficult as you like."

"Who should I slaughter next? Perhaps the hunter?" He leaned closer. "Or maybe the mortal you favor? I can find him." His smug smile returned. "It would be my pleasure."

"Stop. You made your point." She couldn't face another murder, couldn't deal with more blood on her hands.

Paul stroked her cheek with a bloody finger, his expression gloating. "Wise choice, Sarah. Now, you will swear undying devotion, offer yourself to me and embrace your duty to produce heirs of our glory."

Sarah dropped to one knee, her head bowed, one hand on the ground, showing him the defeated posture he so clearly wanted.

Paul leaned over her, his left hand on her head as if she were a prized dog. Using the same knife he had just used to murder Bastien, he began slicing the skin of her neck, marking the same binding rune he had marked on Bastien.

He wasn't going to murder her body. He was planning to shackle her soul.

Sarah suppressed a scream, and formed the image of the cipher she needed, driving away all other thought until it blazed with perfect clarity in her mind.

Eirene shouted, "Wait! Sarah, don't do this!"

"Paul, I'm going to rip your heart out," Gregorios growled.

Paul glanced in their direction. "Your threats are useless now. Be silent."

That distraction was what Sarah needed. She willed her rounon awake and her finger began to glow. The cipher burned in her mind, as if impatient for release.

It was a simple symbol, one of sacrifice, with modifiers directing it away from her and toward Paul.

Paul's grip on her head tightened, fingers digging into her scalp. The blade returned to her neck, poised to make the last mark.

"Swear it," he commanded.

"I swear," she said softly, the words like ash in her mouth.

Paul brought the knife to her neck and cut one last time.

Sarah silently mouthed, "Cross my heart and hope to die." And made an X mark over her heart with her glowing finger just as he completed his rune.

Then she shouted, "I swear by all that's holy to castrate you and shove your balls down your throat!"

Those two glowing marks gave life to the cipher in her mind and bound it to the other four ciphers still intact, spread around the perimeter of the square.

The distributed ciphers merged into a greater rune which linked to the new binding rune as Paul activated it on her neck.

Timing it the way she did, Sarah became the vehicle for Paul to bind himself to her greater cipher instead of her soul. It was like binding himself to the tracks in front of a runaway train.

The resulting battle cipher hummed in her rounon ears like a thousand growling cats as Paul's soul force fueled it. His shocked gazed locked on her.

Then all Paul's power backlashed against him.

The soundless explosion of soul force struck like a runaway truck, shattering statues and sending everyone tumbling away from Paul like tumbleweeds in a hurricane.

It blasted Paul off his feet, straight up, two hundred feet. He collided with the top of his spherical shield and rebounded even faster.

He struck the ground so hard he shattered stone and sank eight inches into the earth. The huge perimeter shield darkened, then exploded, shards of shimmering amber tearing out with destructive force.

The sweeping arms of both colonnades around the square shattered under the onslaught, sending stone debris blasting even farther to rain down over nearby military and police forces.

Much of the force of the exploding shield flew upward, shredding hovering military and news helicopters and raining burning debris for a mile around the square. The blast rocked the Basilica, crumbling the facade of the nearby entryway and tearing entire sections off the outer layer of the towering dome.

Sarah crashed down onto a pile of rubble on the south side of the square where the colonnade had stood just moments ago. Groaning, she sat up.

Every inch of her ached, and she was amazed she hadn't broken a dozen bones. Her enhancements burned against her skin, drawing deep from the precious well of her soul strength.

She'd already used so much to power her ciphers, a deep exhaustion had settled over her limbs. Even as her enhancements bled away the pain, she could feel the end of her strength approaching. She couldn't take much more.

Strong hands lifted her from behind and she turned to find Tomas had arrived. She threw herself into his arms and drank in the feel of him. His solid presence helped hold at bay the horrors she'd just witnessed.

She only allowed herself to hold him for a couple of seconds. Paul was too much of a threat to ignore.

"You're late," she said as she pushed away.

He grinned. "Arrived in time to see you blow up Paul. That was awesome!"

She turned and looked across the square. Paul still lay unmoving in the little hole he'd driven into the ground, surrounded by the shattered remains of his animated statues.

"Can someone please kill him now?" she asked.

Tomas tapped his earpiece. "All units. Open fire."

101

Vercingetorix manipulated all of us! Trusting any facetaker demon is a mistake, even one sworn as an enemy to Shahrokh and his new-found council.

He took advantage of our support, abandoned three of our brothers to death, and employed kashaph enchanters, despite our treaty. The joy I feel at his death is turned bitter by the knowledge that Gregorios was the one who destroyed his rune web and executed the abominable kashaph.

To add insult to our failure, Gregorios sought me out and extended a hand of friendship and an offer of a joint corps to hunt kashaph together.

~HAYYIM, HUNTER TEAM LEADER, AFTER THE BATTLE OF
ALESIA DURING THE GALLIC WARS, 52 A.D.

MOST OF THE Italian forces were still struggling to rise when enhanced soldiers from the Tenth and from Yurak opened fire. Fifty-caliber rounds raked Paul's prostrate form, and for the first time, they broke the skin.

Sarah gripped Tomas' hand hard as she watched, willing the bullets to destroy the monster. Grenades and mortars began falling in waves, the explosions rolling across the square in ever-growing echoes. The blasts sprayed dirt and debris and smoke into the air, temporarily obscuring visibility.

"Cease fire," Tomas ordered.

"Why?" Sarah demanded.

"Gregorios is going in. You lost your earpiece."

He pointed across the square and Sarah noticed Gregorios and

Eirene rushing toward the fallen cui dashi. Eirene had found her repeating grenade launcher, and its smoking barrel testified that she'd participated in the barrage. Gregorios ran in front of her, wielding a gladius.

"Go help him," Sarah said, pushing Tomas forward. "Get everyone to go help."

He shook his head. "It's Gregorios' right. For Bastien."

Alter arrived then, skidding to a halt in the rubble. He was grinning, but still wore a haunted look from what he'd been forced to do to Reuben. "Tomas, call in napalm! Burn him."

"It hasn't arrived yet. Besides, Gregorios will take his head off."

"It should be me," Alter growled, stomping away.

Movement beyond him drew Sarah's gaze and she focused on Spartacus standing close to the ruined entrance to the Basilica.

He saluted after Eirene and Gregorios, then hefted the red porphyry stone that held the forbidden runes. Without a backward glance, he strode into the Basilica and disappeared from view.

Sarah was about to point that out to Tomas, who was peering through the clouds of smoke toward Paul, but instead she gasped. The lines of her latest cipher, which had been glowing across the square, flickered and died.

"No!" she cried in frustration.

"What?" Tomas demanded, scanning the area, raising his rifle. Alter crouched nearby, hands raised to fight.

"My cipher is failing!"

"No," Alter cried, rushing to her and grabbing her arm. "Hold him!"

"I can't. His counter rune is trumping mine."

She caught Tomas' hand. "Get Gregorios out of there."

In the center of the square, Paul rose to his feet. Despite the brutal damage he'd taken and the blood covering him from head to toe, he stood tall and threw out his arms.

"I will raze this city to the ground! The world will tremble and know my rage."

"I'm really starting to hate that guy," Tomas muttered.

Gregorios had stopped and glanced back at Eirene. She fired another grenade.

Paul caught it and threw it back at Gregorios, his arm blurring with fully restored strength. Gregorios ducked the missile and it blew up behind him, knocking him from his feet.

"Get them out of there," Sarah insisted.

Alter snarled, "We have to destroy him."

"How?" Sarah asked, feeling exhausted. No matter what they did, they hadn't managed to do more than anger Paul.

Paul turned toward Sarah, as if he could hear her words. He shouted, his voice so loud it vibrated the rubble at her feet. "You can't stop me! Can't you see that now? You fool! Everyone you've ever loved will suffer for your rebellion."

Tomas placed a strong hand on her shoulder. "Gregorios and Eirene will rendezvous with us on the east end of the square. They've ordered all units to concentrate on protecting you, Sarah."

He led her toward their massed troops near the Via della Conciliazione.

"No. You all have to get away. He'll kill you," she protested.

"Not if we kill him first. Sarah, you hurt him. You have to do it again."

"I don't know how! Everything I do he's undoing."

"You can do it," Tomas said. The honest trust in his gaze bolstered her courage, even though she wanted to scream with terror to think what Paul would do to him if she failed.

"Give us a chance," Alter added. "Please." He looked ready to rush Paul again, even though he lacked any chance to defeat him alone.

Sarah took a deep breath. "All right."

She tried to clear her thoughts as they broke into a run. Something about the greater rune Paul was using to link those three master runes was tugging at her mind. The key was there. It had to be.

Alter shouted, "Think faster. Look out!"

Paul had crossed to the ring of stones set around the hole where the obelisk had stood. They marked the shadow of the obelisk at noon as it entered each of the signs of the zodiac.

Ignoring bullets and mortars that no longer hurt him, Paul ripped one of the stones out of the ground.

"First, witness the death of the man you love!"

He threw the stone at Tomas, and it shot across the distance faster than a professional baseball pitcher could have thrown a fast ball.

Tomas, who was running just ahead of Sarah, barely dove out of the way in time. Sarah skidded to a halt and the large stone hurdled through the air a yard ahead of her.

It careened off a broken column, ricocheting sideways and plowing into the side of a military truck, ripping the back right off and scattering soldiers.

"Look how weak he is, Sarah," Paul cried, ripping another stone out of the ground. "I can give you so much more."

"You can't give anything," Sarah shouted back, wishing for her favorite rifle. Her bullets might not hurt him, but shooting him a few times would have made her feel better. "You only know how to take."

With a furious scowl, Paul threw the heavy stone at Sarah.

She dove out of the way, crashing into Tomas as he rose, and knocking them both back to the ground. The stone tore through the air inches from her legs and bounced off the rubble, arcing high over the city. Sarah hoped it didn't kill anyone when it landed.

She wondered if he'd really intended to kill her with that stone. She preferred dying over giving herself to him as his sex slave, but she didn't want to die yet.

"Come on!" Alter shouted, grabbing Sarah and hauling her to her feet

Harriett arrived to help, but Paul leaped to a third stone and threw it at Tomas, just as he was rising.

"Look out," Harriett shouted, knocking Tomas aside.

The stone caught Harriett in the side. The impact shattered her torso, spraying blood and bits of broken bone across Sarah and the others.

Sarah screamed, horrified by how fast it had happened. Only the sight of Harriett's glittering soulmask slipping free as she abandoned the dying host helped her cope with the gruesome sight. She couldn't bear to see another friend die at Paul's hand.

He needed to die.

Drawing her reignited rage around herself, Sarah slashed her hand in the air, forming a shield barrier. It consumed much of her remaining rounon strength as it rose between them and Paul.

The fourth missile deflected off of it, and she huddled behind it with Alter as Tomas risked a run to snatch Harriett's soulmask from the ground.

Paul shouted, "Enough!ted. "I'll prove to the world my dominance."

"He doesn't get it," Tomas said. "The more he destroys, the more people will resist him."

"Let's hope," Sarah said.

"I don't want to see what he's planning," Alter said. "Come on. We have to get Sarah away."

The three of them ran for the barriers manned by their men, but with every step, Sarah wished she could run somewhere else. Trying to hide among those brave men and women would only get them killed.

Paul completed the new rune in a moment, and Sarah accepted a pair of binoculars to study it. The rune was actually two distinct symbols, marked close together. They were not as complex as his greater rune, but looked unique. They incorporated Hebrew characters within their central foundational strokes.

"What are those?" she asked.

Alter took a look and his grip tightened so hard on the binoculars that they snapped. "Abomination!" he growled. "He's using the forbidden runes."

"What do they do?" Sarah asked, frowning at the broken binoculars.

"They must be the runes he got from Spartacus," Alter said.

"Not good," Tomas muttered. "Sarah, can you use them too?"

As she considered the idea, trying to get a sense of the symbols she'd seen, Paul threw his arms out wide, the forbidden runes burning with pure white intensity.

"I will show you the power of god!"

The sky darkened overhead as roiling, angry clouds filled what had been a clear, blue sky.

"This is going to get ugly," Tomas said. "Get under cover, quick!"

Sarah ran for a nearby truck as Tomas relayed the order and troops scattered to find cover. Within seconds, huge hailstones began falling from the sky. They shattered on the ground with cracks like gunfire. The hail swept across the city, sending everyone scrambling for cover, denting cars, shattering windows, and beating down those too slow or too unlucky to reach safety.

The temperature began to plummet, but Sarah grabbed a clipboard in the truck and sketched out the runes. Alter and Tomas had packed into the front seat of the club cab with her, while five other soldiers had piled into the back seat. The sky darkened and the roar of the hail made speaking difficult. The reinforced windshield of the truck cracked, and Sarah shared a worried look with Tomas.

Alter clicked on a flashlight to illuminate the page while Sarah worked to complete the symbols. She was pretty sure she got it right, but he pointed out a couple of problems with the Hebrew characters.

"Can you use it if you're not sure?" Tomas asked.

"Part of the power of runes is belief that they'll work," Sarah said. "But these runes are specific, so if we mess up, there's no telling what might happen."

The hail ceased and Tomas peered through the ice-splattered windshield. "This can't be good." After a few seconds, he opened the door and stood on the seat to look over the hood.

"Not good," he reiterated, and Sarah joined him just in time to witness the first streak of fire hiss past and splatter flames against the ground.

"He's called down fires from heaven?" Alter exclaimed.

"That's not all," Tomas said.

As fire rained down all around, a deeper rumbling shook the earth and filled Sarah with nameless fear.

"What is that?" she asked.

Tomas motioned her back into the cab, then fired up the engine and pulled it forward around a nearby barricade so they could peer down the nearby Via della Conciliazione toward the source of the noise.

Pouring into the eastern end of the street came a wave of water as high as the houses, sweeping cars and everything else before it.

"Get us out of here!" Alter shouted.

Tomas gunned the engine, racing the truck north toward a side street that circled the square. He tapped his throat and shouted, "All units, run! He's pulled the Tiber off course. Seek shelter to the north."

Fire falling from the sky suddenly didn't seem so bad. Sarah gripped the armrests hard in growing fear as they sped into the cross street, followed by trucks and troops on foot. Debris from the shattered colonnade blocked the road fifty yards ahead, and they leaped from the cab to scramble together up the pile of rubble just as the flood waters burst into the plaza behind them and swept away the trucks and heavy equipment they'd abandoned in their flight.

The ground shook from the raw power of the river unleashed, and spray doused them, slashing at their faces with brutal force. The waters were black from earth and stone scoured from the streets. Sarah caught glimpses of vehicles, and rubble, and corpses, churning in its depths. The feeling of sick revulsion merged with her intense relief that they'd escaped the torrent.

Instead of dispersing through the plaza like any other flood would have, the waters somehow maintained their form and rolled past, a wall of destruction that smashed into the south end of the square, tearing through the Italian forces. With undiminished force, it snatched up vehicles and soldiers too slow to escape its deadly path.

Sarah cried out with horror as she witnessed the destruction and death, her tears mingling with the spray that poured down her face.

Paul had done it. He was an unstoppable madman, intent on nothing but destruction and conquest.

Then she realized, that was the key.

Crouched under a leaning marble column, Sarah pulled out her sketched runes and studied them again. While the ground shook, nearby buildings toppled under the onslaught of the river unleashed, and distant sirens echoed across the city, the uncaring rain of fire sizzled against wet stone.

Sarah ignored it all, grasping at the truth she'd discovered, and her fear faded under renewed hope.

She understood what they had to do.

102

To think a rune of creativity could prove so powerful. Archimedes was so much more than a thinker of maths and frivolous pursuits. His brilliant defenses of Syracuse against the Romans suggests he could have been recruited. I found no evidence of kashaph tendencies, but he was murdered in his workshop by the enforcers before I could speak with him or discover his unique rune.

~MELEK THE BALD, 212 A.D.

"LOOK AT THIS." Sarah drew Tomas and Alter deeper under the leaning column and pointed at Paul's greater rune. "He's combined the three master runes, but the only truth he's using is conquest and destruction."

"Right," Alter said. "We talked about that. He saw the truths he wanted to see, the ones that match his goals."

"Exactly," Sarah said. "But those aren't the truths I saw in the runes."

"What are you saying?" Tomas asked as Gregorios and Eirene joined them. Francesca dropped to one knee beside Tomas and accepted from him the soulmask of her sister. She leaned close and whispered something, a smile flickering across her face.

Sarah wished she could hear what they were saying. She could use a little humor at the moment, but didn't dare waste any time. "Paul is twisting everything from those historical moments to evil purposes, but those moments were stronger than that. In Berlin, Hitler fell, destroying the country's hopes of world domination."

She pointed at part of the greater rune. "Paul's using that part. But the deeper truth of that moment was something different. That day, the world ended a conflict in Europe that had cost millions of lives and would have continued killing had he not fallen. It was a great victory for the forces of peace."

Sarah gestured at the devastation left behind by the out-of-control river. The waters were gone, but they'd wreaked terrible damage. "Paul lives in a world without peace. He can't understand it."

"I don't get where you're going," Alter said. "He's still commanding the power of those moments."

"He's not the only one who can, though."

Eirene crouched beside her. "Are you saying you can access the might of those master runes at the same time he's got an open link to them?"

"I think so."

Gregorios said, "Is that possible?"

Alter frowned. "I don't know. Master runes aren't used, Sarah! He's linked them into a greater rune bonded to his soul. I think he's got them locked down."

"I don't think so," Sarah said, not sure how she knew, but convinced she was right. "If I can tap into a deeper truth, I can shift the balance away from him."

"It might work." Francesca gave Sarah a fierce grin. "If anyone can do it, it's you, girl."

"In every instance, he's focusing on one truth," Sarah said, smiling her thanks. "We need a stronger truth."

Alter shook his head. "It's like a rune duel, Sarah. You can't just ignore what's already been marked. You have to modify it, change it to your purpose."

"Of course!" Another concept clicked into place and Sarah pulled Alter down to her, kissing him on the lips. "Brilliant."

Alter's face lit with a happy smile.

Tomas dropped to one knee, forcing himself between them, looking ready to punch Alter. Sarah kissed him too. "Work with me here, okay?"

"What are you thinking?" Tomas asked, somewhat mollified.

"We can change his rune to a different truth."

"Like what you did in the circus?" Alter asked.

"Not exactly. There, I changed a rune that hadn't activated yet by finishing it with different strokes. Paul's greater rune is fully active, and he's got counter runes in place to block tampering."

Sarah drew the foundational keystone elements of each of the master runes onto the page, reflecting the truths she sought. They fell together easily, forming the periphery of a new cipher. It only lacked the right center to bind them all together.

"He'll never let you get close enough again," Tomas said. "He'll crush your fingers if you try to mark another cipher around him."

"I can't just draw a cipher," Sarah said, frowning again. "We need something to trigger the change, something I can use to link to his rune and twist it."

"Like re-focusing a laser," Tomas said. "You just need a mirror."

"Exactly," Sarah said. "But our mirror has to reflect the truths I need to draw upon. We need love and honor." She added marks into the center of the new cipher. "Those can trump the runes of conquest and fear he's using. Charity trumps cruelty."

She glanced up at Eirene. "Right?"

"Always," Eirene said with quiet confidence.

Sarah added more marks. It was taking shape, and the beauty of it tugged at her heart. It still lacked a final keystone in the center, the deepest truth that would tie it all together.

The symbol came to her and she caught her breath, her finger shaking. She didn't dare draw it.

"What?" Alter asked. "You see it, don't you?"

She nodded, whispering. "Self-sacrifice trumps domination."

Sarah drew the mark, hating herself for what she saw, knowing there was no other way. The final cipher glowed on the page, resonating in her soul with undeniable power. This was her greater cipher, the one that could usurp Paul's control over those pivotal moments in history. A cipher she doubted he could ever imagine existed.

This cipher could defeat him.

She only needed to ask someone to die for her.

103

The legions honor me, and my future is secure. Why do I feel like a fraud? I alone accepted the enhancement Gregorios' men offered, despite my brothers' protests. Now they are dead, their courage insufficient to win the day. I avenged them and secured a great victory for Rome, but am I a hero or a villain?

~PUBLIUS HORATIUS, THE LONE SURVIVOR OF THE
FAMOUS DUEL OF TRIPLETS THAT SETTLED THE WAR
BETWEEN ROME AND ALBA LONGA, 7TH CENTURY B.C.

"IT'S BEAUTIFUL," Tomas breathed, sliding one finger across the new cipher Sarah had just designed.

"It's perfect," Alter said, his eyes shining.

"No." Sarah wanted to crumple the paper, but it wouldn't matter. That cipher had already burned into her heart. She could re-draw it again instantly. "Don't you see, the key is self-sacrifice?"

"No greater love," Alter recited with reverence, nodding slowly.

"It's too much," Sarah said. "I can't."

Tomas kissed her gently on the lips. "It's all right. I've died in battle before. Piece of cake."

"Not this time," she said, gripping his hand and blinking away tears. "This binds to the soul. It'll only work if the sacrifice is made willingly, and there's no going back. It'll drain the soul that binds it."

"But it'll give us the power to kill Paul?"

"It'll give someone the power." Alter pointed at the rune. "Sarah this cipher is more powerful than anything we've ever attempted before."

"I can handle it," Tomas said. "I only need a minute to kill him."

"You won't get a minute," Alter said. "The power of this cipher will snuff out any normal soul, even one with as many enhancements as yours."

He gestured toward the square. "We don't have time to waste, and I'm the only one who can make this work."

Sarah followed his gaze. The floodwaters had receded, bearing with them the untold number of dead caught in their wake. The area south of the square was devastated, buildings shattered, military hardware flattened. Standing water pooled along the streets and the survivors stumbled through it in shock.

The battle was over. Paul had won.

He stood in the center of the square, exultant. He made a beckoning gesture and a single statue strode out of the damaged entrance to the Basilica. Sarah recognized it as Mary from the famous Pieta sculpture. Instead of bearing the body of Jesus, she was carrying the struggling form of the pope.

Sarah's heart sank. She had hoped the pope had escaped. The aged pontiff looked shaken and terrified.

Paul gave him a mock bow. "Thus do I prove my divinity. Grovel at my feet and be my prophet, or die today."

"We have no choice," Sarah whispered, her heart breaking. "Only a living soul, sacrificed to him, bound to this cipher, can redirect the power of those moments. In his moment of victory, we can destroy him."

"You're sure it'll work?" Tomas asked.

Sarah could only nod. The strength of her assurance was killing her.

He saw the truth in her eyes. "I'm sure of one thing. I love you."

"You can't," she said.

"No, he can't," Alter agreed. "I'm the only one who can." He leaned closer, his gaze intent. "Sarah, I have nothing left to lose anyway. My family will hunt me down after today. Let me destroy that monster and die with honor."

Sarah hesitated and glanced at Tomas, who looked ready to argue, but waited for her. "This must be done for love, with a pure willingness to sacrifice, to link your soul to mine and activate the cipher."

"Then I have to do it," Tomas said, his voice determined, but his expression sad. He could do it for her, but once they activated the rune, their hopes of a long life together would be consumed in the fires of destruction.

If they didn't do it, they would both die in moments anyway.

"No," Alter said with equal determination. "Sarah, I love you. I will do this for you."

"Back off," Tomas growled. "This is my duty. It's our love that needs to fuel it."

Sarah placed a restraining hand on Tomas' arm and kissed him tenderly. He looked relieved, but the sadness lingered in his gaze. Alter looked ready to leap upon Tomas' back.

"Alter is right," Sarah said softly. "You're not strong enough to do this alone."

"You can't be serious," Tomas whispered, anguished. "Sarah, listen to what you're saying!"

"I love you, Tomas," she said, fighting back tears at the thought of what she was about to attempt. "But I need Alter too."

"Wait, what?" Tomas asked.

"I need you both," she said. "Only together can we do this."

"I'll do it," Alter said quickly. "My soul is yours, Sarah."

Tomas scowled at him. "Sarah, tell us what you need and we'll do it."

Sarah fought to stay focused. She couldn't bear to lose either of them, but she had to risk them both.

"The mission comes first," Tomas said. "Do it, Sarah. We're out of time."

In the square, the statue of Mary dropped the pope and he stood to face Paul, arranging his ropes with the little dignity that remained to him. Although visibly terrified he spoke loudly. "I defy you, false king. Antichrist."

"Do it," Alter pressed.

They both shed their vests and pulled off their shirts. Sarah placed one hand on Alter's chest, feeling his heartbeat and the warmth of his skin. He did not speak, but stared at her with silent intensity, and his gaze spoke volumes. She wished she could show him how much she cared for him. That fact made the sacrifice all the more difficult because his love could never be reciprocated.

Sarah accepted a slender knife from Tomas and quickly marked a cipher on Alter's chest, above his heart. He made no complaint, his eyes never wavering.

She repeated the process with Tomas, and when she finished, she kissed him tenderly, even though they only had a second.

"If I'm wrong," she whispered. "I'm sending you to die for nothing."

"I trust you," he said simply. "And I love you."

Sarah smiled through the aching grief in her heart, hating Paul more than ever for forcing her to risk the first man she truly loved. "He has to dispossess one of you."

"We'll get it done," Tomas said, giving her a brave smile as he rose and donned his shirt to conceal the rune.

Alter leaped to his feet, but paused, and in his gaze, Sarah read his desire to kiss her again.

"Go," she said. He sighed, then sprinted into the square with Tomas at his side.

As Paul advanced on the pope, Tomas' voice pulled him around. "Face me, coward!"

Paul grinned. "So the mortal comes to make a sacrifice?"

He had never spoken truer words.

104

I found Rome a city of bricks, but in only two lifetimes I have made it a city of marble.

SARAH WATCHED as Tomas and Alter strode into the square to face Paul. Tomas carried a fighting knife, and Alter's hands burst into purple fire. They looked pitiful compared to the bloody cui dashi standing over the pope.

"You think you can just show up and take my girl?" Tomas demanded.

Paul laughed. "Absolutely."

"She won't serve you," Tomas said. "Her soul is free."

"Yours won't be," Paul promised. He didn't even bother to draw a weapon.

"Fight me!" Tomas shouted and charged, blade held high.

"You are unworthy," Paul said, blurring across the distance between them, knocking Tomas off his feet with a brutal blow to the chest.

Tomas struggled back to his knees, his face twisted with pain.

Alter closed in a rush. "I'm worthy!"

Paul laughed and caught him with one hand. "I thought you learned your lesson after what happened to your brother."

"I'm going to kill you, abomination," Alter growled, his eyes flashing with the power of his nevron. "You're fate is sealed."

Paul slapped him so hard, the report echoed across the square. Paul's eyes ignited in turn, and purple fire ringed his hand. "You first, fool."

Tomas leaped upon Paul's back, knife striking uselessly. Paul flung him away. "I'll shatter your soul in a moment, mortal."

Sarah shed her bulletproof vest and pulled down the front of her blouse to expose the skin over her heart. She had to time her move exactly.

Alter's shouted cries faded as Paul severed him from his body and began extracting his soulmask. He took his time, enjoying the process.

With the slender knife, Sarah cut into her chest, the movements fast and sure, while tears dripped down her cheeks. She felt no pain, just a terrible growing sense of loss. There were so many things she longed to say, so much she'd thought they'd have time to do.

In the square, Alter's soulmask popped free and his dispossessed body fell in a heap at Paul's feet. Paul lifted his soulmask high, as if in salute.

Sarah completed the cipher on her chest and activated it. The complex cipher sucked dry the well of her rounon strength and she sagged. Francesca propped her up, speaking words that only sounded like a distant buzzing in her ears.

In the square, Tomas dropped to his knees, the power of his soul meshing with hers, strengthening her, becoming one with her in such a completely intimate level, it filled her with singing joy. She could feel his love, his willingness to yield his soul to her need. The intensity of the contact brought tears to her eyes.

With her rounon replenished by Tomas' strength, the cipher linked across to Alter, and his soulmask glowed with intense light, shifting from its dull shimmer to a brilliant radiance the color of his active nevron. Paul dropped the soulmask and retreated a step, shielding his eyes from the intensifying light.

Alter's soulmask hung in the air, burning like a purple sun, fueled by the purity of his sacrifice.

The greater cipher on Sarah's chest sealed to the combined power of their souls, united through sacrifice, and burned through the conduit to Alter. The brilliant light surrounding his soulmask coalesced into a slender beam that drove into Paul's chest, piercing his greater rune.

Paul convulsed, grabbing at his chest, bellowing with pain. For a moment the torrent of energy he commanded held its own against the force of Sarah's cipher, with Paul's body the battlefield. He shook under the mighty, opposing forces and Sarah wondered how he wasn't ripped apart by them.

She staggered to her feet, and their eyes met across the distance. She read his fury, his defiance and, after a second, his fear.

Her cipher continued to build momentum, like a river swelling with recent rains, while his began to wither.

"I am more than a mortal!" Paul shouted, taking a faltering step toward her.

"You are less than a man," Sarah said, surprised when her voice reverberated through the square with as much force as his.

Paul fell to his knees, threw his head back, and howled with loss as the full measure of those three pivotal moments of history that he had been controlling were snatched away.

Alter's soul acted as the prism to redirect all that power at Sarah.

Sarah rocked backward, every muscle convulsing in unison as the energy struck like a lightning bolt. Her skin cracked and blackened and heat tore through her, threatening to boil her blood. Her hair floated off her shoulders, sparks crackling off the ends, but she lacked the ability to breathe or to scream.

Then a second wave thundered through Sarah like a flash flood, linked back to the shades of millions of souls. The invisible blow threw her off her feet. The world burned around her, and her limbs shook as that soul force overwhelmed her ability to contain it.

Light streamed out of Sarah's open mouth instead of a scream, and flames dripped from her fingertips. The energy consumed her innards, but she couldn't move, couldn't escape. She could barely comprehend what was happening to her.

Eirene stepped in front of Sarah, looking terrified. She grabbed Sarah's arm, then let go with a yelp of pain. "Oh, Sarah, What have you done?"

Sarah wanted to explain, but she couldn't speak. Lying in rigid immobility as the energy tore at her, she wanted to laugh at their surprise. She had needed a sacrifice, but she couldn't bear for Tomas or Alter to give their lives for her.

Vlad's words echoed in her mind. "If I'm not willing to take the risk to protect those only I can protect, then we've already lost."

She needed their sacrifice to break Paul's rune, but she alone would tempt the fates by attempting to control those master runes.

As the energy threatened to tear her apart, Sarah wondered if the world would label her a vampire, a monster as they had Vlad?

Through the conduit she shared with Tomas, she felt his worry, his desire to help, and that eased her pain, confirmed that she'd made the right choice. She couldn't sacrifice Tomas' life, not like that. She had drawn a different rune on him, binding his sacrifice to her.

The strength she drew from him made the critical difference in keeping her alive. Even so, she quivered, on the very cusp of losing control. Had she drawn upon the power of destruction as Paul had, she would have died instantly. Instead she had drawn upon the power of love, committing herself as the sacrificial offering to receive the punishing load.

As the energy reached its apex, the pain that tore at her transformed. The power of the truth she had sought burned through the link to those moments in history with singular purity. Ecstasy swept her away, so intense she could scarce comprehend it. Her muscles relaxed enough for her to move a little, but her physical form lacked the strength to handle the torrent pounding her.

Something had to change.

With agonizing slowness, Sarah dragged down the waist of her pants and cut two marks into the enhancement just below her hip, changing it the way she had in the memoryscape.

It activated instantly and, just as she had in the memoryscape, her body shifted as those marks adjusted the focus of her enhancement. Her form became fluid and her skin took on a quicksilver hue.

The glorious ecstasy filling her became a bit more manageable as her tissue composition altered and strengthened, better able to handle the strain. Sarah flowed to her feet and bounced there, unable to refrain from movement.

The sheer volume of energy filling her was more than even her altered physical form could endure. She could contain it a few seconds longer, could do what had to be done. Then she had to find a way to spend it or release it, or it would consume her.

Her eyes focused and Sarah noticed Eirene, Gregorios, and Francesca standing around her, eyes wide with wonder.

"Well, go get him," Gregorios said, motioning toward the square.

"You look amazing," Francesca added, but her smile looked forced.

"Hurry, dear," Eirene said. "You may not have much time."

Sarah wished she wasn't on the verge of exploding. Normal enhancements would have lacked the ability to foster the quicksilver effect, and she wished she had time to explore how it felt in real life.

She didn't. The force of those master runes were too much to contain. So she raced into the square, moving as fast as Paul had before, her legs flowing effortlessly over the broken stone. She passed Tomas without slowing, ignoring his weak cries for her to release the energy. She focused only on Paul, and nothing was going to distract her again.

Driven by so much soul power, she wanted to laugh at their earlier efforts to stop him. There was no force on Earth as strong as the combined might of millions of souls united together through master runes. She marveled that he could harness it at all. His cui dashi strength was awe-inspiring.

Paul had managed to stagger to his feet. Alter's still-blazing soulmask hung in the air nearby, and the pope stood behind them, so amazed he hadn't even tried to flee.

Paul gaped at Sarah as she approached with stolen super speed. He had been uselessly patting at the broken rune on his chest, but the skin was seared, the rune cloven in two, its power shattered.

Sarah closed in a blur, but her legs began to feel soft, as if the blazing power was beginning to melt her from the inside. It didn't matter. She only needed a few more seconds.

Her hands morphed into shining silver blades.

Paul started to mouth a protest, but Sarah drove her sword hands into his stomach. He screamed, clutching at her silvered arms, terror in his eyes.

"I made a promise," Sarah snarled. "And I keep my word."

She yanked her arms away, and blood and guts poured out of the ghastly wounds. With a slash of her left arm, Sarah castrated him.

He staggered, but instead of screaming like any man would, he laughed, blood dripping out his mouth. "You're killing yourself, you stupid mortal."

"You first."

With all her strength, she slashed again, and her bladed right hand cut his throat with remarkable ease, severing his head, and tumbling it across the square and into the Basilica.

Overbalanced by the lack of the resistance, Sarah stumbled to her knees in front of the pope. He gaped at her, then stared at Paul's headless corpse that fell beside her.

"I'm glad you're safe," she said through gritted teeth.

Then she staggered away, searching blindly for Tomas. Her vision was darkening and her muscles quivering. Even her quicksilver form was too weak to contain all the energy she'd stolen. She needed to release it.

She'd defeated Paul, but that truth didn't help. She'd inscribed the rune of self-sacrifice, had accepted the reality that she would probably die, but now that she faced a torturous end, she yearned for a different way.

Her thoughts scattered as she fell to her knees. Her bladed hands melted under the fervent heat of the master runes. If she could get back to Gregorios or one of the other facetakers, they could save her, but her vision blurred and she wasn't sure which way to crawl.

The torrent of energy tore through her, stronger than ever, the rune blazing so bright against her chest it filled the square with pure-white brilliance. She tried to cut off the rune, to sever her connection to it, but her hands no longer worked. They dripped toward the ground when she lifted them, and she cried with terror.

Sarah pitched to her side, and when she struck the ground, pieces of her skin exploded away like mini missiles, burning with white-hot fire like chunks of magnesium. It didn't relieve the pressure, which continued to build.

Sarah tried to stand, but her legs had turned soft. Her torso began to expand, like a volcano filling with lava. More pieces of her quicksilver flesh erupted away, burning as they arced through the air before exploding with shocking intensity. The thunder of the concussions filled the square and echoed in her ears.

Her final cry for help faded to a bubbling gurgle as her vocal cords melted from the inner fire consuming her. Through her faltering vision, she caught sight of Tomas rushing toward her, dodging the silver missiles shooting off in every direction.

She tried to frown. That wasn't Tomas. It was Alter, but he was wearing Tomas' body.

"Sarah, release it," he repeated. "Hurry!"

He'd tried to warn her, ever since she first started testing her rune gift, tried to explain the dangers. She finally understood.

It didn't matter. She couldn't stop it, couldn't control it. As her body melted into the stones of the plaza, exploding piece by piece like a gruesome fireworks display, Sarah's senses contracted. Everything dimmed until she floated in silence, and pain faded to peace.

While her body disintegrated beneath her, she tried to feel Tomas through the soul connection they shared, but not even that was left to her. She hoped he understood she'd done it for him.

"I love you." The words never left her lips, but she heard them.

Then she heard nothing.

105

SARAH BLINKED eyelids that felt as heavy as stone. She sighed from the loss of remembered ecstasy. That energy had ripped her apart, but it had been sublime, something she doubted any other living person could ever feel.

As her mind came fully awake, she realized she didn't hurt anywhere. She felt so deeply tired that she knew it was an exhaustion of soul more than just physical weariness, and all she wanted to do was sleep.

"Are you going to wake up finally?"

"Tomas." Sarah snapped her eyes open and found him standing over her, smiling. The sight of him filled her with singing joy. She didn't even care that he still wore that hunter's body. What form he wore no longer mattered.

Tomas helped her sit. "How are you feeling?"

"Like I need a vacation," she groaned.

She was about to ask what happened, but the memories poured back, and she clutched at his hand in remembered terror.

"It's all right," he soothed, stroking her hand. "You did it."

"Really?"

"What were you thinking?" he asked more sternly. "I was the one that was supposed to sacrifice myself." After a pause he added, "Or Alter even."

"You did," she said.

"You did too." He spoke lightly, but his eyes were sad.

Sarah rubbed her face and realized with a start that her hand was not her own. She glanced down and a new fear set her pulse racing.

She wore a different body.

She was sitting on a bed in one of the trauma rooms in the Suntara headquarters, dressed in a simple blouse and loose-fitting, cotton stretch pants. Her body was slender and felt young. It looked vaguely familiar, but she'd never looked at the world out of these eyes before.

Sarah had experienced enough new bodies that she handled the shock well, but her hand still trembled in Tomas'. She couldn't voice the question that had to be asked.

Tomas knelt beside her bed, taking her hand in both of his. "We only barely saved your soul. The explosions kept the others back, and only Alter could get through."

"But he was dispossessed," Sarah said with a frown.

"I gave him a lift," Tomas said. "He'd never tried double layering before, but we were motivated." He shivered. "That was a weird experience."

Sarah stared. "You shared a body with Alter?"

"To save you, I'd go to hell and back," he said. "I guess we both would."

"How badly was I injured?" Sarah asked, her mind turning back to the agonizing ecstasy of her quicksilver flesh melting under the fervent heat of those master runes.

Tomas hesitated, and that was all the answer Sarah needed. She fell back against the pillow, unable to comprehend the loss.

She'd fought so hard to escape Alterego with body and soul intact. Those efforts had teamed her up with Tomas, had driven her to learn the truth about facetakers, and risk her life to free Eirene.

All for a chance to live as herself.

She'd defeated Paul, but she'd destroyed herself at the same time.

Francesca swept into the room, wearing a twenty-something body, looking more mature and at the same time more vivacious than ever. She pulled Sarah into a sitting position and gave her a warm hug.

"I'm glad you made it out all right," Sarah said.

"Take good care of that suit," Francesca said, patting Sarah's shoulder. "I enjoyed that one."

That's why she recognized it. "I can't take this from you," she stammered, but felt a new shiver of terror. She couldn't lose this new body so soon. If they took it away, would she ever have another one to could call her own?

"You look lovely in it," Francesca said. "We've already got you a new identity, passport, everything." She added with a wink, "Even transferred all your assets."

"Thanks," Sarah managed, her mind lost in the complexities suggested by Francesca's words. "So I'm ... dead?"

"Martyred," Tomas said. "Pretty impressive, really."

"Don't worry," Francesca said. "You'll get used to it. You'll love this life, Sarah. It's a virgin form, barely lived in."

"But what about you?"

"New life," Francesca said, rising to show off her new form with a spin. She was taller now, with a fuller figure. "Harriett had to change forms and sisters stick together."

"So she's all right?"

"Takes a lot more than dying to kill that girl," Francesca said with a grin, which faded a moment later. Sarah wondered if she was thinking of poor Bastien. The thought of his gruesome death brought fresh tears to her eyes.

Francesca punched Tomas in the shoulder. "You watch yourself, dating such a young girl. Don't take advantage of her."

"I don't think I can take advantage of the Sword of the Deliverer."

"What?"

"It's all over the news," Tomas said, flipping to the local channel on the wall-mounted television. "They're already talking about making you an official martyr for killing Paul and saving the pope."

"You're kidding," Sarah said, her eyes glued to scenes of the aftermath.

Much of the front of the Basilica had been destroyed, and sizable chunks were missing from the outer shell of the dome. The square was a blasted ruin, cordoned off by police tape. In one corner of the screen they were replaying the moment when the Tiber River burst its banks and tore through the area. Sarah looked away.

"I've never been martyred," Francesca said. "Way to end your first life with a bang."

"A sword name?" Sarah asked, wondering if the other rune warriors had gotten theirs by accident too.

"What do you expect after changing your arm into a sword and hacking apart the guy trying to take over the world?" Francesca asked.

"I think you're ready for knife fighting lessons," Tomas added.

Sarah appreciated their attempts at levity, but they didn't help much. She sagged against the bed, too overwhelmed to deal with it.

Tomas kissed her. At least that felt normal. She stroked the back of his head with her new fingers and twined them into his hair.

"I guess I'm dating a celebrity," Tomas said.

"Are you? Do you even want to?"

Sarah scanned her new body. She was a little shorter than before, at least five years younger, more petite. Tomas had fallen in love with a top model. This body was pretty, but not the same. She'd fill out as she finished maturing, but she was consumed by a terrible fear that he wouldn't want her any more.

Francesca brought over a mirror. Sarah studied her reflection, particularly the critical areas around the edges of her face and jaw. She saw none of the telltale marks that signified a poorly aligned soulmask. Her face looked natural and fit the skull extremely well. Her hair hung past her shoulders, thick and silky straight instead of softly curled.

"We took some extra effort to make sure you fit right," Francesca said. "Turned out pretty good, I think."

"Thank you." She was touched by the effort to help her transition smoothly into her second life.

Tomas took her hands in his again. "I love you, Sarah, no matter what you wear."

She had felt the strength of his soul meshed with her own, and perhaps still felt a little of him there with her. She loved him, no matter what suit he wore. Was it too much to ask him for the same commitment?

"But this was Francesca's," Sarah protested.

"She never looked as good in it as you do."

Francesca laughed. "You could only dream of dating me, tough guy."

"Neither one of us is in our first life," Tomas said seriously. "It takes some getting used to, but at least you're here and we're together. You'll be fine and I will always be here for you."

She embraced him and let him hold her for a long moment, breathing slow and adjusting to the feel of his powerful arms holding her slender shoulders.

Francesca wiped a tear with an exaggerated motion. "I'm such a sap. See you later, lovebirds."

106

I will not apologize to the hunters for intercepting their team. How could I have known they were targeting that heka cell instead of me after all the times they've tried to assassinate me? The outbreak of plague from that heka cell is unfortunate. It interrupts commerce, and the stench of the rotting corpses in London has driven me to my summer home in the Alps. However, the death of so many presents a rare opportunity to increase our holdings. Send Eirene to court to investigate acquisition of additional properties.

~SHAHROKH, 1563

MELEK SHOVED a metal ruler under the cast on his leg to reach the maddening itch. For a moment he sighed with relief, but then the itch moved farther down his leg, beyond his ability to reach. He cursed the shortness of rulers and was tempted to shatter the cast to free himself from the torture. Weeks after his injury, and he was still abed. He hadn't been so badly injured since he was a foolish teenager. That time, he hadn't had all of his enhancement runes.

Melek was beginning to worry. Without his enhancements, he would have died for sure, but he should have healed by now. Few things interrupted the bond of a powerful soul with its enhancements, but severe trauma and emotional turmoil could. He'd seen too much of both in recent weeks.

A soft knock came at the door, offering a welcome distraction. At his call, Ira entered the room. The hunter looked fit, having already returned to duty like most of the family. Those who survived, anyway.

"Pardon the interruption," Ira said. "But a package has arrived from your son."

Ira pulled over a wheeled table and deposited a large box onto it. Melek hesitated. He'd heard nothing from Alter in the days since the apocalyptic events of Rome. The surviving members of the team had already returned and filed their reports. It was a miracle any of them had survived. The loss of Reuben weighed him down with constant sorrow.

It was a shame the rune warrior had died. The world owed that brave young woman a debt of honor. Alter had been right to attempt to free her from Gregorios' sway.

The name of his youngest son filled him with conflicting emotions, some of which he was not yet ready to confront. So he cut the tape and opened the box.

Melek grinned. The book of runes, his family's most treasured possession. He lifted it reverently from the box, grunting at its weight. The leather-bound volume looked undamaged, and he breathed a sigh of relief. The loss of this treasure had stung as much as the death of so many relatives.

He leaned back against his pillow, book on his lap, hands atop it, and closed his eyes for a moment of heartfelt prayer.

"Melek," Ira said uneasily after a moment. "You should take a look at this."

Melek opened his eyes and leaned forward to peer into the box.

An ornate wooden box had sat under the book of runes. Melek lifted it out and eased open the lid.

Reuben's soulmask was inside, nestled in folds of satin.

"I will be avenged!" Reuben's helium-high whisper voice sounded shriller than the last time he had returned home dispossessed. His eyes flickered with rainbow lights and his mask quivered in Melek's grasp when he lifted it.

"Oh, my son," Melek breathed. "I am so sorry."

The hunters had related the brothers' failed attack on the cui dashi and Reuben's attempt to harness the forbidden runes. That had been bad enough, but Melek's heart had bled to hear of Paul corrupting those runes, enslaving Reuben to his will and sending him to commit murder.

Alter had stopped him, had saved many innocents.

Alter was cui dashi.

Melek felt as lost as both of his sons were to him. In quiet moments, he wondered how the family had fallen so low.

Ira lifted a letter from the box and Melek motioned him to read the simple note.

"Father, I am sorry."

Melek leaned back against the pillow, holding the letter to his chest, trying to ignore the aching in his leg.

107

Honor and courage amount to less than I thought, at least against a foe enhanced like the Samnites. What has happened to the world when strength of arms and purity of heart matter less than acquiring the best rune?

~QUINTUS AULIUS CERRETANUS, ROMAN COMMANDER, SHORTLY BEFORE HIS DEATH, BATTLE OF LAUTULAE, 315 B.C.

GREGORIOS LOOKED across the conference room at the gathered council members. He hadn't slept much in the three days since Paul's attempt to rise as the king of the world. None of them had.

Harald, at least, had put his slumber time to good use. He had spent hours in the machine, but had found no evidence of any other memory walkers. Already his mental faculty was sharpening, his soul fragmentation healing.

He had made his first transfer in decades this morning. He now wore a powerful young Caucasian form with a bodybuilder's bull neck. He might need to resort to cracking heads again if they had any hope of eventually working themselves back out of the public eye.

Zuri sat beside him, stunning in an athletic, Nigerian body with short hair and a long neck, accentuated by the dazzling new diamond necklace she wore to celebrate the transfer. She too had spent some time in the machine, and planned to make it part of her regular workout routine.

Eirene sat to Gregorios' right, along with their daughters. Bastien's absence still hurt more than he dared acknowledge. Every time he thought of Paul's atrocities, he was filled anew with simmering rage. He was going to need it to sustain him.

"Any word of Spartacus?" he asked.

Francesca nodded. "He's surfaced in Hollywood."

That almost made Gregorios laugh. They still needed to deal with Spartacus, get those forbidden runes from him, and restore Tomas' body, but it looked like he was serious about becoming an actor.

"Keep him there," he said. "Get an agent from one of our subsidiaries to sign him and keep an eye on him for now."

"Will do," Francesca said.

"Harald, what's the status with the media?" Gregorios asked.

"The initial tumult has died down," Harald reported. "So they're moving into serious investigation stage. We've deflected numerous inquiries regarding your identities, but you were front and center on the videos. There's a frenzy to learn everything possible about the Sword of the Deliverer and her heroic companions."

"Keep working at it." One of the few good qualities of news reporters was their hummingbird-short attention spans.

"We've been digging up information about some of the fallen local soldiers," Harald said. "Highlighting the unsung heroes who died defending their homeland."

Zuri looked up from her notes. "The conflict was chaotic, but everything's recorded these days. There are inquiries along official channels also. They know our connection to events and as usual, bureaucrats are hunting scapegoats."

Quentin, who stood in as security spoke, "That's my fault. In gaining permission for our intervention, and during my inquiry with the Vatican, I had to use those official channels."

"There's no helping it," Gregorios said. "Keep them running in circles."

"We released twenty thousand pages of historical documentation about the theories of superhuman enhancements proposed by academics over the past century, all doctored by Harald's department," Zuri said with a wicked grin. "Mind-numbing and completely useless. It'll give them something to chew on without letting them get anywhere."

"We've got a lot of interest in Yurak," Harriett interjected. "There have been several inquiries into our special tactics and battle enhancements."

"Push the special equipment angle," Gregorios said.

"Already doing it. All our gear is custom-made, but we might land several lucrative contracts out of this."

Gregorios considered that. "Not a bad idea for more agencies to have better equipment to deal with heka outbreaks, but that also makes them better equipped to come after us if they decide to."

"We have plans to install remote shut-off devices embedded in everything we ship," she said. "Known only to us, of course."

"It's worth the risk," Eirene said. "We're going to have another outbreak. The only question is when."

"Are you sure?" Harald asked. "Now that Paul's gone and his heka team destroyed, maybe things will settle down."

"You didn't see his mother," Gregorios said. "She's the ultimate threat we have to neutralize, and she made Paul look like a schoolboy."

"At least until he linked those master runes," Eirene added.

"She's out there, the queen mother, and we need to take her down."

"We've already stopped their plot," Harald said. "I bet she'll go to ground."

"She might have the master runes," Gregorios said. "And I didn't get the feeling she's scared of anything."

"Besides, from the nuggets Paul let slip, it sounded like she has bigger plans, like harvesting our nevron."

"Then why didn't she show up during that showdown with Paul?" Zuri asked. "With her help, we'd have folded for sure."

"I don't know," Gregorios admitted. "I worry about that. It makes me wonder if Paul's stunt was just one part of her plan."

"You think declaring himself emperor of the world wasn't his end game?" Francesca asked. "It nearly worked."

"I know," Gregorios said. "But there are some pieces still bothering me. I'm convinced we haven't seen the last of her, and as we just learned, historical approaches to cui dashi problems no longer work. We need to do more while we have a chance."

"Speaking of that," Eirene said. "Where is our rune warrior?"

"Getting used to her new life," Francesca said with a smile.

108

May it be my privilege to have the happiness of establishing the commonwealth on a firm and secure basis and thus enjoy the reward which I desire, but only if I may be called the author of the best possible government; and bear with me the hope when I end this life that the foundations which I have laid for its future government, will stand firm and stable through all of my lives to come.

~CAESAR AUGUSTUS, SECOND LIFE OF JULIUS CAESAR

SARAH SAT across from Tomas at a table outside a little trattoria in Florence, with excellent views of the Duomo. It was a beautiful, mild day and the midday crowds were thinner than normal.

She swirled her soft drink and studied her new hands. They might be a little smaller, but they were very nimble. She might try taking up painting. She'd never been very good at it, but now she suspected she might be able to discover a knack for it. She needed to explore all those aspects of her new self and forge a new identity.

She wasn't the Sarah she'd always been. That Sarah was dead.

She'd seen the video.

Sarah could scarce believe it when she'd watched the footage of herself standing against Paul, momentarily harnessing the power of those three master runes. Seeing it on video drove home just how desperate the situation had been. At the time, she'd been so afraid, so focused on the moment that she hadn't had time to really think it through.

She was Sarah, but she was still figuring out what that meant. That unknown element left her feeling constantly nervous, as if her anchor with reality had broken free.

Tomas took her hand in his, drawing her thoughts back to the present. He was her anchor now. Without him, she wasn't sure if she could cope. She was glad to know Gregorios and Eirene were safe, and she'd seen Harriett in a beautiful new suit very similar to the new one Francesca had acquired. That had helped ease some of her nightmare memories from that horrible confrontation.

She'd spoken with Alter only once, but the moment had turned awkward when she'd hugged him. He hadn't known how to react to her new body, and she wasn't ready to deal with the questions that lingered in his eyes.

"How do you like modern day Florence?" Tomas asked, drawing her back to the present.

"I love it," she said, grateful for the excuse to leave the difficult questions behind for a while. "No breaking statues or running fights through the streets."

"No minotaurs," he conceded.

She shuddered. "None of that."

"No running across rooftops, though," Tomas added.

"I can live without it." Sarah did love the freedom of leaping impossibly far over buildings, but for now one reality was proving hard enough to handle.

They rose and ambled slowly toward the great domed cathedral of the Duomo. Up close, it reminded her of the devastation of the Basilica in Rome, something they had hoped to escape with this trip. So they moved past, toward Ponte Vecchio. They spent a couple hours window shopping, just enjoying each other's company.

Sarah was still adjusting to the slightly different angle on the world from her shorter stature. The changes were subtle at times, but still significant to her. She startled at times to see her new reflection in the mirrored windows. She didn't feel at home yet, and wondered how long it would take before she did.

Tomas slid an arm around her waist and she leaned against his shoulder. Would he ever get his body back? Did it matter?

Tomas drew her to him and she leaned up to kiss him. They lingered over it, despite drawing some looks from other pedestrians. His lips felt the same, as did the feel of his skin on hers. Their shapes might be altered, but she closed her eyes and let the fear go, just enjoying the moment, appreciating the power of a single kiss.

When they resumed walking hand in hand he asked, "How are you doing?"

For the first time since being martyred she could honestly say, "I think I'm going to be all right."

WHERE'S THE NEXT BOOK?

Waiting for you. *Aeon Champion* is the explosive finale to the series, and I believe it's everything you're hoping for. And more.

One second you're a hero . . .

The next, you're hunted by an angry worldwide mob and terrifying new predators. An unknown enemy has infiltrated the highest offices of world power, and they're calling all the shots now.

Sarah wants to use her amazing rune powers to heal, but she's again driven into the memoryscape, hunting for truths concealed for millennia. How can ancient China and ancient Egypt hold the key to solving the current world crisis?

Will they survive long enough to find out?

With the fate of everything on her shoulders, Sarah alone can step into the deepest reaches of history and face a threat thousands of years in the making.

Yeah, you want this. And there's no reason not to pick it up right now.

Get it here: https://smarturl.it/ed2cci

THUMBS UP? OR THUMBS DOWN?

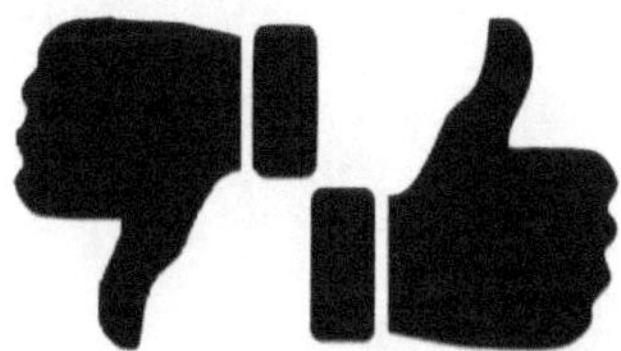

Reviews are still the best way to support your favorite authors (other than buying 5000 copies of all of their books for everyone you know for Christmas).

So are you willing to take 5 seconds and share your thoughts with the world? Now, while it's still fresh?

You love this book, so don't hold back. Tell the world!

Post a review of *Rune Warrior* here: https://smarturl.it/1rms8q

Thank You!

Frank

AUTHOR'S NOTE

I loved writing this book! It's big. It's epic. It's complex.

It's got Spartacus.

I like history, but I've always particularly loved studying Roman history. *Rune Warrior* allowed me to explore and tweak and twist Roman history in fun and fascinating ways. The more I explore history, the more I realize I'm barely brushing the surface. There are so many amazing stories, and real life is often far more interesting than fiction could ever be.

Wrapping so much Roman flavor in with this world-spanning, fast-paced adventure was a special treat. I loved exploring the man-out-of-time concept with Spartacus even more than I had with other characters. The story also offered unique ways to explore questions of identity and how we look at ourselves. Are we physical, spiritual, or a combination of the two? So much fun exploring such ideas.

And the best part is that the story's not complete. *Aeon Champion*, the final chapter in the Facetakers, is going to take the conflict to whole new levels and build upon what we did in *Memory Hunter* and expanded here in *Rune Warrior*.

Buckle in, because this story is still accelerating.

Frank Morin is a storyteller, an outdoor enthusiast, and an eager traveler. He is the author of fast-paced grab-you-by-the-eyeballs-and-don't-let-go adventures, including *The Petralist*, his epic teen fantasy series, full of explosive magic, huge adventure, and brilliant humor. Frank also writes *The Facetakers* fast-action historical fantasy thrillers you've been enjoying.

When not writing or trying to keep up with his active family, he's often found hiking, camping, Scuba diving, or traveling to research new books. Find out more about his novels and his shorter fiction, or join his readers group at: www.frankmorin.org

ABOUT THE AUTHOR

Frank Morin is a storyteller, an outdoor enthusiast, and an eager traveler. He is the author of fast-paced grab-you-by-the-eyeballs-and-don't-let-go adventures, including *The Petralist*, his epic teen fantasy series, full of explosive magic, huge adventure, and brilliant humor. Frank also writes *The Facetakers* fast-action historical fantasy thrillers you've been enjoying.

When not writing or trying to keep up with his active family, he's often found hiking, camping, Scuba diving, or traveling to research new books. Find out more about his novels and his shorter fiction, or join his readers group here.